Page to Stage

Plays from Classic Literature

*Seventeen Full-Length Plays
for Students*

*including information, lessons,
and assignments for understanding and
performance*

Page to Stage

Plays from Classic Literature

Perfection Learning
Logan, Iowa 51546-0500

Editorial Director   Julie A. Schumacher
Senior Editor   Gay Russell-Dempsey
Design   Mary Ann Lea Design
Electronic Technology   Pegi Bevins, Digital Talkies, Stewart Hondros
Permissions   Frances Brown

Cover Images by   Laurie Rubin

Warning
The editors have made very effort to trace the ownership of all copyrighted materials found in this book and to make full acknowledgment for their use.

Acknowledgments
Frankenstein by Tim Kelly Copyright ©1974 by Tim Kelly CAUTION: Professionals and amateurs are hereby warned that *Frankenstein,* being fully protected under the copyright laws of the United States of America, the British Commonwealth countries, including Canada, and the other countries of the Copyright Union, is subject to a royalty. All rights, including professional, amateur, motion picture, recitation, public reading, radio, television and cable broadcasting, and the rights of translation into foreign languages, are strictly reserved. Any inquiry regarding the availability of performance rights, or the purchase of individual copies of the authorization acting edition, must be directed to Samuel French, Inc., 45 West 25 Street, NY, NY 10010 with other locations in Hollywood and Toronto, Canada.

(Continued on page 462.)

Copyright © 2002 by Perfection Learning ® Corporation
1000 North Second Avenue
P.O. Box 500
Logan, Iowa 51546-0500
Tel: 1-800-831-4190 • Fax: 1-800-543-2745

ISBN: 0-7891-5729-2
Cover Craft ® ISBN: 0-7569-0934-1

Contents

Dear Student,

Welcome to *Page to Stage*! The plays in this book were chosen solely with you in mind. They are lively, interesting, and varied, and we think that you will enjoy them. They all originated as other kinds of literature— short stories, novels, myths, fables, and so on. You'll not only be reading about Pip, Estella, and Magwitch in *Great Expectations,* you may actually become them!

Each play is preceded by background information and an excerpt from the original work for you to compare to an excerpt from the play. Having an understanding of the original text will help you in your approach to the play.

After reading each play, you will analyze the play as both a dramatic and a literary work, and try your hand at many different drama-related activities. Our goal is to involve you in all facets of drama and its production. We hope you have fun doing it!

The Editors

Setting the Stage for

Frankenstein

from the novel by Mary Shelley
adapted for the stage by Tim Kelly

Creating Context:
The Birth of a Monster

"We will each write a ghost story," said the poet Lord Byron to his friends. And so began the germ of the idea for *Frankenstein*, written by Mary Shelley in 1816, when she was just nineteen. Mary and Percy Bysshe Shelley were visiting Byron at his villa in Switzerland. The weather had turned wet and gloomy and the small group had been reading gruesome stories. One featured a man who, having deserted his lover, ends up in the arms of her ghost. In another story, a gigantic ghostly form visits his sleeping young offspring and bestows a kiss that causes each to wither like a dead flower. These stories impressed the young Mary, but when she pondered what to write, nothing came to her. Each day she was asked, "Have you thought of a story?" and each day admitted that she had not.

Then one day she heard Lord Byron and Percy Shelley talking about a doctor who was reputed to have stimulated life in a piece of vermicelli. Life in a small glob of pasta! Could a dead human being thus be galvanized into life? Or perhaps a creature might be assembled, pieced together, and animated! That night, Mary could not sleep. When she closed her eyes she saw the image of a man, "a student of unhallowed arts," kneeling beside a creature that he had manufactured. She imagined the creature stirring, mocking "the stupendous mechanism of the Creator of the world." As the story continued in her mind, Mary Shelley felt the terror and thrill of fear, which she immediately began to translate to paper.

Mary Shelley

The next day Mary announced that she had thought of a story. *Frankenstein, or The Modern Prometheus,* was written in daily installments, and was well received by those assembled. It was published anonymously in 1818, and later under her own name. Many consider *Frankenstein* to be the first full-blown science fiction novel—a classic of the genre.

Some people confuse the name of the monster with that of the doctor. Be aware that the doctor's name is Frankenstein and that the monster is never given a name. As you read *Frankenstein,* pay attention to the way Tim Kelly creates and maintains the mood.

As a Reader: Understanding Mood

Authors create mood, or atmosphere, in many ways: by the things the characters say or think, or how they react to events, and by descriptions of the surroundings or other details. Mood is an important part of *Frankenstein*, both in the novel and the play. Compare the two excerpts below and think about the mood they share.

from Page · · ·   · · · to Stage

I became acquainted with the science of anatomy: but this was not sufficient; I must also observe the natural decay and corruption of the human body.... Darkness had no effect upon my fancy; and a churchyard was to me merely the receptacle of bodies deprived of life, which, from being the seat of beauty and strength, had become food for the worm. Now I was led to examine the cause and progress of this decay, and forced to spend days and nights in vaults and charnel-houses .... I beheld the corruption of death succeed to the blooming cheek of life; I saw how the worm inherited the wonders of the eye and brain. I paused, examining and analyzing all the minutiae of causation ... until from the midst of this darkness a sudden light broke in upon me—a light so brilliant and wondrous, yet so simple...

from *Frankenstein* by Mary Shelley

VICTOR. ...I had one passion and only one. To examine the causes of life. And to do that I first had to have recourse to death.

HENRY. Death?

VICTOR. I became acquainted with the science of anatomy in a way that was zealous, accelerated. I observed the natural decay and corruption of the human body.

HENRY. In the dissecting room of the university, you mean.

(*As* VICTOR *is speaking, his passion and emotional involvement is painfully obvious. He rants, he gestures, he pauses ... there is the awesome realization that what he speaks might be true and this horror is conveyed to* HENRY, *who listens in a state of morbid fascination.*)

VICTOR (*contemptuous*). No, I do not mean in the dissecting room of the university.

HENRY. What do you mean, then?

VICTOR. I mean that the charnel-house became my haunt. I lived with the stench of decay in my nostrils. A church graveyard was not a holy place to me. It was, instead, only the receptacle of bodies deprived of life.

HENRY. I don't believe you.

VICTOR. Then you are a fool. I saw how the fine form of man was degraded and wasted. I beheld the corruption of death and studied until my senses no longer knew the hour, the day, the week. And finally in the midst of my darkness a sudden light broke in upon me—a light so brilliant and wondrous, yet so simple....

from *Frankenstein* adapted by Tim Kelly

As a Costume/Makeup Designer: Creating the Mood

Frankenstein takes place in Switzerland in the late 1800s. As you read the play, try to visualize the costumes, including accessories and props. Rid your mind of movie monsters and focus on the creature as Shelley wrote him and Kelley has adapted him.

Frankenstein

Time

Before the turn of the nineteenth century

The Characters

VICTOR FRANKENSTEIN	A young scientist
ELIZABETH	Victor's fiancee
HENRY	Victor's friend, also a scientist
FRAU FRANKENSTEIN	Victor's mother
THE CREATURE	An artificially created man
JUSTINE	A Gypsy girl
ERNST	An inspector-general of police
SOPHIE	A housekeeper

Setting

A chateau on the shores of
Lake Geneva, Switzerland

ACT ONE SCENE 1

SETTING: The study of VICTOR FRANKENSTEIN. *Down Right is a door that leads into an offstage laboratory. Up Center is the main entrance into the room, with drapes that can be pulled across when required. There is a hallway beyond this entrance that leads off Up Right to an unseen door. Left and Right of the main entrance are rows and rows of books. French doors, also with drapes, are Stage Left with some outside garden foliage in view. A sofa is Stage Right and two fine chairs are Stage Left. Sofa and chairs are angled out to the audience for best sight lines possible. There is a desk and chair Down Left with a standing anatomy chart. This describes only the essentials. Naturally, additional stage dressing will greatly enhance the impact of the set; paintings, more books, small tables, occasional chairs, lamps, rugs, hunting trophies, vases, etc. The study is a darkish sort of enclave, shadowy but comfortable, reflecting masculine elegance and an aura of the academic.*

AT RISE: Night. The room is softly lighted. Drapes Up Center and at the French doors are pulled aside. Moonlight illuminates the garden foliage. Stage remains empty for a moment and, then, voices behind the laboratory door.

SOPHIE'S VOICE *(offstage).* I don't understand. I don't understand any of it.

ERNST'S VOICE. It's not important what you do or do not understand.

(ERNST, *a police commandant in uniform, enters Right. He's an exacting man, well disciplined, a dedicated professional. He's followed by* SOPHIE, *the housekeeper. She's nervous and apprehensive.*)

SOPHIE. Police everywhere. In the garden. On the shores of the lake.

(ERNST *has crossed Down Center, takes out his revolver, checks it.*)

ERNST. We've searched the house thoroughly.

SOPHIE. Yes, but why?

ERNST. You ask a great many questions, Sophie.

SOPHIE. I've earned that right.

ERNST. You're certain there's no other room or area of the chateau where anyone might hide? Or any *thing*?

SOPHIE. What *thing*?

ERNST. One question at a time.

SOPHIE (*annoyed*). I've been housekeeper for many years. I know of no other room or area of the chateau.

(ERNST *checks the bullets.*)

ERNST. They say he's afraid of gunfire.

SOPHIE. Who? Herr Frankenstein?

ERNST. No, not him. (*voices from off Up Right*)

ELIZABETH'S VOICE (*offstage*). Victor, what are you doing?

VICTOR'S VOICE (*offstage*). Only what tradition expects of me.

SOPHIE. They're back.

ERNST. Come on. Give them a few minutes of sanity.

SOPHIE. Sanity?

ERNST. Do as I tell you. (ERNST *moves to French doors, exits.*)

SOPHIE (*follows after him*). No reception, no guests, police everywhere. Not my idea of a wedding night.

(*We hear the laughter of* ELIZABETH *and shortly thereafter* VICTOR FRANKENSTEIN *appears Up Center with his bride in his arms.*)

ELIZABETH (*happily*). Put me down, Victor. I'm out of breath.

(VICTOR *is a young man, early twenties. Serious, tense, apprehensive.* ELIZABETH *is younger by a year or so. She wears her bridal gown with style and clutches a bouquet of flowers.* VICTOR *puts her down and she moves toward the sofa.*)

VICTOR. Should I ring for Sophie?

ELIZABETH. What on earth for?

VICTOR. I thought you might want something to eat or drink. (*He glances nervously to the open French doors.*)

ELIZABETH. No, nothing. (*Then:*) Victor, now that we're married—won't you tell me what's been troubling you? (*He moves to the French doors, looks into the garden.*) You've been so distraught. When I speak, I'm not sure you hear what I say. When I look at you, I know your thoughts are elsewhere.

VICTOR. Forgive me, Elizabeth. (*Almost to himself*) I have so much to be forgiven for.

ELIZABETH (*concerned*). Victor? (*He turns.*) You . . . you don't regret marrying me? (*He crosses to her, takes her hand, kisses it.*)

VICTOR. I am afraid.

ELIZABETH. Afraid of what? (*Strong*) Victor, you must tell me. You've lived these past months with some terrible private dread. I want to bring you happiness. (*Proud*) I am Frau Frankenstein, the wife of a brilliant young scientist. Whatever troubles you, has to trouble me. I beg you, Victor. Take me into your confidence. (VICTOR *turns once again to the French doors.*) What's out there that frightens you?

VICTOR (*points*). Tonight . . . this very night . . . the man who will kill me will come through those doors. (ELIZABETH *can barely speak, reacts.*)

ELIZABETH. What are you saying? (*She sits on the sofa, stunned.*)

VICTOR. I know it sounds incredible. Monstrous. All the same, it's true.

ELIZABETH. Who would want to kill you? Why?

VICTOR. *(He sits beside her.)* I ask only that you remember your love for me when you hear my words.

ELIZABETH *(wary).* Go on . . .

VICTOR. Do you remember when I returned from the university at Ingolstadt?

ELIZABETH. Of course. You were in such poor health. We were all so worried for you.

VICTOR. I didn't want to return . . . I wanted to find some icy glacier and build a funeral pyre[1] . . . if not for myself, then for my deeds . . . *(The stage lighting dims down as* VICTOR *recollects the events of the past.* ELIZABETH *gets up and walks stately to the Up Center exit. Even in the dark her wedding gown will be semi-visible, so the actress should make her exit appear as part of the remembrance.* VICTOR'S *words continue in the near-blackness.)* I hadn't slept in days . . . my brain was on fire. . . . I was consumed with guilt and fear . . . and that private dread you speak of. . . .

(The stage now is in total blackness. ELIZABETH *is out. From off Left we hear the voice of* HENRY CLERVAL.)*

HENRY'S VOICE *(offstage).* Victor? Victor, are you in there . . . ? *(Lights dim up for daylight.* VICTOR *is still sitting on the sofa.)* Victor? *(*VICTOR *stands as* HENRY *comes in via the open French doors carrying a book.)* Ah, there you are.

VICTOR. How are you, Henry?

HENRY *(moves Center).* Question is, how are you?

VICTOR. Constant. My temper is almost violent. My mood varies between deep depression and melancholia.

HENRY *(attempts to jar him out of his somberness).* Come, come, Victor, you're away from your gloomy university. What could be more pleasant than a holiday on the shores of Lake Geneva in one's own chateau?

VICTOR. Holiday? Call it retreat. Sanctuary. Anything but holiday. I appreciate your good spirits, Henry. I know you're trying to cheer me up. It can't be much fun for anyone having me about like this.

HENRY. You've had a slight breakdown, that's all. Understandable, considering the way you drive yourself. For a young man, you take life far too seriously.

(By now, Victor has crossed to his desk and sat down. He busies himself with the finishing of some letter.)

VICTOR. Life is serious. What man does with life even more so.

HENRY. Have it your way, but there's no need to be pompous.[2] *(holds up the book)* Perhaps this will cheer you up. A new thesis in biochemistry.

VICTOR. That's your field, not mine.

HENRY. Ah, but this work is by Albertus Magnus. *(*VICTOR *looks up.)* "Natural Philosophy and Chemical Persuasion." The book is quite fascinating, and Magnus *is* your favorite professor.

VICTOR. He was.

HENRY. You ought to read it. You haven't already purchased it?

VICTOR. No.

HENRY. Good.

VICTOR. Peculiar that you should bring up his name.

HENRY. How so?

VICTOR. I'm finishing a letter to him.

HENRY. Indeed.

---

1. funeral pyre, a pile of combustible materials for ceremoniously cremating a body

2. pompous, arrogant; haughty

VICTOR. I'm informing him that I do not intend to return to Ingolstadt.

HENRY. You mean, until you've regained your health.

VICTOR. I mean—never.

(Henry moves to Downstage chair, sits in such a way that his body is angled to face Victor at the desk.)

HENRY. Victor, is this because of your brother?

VICTOR (thoughtfully). I confess William's murder is not a thing I accept easily. To live less than ten years when life holds out so much promise, and die at the hands of an unknown killer, seems to me the height of cosmic cruelty.

HENRY. Cosmic cruelty? The lad was murdered for an expensive gold cross. Obviously by a thief of the lowest kind. Vicious and unfeeling. A monster.

MOTHER'S VOICE (from off Up Right). Victor, may I come in?

VICTOR. It's my mother. Please do not make any mention of William. She holds up extremely well, but—

HENRY. I understand.

(VICTOR rises, takes out a chain of keys, moves Up Center.)

VICTOR. One moment, Mother. I'll unlock the door. (VICTOR exits. HENRY opens the book, reads. FRAU FRANKENSTEIN, VICTOR'S mother, enters Up Center. HENRY stands.)

MOTHER. Ah, Henry, how wonderful that you're here. (HENRY bows politely.)

HENRY. Always a pleasure, Frau Frankenstein. (VICTOR enters Up Center.)

MOTHER. I can't tell you what your visits mean to Victor. You, his best friend, have never deserted him.

HENRY. Boys together, friends together. Comrades always.

MOTHER. Did you hear that, Victor?

VICTOR. I have never doubted Henry's friendship. As I trust he will never doubt mine.

MOTHER (sits on sofa). If you could only persuade him to get out and around. My son does nothing but lock himself here in the study as if the sound of another human voice was more than he could bear.

VICTOR. You exaggerate, Mother. (He moves behind the sofa.)

MOTHER. No, Victor, I do not. (To HENRY) He never sleeps. Sophie is at her wits' end trying to think of something that will tease his appetite. Elizabeth has become his devoted nurse, but I'm afraid my son is a bad patient. (Takes VICTOR'S hand) I do worry about you. The doctor says—

VICTOR (scoffs). The doctor—

MOTHER. You shouldn't scoff like that, Victor. You're a scientific man yourself.

VICTOR. There is a world of difference, Mother, between a doctor and a scientific man.

MOTHER. If there is I'm not aware of it. I only meant that you shouldn't insult him by your indifference. He has your best interests at heart. You know you can't go on the way you have. You must eat, rest.

(Angrily, VICTOR pulls his hand away, turns his back.)

VICTOR. Oh, stop it, Mother.

(HENRY and MOTHER exchange an embarrassed look.)

HENRY (eager to change the subject). And where is Elizabeth this fine day?

MOTHER. She went to the flower market. I believe she could live her life there. But she was that way even as a child. She could tell you the name of any flower that grew. Victor could pull a flower apart and tell you exactly what was inside of it, what made it grow.

HENRY. Some would find that an ideal combination. The pragmatic and the romantic.

MOTHER *(thinks).* Yes, yes. That's very good, Henry. Very good, indeed. *(SOPHIE has entered Up Center.)*

SOPHIE. I'm sorry to disturb you, Frau Frankenstein.

MOTHER. What is it, Sophie?

SOPHIE. It's Ernst Hessler. *(HENRY, VICTOR, and MOTHER tense.)*

VICTOR. I'll see him outside. *(VICTOR moves toward Up Center exit, is stopped by:)*

MOTHER. No, Victor. *(To SOPHIE)* Show him in here, Sophie. *(SOPHIE nods, exits.)*

HENRY. Perhaps I should leave.

MOTHER. Nonsense. It's probably something quite routine about . . . the investigation.

VICTOR. I don't think you should see him. You know how upset you get.

MOTHER. Victor, it is you who gets upset. *(A second passes and SOPHIE again appears Up Center.)*

SOPHIE. Inspector General Hessler. *(ERNST enters Up Center, moves to FRAU FRANKENSTEIN.)*

ERNST. I am sorry to intrude, Frau Frankenstein.

MOTHER. You are always welcome in my house, Ernst. *(She holds out her hand. He kisses it in a perfunctory[3] manner.)* You know Henry, of course. Our neighbor.

ERNST *(slight bow).* Herr Clerval. *(To VICTOR)* Victor. *(VICTOR nods.)*

MOTHER. You'll stay for tea?

ERNST. I'm afraid not.

VICTOR. Then this is a professional visit?

ERNST. Yes.

MOTHER. Something . . . something about William's . . . murder? *(ERNST looks to HENRY.)* Henry is a dear and trusted friend of this family. You may speak freely in front of him.

ERNST. As you wish. *(To business)* We have William's cross. *(Takes it from some pocket. All react.)*

VICTOR. Who had it?

ERNST. A girl by the name of Justine tried to sell it in Geneva. Unfortunately for her, the buyer was one of our informants.

HENRY. A girl?

ERNST. A bad sort. She travels with horse dealers. Gypsies. Her kind would cut a throat for a tablespoon.

MOTHER *(repulsed).* Please.

ERNST. An unfortunate choice of words. Forgive me.

VICTOR. There can be no mistake?

ERNST. They were encamped on the lake shore the day of William's murder. We know your brother visited the encampment. He was seen there. It's a popular spot for local boys. The girl was seen talking to him, admiring the cross at his neck. The night of the murder the Gypsies broke camp and moved on.

HENRY. Hardly seems sufficient to prove this girl guilty.

ERNST. She has a bad record. We have her on file.

MOTHER. She has confessed?

ERNST. Far from it. She denies any knowledge of the crime.

MOTHER. If that is so, how can you be so positive?

ERNST. Because of the absurd story she made up to cover her deed.

VICTOR. What story?

ERNST. She claims a man gave her the cross.

HENRY. Is that so extraordinary?

ERNST. Ah, but this man was no ordinary mortal. He was large and stitched together like a rag doll.

---

3. perfunctory, insincere; mechanical

VICTOR. *What!*

ERNST. She had the impudence to offer that myth to me. I thought I heard them all, but a large man stitched together was a new one.

VICTOR. *No!*

MOTHER. Victor, are you all right?

VICTOR *(to* ERNST *crossing to the French doors).* Why did you have to bring this news?

ERNST. It is my duty. I assure you, Victor, I had no idea it would upset you in this manner.

MOTHER *(stands).* My son has been under a doctor's care. He's not himself at all. Forgive him.

VICTOR *(to* ERNST*).* Get out.

HENRY. Victor, get a hold of yourself.

VICTOR. *Get out, I said.* (ERNST *bows to* VICTOR, *nods to* HENRY.*)*

MOTHER. I'll see you to the door.

ERNST. Thank you, Frau Frankenstein. *(She leads the way.)*

MOTHER. I wonder, Ernst, might I have the cross?

ERNST. I'm afraid not. Evidence.

MOTHER. I understand.

ERNST. When the case is closed, I'll see that it's returned. *(She glances nervously at* VICTOR. MOTHER *and* ERNST *are out.* HENRY *stands.)*

HENRY. Was that necessary? If you go on this way, there's nothing ahead but disaster for you. You've got to take the doctor's advice.

VICTOR. Did you believe him?

HENRY. The doctor?

VICTOR *(bitterly).* No, not the doctor. Ernst. What he said about that girl's story.

HENRY. I have no reason not to believe him.

VICTOR. "Stitched together like a rag doll."

HENRY. The girl was lying.

VICTOR. Was she?

HENRY. It's as simple as that—a lie. Nothing more.

VICTOR. I assure you even simplicity can turn into something twisted and evil. Today's exhilaration can fade quickly into tomorrow's grief.

HENRY *(irritated by* VICTOR's *gloominess).* Can't you say a single sentence without decorating it with crepe?

VICTOR *(directly).* The girl was not lying.

HENRY. Be reasonable.

VICTOR *(furious).* Don't patronize me! I tell you the girl spoke the truth.

HENRY. I will not stand here and listen to this raving. (HENRY *moves to the Up Center exit.)*

VICTOR *(distraught).* Henry, if our friendship means anything at all, I ask you to stay. I plead with you to stay.

HENRY *(turns).* On one condition.

VICTOR. What is that?

HENRY. The Victor Frankenstein who left this chateau for the university was not the same man who returned here for sanctuary as you call it. Something happened to him during that time he was gone. I want to know what it was, and unless you are prepared to tell me of your affliction—

VICTOR *(cutting him off).* Yes, yes. I intend to. I want to. I must. *(Moves to him.)* You are my last hope. What I am going to tell you will chill the marrow of your mortal bones.

HENRY. Let me be the judge of whether or not my "mortal bones" will freeze.

(Quickly, VICTOR *crosses to the desk and from some drawer pulls a ledger, various papers, and documents.)*

VICTOR. If I appear unsettled and half-mad, there is a reason.

HENRY. If you're referring to Ernst's visit, I can only comment that it is unjust to blame the messenger for the message.

VICTOR. You think that's why I cried out?

HENRY. What else am I to think?

VICTOR *(points to ledger, papers, etc.)*. The secret of my unrest lies here. In these documents and papers. The recorded crimes of Victor Frankenstein.

(VICTOR moves toward the center of the room. Curious, HENRY crosses to the desk and looks over the material. Eventually, HENRY sits behind the desk. VICTOR moves about for the best stage picture as he speaks.) You think that whatever happened began at the university. You are wrong. *(Points to laboratory door.)* It began behind that laboratory door. As a boy, science and biology consumed me, as it did you—far more than the fever that now plagues my brain. I was more advanced in my studies than even you realized. The university merely stimulated me to press on into the secret that has baffled men from the moment they first sucked breath.

HENRY. What secret?

VICTOR. I often asked myself from where did the principle of life proceed?

HENRY. A bold question.

VICTOR. Yet we are always on the brink of discovering something new and strange and bold. Our cowardice or carelessness defeats us. We restrain our inquiries in fear of what we might discover. We fear the unknown and long to embrace it. I had one passion and only one. To examine the causes of life. And to do that I first had to have recourse to death.

HENRY. Death?

VICTOR. I became acquainted with the science of anatomy in a way that was zealous, accelerated. I observed the natural decay and corruption of the human body.

HENRY. In the dissecting room of the university, you mean.

(As VICTOR is speaking, his passion and emotional involvement is painfully obvious. He rants, he gestures, he pauses, he speaks clearly, intelligently, persuasively. Always, with his words, there is the awesome realization that what he speaks might be true and this horror is conveyed to HENRY, who listens in a state of morbid fascination.)

VICTOR *(contemptuous)*. No, I do not mean in the dissecting room of the university.

HENRY. What do you mean, then?

VICTOR. I mean that the charnel-house became my haunt. I lived with the stench of decay in my nostrils. A church graveyard was not a holy place to me. It was, instead, only the receptacle of bodies deprived of life.

HENRY. I don't believe you.

VICTOR. Then you are a fool. I saw how the fine form of man was degraded and wasted. I beheld the corruption of death and studied until my senses no longer knew the hour, the day, the week. And finally in the midst of my darkness a sudden light broke in upon me—a light so brilliant and wondrous, yet so simple, that while I became dizzy with the prospect of success, I was surprised that among so many men of genius I alone, Victor Frankenstein, should be reserved to discover so astonishing a secret.

HENRY *(annoyed with VICTOR's mood)*. That again.

VICTOR. I asked for your friendship, not your skepticism.

HENRY. You have both. Go on.

VICTOR. The stages of the discovery were distinct and probable. Others could have discovered what I did. Albertus Magnus, for one. But brilliant minds must match their gifts with boldness and imagination, not be earthbound by the improbable. After days and nights of incredible labor and fatigue, I succeeded in discovering the cause of generation and life. I was capable of bestowing animation upon lifeless matter.

HENRY. That's not possible, Victor.

VICTOR *(laughs)*. You think not? You, too, are earthbound. When I found so astonishing a power placed within my hands, I hesitated a long time before I decided how to employ it.

HENRY. And how did you?

VICTOR *(flat, unemotional)*. I began the creation of a human being.

HENRY *(incredulous)*.[4] You did what?

(VICTOR sits, half-enjoying his dreadful recollection and the effect it's having on HENRY.)

VICTOR. In a solitary chamber at the top of my rooming house, I kept a workshop of filthy creation.

HENRY *(stands)*. How could you "create" another human being?

VICTOR. With considerable dedication and a strong stomach. The city morgue and the charity hospital furnished my materials. From one, I stole a hand. From another, I purchased a leg. On dark nights the graveyard proved productive in direct proportion to the energy I was willing to expend in opening a grave.

HENRY. No more, Victor! Enough!

VICTOR. I became nervous to a painful degree. The fall of a leaf startled me, and I shunned everyone as if I were guilty of a crime. I collected the instruments of life around my table, and when I finished I fell asleep across my cot, troubled by dreams.

HENRY *(moves toward him)*. I should think so. And that was the end of your experiment?

VICTOR. If only it could have been. I dreamed I saw the grave worms crawling in the folds of my father's funeral shroud. I started from my sleep in horror, and I beheld the life I created with these hands staring down at me, one hand outstretched as if the Creature were imploring some aid. *(Deep breath)* There. Now you know.

HENRY *(convinced VICTOR is insane)*. I know what you have told me.

VICTOR. You still don't understand?

HENRY. What more can there be?

VICTOR. Ernst . . . William's murder . . . the Gypsy girl. Think, Henry, think. *(Recalls ERNST's words)* "Ah, but this man was no ordinary mortal. He was large and stitched together like a rag doll." It was he, my Creature, made from the bits and pieces of other men, who murdered little William. *(Rises, seizes HENRY by the shoulders.)* Don't you understand? He's found me! He's followed me here to Geneva.

HENRY. If what you say is true, why would he do that? Why would he murder William? Why would he hate you? You gave him life. No, it's too preposterous.

VICTOR. You must listen!

HENRY *(breaking away)*. I've heard more than enough.

VICTOR. I'm not mad!

HENRY *(exits Up Center)*. You will be if you continue this way.

VICTOR. Henry! *(He moves after him.)* I asked for your help. Do not desert me! *(Suddenly, VICTOR freezes. It's as if a cold wind has blown across his heart. Afraid, he turns and sees the CREATURE, who has entered via the open French doors, standing inside the room, his arms outstretched as if to embrace the horrified FRANKENSTEIN.)* Henry, Henry! *(Turns to CREATURE)* Devil! Murderer! *(CREATURE takes a step toward his creator. HENRY*

---

4. incredulous, in disbelief

returns, sees CREATURE, *reacts.* VICTOR *backs away.)* Do you still doubt me? See for yourself. Stitched together like a demon from hell. Here standing before you is the proof of my infamy!

(HENRY *can't accept it. He's too shocked for any action.)*

HENRY. God help you, Victor. *(Then:)* God help us all.

CREATURE *(slowly, dramatically, an emotional appeal).* Frankenstein . . . help me.

ACT ONE SCENE 2

AT RISE: *Night. Drapes have been drawn across the French doors, giving the study a "closed in" feeling. Lamps glow. The* CREATURE *is seated in the Downstage chair, which has been turned around to face the audience squarely. The anatomy chart has been placed beside the* CREATURE. HENRY, *in shirtsleeves, is examining him. He's wildly excited.*

HENRY *(moving the* CREATURE's *head from side to side).* . . . And to the best of your knowledge, you had no adverse reaction to the anaesthetic?

CREATURE. No.

HENRY. No paralysis of any kind?

CREATURE. No.

(Henry moves to the desk and makes some notes. He picks up a measuring tape or something similar and returns to the CREATURE. *First he studies the chart and, then, he proceeds to take head measurements.)*

HENRY. I'm rather amazed about the eyelids. Moist, lubricated by circulating the tears. And the cornea—clear, transparent. The membrane functions normally. Stand up, please. *(The* CREATURE *obeys.)* Run in place. *(The* CREATURE *begins to run in place, fast.)*

No, no, no. Slowly. *(The* CREATURE *slows down.)* Excellent. You may be seated. *(*HENRY *returns to the desk and picks up a paperweight, crosses back to the* CREATURE, *hands it to him.)* I want to test the strength of your grip. *(The* CREATURE *holds out the paperweight and proceeds to crush it with ease.* HENRY *is amazed, takes back the weight and places it on the desk.)* I would say the end results are not yet cosmetically satisfactory, and there is a decided tendency toward hyperthyroidism, but in all other respects you are remarkable. I would have thought if such an experiment succeeded the conclusion would be a chronic invalid. I was wrong for doubting Victor.

CREATURE. Is that all I am?

HENRY. How do you mean?

CREATURE. An experiment.

HENRY *(puts down his notes).* Far more than an experiment, my strange friend. You are living proof that worn out parts can be replaced. You offer hope for an extended life span.

(VICTOR *enters from laboratory, putting on his jacket. He stands listening, unobserved by the* CREATURE.)

CREATURE. I am a monster. A living thing that is dead. I am alone, lonely. All men shun Frankenstein's creation.

VICTOR. And why shouldn't they? Murderer.

HENRY. Did you sleep at all?

VICTOR. I never sleep. Not any more. All I do is dream of horrors. (VICTOR *sits on the sofa.)*

HENRY *(crosses to* VICTOR). This is no horror. Whatever your technique, you have opened a special field of surgical study.

VICTOR *(unimpressed).* If one is a sadistic vivisectionist.[5]

---

5. vivisectionist, one who dissects animals for research

HENRY. He has the power of locomotion. Complete mastery of speech, reasoning, deduction. His parts will not wear out.

VICTOR. A living machine.

HENRY. Yes, if you will.

VICTOR. Beware, Henry. The excitement in your voice betrays you. You have caught my fever. (HENRY *crosses to the* CREATURE.)

HENRY. No extra fingers, no missing cartilage. Blood pulsates through his veins as it does through yours and mine.

VICTOR. Blood of dead men.

HENRY (*insistent*). This is no monster. You have engineered a finely tooled machine powered by an intricate network of muscles and tendons. The grafting is amateurish, repulsive, but it suffices.

VICTOR. You have forgotten something.

HENRY. I shouldn't wonder.

VICTOR (*stands*). There sits the hideous "thing" that has come to kill me.

CREATURE. That is no longer true.

VICTOR. I curse the day I gave you life.

CREATURE. I expected this reception. All men hate the wretched. How I must be hated then. I am miserable beyond all living things. I did not always hate you, Victor Frankenstein. The night you brought me to life, I rushed from your rooms believing the world would welcome me. I thought myself no different than others. I watched you sleeping and saw no great dissimilarity between us.

VICTOR. That is disgusting.

HENRY. No, it is not. You brought him into existence. It is perfectly natural that he would think you and he were both of a kind.

VICTOR (*incensed*). Both of a kind!

CREATURE. I am one of no kind. An outcast. Wherever I showed myself people ran in terror and repulsion. I had no friend. In the winter I froze sleeping in the hills. In the summer I hid in the woods.

HENRY. Were you harmed in any way? Physically, I mean.

CREATURE. Hunters came into the woods searching for game. I had never seen a gun or heard its sound. It frightened me and I ran, but they followed after. (*Touches his shoulder*) A great pain tore into me, and I saw my own blood for the first time. It sickened me.

HENRY. You hear that, Victor? He felt pain. He knows fear.

VICTOR. As I do. As you should. (*To* CREATURE) Go from this house. Leave me.

CREATURE. Have I not suffered enough? Now you seek to increase my misery?

VICTOR. Is that why you have sought me out? To come here for a hiding place? Is that why you murdered a defenseless boy?

CREATURE (*stands*). I did not murder him. You did, Frankenstein. (VICTOR *stiffens.* HENRY *moves toward the desk, watching the duo confront one another.*)

VICTOR. You dare say that to me?

CREATURE. A creature such as I must dare. I saw a child coming toward me. Suddenly, as I gazed on him, an idea seized me that this little creature had lived too short a time to understand the horror of deformity. If I could educate him before others imparted their prejudice, I should not be so desolate in this peopled earth. I would not be alone. For of all curses, that is the one I loathe above all others.

HENRY (*curious more than accusative*). But why murder?

CREATURE. I had no such intention. At first. I seized him as he passed. As soon as he beheld my form, he placed his hands before his eyes and uttered a shrill cry. "Let me go!" he screamed. "Monster! Ugly wretch! Let me go or I will tell Victor. He will punish you! Victor Frankenstein, my brother, will punish you!"

VICTOR *(visibly shaken).* Poor, poor William.

CREATURE. I swelled with hellish triumph. I thought, I, too, can create desolation. My enemy is not invulnerable. This death will carry despair to him, and a thousand other miseries shall torment and destroy him. Frankenstein will suffer as I have suffered. *(HENRY and VICTOR say nothing for a moment and, then, the CREATURE sits.)* Have you suffered, Frankenstein?

VICTOR. More than I would have thought possible.

CREATURE. Then I am satisfied. You have created me, but your work is not finished.

VICTOR. It is . . . finished.

CREATURE. You have created me. You must destroy me.

HENRY *(alarmed).* What!

VICTOR *(a thoughtful pause).* We are in accord. At last.

CREATURE. Then you'll do it?

VICTOR. Yes.

HENRY. Victor!

CREATURE. When?

VICTOR. Tonight.

HENRY. Victor, I protest.

(VICTOR's manner is deficient and direct. The unemotional scientist. He crosses to the laboratory door, opens it.)

VICTOR. We can't risk having you seen. You'll be safe in there until I'm ready. Make no sound.

(The CREATURE stands, crosses for the laboratory.)

CREATURE. Remember this—my agony is greater than yours. *(The CREATURE enters the laboratory.)*

VICTOR. No one ever goes in there. But to be safe . . . *(VICTOR locks the door.)*

HENRY. You cannot be serious about his request.

VICTOR. Ah, but I am. He has brought me my salvation. *(As they discourse, VICTOR goes to the drapes masking the French doors, opens them. Early morning sun streams in.)*

HENRY. It would be murder.

VICTOR. You cannot murder a walking inventory of borrowed human parts.

HENRY. That's absurd and you know it.

VICTOR. Call it anything you like. Execution, a balancing of the scales. Retribution, if you will. Anything but murder. There is blood on my hands for having created him.

HENRY. And you think that by destroying him you can wash away that blood. Is that it?

VICTOR. It is my only hope.

HENRY. Then I appeal to you as a man of science. I do not speak now as a dear friend. I speak to you as another who is dedicated to pushing back the barriers of ignorance.

VICTOR. Barriers? *(Points to laboratory door)* I crumbled one barrier and look at the result.

HENRY. I have looked and what I've found is both miraculous and marvelous. This "Creature" is not at fault. He was an innocent thrust into a world that has no comfortable place for the unordinary. He had every right to expect gentleness and understanding. Instead, he found that mankind itself is very often monstrous.

VICTOR. There is nothing you can say that I haven't said to myself a hundred times. *(Crosses to desk, grabs some photograph, moves to HENRY, puts the frame into his hand.)* Here, look into the face of William. You speak of an innocent. There is your innocent. My young brother.

HENRY. Victor, be sensible. I am speaking to your intellect, not your emotion.

VICTOR. Damn your intellect.

HENRY. And damn your emotion!

(From off—Up Right)

MOTHER'S VOICE. Victor, Victor?

VICTOR *(takes out his keys).* Say nothing of this. To anyone.

HENRY. For the time being.

VICTOR. Return this evening. I will need your assistance.

MOTHER'S VOICE. Victor? (VICTOR *exits Up Center with the key ready to unlock the hallway door.* HENRY *moves to the desk and puts down the framed photograph.)* I shan't hear another word. If you will not come to the breakfast table, you shall eat in the study. *(By now, she has entered.* VICTOR *stands Left of Up Center entrance.* MOTHER *wears an attractive robe over her nightgown.)* Henry? Here so early?

HENRY. I'm afraid I never left.

MOTHER *(Sees anatomy chart, disorder on the desk. She sighs protectively.)* I was counting on you to help Victor rest. And look at this. It's as if you were boys again. Up all night with your studies and vile smelling test tubes. You'll stay for breakfast?

HENRY. Sleep at the moment is more appealing than nourishment.

MOTHER. I shall be angry with you if you encourage Victor in any work. It would be quite destructive.

HENRY *(meaning the* CREATURE*).* I agree with you. If you'll excuse me? *(Takes his jacket from some chair, puts it on.)* It's a lovely day outside. I'll enjoy the walk home. I have a great deal to think about. Until later, Victor. *(At French doors)* Frau Frankenstein. (MOTHER *nods,* HENRY *exits.* VICTOR *moves Down Center.)*

MOTHER *(touches his face).* If you could see your eyes. I can count every tiny vein.

VICTOR. I would like to be alone, Mother.

MOTHER. No, Victor. I have given in to your whims and ways far too often. Elizabeth is taking you into the city this morning. She has shopping to do.

VICTOR. You think that interests me? Shopping!

MOTHER. No, I'm sure the shopping will bore you, but Elizabeth's company will be pleasant. *(He turns away.)* Won't it? (SOPHIE *enters Up Center with a breakfast tray.)* Ah, Sophie. Good, good. Put the tray on Victor's desk.

VICTOR. I am not hungry.

(MOTHER *ignores him. Moves the anatomy chart back to its proper position.)*

MOTHER. I am going to insist that you allow Sophie in here to clean.

SOPHIE. I haven't been in here for so long, Herr Frankenstein. Everything is covered with dust. It's not healthy to breathe dust.

VICTOR. Is that your medical opinion?

MOTHER. There is no need to be rude.

VICTOR. I have asked that you respect my wishes. Do not enter unless the door is unlocked.

MOTHER. You allow Henry to come and go at will through the garden.

VICTOR. That is another matter.

MOTHER. Neither Sophie, Elizabeth, nor I have ever bothered you about your laboratory. Although at times, the smells have been unbearable. However, other people do come into the study. You're not being fair. Let Sophie clean.

VICTOR *(sits on sofa, resigned).* If only all matters could be reduced to such elements. To eat a breakfast, to go shopping, to clean a room.

MOTHER (*trying to pull him from the doldrums*). Sophie has a surprise for you. (*She crosses back to the chair in which the* CREATURE *was sitting, puts it back into position.*)

SOPHIE. Strawberries. First of the season, Herr Frankenstein.

VICTOR. Leave the tray.

MOTHER. Sophie, bring me the strawberries. (SOPHIE *picks up the bowl, crosses to* MOTHER, *hands her the bowl.*) Eat the strawberries, Victor. (*He laughs.*) Is that so amusing?

VICTOR. Mother . . you're so good . . . so comforting . . . strawberries. Strawberries!

(*He laughs again.* MOTHER *and* SOPHIE *exchange an amazed look and they, too, get caught in* VICTOR's *mood and join in.* ELIZABETH *enters Up Center dressed most attractively. She carries a hat box, looks at the laughing trio, amazed.*)

ELIZABETH (*bright smile*). I'm sorry I wasn't here a moment earlier. I like a good joke as well as the next.

VICTOR (*smiling*). Not that, not that at all. It's just that I was struck by the incongruity[6] of my dark moods and my mother's dish of strawberries.

SOPHIE. They're perfectly good strawberries, sir. The man who sold them to me is reliable. I've never had any complaints about his produce.

VICTOR. I'm sure you haven't. (*He takes the strawberries and begins to eat. The women are delighted.*) Delicious.

MOTHER (*sigh of relief*). Come along, Sophie. We'll leave them alone. (SOPHIE *starts out, followed by* MOTHER, *who turns Up Center.*) And you will let Sophie clean in here?

VICTOR (*eating*). Yes, yes.

MOTHER. When, dear?

VICTOR (*anxious to close the subject*). Soon.

(MOTHER *gives a gesture of resignation to* ELIZABETH, *exits.* ELIZABETH *moves to some table, or the desk, and puts down the hat box.*)

ELIZABETH (*picks up breakfast tray*). I put the bud vase on the tray myself. Did you notice the petals?

VICTOR No. What is the flower?

ELIZABETH. There isn't any. I only wanted to see if you'd notice.

VICTOR (*puts down the dish*). I have been insensitive, haven't I?

ELIZABETH. I understand. No one here but solicitous women who would smother you with trivialities and fresh strawberries.

VICTOR. Most men would find that an enviable condition. (ELIZABETH *opens the hat box, takes out a wedding veil.*)

ELIZABETH. I can't make up my mind about this veil. I thought we might return it to the shop and see what else they had.

VICTOR. Not a subtle hint.

ELIZABETH. Victor, listen to me. I don't pretend I'm not disturbed by your strange moods and temperament. You're different from other men, true. Perhaps that's the very quality that attracts me. We've grown up together and I have always loved you. I don't know what troubles you. You're complex and difficult. I'm not blind to that. But, Victor, don't close your heart to me. Don't keep your love from me.

VICTOR. If only I could be honest.

ELIZABETH (*crosses to him, puts the veil on sofa*). I want to help you in life. I want to be with you. We were companions as children. We'll be companions now. Only closer, dearer.

VICTOR (*recites the cliché with an almost hopeful smile*). And you'll read to me, and cook for me, and comfort me when I'm alone and others might turn against me?

---

6. incongruity, contrast between

ELIZABETH. Don't make light of such things, Victor. They count for something. I would do all those things. Gladly.

VICTOR. Then a wife is truly a wonderful thing.

ELIZABETH. Let me be wonderful for you, Victor. I have never loved anyone else. I never shall. You will never be alone. I promise you that. (VICTOR *stands, takes her hand, kisses it.*)

VICTOR. Dear, dear Elizabeth.

ELIZABETH (*happily*). Come along now . . . we'll have the morning together. We'll visit the flower market. (VICTOR *seems to brighten.*)

VICTOR. My dark moods will soon be at an end. And I promise you that, Elizabeth. Yes, yes, by all means—the flower market.

(ELIZABETH *holds out her hand and* VICTOR *crosses to her and they sweep out the French doors, delighted in each other's company. A moment passes and, then, the door to the laboratory opens. In her happiness,* ELIZABETH *has forgotten the bridal veil. The* CREATURE *has obviously been eavesdropping. He moves to the sofa and picks up the veil. He finds it a thing of wonder and pleasure. Over and over in his hands he turns it, as if he almost expects it to change shape. Tenderly, lovingly, he caresses it to his cheek.*)

CREATURE (*smiles in anticipation*). Wife.

ACT ONE SCENE 3

AT RISE: That evening. Drapes are drawn at Up Center. At the French doors, the drapes are pulled to the sides revealing a moonlit night, one door open. VICTOR *is at his desk, poring over books and assorted notes, a lamp burning beside him. He works at a feverish pace, checking and rechecking, making notations in his ledgers. He wears a white smock.*

VICTOR (*barely audible*). . . . The bronchial tubes and then into the chest cavity . . . the tendons and the attached muscle and tissues . . . the large veins into the muscular structure of the heart . . . no resuturing required . . . totally sever the arm . . . the leg . . . complete reversal of transplantation . . . (*The* CREATURE *quietly comes from the laboratory and stands watching* VICTOR. *The scientist is wholly preoccupied and is unaware of the intrusion.*) . . . the spinal column compressed . . . no attempt to minimize the loss of blood to brain tissue . . . yes, yes . . .

CREATURE. Frankenstein.

VICTOR (*looks up*). It won't be long now. You shall have your wish. I'm waiting for Henry. I'll need his assistance.

CREATURE. How will you do it?

VICTOR. I put you together piece by piece. Your whole anatomical structure is a patchwork of transplanted blood vessels, tissues, bones. I shall simply reverse the process. You will cease to exist piece by piece. You needn't worry. I'll attack the brain first. You'll feel nothing.

CREATURE. And the "pieces."

VICTOR. The disposal of the "pieces" is not the concern of surgery. Still, if you must know—

CREATURE (*interrupts*). Yes . . . tell me.

VICTOR. Several options. Quicklime . . . acid . . . burial.

CREATURE. None of those, Frankenstein.

VICTOR. You have something else in mind?

CREATURE. I will live.

VICTOR (*doesn't understand*). No, you will not live. Once the surgery is finished you will be erased from this earth.

CREATURE (*repeats*). I will live, Frankenstein.

VICTOR. What the devil do you mean?

CREATURE. I have a passion which you alone can gratify.

VICTOR. I have vowed to grant your request. Tonight your agony ends and my life begins anew.

CREATURE. No, Frankenstein. *My* life begins anew. (VICTOR *slowly rises, moves in front of his desk.*)

VICTOR. What are you saying?

CREATURE. We will not part until you grant my wish.

VICTOR. You wish for more than death?

CREATURE. Yes. More than death. Life. This time not for me, but for another.

VICTOR. Another?

CREATURE. I am alone and miserable.

VICTOR. Tonight I end that misery.

CREATURE. Men will not associate with me, but one as deformed and horrible as myself would not deny herself to me. My companion must be of the same species and have the same defects as I.

VICTOR. No such creature exists.

CREATURE. You must create her.

(VICTOR *is struck dumb, he leans back against the desk for support.*)

VICTOR. I thought you sought oblivion.

CREATURE. What I ask of you is reasonable and moderate.

VICTOR. Reasonable!

CREATURE. I demand one of another sex, but as hideous as myself. I demand a *bride* for Frankenstein's Creature.

VICTOR. You *demand*. You have no right to demand anything of me.

CREATURE. If you consent neither you nor any other human being shall ever see us again.

VICTOR (*his hands to his ears*). I won't listen.

CREATURE. You must create a female for me with whom I can live in companionship.

This you alone can do, and I demand it of you as a right which you must not refuse.

VICTOR. *I do refuse!*

CREATURE. Do not incite my anger.

VICTOR. I do not fear your anger, and no torture shall ever extort a consent from me.

CREATURE. Is what I ask so difficult?

VICTOR. For me it is an impossibility. You ask me to create another like yourself.

CREATURE. I do.

VICTOR. Two whose joint wickedness might desolate the world.

CREATURE. We will harm no living thing.

VICTOR. How did you come by this preposterous idea?

CREATURE. By listening to one who loves you.

VICTOR (*understands*). So you were listening at the door when I spoke with Elizabeth.

CREATURE. Her words were gentle.

VICTOR. I have agreed to give you death. By the hands that were responsible for giving you life. Beyond that, I owe you nothing.

CREATURE. Reconsider.

VICTOR. Never.

CREATURE. You are wrong and instead of threatening, I am content to reason with you.

VICTOR. You are malicious.

CREATURE. I am malicious because I am miserable. You, my creator, would tear me to pieces and triumph. Remember that. And tell me why I should pity man more than he pities me. Shall I respect man when he condemns me? Let him live with me in the interchange of kindness, and instead of injury I would bestow every benefit upon him with tears of gratitude at his acceptance. Why cannot that be, Frankenstein?

VICTOR. Human sensibilities forbid it.

CREATURE. Do as I ask. (VICTOR *turns his back.*) If I cannot inspire, I will cause fear, and chiefly toward you, my enemy. I will revenge my injuries. Have a care. I will work at your destruction, so that you shall curse the hour of your birth.

VICTOR (*turns back*). There! Your true nature. Threatening, dangerous, wicked. Your bride would be a monster, too.

CREATURE. It is true we shall be monsters, cut off from all the world; but on that account we shall be more attached to one another.

VICTOR. What happiness could there be in your lives?

CREATURE. Our lives will not be happy, but they will be harmless and free from the misery I now feel. My creator, let me feel gratitude towards you for one benefit. Let me see that I excite the sympathy of some existing thing. Do not deny me my request. I do not ask of you, Frankenstein. I *beg* of you.

VICTOR (*VICTOR is visibly shaken. He moves to the Downstage chair, sits.*) There . . . there is some justice in your argument.

CREATURE. We will go to the forest or some jungle. My food is not that of man. I do not destroy the animals to glut my appetite. Acorns and berries will sustain us.

VICTOR. The noble savage.

CREATURE. Do not mock me.

VICTOR. And do not tempt me. (CREATURE *can sense* VICTOR *is weakening.*)

CREATURE. We shall make our bed of dried leaves. The sun will shine on us as on man. Pitiless as you have been towards me, I now see compassion in your eyes.

VICTOR (*a plea for help*). Why did you have to return?

CREATURE. I swear to you, by the earth which I inhabit, and by you that made me, that with the companion you bestow I will leave the neighborhood of man forever.

VICTOR. That is what you say now, but what guarantee have I that you would not return, more demanding, stronger than ever before?

CREATURE. With another such as I my evil passions and anger will have fled.

VICTOR. Because you will have a bride?

CREATURE (*deeply felt*). Because I will have sympathy.

VICTOR. Forgive me for having created you.

CREATURE. It is too late for forgiveness. Grant me my wish. My life will flow quietly away, and in my dying moments, when that time comes, I shall not curse my maker. (*The* CREATURE *moves to* VICTOR *and puts his hand on* VICTOR's *shoulder.* VICTOR *stiffens, but is not repulsed at this moment.*)

VICTOR. As your maker, perhaps . . . perhaps . . . I do owe you some measure of . . . happiness.

CREATURE. We shall be things of whose existence everyone will be ignorant. The love of another will destroy the cause of my crimes. Pity me, Victor Frankenstein. Pity me.

(VICTOR *is lost in deep thought. The* CREATURE *moves back to the laboratory, turns once to stare at the scientist, exits.* VICTOR *remains seated. Alone, troubled. He stands, paces a few steps.* HENRY *enters via the French doors.*)

HENRY. I'm here as you requested—if only to dissuade you.

VICTOR (*turns slowly*). Always the man of science. Right, Henry?

HENRY. In this matter, yes.

VICTOR. You could never be as persuasive as my Creature.

HENRY. You look distant. What are you thinking?

VICTOR. *Paradise Lost.*

HENRY. Paradise?

VICTOR. The words of Milton: "Did I request thee, Maker, from my clay/To mould me Man, did I solicit thee/From darkness to promote me?"

HENRY (moves Downstage). You gave him life, Victor. And now you want to take it from him.

VICTOR. The Creature has had second thoughts.

HENRY. What do you mean?

VICTOR. Death is no longer to be its destination.

HENRY. He wants to live?

VICTOR. More than that.

HENRY. Surely that's enough.

VICTOR. You don't understand.

HENRY. I'm trying to.

VICTOR. He asks that I create a bride. Yes, a bride.

HENRY (impressed). He's more human than I realized.

VICTOR. A companion to share his wretched loneliness.

HENRY. But it's . . . it's unthinkable.

VICTOR. Aha! So now Henry Clerval has second thoughts. Yet it was Henry Clerval who sought to dissuade me.

HENRY. Dissuade you from destroying what was already in existence. I couldn't condone murder in any form. But to create a second Creature is not the same at all.

VICTOR. Test your fire, Henry. Put your scientific zeal to the crucible. You have marvelled at my "genius." You have been swept up in this bold experiment. You held staunch, while I wavered.

HENRY. For the possibilities the experiment offered.

VICTOR. I cannot do it alone. A second time would be impossible. I must have another with me. The Creature has promised they will live apart from man. Quietly. Without maliciousness.

HENRY. And if you refuse?

VICTOR. The Creature will become a hound of hell. I will be its prey. (Change in mood) Henry, let us give the Creature what it asks. I can't destroy it now, for its appeal was too sincere, springing from its cursed heart.

HENRY (wavering). I . . . I don't know . . .

VICTOR. I can compensate for the wickedness of the first by the creation of a gentler second.

HENRY. Perhaps . . .

VICTOR. Help me. If not for the Creature's wish, then for the experiment itself. You were amazed, fascinated. You, alone, among all others will see how the miracle is accomplished. Will you turn your back on that? (HENRY thinks.)

HENRY. When would we begin . . . if I agreed?

VICTOR (moves to French doors). What better time than tonight? (HENRY doesn't move.) Henry, are you not dedicated to pushing back the barriers of ignorance?

HENRY. Where are you going?

VICTOR. Where else? The church graveyard.

HENRY. Graveyard?

VICTOR (cold, detached, scientific). It will be my warehouse of spare parts. My salvation, my absolution. I offer you a glimpse of the eternal. The choice is yours.

HENRY (pause; then:) I accept.

VICTOR. Splendid. We'll get shovels from the greenhouse. Come along, Henry. (VICTOR exits in excited spirits. Caught up in the fever of the adventure, HENRY moves to follow.)

FAST CURTAIN
END OF ACT ONE

ACT TWO SCENE 1

TIME: A week later.

AT RISE: The room is in shadows. From behind the laboratory door comes the sound of machinery humming. Metallic rumblings coupled with bolts of flashing light that can be glimpsed through cracks in the door give evidence that VICTOR *is experimenting with the* CREATURE's *bride-to-be. Early morning light, that will fade up full as the scene progresses, filters in through the French doors. A few seconds more of laboratory activity and, then, silence. Another moment passes and a weary* VICTOR *enters. He wears a surgical gown, mask, cap. He removes the cap and mask as he crosses to the desk and pours himself a glass of brandy, downs it in a thirsty gulp.* HENRY *enters via the French doors carrying some wrapped article.*

HENRY. Not too late, am I?

VICTOR. I expected you an hour ago.

HENRY. Couldn't be helped. Any difficulties?

VICTOR. None beyond what we already know. We'll need to increase the voltage.

HENRY *(moving in).* How's he behaving?

VICTOR. More like an expectant father than an expectant groom.

HENRY. Understandable.

VICTOR. He sits in the corner of the laboratory like a huge whipped dog. Watching. If I touch a switch his eyes flick to the spot.

HENRY. I've noticed that.

VICTOR. If I rewire the apparatus he takes careful note of how it's done.

HENRY. Testimony to your extraordinary skills.

VICTOR *(moves Center).* Testimony to his craftiness. You've noticed his gift of mimicry. Oh, he watches you, too, Henry. A little while ago I suddenly realized he was unusually quiet.

HENRY. And?

VICTOR. He was studying your notes.

HENRY. My notes?

VICTOR. I think it might be wise if you devised some code or other.

HENRY. If you say so.

VICTOR. It's both touching and horrible to watch him. Whenever I enter the laboratory he's by the surgical table.

HENRY. He never touches anything.

VICTOR. And, yet, he knows every molecule of his bride-to-be. I entered unobserved earlier and found him talking to the incomplete thing.

HENRY. He's never given me a bit of trouble. Undoubtedly, he accepts me as some sort of an apprentice. Nothing more.

VICTOR. Don't be too sure. You've been his champion. He's not likely to forget that.

HENRY. I wonder, Victor, where we would be at this point in our lives if the creature you created had been beautiful instead of ugly.

VICTOR. Don't mistake me for some kind of moral idiot.

HENRY. You know I don't.

VICTOR. Leave speculations of that sort to philosophy. I don't want you to mistake my full motives. I thought, at one time, a new species would bless me as its creator and source. Many excellent natures would owe their being to me.

HENRY. In one case, at least, that is true.

VICTOR. That monster is far from happy and nowhere near excellent.

HENRY. His bride may present a different story.

VICTOR. These experiments with the second creature intrigue you?

HENRY. Beyond words. You know that. Why do you ask?

VICTOR. You feel no animosity[7] toward him?

---

7. animosity, ill will; anger

HENRY. None. And none to his bride.

VICTOR. Because you're a scientist?

HENRY. Why else?

VICTOR. You wear your badge of scientific inquiry like a coat of arms. Take care it doesn't pierce.

HENRY. I leave gloomy speculation to you, Victor. You're a master.

VICTOR. I suppose. Still, I can't forget easily. When I first saw his terrible eyes looking down upon me in my sleep, I knew I had fallen from the autonomy of a supreme artificer to—

HENRY. To what?

VICTOR. The terror of a child of earth.

HENRY. He is your responsibility. Accept that.

VICTOR. I ran from my responsibility once.

HENRY. Surely you won't do it a second time. We've come too far for such thoughts. I believe him. He wants what he says he wants. He'll never harm another human being.

VICTOR. If only I could share your belief. After all, Henry, it was you who called the murderer of William—"Vicious and unfeeling. A monster."

HENRY. Much too early for intellectual exercises. Unlike you, I look at the birth of this additional Creature from a practical view.

VICTOR. What could be more impractical than creating a wife for a Creature that shouldn't exist in the first place? (HENRY *laughs, moves to desk.*)

HENRY. You'll cheer up when you see what I've brought. You don't give yourself enough credit. The safety methods in future surgery that I've learned at your side will help thousands of people. There is a long list of diseases of vital organs for which a healthy transplant would be curative. (*Henry is carefully unwrapping his bundle.*)

VICTOR. I marvel at your ability to find merit in this enterprise.

HENRY (*annoyed*). And I marvel at your perpetual vacillation. Your self-induced depressions. You love this Creature and you hate him. You have made your bargain. Stick to it.

VICTOR. What have you there?

HENRY. You'll see. Imagine the mercy in replacing a worn-out lung with another that is vital and functioning.

VICTOR. In other words, my evil shall henceforth become my good.

HENRY. Think of yourself less a modern Prometheus and more of a humanitarian.

(HENRY *crosses to* VICTOR *with the wrapping paper unfolded. We catch a glimpse of a severed human hand.*)

VICTOR (*looks, interested*). Where did you get this one?

HENRY. City morgue. None of the hands so far have been satisfactory.

VICTOR. They were satisfactory, but they weren't fresh. Both aspects are essential.

HENRY. I think this one will do nicely.

VICTOR. Let me have it. (HENRY *passes him the hand.* VICTOR *crosses back to the desk and studies it with the aid of a magnifying glass.*) Hmmmm. Maybe. I can't be positive. The hands from the graveyard all showed signs of congenital defects. We must give her hands where the skin, tendons, muscles, blood vessels, and nerves are capable of sustaining sensation and accomplishing motion. (*Closer inspection*). She couldn't have been dead for long. Good, good.

HENRY. She was young. A derelict.

VICTOR. No questions?

HENRY. The morgue keeper got his price.

VICTOR. I'll want to test for elasticity. (CREATURE *enters from laboratory.*)

HENRY. Victor.

VICTOR (turns). I warned you to stay out of sight.

CREATURE. How much longer?

VICTOR. All in good time.

CREATURE (insistent). When?

VICTOR. When I decide the time is right.

HENRY (to VICTOR). Will you name her, or will he?

VICTOR. He can call her whatever he likes.

CREATURE. You must hurry.

VICTOR. Must? Is that a word to use to your creator?

CREATURE. Remember, Frankenstein, I am your Creature. I ought to be your Adam.

VICTOR. I see you more as a fallen angel.

HENRY (to CREATURE). We are doing as you requested.

VICTOR. What more can you want?

CREATURE. Haste.

MOTHER'S VOICE. (from off—Up Center). Victor?

VICTOR. (turns to French doors). Morning comes so quickly. (To CREATURE) Stay back. Out of sight. And quiet. (CREATURE moves to laboratory door, turns.)

CREATURE (the final word). Haste. (He exits.)

HENRY. I'll make a few more tests. (He crosses for the door.)

VICTOR. Henry. (HENRY turns back. VICTOR picks up the wrapping paper with the severed hand.) Take this with you.

HENRY. Careless of me. (He takes the hand from VICTOR, exits into laboratory.)

MOTHER'S VOICE. Victor? (VICTOR doesn't want to admit her, but he has no choice. He takes out his keys, exits Up Center. A moment of silence as VICTOR unlocks the door.) Why you should prefer to sleep in your laboratory is something I'll never understand.

VICTOR'S VOICE. The cot is comfortable. (By now both have moved into the study. MOTHER moves to sofa.)

MOTHER. I don't know why I should even bother to be concerned. You ignore my advice in all things.

VICTOR. I'm preoccupied. Is that so difficult to understand?

MOTHER (sits). I thought you returned from Ingolstadt because you were exhausted.

VICTOR. I was.

MOTHER. And now?

VICTOR. I'm still exhausted, but the exhaustion is of a different sort.

MOTHER. What rubbish. (Throws up her hands) And what is that supposed to mean—"The exhaustion is of a different sort"?

VICTOR (sitting). Mother, I must ask that you leave me to my work.

MOTHER. And what is that work, Victor?

VICTOR. Why do you ask?

MOTHER. Can't I be curious? You're curious. And cautious. You always seem to fear someone will discover a secret about you.

VICTOR. Nonsense.

MOTHER. Delivery men at the door day and night with boxes of who-knows-what. Henry Clerval creeping through the garden at all hours. You think I haven't worried about it all? (Stands, moves to laboratory) The sounds, the lights. What do you hide behind this door, Victor?

VICTOR. Nothing that could possibly interest you.

MOTHER. Let me be the judge. (She goes to open the door.)

VICTOR (Springs to his feet). No!

MOTHER (turns, startled). What is it? (Looks at the door and, then, worried, backs off) There is something . . . very wrong.

Whatever it is you're up to, Victor, it frightens me. (VICTOR *tries to calm the waters.*)

VICTOR. Nothing to be concerned about. You know how I am about my work.

MOTHER (*crosses back to him*). I worry about you. You are the man of this household, Victor, but I can feel you moving farther and farther away from me. (*Sits on sofa again*) I don't speak much of your brother. I try not to. It was a terrible sorrow when your father died, but I had William and I had my Victor. And, cruelly, William was taken from me. You are the only flesh and blood I have left. (VICTOR *sits beside her.*) Take care not to break my heart. After William, I couldn't stand losing you.

VICTOR. I'm sorry for any pain that I've caused.

MOTHER. You act so unsettled. Angry. (*Then:*) Elizabeth worries, too. She's in love with you. Why do you not marry her?

VICTOR. I love Elizabeth tenderly and sincerely.

MOTHER. Then prove it. Why do you delay?

VICTOR. I've never know anyone who excited my warmest admiration and affection as Elizabeth does.

MOTHER. One might say the same thing about a piece of porcelain.

VICTOR. I mean my words.

MOTHER. I confess, my son, that I have always looked forward to your marriage. It would give me strength in my declining years.

VICTOR. Declining years? You are still a young woman.

MOTHER. You and Elizabeth were attached to one another from your earliest childhood. You studied together and always seemed suited to one another.

VICTOR. What is it you're trying to say?

MOTHER (*cautiously*). I fear, perhaps, you regard her as a sister, without any wish that she might become your wife. (*Sighs, as if a great burden had lifted from her mind*) There. That is what I fear. (*Almost lightly*) That and whatever lies behind that laboratory door. (*Concerned*) Perhaps . . . you may have met another whom you love. Perhaps you consider yourself bound in honor to marry Elizabeth and this brings you pain.

VICTOR (*stands*). I vow to you. My future hopes are entirely bound up with Elizabeth.

MOTHER (*stands, faces him*). If you feel this way about her, marry quickly. And this sullenness which appears to have taken so strong a hold of your mind will dissipate itself.

(*Door to laboratory opens and* HENRY, *coatless but wearing a white smock, thunders in. He holds the severed hand in the wrapping paper.*)

HENRY. Victor, it won't do after all. It bruises too easily. (*Sees* MOTHER, *reacts*). Oh, forgive me, Frau Frankenstein.

MOTHER. What do you have in that wrapping paper?

(HENRY *quickly folds the paper around the severed hand.* MOTHER *has seen something, but what she isn't quite certain.*)

HENRY. Oh, uh . . . an idle experiment.

MOTHER. With bruises?

HENRY. It would be of no interest. (MOTHER *can feel the tension in the air.*)

VICTOR. Then I think it would be best if we went into town together. We might "exchange" it for one more suitable.

HENRY. Yes, yes. Good idea. I'll get my coat. (*Returns to laboratory*)

MOTHER. If you're going shopping, take Elizabeth. She'd enjoy the walk.

VICTOR. This is not a shopping trip. At least, not the kind Elizabeth would appreciate.

MOTHER. If you say so, Victor. (VICTOR *smiles, kisses her on the forehead.*)

VICTOR. Trust me.

MOTHER. I try. (HENRY *returns carrying his jacket.*)

HENRY. I'm ready.

VICTOR. Then we're off. (HENRY *crosses to French doors, putting on his coat, exits. VICTOR crosses to the laboratory door and locks it with his key.*)

MOTHER. Will you be back for lunch?

VICTOR. Depends on our trip into town.

MOTHER. You're the despair of Sophie.

VICTOR. And of you, and of Elizabeth, and of Henry, and of myself. But, soon, all that will pass.

MOTHER (*sits*). I pray for it. (VICTOR *crosses to the French doors.*) Enjoy the day.

VICTOR (*turns, smiles*). Remember—trust me.

(*She blows him a kiss. He exits.* MOTHER *remains alone Onstage. Slowly, she turns her head to the laboratory, rises and cautiously moves to it. There is a determination in her maneuver. Warily, she tries the door—as if hoping* VICTOR *hadn't locked it after all. She crosses to some bell rope and pulls it. She's nervous, apprehensive.* ELIZABETH *enters Up Center.*)

ELIZABETH. I thought I'd find Victor in here.

MOTHER. He's gone into town with Henry. They had to exchange something.

ELIZABETH. What?

MOTHER. When it comes to Victor's and Henry's experiments, I think it's best not inquire too closely. Many years ago, I entered that room and was met by a small army of leaping frogs. And there were some peculiar furry things in cages. I've never been back.

ELIZABETH (*laughs*). That does sound like Victor. Even little William found him

unique . . . (*Breaks off*) I'm sorry . . . I didn't think.

MOTHER (*touched*). I understand, dear. Happens to me all the time. When I'm alone mostly. (*She fights to hold back a tear, uses her handkerchief.* SOPHIE *enters.*) Oh, Sophie, be kind enough to go into the cellar.

SOPHIE. The cellar?

MOTHER. My husband's carpentry table. You'll find an old metal box there. Bring it here.

SOPHIE. Yes, Frau Frankenstein. (*She exits.*)

MOTHER. She doesn't like to go down there. She's afraid of spiders.

ELIZABETH. I share her phobia.

MOTHER (*to business*). Elizabeth, you know my feelings toward you. When my late husband and I took you into our house, you were a beautiful child. Abandoned, unloved.

ELIZABETH. No, not unloved. You took me to your hearts.

MOTHER. And there is no doubt in my mind that you love Victor.

ELIZABETH. Nor in my mind.

MOTHER. You're good, you're gentle, you're understanding.

ELIZABETH. You make such virtues sound like liabilities.

MOTHER. I don't mean to, only I think there is a great danger in being sisterly.

ELIZABETH. You think Victor looks upon me as a sister?

MOTHER. He will always consider you such unless you give him greater cause to look upon you as a wife. You must be more aggressive with him. Unlike most women you'll have to compete with science. With a man like Victor science can be a formidable rival.

ELIZABETH. If my rival is to be science, I fear I'll always come in second best.

MOTHER. You understand him. As I do. But understanding Victor is not enough. Set your mind to your marriage and let nothing stop you. Don't wait for Victor to see his folly. Marry him. That is the only way. Quick, decisive, total victory.

ELIZABETH *(laughs).* You should have been a matchmaker.

MOTHER. That is exactly what I'm trying to be. Your marriage to my son will be my happiest moment. *(Stands)* Go after him. Run if you have to. If they suggest you're intruding, then intrude. Hurry. They couldn't have gotten far.

ELIZABETH. But Victor will want to be about his business.

MOTHER *(pushes her to the French doors).* Make his business you, Elizabeth. Do as I say.

ELIZABETH. But, I've never forced myself on Victor.

MOTHER. Exactly. Remember, quick, decisive.

ELIZABETH *(smiles brightly, turns).* Total victory!

MOTHER. Bravo! *(ELIZABETH dashes out. MOTHER waves after her. SOPHIE returns carrying a metal box.)*

SOPHIE. Is this what you wanted?

MOTHER *(crosses over, takes box).* Yes.

SOPHIE. It's awfully dusty.

MOTHER Close the door into the garden and draw the drapes. *(MOTHER blows off some dust, moves down to desk, sets the box on top.)*

SOPHIE. The delivery men were here again. There's a package in the hallway addressed to your son.

MOTHER. Who is it from?

SOPHIE. Some chemical shop in Zurich. I think it's glass tubing. *(The French door is shut, the drapes pulled.)*

MOTHER. You can go. I'll call if I need you for anything. *(SOPHIE can see FRAU FRANKENSTEIN is nervous about something.)*

SOPHIE. Are you all right, Frau Frankenstein?

MOTHER. Yes, yes. Do as I say. Go about your business, and close the hallway door on your way out.

(SOPHIE exits looking back, concerned. MOTHER has opened the box and rummages through until she finds a ring of old keys. She holds them up, looking for a particular one. When she has it, she crosses to the laboratory door. She pauses, reflecting on the merit of her action. She tries the key. It doesn't fit. She tries a second key. Same thing.) Oh, dear. *(The third key works. She pushes open the door and, apprehensive, enters. Stage remains empty.)*

CREATURE'S VOICE. No! No! Go back! Go back!

(A terrible scream from FRAU FRANKENSTEIN. And another. She stumbles back into the study, disoriented, horrified, afraid. CREATURE looms up in the doorway. MOTHER backs away from him, mesmerized.)

MOTHER. Get away from me.

CREATURE *(CREATURE comes after her, pleading, hoping, begging for understanding.)* Do not fear me. Do not scream.

MOTHER *(MOTHER backs Up Center, her breathing coming in tiny gasps, her words tortured. She clutches at her heart.)* Sophie! Let me be, please! Sophie!!! *(She drops to the floor in a spasm of pain, crying out.)*

(CREATURE drops to his knees and takes her in his arms, sees that she's been frightened to death.)

CREATURE *(sorrowful).* I meant you no harm. *(He closes her opened eyes and sits there holding the dead woman in his arms as if she were a large broken toy.)* No harm. *(Deeply felt)* Forgive . . . the Creature.

ACT TWO   SCENE 2

TIME: Two days later. Rain.

AT RISE: ERNST *stands at the closed French doors looking into the dark garden. Sound of the rain is soft but audible, on and off, during scene. The room is dark and lamps glow.* SOPHIE *enters Up Center.*

SOPHIE. The carriage is turning into the drive.

ERNST. Nasty weather for a funeral.

SOPHIE. Nasty weather for anything.

ERNST. How is it you didn't go to the cemetery, Sophie?

SOPHIE *(emotional).* I couldn't. I've only been to one funeral in my life. A school friend. I've never forgotten it. I couldn't bear the thought of going through that again with anyone. *(Looks around the room)* I'd rather remember Frau Frankenstein the way she was.

ERNST. I understand. *(Moves to place where* MOTHER *died)* You found her here?

SOPHIE. Yes. I heard her cry for me and when I came in she was sprawled out on the floor, her hand over her heart and her face the color of ash.

ERNST. I was unaware that she had a weak heart.

SOPHIE. So was everyone else. But that would be like her. She never was a complainer.

ERNST. Spine like whalebone. She held up like a Prussian during that awful business with little William.

SOPHIE *(wipes away a tear).* In front of people, yes. She cried herself to sleep many nights, though.

ERNST. Still, the attack came on suddenly, didn't it?

SOPHIE. I got the metal box with the keys from the cellar.

ERNST. Keys?

SOPHIE. She wanted them for something. I found them on the floor.

ERNST. And what became of them?

SOPHIE. I don't know. Herr Frankenstein took them, I think.

ERNST. It's been a strange time. Would you believe there are ghouls at work?

SOPHIE. Ghouls? What kind of ghouls?

ERNST. How many kinds are there? Several graves have been broken into recently.

SOPHIE. That's horrible. Stealing jewelry, I suppose.

ERNST. That I could understand. No, the ghouls didn't take any jewelry—at least in one case.

SOPHIE. What did they take?

ERNST. A foot.

SOPHIE *(feeling faint).* Oh . . .

ERNST. I imagine Victor took the death of his mother hard. *(Sees that* SOPHIE *is faint.)* Are you all right?

SOPHIE. I will be, I think.

ERNST. Didn't mean for my story to upset you.

SOPHIE *(frowns).* Herr Frankenstein's barely spoken a word in two days. And he works so hard. He and Herr Clerval.

ERNST. Work?

SOPHIE *(nods to door).* The laboratory.

ERNST. And what is their project?

SOPHIE. Oh, I wouldn't know. No one is permitted in there. It's the one room in the chateau that belongs to Herr Frankenstein alone. I don't know how they manage to get all the machinery in.

ERNST. Machinery? What kind of machinery? *(As the dialogue continues,* ERNST *crosses to the laboratory door.)*

SOPHIE. Wires and rods and electrical bulbs. Things like that. I don't know much about such matters.

ERNST *(tries door).* And you say he's secretive about what he's doing?

SOPHIE. Oh, yes. It's his way. When he gets involved in his work he's like a machine himself.

ERNST. Still, it can't do his health any good. Odd. This door is locked from the outside.

SOPHIE. He refuses to take care of himself. Eats almost nothing.

ERNST. When I last saw him I had the impression he was on the verge of a collapse. Seemed exhausted.

SOPHIE. That hasn't changed, I'm afraid.

ERNST *(moves back to* SOPHIE*).* It's been a bitter season for Victor Frankenstein. His brother murdered, his mother taken so suddenly. I was fond of Victor's mother. A fine woman.

SOPHIE *(chokes back another tear).* Yes, sir.

*(*VICTOR *and* ELIZABETH *enter Up Center.* ELIZABETH *wears black with a mourning veil.* VICTOR *has a black armband on.* HENRY *follows them into the room.)*

ELIZABETH. You here, Inspector General?

ERNST *(bows and salutes).* Allow me to extend my deepest sympathy to you, Fraulein, and to you, Victor.

VICTOR. Thank you, Ernst. *(*ELIZABETH *throws back her mourning veil.)*

SOPHIE. Should I make tea?

ELIZABETH. Please do, Sophie. We're all chilled. So dark, so cold out.

SOPHIE. I'll make some biscuits, too.

ELIZABETH. You might take the umbrellas to the kitchen and dry them. *(To* VICTOR*)* Your mother never liked to dry them out in the hallway. *(*SOPHIE *begins to sob.* ELIZABETH *moves to her.)*

SOPHIE. Poor, poor Frau Frankenstein.

ELIZABETH *(comfortingly).* Now, now, Sophie.

SOPHIE. I am sorry. Forgive me. I . . . I can't believe she's gone. I can't.

ELIZABETH. None of us can. Pull yourself together and go along to the kitchen.

SOPHIE *(exiting).* Yes, Fraulein. Tea won't be long.

ELIZABETH. She's taken it hard. Sophie was so devoted. *(Takes out handkerchief, sits on sofa)* I know what she feels. I can't get used to the idea myself. Doesn't seem possible. So unreal. I can't understand it. Alive and vibrant one moment—gone the next.

HENRY. Sudden heart failure. Not uncommon.

ELIZABETH. I leave the medical reasons to you, Henry. There's no comfort in them for me. I shall always remember her as the dearest, kindest woman I have ever known. *(*VICTOR *crosses to sofa, takes her hand.)*

VICTOR. I'll need your strength, Elizabeth.

ELIZABETH *(forces a brave smile).* And you shall have it. The memory of your mother sustains me.

VICTOR. This is most kind of you, Ernst, to stop by.

ERNST. Actually, I am here for two reasons.

HENRY. Two?

ERNST. The first you know. My sympathy.

VICTOR. Yes, yes.

ERNST. And the second—*(He breaks off.)*

VICTOR. Well?

ERNST. The girl—

VICTOR. What girl?

ERNST. Justine.

HENRY. You don't mean the Gypsy girl?

ERNST. I do.

VICTOR. What about her?

ERNST. Ordinarily, I'd deny her request, but since we're transporting her to prison today and the wagon had to come this way, I thought—

HENRY *(infuriated).* You thought what?

ERNST. She begs to speak with you, Victor. I agreed. Her hanging is scheduled within the week. A last request you might say.

VICTOR. You want me to see her—in here?

HENRY. That's outrageous.

ERNST. You could come to the prison if you prefer. However, it's a forbidding place. I thought this would be more convenient.

HENRY *(still annoyed).* Perhaps Victor does not wish to have the girl in his home. Or to visit her in prison. You come here because of her request on this day of all days?

ERNST. If I've offended, forgive me. I shall, of course, continue the journey without further interruption.

VICTOR. Why does she want to see me?

ERNST. I'm not sure, but she's asked for this meeting many times.

VICTOR. I'll see her.

HENRY *(alarmed).* Victor.

ELIZABETH. Do you think that's wise?

HENRY. I forbid it. I absolutely forbid it.

VICTOR *(insistent).* I will see the girl.

ERNST. She's an interesting case.

HENRY. Your most interesting, I imagine.

ERNST. Not really. There's been a rash of grave robbery lately.

ELIZABETH *(upset).* Oh.

ERNST. I'm afraid I've done it again. I'm not what you'd call a sensitive man.

HENRY. Do you expect an argument on that point?

ERNST *(anxious to retreat).* The wagon is on the side road. I'll bring her myself. *(At the French doors)* May I go through the garden?

VICTOR *(lost in his thoughts).* What?

ERNST. The garden. Would that be all right?

VICTOR. Certainly. *(ERNST exits. HENRY moves towards VICTOR and ELIZABETH.)*

HENRY. The Inspector General is a lout.

ELIZABETH. He means well.

HENRY. There is absolutely no excuse to bring her here.

VICTOR. He's only trying to do his duty.

HENRY. Duty!

ELIZABETH. Henry, what's come over you?

HENRY *(quiets down).* I'm upset. Forgive my outburst.

ELIZABETH. Shouting won't help any of us.

HENRY. I don't think it's wise to see this girl.

VICTOR. I want to see her.

ELIZABETH *(stands).* I'll ask that you excuse me, Victor.

VICTOR *(walks with her to Up Center).* You'd better lie down. Rest.

ELIZABETH. I'll try. *(Emotionally drained, she exits.)*

HENRY. It's madness for you to see the girl.

VICTOR. Poor thing.

HENRY. She's a bad sort. Ernst said so himself.

VICTOR. I was referring to Elizabeth. I know her so well. When no one is looking she'll cry. Like my mother. That's why she's gone to her room.

HENRY. She's gone to her room to avoid seeing this Justine.

VICTOR. Did you notice Elizabeth at the graveside? Standing straight. Strong. As if she were telling my dear mother that she was here to carry on and to rest easy.

HENRY. First time I've ever heard you wax sentimental.

VICTOR. First time I've ever felt sentimental.

HENRY. You've taken it all remarkably well.

VICTOR (*cynical*). Have I?

HENRY. I admire you for it.

VICTOR. Do you think because I haven't cried that I've felt nothing?

HENRY. I didn't mean to imply that.

VICTOR. My unseen tears are angry feelings. (*Points to lab door*) Birth, life, death—stitched together without seam. If that "thing" had never been born, my mother would be with us now.

HENRY. Don't start that again.

VICTOR. Who is responsible? I am, Henry. I am.

HENRY. What ever could have possessed her to go into the laboratory?

VICTOR. Curiosity, a desire to discover. We, of all people, should understand that. Can she ever forgive me?

HENRY. I'm sure she does.

VICTOR. And the Creature, the monster, the devil—do you know what he thinks of? My pain? No. He thinks only of his bride. He tells me, "The sooner she is ready, the sooner I am out of your life. Work faster and avoid future misfortune."

HENRY. Perhaps we should heed those words.

VICTOR. He has no more feeling for my mother's death than I would have for a dying flea. He is a thing of stone.

HENRY. He's right. The sooner we get to work, the sooner all this is ended.

VICTOR. I wonder at you, Henry. More and more. From your honest scientific inquiry has come a mirror image of myself. Do you not fear him now?

HENRY (*doesn't want to answer*). I . . . I . . .

VICTOR. You do fear him. (ERNST *returns with* JUSTINE. *She's young, pretty, forceful. She wears a colorful Romany or Gypsy costume.*)

ERNST (*holding her tightly by the arm*). No trouble or tricks. Say what you have to say and be quick.

(JUSTINE *pulls away from* ERNST *and moves to* HENRY.)

JUSTINE. I was afraid you wouldn't see me. You must believe me, Herr Frankenstein. No one else will. That is why I come here. I wanted to speak to your mother, but they tell me she, too, is dead. For that, I am sorry and sorry again.

HENRY. I am not Herr Frankenstein. (*Nods*) That is he. (*She turns to* VICTOR.)

JUSTINE. No one will believe my story.

VICTOR. And if I did?

JUSTINE. Do not make fun of me, sir.

VICTOR. I do not, I assure you.

JUSTINE. There was a man. A terrible man. With great stitches across his face. I screamed when I saw him, and he held out the cross. It was as if he wanted to give me something to stop my screaming.

ERNST (*scoffs*). And, of course, he said nothing.

JUSTINE. No, nothing. Once I had the cross in my hand, he turned and ran into the woods.

ERNST. Naturally, it was your impulse to strike camp, come into the city, and attempt to sell the gold cross.

VICTOR. Let her tell it in her own words, Inspector General. (ERNST *frowns.*)

JUSTINE. I wanted no part of that cross.

HENRY. You could have thrown it away.

ERNST. No profit in that. (*Sees* VICTOR's *irritation*) Sorry.

VICTOR. You're certain he said nothing to you?

JUSTINE. I am, sir.

HENRY. He made no attempt to harm you, that's correct, isn't it?

JUSTINE (*brightens*). Then you do believe me?

HENRY. I . . . I . . .

ERNST. Her sort knows how to play on one's emotions, Herr Clerval. Come along, you've had your visit.

VICTOR. Wait. *(Concerned)* When will you be hanged?

JUSTINE. I have only a few days more of life. There is no hope for me. The insides of jails and prisons are familiar to me, sir. I've known them ever since I can remember. I was born in a prison. My mother died in one.

ERNST. Bad blood.

JUSTINE *(flashes anger)*. My blood is as good as yours and better than most.

ERNST. Mind your tongue.

JUSTINE *(takes VICTOR's hand)*. I have come here, sir, knowing that my life is to be a short one. But wicked as some may think I am, and I won't deny I've done things I'm ashamed of, I have some decency. Before my maker in heaven and before you, Victor Frankenstein, I swear I am innocent. Look into my face, into my eyes, into my soul and tell me if what you see is murder? *(VICTOR cups her face in his hands.)*

VICTOR. Into your face . . . into your eyes . . . into your soul . . . what do I see? Yes, I see murder! *(Louder)* Murder! *(Louder still)* Murder!

HENRY *(to ERNST)*. Get her out of here.

JUSTINE *(pulling at VICTOR)*. I swear it! It's the truth! I didn't kill anyone! You must believe me! Someone must believe me! Have pity! Pity! *(ERNST pulls her toward the French doors.)*

ERNST. What I get for being soft-hearted. Come along. Leave these gentleman to their business.

JUSTINE *(as ERNST drags her off)*. I am innocent!

(VICTOR is shaken. He slaps his hands to his ears to block out her cries. HENRY crosses to the decanter, pours a glass, and returns to VICTOR who gulps down the liquid.)

HENRY. Are you all right?

VICTOR. You still don't see the ugliness of it? The cruel shame? Now that girl will hang because of the Creature.

HENRY. Circumstances.

VICTOR. She cried "pity" asking for life. So did he. His word has come back to haunt me.

HENRY *(shift in mood)*. My notes are almost complete. Let's move quickly, without thinking, pushed on by the knowledge some good will come of all this.

VICTOR. You'll let him go? Escape?

HENRY. I trust his word. I have no reason to doubt it.

VICTOR. Knowing him to be destructive and wrathful?

HENRY. Only because man has made him so. Let them go and find whatever Eden will have them.

VICTOR *(low, flat)*. No.

HENRY. What?

VICTOR. I said—no.

HENRY. What do you mean?

VICTOR. You haven't lived with him as I have. Sensing his moods, his unspoken questions. Knowing, always knowing, that if he were ever to gain an upper hand, he wouldn't hesitate to use it.

(Door to laboratory opens. VICTOR and HENRY turn. A second or two passes and the CREATURE enters.)

Listening at the door again?

CREATURE. Yes.

VICTOR. Did you hear the girl?

CREATURE. I remember her.

VICTOR. Now another will die because of you.

CREATURE. You had only to point to your laboratory and the girl would have gone free. I remained quiet. But so did you.

HENRY. Victor, when we have finished with our task we'll see what can be done about the girl.

VICTOR. What can be done?

HENRY. I don't know, but we'll think of something.

VICTOR. So easy. Simple. "We'll think of something." And if we don't?

HENRY. I suggest we continue our work.

VICTOR. I no longer have the strength. I would advise you to seek happiness in tranquillity, Henry. Avoid ambition.

HENRY. You have no right to say that, Victor. Because you have been blasted in your hopes, is no reason to assume another may not succeed.

VICTOR. I will not continue.

CREATURE (angry). I can make you so wretched that the light of day will be hateful to you.

VICTOR. You have already succeeded in that.

CREATURE. You are my creator, but I am your master.

VICTOR. Never.

CREATURE. Return to the laboratory.

VICTOR. No.

CREATURE. Continue the work.

VICTOR. I refuse.

CREATURE (menacingly). You will not deny me my bride.

VICTOR. There, Henry. Did you hear it? The tone of those words. Low, threatening, dangerous. Your "victim" can be your victimizer very quickly. Oh, he's sly, and clever, and quick. He can argue and stroke and persuade, but if the winds turn against him how quickly the devil in the monster shines out.

CREATURE. Keep your vow. Create for me a bride. (VICTOR *shakes his head. Negative.*) Shall each man find a wife for his bosom, and each beast have his mate, and I be alone? (*His fury intensifies.*) Are you to be happy while I grovel in despair?

VICTOR. How can I be happy, how can I be content when all the horror of my misguided zeal stands before me—threatening and evil?

HENRY. Victor, calm down. (*To* CREATURE) Both of you.

CREATURE (*furious*). Silence. (*To* VICTOR) You can blast my other passions, but take care. Revenge will remain.

VICTOR. So be it! (*With that,* VICTOR *darts across the room to the laboratory door, opens it, disappears inside, bolting the door behind him.*)

HENRY (*runs to the door*). Victor, Victor!

CREATURE. I will kill you, Frankenstein!

HENRY (*pounding at the door*). Victor, no! No! Victor, Victor!

(*Sound of mechanical apparatus. Flashes of light from laboratory. The* CREATURE *moves to the door.*)

CREATURE. I will kill!

(*Quickly,* HENRY *turns, hoping to placate the* CREATURE. *The flashing lights and the noise of the machinery grows louder and louder.*)

HENRY. Let me talk to him, let me persuade him.

CREATURE. Kill him!

HENRY. I beg of you. Listen to me! (HENRY *attempts to push the* CREATURE *back.*) Listen!

CREATURE. Kill! (*With that the* CREATURE *shoots out his arms and throttles* HENRY *by the neck.* HENRY *gags, making horrible choking sounds. The* CREATURE *smashes his fist into the back of* HENRY's *neck and he crumples to the floor in a dying gasp. Suddenly there is a terrific roar from behind the laboratory door* and the stage lighting flashes up and down wildly. The CREATURE looks all around bewildered, stunned, realizing that the sound and lights indicate that his bride is forever doomed. The CREATURE lifts his arms to the insane flickers of light as the noise continues to grow in volume. His cry is painful, awful in its pathetic appeal.) Wife . . . companion . . . friend . . . No-o-o-o-o-o . . . (His cry fades like an echo. The CREATURE buries his face in his hands and drops to his knees. The lighting returns to normal. A few seconds pass and we realize the CREATURE is sobbing. Laboratory door opens and VICTOR steps out.)*

VICTOR. Finished . . . ended.

CREATURE *(Slowly, the CREATURE lowers his hands. There is a look of almost unbelievable hatred and rage on his face.)* For this, you will pay even more.

VICTOR. Do not poison the air with your malice.

CREATURE *(low, growling).* You will pay.

VICTOR Leave me. *(CREATURE stands, moves to French doors. VICTOR sees the prostrate form of HENRY.)* Henry . . . *(Crosses to the body, kneels beside it. He turns HENRY over in his arms, reacts.)* Dead . . . Henry, too . . . dead . . .

CREATURE. I go, Frankenstein, but remember—I shall be with you on your wedding night. *(Sound of rain increases. The CREATURE steps into the windswept garden.)*

ACT ONE   SCENE 3

AT RISE: Sound of wind. Scene begins as a continuation of the play's opening with VICTOR and ELIZABETH, in her wedding gown, seated on the sofa. VICTOR is finishing his strange story.

VICTOR *(recalling CREATURE's prophecy).* "I shall be with you on your wedding night." *(Repeats)* "On your wedding night."

ELIZABETH *(ELIZABETH stands, moves Center.)* If only you had confided in me earlier.

VICTOR. I was afraid.

ELIZABETH. Of what I would think?

VICTOR. And of what you would say. A thousand other fears, too. Most of all—that you would judge me mad.

ELIZABETH. What torture it must have been for you.

VICTOR. You can never know.

ELIZABETH. Poor darling.

VICTOR. Don't waste sympathy on me. If I had been content to search for the philosopher's stone, or the elixir of life, our wedding wouldn't be like this.

ELIZABETH. He hates you so much that he would kill you on this night of all nights?

VICTOR. What better night to destroy his maker? I denied him his bride and, now, he will deny me my life.

ELIZABETH. It will never come to pass.

VICTOR. I wish I could believe that.

ELIZABETH. You must. I believe it and so must you.

VICTOR. Oh, Elizabeth, I am truly blessed. If only this horrid vision of his return could be wiped away.

ELIZABETH. Do you recall "The Ancient Mariner"?

VICTOR. Coleridge? We read it one summer.

ELIZABETH. Yes. *(Recites)*
"Like one who, on a lonely road,
  Doth walk in fear and dread,
    And, having once turned round, walks on,
    And turns no more his head."

VICTOR.
"Because he knows a frightful fiend
  Doth close behind him tread."

(He stands, takes ELIZABETH in his arms.)

Ernst has the chateau surrounded.

ELIZABETH. Then you're safe.

VICTOR. Perhaps.

ELIZABETH. They'll see him if he comes close to the house.

VICTOR. I hope so.

ELIZABETH. Victor, you must always trust me. Never keep anything from me.

VICTOR. If I live through this night.

ELIZABETH (*covers his mouth with her hand*). Never, never say that again.

VICTOR. Do you realize that if he does kill me, the Creature will have succeeded in destroying the House of Frankenstein? (ERNST *has entered through the garden in time to overhear this remark.*)

ERNST. I assure you, Victor, the Creature will not elude my net. I have a dozen men staked around the chateau with shotguns that would bring down a charging rhinoceros.

VICTOR. You do not know him as I do. He's brilliant in his strategies.

ERNST. I flatter myself that I, too, have considerable skills in that direction.

ELIZABETH. There is no danger, then?

ERNST. The minute the Creature is sighted an alarm will go up. After that, it is merely a matter of seconds before I bring the beast to his knees.

ELIZABETH. Perhaps he won't show up.

ERNST. We've considered that. For his sake it would be better if he didn't. From my point of view I would not wish it. It will give me considerable pleasure to either destroy him, or chain him to the wall of a madhouse or an asylum for the criminally insane.

VICTOR. And the Gypsy girl?

ERNST. We haven't released her yet. No telling what stories she'd carry. No need to unduly alarm the citizenry.

VICTOR. But she will go free?

ERNST. All in good time. (SOPHIE *enters Up Center.*)

ELIZABETH. You see, Victor, you have nothing to fear.

ERNST. Stay in the house. Don't venture outside under any circumstances. I must insist on that.

VICTOR. You have our word. (ERNST *exits Up Center.*)

SOPHIE. Can I get you anything, Frau Frankenstein?

ELIZABETH. "Frau" Frankenstein. How odd that sounds. My married name. (*Lighter mood*) No, Sophie, thank you. Nothing. Oh, draw the drapes. It's so chilly in here.

SOPHIE. Would you like a fire?

ELIZABETH. No. The drapes will be fine.

(SOPHIE *sets about the business of pulling shut the drapes Up Center. When this is done she draws the drapes at the French doors, closing them, too. Dialogue continues through this business.*)

VICTOR. I was thinking something quite terrible. Yet, it may have ended for the better.

ELIZABETH. You're thinking of Henry.

VICTOR. Yes. I don't think anything but death would have stopped his quest. I infected him as surely as if I had injected him with a strange and forbidden venom. Once he tasted what I had savored his doom was sealed. Odd that I have survived and he has not.

ELIZABETH. I shan't listen to any more of this. (*Strong, resolute*) We will get through the night. And tomorrow we will make plans for travel. Greece would be lovely this time of the year. Maybe Italy.

VICTOR. There are a few things I must do.

ELIZABETH. When?

VICTOR. Now. In the laboratory.

ELIZABETH (*stunned*). You can't be serious.

VICTOR. I have many things to destroy. The machinery, the lighting panels, the generator. (*Crosses to his desk and picks up ledgers, papers, etc. When* SOPHIE *is through, she waits by the French doors.*) And these. Most of all these. The ledgers, the notebooks.

ELIZABETH. Must you do it now?

VICTOR. You needn't be afraid. Come with me to the laboratory.

ELIZABETH (*recoils*). No . . . I never want to go in there. I think I shall seal the room forever. Wall it up or tear it out.

VICTOR. Sophie.

SOPHIE. Yes, sir.

VICTOR. Go into the garden and ask one of the men to stay here with my wife.

SOPHIE. You want me to go out there?

ELIZABETH. I'll be quite all right.

VICTOR. Sophie, do as I ask.

SOPHIE. Yes, sir. (*Terrified, she turns and exits through the drapes at the French doors and into the garden.*)

VICTOR (*crosses for the laboratory, ledgers, etc., in his arms*). When these go up in flames I will have made some amends for my sins.

ELIZABETH. Then it should be a private act. Do it quickly, Victor. Hurry back to me. (VICTOR *looks at her lovingly, exits into the laboratory.* ELIZABETH *is left Onstage. Suddenly, it dawns on her that being alone on such a night has slight compensation. She looks about nervously. Sound of wind whips up. The curtains at the French doors rustle.*)

ELIZABETH. Sophie? (*She turns. Nothing. She talks to herself.*) Must get hold of myself. There is nothing to fear. Nothing. (*From the laboratory comes the sound of the machinery, as if* VICTOR *were, once again, up to something questionable.* ELIZABETH *reacts.*) Victor? (*She crosses to the laboratory door and rattles it. It's locked.*) Victor? (*Now comes the unmistakable sound of someone moving behinds the*

drapes *Up Center. The drapes rustle.* ELIZABETH *sees the movement.*) Who's there? (*Nothing. As the sound of the machinery hums from behind the door, the lighting in the shadowy room dims up and then down, up and down.*) Who's there? Who is it? Ernst? (*Mesmerized,* ELIZABETH *moves toward the drapes Up Center. Sound of the laboratory business continues.* ELIZABETH *walks like a somnambulist.[8] Closer and closer to the drapes. Her breathing is heavy, audible. Her hand reaches for the drapery and just as she's about to pull the sections apart—*SOPHIE *darts in via the French doors.*)

SOPHIE (*fast*). Frau Frankenstein. (*Startled,* ELIZABETH *gives a startled half-muted scream.*)

ELIZABETH. Sophie . . .

SOPHIE. The policeman will be here in a moment. I'll go and show him the way. (*With that,* SOPHIE *turns and hurries out.* ELIZABETH *is still frightened, barely able to get out her words.*)

ELIZABETH. Sophie . . . no, wait . . . Sophie . . . (ELIZABETH *turns, moves for the laboratory, set on getting* VICTOR *to open the door.*) Victor, Victor! (*Up Center draperies are flung apart revealing the* CREATURE. *With his wild hateful stare, and his arms spread wide he is a horrifying figure, made all the more so by the dimming up and down of the room's lighting and the constant hum of the laboratory apparatus.* ELIZABETH *turns, sees him in one fast movement, screams.*)

CREATURE. There is a better way to make Victor Frankenstein suffer. (*Points*) You, you the bride of my maker, shall die in his place!

ELIZABETH. Victor, Victor! (ELIZABETH *runs for the laboratory door. The machinery and the lights are still performing. She bangs on the*

---

8. somnambulist, sleepwalker

door.) Victor, he's here! He's here. (The CREATURE *advances and* ELIZABETH *moves into the center of the room.*)

CREATURE. I have never left this house. I have lived under the eaves of the attic . . . waiting . . . waiting. I shall be with you on your wedding night.

ELIZABETH. Please . . . spare us.

CREATURE. Even your cries for mercy give me pleasure, for I think of the words of my bride that I shall never hear. You must die and Frankenstein must suffer! (*He reaches out and grabs her by the throat, his back to the laboratory door.*)

ELIZABETH (*struggling*). No, no—Victor, Victor!!!

CREATURE. Die, die, die! (*Suddenly, the door to the laboratory flings open and* VICTOR *enters with a revolver. He fires. Once . . . twice . . . three times. Each time the hot lead supposedly tears into the* CREATURE *he recoils as if taking the impact. He lets go of* ELIZABETH *who, choking, her hand at her throat, struggles to the Upstage chair. The* CREATURE *makes his way to the drapes at the French doors, clutching his side. He turns once to look at* VICTOR *and holds one hand out as if pleading. Sorrowfully.*) Frankenstein . . . (VICTOR *fires again. The* CREATURE *bares his teeth viciously, stumbles into the garden.* VICTOR *moves quickly to* ELIZABETH.)

VICTOR. It was you he was going to destroy. He would let me live knowing what my life would be like. (*Close to her*) Elizabeth, forgive me.

(*By now, the stage lighting is back to normal.*)

ELIZABETH (*gasping for breath*). I'm . . . all right . . . all right . . .

(VICTOR *quickly moves to the decanter and pours her a glass.*)

VICTOR. His mind is as keen and bright and crafty as ever. I should have guessed what he planned.

ELIZABETH. It's over . . .

(VICTOR *moves to her with the glass.*)

VICTOR. Here, drink this.

(*From Offstage Left we hear the distant sounds of gunfire.* VICTOR *and* ELIZABETH *exchange a worried look. The brandy.*)

Finish it. (ELIZABETH *empties the glass.*) More? (*She shakes her head no.*)

SOPHIE (SOPHIE *runs in through the French doors.*) They are after him!

VICTOR. Did you see him?

SOPHIE. Only as he ran past the police. Who was he? No one will tell me a thing.

VICTOR. Which path did he take?

SOPHIE. He ran toward the water. The lake.

VICTOR. Get some smelling salts.

SOPHIE. I don't need them.

VICTOR (*irritated*). Not for you. For my wife.

SOPHIE. Yes, sir. Right away. (SOPHIE *exits Up Center.* ELIZABETH *takes* VICTOR'*s hand.*)

VICTOR. Why didn't you call out?

ELIZABETH. I did. Over and over. But the laboratory door was bolted and there was so much noise from the machinery.

VICTOR. You'll never hear that sound in this house again. I have destroyed my records, the apparatus, all that remains is the memory.

(ERNST *enters via the French doors.* ELIZABETH *and* VICTOR *stand together, close.*)

Well?

ERNST. He ran into the lake.

VICTOR. He's dead?

ERNST. Nothing could have survived my fusillade.[9]

---

9. fusillade, burst of gunfire

VICTOR. But did you see him fall, or go beneath the water?

ERNST. He was stumbling, mortally wounded. My men will drag the lake for his body. You may rest easy, Victor. Elizabeth, the Creature is no more. If you'll excuse me, I'll return to my men. *(He salutes, bows professionally in the military manner, exits.)*

(VICTOR moves to the French doors, pulls aside the drapes, peers out. ELIZABETH moves Up Center.)

VICTOR. The work of my hands is finished. I have destroyed what I have created. Full circle.

ELIZABETH. Come along.

VICTOR. I could almost feel compassion for him.

ELIZABETH. I do feel it.

VICTOR. You, too?

ELIZABETH. It's ended, Victor. Forever.

VICTOR *(Still looking toward the lake. Thoughtfully—)* I wonder.

(He turns, sees ELIZABETH smiling gently. He smiles in return, moves toward her. They exit Up Center. Curtain.)

END OF PLAY

Frankenstein

Play Analysis

1. Was there any point in the play where you felt Victor Frankenstein could have turned events around and headed down a more positive path? Explain.

2. In the Greek myth, Prometheus brings fire to help maintain human life. Zeus punishes Prometheus by chaining him to a rock, where an eagle feeds upon him. What do you think Shelley's original subtitle, *The Modern Prometheus*, signified?

3. The Creature tells Victor that he is malicious because he is miserable. Do you think there is truth in that statement? Explain.

4. In the original novel, Victor's mother dies of scarlet fever when he is just a teenager. What reasons might Tim Kelly have had for giving her such an important role in the play?

5. **Thematic Connection: Who Am I?** The Creature says to Victor, "Remember this—my agony is greater than yours." Do you agree? Explain.

Literary Skill: Critiquing the Adaptation

In Mary Shelley's novel the entire story of Frankenstein, his family and friends, and the Creature he pieces together, is told in the form of letters from Robert Walton to his sister Margaret. While exploring in the North Pole, Walton sees the Creature in the distance. Shortly thereafter, he rescues Victor from certain death. Victor then tells his tale to Walton, including a section in which the voice of the Creature takes over to tell the story from his perspective. By the end of the novel, Justine has been executed, Henry and Elizabeth are dead, and Victor has just died. The final monologue of the novel belongs to the Creature, who says:

> "I shall die, and what I now feel be no longer felt. Soon these burning miseries will be extinct. I shall ascend my funeral pile triumphantly, and exult in the agony of the torturing flames. The light of that conflagration will fade away; my ashes will be swept into the sea by the winds. My spirit will sleep in peace; or if it thinks, it will not surely think thus. Farewell."

Write a short critique of the events of the play, including an analysis of why you think Kelly changed the ending.

Performance Element: Costumes and Makeup

Frankenstein's Creature is described in the play as a "large man stitched together." How would you make up and costume the actor who is to play the Creature? Write a short list of his attributes, and then draw a picture of the fully made-up and costumed character.

Stand and Deliver

inspired by the life of Jaime Escalante
written by Ramón Menéndez and Tom Musca
adapted for the stage by Robert Bella

Creating Context:
Conflict Resolution

Conflict is a part of life. We can't always avoid disagreements with parents and friends, struggles with teachers, or the battle between the sexes—nor would we want to. Life without conflict would be rather dull. But when conflict shoves us toward violence, we have to know what to do. Learning how to avoid violence and resolve conflicts can be learned. It takes the right tools and a bit of practice. By understanding what causes conflict and using resolution strategies, students can help their schools become safe places to learn and have fun. Many conflict resolution programs offer the following advice:

- Speak to others using polite language and good manners. Words such as "Please," "Thank you," Excuse me," and "I'm sorry" help gain others' respect and trust and set everyone at ease.
- Use active listening techniques to really hear what others are saying. Rephrase what you hear and look into the eyes of the speaker to encourage further communication.
- Focus on the problem rather than the person. Do not lay blame. This helps you diffuse the tension and solve the problem at hand.
- Build power "with" others, not "over" them. Relax and open your mind to other viewpoints.
- Be honest about your part in any conflict.
- Try to share strategies to reach mutually agreeable solutions.
- Come up with a few options you can choose together.

    In the play *Stand and Deliver*, high school mathematics teacher Jaime Escalante must deal with various forms of conflict—from students, fellow teachers, and others. As you read, note how he deals with conflict.

As a Reader: Interpreting Conflict

Conflict is not only one of the moving forces in drama, it is a daily condition of life for Jaime Escalante. One major conflict involves Escalante's assessment of what is best for his students as opposed to that of his department chairperson.

Look at the two excerpts below. Compare Escalante's own words, at the left, to the dialogue at the right, written by Robert Bella. Does the character on the stage seem to you to capture the essence of the man being interviewed?

from Page · · · · · · to Stage

"We have great teachers in America, teachers who can really motivate and do the job. What we have to emphasize is the motivation of the students to do the work, to work together and to share ideas. And we must teach in a classroom what these kids are going to be using in real life.... I'm just a coach. I do ask them to have determination and to believe in themselves, to be disciplined and to put in hard work—and that's the only way they'll succeed....Respect yourself and respect the integrity of others as well."

from *Interview with Jaime Escalante* by Carole Novak

ESCALANTE. No. Here. I want to teach calculus to this class.

MOLINA (*chuckling*). Calculus? Oh, boy, that's a jump.

ORTEGA. That's ridiculous. They haven't had trig or math analysis.

ESCALANTE. They can take them both during the summer.

ORTEA. You expect our best students to go to summer school?

ESCALANTE. From seven to 12...

ORTEGA. Out of the question.

MOLINA. Our summer classrooms are reserved for remedial courses.

ESCALANTE.. Mr. Molina, if you want to turn this school around you're gonna have to start from the top. You have to motivate them every minute, every day, even the best students.

ORTEGA. Our kids can't handle calculus. We don't even have the books.

ESCALANTE. Books are not the problem. I'll teach Bolivian-style. Students copy from the board. Step by step. Inch by inch....

from *Stand and Deliver* adapted by Robert Bella

As a Director: Working with Conflict

As you read *Stand and Deliver*, be aware of the various conflicts in the play—between teacher and administrators, between students and teachers, and between the students and the A.P. examining board, among others. Think about how you would describe the central conflict—the major struggle between opposing forces. As the director, how would you convey to the actors playing Escalante, Ortega, and Molina creative ways to approach their parts in this struggle?

Stand and Deliver

Time
The 1980s

The Characters

THE FACULTY
JAIME ESCALANTE   Teacher, one of a kind

PRINCIPAL MOLINA   Tough guy with a heart

RAQUEL ORTEGA   Self-assured teacher

THE STUDENTS
JAVIER PERALES   Slim, middle-class boy

TITO GUITANO   New-wave math student/musician

CLAUDIA CAMEJO   Moody fashion plate

FRANCISCO "PANCHO" GARCIA   A car freak

LUPE ESCOBAR   Outspoken flirt

ANA DELGADO   A flower ready to bloom

RAFAELA FUENTES   Recent immigrant from Guatemala

ANGEL GUERRA   Member of the Maravilla Gang

THE COMMUNITY
CHUCO   Macho leader of the Maravilla Gang

ARMANDO   The janitor

HECTOR DELGADO   Ana's father

DR. RAMIREZ   A yuppie Latino ETS official

DR. PEARSON   An African American ETS official

and...
the SECRETARY, SECURITY GUARDS, POLICE OFFICER, VARIOUS STUDENTS, MARAVILLA GANG, TOUGH BOY, PREGNANT GIRL, ESLs, etc.

Place
Garfield High School, East Los Angeles

ACT ONE JUNIOR YEAR

—— SCENE ONE ——

AT RISE: *A police siren wails, closer and closer, flashing lights bouncing off the walls of the theatre. The sirens fade out as the lights onstage shift to early morning. Students start filing into the space. While there is excitement in the air, it's muffled by the inertia of barrio life. These are inner-city kids, predominantly Latino; many are poor. The students range in types, a mixed bag of jocks, heavy metal aficionados, ROTCs, new-wave punkettes, cholos (gang members), a few straight arrows, and ESL (English as a Second Language) students. Security guards scan students with metal detectors as they enter the space. Some students are smoking, some hang out by their lockers or the pay phone, others cross on their way to classes. Off in a corner, a tough boy is selling drugs. In another corner, some girls are gathered around a pregnant girl, feeling her stomach and gossiping.* JAVIER PERALES *enters the classroom. The desks are arranged haphazardly. He slides one toward the front and sits in it. He opens a copy of a science-fiction novel and reads intently. A few students enter the classroom. One grabs* JAVIER's *book and throws it in the trash.* JAVIER *gets up and retrieves it. General mayhem. A Latino rap beat comes from the boombox of a just-entering* TITO GUITANO. TITO *wears a jeans jacket with the image of Christ painted on the back. He coolly enters the classroom and sits, still lightly bopping his head to the music. Enter* JAIME ESCALANTE. *There's a slight stoop to his rolling walk but there is nothing weak about him. He is met by one of the security guards.*

SECURITY GUARD. Are you a teacher?

ESCALANTE. Yes, I am. I'm new.

SECURITY GUARD. Gotta see an ID.
(*Bewildered,* ESCALANTE *gets his driver's*

license *out and gives it to the* GUARD. *The* GUARD *refers to a clipboard.*) You're not on my list. (*Into radio*) Uh, Main Office, got a guy here says he's a teacher … "Jaymee" Escalante …

ESCALANTE (*leans toward the walkie-talkie, saying his name with the correct Hispanic pronunciation*). Jaime Escalante. I am here to teach computer science.

SECURITY GUARD. No computers here. (*Chuckling*) Sure you're at the right school?

(*Enter* RAQUEL ORTEGA *with a Los Angeles* POLICE OFFICER. *Abrupt and charming at the same time, she is used to dealing with problems in a no-nonsense way.*)

POLICE OFFICER. Anything else missing?

ORTEGA. Just the key to the ladies' room. (ORTEGA *spots* ESCALANTE *and comes to his rescue.*) Mr. Escalante, glad you made it! Raquel Ortega, chairwoman of the math department. (*To* SECURITY GUARD) He's on the faculty.

POLICE OFFICER. And where exactly was the fecal material found?

ORTEGA. In my office. You'll know when you're near it. (*The* POLICE OFFICER *makes a note.* ORTEGA *starts leading* ESCALANTE *off.*)

ESCALANTE. The computers? They weren't stolen, were they?

ORTEGA. I'm sorry, Mr. Escalante. We were supposed to get computers last year and the year before and there's no funding again for them this year. Let me show you to your classroom.

ESCALANTE. But, you don't understand. I was supposed to teach computers.

ORTEGA. Welcome to Garfield, Mr. Escalante. (*They exit. A bell rings. The behavior of the kids in the classroom grows more chaotic with the sounding of the bell.* CLAUDIA CAMEJO *crosses near* TITO's *desk.*)

TITO. So, where were you last night?

CLAUDIA. What do mean, where was I?

TITO. I was waiting.

CLAUDIA. Oh, you were waiting, huh?

TITO. Yeah, and I was dreaming about you.

CLAUDIA. Good. Keep dreaming. (CLAUDIA *gives him a playful slap and wanders off.*)

(*Enter* ESCALANTE. *His entrance has absolutely no effect on the kids. If anything, they become more rowdy.* PANCHO GARCIA *slides over to* ESCALANTE *and imitates every gesture the teacher makes.*)

PANCHO. You our new teacher, man? Hey, you the teacher?

ESCALANTE. Will everyone please try to find a seat?…

PANCHO. Hey, what are we gonna do today?

ESCALANTE. Please take a seat.

PANCHO. Sure, no problem, "Teacher Man." (*The students heckle* ESCALANTE's *efforts.*)

ESCALANTE. For those of you who cannot find a seat, please stand against the wall. (*There are about 25 students and only 15 desks.* TITO *grabs a passing* CLAUDIA *and sits her on his lap.*)

TITO. Hey, let's put our desks in a circle and discuss our feelings, huh?

ESCALANTE (*overlapping*). Okay, all right. One body to a desk.

CLAUDIA. Could we talk about sex?

ESCALANTE. If we talk about sex, I have to give sex for homework. (*The students react with catcalls, laughs, and whistling.* CLAUDIA *gets off* TITO's *lap.*)

CLAUDIA. You know, I could get you fired for saying that.

ESCALANTE (*overlapping*). Stand back everyone, please … Move back.

ESL STUDENT #1. *Que dijo?*

ESL STUDENT #2. *No sé.*

ESCALANTE (*to ESL students*). *Entienden inglés?*

PANCHO. Sometimes … (*Some students laugh.* ANA DELGADO *tries to defend the ESLs.*)

ANA. Come on, you guys … (*More laughter*)

ESCALANTE. *Los que no entienden inglés, por favor levanten la mano.* (*More hooting from the students and most raise their hands in a pretense of ignorance.*) Please move forward if you do not speak English. *Los que no hablan inglés, por favor, pasen al frente.* Please, for all the first row, please stand up.

ANA (*relinquishes her seat, turns to* JAVIER). Javier.

JAVIER. No. (JAVIER, *in his front row seat, does not move. Several* ESL STUDENTS *move forward and sit in the front row.*)

ESCALANTE (*to* JAVIER). What's the problem?

JAVIER. I was the first one here.

ESCALANTE. I'll find you another seat, okay, Johnny?

JAVIER. My name's not Johnny. (ESCALANTE *erases graffiti in order to write his name on the board.*)

ESCALANTE. Okay, okay, I make a mistake. No problem. My name is Mr. Escalante and I teach … (*Refers to course description*) Arithmetic 1-A. (JAVIER *stubbornly reads from his book.* ESCALANTE *closes* JAVIER's *book and points to the back of the class.* JAVIER *reluctantly gives up his seat. Jeers and whistles from the other students.* ESCALANTE *picks up a textbook and writes on the blackboard: 31 lbs. - 19 oz. = ? While writing:*) Okay. Chapter 1. Weights and measures. Start simple: 31 pounds minus 19 ounces equals what?

TOUGH BOY. Pounds of what?

ESCALANTE. Whatever you want.

TOUGH BOY. I have 31 pounds of dope and sold 19 ounces.

TITO. If you had 31 pounds you'd be pretty stupid to be here in school. (*The class breaks into laughter.*)

ESCALANTE (*to* CLAUDIA). Do you have the answer?

CLAUDIA. I don't have to buy drugs, he gives them to me. (*More catcalls and laughter*)

ESCALANTE. If he gave her 19 ounces, how

much would he have left? Anybody? (JAVIER *raises his hand.* ESCALANTE *nods to him.*)

JAVIER. Twenty-nine pounds, 13 ounces. (*Some students smack their lips and hiss "Lambe" to* JAVIER. *He shoots them dirty looks.*)

ESCALANTE. That's right. Way to go, Johnny. (ESCALANTE *writes on the board: 1,872 ÷ 23. While writing:*) You keep that up and you'll go back to head of the class. Invent the hyper-drive for a spaceship. Computers. Science fiction, science fact. Okay. 1,872 inches divided by 23 inches. (*Students snicker. Someone burps loudly.* ESCALANTE *turns to the class, no hands are raised.*) Who's got the answer? C'mon, this is easy. Anyone can do. You, in the plaid shirt.

PLAID SHIRT (*mischievously*). 1,895.

ESCALANTE. Why did you add them? How many of you don't know what this means? (ESCALANTE *points to the long division sign.*)

PANCHO. I don't need no math. I got a solar calculator with my dozen doughnuts.

LUPE. The bus is exact change, no big deal. (*Laughter from the class*)

ESCALANTE. Okay, okay. Quiet! (*The bell rings. The students rush out of the classroom, cheering and laughing. They nearly trample a confused* ESCALANTE. *He checks his watch, then hears a voice offstage.* ESCALANTE *crosses out into the hallway.*)

MOLINA (*offstage*). Everyone back in their classroom!

(PRINCIPAL MOLINA *enters the hall. The students groan and start to clamor as he ushers them back into the classroom.*)

MOLINA. Back! Back in class! That was a premature bell!

PANCHO. Premature bell? I thought we weren't supposed to discuss sex in class.

MOLINA. All right, sit down. Sit down! Stop talking! (MOLINA *goes to the window and looks out through binoculars.*)

ESCALANTE (*joins* MOLINA). Principal Molina.

MOLINA. Mr. Escalante, please, call me Hugo.

ESCALANTE. Is it a fire drill?

MOLINA. No. Little sneaks rigged the bell. (*The bell rings again and students break for the doors, screaming and laughing.* MOLINA *races after them shouting. The halls fill up as if the day was just beginning.* MOLINA *continues from offstage.*) Class is not over yet! Get back inside!

(*Alone in the classroom,* ESCALANTE *surveys the damage. The walls are filthy and covered in graffiti. He shakes his head and slowly starts to pick up the trash the students left on the floor. The lights fade up into a tableau of the school. A spot comes up on* PANCHO. *As* PANCHO *speaks, we see* ESCALANTE *straightening up the desks and cleaning up the classroom in the background.*)

PANCHO. Let me tell you something about school. Besides the fact that it sucks—you got all these dense teachers tryin' to brainwash you into thinkin' the way they do. I mean, like I really want to think like them. "Those who can, do. Those that can't, teach." That's what Uncle Nando says. He dropped out of school when he was younger than me. Talked himself into a job as a carpenter's apprentice. Now, Uncle Nando's like 32, and runs his own construction company. I mean, he's got it made. He don't even gotta work Saturdays if he don't wanna. Got a big-screen TV right in his office. Drives a bitchin' Trans Am that's already paid off. I'm tellin' you, the chicks are all over him. As soon as I get a decent job, I'm outta here. Probably start as an apprentice mechanic. This way I can get parts for my car at a discount. I got a '74 Mustang, and as soon as I start bringing in the dough, I'm gonna fix the body, paint it candy-apple red, turn the rims inside out, install a stereo system you can hear a block away, and get my engine purring like a tiger. Roaaaow!! By the time I'm Nando's age, I'll be the boss of my own body shop.

(Like an exaggerated TV commercial) "You got a problem with your car, take it down to Pancho's. Ten percent off to any woman who wears a dress up to here." *(Laughs at his own joke)* Hey, I know some of you are thinkin', this carnal[1] up here is full of himself. But I really know how to get around. I'm a walking road map. Ask anybody in Garfield. I get anyone anywhere fastest way possible, guaranteed. *(Rapid fire)* El Dorado Disco in Long Beach? Even though it seems out of the way, jump on the 5 to the 710. Unless it's rush hour. Then you take Soto to Slauson, left on Atlantic but skip the light and cut through the Thrifty's parking lot, then you're on Atlantic all the way out to Ocean, make a right and then you hit Shoreline. And you can put pedal to the metal on the way home 'cause the cops don't use radar at night. See? That's why I'm in no hurry. 'Cause I know where I'm going. Won't be long 'fore I'm cruising around in the fiercest piece of machinery in East Los. Pick up any ruca[2] I want. That's right, man. Don't need no high school diploma for that. *(Lights fade out.)*

SCENE TWO

AT RISE: *The first day of school is long over. The students have left and so have most of the faculty.* ESCALANTE *has spread out newspapers on the floor of his classroom. He's surrounded by painting supplies.* MRS. ORTEGA *stops by and peeks into the classroom.*

ORTEGA. Mr. Escalante, is everything okay? The security guard told me you were staying late.

ESCALANTE. Needs some paint. Then it will only smell bad.

ORTEGA *(smiling)*. Be careful. If the school board sees the faculty making repairs, pretty soon they'll have us sweeping the hallways.

ESCALANTE *(smiling back)*. It'll be Top Secret.

ORTEGA. Bear with us, Mr. Escalante. Students can sense a new teacher's frustration. I'd hate for them to take advantage of you.

ESCALANTE. Mrs. Ortega, I'm not a new teacher. I taught for years at a Jesuit school in Bolivia.

ORTEGA. Yes, of course. But Garfield students are a bit different than Jesuit students. You can see for yourself, it's a tough school.

ESCALANTE. I like tough schools. It's no good unless the kids work hard.

ORTEGA. By "tough" I mean …Mr. Escalante, one of our "kids" tried to stab another kid in the schoolyard today with a compass he stole from geometry class … A lot of them only show up because they get a free lunch … By next year, half your class will be dropouts. *Desaparecidos.*

ESCALANTE *(gently)*. Mrs. Ortega, if these kids are in school I can teach them more than adding and subtracting. You have me teaching basic arithmetic five periods in a row. I taught physics to barefooted Indians in the Altiplano.

ORTEGA. If we can teach them to count their change, balance their checkbook, maybe learn a trade, then we've educated them. With these kids it's not like—are they going to college, it's more like—are they going to make it home? *(Beat)* Mr. Escalante, I hope coming back to teach wasn't a rash decision on your part. Every year we get well-intentioned people going through a mid-life crisis. They want to do something meaningful with their lives, then quit on us after two weeks …

ESCALANTE *(looking at the walls)*. Might need two coats.

ORTEGA. Mr. Escalante, next time you want

---

1. *carnal,* blood brother
2. *ruca,* girl

to do something outside your job description, please, check with me first. Good night. (ORTEGA *exits.* ESCALANTE *looks at the painting supplies, a bit disappointed. He sighs, then starts to prepare the walls to be painted. The lights slowly fade out.*)

SCENE THREE

AT RISE: *The bell rings and the lights come up on the classroom. The newly painted walls are in stark contrast to the graffiti in the hallway. Students are filtering into the room.* ESCALANTE *is at the head of the class looking over a seating chart. The students pay little attention to their teacher.*

ESCALANTE. … Garcia, Guitano, Perales, and Santos. All right, these are your permanent seats for the rest of human history. Any problems with this, too bad. (*The students begin to settle into their newly arranged seats, but the chatter continues nonetheless.*) 2x plus x plus 1. Who's got the answer?

PANCHO. We're supposed to add the alphabet? (*Snickers and chattering*)

ESCALANTE. Too hard for you *burros*? Okay. How about 9 squared?

TITO. The only square around here is you, man. (*Laughter and more talking*)

ESCALANTE. All right, all right…You like to talk, that's okay … Let's talk numbers. C'mon, you like to talk. Give me some numbers! C'mon! (*Some students continue to talk, some throw out numbers, being as disruptive as they can.* PANCHO *is reading a car magazine.* TOUGH BOY *stands on his desk and screams.*)

TOUGH BOY. 738!

ESCALANTE. More!

PREGNANT GIRL. 365. (ESCALANTE *lists the numbers on the board as they are called out, some in English, some in Spanish. Part of the class begins to get caught up in the game and the room fills with shouted numbers and laughter.*)

ESCALANTE (*overlapping*). More! More!

STUDENTS. 433. 327. 634! 248! 751!

ESCALANTE. Okay! Okay! Okay! Stop! (*The class briefly settles down.* ESCALANTE *prowls around the room looking for a victim. He spots* PANCHO *reading his magazine.*) Hey, Motorhead! You bring your calculator today? (*Some students laugh and repeat the nickname.* PANCHO *pulls out a solar calculator.* ESCALANTE *walks back to the board.*) Okay. I'll make you a deal. You add these numbers faster than me and you can read your magazine. I win, I get the magazine and the calculator. (*Students giggle and ad-lib, "Yeah right," "Go ahead," "Go for it, Pancho," "Motorhead."* PANCHO *smiles, contemplating his victory.*) It's a deal? All right. Go! (PANCHO *quickly enters the list of numbers into his calculator.* ESCALANTE *adds the numbers on the board, writing the answer, but starting with the numbers in the left hand column instead of the right. Students egg* PANCHO *on, but* ESCALANTE *finishes long before him: 3,496.*) Motorhead, you done yet? What'd you get? 3,496! Is it right? Is it right?

PANCHO (*looks up from his calculator, annoyed*). Okay, yes! It's right!

ESCALANTE (*patting* PANCHO's *belly*). Stay away from those doughnuts, they slow you down. (*Some students groan, some cheer and laugh as* ESCALANTE *takes* PANCHO's *magazine and calculator.*)

VARIOUS STUDENTS (*overlapping*). You cheated! You did it backwards. No way! How'd you do that?

ESCALANTE. I can tell you the secret!! But you guys don't like math. You like Mickey Mouse classes. You want me to tell you? Okay! Math is simple. Anyone can do!

LUPE (*to* CLAUDIA). This guy's loco. (*A paper airplane whizzes by* ESCALANTE's *head. Students are still giggling and heckling.*)

ESCALANTE. You see! You don't like math! You like airplanes! But you know what an airplane is? It's math. It is! Aerodynamics. Relation to forces! G-loads! What else you like? (*Students shout out things, laughing and teasing each other. "Cars," "Basketball," "Drugs," "Cellular phones," "Girls," "Roller-coasters."* ESCALANTE *prowls the room, like a cross between a cheerleader and a bulldog; always in motion, cajoling, mischievously feigning punches, teasing.* ESCALANTE *continues, overlapping.*) Cellular phones! For cellular phones you need to know about math! They cost so much! Okay, c'mon! Give me an example of something where you don't need math.

PANCHO. Race car driver.

ESCALANTE. Power-to-weight ratio …Race cars use down-force, upside down aerodynamics, to get more grip from the tires. More grip—more speed—better handling. Talk to the girls, they know. Better handling, you win the race!

CLAUDIA. You got that right. (*Some students make catcalls.*)

ESCALANTE. Engineering, astrophysics. Anything you do, you're going to need math. It's the language of the future! They're gonna outlaw words. Only gonna use numbers! Name something else!

TITO. Rock star! (*The kids laugh and cheer.*)

ESCALANTE. Math is the foundation of music. Tempo! Quarter notes, eighth notes, half notes. Beethoven was my first student! Try again, Johnny. (*The students begin drumming on desks to "Oye Como Va," or making any kind of musical noise they can think of.* ESCALANTE *dances to his desk. He opens his briefcase and puts on a chef's hat.*) All right, all right, quiet. Quiet! I'm a bad man. Could hurt you good. (*With some ceremony, he pulls a meat cleaver from the briefcase, and thwacks it down into his wooden desk.* students *snicker and heckle.*) Okay. I warned you. This is serious business. (ESCALANTE *puts on an apron. With the cleaver he goes at several apples like a sushi chef. Some giggles and ad-libs.*)

PANCHO. Looks like Julia Child. (*Finished,* ESCALANTE *cleans the blade with a small towel and places the cleaver on his desk. He moves about the room distributing pieces of apple.* ESCALANTE *walks with a sense of purpose, never smiling or breaking the mood. He ends up near* CLAUDIA *and quickly asks her:*)

ESCALANTE. What you got?

CLAUDIA. It's an apple. (*Everyone laughs.*)

ESCALANTE. How much?

CLAUDIA. What do you mean? (*A few students giggle.* ESCALANTE *moves quickly to* LUPE.)

ESCALANTE. What you got?

LUPE. Half.

ESCALANTE. Goot. Excuse me my German accent. (*More giggling.* ESCALANTE *approaches* ANA DELGADO *at the back of the class.*) What you got? (ANA *draws into herself as her teacher gets closer.*) What you got?

ANA (*whispering*). Missing 25 percent.

ESCALANTE. What? I got wax in my ears.

ANA. Missing 25 percent.

ESCALANTE. That's right. Missing 25 percent. Is it true intelligent people make better lovers? (*This breaks the kids up.* ESCALANTE *turns quickly to* PANCHO. PANCHO *is devouring his apple.*) Hey, what you got?

PANCHO (*the core in his mouth*). I got a core. (*More laughter*)

ESCALANTE (*overlapping*). You owe me a hundred percent. And I'll see you in People's Court. Everyone, please open your book, Chapter 2, page 26. Multiplication of fractions and percentages.

(*The class is interrupted by the entrance of* ANGEL GUERRA *and* CHUCO. CHUCO'*s got a hard look, baggy pants, white shirt buttoned at the collar, long black coat and sneakers.* ANGEL *wears a t-shirt and a net on his head. The room gets quiet.*)

ESCALANTE (*pointing to apples*). Twenty-five percent, fifty percent, seventy-five percent, and a hundred percent. (CHUCO *and* ANGEL *approach* ESCALANTE *with the casual swagger of gang kids.*)

CHUCO. Who's calling the shots, *ése*?[3]

ESCALANTE. Got a slip? (CHUCO *holds out his slip to* ESCALANTE. *Before the teacher can take it,* CHUCO *lets it fall to the floor.* ESCALANTE *picks it up. To* ANGEL:) You got a slip? (ANGEL *just sniffs and looks at the ceiling. The class silently observes the confrontation.*) Okay, you'll have to stand in the back until I get another desk. (*To* CHUCO:) You sit right here, okay? (ESCALANTE *makes* JAVIER *give up a front row seat.* JAVIER *grimaces, but doesn't fight. He stands and joins a few other students standing against the wall. Over* JAVIER's *cross:*) Everyone please read the first paragraph. (*Softly to* CHUCO) Where's your equipment?

CHUCO. What you mean?

ESCALANTE. Paper?

CHUCO. Don't got any.

ESCALANTE. Pencil?

CHUCO. Don't got any.

ESCALANTE. Got to come to this class prepared.

CHUCO. Do the work in my head.

ESCALANTE. Ohhhh. You know the times table?

CHUCO. I know the ones, the twos, and the threes … (*On "threes,"* CHUCO *flips* ESCALANTE *the finger. A few gang members laugh, egging* CHUCO *on.*)

ESCALANTE. Finger Man. I heard about you. Are you the Finger Man? I'm the Finger Man, too. Do you know what I can do? I know how to multiply by nine! Nine times three. What you got? (ESCALANTE *holds up 10 fingers, with his palms toward* CHUCO. *Then, with his left hand he counts off three fingers. The third one he bends in half. He wiggles the two fingers on one side of the bent*

middle finger, and the seven fingers on the other side during the part of the answer that corresponds to the number of fingers held up.*) Twenty-seven. Six times nine. (*Counting fingers*) One, two, three, four, five, six. What you got? Fifty-four. You wanna hard one? How about eight times nine? One, two, three, four, five, six, seven, eight, what you got? Seventy-two. (*The bell rings.* ANGEL *and the rest of the students begin to file out. To* CHUCO.) Stay put. I want to talk to you, man. (*To class*) Please make sure you do problems one through twenty. Page 26.

PANCHO. Can I have my magazine, Mr. Escalante?

ESCALANTE. Don't bring it to class again, all right? (*As* PANCHO *exits,* ANGEL *deliberately bumps him. The Maravilla Gang,* CHUCO's *army, has followed* ANGEL *back into the room.* ESCALANTE *notices that he is alone with the gang, cut off from the exits.*)

CHUCO. *Sabe qué, ése*?[4] Don't get excited. (CHUCO *walks past* ESCALANTE *to the desk and picks up the meat cleaver. He fingers it during his lines, smiling.*) Y'know, cut me a "D" like the other profes. I'll read my funny books, y'know, count the holes in the ceiling. Kick back.

ESCALANTE. First thing I can teach you is some manners. (ANGEL *steps forward and mischievously reaches for a pencil in* ESCALANTE's *pocket.*) I wouldn't do that if I was you. Might lose a finger. Won't be able to count to 10.

CHUCO. We've seen *vatos*[5] like you before. (CHUCO *slams the cleaver down into desk.* ESCALANTE *flinches.* CHUCO *smiles easily.*) You'll be hurting soon.

ANGEL (*tap-slaps* ESCALANTE *on the cheek*). *Ponte trucha*,[6] huh? (*Exit* ANGEL, CHUCO,

---

3. *ése*, dude

4. *Sabe qué, ése?* You know what, dude?

5. *vatos*, guys

6. *Ponte trucha*, Get with it.

and the gang. ESCALANTE *removes the cleaver from the desk and returns it to his briefcase.)*

(Lights shift. ANGEL *appears downstage in a pool of light. He is smoking. Upstage,* ESCALANTE *begins to hang posters of famous sports figures on the walls of the classroom.* ANGEL *watches him, then faces the audience.* ANGEL *snaps his fingers and causes the lights to fade down on* ESCALANTE. ANGEL *smiles at his power.)*

ANGEL. Now you in my classroom. Ain't teachin' no stupid math, y'know. Not here, homes. Not in East Los … (ANGEL *looks around the room.)* Ever see somebody die? Bam! Bam! Bam! And the *carnal's* dirt nappin'? I don't think so. Man, sometimes a *vato* gets killed, he don't die. Not right away. Had to steer my bike through three different gang territories just to make it to sixth grade. I was still a *moscoso*[7] when I started out a baby tagger. My homey did buses, but I could climb … reach the heavens, spray paintin' the signs over the freeway. It was a joke, a game that turned to war. (*He assumes a gang pose.)* You've seen the stare. You return the stare, you challenge me … Your fear is my friend. Night my homey got permanently taxed, we were down by the street corner. Having a good time, brown-baggin' some brew, forgettin' our cares … A car drives up slow … Shots ring out—one, three, two loose *balas.* My homey shot in *el pecho*[8] and shoulder. My carnal, who had never let me down, was next to me *sufriendo* and all I had was a bruised elbow … I held him tight and tighter … Tryin' to keep him *vivo,*[9] y'know, puttin' up a big "stay away" sign, flashin' "no trespassing," so *la muerte* would not take him away … Took three hours to die. Three hours. Cursing. Crying. Hurt so bad, he started laughing. Made me laugh. Till his insides started spillin' out … Coughing blood on my face that I was too afraid to wipe off. I actin' like it don't hurt. (*He assumes his gang pose.)* Everybody gotta die sometime … Life goes on … Blood in, blood out, *sangre por sangre, carne de mi carne, vida por vida* … Barrio … Where you feel *bienvenido* … Wanted, *como en tu casa.* Think some math teacher's gonna cover my ass? Or give me the respect I get from my homeys? The pride? Not in this life. You wanna talk numbers? Three thousand gang deaths a year in the City of Angels—*Nuestra Señora la Reina de los Angeles.*[10] You wanna talk math? Homes plus Homes plus Homes equals Strength. *Familia. Mi familia.* And you don't turn your back on that, *ése.* Not on blood. Not when it's your homey who's bleedin'. That's the truth, homes. That's education. (*Blackout)*

SCENE FOUR

*A**T RISE: Recess, a few weeks into the semester. Students are goofing around in the hallway.* PANCHO *is near a door to the class as he and* TITO *check out* CLAUDIA *and some other girls.*

PANCHO. Claudia thinks she's so hot just because she dates *gabachos.*[11]

TITO. You jealous, man?

PANCHO. No, I mean, just 'cause she's fine, doesn't mean I want her.

TITO (*laughing).* Oh, man. You're so full of it! You know you dig her.

*(*ESCALANTE *enters the hallway on his way to class. He spots the boys and casually strolls up beside* PANCHO.)*

PANCHO. Shut up, homes.

TITO. Yeah, well, just don't let her know. That's like the worst thing you can do with a woman.

ESCALANTE. You're in love, huh?

---

7. *moscoso,* snot-nose (kid)

8. *el pecho,* the chest

9. *vivo,* alive

10. *Nuestra Señora la Reina de los Angeles,* Our Lady Queen of the Angels

11. *gabachos,* white boys

TITO (*laughing*). He's buggin'.

ESCALANTE. Let me know … Which one?

PANCHO (*walking off*). C'mon. Let's go.

ESCALANTE (*to* TITO). How 'bout you, Johnny? C'mon, don't be afraid.

TITO (*laughing*). I'm not Johnny, man. (TITO *walks off after* PANCHO. ESCALANTE *heads to his class.*)

ESCALANTE (*to himself*). I know, Tito. Tito el Grande.

(TITO *blasts his boombox. Students start dancing wildly.* PRINCIPAL MOLINA *and* MRS. ORTEGA *enter the hall. They're in the middle of a heated discussion.*)

MOLINA (*entering*). That's exactly the point I'm trying to make, Mrs. Ortega. (*To* TITO.) Tito, turn that thing off, or I'll confiscate it!

TITO (*turning off the box*). It's recess. We're supposed to be relaxing.

MOLINA (*back to* ORTEGA). I'll tell you now, I will not be the principal of the first school in the history of Los Angeles to lose its accreditation.

ORTEGA. I'm the last person to say that this school doesn't need to improve. But, if you want higher test scores, start by changing the economic level of this community.

(ESCALANTE *re-enters the hall.*)

ESCALANTE. Good morning, good morning. Excuse me, please, but I need more chalk for the classroom.

ORTEGA (*to* MOLINA). As I said before, we lack the resources to implement the changes the district demands.

MOLINA. Yes, I know that, Mrs. Ortega. I also know that if we don't try *something*, we are certain to fail.

ESCALANTE. Forgive me, I'm sorry. I didn't mean to interrupt.

MOLINA. No, it's fine, Mr. Escalante. This is as good a time as any … Garfield High has been put on academic probation. If we

don't turn things around this year, we'll lose our accreditation.

ORTEGA. If *we* fail? You can't teach logarithms to illiterates. Look, these kids come to us with barely a fifth grade education. There isn't a teacher in this school who isn't doing everything they possibly can.

ESCALANTE. I'm not. I could do more.

ORTEGA. I'm sure Mr. Escalante has good intentions, but he's only been here a short while.

ESCALANTE. If you treat them like losers, they act like losers. Hold them accountable, ask for more, and they will deliver.

MOLINA. You really think our students can do better?

ESCALANTE. Students will rise to the level of expectation, Señor Molina. (*Pause*)

MOLINA. All right. What do you need, Mr. Escalante?

ESCALANTE. *Ganas*[12] … That's all we need … *Ganas*.

(*Offstage, we hear shouting and a crash—a fight is breaking out.* CHUCO *and a couple of the Maravilla Gang race across stage to join in. Some of the students follow them out of curiosity. There are gunshots and screams. Pandemonium.* MOLINA *chases after* CHUCO. ORTEGA *huddles down in a corner.* ESCALANTE *spots* ANGEL *racing across stage to join* CHUCO. ESCALANTE *grabs him and puts him against the wall.*)

ANGEL. Let go! Let go! (ESCALANTE *struggles to keep* ANGEL *from escaping. He works him into an arm lock. Offstage, a whistle blows. We hear the security guards shouting.*)

CHUCO (*offstage*). Angel! … Angel!

ANGEL. Let go! That's my homey! (*The offstage commotion starts to die down. When it does,* ESCALANTE *finally loosens his grip on* ANGEL. ORTEGA *stands to watch* ESCALANTE *confront* ANGEL.)

---

12. *ganas,* desire

ESCALANTE. You need to hit someone, hit me, Mr. *Manos de Piedra*.[13] (ANGEL *cocks his arm, but cannot bring himself to hit* ESCALANTE) You pretend not to hear, Johnny, but I know you're listening. (ANGEL *storms out.* ORTEGA *hands* ESCALANTE *the glasses he lost in the scuffle.*)

ORTEGA. I think you're going to need more than just *ganas*, Mr. Escalante. A lot more. (*She exits.* ESCALANTE *looks around the halls and slowly heads into his classroom. The school bell rings. The hallway empties of students.*)

(*The lights shift.* ESCALANTE *writes on his blackboard: 1/4 + 1/4 = 2/4 = 1/2. Students file into the classroom, laughing and chattering. There are about 20 kids left. Some have dropped the class.*)

ESCALANTE. As soon as the bell rings from now on I want you in your seats ready for action. We will start each day with a quiz.

TITO. Oh, c'mon.

ESCALANTE. There will be no free rides, no excuses. Already have two strikes against you. Already behind. Have to play catch up. Take short cuts. Fast break on them. There are some people in this world who will assume that you know less than you do because of your name and complexion. But math is the great equalizer.

PANCHO. … guy's dreamin' …

ESCALANTE. Add and subtract, divide and conquer! When you go for a job the person giving you that job will not want to hear your problems, and neither do I. (ESCALANTE *strolls down the aisle. He thumps a sleeping* CLAUDIA *on the head. She snaps out of it.*) Hello, Señorita, you certainly have on a lot of makeup today. You have a contract with Dracula? (PANCHO *is reading a car magazine hidden in his notebook.*) Francisco García?

PANCHO (*with Anglicized pronunciation*). It's Garcia.

ESCALANTE. Well, when I say García you answer, okay, Pancho? … What you looking at García?

PANCHO. I'm not looking at nothing.

ESCALANTE. Okay. That's it. I warned you. No hot rod magazines in math class. (ESCALANTE *throws the magazine into the trash. He takes a tiny blue chair and places it in front of the students. There's some heckling, laughter.*)

LUPE. Ooooo, we're in trouble now. (*More laughter*)

ESCALANTE (*to* PANCHO). Sit.

PANCHO. Me?

ESCALANTE. Nobody else.

PANCHO. No. I don't think so …

CLAUDIA. Go on, Motorhead. (*More laughter, name calling.* ESCALANTE *moves from desk to desk, sometimes whispering, sometimes challenging, always inspiring.*)

ESCALANTE. I run the show. You're gonna do what I say. Don't do what I say, you gonna fly. Got other schools we can send you to. You won't like them. Gonna have to take three buses to get there. (PANCHO *considers this. Then, he clowns his way into the chair.*) Welcome to the show.

TITO. Some show. Can I get my money back? (*The kids laugh and begin to heckle* PANCHO.)

A FEW STUDENTS. Awwww. Look at the little baby in the chair! Where's your milk bottle? (*More laughter. A sign is hanging underneath the clock. It reads: "Determination + Discipline + Hard Work = The Way to Success."*)

ESCALANTE. Okay. Okay. See the sign? Goot. Read the sign … Go on.

PANCHO. "Determination."

ESCALANTE. Determination means you refuse to quit. Never give up. Very goot. What else it say?

---

13. *Manos de Piedra*, hands of stone

PANCHO. C'mon …

A FEW STUDENTS. Ohhhh. What's the matter, baby, gotta go pee-pee? *(More laughter)*

ESCALANTE. Better read quick.

PANCHO. "Discipline."

ESCALANTE. Discipline means you follow instructions. From your mom, your dad, your coach. I'm just a coach. And if you guys are my team, then I'm in big trouble. What else does it say? … C'mon …

PANCHO *(softly)*. "Hard work."

ESCALANTE. Hard work is the future. You are the future. You can do it. Anybody can do … Then? … Let's go, Motorhead, not done yet.

PANCHO. "The way to success."

ESCALANTE. Success. Success means victory. Does not come easily. Don't find it in a box of Cracker Jacks. No. Too bad . . . Where do you find it? Huh? *(To ANA)* Smart Lady, you know. Tell them, where do you find it? *(ANA looks down and shrugs her shoulders. ESCALANTE smiles)* In yourself. Believe in yourself, you're gonna do it. Means you're building confidence. You're gonna do it. You're gonna do it, Johnny. You're the best … Now I got a new sign. Motorhead, go hang it up. *(ESCALANTE points to a rolled banner on his desk. PANCHO crosses to it and picks it up.)*

PANCHO. Where you want it?

ESCALANTE *(smiling)*. You decide, Johnny. *(PANCHO stands on a chair and hangs one side of the banner. He moves the chair and hangs the other side. Over sign-hanging:)* You're gonna work harder than you ever worked before. You need the tools. Gotta get good. Gonna have to practice. *(PANCHO jumps down and the banner unfurls. It reads: GANAS—THAT IS ALL I NEED. The students cheer and clap sarcastically. PANCHO takes a bow. To PANCHO.)* Way to go, Johnny, now take your seat. *(PANCHO rolls back to*

his desk. ESCALANTE moves among the kids.) You have entered Garfield but Garfield has not entered you. You are murderers. You kill time. Now—that's finished. You late, you get the chair. Don't come prepared—chair. Miss class, you see the principal. Don't like the rules, you fly. Easily understood? Good. In order to get good, there has to be the desire. The ganas. That's the only thing I ask of you. Ganas. And a haircut. *(Tugs TITO's hair)* If you don't have the ganas I will give it to you. Because I am an expert. Today is Monday, tomorrow is Wednesday, Friday is payday. The weekly test. There will be no diagonal vision. Eyes on your own paper. Cheating is not tolerated. *(ESCALANTE starts handing out quizzes. The students groan.)*

TITO. You gotta be kidding!

ESCALANTE. You will have ten minutes to finish a quiz. You finish early, you work on whatever problem is on the board. No questions? Goot. *(The students resign themselves to working on the quiz. ESCALANTE smiles.)* And you're not students anymore. This is Garfield High. That means you're *Bulldogs.* Dog-dog-dog-dog-dog-dog …

(ESCALANTE continues his chant, prowling the room as the students work on the quiz. Enter CHUCO, ANGEL, and the Maravilla Gang. ESCALANTE stops his chant. Everyone stops working.)

TITO *(softly)*. The chair, give 'em the chair …

ESCALANTE *(to TITO)*. Okay, okay. *(To CHUCO)* Are your friends auditing?

CHUCO. Yeah. I "audited" them to come with me.

ESCALANTE. You see? Safety in numbers. *(CHUCO does his strut and sits. ANGEL follows. The rest of the Maravilla Gang remains standing. No one works on their quiz. ESCALANTE takes off his tie and wraps it around his head like a gang member. He starts imitating the walk and talk of CHUCO.)* I am

"El Ciclón," from Bolivia. One man gang. This is my domain. *Pues ni modo.*[14] *(In* CHUCO's *face)* Don't give me no gas. I'll jump on your face. Tattoo your chromosomes. *(Some students laugh.* CHUCO *ignores* ESCALANTE. ESCALANTE *resumes his own style. He crosses up to the board and erases the problem. He writes in its place: -2 + 2 = ?)* Okay. This is basic math, but basic math is too easy, even for you *burros*. So, I'm going to teach you algebra, because I'm the champ. If the only thing you know how to do is add and subtract, you will only be prepared to do one thing. Pump gas—

CHUCO. Hey, ripping off a gas station is better than working in one, *que no?*

ANGEL. *Orale!*[15] *(*ANGEL *and* CHUCO *shake hands, cholo-style.)*

ESCALANTE. *Orale!* I'm a tough guy. Tough guys don't do math. Tough guys deep-fry chicken for a living. Work at Pollo Loco. You want a wing or a leg, man?

TITO. I want a thigh. *(The students laugh at* CHUCO's *expense.)*

ESCALANTE. *Orale.* Whoever heard of negative and positive numbers? Anybody?

PANCHO. Yeah, negative numbers are like unemployment. Ten million people out of work. That's a negative number.

ESCALANTE. We're gonna need a lot of Kleenexes. There's gonna be a lot of bloodshed here. *(to* LUPE*)* You been to the beach?

LUPE. Yeah.

ESCALANTE *(to* PANCHO*).* You ever play with the sand?

PANCHO. C'mon, man …

ESCALANTE *(to* CHUCO*).* Finger Man! … Come on, Finger Man, did you ever dig a hole? The sand that comes out of the hole, that's a positive. The hole … is a negative. That's it. Simple. Anybody can do. Minus two plus two equals? *(To* ANGEL*)* Hey, Nethead, how about you? *Orale!* Answer it.

Come on, you know the answer. Minus two plus two. Fill the hole. What's that on your knuckles? *(The class has gotten very quiet.* ESCALANTE *holds up* ANGEL's *hands and reads the tattooed knuckles. Spelling it out.)* L-O-V-E H-A-T-E. If I had that on my hands I wouldn't raise them either. *(*ESCALANTE *gets next to* ANGEL's *ear.* ANGEL *just stares ahead.)* Hey, tough guy. *Orale!* Come on. Negative two plus two equals … Anyone can do. Fill the hole. *(*ANGEL *is still.* PANCHO *snickers.)*

CHUCO. I don't think so, *ése.*

ESCALANTE. Come on, just fill the hole. You gonna let these *burros* laugh at you? Minus two plus two equals … *(*ANGEL *turns his back to* ESCALANTE*.)* I'll break your neck like a toothpick. *(Makes crunching sound.)* Orale. Minus two plus two equals … *(*ANGEL *continues to defy his teacher.* ESCALANTE *stays close to* ANGEL's *ear. He waits.* ANGEL *barely moves his mouth.)*

ANGEL. Zero.

ESCALANTE. Zero? You're right. Simple. That's it. *(*ESCALANTE *skips to the board and finishes the problem.)* Minus two plus two equals zero. He just filled the hole. Did you know that neither the Greeks nor the Romans were capable of using the concept of zero? It was your ancestors, the Mayans, who first contemplated the zero. The absence of value. True story. You *burros* have math in your blood.

ANGEL. Hey, Kimo Sabe *todo!* It's the Lone Ranger! The man knows everything! *Orale!* Kimo Sabe!

CHUCO. Kimo Sabe *nada!* (CHUCO *stands. Everything stops for a moment.* CHUCO *stares at* ANGEL, *then gestures to a door. Exiting.)* Angel! *Vámonos!* (CHUCO *heads out with his gang in tow.* ANGEL *rises from his chair, reluctantly following.)*

---

14. *Pues ni modo,* No way.
15. *Orale!,* All right!

ESCALANTE. Nice knowing you. Have a nice day. *Arrivederci! (The gang has left except for* ANGEL. *He stops and looks to* ESCALANTE.)

ANGEL. Kimo Sabe *todo. (*ESCALANTE *watches* ANGEL *exit. A few students repeat the nickname "Kimo Sabe.")*

*(*RAFAELA FUENTES *enters.)*

RAFAELA *(hesitantly).* I was said to go here.

ESCALANTE. Goot. Another customer … You're in luck. I've got two seats. Take your pick. Relax, take Sominex. Don't sleep in my class. I take that as an insult. *(The bewildered* RAFAELA *takes* CHUCO's *old desk.* ESCALANTE *looks at* ANGEL's *vacant spot and sighs. He writes a set of parentheses on the board. He points to them, then fills in the equation:* $-(-2) = +2$. *Over the above:)* Okay! Parentheses mean multiply. Every time you see this, you multiply. A negative times a negative equals a positive … A negative times a negative equals a positive, say it. *(Silence)* A negative times a negative equals a positive. Say it!

ANA. A negative times a negative equals a positive.

ESCALANTE. Again! *(Silence)* There's beauty in silence. I like it. Okay. Everyone!

ANA AND JAVIER. A negative times a negative equals a positive.

ESCALANTE. I can't hear you!

CLAUDIA, TITO, ANA, AND JAVIER. A negative times a negative equals a positive.

ESCALANTE. Louder!

THE WHOLE CLASS. A negative times a negative equals a positive.

ESCALANTE. Louder!

THE WHOLE CLASS *(louder).* A negative times a negative equals a positive!

ESCALANTE *(with the students).* A negative times a negative equals a positive! A negative times a negative equals a positive! *(The refrain continues a few more times and then:)*

Why? *(Lights fade to black as the students ponder* ESCALANTE's *question.)*

SCENE FIVE

AT RISE: *A spot comes up on* RAFAELA *holding writing paper, an envelope and some photos. She sits at a desk and begins to write. In the background, light comes up on* ESCALANTE, ANA, *and* JAVIER. *They are putting up Christmas decorations.*

RAFAELA *(halting English).* Dear Mama. My teacher say to write always the English so to get good. *(She stops writing and addresses the audience.)* Takes many weeks before Mama gets letter in Guatemala. Then she needs carry letter to next town, whole day on bus. She pay *abogado* 18 *quetzales* to read the English. Ten cars I need clean by hand so to mail three American dollars to Mama and make happy at how good is my English she hear in Spanish. *Loco* … Mama speak *Quiché* then she learn Spanish from the nuns. Until *mi abuelo*[16] was killed by *un soldado* who steal his *burro*. Mama leave school so to cut the sugar cane. But she make promise to The Virgin, her child go to school even if the earthquake … "Work hard, speak the English, every day be gifts and blessings. Better than home, much better" … Last thing Mama say before I come to *El Norte. (*RAFAELA *resumes writing the letter.)* Here for you is pictures of me and Teresita. Would you like dress like she wear? I lucky to be staying in house so nice. *(*RAFAELA *again confides in the audience.)* How I tell Mama that Teresita only talk about American dollars? She is left by husband alone. She say if I make no more contribution I am to go. So I pay more so Mama don't feel Teresita move me out because I was disrespect to her friend

_____

16. *mi abuelo*, my grandfather

she have from when they were children. "Send Mama pictures of us on new sofa by Christmas tree," Teresita tell to me. *(Pointing at photo)* This new sofa took away by Sears men because her plastic money run off. *(Another photo)* We take photo in front of big car in Hollywood Boulevard that belong to long-haired man with guitar, not Teresita. Many things I do not understand in this strong country. Who in *mi pueblo* believe students paint ugly the school? Break the books? Point guns at teachers? Why someone not want something they get for free? *(RAFAELA resumes writing the letter.)* I am happy, Mama. I eat meat every day. I have luck to make many friends. It is always new thing I see and always I am thanking you for the life I am making. All my love, and God watch over you. Rafaela. *(She folds the letter and seals the envelope.) Con todo me amor y que Dios te bendiga.*[17] *(Lights fade down on* RAFAELA. *In the blackout we hear:)*

SECRETARY. *(over P.A. system).* Your attention, please. All undocumented aliens who wish to remain in school must have INS form 11E filled out and signed by a parent or guardian by Monday. *(The* SECRETARY *repeats the message in Spanish:) Atención, por favor. Todos los estudiantes extranjeros e indocumentados que deseen permanecer en esta escuela deben llenar el formulario once-E de Inmigración y traerlo firmado por padre, madre o guardián legal a más tardar el lunes próximo.*

(The lights come up on ESCALANTE'*s classroom. It is December, the end of a school day. The walls of the classroom have more pictures of inspirational people and Christmas decorations.* ESCALANTE *is grading papers in the classroom.* ANGEL *enters, making sure that no one sees him do it.* ESCALANTE *looks up.)*

ESCALANTE. What's the matter, Johnny? You an empty set?

ANGEL. Hey, Kimo man, I want to talk to you about the class. Y'know, maybe we can do a deal here—

ESCALANTE. You already lost your seat. Don't give me no gas.

ANGEL. I know about that. That was a mistake. I'm gonna play it straight with you, man. I got a little problem, though.

ESCALANTE. Yeah. Me.

ANGEL. No, no, no, seriously, man. Books. Can't have the homeys see me haul them around.

ESCALANTE. You wouldn't want anyone to think you're intelligent, huh?

ANGEL. So, maybe I could have two books. Keep one stashed at home, huh? *(*ESCALANTE *goes to his desk drawer and takes out several books. He opens each and removes a small card.)*

ESCALANTE. I'll cut you a deal. I'll give you three books. One for class, one for home, and one for your locker. So people know you never take it out.

ANGEL. Hey, man, this one's broken. *(*ESCALANTE *replaces the broken book. He hands the cards to* ANGEL.*)*

ESCALANTE. Sign each.

ANGEL. What's this for?

ESCALANTE. That's how much the book cost. That's how much you pay if you mess me up, put in the graffiti. Easily understood?

ANGEL *(signs each of the cards).* Yep.

ESCALANTE. So. What do I get?

CHUCO *(offstage).* Angel!!!

ANGEL. Protection, Kimo … *Protección* … understand?

ESCALANTE. Yep. I understand … I understand. *(*ANGEL *makes for an exit, stashing the books under his jacket.* ESCALANTE *remains in the classroom, humming to himself. Singing.)*

---

17. *Con todo me amor y que Dios te bendiga,* With all my love and may God bless you.

On the first day of Christmas, a *cholo* came to me ...

(*Enter* ANA *and her father,* HÉCTOR DELGADO)

ANA. Papa, this is Mr. Escalante, my math teacher.

ESCALANTE (*smiling*). Mr. Delgado. How are you?

DELGADO. *Mucho gusto.*

ESCALANTE. To what do I owe this pleasure?

ANA. I can't stay in your class.

ESCALANTE. Why not?

ANA. My—

DELGADO. Anita ... Señor Escalante, I have a family restaurant. Already she spends too much time studying. Now, with the extra work from your class, *imposible* ... So. Señor Molina said we need your signature—

ESCALANTE. No way. I won't sign. Ana should stay in this class. She's top kid.

DELGADO. The restaurant needs her.

ESCALANTE. You should hire another waitress. Ana can be the first one in your family to graduate from high school. Go to college.

DELGADO. I thank you for your concern, Mr. Escalante. But, her mother works there, her sisters, her brothers. This is a family business. She has responsibilities.

ESCALANTE. What about responsibility to her future? She could help the family more by getting an education.

DELGADO. Ahhh, probably get married. She wouldn't finish college.

ANA. Papa.

DELGADO. Ana! *Espera afuera.* (ANA *is close to tears as she leaves the classroom. She waits in the hall as the men resume the debate.*)

ESCALANTE. She talks about going to medical school.

DELGADO. No. I don't think so.

ESCALANTE. She should make her own choices.

DELGADO. *Un momento! Yo soy el padre de la niña, no usted!*

ESCALANTE. She'll just get fat and stupid. She'll waste her life away in your restaurant. She's top kid!

DELGADO. I started washing dishes for a nickel an hour. Now, I own that restaurant. Did I waste my life?!

ESCALANTE. I washed dishes too, when I first came to this country. But that—

DELGADO. Good! Strap on an apron. Come by and give us a hand.

ESCALANTE (*overlapping*). She could go to college, come back and teach you how to run the place.

DELGADO. *Profesor*, I know how to run my own family! Now, please, the signature. (*Reluctantly,* ESCALANTE *signs the paper.*)

ESCALANTE. Mr. Delgado, you've obviously done well for your family. If you believe yourself to be a good father, you must believe you raised your daughter to make the right decisions on her own ... Please sir, I just want what's best for Ana.

DELGADO. So do I, Mr. Escalante. So do I.

(*The* DELGADOS *exit. Exhausted,* ESCALANTE *returns to his desk and packs up his papers. He turns off the classroom light and starts into the hallway.* ARMANDO, *the janitor, is sweeping the trash-filled hall.*)

ARMANDO. You leaving, Mr. Escalante?

ESCALANTE. *Sí,* Armando. My wife's gonna kill me. I'm already late for dinner.

ARMANDO. Oh, all right.

ESCALANTE. Why?

ARMANDO. No, that's okay. Never mind.

ESCALANTE. Hey, Armando. *Qué te pasa?*

ARMANDO. No, it's just, you see, I'm taking this night class so I can get my G.E.D. diploma? And I'm having a hard time with the math.

ESCALANTE. Math? I'm the champ. Let's see

what you got, Johnny. (ARMANDO *pulls a piece of paper out of his pocket and hands it to* ESCALANTE. ESCALANTE *puts down his brief-case and takes a look at the paper.*) No problem. Piece of cake. (*Lights fade down on* ESCALANTE *and* ARMANDO.)

(*Lights up on* LUPE. *She is kneeling down, praying.* ESCALANTE *and* ARMANDO *are in the classroom taking down the Christmas decorations and hanging signs.*)

LUPE. Dear Lord … It's me, again. I wanted to thank you for helping Mama get her new cleaning job at the convention center. Papa's not so happy that she's working nights, but now he can get that new grass blower, 'cause the old one was giving him kidney problems. Thank you for keeping Margarita safe when she ran into the street. I should have been paying more attention, but Tomás, Jose, and Flaco were fighting, and there's just too many kids in one room …*Diosito Mio*, I know I should be happy with the way things are, but you're going to have to give me the strength of Mother Teresa so I can maintain my diet. Please, please, please, allow me not to fall into temptations like *carnitas de puerco*, French fries, and all the *helado de chocolate* in your creation. Give me the taste buds for the fruits and veggies that are gonna make me skinny in the eyes of this world. I guess it could be worse. I could be stupid and fat … Then, I wouldn't care about my hair, my clothes. I'd be too dumb to notice if some guy was into me. Not like there are any. Except, maybe Pancho … He likes me, he just don't know it, yet. Not that I'm desperate or anything. But, it would be nice to be close to someone … When you're tired or depressed, somebody to hold onto … Would that be okay with you? I understand the whole thing about pre-marital sex, but *Diosito Mio*, does being a virgin mean the only thing I can hug is my pillow? … I mean, I could just fall asleep in his arms … Please watch over Grandma, and Mama and Papa … Please make sure the little monsters stay healthy and safe … Please forgive me for always being such a smart-mouth. (*She begins to quietly say the "Our Father" in Spanish. As she prays, the lights fade to black.*)

SCENE SIX

A T RISE: *It is January.* ESCALANTE, ARMANDO, *and the Christmas decorations are gone. On the walls, more inspirational slogans: "What is mediocre is useless," "If you've tried to do something and failed, you are much better off than if you had tried to do nothing and succeeded." The students are hanging out in the classroom. Some of them are eating lunch. A few are tossing a ball around, others are just goofing off. The room has become a safe haven for them. In one corner,* JAVIER *and* ANA *are going over an assignment together.* RAFAELA *sits by herself.* TITO *and* PANCHO *are off together.* TITO *is playing an instrument and singing.* LUPE *and* CLAUDIA *are on the other side of the room, fixing their makeup.*

TITO. Pancho, man, you're always checking out Claudia.

PANCHO. You know that's the only reason I'm still in Kimo's class.

TITO (*sings*). Pancho's in love …

PANCHO. Shut up, shh, man! She's looking over here.

CLAUDIA (*looks over to* PANCHO *and* TITO). Look at Pancho. Slobbering like a dog.

LUPE (*turns away fast when she sees* PANCHO *looking their way*). Shh, quiet! I think he heard you!

CLAUDIA. Jesus, girl, don't tell me you're into Pancho Villa.

LUPE. Don't embarrass me, Camejo.

CLAUDIA. Come on, don't be shy, talk to him. (CLAUDIA *starts toward the boys,* LUPE *slowly joins her. They saunter over to* TITO *and* PANCHO. CLAUDIA *breaks the ice.*) I'm pretty fed up with that *pelón*[18] we got for a teacher.

PANCHO. Yeah, Escalante's got a real bug up his butt, giving us homework over vacation. (PANCHO *nudges* TITO.)

TITO. Oh, yeah. He's from Bolivia, South America, man. Probably some Nazi come out of hiding or something.

PANCHO (*begins to mimic* ESCALANTE's *walk and talk*). Whatsamatter, Johnny, you don't like my class? Too bad. Go work for Burger King.

(*A few more students enter the classroom. There are about 14 now, only the core group remains.*)

LUPE. Don't you guys know what's happening? Garfield's losing its accreditation.

PANCHO. So only teachers who act like jerks are gonna keep their jobs.

CLAUDIA. Well, what if we all decide not to take his tests? I mean, he can't fail the whole class.

TITO. Mutiny? That's cool. (*The conspirators nod and smile. They whisper their plans to the rest of the class.*)

PANCHO (*imitating* ESCALANTE). Okay, Johnny! You do the work or you take a hike because I am the champ! Dog-dog-dog-dog …

(ESCALANTE *enters.* PANCHO *doesn't see him but the others do. Everyone finds a seat.* PANCHO *finally sees* ESCALANTE, *and tries to cover his embarrassment. Sheepishly, he heads to a desk.* ESCALANTE *smiles at* PANCHO.)

ESCALANTE (*handing out tests*). Welcome back! Happy New Year! You're still failing! Got your algebra test results. We don't do better today, heads are gonna roll.

JAVIER (*looks at his test grade*). I've never gotten anything lower than a B+ in my life.

ESCALANTE. Because you take those Mickey Mouse classes. Always get an A. Here you got another chance to do a solid D. All right, let's see the homework. (*Some students groan.* ESCALANTE *hands out a stack of new quizzes. The students pass them around.* ESCALANTE *moves from student to student, collecting homework.*) Okay, first quiz. New semester, new rules. Today you got five minutes. Gotta hurry, running outta time. Gotta move faster. (*The mutineers look to each other for the signal.* PANCHO *looks over to* CLAUDIA *and grins.*)

PANCHO (*whispering*). Here he comes.

LUPE (*whispering*). Watch this. (LUPE *launches the mutiny by turning her quiz over.* CLAUDIA *does the same.* PANCHO, TITO, *and a bunch of others follow along.* ESCALANTE *goes to* LUPE.)

ESCALANTE. You finished already?

LUPE. I'm not taking the test.

ESCALANTE (*softly*). What's the matter with you? You didn't turn in your homework, either.

LUPE. My goat ate it. (CLAUDIA, PANCHO, TITO *and a few others laugh.*)

ESCALANTE. You don't do your homework, you don't get a ticket to watch the show.

JAVIER. Give her the chair! (ESCALANTE *takes out the chair.*)

LUPE. No way.

ESCALANTE. The longer you wait, the longer you sit.

JAVIER AND A FEW OTHERS (*softly*). Chair, chair, chair …

LUPE. Come on, you guys!

HALF THE CLASS. Chair, chair, chair! (LUPE *looks around at her fellow mutineers, but they offer her no support.*)

ESCALANTE. Either you get in the chair or you fly. Lots of things you can do. Sombrero weaving, making license plates. Your choice.

---

18. *pelón,* baldy

MOST OF THE CLASS (louder). Chair! Chair! Chair! (LUPE *finally gets up and sits in the blue chair.*)

VARIOUS STUDENTS. Ha, ha. That's what you get. You're the show!

LUPE. Shut up.

ESCALANTE. Anybody else not doing the quiz, I got plenty of chairs… All right, back to work. You don't have much time left. (*All turn their quizzes right side up and begin working. Softly to* LUPE.) See, now you're the show. (ESCALANTE *briefly prowls the aisles, then returns to* LUPE's *side.*) What's the matter with you? You're top kid. Come on, you're the best! You're gonna have to take the quiz anyway. You're in quarantine. Back here, 3 o'clock. Go on, back to your seat. (LUPE *obeys and is heckled back to her seat. On passing* PANCHO, *she whacks him on the head.* ESCALANTE *writes a problem on the board while the class works on the quiz.*)

(ANGEL, *sans hair net, tries to slip into the room.*)

SCATTERED VOICES. Late, late, late …

ESCALANTE. Whoa, no way, Angel. No chair for you. Go find yourself a Mickey Mouse class. Go to woodshop, make yourself a shoeshine box. You're gonna need it. (*The students heckle* ANGEL. *He walks to the front of the class.*)

ANGEL. Okay, Kimo. You're the man, you know best … Why don't you put them all in college, huh? Then let dumb taco benders like me pick their vegetables for them, collect their garbage, clip their poodle's toenails.

ESCALANTE. You're off the team. Goodbye. Have a nice day. (ANGEL *throws his hands up and backs into the blackboard, taking the pose of Christ on the cross.*)

ANGEL. I may be sinner, but, I'm willin' to pay for my sins … (*Some laughter. Everyone waits to see what* ESCALANTE *will do.*)

ESCALANTE. Okay, one shot deal. See you at 3 o'clock. Make-up quiz. Sit down. (*As* ANGEL *heads to his desk he flashes his tattooed knuckles in* PANCHO's *face.*)

PANCHO. Get out of my face.

ANGEL. I got more bad news for you, profess. Now, I know what I'm gonna say is really gonna trip you out, but I expect you to take it like a man … Mr. Escalante, I forgot my pencil. (*The class breaks into laughter.* RAFAELA *hands* ANGEL *a pencil.*)

ESCALANTE. Okay, time is up. Pass 'em forward. Thank you, thank you, thank you. Everyone look at the board. Will someone please read for me this problem? Anybody? (ESCALANTE *collects the quizzes and puts them on his desk.*)

STUDENTS (*in unison*). Juan has five times as many girlfriends as Pedro. Carlos has one girlfriend less than Pedro. If the total number of girlfriends between them is 20, how many does each gigolo have? (*The students laugh.* ESCALANTE *roams the aisles. The students can't take their eyes off him.* JAVIER *and* TITO *raise their hands.*)

ESCALANTE. Okay, okay. How many girlfriends does each gigolo have? Anybody? (*To* TITO) Think you got it, Einstein? Do you think you're gonna do it?

TITO. Juan is x, Carlos is y. Pedro is x plus y. Is Pedro bisexual, or what? (*Students laugh and snicker.*)

ESCALANTE. I have a terrible feeling about you, Tito. Camejo, stand and deliver!

CLAUDIA. 5x equals Pedro's girlfriends?

ESCALANTE. You're pretty now, but you're gonna end up barefoot and pregnant, in the kitchen. (*He imitates a plane flying and crashing with his hand and voice.*) Yeooow!! … Dog-dog-dog-dog …

CLASS (*picking up chant*). Dog-dog-dog-dog-dog-dog-dog …

(PRINCIPAL MOLINA *and* MRS. ORTEGA *enter. They look around the room.*)

ANGEL. Late, late, late.

ESCALANTE (*overlapping*). Okay, okay, okay, okay. How many girlfriends? What's the answer? (MOLINA *and* ORTEGA *take seats in the back.*)

PANCHO (*guessing*). Subtract Carlos from Pedro and divide by Juan?

ESCALANTE (*squeaky voice*). Some of these kids are in love, they're going to need heart transplants. Make me look bad in front of the boss.

RAFAELA. Can you have negative girlfriends?

ESCALANTE. No. Just negative boyfriends. (*As if to God*) Forgive them for they know not what they do!

ANGEL. Carlos has x minus 5 girlfriends, *qué no?*

ESCALANTE. "*Qué no?*" is right, *qué no.* (*Some laughter.* LUPE *raises her hand.*) The answer to my prayers! Yes?

LUPE. May I go to the restroom, please? (*Laughter*)

ESCALANTE. Hold it. You got two minutes. (*To* JAVIER) Señor Maya? My job is in your hands. Hit it.

JAVIER. It's a trick question, Mr. Kimo. You can't solve it unless you know how many girlfriends they have in common. Right?

ESCALANTE (*to* MOLINA *and* ORTEGA). It's not that they're stupid. It's just that they don't know anything.

(*The kids laugh.* ANA *enters the room unbeknownst to* ESCALANTE. *She studies the problem on the board.*)

JAVIER. I'm wrong? (ESCALANTE *attacks him with mock karate chops to the head.*)

ANA. X equals Pedro's girlfriends. 5x equals Juan's girlfriends. X minus 1 equals Carlos' girlfriends. X plus 5x plus x minus 1 equals 20, so, x equals 3. (*The class applauds.* ANA *smiles and sits.*)

ESCALANTE (*to* ANA). Good to see you.

PANCHO. Hey, Kimo, this stuff makes no sense half the time. You gotta show us how it works in the real world.

ESCALANTE (*to* MOLINA). Do you think it would be possible to get a couple of gigolos for a practical demonstration? (*The students laugh.*) No, no, no, just kidding, just kidding. (*The bell rings and students file out.* ESCALANTE *catches up with* ANA.) Your father changed his mind?

ANA. I told him if he didn't let me come to your class I would get pregnant before my 18th birthday. He bought me a desk so I can study at the restaurant!

ESCALANTE. That'll do it.

ANA. *Hasta mañana!* (ESCALANTE *smiles and shakes his head as* ANA *exits. He returns to his desk.* ORTEGA *and* MOLINA *walk over.*)

ESCALANTE. So. Do I pass the test?

MOLINA. You have some unusual methods, Mr. Escalante.

ESCALANTE. Thank you very much.

ORTEGA. But are they learning?

ESCALANTE (*opens his briefcase and takes out some papers*). Their algebra midterms. (Putting them down) B+, A-, B, C+, A-, B-, C, B+, A, A, A …

ORTEGA. This is just one class.

ESCALANTE. I want to teach calculus next year.

MOLINA. What, you're leaving us, Kimo? You got a college job?

ESCALANTE. No. Here. I want to teach calculus to this class.

MOLINA (*chuckling*). Calculus? Oh boy, that's a jump.

ORTEGA. That's ridiculous. They haven't had trig or math analysis.

ESCALANTE. They can take them both during the summer.

ORTEGA. You expect our best students to go to summer school?

ESCALANTE. From 7 to 12 … Every day, including Saturdays. Yep. That'll do it.

ORTEGA. Out of the question.

MOLINA. Our summer classrooms are reserved for remedial courses.

ESCALANTE. Mr. Molina, if you want to turn this school around you're gonna have to start from the top. You have to motivate them every minute, every day, even the best students.

ORTEGA. Mr. Escalante, please don't lecture us. I've been teaching here for 15 years, I think I know our students better than—

ESCALANTE (*interrupting*). We're not teaching the right stuff!

ORTEGA. Our kids can't handle calculus. We don't even have the books.

ESCALANTE. Books are not the problem. I'll teach Bolivian-style. Students copy from the board. Step by step. Inch by inch, I'll mimeograph pages from a college text.

MOLINA. College calculus?!

ESCALANTE. Of course. They can take the Advanced Placement Test. Get college credit.

ORTEGA. There are some teachers who would have trouble passing the Advanced Placement Test.

MOLINA. You really think you can make this fly? (*Pause*)

ESCALANTE. I teach calculus next year, or, have a good day.

ORTEGA (*to* MOLINA). Well, if this man can walk in here and dictate his own terms over my objections, I see no reason for me to continue as department chair.

MOLINA. Raquel, you're taking this far too personally—

ORTEGA (*interrupting*). I am thinking about those kids! Fewer than two percent of the seniors in this entire country even attempt the A.P. tests. This isn't Andover or Exeter

… If our kids try and don't succeed, you'll shatter what little self-confidence they do have. These aren't the types that bounce back … Have a good day. (ORTEGA *exits. Pause.*)

MOLINA. You've got a way of putting people off …

ESCALANTE. The truth can do that …

MOLINA. Jaime, has it occurred to you that she may be right? Kids are dropping your class already. And now you want them to give up summer vacation?

ESCALANTE. Hugo, if my kids can pass the Advanced Placement Test, they'll get college credit. Be a big plus for your school. For the whole community. (ESCALANTE collects his belongings. MOLINA *sighs.*)

MOLINA. Are you sure these kids will go to summer school?

ESCALANTE. Yep.

MOLINA. I certainly hope you're right. (MOLINA *exits, leaving* ESCALANTE *alone onstage. Lights fade down.*)

SCENE SEVEN

A T RISE: *Lights fade up on the first day of summer school. It is early in the day and already it's oppressively hot. The classroom now has pictures of the space shuttle and Mayan pyramids. The newest incentive banner reads: "Calculus wasn't meant to be easy. It already is."* ESCALANTE *is onstage alone, waiting. He checks his watch and then crosses over to the air conditioner. He tinkers with the controls. Nothing. Frustrated, he gives it a kick. It starts momentarily, then dies abruptly.* ESCALANTE *draws a circle and then a cross inside it, so it looks like a pie with four slices. He writes the letters S, A, C, T, one in each section, starting in the top left section, moving clockwise. Next to the S he writes:* Sin +. *Next to the A:* All +. *Beside the C:* Cos +, *and next to the T:* Tan +. *Then, in big letters, the phrase:* All Seniors Turn Crazy! *Some of this can occur underneath the following dialogue.* ARMANDO *enters.*

ARMANDO. I made sure the gate was unlocked.

ESCALANTE. *Muchas gracias.* (ESCALANTE *checks his watch.*)

ARMANDO. It's tough to get kids in school during the summer.

ESCALANTE. They still got one minute.

(ANGEL *enters.*)

ANGEL. Hey, Kimo. You proud of me? I'm the first dude here. *(Pointing to the sign)* What's calcoolus?

ARMANDO *(correcting* ANGEL*).* It's *calculus.* (ARMANDO *exits.*)

(JAVIER *and* ANA *come running in, out of breath.*)

JAVIER. Sorry we're late, Kimo. We thought we'd give everybody else a head start. *(They see the empty classroom.* ESCALANTE *smiles at them as they take two desks up front.*)

(*A few more students trickle in. They all open their notebooks.* ana *looks around at the empty desks.* TITO, CLAUDIA *and a few other students come running in.*)

ESCALANTE. You're late.

TITO. By whose clock? *(They're frozen at the doors, waiting to see if* ESCALANTE *will let it slide.*)

(PANCHO *and* LUPE *have entered the hallway holding hands. They stop in front of the classroom and kiss gently.*)

ESCALANTE. My class, my clock. Everyone, synchronize the watches: Now. 8:01 and 29 seconds. (ESCALANTE *smiles and everyone laughs as they take their seats.*) All right, let's go. Plenty of good seats left. Hey, where's Motorhead?

CLAUDIA *(slyly).* He's with Lupe. (ESCALANTE *makes his way to the door. When he spots the kissing couple, he motions for a*

few kids to come watch. Soon there is a small cluster watching LUPE *and* PANCHO *kiss.*)

ESCALANTE. Careful. You can make babies from doing that. Just kidding, just kidding. *(Everyone breaks out laughing, including* ESCALANTE *as they pile back into their desks.* ESCALANTE *gives* PANCHO *a swat on his way past.*)

(RAFAELA *knocks gently and enters.*)

RAFAELA. Excuse me, Kimo. I sell oranges on freeway ramp. There was accident, traffic slow down, lots of business. (ESCALANTE *waves her in and she takes her seat, passing out oranges on the way.*)

ESCALANTE. Okay, okay. Sit down. Do you think I want to do this? The Japanese pay me to do this. They're tired of making *everything.* They want you guys to pull your own weight. So they can take vacations on Mount Fuji.

CLAUDIA. Kimo, it stinks in here.

ESCALANTE. Somebody give Claudia an orange. *(She is quickly surrounded by outstretched hands, each holding an orange.* ESCALANTE *refers to the board.*) All right, here's a shortcut for you *burros,* so you remember what's positive in which quadrant. Here, All are positive; here, *Sine* is positive; here, *Cosine;* here, *Tangent.* Got it? No? What's the matter? You lost? Don't like summer school? You think this is bad? You guys have it easy! *(Melodramatically)* When I was your age, one day on my way to school I got lost in the hot, steamy Amazonian jungle. It was 120 degrees. I started hallucinating, wandering in circles, within the grasp of *los animales salvajes. (Collapsing to the floor)* To keep my sanity, I said this axiom, over and over in my head, until I was able to claw my way back to civilization. All Seniors Turn Crazy … All Seniors Turn Crazy …. *(Referring to the board)* All, Sine, Cosine, Tangent. *All Seniors Turn Crazy* … A-S-T-C. A-S-T-C!! If it wasn't for trigonometry, none of us would be here now. *(The kids applaud* ESCALANTE'S *performance. He stands up and takes a bow, then crosses to the board.)*

ANGEL. Kimo, I thought this room was supposed to have an air conditioner, man.

ESCALANTE. It does have an air conditioner. Just doesn't work.

ANGEL. Great.

ESCALANTE. You should think, cool, man. Think … like a cool calculus team. Think … *(Slowly the class fills in the blank.)*

STUDENTS *(in unison).* … Cool …

ESCALANTE. Think …

STUDENTS *(in unison).* Cool … *(ESCALANTE mouths the word, "Think," and gestures for them to continue. Soothingly:)* Cool … Cool … Cool … Cool … Cool … *(The lights fade to black.)*

END OF ACT ONE

ACT TWO SENIOR YEAR

— SCENE ONE —

(In the blackout we hear:)

SECRETARY'S VOICE *(over P.A. system).* On behalf of the principal and the faculty, we'd like to welcome you back from summer vacation. Anyone caught smoking on school property may face suspension. Also, for safety reasons, it is advised that female students should only use the restrooms in pairs. Please make sure to inform your teachers that you need accompaniment and they will provide the proper hall passes. Thank you. *(The secretary repeats the announcement in Spanish as the lights come up on the beginning of the new school year.)* *En nombre del director y la facultad deseamos*

darle la bienvenida a un nuevo año escolar. El que sea agarrado fumando será suspendido. Por motivos de seguridad recomendamos que las estudiantes femeninas no vayan al baño solas. Infórmenle a sus maestros que necesitan un acompañante y ellos les darán el permiso requerido. Muchas gracias.

(The hallway is filled with the usual pandemonium. Kids smoking, listening to music, clusters of girls and boys scoping each other out. CHUCO *and the Maravilla Gang are gathered off to one side. One of the gang is spray painting their* placa[19] *on a wall.* ANGEL *enters, reading from his class schedule.* CHUCO *spots him.)*

CHUCO. *Orale!* Homes … *(ANGEL stops when he sees* CHUCO *and the gang.* ANGEL *puts away his class schedule as* CHUCO *waves him over.)* Where you been, man? All summer, hide and seek with you.

ANGEL. Been busy … What you doing here? Thought you dropped out.

CHUCO *(smiling).* Yeah, well, thought I'd pay a little visit to the school. *(CHUCO takes the schedule from* ANGEL'S *pocket and looks it over.)* Oh, man. You still in Kimo's class? That *pelón* has you goin' good … You should dump math and come hang out with *la clica,* get stoned, cruise Whittier. *(He puts the schedule back in* ANGEL'S *pocket and fixes* ANGEL'S *collar.)*

ANGEL. Yeah. Maybe.

CHUCO *(gives* ANGEL *a long, hard look).* What's with this maybe stuff? Man, we're *carnalitos … Mi misma sangre.*

ANGEL. We're still blood, homes. *(They shake hands,* cholo-*style.)*

CHUCO. Okay, so listen, bro, I got a little business to take care of. Why don't you keep an eye out for me, okay? *(CHUCO takes out some drugs and shows them to* ANGEL.*)*

ANGEL. Man, you can't be selling that here.

---

19. *placa,* symbol

CHUCO. Just take a second—

ANGEL. No way, *ése*, no way.

CHUCO. What's with you, bro?

ANGEL. The principal will have my little *culito*[20] on the street, homes.

CHUCO (*stares down* ANGEL). What's the matter, *Mamasita*? … (ANGEL *looks at* CHUCO *and shakes his head. Almost the entire Maravilla Gang is watching.*) C'mon, *tirame un beso.*[21] (ANGEL *turns to walk away.* CHUCO *shoves him from behind and* ANGEL *falls to the ground. His pencil falls from behind his ear to the floor beside him.* ANGEL *picks it up in a threatening manner.*) What's the matter? Gonna stab me with a pencil? Not man enough to use a knife?… (*A small crowd has gathered, looking for a duel.* ANGEL *thinks about fighting, then breaks the pencil with one hand. He gets up and walks away, ignoring* CHUCO.) Where you going? Come back! … Angel? … Angel!!

(CHUCO *watches as* ANGEL *walks off. Upstage, there is a crash of breaking glass and some screaming and shouting. A Maravilla Gang member comes racing down the hall, a security guard not far behind.* CHUCO *and the rest of the gang tear out through the audience, laughing and screaming.* ESCALANTE *enters.*)

GANG MEMBER. Welcome back, *pelón*!! (*The gang member crashes into* ESCALANTE *while trying to escape. The security guard catches the gang member and takes him off in handcuffs.*)

(ESCALANTE *collects his books, dusts himself off, and enters the classroom. The desks have been rearranged into clusters. He writes on the blackboard: A.P. Calculus.* CLAUDIA, RAFAELA, *and* TITO *all spill into the classroom.* JAVIER, ANA, *and the rest of the class make their way in.* ANGEL *comes in last. While the rest of the school appears unchanged, there is a bit more enthusiasm within* ESCALANTE's *group. By now however, there are more desks than students.*)

ESCALANTE (*overlapping entrances*). Welcome back, welcome back. Everybody still alive, that's a plus. You're still failing, though. (*Students groan and laugh.* ESCALANTE *moves amongst them playfully.*) Remember the good times we had over the summer? Remember trigonometry? Math analysis? Do you remember when things were really jumpin' good, oh yeah. Well, the good times are gone with the wind. It's now the good, the bad, and the ugly. (*The class groans.* ESCALANTE *takes out a stack of forms and passes them out.*) We'll go step by step. Inch by inch. Calculus was not made to be easy. It already is.

JAVIER (*reading form*). Oh, come on! Contracts? You mean you can't trust us by now?

ESCALANTE. For those of you making the commitment, you will be preparing yourselves for the Advanced Placement Test. Make sure a parent or guardian signs it before you come to class tomorrow.

TITO. Wait, wait, wait. We have to come an hour before school, take your classes two periods, and stay until five?

ESCALANTE. Believe it or don't.

PANCHO. Saturdays? We have to come on Saturdays? (PANCHO *looks at the contract long and hard, then puts his head on his desk.*)

LUPE. And no vacations?

ESCALANTE. Yep. If you want to be on the calculus team.

ANGEL. *Orale*, Kimo! This is worse than juvy.

TITO. Kimo, we're seniors. This is supposed to be our year to slack off.

ESCALANTE (*tugs at* TITO's *hair*). What's the matter, Johnny? Think you won't be able to make it Saturday morning after playing in your band Friday nights?

TITO. Look, you love scarin' us into doing

---

20. *culito,* behind

21. *tirame un beso,* throw me a kiss

stuff, Kimo, I know. But that gets old real fast.

ESCALANTE. Hey, Motorhead? What about you?

PANCHO (*looks up from his desk*). Kimo, I don't want to let you down, but I gotta put school on hold.

ESCALANTE. What're you talking about?

PANCHO. My uncle offered me a job operating a forklift on Saturdays and Sundays. I'll be making time and a half.

ESCALANTE. So what?

PANCHO. So, two years in the union and I'll be making more than you. I'll be able to buy a new Trans Am.

ESCALANTE. Can't cruise through life, Pancho. Wouldn't you rather design cars than repair them? Can't even do that if they got fuel injection. Cars get old. Jobs come and go. An education lasts forever. Get it signed.

PANCHO. Kimo, I can't—

ESCALANTE (*tosses a clown's mask over to PANCHO*). For you, Johnny. For when you work at Jack-in-the-Box. Fit right in.

PANCHO (*tosses the mask to the floor*). Man, you're not gonna strip my gears. (*PANCHO walks out.*)

ESCALANTE. Anybody else jumping ship? Okay, let's go.

(*The kids all eye each other for a moment and then slowly open up their notebooks. The bell rings to signal the start of class. Lights fade to a transition. The students spill out of the class and down the halls. LUPE and CLAUDIA enter the hallway. CLAUDIA is reading from a book.*)

CLAUDIA. Originally referred to as the calculus by Sir Isaac Newton.

LUPE. The calculus? Sounds like a disease.

CLAUDIA. It says he invented it so he could figure out planet orbits, but he never bothered to tell anybody about his discovery.

LUPE. So how they know he discovered it?

CLAUDIA. 'Cause this other guy went around claiming *he* had invented it. But this guy was so stupid, he got it all wrong. So Newton had to go public and correct all his mistakes …

LUPE. For a genius, Newton was an idiot.

CLAUDIA. Yeah. I mean if I invented something I'd make sure everybody knew about it. That way I'd get paid. (*They laugh and LUPE tosses the book aside. CLAUDIA takes out her contract and looks at it.*)

LUPE. I can't believe we just lost summer vacation, and now Kimo wants us to come in morning, noon, and night.

CLAUDIA. My mom already thinks I'm crazy … She says, "Boys don't like you if you're too smart." She's never gonna sign this contract.

(*PANCHO enters. He's still brooding.*)

LUPE. You gonna come back to class, or what?

PANCHO. I don't know. My uncle's doing me a *favor*.

LUPE (*sidles up to him and strokes his back patiently*). But that job will always be there for you.

PANCHO. No, it won't! He'll hire somebody else! Man, Kimo's messin' up my plans.

LUPE. But I thought we were going to go to college together. (*LUPE strokes PANCHO's face. He pulls away.*)

PANCHO. Lupe, don't tell me what to do. I don't need you to think for me.

LUPE. I was just tryin to help—

PANCHO. Maybe I don't want your help, okay? (*LUPE turns and walks away.*) Oh, come on. Lupe! (*PANCHO stops her before she can exit. They talk silently upstage. A spot comes up on CLAUDIA, off by herself.*)

CLAUDIA. Pancho. He doesn't even know how good he's got it with Lupe. She's perfect for him. And all he can think about is what he doesn't have. Men think they're so smart 'cause they run everything, but really, they're just plain stupid. And they don't even realize it. Like, like what're those dogs called, the ones that hunt birds? They bark and bark, running around chasing after the bird, then, when they finally catch it—they spit it out. And then they start running around again, barking and stuff, wondering what happened to the bird. *(She looks over at* PANCHO *and* LUPE. *They have made up and are hugging.) Men.* Sometimes I wish I didn't think they were so sexy. Like if I was into girls or something. At least I can understand them. I mean, this guy I was dating once? He didn't like to mess around before he played basketball. Said he had to channel himself or something. And that's cool, except, if the team lost a game? Then he'd wanna go at it *hot and heavy.* 'Cause he was gettin' his energy flowing the *right* way. One day he's *blocked,* next time he's *flowing.* Like a toilet or something. If he hadn't been such a good kisser, I woulda never put up with his crap. *Stupid.* Bark, bark, boss, boss. Always giving orders, making rules … I'm sick of it. All the pushing … Is it genetic or something? Guys have genes that make them such jerks? … My stepfather doesn't like dinner, so he yells at my mom. He gets drunk at night and yells some more. You try and say something to him, make some sense, and *smack.* Like it's a game or something. "Shut up or I'll smack ya," so I shut up and get smacked anyway. Smacking, barking, pushing. Almost wish I was a guy, so I could smack him around. But like, I want to be like that? *Please.* Nobody has the right to push anybody around. That might work with my mom, but not me. Told him that right to his face. I am woman, hear me roar. I'm gonna be somebody. I can take care of myself. I'll

sign my own *contracts.* I'll make my own way. Get my own place. Where nobody's yelling and nobody's pushing and nobody's getting hit … Someplace where *I* make the rules … You don't like them? Fine. You can split … It'll be a peaceful place. Somewhere a woman can relax … And be happy … And be safe … And not have to hide from no dog that don't know no better than to leave the birds alone. (CLAUDIA *looks down at the contract. She forges a signature on the contract and puts it in her pocket. Lights fade down on her and up on the classroom.)*

(It is 7 A.M. ESCALANTE *is alone in the room, preparing for early morning class. He takes out a tape player, puts on some classical music and then crosses to the board. He writes out a problem.* ARMANDO *is mopping the hallway.* ANA, JAVIER, *and* TITO *wander in.* TITO *is practically sleepwalking.)*

ARMANDO. What're you doing here so early?

ANA. Mr. Escalante's class, remember? (ARMANDO *nods his head.* ANA *and* JAVIER *head to the classroom.* TITO *wanders down the hall.)*

ARMANDO. Yo, Tito. Wrong way, man.

TITO. What? … Oh … Thanks. *(*TITO *heads toward the class.)*

(Other students are filtering in. Because of the early hour, they are less than enthusiastic. ESCALANTE *is waiting by the door receiving contracts from the students as they enter.)*

ESCALANTE. Thank you, thank you very much. You don't got it signed, you don't get a ticket to watch the show. Thank you, Mr. Kung Fu. *(To* TITO*)* Hey, get a haircut, one more time I gotta tell you. Good morning, good morning. Mr. Blue Eyes, thank you very much. Elizabeth, my Taylor! Sophia, My Loren! Red, get a new jacket. Thank you, very much. *(To* ANGEL*)* Clint, forget your gun? (ANGEL *hands him his contract.*) Unfold it. Good. (*Everyone has returned except for* PANCHO. ESCALANTE *puts the contracts in his briefcase and heads to the blackboard.*) Hey, how come it's so quiet?

JAVIER. It's 7 A.M., Kimo.

LUPE. Yeah, my rooster's still sleeping.

ESCALANTE. Okay, you see this problem on the board? (ESCALANTE *points to the board. No reaction from the students.*) Come on, *wake up*, drink coffee. You see this? One, you got the graph, right here. Two, this is it. The most important part. This, right here. It's a radius of rotation. That's it. Anybody got any questions? Anybody can do it … (ESCALANTE *prowls the room.* ANGEL *raises his hand and points out a sleeping* TITO.) As long as you remember one basic element, and that is—the element of surprise. (*He thwacks* TITO *on the head with a small red pillow.* TITO *awakens with a start.*) Stay awake! I take it personally. Oh, you're waking up, good morning! How are you? Bring toothpicks to pinch your eyes open. Easily understood, Johnny?

TITO (*still sleepy*). Me and my band were swimming with dolphins, whispering imaginary numbers, lookin' for the fourth dimension …

ESCALANTE. That's good. That's very good. Go back to sleep. Okay … (*Scattered laughs.* TITO *puts his head down on the pillow.*)

(PANCHO *enters and* ESCALANTE *stops teaching.* PANCHO *drops off his signed contract on the desk and takes his seat.* ESCALANTE *has a smile on his face.*)

PANCHO. What you smilin' about?

ESCALANTE. Who me? It's a beautiful morning. I love the morning. (ESCALANTE *takes in the ragged group. He turns off the music coming from his tape player.*) Hey! What're you gonna do, sleep while Rome's burning? Let's go. Wake up! Yeooowww!! Dog-

dog-dog … (ESCALANTE *bounces around the room. The students halfheartedly respond.*)

STUDENTS. Dog-dog-dog-dog …

(ESCALANTE *heads back to the blackboard. The students continue the chant.* ESCALANTE *turns to them with a scowl.*)

ESCALANTE. Okay, okay. Enough fun. Back to work. (*The class groans. The lights fade out.*)

SCENE TWO

AT RISE: *Lights up. Most of the students are still in their desks, working hard. Some are hanging up the Christmas decorations.* ESCALANTE *is quietly helping a couple of them off to one side. A bell rings signifying the end of the school day. We hear* PRINCIPAL MOLINA *over the P.A. system. The hallway fills with screaming and laughing students on their way home.* ESCALANTE'*s class stays at their desks.* ARMANDO *enters the classroom.* ESCALANTE *nods at him, and* ARMANDO *proceeds to sweep the floor. The students are used to the routine and lift their feet for him. For the most part, the kids in the hallway ignore* MOLINA'*s speech. Those that do pay attention do so only to heckle or cheer at inappropriate times. Everyone else is gleefully preparing to leave.*)

MOLINA'S VOICE (*overlapping above*). Testing … testing … What? … Oh, thank you … (*Clears his throat*) As you leave for vacation, I just wanted to wish everyone a Merry Christmas and a Happy New Year. I hope you all enjoy a happy and healthy holiday vacation … Oh, also. If anyone has information regarding the missing typewriters, I would greatly appreciate it. There will be no questions asked. Thank you … How do you turn this off? … Oh, thank you.

(*There is some static and the intercom cuts off.* CLAUDIA *and a few others look up from their work and longingly watch everyone leave. A group of students walk by the class. Someone says, "Don't they ever leave?" The others laugh and joke as they walk off.* ESCALANTE *reads out loud from a test booklet.*)

ESCALANTE. Okay, see all those kids leaving school, climbing the hill to go home. Okay, that may be considered as a combination of two motions, horizontal and vertical. If the slope of the hill varies, the relation between the two rates of motion becomes complex. Got it? I doubt it. Who can explain this to me? Anybody? Come on, use the shortcut.

ANGEL. Kimo, this shortcut put me in the wrong neighborhood.

ESCALANTE. How 'bout you, Claudia?

CLAUDIA. Call on someone else, Kimo.

ESCALANTE. Come on, we're going backwards. This is ancient history. You can't forget what you learned last month. Come on, Claudia, think!

CLAUDIA. I don't feel like thinking.

ESCALANTE. You're foolin' around too much during the weekend. Girl's gotta do some work from the neck up. (*The students laugh.*) We're gonna have to work straight through Christmas break. (*The students groan.*)

CLAUDIA. Not me. (*She grabs her things and makes for an exit.*)

ESCALANTE. Where are you going? You late for another date? (*To class*) Girl's got more boyfriends than Elizabeth Taylor.

CLAUDIA (*at the door*). I don't appreciate you using my personal life to entertain this class! (*She storms out.* ESCALANTE *signals for* JAVIER *to lead the lesson, then heads out after* CLAUDIA.)

ESCALANTE. Claudia … (*Some students rest their heads on their desks while others continue working. Maybe some take down the Christmas decorations.* ESCALANTE *runs over to* CLAUDIA, *who is crying in the hall.*) It's

okay. It's okay. Talk to me … Shhh. It's okay. (*He takes* CLAUDIA *by the arm and they walk farther away from the class.*)

CLAUDIA (*still crying*). Everything is falling apart right now. My boyfriend's freaking out, my mom. School sucks. I'm in that classroom all day, Kimo. Look at my clothes! And my hair. I can't even comb it! I hate my life.

ESCALANTE. At least you have hair to comb.

CLAUDIA. I hate math! I hate calculus!

ESCALANTE. No problem. I hate it, too. (*She laughs through her tears.* ESCALANTE *opens his arms and they hug. He smiles at her.*) Okay, get back in class before I get in trouble.

(CLAUDIA *heads back to the classroom, wiping away the tears.* MOLINA *passes her as he crosses to* ESCALANTE.)

MOLINA. Jaime, listen, I need a favor. Mr. Sanzaki resigned. He got his job back in aerospace. I need someone to cover his night school class.

ESCALANTE. No, no, Hugo, the test is a month away …

MOLINA. Jaime, I'm in a jam. It's just until I replace him, okay?

ESCALANTE. I'm not going to be through with my calculus team till seven.

MOLINA. Great! The class starts at eight. Can you start tonight?

ESCALANTE. Eight o'clock? … My family's never gonna forgive me. (ESCALANTE *starts for his class again.* MOLINA *calls after him.*)

MOLINA. Jaime, think they'll pass the A.P. test?

ESCALANTE. Sure, sure. They're top kids.

MOLINA (*exiting*). Got my fingers crossed. Keep up the good work. (MOLINA *strides off.*)

ESCALANTE (*to himself*). Eight o'clock. Got a new class. Eight o'clock. (ESCALANTE *heads back to the class. Blackout.*)

SCENE THREE

AT RISE: *The Christmas decorations are gone. The students are all in their desks, looking more run-down than before.* PANCHO *is at the blackboard, working on a problem.* ESCALANTE *paces the room. He's agitated. He looks at* PANCHO's *attempt at an answer.*

ESCALANTE. Come on, Pancho. No way. This is easy. (PANCHO *tries again, stops, erases his work and begins again. He is getting frustrated and so is* ESCALANTE.) Put some energy into the upper quadrant of your stomach. Only got three weeks before the test. Use the shortcut! (PANCHO *stares intently at the problem. He takes another shot.*) No, no, no. C'mon! This is baby stuff, for Boy Scouts!

PANCHO. You know my mind don't work this way.

ESCALANTE. No excuses, Pancho. Tick-tack-toe. It's a piece of cake, upside down. Watch for the green light! (PANCHO *is exasperated. He stares at the board. Finally, he can't take it anymore and he punches the blackboard.*)

PANCHO. I been with you guys two years! Everybody knows I'm the dumbest! I just can't handle calculus, okay?! These guys have a better chance of making the A.P. test without me. (JAVIER *snickers.*) Don't laugh!

ESCALANTE. How can we laugh? You're breaking our hearts.

PANCHO. Don't do this, Kimo.

ESCALANTE. How noble. To sacrifice himself for the benefit of the team … Do you have the *ganas*? Do you have the desire?

PANCHO. Yes, I have the *ganas*!!

ESCALANTE. Do you want me to do it for you?!

PANCHO. Yes!!

ESCALANTE (*Takes the chalk from him. To* PANCHO) You were supposed to say no. (PANCHO *goes to his seat.* ESCALANTE *draws a graph on the board as he talks to the class.*)

I'm gonna have to get tough. Bullets are gonna have to start flyin'. Gonna have to stay late again. (*Everyone groans.*)

(ANGEL *enters. He's out of breath as he takes his seat in the back.*)

ANGEL (*whispering to* TITO). What I miss?

ESCALANTE (*to* ANGEL). The counselor was just here looking for you.

ANGEL. Hey, Kimo, it's cool, I was at the hospital …

ESCALANTE (*overlapping*). Something about some cosmetology classes. He says there's three different levels. One for boys, one for girls, and one for, I don't know what kind. Why don't you go find out?

ANGEL (*overlapping*). Oh, Kimo. Please listen, man. *Mi abuelita* fell down, hurt her hip, I had to get her taken care of—

ESCALANTE (*Returns to the board. Overlapping.*) Check out. Game's over. You lose.

ANGEL. You never listen, man! You never listen to nobody!! *Te crees el más chingón!*[22]

ESCALANTE. *Adiós.* Why don't you send me some postcards? Or call me on the telephone, let me know how you're doing. We love you.

ANGEL (*throws his desk over and grabs his crotch*). Kimo Sabe this, *cabrón*! Huh?! (ANGEL *exits.*)

ESCALANTE. Hey, Pancho, I think that guy's got a bigger problem than you. (*He finishes drawing the graph.*) Tick. Tack. Toe. Simple. (ESCALANTE *looks around the room. No one is smiling. The lights fade into night.*)

(*It is clearly after hours and the mood is subdued. The kids are sprawled all around the classroom, studying in pairs or small groups. They look ragged.* ARMANDO *is sitting on the hallway floor, working out a math problem.* ESCALANTE *is standing beside him. He seems tired and distracted.*)

ESCALANTE (*re:* ARMANDO's *work*). That's the

---

22. *Te crees el más chingón!,* You think you're the biggest stud!

wrong number, but you put it in the right place. You've got to watch the negative sign. Remember, it's a little stick that might trip you up. (ARMANDO *nods his head, crosses out a number, then puts in the right answer. He shows it to* ESCALANTE.)

ARMANDO. Like this?

ESCALANTE. That's it. You're the best.

ARMANDO. Thanks, Kimo. (ESCALANTE *wanders over to the class and peeks his head in the door.*)

ESCALANTE. All right. Synchronize watches, ready? Start the practice test: now. (*The kids mumble an acknowledgment and begin taking the practice test.* ESCALANTE *winces and massages his chest. He heads back over to* ARMANDO.)

ARMANDO. Working too hard, Mr. Escalante.

ESCALANTE. They'll be okay. They're tough kids.

ARMANDO. I was talking about you, Kimo.

ESCALANTE. No, come on, I'm the champ.

ARMANDO. You're working seven days a week. You should take a night off, take your wife and sons to the movies.

ESCALANTE. Twelve more days they got the test. Then, I go to junior high school to recruit for next year's class.

(ARMANDO *returns to his work.* ESCALANTE *spots* ANGEL, *who has just entered the hallway. He's carrying some food.*)

ANGEL. Heard there was some crazy vatos studying here late.

ESCALANTE. You're off the team. You blew it.

ANGEL. *Mi abuelita* thought they might be hungry. (ANGEL *holds up the food as a peace offering.* ESCALANTE *turns away, but then catches a whiff of the food.*)

ESCALANTE (*interested*). *Lomo montado? Pica a lo macho?* Where did your *abuelita* get the recipes for this?

ANGEL. I went to the library. Looked it up

under Bolivian brain food. We're gonna need it.

ESCALANTE (*gives* ANGEL *a long, hard look*). You gonna play by the rules?

ANGEL. I need calculus to get me a good job, Johnny …

ESCALANTE. You pull any tricks on me, I'll eat you for dinner … Get in there, you're way behind. (ESCALANTE *takes the food from* ANGEL. ANGEL *runs enthusiastically toward the classroom, then slams on the brakes, reverting back to his slow gang strut in front of the other kids.* ESCALANTE *sits beside* ARMANDO. ARMANDO *reaches for some food.*)

ARMANDO. Smells good. I hope they finish the test ahead of time.

ESCALANTE (*massaging his stomach*). I've lost my appetite, lately.

(*The lights fade into a tableau on the class A solo spot comes up on* JAVIER.)

JAVIER. Kimo reminds me a lot of my father … Not that they look alike, but that they're both so single-minded. My father started out picking grapes and nectarines in the San Joaquin valley—12 hours a day, six days a week. He taught himself at night by a kerosene lantern at migrant labor camps and succeeded in earning a G.E.D. by his 21st birthday. That's when he enrolled at Fresno State and met my mother. Seven years to obtain his degree. Five days of harvesting to afford two days of higher education. On the day he graduated, he proposed to my mother, only he insisted on becoming a C.P.A. before raising a family. He made her wait four years before she finally heard her wedding bells. You have to admire a man with his patience and fortitude. But my father doesn't understand that what worked for him isn't necessarily gonna work for me. Back in his day, you could look down the road, see something in the distance, and be reasonably assured it would still be there when you arrived, no matter how long it took. But the world I live in isn't grapes and nectarines. It's two-way television, talking computers, genetic engineering—stuff that's gonna feel like ancient history by the time I graduate college. So I'm busy preparing myself for a future that's hard to see. I imagine worlds where cars skim through the air like boats on water. Sailing up to cities built a mile high, so that you can't tell the difference between clouds and windows. And everything self-cleaning, by design. Designs pioneered by Javier Perales … This my father calls daydreaming. My father's centrifugal force keeps me earthbound while I gaze upward to the heavens, through the prism of my own inner scope, imagining whole new worlds. In the time it takes to walk between social studies and gym class.

(*The lights change back to daytime. The students are still in their seats. They're exhausted.* ESCALANTE *is writing a problem on the board, pressing so hard that he breaks the chalk. He starts roving the aisles as he waits for the answer, his impatience mounting.*)

ESCALANTE. We're looking for the area in the first quadrant bounded by the curve. What are the limits? Anybody?

CLAUDIA. Zero to pi over two, sir?

ESCALANTE. Wrong. Lupe?

LUPE. Uh, zero to pi over two?

ESCALANTE. What's wrong with you? This is review.

LUPE. Kimo, I checked my work twice.

ESCALANTE. I'm giving you the graph. Check it again.

TITO. No, Kimo. I got the same answer as the *gordita*.

LUPE. Don't call me *gordita, mocoso*.

ANA. It's zero to pi over two, sir.

JAVIER. Yeah, I got the same thing.

ESCALANTE. You guys should know this. No way! No way! You all took the shortcut, but you all took the same wrong turn! Green light means you add. Zero to pi over four. You should know this! What's wrong with you? This is review! You're acting like a blind man in a dark room looking for a black cat that isn't there! What's wrong with you guys?! I don't believe it! It's giving me a shot from the back! NO WAY! NO WAY!! (ESCALANTE *storms out. Silence.*)

PANCHO. Man, Kimo finally blew a head gasket. (ESCALANTE *enters the hallway, extremely upset. Suddenly, he grabs his arm and starts to massage it. He's in some pain. He stops short and massages his chest. He falls to his knees, clutching his chest.* ESCALANTE *collapses to the floor, gasping for air. He crawls a little way and then lies motionless, his breathing labored.* RAFAELA *has wandered out of the classroom to find* ESCALANTE. *She spies him on the floor.*)

RAFAELA. Ayudenme … por el amor de Dios!![23] (*The others run from the classroom to see what the problem is. They find* RAFAELA *kneeling beside* ESCALANTE. *They gather around their fallen teacher.*)

LUPE. Somebody get a teacher!! (PANCHO *races off down the hallway. Blackout*)

SCENE FOUR

AT RISE: *The students hang out in the classroom. The team spirit is low.* CLAUDIA *is staring off into space.* LUPE *paces,* PANCHO *watches her.* ANGEL *is off by himself.* TITO *is quietly playing an instrument.* RAFAELA *looks as if she's been crying.* ANA *reads intently.* JAVIER *goes to* ESCALANTE's *desk and opens a book.*

JAVIER. Page 456, please … Come on, you guys. Four-fifty-six.

TITO. Will you shut up and sit down, man. (*Pause.* JAVIER *sits back down.*)

---

23. *Ayudenme … por el amor de Dios!!,* Help me … for the love of God!!

LUPE. He should have taken it easier.

RAFAELA. It's our fault. We just sit back and watch him burn in.

CLAUDIA. It's burn out.

PANCHO. He looked fine to me.

ANGEL. The man brought it on himself. He was asking for trouble.

ANA. How can you say that!?

PANCHO. What do you know? You're nothing but a wannabe *cholo*.

ANGEL. At least I'm not a whimp! (PANCHO *shoves* ANGEL. *They start fighting.*)

CLAUDIA (*overlapping*). Stop it, guys!

ANGEL (*overlapping*). You want me, Motorhead? Come on!

PANCHO (*overlapping*). Come on, man, I'll kick your butt!

RAFAELA (*overlapping*). Please, don't fight, please.

TITO (*unable to separate them, overlapping*). Pancho! Cool out! Just cool out!

(MOLINA *enters.*)

MOLINA (*overlapping*). All right, all right! Break it up! Pancho! Just break it up. Now, settle down. (*The fight stalls. Everyone takes a deep breath and settles down.* PANCHO *shoots a dark look to* ANGEL.)

ANGEL (*to* PANCHO). We'll talk later, *ése.*

MOLINA. All right, settle down, Angel, everybody, just sit down … Mr. Escalante is okay. He's recovering from a mild heart attack and he'll be under observation for the time being … I know there's only a couple of days before the A.P. calc exam, so Mrs. Ortega will be taking over the review. And I don't want to hear about any more trouble from this room … Angel, Pancho— I want you on your best behavior. You owe that much to Mr. Escalante. Now, can I trust you guys? … (PANCHO *and* ANGEL *nod.*) Okay. Get in your seats. (*The boys take their seats and* MOLINA *exits. The lights fade to a tableau. A spot comes up on* TITO.)

TITO. All I can hear is this white noise reverbing in my skull, ringing in my ears … Waves of sound that echo out of my body. Leaving me … Alone … Hollow … Empty … Except for one chord … One feeling. A whisper. Trying to get out. Making it hard to breathe … One chord … One song …

(*He picks up an instrument and starts to play a jarring, painful riff which slides into a soulful melody. When the music is done, the lights in the class return to normal.* ORTEGA *is at the front of the class. The students are deadly silent.*)

ORTEGA. Now, I know you're all a bit upset over Mr. Escalante's condition and so am I. Personally, I feel very badly about the whole thing … I warned Mr. Molina something like this was bound to happen … All we can do now is pray for a full recovery for Mr. Escalante … And I hope the rest of us can learn from this experience … Life is ultimately about balance. And compromise. It's important to set goals, even ones that are difficult to attain. But finally, it's even more important to keep things in perspective. You have already accomplished far more than most high school seniors. In fact, if any student in this room were to decide not to take the A.P. test, no one could possibly hold it against you … (*The students eye each other. No one speaks.*) Unless anyone has any questions, why don't you all take the rest of this period off.

JAVIER. But the test is the day after tomorrow.

ORTEGA. I'm aware of that, Javier. But I think in this case, it couldn't hurt to take a little time away from calculus.

(ESCALANTE *pokes his head into the room.*)

ESCALANTE. Hi!

STUDENTS. Kimo! How are you?! Hey, Kimo Sabe! Kimo! (*They applaud as he enters.*)

ESCALANTE. I'm still alive! I'm a hard dyin' type of guy.

LUPE. Shouldn't you be in the hospital?

ESCALANTE. No, I should be here with you. Yeooowww! (ESCALANTE *crouches down and growls like a dog.*)

STUDENTS. *Bulldogs!!!!*

ESCALANTE. Thank you for baby-sitting my *canguros.*

ORTEGA. Well … It seems as though I'm no longer needed here. Good to have you back, Mr. Escalante. (ORTEGA *exits.*)

ESCALANTE. Have a good day, Mrs. Ortega. (*The students laugh.* ESCALANTE *roams the room like his old self.*) How are you? How are you?

TITO. Hey, you should be taking it easy, man.

ESCALANTE. Had to leave the hospital before they added up the bill.

ANGEL. Kimo, back to bed, homes.

ESCALANTE. No, I should be here with you guys. I mean, you already forgot to stand up! Come on! Come on! Stand and deliver. Everybody! Come on! (*The students jump out of their chairs.*) No, no! Against the wall, like a snake! Hurry! (*The students laugh and shout as they form a chain and snake around the room. The snake runs its course and stops with a line against the wall.* ESCALANTE *steps up to the front of the line. Overlapping above:*) Okay! We've been practicing for this all year. You're the best. You guys are the best! This is going to be a piece of cake!

STUDENTS (*in unison*). Upside down!

ESCALANTE. And?

STUDENTS (*in unison*). Step by step!

ESCALANTE. All right! You got it now. Get ready, keep your eyes open. (*To* LUPE) Y equal to 1 n quantity x minus 1. What's the domain?

LUPE. X is greater than minus 1. (ESCALANTE *shoots* LUPE. *She goes to the end of the line.*)

ESCALANTE (*overlapping*). No! I been gone one day and you forget already. Tito?

TITO. X is less than minus 1?

ESCALANTE (*gasping*). No! End of the line! You're going to kill me, give me another heart attack. (TITO *goes to the end of the line. It's* PANCHO*'s turn next.*) What's the domain?

PANCHO. All real numbers greater than 1. X is greater than 1.

ESCALANTE (*shakes* PANCHO*'s hand*). I told you you could do it! Okay, Kimo Sabe! You're the best!

PANCHO. All right! (PANCHO *proudly retains his place in line.* ESCALANTE *continues on.* ANGEL *is next. They stare at one another for a long moment.*)

ESCALANTE. Dog.

ANGEL. Dog.

ESCALANTE AND ANGEL. Dog … Dog … Dog-dog-dog-dog …

STUDENTS (*joining in*). Dog-dog-dog-dog … (*Lights down. The refrain continues through the blackout. End refrain.*)

SCENE FIVE

A T RISE: *Lights come up on the classroom. The desks have been straightened. The students are seated, neatly spaced in rows.* PRINCIPAL MOLINA *is passing out test booklets.*

MOLINA. Anyone not here to take the Advanced Placement Test in calculus should now leave. All right, be sure that each mark is black and completely fills the answer space. If you make an error, you may save time by crossing it out rather than trying to erase it. It is not expected that everyone will be able to answer all the multiple choice questions … You may not use calculators, slide rules, or reference material. When you're told to begin, open your booklet, carefully tear out the green insert, and start to work … You may begin—now.

(*The students open the booklets and begin. They*

look intense, tired and under pressure. MOLINA *prowls up and down the aisles. Perhaps there is a sound cue which helps indicate the excruciatingly slow passage of time … like a metronome. The students work in total silence. We hear the occasional cough … A chair shifts … The lights fade to a tableau with a spot on* TITO. *He starts tapping his desk nervously.* MOLINA *stands near him.* TITO *stops … Two more lights come up, one on* ANA, *one on* JAVIER. ANA *fills in the correct answer and turns a page.* JAVIER *thinks for a moment, then writes in his test, trying to keep up with* ANA … *A light comes up on* PANCHO. *He's a little perplexed. He sighs, and erases an answer from his test booklet … A light comes up on* RAFAELA. *She is speaking softly to herself in Spanish.* MOLINA *crosses to her side, puts his finger to his lips and gently cautions her … Three more lights come up on* ANGEL, CLAUDIA, *and* LUPE. CLAUDIA *has her head in her hands.* LUPE *is chewing her nails.* ANGEL *takes a deep breath, and plunges into the problem. Some of the kids are stuck, others start writing.* MOLINA *continues his vigil as the students continue their painstaking work. After a while, the lights slowly fade out.)*

(The lights fade back up on MOLINA *speaking. The classroom is full with students, teachers, and family. There is a strong current of excitement throughout the room. Everyone is beaming.)*

MOLINA. We, being teachers, know the Advanced Placement Tests are very difficult, especially in mathematics. Less than 2 percent of all high school seniors nationwide even attempt the A.P. test in calculus … I am proud to announce that no other school in Southern California has more students passing than Garfield High School. *(The guests clap respectfully for the students' achievement.* ESCALANTE *remains quietly proud.* MR. DELGADO *shakes his hand.)* Eighteen students took the test and eighteen passed. Many with the highest score possible.

*(*ANGEL *enters. He's drunk and wobbles as he walks, a big smile on his face. He bumps into a*

desk. *Everyone notices him.* ARMANDO *nudges* ESCALANTE.)*

ARMANDO *(softly).* Is he drunk?

ESCALANTE. No, he just walks like that. *(*ANGEL *joins his classmates.* MOLINA *tries to recover the moment.)*

MOLINA. It's because of the caliber of this graduating class that Garfield High is no longer under academic probation—Yes?

*(*RAFAELA *has sidled up to* MOLINA. *She whispers in his ear.* MOLINA *steps aside and* RAFAELA *takes his place.* TITO, CLAUDIA, ANGEL, LUPE, JAVIER, ANA, *and* PANCHO *line up behind her. The girls are holding* ANGEL *steady.)*

RAFAELA *(slowly).* We have an announcement to make.

MOLINA. It's all right. *(Encouraging her)*

RAFAELA *(smiling).* Okay. We, the A.P. calculus class, would like to present this plaque to our teacher, Jaime A. Escalante.

*(*ESCALANTE *makes his way to the students. They surround him as he reads the plaque. Embarrassed,* ESCALANTE *smiles and nods thankfully to the crowd. He tries to return to his place in the back. The kids don't let him leave.)*

RAFAELA. No, no. Read it out loud. Go ahead, don't be afraid.

ESCALANTE. "For improving our past, working tirelessly with the present, and shaping our future." *(*ESCALANTE *gets choked up. The students laugh and give him a group hug, as everyone else applauds respectfully. Lights down.)*

SCENE SIX

AT RISE: *The clapping continues through the blackout as the actors clear the stage. Lights come up on* ANA, *alone downstage, holding a letter.*

ANA. In most European nations, students

attend classes six days a week. In Japan, they also attend classes at night. The average American student spends 2,000 more hours in front of the television than in school. Every six seconds a crime occurs on or near an American campus … In one year, 338,000 students carried handguns into school at least once. More than 100,000 were armed every day. Approximately one quarter of all major urban school districts are now using metal detectors and 74 percent of the students in those districts have witnessed either a killing, stabbing, or shooting … Nine of every ten young people murdered in an industrialized nation are slain here in this country. In California, murder, theft, arson, and robbery are committed more often by juveniles than by adults. And in many cities, homicide is now the leading cause of death among children. In half those cases, the killers are also children. Gang participation has become the urban poor's version of teenage suicide. According to the National Commission on Secondary education for Hispanics, 40 percent of all Latino youths who drop out of U.S. schools, do so before the 10th grade … Forty-five percent of Mexican American children never finish high school. When I started at Garfield High the dropout rate was 55 percent … You can understand why graduation day was the most exciting day of my life … Rafaela in her new dress … Javier surprised me with a corsage. And Papá invited the whole class to dinner at the restaurant. You should have seen how proud Papá was of me when U.S.C. offered me a full academic scholarship. I calculated that it would cost more for my college diploma than my grandfather had earned in his entire life. As hard as it was, my straight A's were definitely worth the effort. I knew that I was not going to become just another statistic … Three days after graduation, the letter came in the mail. *(She begins to read from the letter.)* "Dear Ms. Delgado … I am writing to you because the Educational Testing Service Board of Review believes there is reason to question your Advanced Placement calculus grade."

(Lights come up on RAFAELA, TITO, LUPE, *and* PANCHO. *They too are holding letters.)*

RAFAELA. What?

TITO. They gotta be kidding.

LUPE. Oh, please no, don't let it be true.

(Lights come up on CLAUDIA, ANGEL *and* JAVIER, *also with letters. It is early summer, the students have graduated. They should be happy, but they're not. Everyone is tense. The students make their way into one group downstage.)*

CLAUDIA *(reading).* "Based on the unusual agreement of incorrect answers, the Educational Testing Service has no alternative but to question the scores of all the students with such unusual agreement."

PANCHO. English. What does it mean in English?

JAVIER. They're saying that we copied from each other, because we all had the same wrong answers.

LUPE *(sarcastically).* We're too stupid to know how to cheat correctly.

ANA. Those letters don't go to our colleges, do they?

JAVIER. Of course they do. These are the guys who do the SATs.

ANA. But once they give you a scholarship, they can't take it back, can they?

ANGEL *(reading).* "It's standard procedure to grade the test with the identity of the students concealed. Only after irregularities were found was it determined that the students who were in question were all from Garfield High School." *(CLAUDIA suddenly breaks down into tears.* LUPE *consoles her. Some of the kids head toward the classroom.* JAVIER *crosses over to* ANA.)*

JAVIER *(softly).* Anyone could have cheated. Pancho was way behind. Claudia freaking out all the time. Do you think someone got the test ahead of time?

ANA *(softly).* No, but my father does.

(The lights crossfade as they make their way into the class and sit down. During the transition, ESCALANTE reads out loud from a letter.)

ESCALANTE *(reading).* "This is a serious problem, and the E.T.S. would like to meet with you after you have read this letter and the enclosed pamphlet." You all received the same thing?

JAVIER. We can fight it. Take 'em to court. There's the Mexican American Legal Defense Fund and the A.C.L.U.

ANA. I'm supposed to start college in the fall.

RAFAELA *(quietly).* We could retest. *(Everyone turns to her.)*

CLAUDIA. Taking the test again is like saying we cheated. It's an admission of guilt!

TITO. No way! I'm not gonna do it! I don't need to prove nothing to nobody.

ESCALANTE. These people are human. They could make mistakes, too.

JAVIER. Kimo, they're calling us cheaters! *(ESCALANTE looks at them one by one, looking for the truth in their eyes.)*

ESCALANTE. There was no need to cheat. You guys are the best. I'm gonna clear this up. *(ESCALANTE exits.)*

PANCHO. Damn! If I had taken that job with my uncle, I could have had a brand new car by now!

LUPE. Hey, it's okay. You're good with cars. You can fix yours.

CLAUDIA. Your girlfriend's accused of cheating and all you can talk about is your lousy car?

PANCHO. At least my car puts out! *(LUPE starts to cry. CLAUDIA comforts her.)*

CLAUDIA. You are such a jerk, Pancho!

(A deadly silence takes over the room. The group is broken up into factions—everyone eyeing one another. No one talking. PRINCIPAL MOLINA and DRS. PEARSON and RAMÍREZ enter the hallway. They cross toward the classroom.)

MOLINA. We would like to resolve this with as little publicity as possible.

PEARSON. Certainly, that is our intention as well.

MOLINA. I proctored the test. Everything was done according to your specifications. The desks were the required three feet apart. Here's a chart of where each student sat. *(MOLINA hands the chart to PEARSON.)*

RAMÍREZ. Mr. Molina, we understand this school has a history of break-ins.

MOLINA. That's true. But, no one ever broke into the safe. It's impossible. I assure you, only my secretary and I know the combination.

(ESCALANTE catches up with them.)

ESCALANTE. Hugo!

MOLINA. Jaime, this is Dr. Pearson and Dr. Ramírez of the Educational Testing Service. Gentlemen, Jaime Escalante. The A.P calculus teacher.

PEARSON. Mr. Escalante.

RAMÍREZ. *Qué tal? Un placer.*

ESCALANTE. *El gusto es mío, Señor.*[24]

MOLINA. We were just on our way to the students.

ESCALANTE. Good. Let's go. *(ESCALANTE starts to lead them off.)*

PEARSON. I'm sorry, Mr. Escalante, but that's just not possible. E.T.S. policy.

ESCALANTE. But, they are my kids. I should be there.

RAMÍREZ. Mr. Escalante, this controversy is officially between the Educational Testing Service and the students. *(PEARSON,*

---

24. *El gusto es mío, Señor,* The pleasure is mine, Sir.

RAMÍREZ, *and* MOLINA *head to the classroom.* ESCALANTE *starts to follow them.* MOLINA *stops him. Exasperated,* ESCALANTE *relents. After a beat, he exits offstage.)*

(PEARSON, RAMÍREZ, *and* MOLINA *enter the classroom. The room gets very quiet.)*

MOLINA. These gentlemen are from the Educational Testing Service. They've come a long way, so, let's cooperate with them as much as possible. *(More silence)*

RAMÍREZ. Well … Does anyone have anything to say? *(Silence.* MOLINA *crosses to* ANA.*)*

MOLINA. Ana. I've known your family for years. Tell us the truth.

ANA. Nothing happened.

MOLINA *(bluffing).* Now, don't lie to me.

ANA *(near tears).* I'm telling you the truth! Nothing happened!

JAVIER. Why don't you just leave her alone? She didn't do anything wrong.

PEARSON. Then tell us who did. *(JAVIER gets out of his chair and walks out, slamming a door.)* We're not cops. We're not here to put anyone behind bars. If you cheated, let us know so you can go home and enjoy the rest of your summer. *(Silence.* RAMÍREZ *sits down next to* RAFAELA.*)*

RAMÍREZ. *Permiso* … I come from this neighborhood. *Yo vengo de este barrio.* And I know that sometimes we're tempted to take shortcuts. Just tell me the truth. What happened? *Dime la verdad.*

(RAFAELA *looks around fearfully.)*

ANGEL. Okay. *(Pause. The students look at him.)* We're busted. Why don't we just admit it?

RAMÍREZ. How'd you do it? *(Pause.* ANGEL *stands.)*

ANGEL. You sure no one gets in trouble, right?

PEARSON. As long as you tell us the truth.

(ANGEL *looks around the classroom. Everyone waits expectantly.)*

ANGEL. I got the test ahead of time. I passed it around to everyone.

PEARSON *(pulls out a notebook, preparing to gather evidence).* How did you get the test?

ANGEL. The mailman. I strangled him. His body's decomposing in my locker. *(The students start laughing so hard they are practically on the floor.* PANCHO *crosses to* ANGEL *and gives him a high-five.* TITO, ANGEL, *and* PANCHO *hug. The team is reunited.* PEARSON *and* RAMÍREZ *exchange a look.)*

RAMÍREZ *(to* MOLINA*).* There's no sense in continuing if they won't cooperate. *(ANGEL thrusts his tattooed knuckles in* RAMÍREZ's *face.* PEARSON *and* RAMÍREZ *leave.* MOLINA *glares at the laughing students.)*

MOLINA. If that's how you're going to behave, then just go home. *(The students spill out of the classroom. Lights down.)*

SCENE SEVEN

AT RISE: *Lights come up on* MOLINA *and* ESCALANTE *in the classroom.* ESCALANTE *is pacing like a caged animal.* MOLINA *is holding a letter.*

MOLINA. Jaime, please, let me take care of this. It's an administrative problem. You're only the teacher.

ESCALANTE *(takes the letter from* MOLINA*).* This I take care of myself.

(MRS. ORTEGA *walks into the room.)*

ORTEGA. You wanted to see me?

ESCALANTE. Do you know how this got in my box? *(Hands her the letter)*

ORTEGA. What is it?

MOLINA. A letter of resignation … Unsigned … Anonymous.

ORTEGA. My guess is that it could have something to do with the scandal this school is facing.

ESCALANTE. Do you think they cheated? *(Pause)*

ORTEGA. Mr. Escalante, you put those kids under an awful lot of pressure. They would have gone to any lengths to please you.

ESCALANTE. Do you think they cheated?

ORTEGA. I don't take any joy in your failure, Mr. Escalante. I recommended you for this job. On some level, I share the responsibility. The whole school does.

ESCALANTE. You didn't answer my question.

ORTEGA. All right. Well … Every night when I go to bed, I watch the television news. I see a lot of people go on trial. They deny everything or their lawyers say they were insane when they did it. A lot of them get off … But, I believe that most people who get caught today are guilty. Don't you, Mr. Molina? *(ORTEGA exits. ESCALANTE crumples up the letter.)*

ESCALANTE. Yep, it's true. Teaching dulls the senses …

MOLINA. Jaime … *(ESCALANTE doesn't say anything. MOLINA crosses to his side. They stand that way for a moment.)*

ESCALANTE. I may have made a mistake trying to teach them calculus.

MOLINA. Regardless of whether they passed that test or not, Jaime, they learned.

ESCALANTE. Yeah, they learned if you try real hard, nothing changes.

MOLINA. That's what you think? … Then quit … If that's all you have left to teach … Quit.

ESCALANTE. You know what kills me, that they lost the confidence in the system that they're now finally qualified to be a part of … I don't know why I'm losing sleep over this. I don't need it. I could make twice the money, in less hours, and have people treat me with respect.

MOLINA. Respect? Jaime, those kids love you.

They love you. *(They embrace. MOLINA exits.)*

(ESCALANTE slowly begins to organize his papers. A Maravilla Gang member drifts in. ESCALANTE eyes him. Neither of them speak. One by one the entire gang makes their way in. The classroom is deadly silent. CHUCO and ANGEL enter and cross to ESCALANTE.)

CHUCO. *Orale, Kimo sabe … Kimo sabe todo.* *(CHUCO holds out his hand. He and ESCALANTE shake hands,* cholo-style.*)*

ESCALANTE. *Orale.*

CHUCO. Homes told me you're havin' some problems. Just wanted to say, we got you covered.

ESCALANTE. Thank you very much.

CHUCO. We gonna cruise downtown, take action on those E.T.S. boys. You gotta throw down, homes. Hit them where they live. Like you say, *ése*, teach them some manners.

ESCALANTE. I see … Tell you what. Let me try it my way first. That doesn't work, I'll let you know. Okay, Johnny?

CHUCO. Put the word out, bro. We'll back your play.

MARAVILLA GANG *(exiting).* *Orale!* Kimo Sabe! *Orale! Orale!!*

ESCALANTE. *Orale.* Okay. *(They all head into the hall. ESCALANTE pulls ANGEL aside).* Just tell me that wasn't your idea.

ANGEL *(conspiratorially).* It was Chuco's idea.

ESCALANTE. Goot. *(ESCALANTE pats ANGEL on the back. ANGEL follows the Maravilla Gang off.)*

(PEARSON and RAMÍREZ have entered the classroom. They are looking over the "scene of the crime.")

PEARSON. We're going nowhere here. I say we wash our hands of it.

RAMÍREZ. I think our best course of action is to turn the whole dispute over to the universities. Let the students appeal to whichever ones they've applied to.

(They start to exit. ESCALANTE *enters the class-room.)*

ESCALANTE. Good afternoon, Doctors ... I feel I have the right to know why you think my students cheated.

PEARSON. Mr. Escalante, I appreciate your concern, but we're not at liberty to discuss the controversy with you.

ESCALANTE. Principal Molina proctored the test himself. His integrity has never been called into question and he has verified that nothing unusual took place. You investigated the test site personally. What have you found? Was anything out of order?

RAMÍREZ. It's an internal investigation for E.T.S. purposes only.

ESCALANTE. I would just like to see the test, that's all.

RAMÍREZ. Mr. Escalante, I understand what you're going through here, but, I repeat, the problem is between the E.T.S and your students. It doesn't reflect upon the school or its administration.

ESCALANTE. I would just like to see what kinds of mistakes were made. Once again, I'm their teacher. I know my kids.

PEARSON *(to* RAMÍREZ*).* If you're finished, we can leave. *(*PEARSON *and* RAMÍREZ *move to exit.* ESCALANTE *cuts them off.)*

ESCALANTE. Excuse me, but I'm not finished.

PEARSON. Mr. Escalante, as a mathematician, you're doubtlessly aware of the statistical improbability of having that many tests with identical wrong answers.

ESCALANTE. Maybe they all made the same mistakes because they all had the same teacher, teaching them the same program. I taught them step by step, inch by inch, all the way.

PEARSON. There were some ... unorthodox, even illogical, computations for students of this caliber. Mistakes in simple math.

ESCALANTE. I may have made mistakes. They were way behind. We had to cram five years inside two. I had to teach them shortcuts.

PEARSON. Look, your students averaged fewer than four wrong on the multiple choice, while other schools average, what, fourteen to eighteen incorrect answers? And we found out that most of your kids finished the test with time to spare.

ESCALANTE. They should be rewarded, not punished.

RAMÍREZ. Mr. Escalante, the Educational Testing Service does not act capriciously.[25] Every major university in the United States subscribes to our service.

ESCALANTE. I would just like to see the proof of wrongdoing. I would like to see the tests.

RAMÍREZ. Let me reiterate. There has been no proof of wrongdoing here. Only a suspicion of cheating.

ESCALANTE. In this country, one is innocent until proven guilty. Not the other way around.

RAMÍREZ. Just because we can't prove guilt doesn't mean we can sanction those scores.

PEARSON. If you're so confident of your students' abilities, why not encourage them to retest?

ESCALANTE. Why should I?

PEARSON. If they don't retest, everyone will assume they cheated.

ESCALANTE. Everyone will assume they cheated if they *do*! I want to see the tests, please!

RAMÍREZ. We're going around in circles here. Mr. Escalante, we're psychomatricians, thorough to the point of boredom. We're

---

25. capriciously, impulsively; irresponsibly

not out to get anyone here. (PEARSON *and* RAMÍREZ *try to exit, but again,* ESCALANTE *blocks the way.)*

ESCALANTE. Not so fast! If this was a simple situation of two students cheating, that's one thing. But, by making a blanket accusation, you're saying that there was a conspiracy. Every conspiracy has a leader! Who better qualified to be the leader than the teacher?!

RAMÍREZ. Mr. Escalante, nobody's accusing you of anything.

ESCALANTE. Not only me! The school, the parents, the entire community!

RAMÍREZ. Scores this high, I guarantee you, would be questioned regardless of the school.

ESCALANTE. Yes, but if this was Beverly Hills High School, they wouldn't have sent a black and a Latino to investigate.

RAMÍREZ. Mr. Escalante, I hope you're not insinuating that we haven't earned our positions here, 'cause no one's given me a damn thing ... I suggest you're letting your emotions get the best of you.

ESCALANTE. If no one has given you a damn thing, you should not be taking away from my kids!

RAMÍREZ. The *identities* of the students were concealed until it was determined that irregularities existed.

ESCALANTE. Those scores would never have been questioned if my kids did not have Spanish surnames and come from *barrio* schools! You know that!

RAMÍREZ. All right. We've been patiently explaining our position and listening to your complaints. But *now,* our conversation is over.

ESCALANTE. There's something going on here that nobody is talking about! And you know what it is!

RAMÍREZ. No one has the right ... to accuse me ... of racism. *No* one has the right to accuse *me* of racism!

ESCALANTE. I know well how to spell discrimination! I thought this was over a long time ago. Why are you doing this to my kids?!

PEARSON. There are two kinds of racism, Mr. Escalante. Singling out a group because they're members of a minority and *not* singling out a group because they're members of a minority.

ESCALANTE. My kids could teach you a thing or two, Johnny!

PEARSON. All right. Enough is enough. It's high time we left.

ESCALANTE. Go for it! You didn't show me the tests. You didn't prove anything. My kids didn't do anything! I'm gonna prove you guys wrong! (PEARSON *and* RAMÍREZ *exit. Lights down.)*

SCENE EIGHT

AT RISE: *Lights come up and a few of the students are in the classroom. More are wandering in.* ANGEL *enters and walks to where* TITO *is sitting.*

ANGEL. My desk, man.

TITO. No, it was mine. (ANGEL *reaches underneath the desk and pulls something out from below. He rolls his fingers in front of* TITO's *face.)*

ANGEL. My boogers. My desk.

TITO. Your desk. (TITO *gladly moves. Most of the students have gathered in the classroom.)*

(LUPE *enters the hallway.* PANCHO *runs to catch up with her.)*

PANCHO. Lupe, please, wait!

LUPE (*stops, but remains faced away from* PANCHO). What do you want?

PANCHO. I need to talk.

LUPE. Now is not the time for this, Pancho. *(She starts to walk away.* PANCHO *musters his courage.)*

PANCHO *(slowly).* I think about you every day … I can't get you out of my head … And … I'm afraid I'm never gonna see you again.

LUPE. You can't expect me to be your girlfriend at your convenience.

PANCHO. I'm a jerk. Sorry.

*(*PANCHO *leans in to kiss her and* LUPE *melts into his embrace.* CLAUDIA *enters the hallway and sees the couple. She smiles as she passes by them and into the class.)*

CLAUDIA. I thought I'd seen this place for the last time. *(*PANCHO *and* LUPE *break off the kiss and enter the classroom holding hands.)*

*(*ESCALANTE *enters the hallway, heading for the class. The students look up expectantly when he enters.)*

PANCHO. Kimo, we graduated two months ago. What're we doing here?

ESCALANTE. Still somethin' I gotta teach you *burros*. Back in Bolivia, I was a professor in the top school. I emigrated to this country because I wanted my children to have a shot at the American dream. Not so easy. No one here understood me when I opened my mouth because "I mess up with the language." No matter how well I knew my subject, no matter how much I had to offer, there wasn't a single school which recognized my degrees from Bolivia. Everything I had accomplished back home added up to a big zero. Whole new ballgame. Mopped the floors at Van De Kamps cafeteria. Bus tables in the day, learn English at night. I became cook in the restaurant. Two eggs and bacon, Bolivian-style. It would have been easy to give up. But I'll tell you what … I would not give in to their ignorance. Or to my own fears. I swallowed my pride. I enrolled at city college taking courses about subjects which I'd already taught. it was harder the second time, because now I had to support a family. I felt as if I was going backwards. And at times I was afraid I didn't have the *ganas* anymore. But I never thought I was beat. *Never* … Because I had a secret weapon … Knowledge … Knowledge is power … It's something that can never be taken away from you … Like it or not, you're gonna be tested the rest of your lives. And the only time you fail is when you quit. When you let them take away your spirit … Your desire … Your *ganas*. *(The students look at each other. Silence.)*

RAFAELA *(softly).* I want to take the retest.

ANA. Me too. *(They look around to their classmates.)*

JAVIER. I won't do it. I won't retest. *(*JAVIER *gets up to leave.)*

ESCALANTE. We go as a team, or we don't go at all. *(*JAVIER *freezes at the door.* ANA *crosses to* JAVIER, *takes his hand and leads him back to his desk. Everyone looks to* JAVIER.*)* What do you say, Mr. Perales. In, or out? *(*JAVIER *looks at their expectant faces. He gives them the thumbs-up sign.)*

JAVIER. Count me in, Kimo. *(The students wait nervously as* ESCALANTE *heads out to the pay phone. He puts in a quarter and dials.)*

CLAUDIA. What's he doing?! What's he doing?! *(*LUPE *runs to the classroom door and relays the phone call to the kids.)*

LUPE. Shhh!!! He's on the phone!

ESCALANTE. Hello? This is Jaime Escalante … My students have decided to take the test again … You're kidding! … Tomorrow? …

LUPE *(relaying the info).* They say we gotta take it tomorrow! *(She looks fearfully to* ESCALANTE.*)*

VARIOUS STUDENTS *(overlapping).* No way!

One day? How we gonna do it in one day?

LUPE (*to the class*). Shhh!!

ESCALANTE (*considers, then gives* LUPE *the thumbs-up sign*). Eight A.M., tomorrow. Thank you. (*He hangs up the phone.* TITO, LUPE, *and* CLAUDIA *have spilled out into the hall.*)

TITO. No, Kimo. One day?

ESCALANTE. Can't do it in any less. I didn't make the rule. Gonna have to review the entire course in one shot. Okay, let's go! (ESCALANTE *ushers them back into the class.*)

CLAUDIA. Kimo, you're afraid we're gonna screw up royally tomorrow, aren't you?

ESCALANTE. Tomorrow's just another day, honey. I'm afraid you're gonna screw up the rest of your lives.

PANCHO. Maybe they'll give us the same test.

ESCALANTE (*gently*). Uh-uh. It'll be harder. You can count on that. Just go step by step and play defense. Don't bring anything. No pencils, no erasers, nothing. Don't wear clothes with too many pockets. Don't let your eyes wander. No spacing out. Don't give them any opportunity to call you cheaters. You are the true dreamers. And dreams accomplish wonderful things. You're the best. Tomorrow you'll prove that you're the champs. We're gonna start with Chapter 1 … (*Lights slowly fade out.*)

SCENE NINE

AT RISE: *Lights up.* PEARSON *and* RAMÍREZ *are in the classroom along with several of the students.* PANCHO *and* LUPE *are sitting near each other.* RAMÍREZ *places tests down on their desks.* JAVIER *enters along with a few others. As they enter,* PEARSON *gives each a pencil. Each student finds a desk.*

RAMÍREZ. Sit anywhere you like.

(*The group is almost complete.* ANA *enters.*)

ANA. Excuse me? I'm going to have to leave early.

RAMÍREZ. What's wrong?

ANA. I have an appointment at U.S.C. It's related to my scholarship.

PEARSON. Can't it wait?

ANA. No, it can't. (PEARSON *and* RAMÍREZ *exchange a look.*)

RAMÍREZ. Okay. Just do as much as you can.

(ANGEL *arrives barechested, wearing only shorts with the pockets turned inside out. He throws his hands over his head like a prisoner being searched.* PEARSON *shakes his head and hands him a pencil.* ANGEL *accepts the pencil and flashes his knuckles at* PEARSON.)

PEARSON. Please take a seat. (ANGEL *sits.* PEARSON *closes the doors.* RAMÍREZ *directs* ANA *to a seat near the door and counts the students.*) I'm sure you are all familiar with the procedure. You have 90 minutes to complete the multiple choice section. Do not fill in answers by guessing. Wrong answers will be counted against you. Credit will be given for partial solutions. Do not spend too much time on any particular answer. You may open the booklet, and, begin. (*The students do so. This test is far more daunting than the first test.* RAMÍREZ *and* PEARSON *constantly prowl up and down the aisles.*)

(*A light comes up on* ESCALANTE. *He's alone, pacing nervously, talking to himself, willing the students to do their best.*)

ESCALANTE. It's okay … You're the best … Just go step by step … Play defense … (*As if in response to* ESCALANTE, *the students begin to tackle the problems. During the following dialogue* RAMÍREZ *and* PEARSON *should never acknowledge that any of the students are speaking out loud.*)

JAVIER (*slowly*). One. A particle moves along the x-axis so that its acceleration at any time t is given by a(t) equals 6t minus 18 …

CLAUDIA *(softly)*. I hate math … I hate calculus …

ESCALANTE. No problem, I hate it, too … Stay calm.

ANA *(softly)*. Not enough time, not enough time …

ESCALANTE. You can do it …

JAVIER AND CLAUDIA. At time t equals 0 the velocity of the particle is v(0) equals 24, and at time t equals 1 its position is x(1) equals 24 …

TITO. White noise, ringing in my ears …

ESCALANTE. You're the champs.

RAFAELA. I tried so hard, Mama, I really did …

ESCALANTE. You can do it …

TITO. Waves of sound … Empty … Alone …

JAVIER, CLAUDIA, ANA, AND ANGEL. (a) Write an expression for the velocity v(t) of the particle at any time t …

PANCHO. You know my mind don't work this way! Everybody knows I'm the dumbest! I just can't handle calculus, okay?!

ESCALANTE *(gently)*. Come on, Pancho. Tick-tack-toe. Piece of cake.

CLAUDIA, ANA, ANGEL, TITO, AND RAFAELA. (b) For what values of t is the particle at rest?

LUPE. *Diosito Mio, por favor,* I'm just so tired …

ESCALANTE *(teasing)*. Hey, *Señorita*, no spacing out, tomorrow you sleep.

CLAUDIA, ANA, ANGEL, RAFAELA, AND TITO *(overlapping)*. (c) Write an expression for the position x(t) of the particle at any time t.

ESCALANTE *(overlapping)*. Watch for the stick, it'll trip you up …

JAVIER *(overlapping)*. I can see worlds where cars skim through the air like boats on water …

ESCALANTE *(overlapping)*. Knowledge is power. Your secret weapon …

CLAUDIA *(overlapping)*. Someplace to relax, someplace to breathe, pushing, pushing …

ANGEL, TITO, RAFAELA, JAVIER, LUPE, AND PANCHO *(overlapping)*. (d) Find the total distance traveled by the particle from t equals 1 to t equals 3.

ANA *(overlapping)*. Dear Ms. Delgado, The E.T.S believes there's reason to question your A.P. test grade …

ANGEL *(overlapping)*. Not around here, homes. Not in East L.A.… .

LUPE, PANCHO, RAFAELA, TITO, AND CLAUDIA *(overlapping)*. The Board doubts that the grades are valid due to these unusual circumstances …

ESCALANTE *(overlapping)*. You don't ever give up! You don't ever give in!

ALL STUDENTS *(overlapping)*. It's standard procedure to grade the test with the identity of the students concealed …

ANGEL. Fear is my friend.

ALL STUDENTS. Step by step, inch by inch, no free rides.

ESCALANTE. You are the true dreamers, and dreams can accomplish wonderful things …

ESCALANTE AND STUDENTS. Step by step, inch by inch, no free rides. *(The chant continues as the lights fade out.)*

SCENE TEN

A T RISE: Lights up. The kids are scattered around the class, anxiously awaiting the results. PRINCIPAL MOLINA *and* ESCALANTE *are in the hallway.* ESCALANTE *is pacing.*

MOLINA. They probably got stuck in traffic.

ESCALANTE. I didn't get stuck.

MOLINA. Do you want to send the kids home?

ESCALANTE. No. We wait. (*Checks his watch.*)

MOLINA. Oh! Did I tell you? There's good news. The computers arrived!

ESCALANTE. Yep. That'll do it.

(*He and* MOLINA *continue waiting. Finally,* PEARSON *and* RAMÍREZ *stride down the hall. They stop in front of the classroom.*)

ESCALANTE. Do you have a late pass? No? Too bad. (*The E.T.S men share uncomfortable smiles. The four head into the class. A few kids discreetly whisper, "Late. Late." Someone calls out, "Give 'em the chair."* RAMÍREZ *opens his valise and takes out the results. The room gets deadly silent.*)

RAMÍREZ. As you know, A.P. tests are graded on a scale from one to five. A grade of one or two is failing. Three or four is passing. Five is a perfect score. (*Pause*) Delgado, Ana: 4. (ANA *and* JAVIER *hug.* RAFAELA *stands when her name is called.*) Fuentes, Rafaela: 4. (*The class lets out a small cheer.* RAMÍREZ *has to speak up. A bit louder.*) Escobar, Guadalupe: 4. (LUPE *jumps up and screams. She and* CLAUDIA *jump up and down in each other's arms. The excitement builds.* RAMÍREZ *continues, louder.*) Guitano, Tito: 4. (TITO *shouts and does a drum roll on his desk. Louder.*) Perales, Javier: 5. (*The class roars its approval.* ESCALANTE *goes over to* JAVIER *and shakes his hand.*)

PEARSON. Quiet! Please! Just a few more. (*The class settles down a bit.*)

RAMÍREZ. Camejo, Claudia: 4. (CLAUDIA *rejoices.*) Garcia, Francisco: 3. (PANCHO *jumps up and shouts. He and* LUPE *kiss.*) Guerra, Angel: 5. (*The students cheer. The*

celebration gets out of control. RAMÍREZ *hands the results to* MOLINA. MOLINA *shakes hands with* PEARSON *and* RAMÍREZ. *The three of them exit.*)

ANGEL. Kimo, Kimo, Kimo, Kimo … (*The students join the chant and pick up* ESCALANTE *onto their shoulders.*)

STUDENTS. Kimo, Kimo, Kimo, Kimo, Kimo … (*The chant fades out as each student steps forward to deliver the tally for Garfield High's calculus program.*)

LUPE. In 1982 Garfield High School had 18 students pass the A.P. calculus exam.

PANCHO. In 1983 Garfield High School had 31 students pass the A.P. calculus exam.

RAFAELA. In 1984, 63 students.

TITO. 1985, 77 students.

CLAUDIA. 1986, 78 students.

JAVIER. In 1987 Garfield High School had 87 students pass the A.P. calculus exam.

ANA. When I started at Garfield it was in danger of losing its accreditation. By 1988 it had produced more Advanced Placement calculus students than all but three public schools in the entire nation.

ANGEL. If the average spray can covers 22 square feet and the average letter is three square feet, how many letters can a tagger spray with 3 cans of paint?

ESCALANTE (*overlapping*). Okay, that's it, the chair for you, Johnny.

ANGEL. Just kidding, just kidding. (*Lights out*)

END OF PLAY

Discussing and Interpreting
Stand and Deliver

Play Analysis

1. Do you think Jaime Escalante could teach anyone A.P. calculus? Why or why not?
2. Make a list of the various conflicts that arise throughout the play. Choose one and discuss it with the class.
3. Edward James Olmos played Jaime Escalante in the movie. Who would you cast in the role and why?
4. Write a short biography of two of the characters, describing them as they appear in the play and revealing what they have done in the years since.
5. **Thematic Connection: Who Am I?** Chose one of Jaime Escalante's students and write a first-person essay titled "Who I Am" in the voice of that student.

Literary Skill: Analyze the Script

In the scene below, Escalante answers Chuco very simply each time he speaks. The script does not indicate what Escalante is thinking, or how he moves or gestures. Rewrite the scene to include all these details.

> **CHUCO.** *Orale, Kimo sabe...Kimo sabe todo (CHUCO holds out his hand. He and* ESCALANTE *shake hands,* cholo-style.)
>
> **ESCALANTE.** *Orale.*
>
> **CHUCO.** Homes told me you're havin' some problems. Just wanted to say, we got you covered.
>
> **ESCALANTE.** Thank you very much.
>
> **CHUCO.** We gonna cruise downtown, take action on those E.T.S. boys. You gotta throw down, homes. Hit them where they live. Like you say, *ése,* teach them some manners.
>
> **ESCALANTE.** I see...Tell you what. Let me try it my way first. That doesn't work, I'll let you know. Okay, Johnny?
>
> **CHUCO.** Put the word out, bro. We'll back your play.
>
> **ESCALANTE.** *Orale.* Okay. *(They all head into the hall.* ESCALANTE *pulls* ANGEL *aside.)* Just tell me that wasn't your idea.
>
> **ANGEL** *(conspiratorially).* It was Chuco's idea.
>
> **ESCALANTE.** Goot....

Performance Element: Direct the Scene

You are directing two actors in the scene above. What ideas might you share with the actor playing Chuco as to his attitude, motivation, and body language? What questions would you ask the actor playing Escalante about his feelings during this scene? How would you expect the actor playing Angel to deliver his one line?

Selkie

based on a myth from the Orkney Islands
adapted for the stage by Laurie Brooks Gollobin

Creating Context:
The Fin Folk

Stories about fin folk, mythical sea creatures who shed their skins and come to shore in human form, are popular in many island nations. Leaving their homes in underwater caverns and sunken islands, these water folk visit humans, watch them dance, and sometimes even join the dancing.

Selkies are popular fin folk in the folklore of the Orkney and Shetlands Islands, located off the northern coast of Scotland. Selkies, also called seal people, are beautiful and doe-eyed. Thought to have been fallen angels who were too good to be sent to hell, they fell instead to earth and were taken in by the sea. Sometimes persecuted by humans, they also inspire human love and affection. Tales are told of humans who steal a selkie's seal pelt in order to insure that the selkie cannot return to the sea. In this way many a man and woman in Scottish mythology secures a husband or wife who must remain on land until the pelt is discovered.

People of Micronesia, an island nation in the North Pacific, tell a similar story about Porpoise Girl, who leaves her porpoise tail hidden in the rocks only to have it stolen by a man she ultimately marries. He keeps her tail hidden until one day she finds it, puts it on, and rushes back to the sea. But first she warns her children never to eat porpoise.

The Irish tell of the merrow, sea people with fish bodies. The merrow maid, or mermaid, is beautiful and pale with dark eyes and long hair. The merman has green teeth and skin, a sharp red nose, and tiny eyes. They shape shift by using a red cap. If the cap is stolen, they cannot return to their underwater world. Humans gain mermaid brides by stealing this cap. Children of such couples have webbed fingers and toes.

Laurie Brooks Gollobin traveled to the Orkney Islands to research the selkie. There she discovered the people's musical language, called Norn. Listen for the lilt of Norn as you read.

As a Reader: Exploring Language

As you read the play *Selkie,* you will quickly become aware of words and turns of phrase unlike any of those in Standard English. This is the language of people who live on islands near Scotland—a language that seems as liquid and forceful as the sea itself. To fully appreciate it, read the passages below out loud and compare their sounds. The translations at left (in parentheses) should help you.

from Page · · · · · · to Stage

"Bit Mam," said the bairn. "I ken fine whar hid is. Wan day when ye war oot and me Fither thowt I wis sleepin' i' the bed, he teen a bonnie skin doon, gloured at hid for cheust a peedie meenit, then foldit hid an' laid hid up under dae aisins abeun da bed." ("But Mom, I know well where it is. One day when you were out and my Father thought I was asleep in bed, he took a pretty skin down, glowered at it for a short time, then folded it and put it away in the aisins over the bed.")

When the selkie-wife heard this she clapped for joy and rushed to the place where her long-concealed skin lay.

"Fare thee weel, peedie buddo," she said to her child and ran from the house. (*Peedie buddo* is a term of endearment meaning "little friend.")

Rushing to the shore she threw on her skin and with a wild cry of joy, plunged into the sea. . . .

And that was the last the Goodman ever saw of his sea-wife. Often though, in the twilight of his years, he could be seen wandering on the empty seashore, hoping once again to meet his lost love. But never again did he look upon her fair face.

from *The Goodman of Wastness*, a selkie myth

ELLEN JEAN. And …and look … I found yer pelt.

MARGARET. Ahhhh. Me pelt! Ye found me pelt! (*Laughing,* MARGARET *falls to her knees on the beach, caressing* the pelt….)

ELLEN JEAN. Mither ye're laughin'.

MARGARET. Oh, Peedie Buddo, ye've given me back me life.

ELLEN JEAN. Yer sisters said ye'll leave me fer the sea.

MARGARET. Leave ye? No, Peedie Buddo. I'll alus be with ye. Come…Fourteen years I have been captive on the land. In that time I have grown old and stiff. Me skin is dry and cracked fer want o' the sea. Me bones are as brittle as driftwood lyin' on the shore. Ye have brought me what I need. It is me time tae return home.

ELLEN JEAN. Mither, please, dunna leave me!

(*The sound of the wind and the sea*)

MARGARET. I will alus be with ye. Look tae the sea, and ye'll see me there. In the waves breakin' on the shore, the sun glitterin' on the sea foam. Precious shells will wash up on the beach. Fish will leap intae yer nets, and the selkies will guide ye safely through the tides in the sea.

from *Selkie* by Laurie Brooks Gollobin

As a Sound Technician: Music and the Sea

This play calls for many special sounds: fiddle music, selkie music, the sea, and the wind. As you read, try to imagine the place and the people, and all the sounds that go on around them.

Selkie

Time

Over a hundred years ago on Midsummer's Eve (June 21), when the people of the Orkney Islands herald the coming of summer with a celebration called the Johnsmas Foy. They call this time the simmer dim, when there is daylight even at midnight.

The Characters

DUNCAN
A crofter (tenant farmer) in his thirties

MARGARET
A lovely, pale-skinned woman with brown hair, in her late twenties

ELLEN JEAN
Brown-haired daughter of Duncan and Margaret, thirteen years old.

PA
Duncan's father, a fisherman

TAM
A traveller (gypsy) lad of fourteen, with black eyes and a keen sense of mischief

BLACK HAIR
One of the selkie-folk women with long, black hair

RED HAIR
One of the selkie-folk women with long, red hair

Setting

The Orkney Islands north of the wild, rocky coast of Scotland. The stage is set to suggest the rocky seacoast as well as the interior of a farmhouse.

Fiddle music. Dim daylight. The beach. It is Midsummer's Eve, when there is light for twenty hours a day. PA is downstage, playing his fiddle. He is scruffy and bearded, with a kind voice and warm ways.

Through the thick fog, called "the har," a large flat rock can be seen at center. Rippling lights create the sea downstage of the rock. Sounds of the wind and the sea. The sounds of the selkies singing in the distance. PA *tucks his fiddle under his arm.*

PA. There was alus the sound of the sea *(He imitates.)* and the sound of the wind. *(He imitates.)* Aye, and the selkies singing. *(He imitates the selkies.)*

*(*DUNCAN, *as a young man of about eighteen, enters, carrying a rake and a bag for gathering seaweed.)*

There was also a young crofter named Duncan who lived by the sea. Through the thick fog he could see them approachin' the rocks—the selkie folk—seals that live in the water, but change into humans one magical night each year. It was that night . . . Midsummer's Eve, the night o' the grand celebration called the Johnsmas Foy.

(Three selkies, BLACK HAIR, RED HAIR, *and a brown spotted selkie enter and move in the sea area toward the rock at center.* DUNCAN *hides himself behind upstage rocks. The selkies emerge onto the rock at center.)*

He'd heard the stories told round the peat fires of the gray seals that shed their pelts and become beautiful lasses, but he niver believed them. Yet here, before his own eyes were three selkies on the shore and as he watched, they shed their skins.

(Selkie music. Joyously, the three throw off their skins and are transformed into beautiful young women; one red-haired, one black-haired, and one brown-haired.)

PA. One was a fair lass with golden-red hair,

another a young lass with shinin' black hair, and last . . . the fairest lass he had ever seen, with brown hair shimmerin' in the dim northern lights.

(As the music soars into the night, the selkie girls leap off the rock and do a wild dance on the beach as DUNCAN *watches unseen in the shadows.)*

They danced, the three selkie lasses, danced on the land, like waves on the sea. As he watched them leap wildly aboot the beach, he looked at the brown-haired selkie lass with all the eyes in his head. A strange feelin' came over him, a powerful feelin'. He knew he must take her, the brown-haired selkie lass, take her home tae be his sea-wife. Yes, and he knew he must steal her pelt, like in the stories. Withoot her pelt, she could niver go back tae the sea, but must follow him wherever he might lead her.

*(*DUNCAN *comes out of his hiding place and approaches the women. The black-haired girl sees him and cries out a warning to the others. The selkie folk grab their pelts and enter the sea area.* DUNCAN *runs forward and takes up the pelt of the brown-haired girl. She reaches out her arms, imploring him to give back her pelt.* DUNCAN *firmly tucks the pelt underneath his arm. The girl slowly collapses on the beach, crying bitterly.* DUNCAN *offers his hand to the selkie girl. She hesitates.* DUNCAN *takes her hand, kisses it, and never taking his eyes from her face, leads her offstage.)*

'Tis true. It happened. The crofter was my son, Duncan, and because she wouldna say her name, we called his sea-wife Margaret. Their only bairn, a daughter— was named Ellen Jean.

*(*ELLEN JEAN *enters and runs forward onto the rock at center. She gazes out to sea as if looking for something, then swiftly enters the water and exits.)*

(Lights fade on beach and come up on the interior of the crofthouse. MARGARET *sits on a stool,*

winding wool, working the yarn carefully between her fingers. She is much changed from when we saw her in the first scene. Her body is bent and she wears a shapeless homespun dress with an apron. She moves with an odd, shuffling gait, as though her limbs are too heavy for her body.)

(PA begins to play a lively tune on his fiddle. He enters the crofthouse, fiddling, as ELLEN JEAN enters and begins to dance about the room. The dancing is similar to the dancing performed by the three selkies in the first scene. ELLEN JEAN's long, brown hair swings about her as she dances. She wears a nondescript homespun dress tied at the waist, with unusually long sleeves which hang down, covering her hands. She shouts for punctuation as she dances. PA ends the tune as ELLEN JEAN leaps into the air and lands gracefully on the floor in a heap.)

PA *(laughing).* Well done, bonny lass! There's none can dance the music tae life as yerself.

MARGARET. Aye. She's the gift in her, our Ellen Jean.

ELLEN JEAN. 'Tis no' guid yet, fer all the tryin'.

PA. It'll come tae ye, in time, if ye wait.

ELLEN JEAN. Waitin' fer this, waitin' fer that. When will all the waitin' be over?

PA. When ye're stone dead, buried in the ground, and cold as the fishes.

MARGARET. Then ye're wishin' ye had the waitin' tae do.

ELLEN JEAN. Sometimes I have the strangest feelin', walkin' through the days sleepin' like. One day I'll wake up, an' everything'll be different.

PA. Different? Worse is more likely.

ELLEN JEAN. Oh, Pa, ye canno' tell the future. Mither, will ye do up me hair? It always comes all far-flunglike when I'm dancin' wild.

MARGARET *(smiling).* A fine nest fer the birds ye have there. (MARGARET *combs*

ELLEN JEAN's *hair, fastening it with a clasp.)*
Voices whisper with the wind
Of places ye have niver been.
Singin' songs of ebb and flow
Of secrets ye will someday know.

Listen tae the sea,
There is a land far beneath.
Awaken from yer sleep
Tae the mysteries doon below.

Selkies glidin' in between
Tides that play upon the sea
Callin' ye tae come along,
Beckon ye tae sing the song.

Listen tae the sea,
There is a land far beneath.
Awaken from yer sleep
Tae the mysteries doon below.

ELLEN JEAN. Thank ye, Mither, ye alus do it best.

(MARGARET *kisses* ELLEN JEAN's *forehead.)*

MARGARET. Eyes green as the sea.

PA. A brown-haired lass, there's none so fair Neither golden nor black locks can compare.

ELLEN JEAN. Dunna be sayin' that. Ye're only feelin' sorry fer me.

PA. I like rhymin' is all.

Eetam, peetam, penny pie, Pop-a-larum, jinkam jie.

Stand thoo there til I come by.

(Angrily, ELLEN JEAN *starts to leave.)*

Dunna be goin' off in a huff! What's got ye so ill-bisted?

ELLEN JEAN. I canno' abide rhymin' is all.

PA. I meant ye no disrespect.

ELLEN JEAN. Day after day I got tae hear the others sayin' hateful rhymes aboot me.

PA. What a bulder o' nonsense! Dunna be payin' attention tae what the others say. It's the inside o' ye that matters.

ELLEN JEAN. No one wants to know me inside, they're too busy gawkin' at the outside.

MARGARET. People's afraid o' what's different, fearin' what they dunna understand.

ELLEN JEAN. None o' them others wants tae be wi' me.

PA. I do.

ELLEN JEAN. I dunna care fer that.

PA. Dunna care fer yer old Grandpa?

(He takes a stance like a puffin, and waddles about the room, making the high-pitched "hey-al" sound of the puffin breed. ELLEN JEAN scowls.)

I remember when 'at sent ye rollin' on the floor wi' laughin'.

ELLEN JEAN. When I was a bairn.[1]

PA. How aboot this?

(He configures his body to imitate a sheep and makes ridiculous bleating sounds.)

ELLEN JEAN. Ye've gone daft.

PA *(Physicalizing himself into a cat. Cat voice.)* Rrrrrrrrrrr. Meow. Skim off the cream fer me dinner. I'm a peedie bit hungry.

(PA rubs his shoulder up against her, knocking her down. ELLEN JEAN laughs.)

There. I've made ye laugh.

ELLEN JEAN. Pa, ye're me family. Ye've no choice but tae be with me.

PA. Buy, buy, that's no way tae talk.

ELLEN JEAN. It's the others—I wish the others liked me.

MARGARET. The lads and lasses'll take notice when they see yer dancin' at the Foy this night.

PA. It'll be a celebration like none afore it. The torches o' heather cracklin'. The dancin' and singin' till dawn. I can see the looks on 'em. Eyes wide as saucers with the surprise.

(ELLEN JEAN hangs her head and is silent.)

O Look! Have ye niver seen the like o' the dancin'! More wondrous than the skelly sun hittin' the cliffs o' Hoy! Who is she, 'at bonny lass?

ELLEN JEAN. I'll no' be dancin' at the Foy.

PA. Ye're thirteen. Yer fither expects ye tae dance. He's bragged aboot it from Kirkwall tae Stromness.

MARGARET *(caressing ELLEN JEAN's hair).* Yer dancin' is a gift. Ye must no' hide what is worthy in yerself. Perhaps when the others see 'at side o' ye . . .

ELLEN JEAN. They'll hate the dancin' and think me a fool!

(ELLEN JEAN turns in anger and charges for the door. The door opens and DUNCAN enters. DUNCAN is tall and dark-haired; a lanky, awkward man who looks as though he isn't quite comfortable in his skin.)

DUNCAN *(stopping ELLEN JEAN at the door).* Hover ye noo, lass. What's yer hurry?

ELLEN JEAN. No hurry, Fither.

DUNCAN. Sit ye doon then. I'd be havin' a word wi' ye.

(DUNCAN goes to MARGARET and kisses her lovingly.)

DUNCAN. Pale as the winter sky and twice as lovely.

(ELLEN JEAN tries to slip out of the room unnoticed.)

MARGARET. A lie is harder tae tell in the long haul than the hardest truth.

PA. The truth! There's a slippery fish, just when ye've caught it up, it slides away from ye.

DUNCAN. Tae me ye're bonny as ever. Workin' each day I'm only waitin' fer evenin' tae be home with ye . . . and Jean. (DUNCAN spots ELLEN JEAN leaving.) Jean! Come hither, lass. James Leslie saw ye yesterday swimmin' oot beyond the voe. Ellen Jean, I've told ye and told ye no' tae swim oot beyond the voe.[2] Even the finest swimmer

---

1. bairn (*Scottish*), child; baby

2. voe, an inlet of the sea

in Orkney must respect the tides. They change in a peedie minute and pull the strongest swimmer doon into the blackness.

ELLEN JEAN. I know the tides.

DUNCAN. Then why do ye swim oot beyond the voe? Is it a watery grave ye'd be after?

ELLEN JEAN. I canno' help meself. Somethin' pulls me doon tae the beach and in tae the sea.

DUNCAN. I'll no' have ye riskin' yer life when the har rolls in and ye canno' see beyond yer nose. None o' the others would dare swim in these waters. I dunna understand. Why do ye no' stay on land with the others?

ELLEN JEAN. I had tae swim oot tae the skerrie.

DUNCAN. What were ye thinkin', lass? 'At's near two miles oot tae sea.

MARGARET. 'Twas the selkies callin'. The red and the black.

ELLEN JEAN. They came back, Mither, just as ye said they would.

MARGARET. Aye, at Midsummer's tide.

ELLEN JEAN. One red as the sun goin' down, the other dark as peat.[3]

MARGARET. Noses lifted straight oot o' the water, like they'us lookin' fer somethin'.

(MARGARET *looks toward the sea.*)

DUNCAN. There are hundreds o' selkies swimmin' in these waters, alike as one another.

ELLEN JEAN. I knowed 'em straight away and no mistake. I saw their eyes up closelike. Human eyes, they were. They'us cryin'.

DUNCAN. Ach, 'twas only sea water drippin'.

MARGARET. Selkies cry just as humans do. And fer the same reasons. Longin' fer what's been lost and canno' be found.

ELLEN JEAN. They'us callin' me. They wanted me tae follow 'em.

DUNCAN. I'll no' ask ye tae explain it. Just no' tae do it.

ELLEN JEAN. I try tae stay on land, Fither, but then I'm achin' fer the feel o' the water and the pull o' the waves.

(ELLEN JEAN *moves her arms to illustrate her thoughts and her long sleeves fall back to reveal her hands. The crofthouse grows silent as* ELLEN JEAN *realizes she has shown her hands to her father. She instinctively hides them behind her back.*)

DUNCAN. Sha' me yer hands.

PA. Giddy God, noo ye've done it.

MARGARET. Duncan, come have yer ale. It's waitin'.

PA. Aye. I'm thirsty as a landlocked fisherman.

MARGARET. I've fresh baked bannock.[4] Ye must be hungry.

DUNCAN (*to* MARGARET). I'll no' be dissuaded. I'm waitin', lass.

(ELLEN JEAN *slowly holds out her hands for* DUNCAN.)

Webbed, they have grown webbed again. Where's me gully knife?

(DUNCAN *pulls the knife out of the back of his belt and, using his belt, sharpens it with a stropping motion.*)

MARGARET. They'll only grow back, like alus.

PA. Leave her hands alone, won't ye? There's naught tae be done fer it.

MARGARET. Aye. 'Tis no guid tae cut 'em.

ELLEN JEAN (*bravely*). It doesna' hurt too much, Mither.

(PA *gets up and reaches for his coat.*)

PA. 'At pony'll be wantin' tae be fed.

MARGARET. Dunna run from it, Pa. Help me.

PA. Dunna cut her, man. There's naught tae be done fer it.

MARGARET. Even if ye cut 'em clean off, she'll niver be like the others.

DUNCAN. Who will she be like, then? She's

---

3. peat, partially rotted plants found in marshes. Very dark in color, peat can be used as fuel.

4. bannock, flat bread or biscuit

thirteen now, time tae think o' makin' a guid marriage to a crofter with land, home and hearth. She'll need more than a dowry tae fetch a husband.

MARGARET. Let the future be takin' care o' itself.

DUNCAN. Ye'd have me do nothin'! I canno' bear tae hear the others laugh and make sport o' her. I wilna' stand idle, seein' her married off tae some tinker like that dirty Tam McCodrun without a sturdy tub fer washin' or a strip o' land tae keep his family fed.

MARGARET. I've heard tell o' him who took a stunder tae love a lass wi' naught but hersel' tae offer.

ELLEN JEAN. Cut them, Fither. I want tae be like the others.

(ELLEN JEAN *obediently lays her hands on the table.*)

DUNCAN. 'At's a good lass. Hold yer hands steady.

(ELLEN JEAN *turns her head away.* DUNCAN *positions the knife to cut the first web.* MARGARET *rushes forward and stops* DUNCAN.)

MARGARET. No! Cuttin' her hands wilna keep her from the sea! Ye canno' shape her intae yer dreams o' what's tae come or cut her tae fit ye like a bit o' cloth. Look at her! Do ye no' see she's bonny as she is?

(DUNCAN *drops the knife as* MARGARET *sobs. He gathers* MARGARET *into his arms.*)

DUNCAN. There, there, darlin'. Dunna cry. I canno' bear tae hear ye cry. I'll no' cut 'em. I'll no' cut 'em.

(ELLEN JEAN *quietly picks up the knife.*)

PA. Ellen Jean, go oot tae the byre. 'At pony wants feedin'.

(ELLEN JEAN *looks toward her parents and hesitates.*)

ELLEN JEAN. Then I'll cut them meself!

(ELLEN JEAN *slashes the largest web. She cries out and drops the knife, holding her cut hand high in the air.*)

(*Blackout*)

Dim *daylight. The beach. Sounds of the sea and the wind. Sounds of the selkies.* ELLEN JEAN *sits on the rock at center, looking out to sea. Enter* TAM. *He wears dirty trousers, a dingy white shirt, and a faded vest that might once have been colorful. His hair hangs long and stringy, falling often and annoyingly into his eyes. His face, hands, and bare feet are streaked with dirt and he carries a tin pail.* TAM *begins to dig for limpets, then sees* ELLEN JEAN.

TAM. Look what the sea washed up on the beach. A young bit o' skirly-wheeter.[5]

ELLEN JEAN. Go away and dunna daive me with yer gabbin'.

TAM. I warn ye once, I warn ye twice,
I warn ye oot the glowrie's[6] eyes.

ELLEN JEAN. Stop 'at! Stop sayin' 'at hateful rhyme!

(ELLEN JEAN *puts her hands covered by her long sleeves over her ears to block out the sounds.*)

TAM. Hie thee lass 'at swims in the sea,
Stay away from thee and me!

(ELLEN JEAN *ignores him. He laughs.*)

TAM. What're ye doin' here? Waitin' fer the King o' the Sea tae come courtin' ye?

ELLEN JEAN. If he wus, ye'd likely bash in his head with a club, skin 'im alive on the beach, an' sell his pelt.

TAM. Fetch a pretty penny, too, more'n likely.

ELLEN JEAN. Ye're an evil lad. I saw ye doon on the skerrie yesterday ballin' stones at the selkies.

---

5. skirly-wheeter, a type of bird; oystercatcher

6. glowrie, a drunk person

TAM. Aye, me and the lads. Missed 'em clean away, too. More's the pity.

ELLEN JEAN. How can ye be so cruel tae harmless creatures?

TAM. Harmless! Witches they are. Condemned fer their sins tae live in the sea.

ELLEN JEAN. That's no' true.

TAM. Eatin' up the herrin' an' starvin' honest fishin' folk.

ELLEN JEAN. The selkies have a right tae eat as much as any creature.

TAM (*mysteriously*). Comin' up on the land tae steal the peedie bairns from their mithers, just like the trolls.

ELLEN JEAN. That's a lie! The selkies have done naught but kindnesses fer folk, savin' 'em from drownin' and the like.

TAM. Ye like the selkies so much, why dunna ye go live in the sea with 'em!

(ELLEN JEAN *is silent.*)

Cat got yer tongue, Selkie Lass? Got nothin' tae say?

ELLEN JEAN. Nuthin' tae say tae the likes o' thee.

(TAM *lifts a handful of* ELLEN JEAN's *hair and flips it playfully.*)

ELLEN JEAN (*recoiling*). Dunna touch me.

TAM (*becoming aware of his dirty hands*). Ye'd think I had the pox, instead o' a bit o' honest dirt.

ELLEN JEAN. Honest dirt washes off. It's the dirt inside I'm thinkin' of.

TAM. Miss high and mighty. Stickin' yer nose up, keepin' away from me like I'm lower'an sheep filth. Because yer fither's got a bit o' land and a byre doesna make ye so grand.

ELLEN JEAN. I didna say 'at.

TAM. Ye hate me because I'm a traveller, don't ye. A wanderin' gypsy withoot a home. Ye're like all the others.

ELLEN JEAN. I'm no' like the others.

TAM. Get off this beach and leave me tae gather me limpets fer supper.

(TAM *begins to forage among the rocks for limpets to fill his pail.*)

ELLEN JEAN. I have a right tae be here.

TAM. Get off, I said.

ELLEN JEAN. No. I wilna be bullied aboot.

TAM (*threateningly*). Get off afore I run ye off . . . or worse!

ELLEN JEAN. I'll no' give in tae the likes o' thee, Dirty Tam McCodrun!

(TAM *runs to* ELLEN JEAN, *grabs her by her upraised wrists and shakes her.*)

TAM. Dunna call me 'at! Dunna ever call me 'at!

ELLEN JEAN. Let me go! Let me go!

(In the struggle TAM *loses his footing and nearly falls into the sea.* ELLEN JEAN *instinctively reaches out and grabs* TAM *to save him from falling. For a moment it looks as though they will both fall, then they regain their balance.* TAM *looks down at her hands. The long sleeves of her dress have fallen back to reveal her bloody fingers.* ELLEN JEAN *breaks free of* TAM's *grasp and cradles her hurt hand.*)

TAM (*looking at his hands*). Blood! Ye're hurt! Damn me ill-bisted temper!

ELLEN JEAN. Hie thee away from me!

TAM. I didna mean tae hurt ye, only ye called me . . . that name. No one calls me Dirty Tam tae me face.

ELLEN JEAN. 'Tis none o' yer doin'.

TAM. How did ye hurt yer hand then?

ELLEN JEAN. 'Tis nothin'. An accident.

TAM. A bad one, by the looks o' it.

ELLEN JEAN. A slip o' the hand is all.

(TAM *pulls a crumpled cloth from his pocket.*)

TAM. Here. Let me bind 'at up fer ye.

ELLEN JEAN. 'Tis nothin', I said.

TAM. Garn. Ye musn't be so stubborn.

(TAM *takes her hand to wrap the bandage, then stops and stares at her webbed fingers.* ELLEN JEAN *pulls her hand away.*)

ELLEN JEAN. What are ye gleerin' at?

TAM. Yer hands, I … I niver saw the like o' them.

ELLEN JEAN. Then run and tell the others what ye've seen! Tell 'em ye've seen the webs. Tell 'em! (*She angrily shoves her hands in his face.*) Look! Green and slimy like seaweed, they are. They say she has horned skin on her palms. Tell 'em she goes doon tae the beach tae meet the King o' the Sea behind the rocks! Tell them! They'll think ye're a fine one fer knowin'.

(ELLEN JEAN *turns to run away, but* TAM *catches her arm.*)

TAM. Wait! I'm sorry!

ELLEN JEAN. I hate ye, Tam McCodrun, and all the others! (ELLEN JEAN *breaks away and exits, running.*)

TAM (*calling after her*). Wait! I'm sorry! I said I'm sorry! Devil take ye, then. (TAM *picks up his pail.*)

Devil take any who call me Dirty Tam! Devil take the limpets!

(TAM *throws the tin pail into the rocks with a crash.*)

Devil take the selkies! (TAM *looks after* ELLEN JEAN. *Quietly.*) I didna mean it. I didna mean tae hurt ye.

(*Lights shift.*)

Interior of the croft. DUNCAN *kneels before the fire, brushing a selkie pelt with great tenderness. The sounds of the selkies can be heard in the distance.* PA *stands outside the crofthouse watching* DUNCAN.

PA. Ye see, Duncan couldna destroy Margaret's pelt, or she would die. But he lived alus wi' the fear 'at she would discover it and return tae the sea. So he hid Margaret's skin careful-like aboot the croft, first in one place, then another, tae keep it from her searchin' eyes, oilin' and brushin' it each year so it wouldna crack or dry up. It was as though he was carin' fer Margaret herself.

(PA *enters the crofthouse and sits in the rocking chair, which squeaks noisily as he rocks back and forth.* PA *opens his mouth as though to say something, then stops.* PA *heaves a huge, audible sigh.* DUNCAN *looks at* PA *sharply.*)

PA. I didna say a word.

DUNCAN. Yer gettin' ready.

(PA *rocks furiously in the squeaky rocking chair.*)

DUNCAN. Get on with it then.

PA. When I'm ready. When I'm ready.

DUNCAN. I'm in no rush.

(PA *rocks his chair with a vengeance to the rhythm of* DUNCAN's *brush strokes on the pelt.*)

PA. Deer, Sheer, bret and smeer,
       What shall ye have fer dinner?

(DUNCAN *stops brushing and gives* PA *an annoyed look. He begins his rhythmic brushing again.*)

Minch meat small or none at all,
Tae make ye fat or thinner.

DUNCAN. Ye'd best be ready soon, afore ye rock that chair intae the ground!

PA. Ye coulda had yer pick o' island lasses, fine and strong.

DUNCAN. Aye, 'at's the familiar tune.

PA. How could ye have done it, man? Ta'en one o' the selkie-folk tae wife?

DUNCAN. I didna choose it.

PA. And who forced ye?

DUNCAN. The first time I laid eyes on her sittin' on the skerrie, hair blowin' out around her like the mist, I knew I couldna rest 'til I brought her home tae wife.

PA. Now she canno' rest. Walkin' doon tae

the sea night after night. An' Ellen Jean, hidin' herself away on the croft, ashamed o' her hands.

DUNCAN. Things change. This year she'll be goin' doon tae the Foy with me tae dance.

PA. Ye'll be goin' alone tae the Foy this year. She's ta'en herself off tae bed.

DUNCAN. Tae bed? At this hour?

PA. She wilna dance at the Foy. She's afraid the others'll laugh. She canno' find her place among the lads and lasses.

(From the sea comes the sounds of the selkies.)

DUNCAN *(shouting to the selkies).* Leave off yer hoolan'. I canno' think wi' the sound o' ye!

PA. The selkies're callin' tae Margaret, callin' her tae come away wi' 'em. Ye've grown careless. Best be hidin' her pelt away afore she comes back. If she finds her skin, she'll be goin' back to the sea in a twinklin'.

DUNCAN. She wouldna leave me.

PA. She couldna help herself. It's inside her, like Ellen Jean swimmin' oot beyond the voe.

DUNCAN. No! She wouldna leave us, man, after fourteen years!

PA. Then why do ye no' give back her skin?

(There is a moment of silence.)

There's trouble in what ye've done. Ye canno' run from a wrong.

DUNCAN. Are ye through?

PA. It's the bairns that pay fer the wrongs o' the ones gone afore. Ellen Jean'll be livin' wi' yer sin fer the rest o' her life. I shoulda beat ye wi' a stick 'til ye came to yer senses afore I let ye take yer wife from the sea.

DUNCAN. Ye shouldna blame yerself.

PA. I didna stop ye, noo, did I? 'At's me own wrong.

(PA exits. The sound of the selkies calling grows louder and more plaintive. DUNCAN raises his fists in anger. He folds up the pelt and shoves it back into its hiding place above the aisins.[7])

DUNCAN *(shouting out the door toward the sea).* Be off noo! Stop yer callin'!

(DUNCAN slams the window shutters closed as though to lock out the sound. The moaning of the selkies grows even louder. DUNCAN opens the door and yells into the night.)

Go back tae the sea an' leave us alone. She belongs tae me. Do ye hear? She belongs tae me!

(DUNCAN slams the door and exits. The sound of the selkies continues to fill the crofthouse. Within their moaning sounds can be heard the sound of the selkies calling ELLEN JEAN's name. ELLEN JEAN enters, rubbing her eyes. She is wearing a white night dress, and her hair hangs long down her back. She hugs herself and, closing her eyes, sways in response to the selkie sounds. She opens the door, and the selkie sounds grow louder. Her body moves instinctively to the sounds. As though directed to do so, ELLEN JEAN looks in the direction of the pelt. She tries to reach it, but it is too high. She drags over a stool and stands on it. ELLEN JEAN lifts the pelt down from its hiding place and hugs it to her body. She closes her eyes, and swaying back and forth, imitates the selkies' moaning with her own voice. She loses her balance and falls off the stool onto the floor with a crash. The selkie sounds stop. PA enters.)

PA. Ach, Jean! I thought it was the bawkie man come tae steal us away. What're ye aboot?

ELLEN JEAN. Look. A selkie skin. I found it hidden up in the aisins.

PA. What're ye doin' searchin' up in the aisins?

ELLEN JEAN. The selkies woke me. Did ye no' hear 'em?

PA. Ye'd have to be stone deaf or dead no' tae hear their bellowin'.

ELLEN JEAN. No. No. The selkies were callin' me, callin' me name over and over.

---

7. aisins, the eaves of a building

PA. Selkies talkin'. What a bulder o' nonsense!

ELLEN JEAN. Clear as the broonie lights, they'us callin' me name. It was they made me look up in th' aisins. They wanted me tae find the pelt.

PA. Ye're dreamin', Jean. And walkin' in yer sleep by the look o' ye.

ELLEN JEAN. This selkie pelt is no' a dream. Maybe it belongs tae one o' the selkie-folk . . . like in the stories.

PA. More likely stuffed up there tae keep oot the drafty air.

ELLEN JEAN. Oh, Pa, think o' the poor creature withoot its skin.

PA. Long dead noo. They canno' live withoot their skins.

ELLEN JEAN. But it feels warm. Not like somethin' dead at all. I'll be goin' doon tae the sea.

PA. I'd think atifer doin' 'at, if I were thee. It's trouble ye're askin' fer. Return the pelt tae where ye found it. It doesna belong tae ye noo, does it?

ELLEN JEAN. No.

PA. Then ye're no' tae be takin' it.

(ELLEN JEAN *lays the pelt against her cheek and breathes in the smell.*)

ELLEN JEAN. There's somethin' aboot the smell. (ELLEN JEAN *holds out the pelt to* PA's *nose.*)

PA (*making a face*). I'll no' be smellin' any old selkie skin!

ELLEN JEAN. I know the smell. It's … familiar.

PA. Ach, ye know the smell o' the sea, like all the Orkney folk.

ELLEN JEAN. I was meant tae find it, Pa. I know it.

PA. Ye were meant tae dance at the Johnsmas Foy, but ye're no' doin' it, then, are ye?

(ELLEN JEAN *is silent.*)

Come tae the Foy an' dance the music tae

life with yer old Pa. Give the others a chance tae know who ye are inside.

ELLEN JEAN. I canno' dance fer the others. I canno'.

PA. And I canno' force ye tae dance. Sha' me the pelt, and I'll return it tae where ye found it.

(ELLEN JEAN *sighs and gives* PA *the pelt. He puts it back up in the aisins.*)

ELLEN JEAN. I'll ask Mither. She'll know what tae do about the pelt.

PA. No! Dunna be botherin' yer mither. Listen tae yer old Pa. Ferget ye ever saw the pelt.

ELLEN JEAN. But Pa, the selkies . . . they'us callin' me.

PA (*sharply*). 'Twas a dream, I tell ye. Ferget it, and dunna be borrowin' trouble. Things're likely tae be lookin' different in the mornin'. (ELLEN JEAN *hesitates.*) Go on with ye, I said. (ELLEN JEAN *goes toward the door.*) Ellen Jean. (ELLEN JEAN *turns back to* PA.) Dunna be muckin' aboot with what ye dunna understand and canno' finish, do ye hear me?

ELLEN JEAN. Aye, I hear ye, Pa.

PA. Sleep well.

(*Exit* ELLEN JEAN. *The selkie sounds begin again.*)

Sleep well! That's no' likely, fer none this night.

(*Exit* PA. ELLEN JEAN *peeks around the doorway and sees* PA *has gone. She enters and takes the pelt from its hiding place. The sounds of the selkies calling fills the room.* ELLEN JEAN *hugs herself and sways as if in ecstasy. Then she tucks the pelt under her arm and exits into the night.*)

(*Lights shift. Music.*)

T*he beach. Dim light. Music fades. Sounds of the sea and the wind.* ELLEN JEAN *sits at center, looking out to sea. She wraps herself in the pelt, sways to and fro and smiles. For the* *first time she seems happy and at peace. Sounds of the selkies approaching.* ELLEN JEAN *tries to fit herself into the pelt. She tries to put her foot into it, while her arms, attempting several styles of drapery, cannot quite manage to decipher its mystery. Enter the two selkie sisters,* RED HAIR. *and* BLACK HAIR. *The two selkies glide in the sea toward the shore.* ELLEN JEAN *sees their approach and, frustrated by her inability to wear the pelt, folds herself as small as she can, hiding herself beneath it. The selkies haul out on the beach and cautiously move nearer to* ELLEN JEAN. *Enter* TAM *from behind the rocks, carrying a club.* TAM *wears the same dirty trousers, dingy white shirt, and vest. He is barefoot. He sees* ELLEN JEAN *and the two selkies, and runs toward them, lifting the club high over his head to strike. The selkies bellow and escape into the sea.* ELLEN JEAN *jumps up and sees* TAM *about to hit her.*

ELLEN JEAN. No! Dunna strike me!

TAM *(jumping up in shock and dropping the club).* Selkie Lass!

(TAM loses his footing on the slippery rocks.)

Help me! Help!

(TAM falls into the water and lies still.)

ELLEN JEAN *(calling after him).* I hope ye drown. Ye deserve tae drown. Then no more selkies will die from the likes o' Dirty Tam McCodrun! *(When there is no answer,* ELLEN JEAN *looks down into the water.)*

Why dunna ye swim? Afraid they'll say ye've a bit o' the selkie in ye? I hope ye go straight doon tae…

(The selkies bellow and yelp again.)

ELLEN JEAN *(realizing).* Giddy God! He's drownin'!

(ELLEN JEAN, leaving the pelt behind on the rock, enters the water. She moves to TAM, *floating on the surface as if dead.* ELLEN JEAN *drags* TAM *onto the beach with help from the two selkies.)*

I'm sorry. I didna mean what I said. I dinna want ye tae die!

(Selkie music. ELLEN JEAN *looks up and sees the two selkies behind her throw off their pelts. They are transformed into the two beautiful women seen with* MARGARET *at the beginning of the play. Throughout the scene, the two selkies move in tandem as though connected.)*

Giddy God!

BLACK HAIR. Hush yer cryin'. He will no' die.

RED HAIR. Ye have saved him this night. 'Tis the way o' the selkies tae save drownin' men, even the killers.

BLACK HAIR. He'll wake soon enough with an achin' head.

RED HAIR. None the worse fer the baffin.

ELLEN JEAN. I knowed ye would come when I saw ye oot on the skerrie.

RED HAIR. Ye found the pelt.

ELLEN JEAN. I heard ye callin' me. Tellin' me tae bring it.

BLACK HAIR. Ye have the ears tae listen this night and the heart tae tell ye what tae listen fer.

RED HAIR. Aye, and look. She has her mither's eyes.

BLACK HAIR. Green as the sea.

ELLEN JEAN. Do ye know Mither?

BLACK HAIR. Aye, as we know the flow o' the tides and the feel o' the warm sun.

RED HAIR. Ye're very like her, yer mither.

BLACK HAIR. Sha' me yer hands.

(BLACK HAIR takes ELLEN JEAN's *hands and lifts back the long sleeves.* ELLEN JEAN *pulls her hands away and hides them both behind her back.)*

ELLEN JEAN. They're ugly.

(BLACK HAIR takes ELLEN JEAN's *hands in her own and caresses them.)*

BLACK HAIR. They are webbed.

RED HAIR. Made fer the sea.

(RED HAIR embraces ELLEN JEAN.)*

ELLEN JEAN *(to* RED HAIR*).* Dunna be afraid. I'll keep ye safe. No hunters will find ye.

BLACK HAIR. She weeps fer one ta'en by a crofter fourteen years ago an' kept from her home an' family in th' sea.

ELLEN JEAN. Like in the stories.

BLACK HAIR. 'Tis no story. 'Tis true as ye're standin' there. The pelt belongs tae yer mither, our sister.

ELLEN JEAN. Mither? But she canno' be one o' the selkie folk. She's … old.

BLACK HAIR. Fourteen years kept from the sea has made her old.

RED HAIR. Every year at Midsummer, we return tae be wi' her. Seven children she has in the sea, a fither, mither, and we two sisters.

(ELLEN JEAN *pulls back her sleeves and looks with new eyes at her webbed hands.*)

ELLEN JEAN. I'm one o' the selkie folk.

BLACK HAIR. No, lass. Yer part o' yer mither and part o' yer fither. Sea and land. The first of a kind.

ELLEN JEAN (*taking up the pelt and holding it close*). I hate the land. I'm different from the others. I want tae be in the sea.

BLACK HAIR. Yer mither belongs in the sea, but it is no' yer home.

ELLEN JEAN. I have no home. I dunna belong anywhere!

BLACK HAIR. Belongin's no' a place, it's inside ye. Ye will find the knowin' in time.

ELLEN JEAN. More waitin', alus waitin'. I canno' wait any longer.

RED HAIR. Ye must give yer mither back her pelt.

BLACK HAIR. So she can return tae her home in th' sea.

ELLEN JEAN. Return tae the sea? But will she come back?

(TAM *begins to stir. He coughs.*)

BLACK HAIR. He's wakin'.

RED HAIR. Quickly! The sea!

(BLACK HAIR *and* RED HAIR *run to grab their pelts.*)

ELLEN JEAN. Wait! If I give Mither the pelt, will she come back tae me? I need tae know!

BLACK HAIR. Give her the pelt!

RED HAIR. Give her back tae the sea!

(BLACK HAIR *and* RED HAIR *throw on their pelts, and, entering the sea, are transformed into selkies. They swim away from shore and exit.* ELLEN JEAN *stands looking out to sea, watching the selkies.* TAM *sits up, sees her and smiles, then lies back down before she sees him awake.* ELLEN JEAN *goes to* TAM, *who moans loudly.*)

ELLEN JEAN. Please. Wake up. I didna mean fer ye tae die, just no' tae hurt me.

(TAM's *arms go around her. He pulls her to him and kisses her.*)

ELLEN JEAN (*jumping up*). Oh!

TAM (*laughing*). A kiss from the Selkie Lass. Almost worth drownin' fer.

ELLEN JEAN. I hate ye, Tam McCodrun.

TAM. What? Fer a kiss?

ELLEN JEAN. Ye tried tae kill me. Again.

TAM. No. I was after the pelt. How was I tae know ye were darned doon in it?

ELLEN JEAN. Killin' was all ye were after. What kind o' man would club an innocent selkie?

TAM. The hungry kind.

ELLEN JEAN. The night of the Johnsmas Foy? There'll be plenty tae eat.

TAM. There's other kinds o' hunger than in the stomach.

ELLEN JEAN. What other kinds?

TAM. Did ye niver feel fairly silted[8] tae have somethin', wantin' it so much ye can think o' naught but that?

---

8. silted, choked; overwhelmed

ELLEN JEAN. Waitin' fer it tae happen, deathly afraid it niver will?

TAM. Aye, that's the feelin'.

ELLEN JEAN. What are ye silted fer?

TAM. Tae wake up every dawn in the same place. Tae have a place tae call home.

ELLEN JEAN. A place tae belong?

TAM. Aye, 'at's it. Even the feast at the Foy canno' fill up 'at yawnin' hole.

ELLEN JEAN. I know. I want tae belong, too.

TAM. Ye have a home. A fine croft wi' a byre full o' sheep and ponies, too.

ELLEN JEAN. What guid is it if none o' the others wants tae be with me?

TAM. I do.

ELLEN JEAN. Ye do?

TAM. Aye.

ELLEN JEAN. But ye're alus callin' me names and sayin' 'at hateful rhyme.

TAM. Ach, it's fer the lads. There's no meanin' in it. I'll no' be makin' sport o' ye ever again, if ye ask me.

ELLEN JEAN. Why should I believe ye?

TAM. Ye saved me miserable life, did ye no'?

ELLEN JEAN. Aye, more's the pity.

TAM. Ask me, then.

ELLEN JEAN. I'm askin' ye. Dunna be callin' me names.

TAM. Niver again.

ELLEN JEAN. Swear it tae me.

TAM. I swear I'll niver call ye names again.

ELLEN JEAN. And ye'll no' be sayin' 'at hateful rhyme?

TAM. I swear I'll no' say 'at rhyme ever again.

ELLEN JEAN. And swear tae me from this day on ye'll niver raise a hand tae hurt the selkies as long as ye live.

TAM. I've done enough swearin' fer one day.

ELLEN JEAN. Please. 'Tis all I'm askin' fer.

TAM. Do ye know the price 'ats paid oot fer a single selkie pelt?

ELLEN JEAN. There's other ways tae earn yer keep.

TAM. I'm savin' up fer somethin'.

ELLEN JEAN. What're ye savin' up fer, Tam McCodrun?

(TAM *looks at her sharply, realizing she has said his name with respect.*)

TAM (*eagerly*). A bit o' land—a home. A lass tae love me as brave and true as yerself.

ELLEN JEAN. Are ye sayin' 'at because I saved yer miserable life?

TAM. Better ye let me die.

ELLEN JEAN. Niver say such a thing. It might come true. Did yer mither never tell ye?

TAM. She's long dead. The day I wus born.

ELLEN JEAN. I'm sorry. I canno' imagine a life withoot Mither.

TAM. Ach, who wants all that fussin' over.

(TAM *sighs and takes up the pelt.*)

I'll content myself wi' this spotty pelt.

ELLEN JEAN. No. It belongs tae me.

TAM. I can take this pelt if I want. Ye canno' stop me. And maybe if I keep it, ye'll follow me.

ELLEN JEAN. I'll no' follow a thief. The pelt belongs tae me. Ye canno' have it.

TAM. I'll no' take yer pelt . . . if ye'll dance with me at the Foy this night.

ELLEN JEAN. Ye want tae dance wi' me? At the Foy?

TAM. Aye, that's the trade. The pelt fer a dance.

ELLEN JEAN. Dance at the Foy! Aye, I'll dance with ye! (*Suddenly shy*) If that's what ye want.

TAM. I said it, did I no'?

ELLEN JEAN. Will ye promise no' tae harm the selkies?

TAM. It's a hard bargain yer askin' fer, Lass.

ELLEN JEAN. Aye.

TAM. Aye.

ELLEN JEAN. Done?

TAM. Done. *(TAM hands ELLEN JEAN the pelt, and she rolls it into a bundle.)*

ELLEN JEAN. I have somethin' important tae do. Be off with ye noo.

TAM. What's makin' ye so foreswifted tae be rid o' me?

ELLEN JEAN. I have something tae do before the Foy. Get on with ye.

TAM. Ye're mighty mysterious. What're ye aboot?

ELLEN JEAN *(casting about for an excuse)*. Oh. Well, I canno' go tae the Foy in me night-dress, can I?

TAM *(He looks down at his dirty hands and feet.)* Oh, I'm thinkin' I have somethin' tae do, too.

ELLEN JEAN. Dunna ferget yer promise.

TAM. I swear I'll no' hurt the selkies.

ELLEN JEAN. Ferever, no matter what comes.

TAM. I said it, did I no'?

ELLEN JEAN *(taking hold of his arms)*. Say it.

TAM. Ferever, no matter what comes.

ELLEN JEAN. Niver—niver forget yer promise.

(TAM reaches out his hand and touches her.)

TAM. I'll no' ferget.

ELLEN JEAN. Run. Dunna come back until midnight! Until the Foy!

TAM. Until the Foy!

(Giving a joyous shout, TAM turns and runs off-stage. ELLEN JEAN looks up and down the beach, then dances around the beach whirling and high stepping with joy. As she dances, MARGARET enters, and quietly watches her daughter.)

ELLEN JEAN. I'll dance—dance at the Foy! And be one o' them!

(Panting, ELLEN JEAN hugs herself with pleasure.)

MARGARET. 'Tis guid tae see ye smilin', Peedie Buddo.

ELLEN JEAN. Mither!

(ELLEN JEAN runs to her MOTHER, throws her arms around her MOTHER's waist, and holds her.)

ELLEN JEAN. Oh, Mither, I'm goin' tae dance at the Foy—with Tam!

MARGARET. A smart lad, that Tam. And lucky, too.

ELLEN JEAN. And … and look … I found yer pelt.

MARGARET. Ahhhh. Me pelt! Ye found me pelt! *(Laughing, MARGARET falls to her knees on the beach, caressing the pelt and breathing in the familiar smell.)*

ELLEN JEAN. Mither, ye're laughin'.

MARGARET. Oh, Peedie Buddo, ye've given me back me life.

ELLEN JEAN. Yer sisters said ye'll leave me fer the sea.

MARGARET. Leave ye? No, Peedie Buddo. I'll alus be with ye. Come.

(MARGARET holds out her hand, and ELLEN JEAN takes it in her own. MARGARET leads ELLEN JEAN down to the sea.)

MARGARET. Fourteen years I have been captive on the land. In that time I have grown old and stiff. Me skin is dry and cracked fer want o' the sea. Me bones are as brittle as driftwood lyin' on the shore. Ye have brought me what I need. It is me time tae return home. *(MARGARET folds her arms around ELLEN JEAN and holds her.)*

ELLEN JEAN. Mither, please, dunna leave me!

(The sound of the wind and the sea)

MARGARET. I will alus be with ye. Look tae the sea, and ye'll see me there. In the waves breakin' on the shore, the sun glitterin' on the sea foam. Precious shells will wash up on the beach. Fish will leap intae yer nets, and the selkies will guide ye safely through the tides in the sea.

(MARGARET kisses ELLEN JEAN on each cheek.)

ELLEN JEAN. No! Mither! Take me with ye! I want tae go with ye!

MARGARET. Are ye no' afraid?

ELLEN JEAN. Aye. Afraid o' bein' left behind among the others.

MARGARET. Listen well then, Peedie Buddo. I give ye the gift o' the wind tae travel beneath the tides. Only do as I do, and ye will have the way tae find the knowin'.

(Music. ELLEN JEAN *follows her* MOTHER's *lead as she dances the journey beneath the sea and, in a rhythmic exchange of breath, bestows the gift of the wind upon her daughter.*)

MARGARET. Me heart is turned inside oot with the pain o' leavin' ye, but it is me time tae go.

(MARGARET *turns and walks into the sea with the pelt. She puts it around her body and is transformed into a selkie. She glides swiftly into the sea and, without turning back, exits.* ELLEN JEAN *runs onto the rock at center.*)

ELLEN JEAN. Wait! Wait fer me! Dunna leave me behind!

(*Music from the Foy can be heard in the background. Enter* PA.)

PA. Ellen Jean. Hover thee, Lass. Ye canno' follow her. Stay and dance fer yer old Pa at the Foy.

(*Sounds of the selkies calling.* ELLEN JEAN *looks toward the sea.*)

ELLEN JEAN. Can ye no' hear 'em callin' me? I canno' stay on land.

PA. But the tides, Jean.

ELLEN JEAN. Dunna be afraid fer me, Pa. I'll find it. I'll find the knowin'.

PA. Jean, I canno' let ye go.

ELLEN JEAN. Dunna try tae stop me. If ye hold me here I'll hate ye ferever. (PA *embraces* ELLEN JEAN.)

PA. Go then and St. Magnus be wi' ye. Quickly! Duncan's comin' fer the Foy.

ELLEN JEAN. I love ye, Pa.

(*Enter* TAM. *He wears the same dirty clothes, but his face, hands, and bare feet are clean and his hair is combed and tied back neatly. He carries a bunch of heather.*)

TAM. Selkie Lass! I've come fer me dance! Listen! They're comin' up the beach fer the Foy!

(ELLEN JEAN *looks toward* TAM, *then toward the sea.*)

ELLEN JEAN. Dunna ferget yer promise, Tam McCodrun! Dunna ever ferget!

(*The sound of the wind increases.* ELLEN JEAN *runs to the water's edge and enters the sea. She swiftly follows the path her mother has taken.* TAM *runs forward onto the rock.*)

TAM. No! Wait! Ye promised me a dance!

(*Exit* ELLEN JEAN)

TAM. Come back! Come back! Ye'll drown!

(*Sounds of the wind as though a storm is approaching.* TAM *removes his vest, and prepares to leap into the sea to save* ELLEN JEAN.)

PA. Hover thee, Lad.

TAM. I've got tae find her!

PA. Ye canno' swim.

TAM. I canno' stand here like a fool and do nuthin'.

PA. There's naught tae be done fer it. Drownin' yerself oot there wilna bring her back. She's gone. She heard the selkies callin' her. It was her time, just as it was her mither's time tae go.

TAM. God fergive me! I made sport o' her.

PA. There, Lad, tis none o' yer doin'. It's no' yer fault.

TAM. But why did she run from me?

PA. 'Twas no' a runnin' from, Lad, but runnin' to. Ach, ye'd no' believe me if I told ye.

TAM. I want tae know.

PA (*struggling to find the words to explain*). Sometimes ye have tae lose somethin' terrible dear tae gain what ye want most.

TAM. I dunna understand.

PA. Might do me some guid tae tell ye all o'
it. Ye'll stay this night at the crofthouse.
With a roof over yer head and a fire
warmin' me bones, I'll tell ye the tale.
Perhaps we need each other.

*(The music of the Foy rises in the distance. The
sound of the wind howling and the sea waves
crashing.)*

TAM *(looking toward the music).* What will we
tell the others at the Foy?

PA. We'll tell 'em a wrong was done afore ye
were born. And this is the price tae be paid
oot fer it.

TAM *(looking toward the sea).* Will she come
back?

PA *(crossing himself).* Only St. Magnus knows,
Lad. But if she does return, she'll have a
knowin' beyond all the others.

(Lights shift. SELKIE sounds. Music.)

*(BLACK HAIR, RED HAIR, and the selkie MAR-
GARET, wearing their pelts, enter the sea area,
doing a version of the dance seen at the beginning
of the play that suggests the denser movement
beneath the sea. They are celebrating MARGARET's
return home.)*

DUNCAN *(offstage voice, calling from a distance).* Margaret!

*(MARGARET responds to the sound of DUNCAN's
voice, then slowly returns to the dance. With each
sound of DUNCAN's call, she reacts less and less
until she is deaf to his cries.)*

Margaret! Margaret! Come back! Margaret!

*(MARGARET and the two selkie sisters exit. DUN-
CAN enters, running.)*

Margaret! Margaret!

(DUNCAN collapses onto the rocks.)

(Lights shift.)

Dim light. The beach. One year later.
Midsummer's Eve, the night of the
Johnsmas Foy. Sounds of the wind and the
sea. At center sits TAM, looking out to sea. He
wears clean trousers, a shirt, and a new colorful
vest. His hair is combed neatly. Fiddle music. PA
enters, carrying his fiddle.

PA *(to the audience).* Listen. Can ye no' hear
the music? *(He listens.)* A year has passed.
It's Midsummer's Eve, the night o' the
Johnsmas Foy, one year ago since our Ellen
Jean was lost tae the sea. It's nearly midnight. Soon the torches'll be lit and the
dancin' on the beach'll last til the cock
crows. It'll be a guid harvest this year.
Plenty tae eat fer everyone, rich and poor
alike. But there's some hunger canno' be
satisfied wi' food, no matter how rich and
fine.

(The sound of the selkies singing)

TAM. Pa, look! There's selkies swimmin' in.

PA. Aye. Like alus they come back at
Midsummer's Eve.

TAM. How do they know it's Midsummer's
Eve?

PA. The light. The tides. The heat in the air.
It's in their blood.

TAM. Do ye think they know aboot Ellen
Jean?

PA *(crosses himself).* Only St. Magnus knows,
Lad.

TAM. There's somethin' aboot Midsummer. It
alus feels like the beginnin' o' things.

PA. 'Tis a beginnin'. Yer a fine one noo, ye
are, workin' yer own bit o' land.

TAM. Thanks tae yer kindness.

PA. What a bulder o' nonsense! Ye earned the
land wi' hard work. Ye're like me own
family, Lad.

*(Enter DUNCAN, disheveled and dressed in rags
as though he can no longer care for himself.)*

DUNCAN. There she is! 'Tis Ellen Jean comin' up the beach.

PA. No, no, Duncan, that's the others comin' fer the Foy.

DUNCAN. I see her. She's comin'. She's put on her bonny dress, and Margaret's done up her hair with ribbons. Jean!

PA. No, Duncan. Ellen Jean's drowned followin' her mither oot tae sea. Ye know that, man.

(DUNCAN *hangs his head and moans.*)

DUNCAN. She'll come. She'll come tae dance.

PA (*to* TAM). Poor guid man. He wilna give up hopin' she'll come back.

TAM. Aye. Waitin' each day on the beach fer her.

PA. He's near lost his mind wi' the sorrow.

DUNCAN. Jean! Jean! She's comin'. She's only waitin' fer the torches tae be lit, and the music tae start. Pa! Play yer fiddle. Then Ellen Jean'll dance!

TAM (*to* DUNCAN). Sir, come wi' me tae the crofthouse. We'll pour ye some ale and sit ye by the fire.

DUNCAN. Play yer fiddle, Pa! Play and she'll come. She's only waitin' tae hear the music.

(*Shaking his head,* PA *takes up his fiddle and plays a tune.* DUNCAN *goes round the beach lighting the torches of heather. When the torches are lit,* PA *ends the music.*)

DUNCAN. Where is she? Where's me daughter? Where's Ellen Jean? Margaret, give her back tae me! I canno' undo what I have done. Give me back me daughter!

(DUNCAN *falls to his knees on the beach. Selkie music.* ELLEN JEAN *rises from behind the rocks at the side of the stage, bathed in golden light. Her nightdress is changed to shimmering luminescent material the color of the sea, with sleeves short enough to reveal her hands.*)

ELLEN JEAN. Tam! Tam McCodrun. I've come fer me dance.

TAM. Giddy God! Ellen Jean!

DUNCAN. Jean! Me own darlin' daughter! Ye've come back!

(DUNCAN *runs to* ELLEN JEAN *and throws his arms around her.*)

I thought ye were lost, lost tae the sea ferever.

ELLEN JEAN. Lost? No, I am found. I've been tae the bottom o' the sea. Mither breathed intae me the wind tae travel beneath the tides. I have known the selkie-folk, me other family. Seven fine brothers and sisters I have below.

DUNCAN. And yer mither?

ELLEN JEAN. She fergives ye.

DUNCAN. Will she come back tae me?

ELLEN JEAN. She will alus be with ye. Look tae the sea. If ye're hungry, the fishes will leap intae yer nets. Precious shells will wash up on the beach. Yer boat will glide safely through the tides in the ocean and the rocks on the shore. Mither will be yer guide.

DUNCAN. Jean, Jean, I knew ye'd come back.

(ELLEN JEAN *goes to her* GRANDPA *and kisses him.*)

ELLEN JEAN. The waitin' is over, Pa. I've found the knowin'.

PA. Dance, Ellen Jean! Dance the stories tae life!

(*The music of the Foy swells.*)

ELLEN JEAN. Have ye kept yer promise, Tam McCodrun?

TAM. Aye, I said it, did I no'? Will ye be keepin' yers?

ELLEN JEAN. I choose tae dance. I'm fairly silted tae dance wi' ye, Tam!

(ELLEN JEAN *holds out her hand to* TAM. TAM *takes her hands. They look to* PA. PA *takes up his fiddle and begins to play.* TAM *and* ELLEN JEAN *do a version of the dance done by* ELLEN JEAN *earlier in the play,* TAM *following* ELLEN JEAN'S *lead. As they dance,* DUNCAN *fades offstage. As the lights dim,* PA *ends the tune and walks downstage.)*

PA. And so it was tha' the sea married the land. And in the union the island folk saw the birth o' a new kind o' folk—called the clan McCodrun. Across the islands their stories o' the sea and the land can be heard round the peat fires and the Johnsmas Foy is the merrier fer their dancin'. And on Midsummer's Eve, the seventh tide o' the seventh tide, the spirit o' Ellen Jean can still be seen sittin' on the skerrie, whisperin' softlike tae one beautiful, brown-spotted selkie with eyes green as the sea. And tae this day if ye come tae Orkney ye might see a lad or lass with the webbed hands. Dunna be surprised. They're the children o' the children o' the children o' the traveller Tam and Ellen Jean, the Selkie Lass.

(Fiddle music. Lights fade to blackout.)

CURTAIN

Discussing and Interpreting
Selkie

Play Analysis

1. Do you think that Duncan really loved Margaret? Explain your answer.
2. Myths are born of a place and a people. Think of an original myth that might be told in your part of the country based on your location, weather, terrain, and customs. Share your idea with the class.
3. Discuss with the class the Norn language used throughout the play. Compare it to English or other languages you are familiar with.
4. Imagine that you are of the clan McCodrun. Write a short poem or song telling about your ancestry. Try to use the vocabulary used in the play.
5. **Thematic Connection: Who Am I?** Ellen Jean must go through a process of unusual discoveries to find out who she is. How can her story help you understand who you are?

Literary Skill: Write a Myth

Below is a story that was told so often in the 50s and 60s that it became what is called "an urban myth." Read the story and write a short television script incorporating the myth.

Alligators in the Sewers of New York

New Yorkers are famous for flying to Florida in the winter months to trade sleet and frost for heat and humidity. In the 1950s and 60s alone thousands upon thousands of Manhattan dwellers arrived in Miami Beach and vicinity every week during winter. And in those years untold hundreds brought back baby alligators for their children. Not surprisingly, after a time these small lizards began to grow, and as they grew the New Yorkers worried. "What if the alligator hurts the children?" So, with sadness and regret these same New Yorkers flushed the young alligators away—down into the sewers and out of their lives. Or so they thought. Years later, sewer workers began to encounter fierce, gigantic gators—eating mice, rats, anything they could get their huge jaws around. Finally, these monstrous reptiles began to crawl up from their dank environment, looking for more and better nourishment on the streets of the city. Pets began to disappear. Then people turned up missing.

Performance Element: Sound

Go back over the script and look for music cues and other sound effects called for. Make a chart listing the titles of the music you would use, the sounds you would find or record, and the point in the play when you would use them. Share your ideas for sound effects with the class.

Setting the Stage for

Great Expectations

from the novel by Charles Dickens
adapted for the stage by Barbara Field

Creating Context:
Victorian London

Charles Dickens lived from 1812 to 1870. He called the London of his time "The Great Oven" and "The Fever Patch," but he also declared that London was the place that "made me what I am." To a great degree, Dickens helped create for generations of readers a London so vibrant and unique that it remains as real today as it was over 150 years ago.

a London chimney sweep

Dickens was twenty-five years old when the eighteen-year-old Victoria ascended to the throne of England. History would later call the time of her reign (1837-1901) the Victorian Era, and literature would deem any writing that exposed a society's moral failings, social ills, and amusing foibles Dickensian.

In Victorian times, thousands of working people trudged into London daily, many of them poorly paid clerks who copied letters, bills, and documents by hand and in triplicate in the days before typewriters or copiers. Coachmen and grooms lived above stables in places called *mews*. Butcher shops slaughtered animals on the premises, and dairies offered cows' milk on tap— straight from the cow. Knife-grinders and chair-menders hawked their skills along the streets. Chimney sweeps, washerwomen, and tinkers traveled the back streets. Children sold matches or flowers, when they could get them. As a boy, Dickens himself was put to work in a factory while his family languished in a debtor's prison. In those days nonpayment of bills landed you in jail until someone paid your way out.

Often shrouded in a fog created by smoke spewing from factories and from homes that heated and cooked with coal, London's crowded tenements, called *rookeries*, gave rise to crime and sickness. People threw sewage into the street or into ancient cesspits, which seeped into wells and groundwater. Crumbling sewers emptied into the Thames River running through the city. In 1844 it was found that a quarter of London's deaths were caused by bad water and filth.

To the Victorians, all of London was a theatre. They were as likely to attend public hangings, visit opium dens, or take excursions to Bedlam Asylum to stare at the insane as to enjoy pubs and music halls. It was the best of times and the worst of times, and Charles Dickens captured it all.

As a Reader: Understanding Setting

The first act of this play begins in a small English village. Long before act two begins, however, the main character, Pip, is transported to London. Compare the detailed description of Pip's first sight of London as written by Dickens, at the left, to Barbara Field's abbreviated version, at the right. Do you think reading the original novel would help in understanding the story?

from Page • • • • • • to Stage

So, I came into Smithfield; and the shameful place being all asmear with filth and fat and blood and foam, seemed to stick to me. So I rubbed it off with all possible speed by turning into a street where I saw the great black dome of Saint Paul's bulging at me from behind a grim stone building which a bystander said was Newgate Prison. Following the wall of the jail, I found the roadway covered with straw to deaden the noise of passing vehicles; and from this, and from the quantity of people standing about, smelling strongly of spirits and beer, I inferred that the trials were on ... .

"So you were never in London before?" said Mr. Wemmick to me."

"No," said I.

"I was new here once," said Mr. Wemmick. "Rum to think of now!"

"You are well acquainted with it now?"

"Why, yes," said Mr. Wemmick. "I know the moves of it."

"Is it a very wicked place?" I asked, more for the sake of saying something than for information.

"You may get cheated, robbed, and murdered in London. But there are plenty of people anywhere, who'll do that for you."

from *Great Expectations* by Charles Dickens

COACHMAN. London!

PIP. London! (*PIP climbs off the "coach," clutching his valise. He stares around him at the crowd.*)

NARRATION. Not far from the great dome of St. Paul's, in the very shadow of Newgate Prison, Pip alighted and stood before an ugly stone building... .

WEMMICK. So you've never been to London? I was new here, once, myself. But now I know the moves of it.

PIP. Is it a very wicked place?

WEMMICK. You may get cheated, robbed, and murdered in London. But there are plenty of people anywhere, who'll do that for you. Here we are, "Mr. Pocket, Jr."

from *Great Expectations* adapted by Barbara Field

As a Set Designer: Using One Stage for Many Settings

A set designer often has limited space in which to create sets for an expansive play, as is the case with *Great Expectations*. There are eight different settings in the first act alone. As you read, think how you might convey the quiet simplicity of the country as well as the hustle-bustle of a big city on one small stage.

Great Expectations

Time
Around 1860

The Characters
YOUNG PIP

MAGWITCH

JOE GARGERY / AGED PARENT / PORTER / PRISON DOCTOR

MRS. JOE / MOLLY

PUMBLECHOOK / WEMMICK / DRUMMLE

LIEUTENANT / TAILOR / HERBERT POCKET

JAGGERS / COMPEYSON

ESTELLA

MISS HAVISHAM / MISS SKIFFINS

BIDDY / CLARA

YOUNG HERBERT POCKET

PIP

JOE'S BOY

Setting
England

ACT ONE

The entire company is assembled onstage, except for the actor playing MAGWITCH, *who is already hiding behind the tombstone.*

NARRATION. His family name being Pirrip and his own name being Philip, in the beginning the boy could make of both names nothing longer than . . . Pip. So he called himself Pip, and came to be called Pip. The family name, Pirrip, he had on the authority of a certain tombstone, his father's, and on the authority of his older sister, Mrs. Joe Gargery, who was married to the town blacksmith. They lived in the marsh country of Kent, where the Thames ran down to the sea.

In that dark, flat wilderness was a village churchyard where, one day, Pip found his parents.

Churchyard. A few tombstones. PIP *kneels in front of one of them, reads haltingly.*

PIP. "Philip Pirrip, late of this parish." *(Pause)* "Also Georgiana, wife of the above . . ."

NARRATION. The boy, a small bundle of shivers, began to cry, when—(MAGWITCH *pops up from behind a tombstone.*)

MAGWITCH. Keep still, you little devil, or I'll cut your throat!

PIP. Oh don't, sir!

MAGWITCH. Tell us your name quick, then!

PIP. Pip, sir. (MAGWITCH *lifts him abruptly, sets him atop the stone, searches him. He finds a crust of bread, which he gnaws.*)

MAGWITCH. Lookee here, then—where's your mother?

PIP. There, sir. (MAGWITCH *starts.*) There—"Also Georgiana." That's my mother.

MAGWITCH. Hah. And that's your father, alonger your mother?

PIP. Yes, sir. "Late of this parish."

MAGWITCH. Hah. And who d'ye live with now, supposin' I kindly let you live, which I haven't made up my mind about?

PIP. My sister, Mrs. Joe Gargery. She's wife to the blacksmith.

MAGWITCH. Blacksmith, eh? *(He looks down at his leg irons.)* Lookee here: the question being whether or not you're to be let live— you know what a file is?

PIP. Yes, sir.

MAGWITCH. And you know what wittles[1] is?

PIP. Wittles is food, sir.

MAGWITCH. You bring me a file and you bring me some wittles, or I'll have your heart and liver out. Bring 'em tomorrow at dawn—and don't say a word about having

seen me—and I'll let you live. (PIP *nods.*) But mind, I'm not alone, if you're thinking that. No indeed, there's a young man hid with me, in comparison with which young man I am an angel. So you must do as I tell you.

PIP. Yes, sir.

MAGWITCH *(pulls out a little Bible).* Swear— say "Lord strike me dead if I don't."

PIP. "Lord strike me dead if I don't."

(MAGWITCH *gives him a dismissing nod. The boy backs away, then bolts.* MAGWITCH *huddles by the tombstone.*)

The Forge Kitchen.

NARRATION. Pip's sister, Mrs. Joe Gargery, was more than twenty years older than the boy. She had established a great reputation as a foster parent, because she had brought the boy up by hand. (*As* PIP *races in, she slaps him.*) She was neither a good-looking woman, nor a cheerful one. (JOE *steps in to protect* PIP.) Pip had the impression that she must have made Joe Gargery marry her by hand, too. (*She slaps* JOE, *as well.*)

MRS. JOE. Where've you been, young monkey? I'm worn away with fret and fright over you.

PIP. I've only been to the churchyard.

MRS. JOE. Churchyard! If it weren't for me you'd have been in the churchyard long ago. Bad enough being a blacksmith's wife, and him a Gargery, without being your mother as well. You'll drive *me* to the churchyard one of these days, between the two of you. (*As she talks, she butters a slice of bread, hands it to*

---

1. wittles (vittles/victuals), food

PIP *with another slap. He takes a bite, then when she isn't looking, he secretes the rest in his pocket.* JOE *notices, however.* MRS. JOE *turns to* PIP.) Where's your bread? Did you swallow it whole? This boy has the manners of a swine!

JOE. Oh no, my dear, I don't think he—

MRS. JOE. Don't my dear me! I'm not your dear. (*She hands* PIP *a slate, some chalk.*)

NARRATION. Pip felt little tenderness of conscience toward his sister. But Joe he loved. (JOE *watches* PIP *writing laboriously on the slate.*)

JOE. I say, Pip, old chap, what a scholar you are!

PIP. I'd like to be. (*He writes.*) How do you spell Gargery?

JOE. I don't spell it at all.

PIP. But supposing you did?

JOE. It cannot be supposed—though I am oncommon fond of reading.

PIP. Are you, Joe? I didn't know that.

JOE. Oncommon—give me a good book and I ask nothin' better.

PIP (*pause*). Did you ever go to school?

JOE. My father, he were given to drink, Pip; and whenever he were overtook with drink, he'd beat my mother and me, most onmerciful. We ran away a time or two, and my mother would find a job. "Joe," she'd say, "now you shall have some schooling, please God." And so I'd start school. But my father was such a good-hearted man, he couldn't bear to live without us, so he'd hunt us down and drag us home. Then he'd beat us up again to show how he'd missed us. Which you see, Pip, were a serious drawback to my learning. (MRS. JOE *takes* PIP's *slate away.*)

MRS. JOE. Time for bed, boy. (*She gives him a slap for good measure.*)

JOE. Time for bed, Pip, old chap. (*Whispers*)

Your sister is much given to government, which I meanter say the government of you and myself. (*He hugs* PIP. *There is a distant boom of a cannon.*)

MRS. JOE. Hark, the guns.

JOE. Ay. It must be another conwict off, eh?

PIP. Off?

MRS. JOE. Escaped, escaped.

PIP. Please, Joe, where's the shooting come from?

MRS. JOE. Ask no questions, you'll be told no lies.

JOE. It comes from the Hulks, Pip, old chap.

PIP. Please, Joe, what's the Hulks?

MRS. JOE. This boy! Answer one question and he'll ask a dozen more!

JOE. Hulks is prison ships.

PIP. And please, Joe—

MRS. JOE. No more! Time for bed! Bed! Bed! Bed!

NARRATION. Conscience is a dreadful thing when it accuses a boy. Pip labored with the thought that he was to become a thief the next morning . . . which was Christmas Day. (*The cannon booms.*) Pip scarcely slept that night. When pale dawn came he crept into the forge where he stole a file, and thence into the pantry where he stole a loaf of bread, some brandy, and a beautiful, round, firm pork pie. As he ran toward the marshes, the mist, the wind, the very cattle in the field seemed to accuse him. Stop thief! Stop that boy!

The Churchyard. PIP *runs toward the convict, whose back is to* PIP. *The man turns at* PIP's *whistle—but it is not the same man! Both gasp, then*

the man runs off. PIP *empties his pockets, then* MAGWITCH *appears. He grabs the brandy.*

MAGWITCH. What's in the bottle, boy?

PIP. Brandy. (MAGWITCH *stuffs the food into his mouth. He shivers as he eats.*) I think you've caught a chill, sir.

MAGWITCH. I'm much of your opinion, boy. (*He pauses, listens.*) You brought no one with you? (PIP *shakes his head.*) I believe you. You'd be a mean young hound if you could help hunt down a wretched warmint like me, eh? (PIP *watches him eat.*)

PIP. I'm glad you enjoy your food, sir.

MAGWITCH. Thankee, boy, I do.

PIP. But I'm afraid you haven't left much for him.

MAGWITCH. Who's him?

PIP. That young man you spoke of, who's with you.

MAGWITCH. Oh, him. (*He grins.*) He don't want no wittles.

PIP. He looked as if he did—

MAGWITCH. —Looked? When? (*He rises.*)

PIP. Just now.

MAGWITCH. —Where?!

PIP. Right here, a few minutes ago. I thought it was you—he wore gray, like you, and he wore … he had the same reason for wanting a file. He ran away.

MAGWITCH. Did he have a scar on his face?

PIP (*nods*). Here.

MAGWITCH. Give us that file, boy. (MAGWITCH *starts to file his leg irons.*) And then ye'd best go—they'll be missing you! (PIP *nods, then runs off.*)

NARRATION. As Pip ran home, he could still hear the file sawing away at the convict's fetters. He fully expected to find a constable waiting to arrest him when he got home. But there was only Mrs. Joe, readying the house for Christmas dinner.

The Forge Kitchen.

MRS. JOE. —And where the deuce ha' you been now? Company's expected!

PIP. I was … down to hear the carolers. (*She gives him a crack on the head.*)

JOE. Merry Christmas, Pip, old chap.

NARRATION. Dinner was set for half-past one. There was one guest … Mr. Pumblechook, wealthy seed-and-corn merchant in the nearby town. He was Joe's uncle, but he was Mrs. Joe's ally.

PUMBLECHOOK. Mrs. Joe, I have brought you a bottle of sherry wine, and I have brought you a bottle of port wine, in honor of the Day.

MRS. JOE. You was ever the soul of generosity, Uncle. (*They sit at table. She cuffs* PIP.) Stop fidgeting, boy—he wriggles as if he had a guilty conscience.

PUMBLECHOOK. Then he must indeed have one. Boys, Joseph— a bad lot!

MRS. JOE. Will you say the blessing, Uncle Pumblechook?

PUMBLECHOOK. For that which we are about to receive, may the Lord make us truly thankful.

ALL. Amen.

PUMBLECHOOK. D'you hear that, boy? Be ever thankful to them what has brought you up by hand.

PIP. Yes, sir.

PUMBLECHOOK. Joseph, why is it the young are never thankful? I declare, boys are naturally wicious!

MRS. JOE. Too true, Uncle Pumblechook.

JOE. Have some gravy, Pip? (*He ladles it onto* PIP's *plate.*)

PUMBLECHOOK. Not too much—the Lord

invented the pig as an example of gluttony to the young. (*To* MRS. JOE) He's no end of trouble to you, is he, ma'am?

MRS. JOE. Trouble? You cannot know what trouble he's been.

JOE. More gravy, Pip old fellow, old chap, old friend?

PUMBLECHOOK. I suppose this boy will be apprenticed to you, soon, Joseph?

MRS. JOE. Not for another year. Till then he'll eat me out of house and home—but I'm forgetting! I've a delicious pork pie, yet! (PIP *drops his fork.*)

PUMBLECHOOK. Ah, pork pie! A morsel of pie would lay atop any dinner you might mention, and do no harm, eh?

MRS. JOE. I'll just go fetch it. (*She goes.* PIP *rises in terror, rushes to the front door to escape. Simultaneously, a sharp knock at the door, and a scream from* MRS. JOE. *At the door,* PIP *is confronted by a pair of handcuffs, held by a soldier.*)

LIEUTENANT. Hello, young fellow— Does the blacksmith live here?

MRS. JOE (*off*). Stop! Stop, thief, my pie—it's been stolen.

LIEUTENANT. Well?

PUMBLECHOOK. This is the blacksmith's, yes.

LIEUTENANT. Sorry to disturb your Christmas dinner—

PUMBLECHOOK. Think nothing of it, my good man.

LIEUTENANT. —But we've caught two convicts, and need these irons repaired. Can you do it?

PUMBLECHOOK. Not me, him. He's the smith. Certainly he can do it. (MRS. JOE *enters, distraught.*)

MRS. JOE. My pork pie—it's gone—

LIEUTENANT (*to* JOE). By the way, is this your file?

JOE (*examines it*). Which it are!

LIEUTENANT. It was found in the church-yard—

MRS. JOE. Thieves, thieves …

(PUMBLECHOOK *is already pouring port wine down her throat.*)

***

NARRATION. Christmas dinner was over. When Pip arrived at the boat landing with Joe, he recognized *his* convict—and the other, with the scarred face.

(*The convicts glare at each other.* THE LIEUTENANT *takes the handcuffs from* JOE, *snaps them on* MAGWITCH. *The other man,* COMPEYSON, *lunges at* MAGWITCH, *is pulled off by soldiers.*)

MAGWITCH. I took 'im! I caught the villain! I turned 'im in, don't forget.

COMPEYSON. This man—this man has tried to murder me!

MAGWITCH. See what a villain he is! Look at his eyes! Don't forget, I caught 'im for ye! (MAGWITCH *turns, notices* PIP. PIP *gives him a tiny shake of the head.*) I wish ter say something respectin' this escape. It may prevent some persons from lying under suspicion alonger me.

LIEUTENANT. You'll have plenty of chance later—

MAGWITCH. —But this is a separate matter. I stole some wittles up in the willage yonder. Likewise a file—

JOE. Halloa, Pip?

MAGWITCH. And some liquor. And a pie. (*To* JOE) Sorry to say, I've eat your pie.

JOE. God knows you're welcome to it, as far as it was ever mine. We don't know what you have done, but we wouldn't have you starved to death for it, poor miserable fellow. Would us, Pip? (PIP *shakes his head.*

THE LIEUTENANT *calls out, "Ready! Move!"* *The prisoners are marched off,* MAGWITCH *stops, turns back. He and* PIP *stare at each other for a moment, then he goes off. Darkness.)*

The Forge Kitchen.

NARRATION. It was not long after the incident on the marsh that Mrs. Joe returned home in the company of Mr. Pumblechook, in a state of rare excitement.

*(*JOE *smoking his pipe in a chair,* PIP *on the floor beside him.* MRS. JOE *and* PUMBLECHOOK *burst in.)*

MRS. JOE. If this boy ain't grateful this night, he never will be! *(*PIP *tries to look grateful.)* It's only to be hoped she won't fill his head with silly ideas.

PUMBLECHOOK. I doubt it. She knows better.

JOE. Which someone mentioned a *she?*

MRS. JOE. Unless you call Miss Havisham a he—

JOE. Miss Havisham? That odd, solitary lady in the town?

MRS. JOE. She wants this boy to go play there. Of course he's going—and he'd better play, or I'll work him! *(She cracks* PIP *on the head.)*

JOE. Well, to be sure. I wonder how she come to know Pip?

MRS. JOE. Noodle—who says she knows him? *(She cracks* JOE *on the head.)* Couldn't she ask Uncle Pumblechook if he knew of a boy to go play there? Isn't it barely possible that Uncle Pumblechook may be a tenant of hers; and might he go there to pay his rent? And couldn't Uncle, out of the goodness of his heart, mention this boy

here—to whom I have ever been a willing slave?

PUMBLECHOOK. Now, Joseph, you know the case.

MRS. JOE. No, Uncle, Joseph does not know the case. *(To* JOE*)* For you do not know that Uncle, aware that this boy's fortune might be made by Miss Havisham, has offered to deliver Pip to her tomorrow, with his own hands! What do you say to that?

JOE *(mystified).* Thankee kindly, Uncle Pumblechook.

PUMBLECHOOK. My duty, Joseph. *(To* PIP*)* Boy, be ever grateful to those what brought you up by hand. *(He gives* PIP *a box on the ear.)*

NARRATION. Miss Havisham's house was of dismal bricks. Most of its windows were boarded up. There was a tall iron gate before which Mr. Pumblechook and Pip appeared at ten the next morning.

MISS HAVISHAM's. *The garden; then a room.* MR. PUMBLECHOOK *rings the bell.*

PUMBLECHOOK. Right on the dot of ten, boy.

PIP. No sir, I believe we're early. See, her big tower clock says twenty to nine.

PUMBLECHOOK. It must have stopped. My timepiece is always correct. *(*ESTELLA *appears.)*

ESTELLA. What name?

PUMBLECHOOK. Pumblechook

ESTELLA. Quite right. *(She unlocks the gate.* PUMBLECHOOK *pushes* PIP *through.)*

PUMBLECHOOK. This is Pip.

ESTELLA. This is Pip, is it? Come in, Pip. *(*PUMBLECHOOK *tries to follow.)* Do you wish to see Miss Havisham?

PUMBLECHOOK. I'm sure Miss Havisham wishes to see me.

ESTELLA. Ah, but you see, she don't. *(She shuts the gate in his face, leads* PIP *on.)* Don't loiter, boy.

NARRATION. Although she was about Pip's age, to him she seemed years older—Being beautiful and self-possessed—And being a girl.

(She leads PIP *upward, with a candle in her hand. She knocks. A voice says, "Come in."* ESTELLA *gestures* PIP *into the room, then leaves. It is dark. There is a banquet table with a huge cake.* MISS HAVISHAM *is seated before it.)*

HAVISHAM. Who is it?

PIP. Pip, ma'am.

HAVISHAM. Pip?

PIP. Mr. Pumblechook's boy, ma'am. Come to play.

HAVISHAM. Come nearer, let me look at you. Come closer.

NARRATION. Once Pip had been taken to see a waxwork at a fair. Once he had been taken to an old church to see a skeleton in the ashes of a rich robe, which had been dug out of a vault. Now waxwork and skeleton seemed to have dark eyes that moved, and looked at him.

HAVISHAM. Come closer. Ah, you are not afraid of a woman who has never seen the sun since you were born?

PIP. … No.

HAVISHAM. You know what I touch here?

PIP. Your heart.

HAVISHAM. Broken. *(Pause)* I am tired. I want diversion. Play. *(PIP does not move.)* I sometimes have sick fancies; and I have a sick fancy that I'd like to see someone play. Play. Play, play! *(PIP does not move.)* Are you so sullen and obstinate?

PIP. I'm very sorry, but I can't play just now. I

would if I could, but it's all so new here … so strange and fine and … melancholy.

HAVISHAM. So new to him, so old to me; so strange to him, so familiar to me; so melancholy to us both. *(ESTELLA enters.)* Let me see you play cards with this boy.

ESTELLA. With this boy!? Why, he's nothing but a common laboring boy!

HAVISHAM *(aside to* ESTELLA*)*. Well? You can break his heart.

ESTELLA. What do you play, boy?

PIP. Only "Beggar My Neighbor," miss. *(ESTELLA brings out a deck of cards, deals. They play.* PIP *drops some cards.)*

ESTELLA. He's stupid and clumsy—look at his hands, so coarse! *(They play.)*

HAVISHAM *(to* PIP*)*. You say nothing of her. What do you think of her, tell me in my ear.

PIP *(whispers)*. I think she is very proud.

HAVISHAM. Anything else?

PIP. I think she is very pretty.

HAVISHAM. Anything else?

PIP. I think she is very insulting and I'd like to go home.

HAVISHAM. You may go soon. Finish the game. *(They play.)*

NARRATION. The girl won. Her name was Estella. Pip was asked to return the next week. Estella took the candle and led him out.

ESTELLA *(going)*. You're crude. You're clumsy. Your boots are ugly!

NARRATION. The girl saw tears spring to Pip's eyes. Pip saw her quick delight at having been the cause of them. And for the first time, he was bitterly aware that life had been unjust to him. He quickly dried his eyes so she would not catch him weeping.

ESTELLA. Why don't you cry again, boy?

PIP. Because I don't want to.

ESTELLA. Yes, you do. You cried before, and you'll cry again—

NARRATION. Pip headed for home with the shameful knowledge that his hands were coarse and his boots were ugly, and that he was much more ignorant than he had thought himself the night before.

The Forge Kitchen.

(PUMBLECHOOK, MRS. JOE, *and* JOE *wait eagerly.* PIP *enters.*)

PUMBLECHOOK. Well, boy? How did you get on?

PIP. Pretty well, sir.

PUMBLECHOOK. "Pretty well?" Tell us what you mean by pretty well, boy.

PIP. I mean pretty well.

PUMBLECHOOK. And what is she like?

PIP. Very tall and fat.

MRS. JOE. Is she, Uncle? (*Pause.* PUMBLECHOOK *nods vaguely.*)

PUMBLECHOOK. Now, tell us what she was doing when you went in?

PIP. She was sitting in a big black velvet coach. (*His listeners are amazed.* PIP *smiles.*) Miss Estella handed her wine and cake, into the coach. We all had wine and cake—on golden plates! (*Astonished pause*)

PUMBLECHOOK. Was anyone else there?

PIP. Four black dogs.

PUMBLECHOOK. Large or small?

PIP. Immense!

PUMBLECHOOK. That's the truth of it, ma'am. I've seen it myself the times I've called on her. (*He bows, exits with* MRS. JOE. PIP *whistles a tune to himself.*)

NARRATION. After Mr. Pumblechook depart-

ed, Pip—or his conscience— sought out Joe.

PIP. It was all lies, Joe.

JOE. Really? The black velvet coach was a lie?

PIP. Yes.

JOE. Even the golden plates?

PIP. I wish my boots weren't so thick, Joe, I wish—(*He throws his arms around* JOE, *buries his face in* JOE's *shoulder.*)

NARRATION. He told Joe how miserable he'd been made to feel, by Uncle Pumblechook and Mrs. Joe, and by the very beautiful young lady who had called him common.

JOE. One thing, Pip, lies is lies and you mustn't tell any more of 'em. That ain't the way to stop bein' common. As for that, in some ways you're most oncommon. You're oncommon small. You're an oncommon scholar.

PIP. I'm not, I'm ignorant and clumsy.

JOE. Pip? Even the four black dogs was lies?

NARRATION. Although Pip could not improve the quality of his boots, he set about to remedy the quality of his education by taking lessons from Mr. Pumblechook's great-aunt's grand-niece—Biddy—who lived in the neighborhood.

BIDDY (*holds up a slate to* PIP). Six times four.

PIP. Twenty-four.

BIDDY. Seven times four?

PIP. Twenty-eight.

BIDDY. Eight times four? (*A pause.* PIP *isn't sure of the answer and, to tell the truth, neither is* BIDDY.)

PIP. Thirty-four? (*She nods approval.*)

NARRATION. And a week later he returned to

Miss Havisham's at the appointed hour.

* * *

MISS HAVISHAM's. *The garden, then a room.*

ESTELLA. Follow me, boy. Well?

PIP. Well, miss?

ESTELLA. Am I pretty?

PIP. Very.

ESTELLA. Am I insulting?

PIP. Not so much as you were last time.

ESTELLA. No? (*She slaps his face.*) Coarse little monster, why don't you cry?

PIP. I'll never cry for you again. (*As they cross, they pass* MR. JAGGERS *coming from the other direction.*)

NARRATION. As Estella led him through the gloomy house, they encountered a singular-looking gentleman coming toward them.

JAGGERS. Well, well, what have we here?

ESTELLA. A boy.

JAGGERS. Boy of the neighborhood?

PIP. Yes, sir.

JAGGERS. How d'you come to be here?

ESTELLA. Miss Havisham sent for him, sir.

JAGGERS. Well, behave yourself. I've a pretty large experience of boys, and you're a bad set of fellows. Behave! (*He continues out.* ESTELLA *and* PIP *enter* MISS HAVISHAM's *room.*)

HAVISHAM. So, the days have worn away, have they? A week. Are you ready to play?

PIP. I don't think so, ma'am.

HAVISHAM. Are you willing to work, then? (PIP *nods. She takes his arm, leans against his shoulder.*) Help me to walk, boy. (*They circle the table.*) This is where I shall be laid when I am dead. (*She points with her stick.*) What do you think that is?

PIP. I cannot guess.

HAVISHAM. It's a great cake. A bride-cake. Mine.

PIP. There are mice in it, ma'am.

HAVISHAM. Yes. This cake and I have worn away together, and sharper teeth have gnawed at me.

NARRATION. Breathing the heavy air that brooded in the room, Pip suddenly had an alarming fancy that all was decaying—that even he and Estella might presently begin to decay.

HAVISHAM. Now you must play at cards. (ESTELLA *gets the deck.*) Is she not pretty, Pip? (PIP *sighs, nods.* ESTELLA *deals.*)

NARRATION. And so the visits ran, with little to distinguish one from another. Estella always won at cards. Once, some relations called upon Miss Havisham.

A POCKET. How well you look, ma'am.

A POCKET. Happy birthday, cousin—

A POCKET. —And many happy returns of the day.

HAVISHAM. You see, Pip? The vultures have descended again, my Pocket relations. But the Pockets shall not have a penny of mine, never! You may go, Pip.

NARRATION. Pip was all too glad to take his leave. He was about to let himself out by the garden gate, when he was stopped by a pale young gentleman.

(YOUNG HERBERT *appears, munching an apple.*)

YOUNG HERBERT. Halloa, young fellow. Who let you in?

PIP. Miss Estella.

YOUNG HERBERT (*pleasantly*). Do you want to fight? Come on. (*He tosses the apple over his shoulder, strips off his cap, jacket, and shirt.*) I ought to give you a reason for fighting. There—(*He claps his hands together under* PIP's *nose, gently pulls his hair. He dances around* PIP, *fists doubled.*) Standard rules, is that agreeable? (PIP *nods.* HERBERT *dances around, throwing punches which miss* PIP. PIP *finally gets one off, and it levels* HERBERT. ESTELLA *peeps out to watch.*)

PIP. Oh dear, I'm sorry—

YOUNG HERBERT. Think nothing of it, young fellow! (*He jumps to his feet, squeezes a sponge of water over his head, dances around again.* PIP *lands another punch,* HERBERT *falls.*)

PIP. Oh, look, I'm really so sorry, I—

YOUNG HERBERT. Perfectly all right. (*He gets up, picks up the sponge, throws it.*) See, I'm throwing in the sponge. That means you've won. (*He offers his hand. They shake.*)

PIP. Can I help you?

YOUNG HERBERT. No thankee, I'm fine. (*He picks up his jacket and cap. As he goes off,* ESTELLA *passes him, sticks out her tongue. He shrugs, leaves.* PIP *stares after him.* ESTELLA *comes to him.*)

ESTELLA. You may kiss me, if you like. (*He kisses her on the cheek, then, overwhelmed, he flees.*)

Outside the Forge Kitchen.

NARRATION. If Pip could have told Joe about his strange visits—If he could have unburdened himself about his love for Estella, or even about his fight with the pale young gentleman—But of course he could not, for Joe's hands were coarser and his boots thicker than Pip's own! So Pip confided in Biddy—it seemed natural to do so. He told her everything. And Biddy had a deep concern in everything he told her. (PIP *and* BIDDY *are strolling, sharing a piece of toffee.*)

PIP. Biddy, I want to be a gentleman.

BIDDY. Oh, I wouldn't if I was you, Pip.

PIP. I've my reasons for wanting it.

BIDDY. You know best, but wouldn't you be happier as you are?

PIP. I am not happy as I am! I am disgusted with my life.

BIDDY. That's a pity for you, isn't it?

PIP. I know. If I was half as fond of the forge as I was a year ago, life would be simpler. I could become Joe's partner someday. Who knows, perhaps I'd even keep company with you. I'd be good enough for you, wouldn't I, Biddy?

BIDDY. Oh yes, I am not over-particular. (*Pause*) Is it Estella?

PIP. It's because of her I wish to be a gentleman.

BIDDY. Do you wish to be a gentleman to spite her or to win her?

PIP. I don't know. Biddy, I wish you could put me right.

BIDDY. I wish I could . . .

MISS HAVISHAM's.

NARRATION. But Biddy could not put Pip right. Things went on in the same way. His dreams and discontent remained. Time passed. Finally, one day Miss Havisham looked at him crossly—

HAVISHAM. You are growing too tall! What is the name of that blacksmith of yours?

PIP. Joe Gargery, ma'am.

HAVISHAM. I shan't need you to come play here anymore. So you'd better be apprenticed to Mr. Gargery at once.

PIP. But—

HAVISHAM. But what?

PIP. —I don't want to be a blacksmith! I'd rather come here!

HAVISHAM. It's all over, Pip. You're growing up. Estella is going abroad to school next week. Gargery is your master now. (*She glances at* ESTELLA, *whispers to* PIP.) Does she grow prettier, Pip? Do you love her? Shall you miss her? (PIP *turns away, she crosses to* ESTELLA.) Break their hearts, my pride and hope, break their hearts and have no mercy.

NARRATION. Pip was indentured as apprentice blacksmith to Joe Gargery the following week. Miss Havisham's parting gift of twenty-five pounds was cause for celebration in some quarters. (MR. PUMBLECHOOK *and* MRS. JOE *toast.*) Pip did not celebrate. He had liked Joe's trade once. But once was not now. He was wretched. (*Sound of an anvil. Glow of a forge fire.*) Nonetheless, Pip labored. And Pip grew. Always he would gaze into the fire at the forge and see Estella's face. He heard her cruel laughter in the wind. He was haunted by the fear that she would come home, witness his debasement, and despise him. On the surface, however, Pip's life fell into a routine. Days he worked with Joe at the forge. Evenings he became his own teacher—For he had long outstripped Biddy in learning. Once a year, on his birthday, he visited Miss Havisham.

HAVISHAM. Pip, is it? Has your birthday come round again? Ah, you're looking around for her, I see. Still abroad, educating for a lady … far out of reach and prettier than ever. Do you feel you have lost her?

NARRATION. Time wrought other changes. Mrs. Joe Gargery fell gravely ill, and lin-

gered in a kind of twilight, tended by Biddy, who was more sweet-tempered and wholesome than ever. Pip was now a young man, old enough to accompany Joe to the local public house of an evening. And so, in the fourth year of his apprenticeship, on a Saturday night at the Three Jolly Bargemen ….

The Pub. PUMBLECHOOK, JOE, *and* PIP *sit at a table.* JAGGERS *sits at a distance, in the shadows. Others are also drinking. A barmaid serves.* PUMBLECHOOK *is reading from a newspaper.*

PUMBLECHOOK. "The wictim is said to have spoken the name of the accused before he died, according to a witness for the prosecution. And medical testimony brought out during the third day of the trial by the prosecution points to—"

JAGGERS. I suppose you've settled the case to your satisfaction? (PUMBLECHOOK *peers into the shadows.*)

PUMBLECHOOK. Sir, without having the honor of your acquaintance, I have. The werdict should be "guilty."

JAGGERS. I thought as much. (*He rises.*) But the trial is not over, is it? You do admit that English law supposes each man to be innocent until he is proved—proved—guilty?

PUMBLECHOOK. Certainly I admit it, sir.

JAGGERS. And are you aware, or are you not aware, that none of the witnesses mentioned in that questionable journal you read has yet been cross-examined by the defense?

PUMBLECHOOK. Yes, but—

JAGGERS. I rest my case. (*He peers around the*

room.) From information I have received, I've reason to believe there's a blacksmith among you by the name of Joseph Gargery. Which is the man?

PUMBLECHOOK. There is the man. What have you done, Joseph?

JAGGERS. And you have an apprentice who is commonly known as Pip—is he here?

PUMBLECHOOK. Aha! I knew that boy would come to no good!

JAGGERS. I wish a conference with you two—a private conference. *(The others drift away, grumbling.)* My name is Jaggers, and I am a lawyer in London. I'm pretty well known there. I've some unusual business to transact with you. *(PIP and JOE glance at each other.)* Know first that I act as the confidential agent of another. It is my client's orders I follow, not my own. Having said that: Joseph Gargery, I've come with an offer to relieve you of this apprentice of yours.

JOE. Pip?

JAGGERS. Would you be willing to cancel his indentures, for his own good? *(JOE thinks, nods.)* You'd ask no money for doing so?

JOE. Lord forbid I should want anything for not standing in Pip's way.

JAGGERS. Good. Don't try to change your mind later. *(With great formality)* The communication I have come to make is … that this young man has great expectations. *(PIP rises. He and JOE gape.)* I'm instructed to inform him that he will come into a handsome fortune; that he is to be immediately removed from his present sphere of life and from this place; that he is to be brought up as a gentleman—in a word, as befits a young man of great expectations. *(JOE and PIP stare wordlessly for a moment.)*

PIP. Joe—

JAGGERS. —Later. First, understand that the person from whom I take my instruction requests that you always bear the name of Pip. You've no objection, I daresay? Good. Secondly, Mr. Pip, the name of your benefactor—

PIP. —Miss Havisham—

JAGGERS. —the name of your benefactor must remain a secret until that person chooses to reveal it. Do you accept this condition? Good. Good. I've already been given a sum of money for your education and maintenance. From now on, you will please consider me your guardian.

PIP. Thank you—

JAGGERS. —Don't bother to thank me, I am well paid for my services, or I shouldn't render them. Now then, education: you wish a proper tutor, no doubt? Good. Have you a preference?

PIP. Well … I only know Biddy, that's Mr. Pumblechook's great-aunt's grand-niece—

JAGGERS. —Never mind, there's a man in London who might suit well enough, a Mr. Matthew Pocket.

PIP. Pocket—is he a cousin of Miss Havisham?

JAGGERS. Ah, you know the name. He is. When do you wish to come to London?

PIP. Soon—directly!

JAGGERS. Good. You'll need proper clothes—here is twenty guineas. You'll take the hackney coach[2] up to London— it's a five-hour trip. Shall I look for you a week from tomorrow? Good. Well, Joseph Gargery, you look dumbfounded.

JOE. Which I am.

JAGGERS. It was understood you wanted nothing for yourself.

JOE. It were understood and it are understood and ever will be.

JAGGERS. But what if I was instructed to make you a present, as compensation for

---

2. hackney coach, a four-wheeled carriage drawn by two horses and having seats for six persons

the loss of his services—?

JOE. —Pip is that hearty welcome to go free with his services to honor and fortune, as no words can tell him. But if you think as money can compensate me for the loss of the little child what—what come to the forge and … and … ever the best of friends. *(He weeps.)*

PIP. Oh, Joe, don't … I'm going to be a gentleman! *(Darkness)*

NARRATION. That night Pip sat alone in his little room at the forge, feeling sorrowful and strange that this first night of his bright fortune should be the loneliest he had ever known.

The next morning, things looked brighter—Only seven days until his departure. Seven long days. But there was much to do. First he visited a tailor.

PIP *(rings bell).* I beg your pardon …

TAILOR *(unimpressed).* I beg yours.

PIP. I am going to London.

TAILOR. What of it?

PIP. I shall need a suit of fashionable clothes. *(PIP drops coins one-by-one into the hand of the TAILOR, who becomes obsequious.[3] During the following PIP goes behind a screen and changes his clothes as:)*

TAILOR. I beg your pardon, my dear sir. Fashionable clothes, is it? For London! You've come to the right place, you shall be quite correct, I assure you, quite the thing! Indeed, one might call you the "glass of fashion." We'll turn you out from top to toe as fine as any London gentleman could wish!

NARRATION. And thence, to Mr. Pumblechook's, to receive that great man's blessing.

PUMBLECHOOK *(raising a glass).* Beloved friend, I give you joy in your good fortune. Well-deserved, well-deserved! And to think that I have been the humble instrument leading up to all this … is reward enough for me. So here's to you—I always knew you had it in you! And let us also drink thanks to Fortune—may she ever pick her favorites with equal judgment!

NARRATION. And thence to Miss Havisham's, with barely suppressed excitement … and gratitude. *(PIP emerges from behind the screen. His London suit is almost comical in its exaggeration of high fashion. It is* de trop.[4]*)*

HAVISHAM. This is a grand figure, Pip.

PIP. Oh, ma'am, I have come into such good fortune!

HAVISHAM. I've learned of it from Mr. Jaggers. So, you've been adopted by a rich person, have you?

PIP. Yes, Miss Havisham.

HAVISHAM. Not named?

PIP. Not named.

HAVISHAM. You've a promising career before you. Deserve it! You're always to keep the name of Pip, you know? *(He nods.)* Goodbye then, Pip. *(She puts out her hand, he kisses it clumsily.)*

NARRATION. Finally, the morning of his departure dawned.

The Forge Kitchen.

PIP. You may be sure, dear Joe, I shall never forget you.

---

3. obsequious, overly eager to please; fawning

4. *de trop*, French for "too much"

JOE. Ay, old chap, I'm sure of that.

PIP. I always dreamed of being a gentleman.

JOE. Did you? Astonishing! Now me, I'm an awful dull fellow. I'm only master in my own trade, but … ever the best of friends— (*He flees in tears.*)

PIP (*to* BIDDY). You will help Joe on, won't you?

BIDDY. How help him on?

PIP. Joe's a dear fellow, the dearest that ever lived, but he's backward in some things, Biddy … like learning and manners.

BIDDY. Won't his manners do, then?

PIP. They do well enough here, but if I were to bring him to London when I come into my property, they would hardly do him justice.

BIDDY. —And don't you think he knows that? Pip, Pip …

PIP. Well?

BIDDY. Have you never considered his pride?

PIP. His pride? Whatever do you mean? You sound almost envious, and grudging.

BIDDY. If you have the heart to think so, say so! Can't you see, Joe is too proud and too wise to let anyone remove him from a place he fills with dignity— (JOE *enters, blowing his nose.*)

JOE. It's time for the coach, Pip.

PIP. Well then. (*He picks up his valise.*)

JOE. I'll come wisit you in London, old chap, and then—wot larks, eh? Wot larks we'll have!

PIP. Goodbye, Biddy. (*He kisses her cheek.*) Dear Joe— (JOE *grabs* PIP's *hat, throws it up in the air, to hide his tears.*)

JOE. Hoorar! Hoorar! (*With waves and cheers, the "coach" departs for London.*)

NARRATION. When his coach finally left the village behind, Pip wept. Heaven knows we need never be ashamed of our tears, for they are the rain on the blinding dust of earth, overlaying our hard hearts.

Pip felt better after he had cried—More aware of his own ingratitude, sorrier, gentler. But by now it was too late to turn back to Joe, so he traveled forward. The mists slowly rose and the world lay spread before him. And suddenly there was—

COACHMAN. London!

PIP. London! (PIP *climbs off the "coach," clutching his valise. He stares around him at the crowd.*)

NARRATION. Not far from the great dome of St. Paul's, in the very shadow of Newgate Prison, Pip alighted and stood before an ugly stone building.

JAGGERS's *Office.* WEMMICK *appears at* PIP's *knock.* JAGGERS *is inside the room, washing his hands. He pours water from a pitcher into a basin, as:*

PIP. Is Mr. Jaggers in? (WEMMICK *pulls him inside.*)

WEMMICK. Am I addressing Mr. Pip? He's been expecting you. I'm Wemmick, Mr. Jaggers's clerk. (*He leads* PIP *to* JAGGERS.)

JAGGERS. Well, Mr. Pip, London, eh?

PIP. Yes, sir.

JAGGERS. I've made arrangements for you to stay at Barnard's Inn. You'll share young

Mr. Pocket's apartments.

PIP. My tutor?

JAGGERS. His son. I've sent over some furniture for you. And here's a list of tradesmen where you may run up bills. And you will, you will—you'll drown in debt before the year is out, I'm sure, but that's no fault of mine, is it? Good. Wemmick, take him over to Barnard's Inn, will you? I must get back to court.

(He exits. WEMMICK *picks up* PIP's *valise, they stroll.)*

WEMMICK. So, you've never been to London? I was new here, once, myself. But now I know the moves of it.

PIP. Is it a very wicked place?

WEMMICK. You may get cheated, robbed, and murdered in London. But there are plenty of people anywhere who'll do that for you. Here we are, "Mr. Pocket, Jr." *(He knocks.)* As I keep the cash, we shall likely be meeting often. *(They shake hands.* WEMMICK *goes.)*

❧

Barnard's Inn. HERBERT *comes to the door.*

HERBERT. Mr. Pip?

PIP. Mr. Pocket? *(They shake hands.)*

HERBERT. Pray, come in. We're rather bare here, but I hope you'll make out tolerably well.

PIP. It seems very grand to me.

HERBERT. Look around. It's not splendid, because I don't earn very much at present, still I think … bless me, you're—you're the prowling boy in Miss Havisham's garden!

PIP. And you are the pale young gentleman!

HERBERT. The idea of its being you!

PIP. The idea of its being you! *(They laugh, both strike a boxing pose.)*

HERBERT. I do hope you've forgiven me for having knocked you about. *(They laugh, shake hands again.)*

NARRATION. Dinner was sent up from the coffeehouse in the next road and the young men sat down to get acquainted.

PIP. Mr. Pocket, I was brought up to be a blacksmith. I know little of polite manners. I'd take it as a kindness if you'd give me a hint whenever I go wrong.

HERBERT. With pleasure. And will you do me the kindness of calling me by my Christian name: Herbert?

PIP. With pleasure. My name is Philip.

HERBERT. Philip. Philip … no, I don't take to it. Sounds like a highly moral boy in a schoolbook. I know! We're so harmonious—and you have been a blacksmith … would you mind if I called you "Handel"?

PIP. Handel? Why?

HERBERT. There's a piece of music I like, *The Harmonious Blacksmith*, by Handel— *(He hums the tune.)*

PIP. I'd like it very much. So … we two go way back to Miss Havisham's garden! *(They eat.)*

HERBERT. Yes. She's a tartar,[5] isn't she?

PIP. Miss Havisham?

HERBERT. I don't say no to that, but I meant Estella. You know the old lady raised her to wreak revenge on all the male sex?

PIP. No! Revenge for what?

HERBERT. Dear me, it's quite a story—which I'll begin, Handel, by mentioning that in London it's not the custom to put the knife in the mouth—scarcely worth mentioning, but… . Also, the spoon is not generally used overhand, but under. This has two advantages: you get to your mouth more easily, but to your cravat less

---

5. tartar, a person of irritable or violent temper

well. Now, as to Miss H. Her father was a country gentleman. There were two children, she and a half-brother named Arthur. Arthur grew up extravagant, undutiful—in a word, bad! So the father disinherited him—Have another glass of wine, and excuse my mentioning that society as a body does not expect one to be so strictly conscientious in emptying one's glass as to turn it upside-down.

PIP. So sorry.

HERBERT. It's nothing. Upon her father's death, Miss H. became an heiress. She was considered a great match. There now appears on the scene—at the races, say, or at a ball—a man who courted the heiress. This is twenty-five years ago, remember. Also remember that your dinner napkin need not be stuffed into your glass. At any rate, her suitor professed love and devotion, and she fell passionately in love. She gave the man huge sums of money, against all advice—particularly against my father's; which is why she's never liked us since, and why I wasn't the boy chosen to come play with Estella—Where was I? Oh yes, the marriage day was fixed, the wedding dress bought, the guests invited, the bride-cake baked. The great day arrived—but the bridegroom failed to. Instead, he sent his regrets. That morning a letter arrived—

PIP. Which she received while she was dressing for her wedding? At exactly twenty minutes to nine?

HERBERT. Which is why she had all the clocks in the place stopped at that moment! It was later discovered that the man she loved had conspired with her brother to defraud her. They shared the profits of her sorrow.

PIP. Whatever became of them?

HERBERT. Fell into ruin and disappeared, both of 'em. Not many months after, Miss H. adopted Estella—she was a tiny child. And now, my dear Handel, you know everything I do about poor Miss H.

PIP. But I know nothing of you. If it's not rude to ask, what do you do for a living?

HERBERT (*dreamily*). I'd like to go into business. I'd like to be an insurer of great ships that sail to distant ports.

PIP. I see.

HERBERT. I'm also considering the mining business … Africa.

PIP. I see.

HERBERT. Trading in the East Indies interests me.

PIP. I see. You'll need a lot of capital for all that.

HERBERT. True. Meanwhile, I'm looking about me. Temporarily employed in a counting house, but looking about me for the right opportunity… .

PIP. And then … what larks.

HERBERT. Pardon? (PIP *laughs*, HERBERT *joins him.*)

NARRATION. Pip took up his studies with Herbert's father, Mr. Matthew Pocket. He was joined in his classes by another student, a haughty young man named—

DRUMMLE. —Bentley Drummle, seventh in line for a small baronetcy. And who, may I ask, are you?

NARRATION. Latin, French, history, mathematics in the mornings. In the afternoons sports, of which the favorite was rowing on the river.

DRUMMLE. No, no, no, Mr. Pip. Starboard's there. This is port!

PIP. Thank you very much.

DRUMMLE. Now you dip the blade of the oar into the water—that's the wide part, Mr. Pip.

PIP. You're too kind. But I did grow up near the river.

DRUMMLE. Yes, I've heard about you. Your rowing lacks form, there's no style to it, is there? Still, you're strong. One might say you've got the arm of a blacksmith! *(PIP glares at him.)*

NARRATION. To his surprise, Pip enjoyed his studies with Mr. Pocket. He also enjoyed his tailor, his linendraper,[6] his glove maker, his jeweler—

⁂

JAGGERS's *Office.* JAGGERS *washes his hands.* WEMMICK *watches.*

JAGGERS. Well, how much do you need this time?

PIP. I'm not sure, Mr. Jaggers.

JAGGERS. Fifty pounds?

PIP. Oh, not that much, sir.

JAGGERS. Five pounds?

PIP. Well, more than that, perhaps.

JAGGERS. Twice five? Three times five? Wemmick, twenty pounds for Mr. Pip.

WEMMICK. Twenty pounds in portable property, yes, sir.

JAGGERS. And now excuse me, young man, I'm late to court. *(He goes.* PIP *stares after him.)*

PIP. I don't know what to make of that man!

WEMMICK. He don't mean you to know, either. He always acts like he's just baited a trap. He sits watching, and suddenly— snap! You're caught. By the way, if you've nothing better to do at the moment, perhaps you'd like to come home with me for supper. I live down in Walworth.

PIP. Why, that's very kind of you. Yes.

WEMMICK. You've no objection to an Aged Parent?

PIP. Certainly not. *(They stroll.)*

WEMMICK. Because I have one.

PIP. I look forward to meeting her—

WEMMICK. Him. Have you been to dine at Mr. Jaggers's yet?

PIP. Not yet.

WEMMICK. He'll give you an excellent meal. While you're there, do notice his house-keeper.

PIP. Shall I see something uncommon?

WEMMICK. You will see a wild beast tamed.

⁂

Walworth. The garden, with drawbridge.

NARRATION. And so they arrived at Mr. Wemmick's cottage in Walworth. The place was odd, to say the least.

WEMMICK. Step over the drawbridge, if you will, Mr. Pip. *(PIP crosses over with* WEMMICK, *who has grown very affable.)* I must warn you, our little cannon fires at nine o'clock every evening, Greenwich time, so you won't be alarmed.

PIP. It's wonderfully … original here. *(THE AGED PARENT enters, pulling a small cannon on wheels.)*

WEMMICK. Ah, here's the Aged. *(Very loud)* Well, Aged Parent, how are you this evening?

---

6. linendraper, curtainmaker

AGED PARENT. All right, John, all right.

WEMMICK. Here's Mr. Pip, come to tea. *(To* PIP*)* Nod at him, Mr. Pip, that's what he likes. He's deaf as a post, he is. (PIP *nods at* THE AGED, *who nods back.)*

AGED PARENT. This is a fine place my son's got, sir. (PIP *nods.* THE AGED *nods.)*

WEMMICK. Proud as punch, ain't you, Aged? *(All three nod.)* There's a nod for you, and there's another for you. *(To* PIP*)* Mr. Jaggers knows nothing of all this. Never even heard of the Aged. I'll be grateful if you don't mention it—the office is one thing, private life's another. I speak now in my Walworth capacity.

PIP. Not a word, upon my honor.

WEMMICK. When I go to the office I leave the castle behind me, and vice versa. One minute to nine—gun-fire time. It's the Aged Parent's treat. Ready? Here we go! *(There is a big boom.)*

AGED. It's fired! I heard it! *(All three nod happily.)*

NARRATION. A few weeks later, Pip was invited, along with Herbert and Bentley Drummle, to dine at Mr. Jaggers's.

⸙

JAGGERS's *Home. A dining table.*

JAGGERS *(aside, to* PIP*).* I like your friend Drummle; he reminds me of a spider.

PIP. He's not my friend, we merely study together. He's a poor scholar, and he is incredibly rude.

JAGGERS. Good. You keep clear of him, he's trouble. But I like such fellows. Yes, he's a real spider. (MOLLY *appears.* JAGGERS *turns to her.)* Molly, Molly, Molly, Molly, may we sit down? *(She nods. He turns to the others.)*

Ah, dinner is served, gentlemen. *(They sit. She serves.)*

NARRATION. Pip studied her carefully. The night before, he had been to the theatre to see *Macbeth.* The woman's face resembled those he had seen rise out of the witches' cauldron. She was humble and silent … but there was something about her… .

JAGGERS. So, Mr. Drummle, in addition to conjugating the past conditional tense of French verbs, you gentlemen also go rowing for exercise?

DRUMMLE. We do. And your Mr. Pip's rowing is better than his French—

HERBERT. —I say, Drummle!

DRUMMLE. But I'm stronger with an oar than either of these fellows.

JAGGERS. Really? You talk of strength? I'll show you strength. Molly, show them your wrists.

MOLLY *(cringes).* Master, don't—

JAGGERS. Show them, Molly! *(He grabs her arm, runs his finger up and down her wrist delicately.)* There's power, here. Few men have the sinews Molly has, see? Remarkable force, beautiful power. Beautiful. That'll do, Molly, you've been admired, now you may go. *(She goes.)* To your health, gentlemen. *(Darkness)*

⸙

BIDDY. My dear Mr. Pip: I write at the request of Mr. Gargery, for to let you know he is coming up to London and would be glad to see you. He will call at Barnard's Hotel next Tuesday morning at nine. Your sister continues to linger. Your ever obedient servant, Biddy. P.S. He wishes me most particular to write "What larks!" He says you will understand. I hope you will see him, even though you are a gentleman now, for you had ever a good heart and he is so worthy. He asks me again to write "What larks!" Biddy.

NARRATION. With what feelings did Pip look forward to Joe's visit? With pleasure? No, with considerable disturbance and mortification. What would Bentley Drummle think of someone like Joe? And what would Joe think of Pip's expensive and rather aimless new life?

Barnard's Inn. A knock at the door. JOE *enters, awkwardly dressed in a suit.*

PIP. Joe! (JOE *holds his arms out to embrace* PIP, PIP *sticks out his right hand. They shake.*)

JOE. Pip, old chap.

PIP. I'm glad to see you, Joe. Come in, give me your hat! (JOE *remembers he has one, removes it from his head, but holds fast to it.*)

JOE. Which you have that grow'd and that swelled with the gentlefolk!

PIP. And you look wonderfully well, Joe. Shall I take your hat? (JOE *continues to clutch it.*)

JOE. Your poor sister's no worse nor no better than she was. And Biddy is ever right and ready, that girl. (HERBERT *enters from bedroom.*)

PIP. Here's my friend, Herbert Pocket.

JOE. (HERBERT *extends his hand.* JOE *drops his hat.*)

HERBERT. Your servant, sir.

JOE. Yours, yours. (*He picks up the hat.*)

HERBERT. Well. Have you seen anything of London, yet?

JOE. Why, yes, sir. Soon as I left the coach, I went straight off to look at the Blacking Factory warehouse.

HERBERT. Really? What did you think?

JOE. It don't come near to its likeness on the labels.

HERBERT. Is that so?

JOE. See, on the labels it is drawn too architectooralooral. (HERBERT *nods.* PIP *covers his face in mortification.* JOE *drops his hat.*)

HERBERT. You're quite right about that, Mr. Gargery—he is, Pip. Well, I must be off to work. It's good to have met you. (*He offers his hand.* JOE *reaches, drops his hat.* HERBERT *goes out.*)

JOE. We two being alone, sir—

PIP. —Joe, how can you call me "sir?!"

JOE. Us two being alone, Pip, and me having the intention to stay not many minutes more—

PIP. —Joe!—

JOE. I will now conclude—leastways begin—what led up to my having the present honor, sir. Miss Havisham has a message for you, Pip, sir. She says to tell you Miss Estella has come home from abroad and will be happy to see you.

PIP. Estella!

JOE. I tried to get Biddy to write the message to you, sir, but she says, "I know Pip will be glad to have that message by word of mouth." Which I have now concluded. (*He starts to go.*) And so, Pip, I wish you ever well and ever prospering to greater height, sir—

PIP. —You're not leaving?!

JOE. Which I am.

PIP. But surely you're coming back for dinner?

JOE. Pip, old chap, life is made of ever-so-many partings welded together, and one man's a blacksmith, and one's a whitesmith, and one's a goldsmith. Diwisions among such must be met as they come. You and me is not two figures to be seen together in London. I'm wrong in these clothes. I'm wrong out of the forge. You won't find half so much fault in me if you think of me in my forge clothes, with my hammer in my hand. And so, ever the best of friends, Pip. God bless you, dear old chap. God bless you, sir.

NARRATION. And he was gone. After the first guilty flow of repentance, Pip thought better of such feelings. He dried his eyes, and did not follow Joe into the street to bring him back. The next day Pip took the coach down from London. He did not bother to call in at the forge.

⁂

MISS HAVISHAM's. ESTELLA *waits in the shadows.* PIP *enters.*

HAVISHAM. So, you kiss my hand as if I were a queen?

PIP. I heard you wished to see me, so I came directly.

HAVISHAM. Well? (ESTELLA *turns, smiles at him.*) Do you find her much changed?

PIP. I …

HAVISHAM. And is he changed, Estella?

ESTELLA. Very much.

HAVISHAM. Less coarse and common? (ESTELLA *laughs.*) Go into the garden, you two, and give me some peace until tea time. (ESTELLA *takes his arm. They wander out.*)

PIP. Look it's all still here.

ESTELLA. I must have been a singular little creature. I hid over there and watched you fight that strange boy. I enjoyed that battle very much.

PIP. You rewarded me very much.

ESTELLA. Did I? (*She picks up a clay pot of primroses, smells them, picks one and puts it in* PIP's *buttonhole.*)

PIP. He and I are great friends, now. It was there you made me cry, that first day.

ESTELLA. Did I? I don't remember. (*She notices his hurt.*) You must understand, I have no heart. That may have something to do with my poor memory.

PIP. I know better, Estella.

ESTELLA. Oh, I've a heart to be stabbed in or shot at, no doubt. But I've no softness there, no … sympathy. If we're to be thrown together often—and it seems we shall be—you'd better believe that of me. What's wrong, is Pip scared? Will he cry? Come, come, tea's ready. You shall not shed tears for my cruelty today. Give me your arm, I must deliver you safely back to Miss Havisham. (*They return to* MISS HAVISHAM, *who takes* ESTELLA's *hand and kisses it with ravenous intensity.* ESTELLA *goes out.*)

HAVISHAM. Is she not beautiful, Pip? Graceful? Do you admire her?

PIP. Everyone who sees her must.

HAVISHAM. Love her, love her, love her! If she favors you, love her! If she wounds you, love her! If she tears your heart to pieces, love her, love her, love her!

PIP. You make that word sound like a curse.

HAVISHAM. You know what love is? I do. It is blind devotion, unquestioning self-humiliation, utter submission. It is giving up your whole heart and soul to the one who smites you, as I did. That is love. (*Darkness*)

NARRATION. Love her! Love her! Love her! The words rang triumphantly in his ears all the way back to London. That Estella was destined for him, once a blacksmith's boy! And if she were not yet rapturously grateful for that destiny, he would somehow awaken her sleeping heart!

Barnard's Inn.

PIP. I've got something particular to tell you.

HERBERT. That's odd, I've something to tell you.

PIP. It concerns myself—and one other person.

HERBERT. That's odd, too.

PIP. Herbert, I love—I adore Estella!

HERBERT. Oh, I know that. My dear Handel, you brought your adoration along with your valise the day you came to London.

PIP. She's come home—I saw her yesterday. I do love her so!

HERBERT. What are the young lady's sentiments?

PIP. Alas, she is miles and miles away from me.

HERBERT. If that's so, can you not detach yourself from her? (PIP *turns away.*) Think of her upbringing—think of Miss Havisham! Given all that, your love could lead to misery.

PIP. I know, but I cannot help myself. I cannot "detach."

HERBERT. Well. But perhaps it doesn't matter—perhaps your feelings are justified. After all, it would seem you've been chosen for her. Yes, I'm sure it will work out!

PIP. What a hopeful disposition you have.

HERBERT. I must have— I've not got much else. But since the subject's come up, I want you to know first—I'm engaged.

PIP. My dear Herbert! May I ask the bride's name?

HERBERT. Name of Clara. Clara Barley.

PIP. And does Clara Barley live in London?

HERBERT. She does. Oh Pip, if you could see her—so lovely!

PIP. Is she rich?

HERBERT. Poorer than me—and as sweet as she is poor. I'm going to marry her—

PIP. That's wonderful, Herbert. When? (HERBERT's *face falls.*)

HERBERT. That's the trouble. A fellow can't marry while he's still looking about him, can he?

PIP. I don't suppose he can. But cheer up, it will all work out. Yes, I feel it … it shall work out!

ESTELLA. Dear Pip: I am coming to London the day after tomorrow, by midday coach. Miss Havisham insists that you are to meet me, and I write in obedience to her wishes. Yours, Estella.

NARRATION. And suddenly she was there, in London!

(ESTELLA *hands a valise and hatbox to* PIP.)

PIP. I'm glad, so glad you've come.

ESTELLA. Yes. I'm to live here with a chaperone, at great—ridiculous expense, really. She is to take me about. She's to show people to me, and show me to people.

PIP. I wonder Miss Havisham could part with you.

ESTELLA. It's all part of her great plan. She wants me to write her constantly and report how I get on—

PIP. Get on? Get on? With what? With whom? (ESTELLA *smiles.*)

ESTELLA. Poor Pip. Dear Pip.

BIDDY. Dear Pip: I am writing to inform you that your sister died at peace the night before last. Her funeral was held this morning. We discussed whether to wait until you could attend it, but decided that as you are busy in your life as a gentleman we should go forward with the affair as we are. Yours, Biddy. P. S. Joe sends his fond wishes and sympathy.

NARRATION. As Pip got on, he became accustomed to the idea of his great expectations. He grew careless with his money, contracting a great quantity of debts. And Herbert's good nature, combined with Pip's lavish spending, lead them both into habits they could ill-afford. They moved their lodgings from the spartan Barnard's Inn to more luxurious quarters in the Temple, on the banks of the Thames.

(HERBERT *and* PIP *enter, each holding sheaves of bills.*)

PIP. My dear Herbert, we are getting on very badly.

HERBERT. My dear Handel, those very words were on my lips! We must reform.

PIP. We must indeed. (*They look at each other, toss the bills up in the air, watch them float down.*)

NARRATION. Their affairs went from bad to worse, so they began to look forward eagerly to Pip's twenty-first birthday—In the hope that Mr. Jaggers, by way of celebration, might give Pip some concrete evidence of his expectations.

JAGGERS's *Office.* JAGGERS *is washing his hands.*

WEMMICK. Happy birthday, Mr. Pip. (*To* JAGGERS) He's here.

JAGGERS. Well, well, twenty-one today, is that not the case?

PIP. Guilty, sir. I confess to being twenty-one.

JAGGERS. Tell me, Pip, what are you living at the rate of?

PIP. I … don't know, sir.

JAGGERS. I thought as much. Now it's your turn to ask me a question.

PIP. Have—have I anything to receive today?

JAGGERS. I thought we'd come to that! Take this piece of paper in your hand. Now unfold it. What is it?

PIP. It's a banknote … for five hundred pounds—

JAGGERS. And a handsome sum of money, too, you agree?

PIP. How could I do otherwise?

JAGGERS. It is yours. And at the rate of five hundred per year, and no more, you are to live until your benefactor chooses to appear.

PIP. Is my benefactor to be made known to me today?

JAGGERS. As to when that person decides to be identified, why, that's nothing to do with me, I'm only the agent—

PIP. But she—

JAGGERS. —She?—

PIP. —My patron—

JAGGERS. —Hah! You cannot trick me into giving evidence, young man. Now, excuse me, I'm off to court. (*He goes, followed by* WEMMICK. PIP *stares at the bank-note, holds it up, suddenly starts to smile.*)

NARRATION. The following Sunday Pip made a pilgrimage down to Walworth to see Mr. Wemmick. For he had an idea about how he would like to spend at least part of his money.

Walworth. PIP *crosses over the little drawbridge. The* AGED PARENT *greets him.*

AGED PARENT. Ah, my son will be home at any moment, young man. *(PIP nods.)* Make yourself at home. You made acquaintance with my son at his office? *(PIP nods.)* I hear he's a wonderful hand at his business. *(PIP nods.)* Now to be precise, I don't actually hear it, mind, for I'm hard of hearing.

PIP. Not really!

AGED PARENT. Oh, but I am! Look, here comes John, and Miss Skiffins with him. All right, John?

WEMMICK. All right, Aged P. So sorry I wasn't here to greet you, Mr. Pip. May I present Miss Skiffins, who is a friend of mine, and a neighbor. The Aged and Miss Skiffins will prepare tea, while we chat—

PIP. I wish to ask you—you are in your Walworth frame of mind, I presume? *(WEMMICK nods,* THE AGED *nods, they all nod.)*

WEMMICK. I am. I shall speak in a private and personal capacity. *(MISS SKIFFINS leads* THE AGED *away.)*

PIP. I wish to do something for my friend, Herbert Pocket. He has been the soul of kindness and I've ill-repaid him by encouraging him to spend more than he has. He'd have been better off if I'd never come along, poor fellow, but as I have, I want to help him. Tell me, how can I set him up in a small partnership somewhere?

WEMMICK. That's devilish good of you, Mr. Pip.

PIP. Only he must never know I had any part in it. You know the extent of my resources, Wemmick. Can you help me?

(WEMMICK thinks for a moment.)

WEMMICK. Perhaps … perhaps—yes! Yes, I like it. But it must be done by degrees. We'll go to work on it! *(MISS SKIFFINS appears.)*

SKIFFINS. Mr. Wemmick, dear, the Aged is toasting.

PIP. I beg your pardon, but what did she say?

WEMMICK. Tea is served. *(They go off.)*

NARRATION. Before a week had passed, Wemmick found a worthy young shipping broker named Clarriker—who wanted intelligent help—and who also wanted some capital—

And who might eventually want a partner. Between this young merchant and Pip secret papers were signed, and half of Pip's five hundred pounds disappeared. The whole business was so cleverly managed that Herbert hadn't the least suspicion that Pip's hand was in it.

(HERBERT races in to find PIP reading.)

HERBERT. Handel, Handel, I've the most mighty piece of news! I've just come from an interview in the City—man name of Clarriker—I'm to have a position there and—oh, Handel, I start next week, and I might, in time—

PIP. I'm happy for you, Herbert, so happy—

NARRATION. Pip went quickly into his room and wept with joy at the thought that his expectations had at last done some good to somebody. But what of Estella? She rapidly became the belle of London, seen and admired by all. Pip never had an hour's happiness in her society—Yet his mind, twenty-four hours a day, harped on the happiness of possessing her someday. On the occasion of Miss Havisham's birthday they were asked to come down from London together to visit.

✦

MISS HAVISHAM's. PIP *bows.* ESTELLA *kisses her cheek.* MISS HAVISHAM *clutches* ESTELLA's *hand.*

HAVISHAM. How does she use you, Pip, how does she use you?

PIP. According to your designs, I fear.

NARRATION. And he suddenly saw his fate … In the cobwebs … In the decayed wedding cake … In the face of the clocks that had stopped … And his profound sadness communicated itself to Estella.

(ESTELLA *withdraws her hand from* MISS HAVISHAM.)

HAVISHAM. What, are you tired of me?

ESTELLA. Only a little tired of myself.

HAVISHAM. No, speak the truth, you're tired of me! (ESTELLA *shivers, turns away.*) You cold, cold heart.

ESTELLA. What? You reproach me for being cold? I am what you made me—take all the credit or blame.

HAVISHAM. Look at her, so thankless. I took you to my heart when it was still bleeding from its wounds.

ESTELLA. Yes, yes, what would you have of me?

HAVISHAM. Love.

ESTELLA. Mother-by-adoption, how can I return to you what you never gave me?

HAVISHAM. Did I never give her love? You are so proud, so proud!

ESTELLA. Who taught me to be proud? Who praised me when I learned my lesson?

HAVISHAM. So hard, so hard!

ESTELLA. Who taught me to be hard?—

HAVISHAM. But to be proud and hard to me—to me, Estella!

ESTELLA. I cannot think what makes you so unreasonable, when Pip and I have ridden all the way down here for your birthday. I have never forgotten the wrongs done you. I've learned the lessons you taught me— God knows I wish I could unlearn them! (*Pause.* ESTELLA *comes to her, kisses her.*)

NARRATION. And as soon as the quarrel began, it was over, and never referred to again. (ESTELLA *leads* MISS HAVISHAM *off.*)

✦

NARRATION. The following week, Herbert and Pip were dining at their club.

DRUMMLE. Gentlemen, raise your glasses. I give you Estella.

PIP. Estella who?

DRUMMLE. Estella of Havisham, a peerless beauty.

HERBERT (*to* PIP). Much he knows of beauty, the idiot.

PIP. I am acquainted with that lady you speak of. Why do you propose a toast to one of whom you know nothing?

DRUMMLE. Ah, but I do know her. I escorted her to the opera last night.

NARRATION. Now she was seen around the town with Drummle, at the theatre, at a ball, at the races … But wasn't she destined for Pip? He took comfort in that thought, and in Herbert's happiness—For he had Clara Barley. And so, two years pass.

Temple Gardens pictured in the late eighteenth century, when they opened on to the Thames. (By courtesy of the Guildhall Library, Corporation of London.)

The Temple Apartment. Night. PIP *sits reading.*

NARRATION. It was the night of Pip's twenty-third birthday. The weather was wretched, wet and stormy. St. Paul's had just chimed eleven when—Pip thought he heard a footstep on the stair.

PIP. Who's there? (*He puts down his book, takes up a candle.*) Answer! There's someone down there, is there not?

MAGWITCH (*in shadows*). Yes.

PIP. What floor do you want?

MAGWITCH. The top. Mr. Pip.

PIP. That is my name. Pray, state your business. (MAGWITCH *slowly emerges from the shadows, warmly dressed in seafaring clothes.*

He holds out his hands to PIP.)

MAGWITCH. My business?

PIP. Who are you? Explain, please. (MAGWITCH *advances.*) I don't understand—keep away—!

MAGWITCH. It's disappointing to a man, arter having looked for'ard so distant and come so far, but you're not to blame for that. (*He gazes at* PIP *admiringly.*) You're a game 'un. I'm glad you grow'd up a game 'un. (*He takes off his cap.* PIP *freezes.*) You acted nobly out on that marsh, my dear boy, and I never forgot it! And now I've come back to you! I've come back to you, Pip, dear boy! (*And to* PIP's *horror,* MAGWITCH *throws his arms around him and embraces him. Darkness.*)

End Act One

ACT TWO

The Temple. As it was at the end of Act One. MAGWITCH *embraces the horrified* PIP.

MAGWITCH. I've come back to you, Pip, dear boy!

PIP. I know you now, and if you're grateful for what I did on those marshes years ago, that's fine, but—

MAGWITCH. You look to have done well since then.

PIP. I have—please release me, I beg you. (MAGWITCH *lets go of* PIP.)

MAGWITCH. May I make so bold as to ask how you have done well since you and me was out on those shiverin' marshes?

PIP. How? I've been chosen to succeed to some property.

MAGWITCH. Might a warmint ask what property?

PIP (*brief pause*). I don't know.

MAGWITCH. Might a warmint ask whose property?

PIP (*a long pause*). I … don't know. …

MAGWITCH. Might there be some kind of guardian in the picture, then; some lawyer, maybe? And the first letter of this lawyer's name, could it be … J? For Jaggers?!

PIP. My God—no! No, it can't be … you!

MAGWITCH. Yes, Pip, dear boy, I've made a gentleman on you—it's me wot done it! I'm your second father, lad, and I've come back to you, to see my fine gentleman—(*He embraces* PIP *again.*) Didn't you never think it could be me? (PIP *disengages with a wail.*)

PIP. Never! Never, never, never!

HERBERT (*entering in his dressing gown*). I say, Handel, you're making an awful racket—oh, I beg your pardon, I didn't know you had company.… (MAGWITCH *takes a knife out.*)

PIP. Herbert, this is … a visitor of mine. (PIP *sees the knife. To* MAGWITCH:) He's got every right to be here—he lives here! He is my friend.

MAGWITCH (*puts away knife, takes out little Bible*). Then it's all right, dear boy. Take the book in your hand, Pip's friend. Lord strike you dead if you ever spilt[7] in any way sumever. Kiss the book. (HERBERT *does so.*)

PIP. Herbert, this is my … benefactor. (HERBERT *gapes.*)

HERBERT. Oh … I … how do you do, my name's Herbert Pocket. I hope you're quite well … ?

MAGWITCH. How do you do, Pip's companion. And never believe me if Pip shan't make a gentleman on you, too!

HERBERT. I'll look forward to it. Ah … Pip? (PIP *shrugs at him, bewildered.*)

PIP. Tell me, do you have a name? By what do I call you?

MAGWITCH. Name of Magwitch. Christened Abel.

HERBERT. Abel Magwitch, fancy …

MAGWITCH. I were born and raised to be a warmint, but now I'm Pip's second father, and he's my son. More to me than any son. Every since I was transported to Australia, I swore that each time I earned a guinea, that guinea should go to Pip. And I swore that when I speculated and got rich, it'd all be for Pip. I lived rough so that he should live smooth. (*He admires* PIP *benevolently.*) How good-looking he have grow'd. There's a pair of bright eyes somewheres wot you love, eh, Pip? Those eyes shall be yourn, dear boy, if money can buy 'em. (*He beams at* PIP, *yawns.*) Now then, where shall I sleep tonight?

PIP. Pray, take my bedroom.

MAGWITCH. By your leave, I'll latch the door first. Caution is necessary. (*He does so.*)

---

7. spilt, spill; divulge; tell

HERBERT. Caution? How do you mean, caution?

MAGWITCH *(whispers)*. It's death.

HERBERT *(whispers)*. What's death?

MAGWITCH. If I'm caught. I was sent up for life, warn't I? It's death for me to come back to England; I'd be hang'd for it, if I was took.

PIP *(an anguished explosion)*. Then why in God's name have you come?!!

MAGWITCH. To see my dear boy. To watch him be a fine gentleman. *(He nods, beams, exits into the bedroom.* PIP *buries his head in his hands.)*

PIP. Estella, Estella ... I am lost!

HERBERT. Hold steady—he mustn't hear you.

PIP. The shame of it, Herbert! I always thought Miss Havisham—I thought Estella was intended for me. Fool. Foolish dreamer! And now I awaken to find I owe my fortune to this man, this wretched ... criminal! ... who has risked his life to be with me! It's a terrible joke, isn't it? And you know what's the funniest part? I scorned my most faithful friend for these "expectations!" Joe, Joe....

HERBERT. Take hold of yourself, Handel. There are practical questions to answer. How are we to keep him out of danger? Where will he live? *(Dreamily)* There are disguises, I suppose ... wigs, spectacles. Given his intimidating manner, we can hardly dress him up as a vicar but.... I think some sort of prosperous farmer's disguise would be best. We shall cut his hair! *(He looks at the suffering* PIP.*)* Get some sleep, Handel. You'll need it when morning comes.

PIP. When morning comes, Mr. Jaggers had better have a good explanation!

MR. JAGGERS's *Office.*

NARRATION. The moment Pip walked in, Mr.

Jaggers could see from his face that the man had turned up. Jaggers immediately immersed himself in soap and water.

JAGGERS. Now Pip, be careful! Don't tell me anything—I don't want to be told a thing! I am not curious.

PIP. I merely wish to be sure that what I've been told is true.

JAGGERS. Did you say told or informed? Told would imply verbal communication, face-to-face. You cannot have verbal communication with a man who's still in Australia, can you?

PIP. Lawyers' games!

JAGGERS. Games? The difference between the two verbs could mean a man's safety—his life!

PIP. I shall say "informed," Mr. Jaggers.

JAGGERS. Good.

PIP. I have been informed by a man named Abel Magwitch that he is my benefactor.

JAGGERS. That is the man. In New South Wales, Australia.

PIP. And only he?

JAGGERS. Only he.

PIP. I don't wish to make you responsible for my mistaken conclusions, but I always supposed it was Miss Havisham.

JAGGERS. As you say, Pip, that's not my fault. Not a particle of evidence to support that conclusion. *(*PIP *leaves.)* Never judge by appearances—irrefutable evidence, that's the rule. Evidence!

The Temple.

NARRATION. During the following days, Pip studied Magwitch as he napped in the chair, wondering what evils the man had committed, loading him with all the crimes in the calendar!

(As MAGWITCH *dozes in the chair,* PIP *studies him.* HERBERT *enters, lays a sympathetic hand on* PIP's *shoulder.*)

HERBERT. Dear Pip, what's to be done?

PIP. I'm too stunned to think. I could run away for a soldier.

HERBERT. Of course you can't. He's strongly attached to you.

PIP. He disgusts me—his look, his manners!

HERBERT. But you've got to get him out of England, to safety. And you'll have to go with him or else he won't leave.

PIP. You're right, of course. He's risked his life on my account; it's up to me to keep him from throwing it away altogether.

HERBERT. Well said! We'll see the matter through together—

(PIP *seizes his hand in gratitude.* MAGWITCH *wakes up, smiles.*)

MAGWITCH. Ah, dear boy, and Pip's companion: I was napping.

PIP. Magwitch, I must ask you something. Do you remember that day long ago, on the marshes?

MAGWITCH. I do, dear boy.

PIP. You were fighting with another convict when the soldiers caught you—you recall?

MAGWITCH. I should think so! What of it?

HERBERT. If we're to help you, we must know more about that day … and about you.

MAGWITCH. You're still on your oath?

HERBERT. Assuredly.

MAGWITCH (*He takes out his pipe, the young men sit.*) Dear boy, and Pip's companion, I could tell you my life short and handy, if you like: in-jail and out-of-jail, in-jail and out-of-jail. I know'd my name to be Magwitch, christened Abel—but I've no notion of where I was born, or to who. I first came aware of myself down in Essex, stealing turnips for my food. Thereafter there warn't a soul that seed young Abel Magwitch but wot took fright at him and drove him off. Or turned him in. I can see me, a pitiable ragged little creetur, who everyone called "hardened." "This boy's a terrible hardened one." "This one spends his life in prisons." Then they'd preach at me about the devil and let me go. But wot the devil's a boy to do with no home and an empty stomach? So I'd steal food again, and be turned in again. Somehow I managed to grow up … tramping, begging, thieving … a bit of a laborer, a bit of a poacher. And so I got to be a man. One day I was lounging about Epsom races, when I met a man. Him whose skull I'd crack wi' pleasure if I saw him now. His name was Compeyson. And that's the man you saw me a-pounding in the marshes that day long ago.

PIP. Compeyson.

MAGWITCH. Ay. Smooth and good-looking was Compeyson. He had book-learning, so he set hisself up as a gentleman. He found me, as I say, at the races. "To judge from appearances, you're out of luck," he says. "I've never been in it," I answers him. "Luck changes," he says. "What can you do?" "Eat and drink," says I. So Compeyson took me on, to be his man and partner. And what was his business? Swindling, forgery, stolen banknote passing; suchlike. He had no more heart than an iron file.—There was another man in the game with Compeyson—as was called Arthur. (PIP *and* HERBERT *glance at each other.*) Mister Arthur. Poor fellow was in a sad state of decline. Him and Compeyson had been in some wicked business together—they'd made a pot of money off some rich lady a few years before. (HERBERT *and* PIP *look at each other.*) But Compeyson had gambled it all away long since. Mr. Arthur had the look of a dying man when I first took up wi' them—from which I should have took warning. Soon after I came, Mr. Arthur took very ill and began crying, delirious-like, that he was haunted. "She's coming for me—I can't get rid of her. She's all dressed in white, wi' white flowers in her hair." And Compeyson says to poor Mr. Arthur, "She's alive, you fool. She's living in her wreck of a house in the country." And Mr. Arthur says, "No, she's here, in her white dress; and over her heart there are drops of blood—you broke her heart! And now she's coming to hang a shroud on me!" And so he died. Compeyson took it as good riddance. Next day him and me started work. I won't tell you what we did. I'll simply say the man got me into such nets and traps as made me his slave. He were smarter than me. He used his head and he used my legs to keep his own self out of trouble. He had no mercy! My missus—no, wait, I don't mean ter bring my missus in—(*He looks about him, confused.*) No need to go into that. But Compeyson! When we two was finally caught and put on trial, I noticed what a gentleman he looked wi' his curly hair and his pocket handkerchief, and what a common wretch I looked. Judge and jury thought so too, and even the great Mr. Jaggers couldn't get me justice that day. For when it's time for sentencing, it's him wot gets seven years and me wot gets fourteen! Arter the trial, we was on the same prison ship—I paid him back—I smashed his face in. You seed the scar, dear boy. Then I found a way to escape, and I swam to shore, where I first saw you, in among those old graves.

HERBERT. What an astonishing tale!

MAGWITCH. And true. Little Pip gave me to understand that Compeyson had escaped too, and was out on them marshes. And I vowed then and there, whatever the cost to me, I would drag that scoundrel back to the prison ship. And I did, too. I did.

PIP. Is Compeyson dead?

MAGWITCH. He hopes I am, if he's still alive. Well, I've talked myself near to death. Good night, dear boy. Good night, Pip's companion. (*He exits into the bedroom. Pause.*)

HERBERT. Handel?

PIP. Yes, I know. Miss Havisham's brother was named Arthur.

HERBERT. Compeyson is the man who broke her heart.

PIP. Herbert, before I get Magwitch out of the country, I must try to speak with Estella. I must see her once more.

NARRATION. Pip set off by the early morning coach, and was into open country when the day came creeping on. The fields were hung about with mists. At length the coach stopped at the Blue Boar Inn, which was in the neighborhood of Miss Havisham's house. When Pip alighted, he was amazed to see a familiar figure lounging by the inn door.

PIP. Bentley Drummle!

DRUMMLE. You've just come down? (*PIP nods.*) Beastly place. Your part of the country, I think?

PIP. I'm told it's very like your Shropshire.

DRUMMLE. Not in the least like it.

PIP. Have you been here long?

DRUMMLE. Long enough to be tired of it.

PIP. Do you stay here long?

DRUMMLE. Can't say. And you?

PIP. Can't say. (*DRUMMLE gives a brief, unpleasant laugh.*) Are you amused Mr. Drummle?

DRUMMLE. Not very. I'm about to go riding…to explore the marshes. Out-of-the-way villages, here, I'm told. Quaint little public houses. Smithies, too. Boy! (*A STABLE BOY appears.*)

BOY. Yes, sir.

DRUMMLE. Is my horse ready?

BOY. Waiting in the yard, sir.

DRUMMLE. The young lady won't ride today, the weather is too foul. And boy—

BOY. Yes, sir?

DRUMMLE. Tell the innkeeper I plan to dine at the young lady's this evening.

BOY. Quite so, sir. (*DRUMMLE goes. THE BOY turns to PIP.*) May I help you, sir? (*PIP, in a rage, shies his valise at him.*)

MISS HAVISHAM's. MISS HAVISHAM *is in her bath chair.* ESTELLA *sits a little apart, knitting.*

NARRATION. Pip found the two women seated by the fire. Their faces were lit by the candles which burned on the wall.

HAVISHAM. And what wind brings you down here, Pip?

PIP. I wished to see Estella, and hearing that some wind had blown her here, I followed.

HAVISHAM. Pray, sit down.

PIP. What I have to say to Estella, Miss Havisham, I shall say before you. It won't displease you to learn that I am as unhappy as you can ever have meant me to be. (*MISS HAVISHAM says nothing. ESTELLA knits.*) I have found out who my patron is. It's not a pleasant discovery. It's not likely to enrich my reputation.

HAVISHAM. Well?

PIP. When you first brought me here, when I still belonged to that village yonder that I wish I had never left, I suppose I was picked at random, as a kind of servant, to gratify a whim of yours?

HAVISHAM. Ay, Pip.

PIP. And Mr. Jaggers—

HAVISHAM. —Mr. Jaggers had nothing to do with it. His being my lawyer and the lawyer of your patron is coincidence.

PIP. Then why did you lead me on? Was that kind?

HAVISHAM (*striking her stick upon the ground*). Who am I, for God's sake, that I should be kind?!

PIP. In encouraging my mistaken notion, you were also punishing some of your greedy relations?

HAVISHAM. Perhaps.

PIP. There is one branch of that family whom you deeply wrong. I speak of my former tutor, Mr. Matthew Pocket, and his son Herbert. If you think those two to be anything but generous, open, and upright, you are in error.

HAVISHAM. You say so because Herbert Pocket is your friend.

PIP. He made himself my friend even when he thought I had taken his place in your affections.

HAVISHAM. Yes, well?

PIP. Miss Havisham, I speak frankly: if you could spare the money to do Herbert a lasting service in life—secretly—I could show you how.

HAVISHAM. Why secretly?

PIP. Because I began the service myself, two years ago, secretly, and I don't wish to be betrayed. Why I cannot complete it myself is … it is part of another person's secret. (*MISS HAVISHAM stares into the fire. ESTELLA knits.*)

HAVISHAM. Well, well, well, what else have you to say?

PIP. Estella, you know I've loved you long and dearly. I'd have spoken sooner, but for my foolish hope that Miss Havisham intended us for one another. Whilst I believed you had no choice in the matter I refrained from speaking, but now … (ESTELLA *shakes her head, knits on.*) I know, I know. I've no hope that I shall ever call you mine. (*Again,* ESTELLA *shakes her head. She knits.*) If she'd have thought about it, she'd have seen how cruel it was to torture me with so vain a hope, but she couldn't see. Poor Miss Havisham: enveloped in her own pain, she could not feel mine.

(MISS HAVISHAM *clutches her heart.*)

ESTELLA. It seems there are fancies … sentiments—I don't know what to call them—which I cannot comprehend. When you say you love me, I hear your words but they touch nothing here. I did try to warn you.

PIP. Yes.

ESTELLA. But you wouldn't be warned. I am more honest with you than with other men—I can do no more than that.

PIP. Bentley Drummle is here, pursuing you? (*She nods.*) Is it true you encourage him? Ride with him?—Is it true he dines with you today?

ESTELLA. Quite true.

PIP. You cannot love him.

ESTELLA. What have I just told you? I cannot love!

PIP. You would never marry him?

ESTELLA (*pause*). I am going to be married to him.

PIP. Dearest Estella, don't let Miss Havisham lead you into so fatal a step. Forget me—you've already done so, I know—but for the love of God, bestow yourself on a man worthier than Bentley Drummle!

ESTELLA. Wedding preparations have already begun. It is my own act, not hers.

PIP. Your own act, to fling yourself away on a brute?!

ESTELLA. Don't be afraid of my being a

blessing to him! (*A pause.* MISS HAVISHAM *moans.*) As for you, Pip, I trust you'll get me out of your thoughts within a week.

PIP. Out of my thoughts! You have been in every prospect I've seen since I first met you—on the river, in the wind, on the city streets. To the last hour of my life you cannot choose but remain part of me. O, God bless you. God forgive you! (MISS HAVISHAM *clutches at her heart again.* PIP *kisses* ESTELLA's *hand, leaves.*)

NARRATION. All done, all gone! Pip wandered through the lanes and bypaths around the house … Then he turned and walked all the way back to London.

NARRATION. It was past midnight when he crossed London Bridge, closer to one when he approached his lodgings. He was stopped by the night porter.

PORTER. Urgent message for you, Mr. Pip. (PIP *tears open an envelope, reads, as:*)

WEMMICK. Dear Mr. Pip: Don't go home. Yours, J. Wemmick.

NARRATION. Pip turned hastily away. He spent the remainder of the night in an hotel in Covent Garden.

Footsore and weary as he was, he could not sleep. And after an hour, those extraordinary voices with which silence teems began to make themselves audible.

The closet whispered.

The fireplace sighed.

The washstand ticked.

And they all spoke as if with one voice: Don't go home.

Whatever night-fancies crowded in on him, they never ceased to murmur: Don't go home.

When at last he dozed in sheer exhaustion, it became a vast, shadowy verb he had to conjugate, imperative mood, present tense:

Do not thou go home.

Let him or her not go home.

Let us not go home.

Do not ye or you go home.

Early the next morning Pip went to Walworth to consult Wemmick. This was obviously not a matter for the office.

Walworth. PIP *crosses over the drawbridge.*

WEMMICK. You got my note?

PIP. I did.

WEMMICK. I hope you destroyed it. It's never wise to leave documentary evidence if you can help it. (*He hands* PIP *a sausage speared on a toasting fork.*) Would you mind toasting a sausage for the Aged while we talk?

PIP. Delighted.

WEMMICK. You understand, we're in our private and personal capacities here? (PIP *nods.*) I heard by accident yesterday that a certain person had recently disappeared from Australia, a person possessed of vast portable property. Yes? I also heard that your rooms were being watched, and might be watched again. All right, ain't you, Aged P? (*He takes the toasting fork from* PIP, *puts the sausage on a plate for* THE AGED.)

AGED PARENT. All right, John, all right, my boy! (*They all nod.*)

PIP. Tell me, the disappearance of this person from Australia and the watching of my rooms—are these two events connected?

WEMMICK. If they aren't yet, they will be. (*They all nod.*)

PIP. Mr. Wemmick, have you ever heard of a man of bad character whose name is Compeyson? (WEMMICK *nods.*) Is he living? (WEMMICK *and* THE AGED *nod.*) Is he in London? (*All three nod.*)

WEMMICK. I see you've got the point. When I learned of it, I naturally came to your rooms, and not finding anyone at home— or answering the door, anyway—I went to Clarriker's office to see Mr. Herbert. And without mentioning any names I explained that if he was aware of any Tom, Dick, or Richard staying with you, he had better get him out of the way.

PIP. Herbert must have been mystified.

WEMMICK. Not for long. He conceived a plan. Seems he's courting a young lady who lives in Mill Pond Bank, right on the river. And that's where Mr. Herbert has lodged this person, this Tom, Dick, or Richard! It's a sound idea, because although you're being watched, Mr. Herbert isn't … And as he visits there often, he can act as go-between!

PIP. Good thinking.

WEMMICK. But there's an even better reason for the move. This house is by the river. You understand? (PIP *shakes his head.*) When the right moment comes, you can slip your man aboard a foreign packet-boat unnoticed. Here is the young lady's address in Mill Pond Bank—Miss Barley's the name, and a very odd name it is. You may go there this evening, but do it before you go home, so they won't follow you.

PIP. I don't know how to thank you—

WEMMICK. One last piece of advice. You must get hold of your man's portable property as soon as you can. For his sake as well as yours. It mustn't fall into the wrong hands, must it? Well, I'd better be off to the City. I suggest you stay here until dark—you look tired enough. Keep out of sight and spend a restful day with Aged. Ain't that right, Aged P?

AGED PARENT. All right, John.

WEMMICK. Goodbye then, Mr. Pip. *(He goes. PIP stares into the fire.)*

NARRATION. Pip soon fell asleep before the fire. He and the Aged Parent enjoyed each other's society by falling asleep before the fire throughout the whole day. When it was dark, Pip prepared to leave. The Aged was readying tea, and Pip inferred from the number of cups, three, that a visitor was expected. Could it be that odd lady with the green gloves… Miss Skiffins? Pip made his way to Mill Pond Bank. It was an old house with a curious bow window in front.

⁂

Mill Pond Bank.

HERBERT. All's well so far, Handel. But he's anxious to see you. *(CLARA enters.)* Ah, here's Clara, here she comes.

CLARA. Pip, is it?

PIP. And you're Clara, at last! Herbert's words fail to do you justice. *(He kisses her hand.)*

CLARA. Mr. Magwitch wants to know if he may come down. Let me go fetch him. *(She goes out.)*

PIP. Herbert, she's so lovely.

HERBERT. Isn't she? I know where my good fortune lies, money or no—*(MAGWITCH enters.)*

MAGWITCH. I've brought you nothing but trouble, dear boy.

PIP. You're safe, that's all that matters. You know you'll have to go away?

MAGWITCH. But how—?

HERBERT. Handel and I are both skilled oarsmen—

PIP. And I've just hired a rowboat—I keep it tied up at the Temple stairs, near our rooms.

HERBERT. When the time comes, we plan to row you downriver ourselves, and smuggle you aboard a foreign packet.

PIP. Starting tomorrow I'll go rowing every day. If they see me out on the river often enough, it'll be taken as habit. If I'm out there twenty-five times, no one will blink an eye when I appear the twenty-sixth.

HERBERT. A bit of practice in the evenings won't hurt me, either. I've grown soft, cooped up in that office.

MAGWITCH. Hah. Hah! I like it—I like your plan, lads.

NARRATION. Pip and Herbert went rowing the next day. The young men, it appeared, felt a sudden urge to exercise… And after the first few days, no one seemed to notice.

Pip often rowed alone, in cold, rain and sleet… But no one seemed to notice. At first he kept above Blackfriars Bridge, but as the hours of the tide changed, he rowed further, past the tricky currents around old London Bridge.

Once he and Herbert rowed past Mill Pond Bank. They could see the house with the curious bow window from the river. Magwitch was safe inside that house. There seemed no cause for alarm. But Pip knew there was cause for alarm. He could not get rid of the notion he was being watched.

Meanwhile, Pip's financial affairs began to wear a gloomy appearance, for he had vowed not to accept any more money from Magwitch, given his uncertain feelings about the man. And as the days passed, Pip continued to think of Estella. The impression settled heavily upon him that she was married. But he could not bear to seek out the truth of it, and clung to the last little rag of his hope.

(COMPEYSON *appears directly behind him.*)

He was miserable. And still, he could not get rid of the notion he was being watched.

(PIP *turns around, but bumps into* MR. JAGGERS, *who is walking down the road.*)

JAGGERS. Mr. Pip, is it?

PIP. Mr. Jaggers.

JAGGERS. Where are you bound?

PIP. Home, I think.

JAGGERS. Don't you know?

PIP. I...hadn't made up my mind.

JAGGERS. You are going to dine, you don't mind admitting that?

PIP. I confess it, guilty of dining.

JAGGERS. And you're not engaged?

PIP. I'm quite free.

JAGGERS. Come dine with me. (JAGGERS *takes his arm decisively.*) Wemmick will be joining us, too. (WEMMICK *falls in with them.*)

JAGGERS's *House.* MOLLY *is serving soup from a tureen.*

JAGGERS. By the way, Miss Havisham sent you a message. She'd like to see you, a little matter of business. Will you go down?

PIP. Certainly. (*The three men sit down.* MOLLY *stands behind* JAGGERS's *chair, silently.*)

JAGGERS. When? (PIP *glances at* WEMMICK, *who silently mouths the word "soon."*)

PIP. I...soon. At once. Tomorrow. (WEMMICK *nods.*)

JAGGERS. Splendid. So, Pip, your good friend, the Spider—(*To* WEMMICK)—I refer to one Bentley Drummle—appears to have played his cards well. He has won the pool, eh? (*To* WEMMICK) I refer to a young lady.

PIP. It would seem he has.

JAGGERS. Hah! He's a promising fellow in his own way, but he may not have it all his way. The stronger of the two will win in the end; but who is the stronger, he or she? (*He sips.*) What do you think, Wemmick?

WEMMICK (*shrugs*). Here's to the Spider— what's his name?

JAGGERS (*lifts his glass*). Bentley Drummle: and may the question of supremacy be settled to the lady's satisfaction. To the satisfaction of both of 'em, it never can be. (*He drinks.*) Ah, Molly, the soup is delicious this evening.

MOLLY. Thank you, master.

JAGGERS. Our Molly doesn't like company, she prefers to keep her skills for my palate alone. (*She turns her head to one side, fidgets with an apron-string.* PIP *suddenly stares at her.* JAGGERS *notices.*) What's the matter, young man?

PIP. Nothing—we were speaking of a subject that's painful to me. (PIP *and* MOLLY *lock eyes for a moment.* WEMMICK *and* JAGGERS *attack their soup.*)

NARRATION. The action of her fingers was not unlike that of knitting. The look on her face was intent. Surely Pip had seen such hands, such eyes recently. They were fresh in his mind. He stared at Molly's hands, her eyes, her flowing hair, and compared them with hands, eyes, hair he knew too well. He thought what those dearer hands might be like after twenty years of a brutal, stormy life—And suddenly he felt absolutely certain that this woman was Estella's mother. Pip managed to get through the rest of his meal as best he could. At last, he and Wemmick thanked their host and took to the street.

(PIP *and* WEMMICK *stroll. They pass* COMPEYSON *without noticing him.*)

PIP. Mr. Wemmick, we were speaking of Miss Havisham's adopted daughter at dinner. Have you ever seen her?

WEMMICK. Can't say I have. Something troubling you, Mr. Pip?

PIP. The first time I dined at Jaggers's, do you recall telling me to notice the housekeeper. A wild beast tamed, you called her.

WEMMICK. I daresay I did.

PIP. How did Mr. Jaggers tame her?

WEMMICK. We're in our private and personal capacities? (PIP *nods.*) About twenty years ago she was tried for murder at the Old Bailey, and was acquitted. Mr. Jaggers was her lawyer, of course, and I must say his defense was astonishing. The murdered person was another woman, older than Molly, and even stronger. It was a case of jealousy. Molly was married to some sort of tramping man, and he got too familiar with the other woman. She was found dead in a barn near Hounslow Heath, all bruised and scratched—choked to death. There was no other candidate to do the murder but our Molly. You may be sure Mr. Jaggers never pointed out how strong Molly's wrists were then. He likes to, now.

PIP. Indeed he does. How did he get her off?

WEMMICK. Molly was also suspected of killing her own child by this man of hers, to revenge herself on him. Jaggers told the jury that they were really trying her for that crime; and since there was no child, no body, no trace of a child or a body, they had no proof. I tell you, he got the jury so confused that they capitulated and acquitted her of killing her rival. She's been in his service ever since.

PIP. Do you remember the sex of the child?

WEMMICK. Said to have been a little girl, around three.

PIP. Goodnight, Mr. Wemmick, we part here. (*They go off separately.* COMPEYSON *follows* PIP.)

⚜

MISS HAVISHAM's.

NARRATION. The following morning Pip journeyed down to Miss Havisham. There hung about her an air of utter desolation, an expression, almost, of fear.

HAVISHAM. Thank you for coming. I want to show you I'm not all made of stone. What do you wish me to do for Herbert Pocket?

PIP. I had hoped to buy him a partnership in the firm of Clarriker and Company. He's worked successfully there for the past year or so.

HAVISHAM. How much money do you need?

PIP. Nine hundred pounds.

HAVISHAM. If I give it to you, will you keep my part in it as secret as your own?

PIP. Faithfully. It would ease my mind about that, at any rate.

HAVISHAM. Are you so unhappy?

PIP. I'm far from happy—but I've got other causes of disquiet than any you know.

HAVISHAM. Pip? Is my only service to you to be this favor for young Pocket? Can I do nothing for you yourself?

PIP. Nothing, Miss Havisham. (*She takes pen, paper, writes a note.*)

HAVISHAM. This is an authorization to Jaggers to pay Clarriker nine hundred pounds to advance your friend. (*He takes the paper.*)

PIP. I thank you with all my heart. (*She takes another paper, writes.*)

HAVISHAM. Pip, here is my name. If you can

ever write "I forgive her" under it, even after my death, it would mean so much …

PIP. Oh, Miss Havisham, I can do that now. I want forgiveness myself too much to be bitter with you. *(He reaches for her hand, but she drops suddenly to her knees, sobbing.)*

HAVISHAM. What have I done, what have I done?

PIP. I'd have loved her under any circumstances. Is she married?

HAVISHAM. She is. What have I done? What have I done?

PIP. I assure you, Miss Havisham, you may dismiss me from your conscience. Estella is a different case.

HAVISHAM. I meant to save her from a misery like my own! I stole her heart and put ice in its place.

PIP. Better to have left her a natural heart, even if it were to break.

HAVISHAM. What have I done, what have I done?

PIP. Whose child was she? *(She shakes her head.)* You don't know? But Mr. Jaggers brought her here?

HAVISHAM. I asked him to find me a little girl whom I could rear and love and save from my own fate. One night, a few months later, he brought her … she was fast asleep. I called her Estella. She was about three.

PIP. Good night, Miss Havisham. And thank you for your kindness to Herbert. *(He kisses her hand, goes.)*

NARRATION. Twilight was closing in. Pip went into the ruined garden, and roamed past the place where he and Herbert had had their fight … Past the spot where she had kissed him … Past the little pot of flowers whose fragrance she had once inhaled … He turned to look at the old house once more—When suddenly he saw a great, towering flame spring up by Miss Havisham's window, and he saw her running, shrieking, with a whirl of flame blazing all about her, soaring high above her head.

(Screams. Fire.)

Pip raced back into the house, tore off his greatcoat, and wrapped her in it, beating out the flames with his bare hands.

(Screams. Then they subside. Silence.)

HAVISHAM. What have I done? What have I done? Pip, Pip … forgive me … please, God forgive me … . *(Darkness)*

The Temple. PIP *lies on the sofa,* HERBERT *is dressing his burnt hands.*

HERBERT. Steady, Handel, dear boy.

PIP. You are the best of nurses.

HERBERT. The right hand's much better today. The left was pretty badly burned, it will take more time—

PIP. Time.

HERBERT. Steady on! I saw Magwitch last evening. He sends his love.

PIP. And how is Clara?

HERBERT. Taking good care of him. She calls him Abel—she'll miss him when he goes.

PIP. She's such a darling. You'll be marrying soon, won't you?

HERBERT *(grins).* How can I respectably care for her otherwise? Now, this bandage will have to come off gradually, so you won't feel it. *(He works on it.)* You know what, Handel? Old Magwitch has actually begun to grow on me.

PIP. Yes. I used to loathe him, but that's gone. Don't you think he's become more gentle? (HERBERT *nods.*)

HERBERT. He told me the story of his "missus" the other night, and a wild, dark tale it is. Ah, the bandage is off most charmingly. Now for the clean, cool one.

PIP. Tell me about his woman.

HERBERT. She was a jealous one, vengeful to the last degree.

PIP. What last degree?

HERBERT. Murder—am I hurting you? *(PIP shakes his head.)* She was tried and acquitted. Jaggers defended her, that's how Magwitch first came to learn of him. Is the bandage too tight?

PIP. It is impossible to be gentler. Pray, go on.

HERBERT. This woman had a child by Magwitch, on whom he doted. After she killed her rival, she told Magwitch she would also kill their child. There, the arm's nicely done up. You're sure you're all right? You look so pale.

PIP. Did she kill the child?

HERBERT. She did.

PIP. Magwitch thinks she did. Herbert, look at me.

HERBERT. I do look at you, dear boy.

PIP. Touch me—I've no fever? I'm not delirious?

HERBERT. You seem rather excited, but you're quite yourself.

PIP. I know I'm myself. And the man we have been hiding in Mill Pond Bank, Abel Magwitch, is Estella's father!

JAGGERS'S *Office.*

NARRATION. Pip was seized with a feverish need to verify the truth of it. As soon as he was able to leave his bed he visited Mr.

Jaggers. *(JAGGERS and WEMMICK are busy with paperwork. PIP walks in, hands JAGGERS a note.)*

JAGGERS. And the next item, Wemmick, will be—*(He sees PIP.)* What's this? *(Reads)* An authorization signed by the late Miss Havisham … nine hundred pounds, payable to the firm of Clarriker and Company, Ltd., on behalf of … Herbert Pocket? This must be your doing, Pip. I'm sorry we do nothing for you.

PIP. She was kind enough to ask. I told her no.

JAGGERS. I shouldn't have told her that, but every man knows his own business.

WEMMICK. Every man's business is portable property.

PIP. I did ask her for information, however … regarding her adopted daughter. She obliged, and I now know more about Estella than she does herself. I know her mother.

JAGGERS. Her mother?

PIP. And so do you—she cooked your breakfast this morning.

JAGGERS *(unperturbed).* Did she?

PIP. But I know more, perhaps, than even you do. I also know Estella's father. *(JAGGERS looks up, surprised.)*

JAGGERS. You know her father?

PIP. His name is Magwitch. He … lives in Australia.

JAGGERS. On what evidence does he make this claim?

PIP. He doesn't make it at all—he doesn't even know his daughter is alive.

NARRATION. Then Pip told Jaggers all he knew, and how he knew it. For once the lawyer was at a loss for words.

JAGGERS *(pause).* Hah!—Where were we, Wemmick?

PIP. You cannot get rid of me so easily. I must

confirm the truth from you. Please. (JAG-
GERS *doesn't respond.*) Wemmick, you are a
man with a gentle heart. I've seen your
pleasant home and your old father; I know
your kind and playful ways. Please, on my
behalf, beg him to be more open with
me—

JAGGERS. What's this?! Pleasant home? Old
father?!

WEMMICK. So long as I leave 'em at home,
what's it to you, sir?

JAGGERS. Playful ways?!! *(To* PIP) This man
must be the most cunning impostor in
London.

WEMMICK. It don't interfere with business,
does it? I shouldn't be surprised if, when
you're finally tired of all this work, you
plan a pleasant home of your own!

JAGGERS. Me?!

PIP. The truth, I beg you—

JAGGERS. Well, well, Pip, let me put a case to
you. Mind, I admit nothing.

PIP. I understand.

JAGGERS. Put the case that a woman under
such circumstances as you have named hid
her child away, and only her lawyer knew
where. Put the case that, at the same time,
this lawyer held a trust to find a child for
an eccentric, rich client, a lady, to adopt.

PIP. Yes, yes.

JAGGERS. Put the case that this lawyer lived
in an atmosphere of evil. He saw small
children earmarked for destruction; he saw
children whipped, imprisoned, transported, neglected, hounded, cast out—qualified
in all ways for the hangman. And he saw
them grow up and be hanged. And always,
always, he was helpless to intervene. Put
the case that here was one pretty little
child out of the heap that he could save.
Put the case that the child grew up and
married for money. That the natural mother was still living. That the father and

mother, unknown to each other, were living within so many miles, furlongs, yards,
if you will, of one another. That the secret
was still a secret … until one day you got
hold of it. Now tell me, for whose sake
would you reveal the secret? *(Pause.* PIP
shakes his head.) Now, Wemmick, where
were we when Mr. Pip came barging in?

The Temple.

NARRATION. The next evening, Herbert
came home from the office bubbling with
joy, for Clarriker had offered him—

HERBERT *(rushing in).* —A partnership!
Think of it! We're establishing a branch
office in the East Indies and I—I am to go
out and take charge of it! I'll be able to
take Clara and—it's a miracle! Are you surprised? No, of course not, you've always
had more faith in me than I had in myself.
But my dear Handel, after your commitment to Magwitch is over, perhaps … have
you given any thought to your own future?

PIP. I'm afraid to think further than our project.

HERBERT. You might think of a future with
me—I mean with Clarriker's, for in the
East Indies we'll need a—

PIP. —A clerk?

HERBERT. Yes, a clerk. But Handel, you could
expand into a partnership soon enough—
look at me! Clara and I have talked it
over—she worries about you too, the darling. You're to live with us. We get along so
well, Handel. … (PIP, *deeply moved, hugs
him.)*

PIP. Not yet. Not for a while. After we've
seen our project through there are some
other things I must settle.

HERBERT. When you are ready, then?

PIP. When I am ready. And thank you.

NARRATION. That same evening, Pip received a message.

WEMMICK. Burn this as soon as you read it. Be ready to move your cargo out on Wednesday morning. J. Wemmick.

HERBERT. Wednesday!

PIP. We can be ready. Will you warn Magwitch?

HERBERT. I'll visit Clara tonight. But your burns haven't healed yet—I can tell your arm still hurts.

PIP. I shall be ready.

NARRATION. Tuesday. One of those March mornings when the sun shines hot and the wind blows cold … Summer in the sun, winter in the shade. The plan:

(PIP *and* HERBERT *pore over a map.*)

PIP. The tide turns at nine tomorrow morning—it's with us until three.

HERBERT. Just six hours.

PIP. We'll have to row into the night, anyway.

HERBERT. Where do we board the big ship?

PIP. Below Gravesend—here. See, the river's wide, there, and quite deserted. The packet ship to Hamburg passes at midnight.

HERBERT. Wemmick has booked two passages to Hamburg. The two passengers are expected to make an … unconventional boarding, to say the least. (*They smile at each other.* COMPEYSON *lurks on the sidelines.*)

NARRATION. Wednesday. The relief of putting the plan into action was enormous. The two young men set out in their boat as was their habit. Pip felt sure they went undetected. They soon passed old London Bridge, then Billingsgate Market, with its oyster-boats. The White Tower. Traitor's Gate.

Now they were among the big steamers from Glasgow and Aberdeen. Here, at their moorings, were tomorrow's ships for Rotterdam and Le Havre. And there stood the packet scheduled to leave for Hamburg later that evening. Pip and Herbert rowed past it with pounding hearts. Finally they touched the little dock at Mill Pond Bank, where a man dressed as a river pilot was waiting. He climbed into the boat.

MAGWITCH. Dear boy, faithful boy, thankee. And thankee, Pip's companion.

NARRATION. Herbert and Pip rowed their cargo back out on the river.

MAGWITCH. If you know'd, dear boy, what it is to sit alonger my boy in the open air, arter having been kept betwixt four walls …

PIP. I think I know the delights of freedom.

MAGWITCH. No, you'd have to have been under lock and key to know it equal to me.

PIP. If all goes well you'll be free again within a few hours.

MAGWITCH. I hope so. But we can no more see to the bottom of the next few hours than we can to the bottom of this river. Nor yet can we hold back time's tide than I can hold this water … see how it runs through my fingers and is gone?

NARRATION. The air felt cold and damp. Pip's hands throbbed with pain. In mid-afternoon the tide began to run strong against them, but they rowed and rowed until the sun set.

Night. They passed Gravesend at last, and pulled into a little cove. They waited. Magwitch smoked his pipe. They spoke very little. Once Pip thought he heard the lapping of oars upon the water, and the murmur of voices—but then there was nothing. He credited it to exhaustion and the pain in his hands. They continued to wait silently by the river bank.

Then—they heard an engine! The packet for Hamburg was coming round the bend—even in the dark Pip thought he could see the smoke from her stacks!

PIP. Yes, here she comes!

HERBERT. She's slowing down—start rowing!

NARRATION. They eased out on the river again, and headed toward the packet steamer—when suddenly, a four-oared galley shot out from the bank, toward them. On board were four oarsmen and two other figures. One held the rudder lines, and seemed to be in charge—the other figure sat idle: he was cloaked and hidden. The galley began pulling up fast toward Pip's boat—while Pip and Herbert rowed furiously toward the packet.

VOICE FROM GALLEY. You have a returned convict there—that man in the pilot's coat. His name is Abel Magwitch. I call upon him to surrender, and you others to assist!

NARRATION. With a mighty thrust, the galley rammed Pip's small boat. *(Sound of wood on wood, cries, water)* Magwitch stood in the boat and leaned across, yanking the cloak from the other man's face.

MAGWITCH. Compeyson!

COMPEYSON. Yes, it's Compeyson.

VOICE FROM GALLEY. Surrender!

MAGWITCH. You shan't get away with it, not again, not this time!

VOICE FROM GALLEY. To starboard, to starboard—look out—

COMPEYSON. Help, he's got hold of me—he's pulling me—overboard. . . . help!

VOICE FROM GALLEY. We're going to capsize—watch—*(Screaming. The packet sounds its horn, thrashing in water.)* My God, the

steamer! The steamer's upon us! Help—the steamer—headed toward us—*(The packet horn blows with increasing insistence. Shouts, cries, screams, splintering wood.)*

PIP. Magwitch . . . ! *(Then silence. The lapping of water.)*

NARRATION. As the confusion abated, they saw Magwitch swimming ahead. He was hauled on board and manacled at the wrists and ankles. He had sustained severe injuries to the chest and head. There was no sign of Compeyson.

Magwitch told his captors they had gone down together, locked in each other's arms. After a fierce underwater struggle, only Magwitch had found the strength to swim to the surface.

Pip, shivering and wet, took his place beside the wounded, shackled creature.

MAGWITCH. Dear boy . . . I'm quite content. I've seen my boy. Now he can . . . be a gentleman without me . . .

PIP. I will never stir from your side. Please God, I will be as true to you as you have been to me.

NARRATION. Magwitch was removed to the prison hospital, but was too ill to be committed for immediate trial. Pip tried to think what peace of mind he could bring to the wounded man.

PIP. His money—his property—

JAGGERS. —It will all be forfeit to the crown, Pip. I'm sorry.

PIP. I don't care, for myself. But for mercy's sake, don't let him know it's lost. It would break his heart if he thought I weren't to have it.

JAGGERS. You let it slip through your fingers. Poor Pip.

WEMMICK. When I think of the sacrifice of so much portable property! Your creditors will be after you now, I fear.

JAGGERS. However, I'll say nothing to

Magwitch. Poor Pip. I'm late to court.

NARRATION (*Voices echo:*) Late to court. Late to court. Late to court.

⁓⁓⁓

The Prison Hospital. MAGWITCH *lies on a mattress.* PIP *enters.*

MAGWITCH. Dear boy, I thought you was late.

PIP. It's only just time. I waited by the gate.

MAGWITCH. Thankee, dear boy. You never desert me.

PIP. Are you in much pain today?

MAGWITCH. I don't complain of none.

PIP. You never do complain. (*A prison doctor looks at* MAGWITCH, *shakes his head.*) Magwitch, I must tell you now, at last—can you understand what I say? (MAGWITCH *nods.*) You had a child once, whom you loved and lost? (MAGWITCH *nods.*) She lived. She lives, and has powerful friends. She is a lady, and very beautiful. And I love her! (MAGWITCH *kisses* PIP's *hand. He dies.*)

PIP. Oh Lord, be merciful to him, a sinner. (*Darkness*)

⁓⁓⁓

The Temple. PIP *lies sleeping on a sofa.*

NARRATION. Now Pip was all alone. Miss Havisham and Magwitch were dead. And Herbert had left for the Far East. Pip should have been alarmed by the state of his financial affairs, for he was heavily in debt—but that he scarcely had the strength to notice. For he was ill, very ill with fever. He dreamed he was rowing, endlessly rowing. He dreamed that Miss Havisham called to him from inside a great furnace.

(*Creditors begin carrying off the rug, a chair, etc. In the end there is only the sofa and one chair.*)

He dreamed he was a brick in the wall— the steel beam of a vast engine. He dreamed that the creditors had carried off all his furniture but a bed and a chair—and that Joe was seated in the chair. He dreamed he asked for a cooling drink, and that the beloved hand that gave it to him was Joe's. He dreamed he smelled Joe's pipe. And finally, one day he took courage and woke up.

PIP. Is it … Joe?

JOE. Which it are, old chap.

PIP. Oh, Joe, you break my heart.

JOE. Which, dear old Pip, you and me was ever the best of friends. And when you're better—wot larks! (PIP *covers his eyes for a moment.*)

PIP. How long, dear Joe?

JOE. Which you meantersay, how long have you been ill? It's the end of May.

PIP. And you've been here all this time?

JOE. Pretty nigh. For Biddy said, "Go to him, he needs you!" And I do what she tells me. Now rest, Pip. I must write a letter to Biddy, else she'll worry.

PIP. You can write?

JOE. Biddy taught me.

NARRATION. Pip was like a child in the hands of Joe, who cared for him so tenderly that Pip half-believed he was a child again, and that everything that had happened to him since he left the forge was a dream. Finally the fever was gone. But as Pip grew stronger, Joe seemed to grow less comfortable.

JOE. Dear old Pip, old chap, you're almost come round, sir.

PIP. Ay. We've had a time together I shall never forget. I know for a while I did forget the old days, but—

JOE. Dear Pip…dear sir…what have been betwixt us—have been. You're better now.

PIP. Yes, Joe.

JOE. Then good night, Pip. (*He tiptoes out.*)

NARRATION. And when he awoke the next morning, Joe was gone. (PIP *finds a note on* JOE's *chair.*)

PIP (*reads*). Sir: Not wishful to intrude, I have departed. For you are well again, dear Pip, and will do better without Joe. P.S. Ever the best of friends.

NARRATION. Enclosed with the note was a receipt for Pip's outstanding debts. Joe had paid them. (PIP *puts on his jacket, takes his hat.*)

PIP. I'll go to him—to the forge. Biddy was right, he has such pride, such honor. And Biddy—Biddy is there too. Perhaps she'll find me worthier of her than I once was. Perhaps—(*He rushes off.*)

NARRATION. The first person he encountered when he climbed off the coach was his old mentor, Mr. Pumblechook.

PUMBLECHOOK. So, young man, I am sorry to see you brought so low. Look at you, skin and bones. But I knew it! You were ever pigheaded and ungrateful. I always knew it would end badly. Lo, how the mighty are fallen! How the mighty are—

NARRATION. —But Pip could not wait to hear the conclusion of the greeting. He headed down a country lane to the forge. The June weather was delicious. The sky was blue, and larks soared over the green corn. He felt like a pilgrim, toiling homeward from a distant land.

BIDDY. It's Pip! Dear Pip—Joe, Joe, Pip's come home! Look at you, so pale and thin.

PIP. Biddy, dear girl.

BIDDY. How did you know to come today?

PIP. Today?

BIDDY. It's our wedding day. Joe and I were married this morning! (PIP's *face falls for an instant, then he brightens.* JOE *appears.*)

PIP. Married. Married!

JOE. Which he warn't strong enough fur to be surprised, my dear.

BIDDY. I ought to have thought, but I was so happy—

PIP. —And so am I! It's the sweetest tonic of all. Biddy, you have the best husband in the world; and you, Joe, the best wife. She'll make you as happy as you deserve to be. (*He kisses her.*) And now, although I know you've already done it in your hearts, please tell me you forgive me.

JOE. Dear old Pip, God knows as I forgive you, if I have anything to forgive.

BIDDY. Amen. (*He embraces them both.*)

PIP. And now, I must be off, to catch the coach to London. (JOE *and* BIDDY *watch him go. For a moment, they look after him, arms around each other.*)

❧

WEMMICK. Mr. Pip? I know it's a trying time to turn your mind to other matters, but—

PIP. —What? Anything, Wemmick.

WEMMICK. Tomorrow is only Tuesday…still, I'm thinking of taking a holiday.

PIP. Are you? That's very nice…?

WEMMICK. I'd like you to take a walk with me in the morning, if you don't object.

PIP. Of course not. Delighted.

NARRATION. The next morning early, after fortifying themselves with rum-and-milk and biscuits, they did take a walk, to Camberwell Green. Pip was puzzled.

WEMMICK. Halloa! Here's a nice little church. Let's go in.

NARRATION. And they went in.

WEMMICK. Halloa! Here's a couple of pairs of nice gloves. Let's put them on. *(They do so.* THE AGED PARENT *and* MISS SKIFFINS *[still in her green gloves] appear with a clergyman.)* Halloa! Here is Miss Skiffins. Let's have a wedding. All right, Aged P?

AGED PARENT. All right, John!

CLERGYMAN. Who giveth this woman to be married to this man? *(No response)* Who giveth this woman to be married to this man?

WEMMICK *(shouts).* Now, Aged P. You know, "who giveth."

AGED PARENT. I do! I do! I do! All right, John?

NARRATION. And so Mr. Wemmick and Miss Skiffins were wed, with Pip as witness. *(All kiss the bride.)*

WEMMICK *(to* PIP). Altogether a Walworth sentiment, you understand?

PIP. I understand. Private and personal, not to be mentioned in the office.

WEMMICK. If Mr. Jaggers knew of this, he might think my brain was softening. (THE AGED *nods. They all nod.)*

NARRATION. Within a month Pip had left England. Within two he was a clerk in the Far Eastern branch of Clarriker and Pocket. Three years later he was promoted to associate director of that branch. For many years Pip lived happily with Herbert and Clara Pocket. When at last he returned to England, he hurried to the little village and the forge.

☙❧

The Forge Kitchen. JOE *sits smoking.* BIDDY *sews. There is a small boy with a slate on* PIP's *old stool.* PIP *gazes for a moment, then enters. They embrace him. He picks up the child.*

JOE. We giv' him the name of Pip for your sake, dear old boy, and hope he may grow a little like you.

PIP. You must lend him to me, once I get settled.

BIDDY. No, you must marry and get your own boy.

PIP. So Clara tells me, but I don't think so …

BIDDY *(pause).* You haven't forgotten her.

PIP. I've forgotten nothing that ever meant anything to me. But that poor dream has all gone by, dear Biddy, all gone by.

☙❧

MISS HAVISHAM's *Garden.*

NARRATION. The next evening Pip's steps led him to Miss Havisham's gate. There was no house left, only ruins and a garden overgrown by weeds. *(A figure moves from the shadows toward him.)*

PIP. Estella!

ESTELLA. I wonder you know me, Pip. I've changed.

PIP. How is—

ESTELLA. My husband is dead.

PIP. I'm sorry.

ESTELLA. Don't be. He used me with great cruelty. It is over.

PIP. How strange we should meet here, where we first met.

ESTELLA *(pause).* You do well?

PIP. I work pretty hard, so I do well enough. I want so little.

ESTELLA. I have often thought of you. Once you said to me, "God bless you. God forgive you." Suffering has taught me what your heart used to be—

PIP. God has forgiven you, my dear.

ESTELLA. Ay. I have been bent and broken

but, I hope, into a better shape. Tell me we are friends, Pip.

PIP. We are friends.

ESTELLA. And shall continue friends apart? *(He starts to speak, hesitates, nods. He bends and kisses her hand.)*

PIP. God bless you, Estella. *(She leaves through the garden gate.* PIP *looks around the old place. He sees the little pot of flowers, now broken and charred, but with a few blooms still growing. He picks it up, smells them, picks one and folds it into his breast pocket. He sits on the old garden bench. As he does, voices of the past rise up. They begin slow, but speed up, overlapping.)*

NARRATION. Philip Pirrip, late of this parish.
And then, Pip, wot larks!
Stop, thief, stop that boy!
Be grateful, boy, for them what has brought you up by hand.
Love her, love her, love her!
Wot larks.
Coarse little monster, why don't you cry. Cry. Cry.
This young man has … great expectations.
Wouldn't you be happier as you are?
Did you never think it could be me?
Portable property. My dear Handel.
You've the arm of a blacksmith.
Love her, love her, love her!
I cannot love.
I've come back to you, Pip, dear boy.
A wild beast tamed.
Name of Magwitch.
What have I done? What have I done?
Going to be a gentleman.
Great expectations.

*(*PIP *rises.)*

Great expectations.

(He strides out the garden door. Darkness.)

END OF PLAY

Discussing and Interpreting

Great Expectations

Play Analysis

1. Will Pip and Estella continue to be "friends apart?" Does the play give us any indication that they may become more than friends? Support your answer.
2. Dickens was very concerned with the essential difference between genuine worth and superficial gentility. Name four characters in the play who exhibit either of these characteristics. Describe them in detail.
3. *Great Expectations* tells a story in which "things are not always as they seem." Describe three things in the play that turn out not as they first seem.
4. Research the costumes of the Victorian era. How are they alike and different from the clothes we wear? Write a report on an article of Victorian clothing.
5. **Thematic Connection: Family Matters** Draw four family trees that include all of the characters listed below. Tree # 1 should include Pip; tree #2 should include Herbert; tree #3 should include Magwitch; tree #4 should include Wemmick. A family tree is drawn on marriage and blood lines.

Pip	Herbert	Magwitch	Wemmick
Pumblechook	Estella	Biddy	Molly
Joe Gargery	Aged Parent	Mrs. Joe	Mr. Arthur
Pocket	Joe's Boy	Miss Skiffins	Miss Havisham

Literary Skill: Description

Dickens takes pains to describe the sights and sounds that Pip encounters on his journey from youth to manhood; Barbara Field does not have the luxury of using all of Dickens's language. The use of narration helps give the flavor of the original novel, but much must be inferred. Read the description below from the novel and think about ways narration, staging, and acting might help translate the text to the stage.

> On the Monday morning at quarter before nine, Herbert went to the counting-house to report himself—to look about him, too, I suppose—and I bore him company. He was to come away in an hour or two to attend me to Hammersmith, and I was to wait about for him. It appeared to me the eggs from which young insurers were hatched were incubated in dust and heat, like the eggs of ostriches, judging from the places to which those incipient giants repaired on Monday morning.

Performance Element: Period Style

Analyze the script and work up a list of costumes, furnishings, props, and so on that will bring to the stage the essence of English life in the 1840s. Draw a few colorful sketches depicting these period elements.

Ordinary People

from the novel by Judith Guest
adapted for the stage by Nancy Gilsenan

Creating Context:
Depression and Suicide

Suicide is the third leading cause of death for those between the ages of fifteen and twenty-four. Every year thousands of teenagers, many of them severely depressed, commit suicide. Their depression stems from any of a number of causes— loss of a loved one, feelings of self-doubt or worthlessness, an inability to connect to others, and pressure to succeed, to name a few. Of course, most people experience an emotional "down period" at some point in their lives, but they are usually able to overcome this and move on with their lives. For people suffering severe depression, however, breaking free seems as difficult and grueling as climbing out of a deep, black pit. These severely depressed individuals may see suicide as their only option.

Depression and suicidal feelings are treatable mental disorders, but first the illness must be recognized and diagnosed. Then appropriate treatment can be found. Potential suicides give those around them warnings. If you have a friend experiencing the symptoms below, get help immediately.

Signs of Suicidal Tendencies

- change in eating/sleeping habits
- withdrawal or apathy
- anxiety or anger
- hyperactivity
- physical complaints
- overwhelming sense of guilt
- self-loathing
- alcohol or drug abuse
- grades slipping
- talking or writing about death/suicide
- giving away prized possessions

In the play you are about to read, a young man struggles to fight his way back after a suicide attempt. He is not alone. A sympathetic and knowledgeable doctor, a compassionate father, and caring friends give him a hand. As you read, notice how each character relates to Conrad, the young man, and how his feelings about them change throughout the course of the play.

As a Reader: Thinking About the Characters

Many of the characters in *Ordinary People* are highly complex, very real people. In both the novel and the play, these characters are **dynamic**, that is, they change as a result of their experiences. **Static** characters change very little, if at all. As you read the play, try to determine in what way the dynamic characters change.

Compare the two excerpts below. Notice that in the original novel we are privy to Conrad's thoughts and observations, while the stage version gives physical directions for the characters. Which character seems the more dynamic?

from Page · · · · · · to Stage

"How long were you there?"

"Eight months."

"What did you do? O.D.? Make too much noise in the library?"

"No." Looks steadily at the bookcase in front of him; floor-to-ceiling, jammed with books. "I tried to off myself."

Berger picks up the card again; studies it as he blows his coffee. "What with? Pills? Gillette Super-Blue?"

He sees the way to handle this guy. Keep it light. A joker. Slide out from under without damage. "It was a Platinum-Plus," he says. The eyes are fixed upon his thoughtfully. They hold him still. "So how does it feel to be home? Everybody glad to see you?"

"Yes. Sure."

"Your friends, everything okay with them?"

"Fine."

"It says here, no sisters, no brothers. Right?"

"Right," he says. *Don't squirm don't panic release is inevitable. Soon soon.*

from *Ordinary People* by Judith Guest

BERGER. How long were you in the hospital?

CONRAD. Eight months.

BERGER *(seeing something else he wants to pick up and going after it).* What did you do? O. D.? Make too much noise in the library?

CONRAD. Didn't Dr. Crawford tell you?

BERGER. Not really. Just called and said you might be seeing me. He sent your file over, but I haven't had a chance to read it yet. *(He looks around at the mess still left in the room.)* Better tell me. I may not find it before the next full moon.

CONRAD. I tried to off myself.

BERGER. What with? Pills? Gillette Super-Blue?

CONRAD *(tensing).* It was a Platinum-Plus.

BERGER *(looking directly at* CONRAD*).* So how does it feel to be home? Everybody glad to see you?

CONRAD. Yeah, sure.

BERGER. Your friends? Everything okay with them?

CONRAD. Fine

BERGER. What about brothers or sisters? You got any of those?

CONRAD *(tensing).* No.

from *Ordinary People* adapted by Nancy Gilsenan

As an Actor: Creating a Character

In order to play a character believably, you must try to identify with the character. Actors ask themselves these questions: 1. How does my character see himself or herself? 2. How does my character speak and move? 3. What does my character think about other characters in the play? 4. What motivates my character? 5. How does my character change during the play?

Ordinary People

Time

The present

The Characters

CONRAD JARRETT	A boy in his late teens
CAL JARRETT	Conrad's father
BETH JARRETT	Conrad's mother
JOE LAZENBY	Conrad's best friend
STILLMAN	Conrad's swim team acquaintance
JEANNINE PRATT	Conrad's girlfriend
KAREN ALDRICH	Conrad's hospital acquaintance
DOCTOR BERGER	Conrad's psychiatrist
SALAN	The swimming coach

Setting

A suburb in Illinois

ACT ONE

SCENE: The Jarrett living room

*A*t rise of curtain: CONRAD *sits alone. Slumped in a chair, he stares straight ahead, deep in thought. He wears a shirt and slacks which are slightly too big because he has lost a lot of weight. His hair is short, an institutional cut which he wishes would go away, and he has tried to make it look longer by combing it. Popular, solitary music plays on the stereo.* CONRAD's *schoolbooks are stacked neatly on the table in front of him. The window drapes are drawn, although there is morning light outside. The room is filled with a solemn, heavy blue light which waits to be relieved. The living room door is ajar.* BETH *walks by in the hallway, but does not look into the living room. Because of the position of* CONRAD's *chair, she could not see him even if she did look in.*

BETH *(from offstage, passing the door).* I'm clearing the table, Cal. Do you want more coffee?

CAL *(from further offstage).* No, thanks. Go ahead and clear it. *(After a beat)* Has Connie eaten? (CONRAD *turns his head slightly to catch the conversation.)*

BETH *(from offstage, in the doorway).* I don't know. *(She moves away from the door in the direction from which she came.)*

CAL (*from offstage, crossing past the door after* BETH). He should eat something.

BETH (*from offstage, calling to* CAL). I think he can decide for himself, Cal.

CAL (*from offstage, crossing back to the doorway, concerned*). The doctor says he needs to eat.

BETH (*from offstage, with a note of finality*). I'm clearing the dishes.

CAL (*turns away from the doorway and calls as if to the upstairs*). Con? (*There is no response and he moves away from the doorway.*) Con? (CONRAD *tenses.*) Where are you?

CONRAD (*biting his nails, stopping himself, then in a calm, controlled voice*). The living room, Dad.

CAL (*from offstage, not visible*). What are you doing?

CONRAD (*turning off the stereo and calling out*). Calisthenics. (*He moves to bite his nails again but stops himself.*)

CAL (*from offstage, his voice fading*). Beth, where's my tie? (CONRAD *looks around the living room to determine what he should do to set the room right. Finally, he decides to open the drapes and winces as the sunlight floods the room. He walks over to the table, checks and straightens his schoolbooks. As he stands up from fussing with the books, he catches a glimpse of himself in the mirror over the fireplace. He looks at his image, then walks closer. He stands still and runs his hand deliberately through his hair. He does not approve of the cut and seems saddened by it. He puts both hands to his hollow cheeks, runs his fingers down the side of his face, and lowers his jaw as he does. He studies the image in the mirror.*)

CONRAD (*to himself*). This damn rash. (*His fingers leave his face and he rests his hands, palms up, on the mantelpiece. He studies his wrists, then lifts them up in front of his face.*)

CAL (*from offstage*). You ready, Conrad?

(CONRAD *takes a long-sleeved sweater off the back of the chair he sat on and pulls it on over his shirt. He sits down in the chair, takes a book from the table, and opens it.*)

(CAL *enters the room carrying his briefcase.*)

CAL. You need a ride today?

CONRAD No. Lazenby's picking me up at twenty after.

CAL (*delighted*). Great! (CONRAD *looks away, frowning.* CAL *refers to the book* CONRAD *is reading.*) What is it, a quiz?

CONRAD. Book report.

CAL. What book? (*He reads the title on the cover.*) *Jude the Obscure.* How is it?

CONRAD. Obscure.

CAL. Did you eat? There's bacon and eggs.

CONRAD. No, thanks.

CAL (*with genuine concern*). You feel okay?

CONRAD. Yeah, fine. I just didn't want breakfast.

CAL. You ought to keep trying to put on weight.

CONRAD. You worry too much about what the doctor said, Dad.

CAL. It's good advice. Especially now that you're swimming again.

CONRAD. I'm trying, Dad, believe me. You don't have to be heavy to swim. (*He returns to his book.* CAL *walks over to the window to look at the morning outside.*)

CAL (*turning back to* CONRAD). How's it going?

CONRAD. What?

CAL. How's it going? School. Swimming. Everything okay?

CONRAD. Yeah, fine. Same as yesterday.

CAL. What does that mean?

CONRAD (*smiling faintly*). It means you ask me that every day.

CAL. (smiling). Sorry. I like things neat. All tax attorneys do, you know.

CONRAD. It's all right. Go ahead, check me out.

CAL (sitting down in another chair). So, how come Lazenby's picking you up?

CONRAD. He's a friend of mine.

CAL. I know that. I just wondered if it meant you'd be riding with him from now on.

CONRAD. I don't have a formal commitment yet. I'm gonna have my secretary talk to his, though.

CAL. Okay, okay.

CONRAD. We should have the contract drawn up by the end of the week.

CAL (grinning). Okay! (He tries again.) You glad you're swimming?

CONRAD. Sure. Yeah. I asked the coach to take me back, didn't I?

CAL. I just meant . . . you don't think it's too much?

CONRAD. I did it before. I'll work back into it.

CAL. If it gets to be a strain . . . classes, choir, swimming, you know, if you think you can't handle it . . .

CONRAD (miming CAL's actions). I'll go down to old man Knight's office . . . I'll pull out my hair . . . I'll lay across his desk . . . I'll yell hellllp!

CAL (quietly). You could just tell me, Con.

CONRAD (smiling). Okay, Dad. If it gets to be too much, I'll tell you.

CAL (relieved). Thanks. (He gets up.) Okay, next question.

CONRAD. Geez! You should have been a trial attorney.

CAL (ignoring CONRAD's remark). About that doctor in Evanston. Doctor Berger. Have you called him yet? (CONRAD tenses. He makes a move to bite his nails, then stops himself.)

CONRAD. No. I don't have time.

CAL. I think we ought to stick to the plan.

CONRAD. I can't. I'm swimming every night until six. Nobody said I had to call him.

CAL (gently). I know. But I think you ought to. Maybe you could see him on weekends.

CONRAD. I don't need to see anybody. I feel fine. (He bites his nails.)

CAL (carefully). I want you to call him anyway. Call him today.

CONRAD. I don't finish practice until dinner.

CAL. Call him at school. On your lunch hour.

(BETH enters. She is dressed in a neat-fitting, expensive golf outfit.)

BETH. Haven't you two left yet? I tee off at nine. It would be nice to see you out of here before I leave.

CAL. Con's riding with Joe Lazenby today.

BETH. Oh, good. That reminds me, Con. Mrs. Lazenby wants you to drop by there. She says she misses seeing you around. I think it would be nice if you made the effort to drop by. (She notices something about the way CONRAD looks.) What shirt are you wearing? Not the one you wore all summer, I hope. (A car horn honks outside.)

CAL (looking out the window). Your ride's here.

CONRAD (rising and picking up his books). See you at six. (He leaves.)

BETH (moving to the window to watch CONRAD go). Why does he insist on wearing that shirt he wore at the hospital? I want you to talk to him about his clothes, Cal. He's got a closet full of decent things and he goes off every day looking like a bum.

CAL (joining BETH at the window). That's the style. Decency is out; chaos is in. (BETH *doesn't seem to find that funny.)* Okay, I'll talk to him.

BETH *(walking back to the coffee table where* CONRAD *set his books and straightening the magazines).* He just doesn't look right.

CAL. It's partly the weight. Dr. Crawford said it could take a year to gain it back.

BETH. Even your father says he doesn't look like the same boy he was before.

CAL. He's not the same, Beth. We have to remember that. We can't expect him to be the same person he was before.

BETH. And I want you to talk to him about another thing, too, Cal.

CAL. What?

BETH. Tell him to invite Joe Lazenby over. Carole wants him to drop by their house and I want him to invite Joe over here.

CAL. I don't want to pressure him about that, Beth. He'll do it when he's ready. Carole understands that.

BETH. But when people take an interest, it seems polite to . . .

CAL *(flatly).* We all know he's polite.

BETH. All right. *(She sits down and picks up a handful of brochures from the coffee table. Her mood changes and she seems brighter.)* I've been thinking, Cal. I have an idea.

CAL. What's all that?

BETH. They said it's getting a little late, but there are still openings. If we can let them know immediately.

CAL. Know what? *(He takes the brochures from* BETH *and looks through them.)*

BETH. I remember last year you wanted to go to Yugoslavia. But don't you think London would be fun? Like something out of Dickens; Christmas in London.

CAL. Listen. I don't think we should plan to go away for Christmas this year.

BETH. We go away for Christmas every year.

CAL *(putting the brochures back on the table).* I know, but not this year. The timing just isn't right.

BETH. What does that mean?

CAL. You know what it means.

BETH *(rising, putting away a few more out of place items, then trying again).* Well, they said it would be better to leave in the middle of December and book a flight back after the first week of January.

CAL. We can't go in the middle of December. He'd have to miss a week of school. And another week in January would be two weeks.

BETH. He could meet us there when school got out. He could fly back by himself. Mother and Dad would—

CAL *(interrupting).* No!

BETH *(stopping and looking at* CAL*).* I think you're wrong, Cal. I think it would be good for us all to go.

CAL. No. Just . . . no.

BETH *(trying again from another angle).* Why don't you ask him if *he* wants to go?

CAL. I think that was our mistake, going to Florida last Christmas. If we hadn't done that . . .

BETH. It wouldn't have made any difference. You know that. Don't blame the trip.

CAL. I'm not talking about blame. I'm talking about being available. We were busy down there. Every damn minute. There wasn't time to talk.

BETH. What was there to say? What do you think would have been said?

CAL. I don't know.

BETH. Listen, Cal. I don't think it's a good idea for us to blame ourselves for what he did.

CAL *(curtly).* Don't, then. Fine.

BETH *(turning away).* I've got to get to the club.

CAL (remorsefully). Beth, honey, I'm sorry. I'm sorry.

BETH (turning back to CAL). Then why can't we go? Think of all the wonderful places we've been. Spain. Hawaii. I need to go! I need you to go with me.

CAL. I want to go with you. (He goes to BETH.) I just think that now we should . . . this time we might try handling things differently.

BETH (upset). This time! (She loses her composure.) How long are we going to live like this? With it always hanging over our heads.

CAL (frustrated, trapped, trying to convince himself as well as BETH). Nothing is hanging over our heads. Everything is all right.

BETH. Then I don't understand you at all. (She walks out of the room. The lights dim. CAL exits in the darkness.)

*T*he lights come up on STILLMAN, LAZENBY, and CONRAD, talking in front of their lockers. They have just finished swim practice and are dressed only in their slacks, with no shirts. Their hair is still wet and they have towels around their necks. As they talk, they continue to take clothes from the lockers and dress.

STILLMAN. Well, I'll tell you one thing. I damn near killed myself over this Poly-Sci exam. The guy wants a damn personal analysis of it all. I was up until two o'clock trying to make sense out of the stuff.

LAZENBY. It helps if you read it when it's assigned instead of inhaling it the night before the exam.

STILLMAN. Get a sense of reality, Lazenby. We swim our buns off every stupid day. When are we supposed to study?

LAZENBY. I swim. I study.

STILLMAN. Yeah, you're perfect. I bet they kiss your lousy feet at graduation. (To CON-RAD) What about you, Jarrett? Did you take any of your finals last year? They make you take all your finals over?

LAZENBY. Stillman, you know they don't pass you on breathing in this dump if you don't take the final.

STILLMAN. Boy, there's a year wasted, huh, Jarrett? You miss a semester, they make you eat the whole year over again.

(SALAN enters in a threadbare T-shirt and khakis rolled above the ankles. A stopwatch hangs around his neck. As he enters, CONRAD yawns involuntarily.)

SALAN. Maybe I oughta start a bed check on you guys. Hey, Jarrett, you having fun out there?

CONRAD. Fun?

SALAN. Yeah. You oughta be, you know. (He steps downstage away from the others and motions CONRAD to join him.) The point is lost if it's not fun anymore. Right?

CONRAD. I guess.

SALAN. You guess. (He studies CONRAD.) You on medication, Jarrett? Tranquilizers? Anything?

CONRAD (fearfully). No.

SALAN (removing the stopwatch from around his neck). Did I ask you before if they gave you shock out there?

CONRAD. Yeah.

SALAN. Yeah, what?

CONRAD. Yeah, you asked me before. Yeah, they did.

SALAN (shaking his head and clicking his tongue in disapproval). I don't know. I'm no doctor, but I don't think I'd let them mess around with my head like that. (He shakes his head.) Your timing is lousy.

CONRAD. I know.

SALAN. Look, I don't want to be . . . I'm not being too rough on you, am I? But I'm wondering if it's gonna be too much for you. (*He sits on a riser, pulls up one knee, and wraps his arm around it.*) This is a team effort, Jarrett. I've got room for guys who are willing to work at it. Thing is, I can't figure out anymore . . . if that's you or not.

CONRAD (*letting his breath out slowly, angry but relieved he hasn't been dumped*). I'll work. I want to work.

SALAN (*standing up and replacing the stopwatch*). Okay, then. Better plan to stay after. We'll see if we can get your timing back. (*He starts to leave.*) And get to bed at a decent hour, will you? (*He includes the others.*) You kids stay up until all hours and don't care about your bodies. (*He clicks his tongue and exits.*)

LAZENBY. Salan's too picky. He drives me nuts.

STILLMAN. Everything drives you nuts. The day is not complete without Lazenby telling everybody what a screwed-up state the world is in. (*To* CONRAD) Salan tell you your timing is off? (CONRAD *looks hard at* STILLMAN. LAZENBY *is tense, worried.*) He's got those two sophomores, you know. They'd sure as hell like to have your place.

LAZENBY. They're not that good, Stillman.

STILLMAN. No? They look pretty good to me. (*All open their respective lockers and finish dressing.*)

(JEANNINE *enters downstage near the choir risers.*)

STILLMAN (*to* CONRAD *and* LAZENBY *but not heard by* JEANNINE). Hey, there's Pratt. (CONRAD *can't take his eyes off* JEANNINE.) Gimme room. I need a jump.

LAZENBY. Nice legs.

STILLMAN. Nice bod. Like redheads, Jarrett? Hey, look, Jarrett is interested in something.

LAZENBY. You met her yet, Con? Just moved here last spring. Great voice.

STILLMAN. Great everything! The little lady's hot.

LAZENBY. You're a real comedian, Stillman.

STILLMAN (*in mock apology*). What's the matter? Not funny?

(CONRAD *looks at* STILLMAN. *He loathes* STILLMAN, *but does not say anything. He takes his books from his locker and moves downstage.* STILLMAN *and* LAZENBY *exit.*)

JEANNINE. You're early.

CONRAD. So're you.

JEANNINE. We haven't really met. I'm Jeannine Pratt.

CONRAD. Nice . . . uh, yeah, I'm Conrad Jarrett. (*He gives an embarrassed laugh.*) Hi.

JEANNINE (*giggling*). Hi. (*She and* CONRAD *sit at opposite ends of the risers. She opens her music folder.* CONRAD *keeps busy by arranging his books.*)

JEANNINE. You have a very good voice. You should be singing the solo in the Christmas concert.

CONRAD. Nah, I'm not that good . . .

JEANNINE. Yes, you are. You're a better tenor than any of the other seniors. Are you a senior?

CONRAD. Not exactly.

JEANNINE (*laughing*). What does that mean?

CONRAD (*uncomfortably*). I should be. Only I was out of school for a while last year.

JEANNINE. Oh.

CONRAD. I was sick. (*There is a short, uneasy silence.* JEANNINE *looks through her music folder.*) Lazenby told me you moved in last spring. Where're you from?

JEANNINE. Akron, Ohio.

CONRAD. Your dad get transferred here?

JEANNINE. Not exactly.

CONRAD (*laughing*). What does that mean?

JEANNINE (*uncomfortably*). My parents are getting a divorce . . . well, not really . . . they're just separated. I guess it's sort of in a holding pattern at the moment.

CONRAD. Oh. (*An uneasy silence*) Sorry.

JEANNINE (*laughing self-consciously*). It's always so hard, isn't it? The first time you talk to somebody. You want to be so careful not to say the wrong thing . . .

CONRAD (*grinning at* JEANNINE). Yeah, well . . . coincidentally . . . (*He reaches into his back pocket and mimes pulling out a piece of paper.*) . . . to cover this very situation, I happen to have here . . . a list . . .

JEANNINE (*turning to look at* CONRAD). Of what?

CONRAD. Safe Topics. Capital S. Capital T.

JEANNINE (*laughing*). Really? Terrific!

CONRAD. One hundred and one guaranteed sure-fire safe topics.

JEANNINE. Give me a sample.

CONRAD (*pretending to look down the list*). Okay . . . the war.

JEANNINE. What war?

CONRAD. Any war. You name it. Revolutionary, Civil, First, Second, French and Indian . . .

JEANNINE (*giggling*). I don't want to talk about war.

CONRAD. How about the Chicago Bears? (*He mimics two dumb jocks talking.*) Think the Bears'll win Sunday? . . . Nah . . .

JEANNINE (*laughing*). Where did you get this list? It's terrible.

CONRAD (*miming the tearing up of the list*). You're right. Forget it.

JEANNINE. It's a male list. It's a macho list.

CONRAD. So, okay . . . we'll talk about whatever you want to talk about. What do you want to talk about? Beekeeping . . . knitting?

JEANNINE. Knitting! (*She laughs.*) You're crazy!

CONRAD (*half-seriously*). So they say. (JEANNINE *looks at him questioningly and he raises his hands.*) A joke. Just a joke. (*He holds this position, his hands raised, as the lights fade to black. He and* JEANNINE *exit.*)

T he lights come up on BERGER's office. It's a mess, as if it had been ransacked. BERGER is attempting to clean it up.

BERGER (*to himself*). It is time for a better neighborhood . . . Damn! (*He discovers a book on the floor.*) Now here's something that deserves to be stolen. Why didn't they take this? (*He tosses the book into a wastebasket, then stops to look at the mess. He groans and goes back to work.*)

(CONRAD *enters. He observes the mess and stands silent for a minute before* BERGER *notices him.*)

BERGER. Oh, ah, wait . . . don't tell me. Jarrett, am I right?

CONRAD. Right.

BERGER (*smiling and studying* CONRAD). Yeah, you look like somebody Crawford would send me. A match for my daring wit and firecracker mind.

CONRAD. Are you seein' me? Or am I seein' you?

BERGER (*laughing*). Very good. I knew you were sharp.

CONRAD (*looking around*). You remodelling or what?

BERGER (*gesturing at the mess*). I call it "Contemporary Ripoff." What d'you think?

CONRAD. I think you ought to call the cops.

BERGER. What for? Can't find anything missing. Who knows, maybe they even left something for me.

CONRAD. What'd they want? Drugs?

BERGER. I suppose. Nothing but aspirin here. Sit down. Sit down. Move that junk off the chair. I'm Doctor Berger. (*He extends his hand across the desk to* CONRAD *and they shake.*) Want some coffee?

CONRAD. No, thanks. (*He removes the stuff from the chair and sits.* BERGER *pulls his chair over behind the desk, gets his coffee, and sits.*)

BERGER. So. How long since you left the hospital?

CONRAD. A month and a half.

BERGER. Feeling depressed?

CONRAD. No.

BERGER. Onstage?

CONRAD. Pardon?

BERGER. People nervous? Treat you like you're a dangerous man?

CONRAD. Yeah, I guess.

BERGER. And are you?

CONRAD. I don't know.

BERGER *(seeing something else he needs to pick up)*. God, it's disgusting. Second time this office has been ransacked this year. *(He sits down.)* You look like a healthy kid to me. What're you doing here?

CONRAD. What I'm doing here is that I had to come.

BERGER. Ah, authority reigns. So suppose you didn't have to come. What would you be here for?

CONRAD. I wouldn't.

BERGER. How long were you in the hospital?

CONRAD. Eight months.

BERGER *(seeing something else he wants to pick up and going after it)*. What did you do? O. D.? Make too much noise in the library?

CONRAD. Didn't Doctor Crawford tell you?

BERGER. Not really. Just called and said you might be seeing me. He sent your file over, but I haven't had a chance to read it yet. *(He looks around at the mess still left in the room.)* Better tell me. I may not find it before the next full moon.

CONRAD. I tried to off myself.

BERGER. With what? Pills? Gillette Super-Blue?

CONRAD *(tensing)*. It was a Platinum-Plus.

BERGER *(looking directly at* CONRAD*)*. So how does it feel to be home? Everybody glad to see you?

CONRAD. Yeah, sure.

BERGER. Your friends? Everything okay with them?

CONRAD. Fine.

BERGER. What about brothers or sisters? You got any of those?

CONRAD *(tensing)*. No.

BERGER. So what d'you want to work on?

CONRAD. Pardon?

BERGER. Well, you're here. It's your money, so to speak. What do you want to change?

CONRAD. I'd like to be more in control, I guess. So people quit worrying about me.

BERGER. So who's worrying about you?

CONRAD. My father, mostly. This is his idea.

BERGER. How about your mother? Isn't she worried?

CONRAD. No.

BERGER. How come?

CONRAD. She's . . . . I don't know. She's not a worrier.

BERGER. No? What does she do, then?

CONRAD. Do?

BERGER. Yeah. What's her general policy toward you? You get along with her all right?

CONRAD. Yeah, fine.

BERGER *(eyeing another pile of papers he'd like to pick up, then rising)*. You've got a funny look on your face. What're you thinking?

CONRAD. I'm thinking that if you're a friend of Crawford's, you're probably okay, but I don't like this already. I don't like all this dancing around. Let me tell you some things. I had a brother. He's dead. It was an accident on the lake. We were sailing. He drowned.

BERGER. When? *(He sits down behind his desk.)*

CONRAD. Summer before last.

BERGER. I suppose you and Crawford talked about it.

CONRAD. Every day.

BERGER. And you don't like to talk about it.

CONRAD (shrugging). It doesn't change anything.

BERGER. Okay. Anything else?

CONRAD. No . . . Yeah. About friends. I don't have any. Except Karen from the hospital. She's home now, too. In Skokie. I sort of seem out of touch with everybody else.

BERGER. Oh? (There is no response from CONRAD.) Well, okay, now I'll tell you something. I'm not big on control. I prefer things fluid. In motion. But it's your money.

CONRAD. So to speak.

BERGER (laughing). Yeah, so to speak. (He locates his appointment book in the mess and opens it.) How are Tuesdays and Fridays?

CONRAD. Twice a week?

BERGER. Control is a tough nut.

CONRAD. I've got swim practice every night.

BERGER. Hmmm. That's a problem. So how do we solve it?

CONRAD (irritatedly). I guess I skip practice and come here twice a week.

BERGER. Okeydoke. (He gets up and hands the appointment book to CONRAD.) Write yourself down in here, will you? Tuesdays and Fridays at four. (He resumes his cleaning.)

CONRAD (dryly). Sure thing. (He looks around.) Any other jobs I can do for you?

BERGER (smiling broadly). Wise guy . . . joker. I got your number.

CONRAD (grinning). You ain't seen nothin' yet. (The lights begin to fade on BERGER's office as CONRAD rises and walks to C. BERGER exits.)

*T*he lights come up on a park bench that is downstage center from the lockers. KAREN sits waiting for CONRAD.

CONRAD (taking his seat, a little shy). Hi, Karen. How are you?

KAREN. Fine . . . you?

CONRAD (shrugging). Not bad. Light, scattered paranoia, increasing to moderate during the day. (This momentarily disturbs KAREN and she looks away.) Hey, I'm only kidding. I'm fine. Really. (A short pause) I like your hair that way.

KAREN (touching her hair). Do you? Thanks. (She finally looks at CONRAD.)

CONRAD. It's great to see you.

KAREN (nervously ducking her head just slightly). You, too. Did you come on the train?

CONRAD. No, I drove.

KAREN. Long way from Lake Forest.

CONRAD. Not bad. About forty-five minutes. I found a good station, listened to tunes . . .

KAREN (abruptly). I can't stay too long. I've got a meeting at school. Drama Club.

CONRAD. Oh, yeah?

KAREN (rattling on). I'm secretary this year. We're doing *A Thousand Clowns*. D'you know it?

CONRAD. No.

KAREN. It's a great play. But anyway, with me as secretary, we're pretty disorganized, so I'm always in a hurry.

CONRAD (dryly). Well, don't let me hold you up. (A short silence as he and KAREN look at each other. KAREN drops her glance.)

KAREN. I'm sorry. That was rude. (A pause) I wanted to see you, Connie, but I was afraid. You seemed . . . so down when you called.

CONRAD (quickly). No, no . . . I'm not down. Everything's great. I'm back in school. I'm swimming . . .

KAREN. Really? I'm so glad.

CONRAD. Well, we haven't had any meets yet. I could end up on the bench.

KAREN. Oh, no, you'll do fine, I'm sure. When did you get out of the hospital?

CONRAD. August.

KAREN. You seeing anybody?

CONRAD. You mean a doctor? Yeah. Are you?

KAREN (*shaking her head*). No. I started with one last June, when I got out. But it wasn't doing me any good. Really, the only one who can help you is you. Well, you and God. I still think there's value in it, though, for some people.

CONRAD (*needing to defend himself*). Well, I don't know how long I'll keep it up, either. It's only been six weeks. My father sort of shoved me into it.

KAREN. Things were so different in the hospital. People were, you know, wired all the time. You can't live with all that emotion floating around. It's too exhausting.

CONRAD. This guy I see, Berger, says we all should come equipped with a two-prong plug, and then when our systems get overloaded, we just find ourselves an emotional outlet . . . bingo, juices drained, crisis over. (KAREN *laughs. He is pleased.*) I made you laugh. (*A beat*) We had some good talks on the stone bench. I miss that, don't you? And Leo. Leo would always come and sit with us and crack jokes. You ever miss the hospital, Karen?

KAREN (*uncomfortably*). What's there to miss?

CONRAD. I don't know. It wasn't such a battle there. We didn't have to put up such a front all the time.

KAREN. I'm not putting up a front.

CONRAD. I mean you could relax, let your guard down. I get so tired sometimes, so

tired of working at being healthy, adjusted. It's like the harder you have to concentrate on keeping your balance, the surer you are you're going to slip. Are you ever afraid you're going to slip?

KAREN (*upset*). Con, you shouldn't talk like that. You don't want to go back to the hospital. Nobody does.

CONRAD. I didn't mean I want to go back. I just meant, I miss the times—

KAREN (*interrupting*). Well, I don't! I don't miss any of it, and I don't want to think about any of it. And you shouldn't, either. Try to be less intense.

CONRAD (*pretending to note* KAREN's *remark down on paper*). "Less intense." Gee, you sure do make things sound simple, Doctor Aldrich.

KAREN (*frowning*). It isn't simple. I'm just saying we have to try.

CONRAD. Don't you think I try? (*He makes a face, then smiles a broad, contrived smile to tease* KAREN.) Hey, don't I act like I'm trying?

KAREN (*smiling*). I don't know. (*A beat*) I don't really know you, Con.

CONRAD (*hurt*). Oh.

KAREN. I mean, we haven't known each other that long. And only in the hospital. We don't really know each other, do we?

CONRAD (*disappointed, feeling that he's lost something*). No, maybe not. (*An uneasy silence*)

KAREN (*looking at her watch*). I'm late. I've got to go.

CONRAD. So, okay, go.

KAREN (*rising*). The thing is, we should both be careful about who we see. It isn't good for either of us to get down.

CONRAD. I'm not down! (*He calms himself.*) I'm not down, Karen.

KAREN. Well, it's contagious, you know that. We can't risk it, either of us. You see?

CONRAD *(rising).* Sure. I see.

KAREN *(moving to go).* You look great, Con. You really do.

CONRAD. Yeah. You, too.

KAREN. Call me again sometime, will you?

CONRAD. Yeah. Sure. *(The lights begin to fade as* KAREN *exits.* CONRAD *sits back.)* Just not too soon, huh? *(He looks thoughtful and upset as the lights fade out. He exits.)*

B*efore the lights come up on the Jarrett living room,* BETH *and* CAL *are heard offstage. The door opens and* CAL *turns on the lights.* BETH *follows him into the room and both remove their coats.* BETH *folds the coats neatly over a chair as* CAL *moves toward the bar.*

BETH. Do you really need another drink, Cal? You had three at the party.

CAL *(taking out a bottle).* Is that a hint?

BETH. It's not a directive, if that's what you mean.

CAL *(deciding to just put the bottle away).* Okay, I'll take it then. *(*BETH *walks around straightening up the room. He sits idly, picks up the paper, and starts leafing through it.)* Ray and Nancy Hanley looked good. He's put on twenty pounds, I think.

BETH. She's thin. As thin as I've ever seen her. She said it was worry and a bad marriage that keep her in size seven. *(She pauses.)* She told me how lucky I was.

CAL. Hmmm?

BETH. To have you . . . to never have been disillusioned.

CAL. *(looking up from the paper, interested).* Geez, it's been seven years since all that happened. Ray's not such a bad guy. And people make mistakes.

BETH. It was an affair, Cal, not a mistake.

CAL. Yes, but she decided to come back to him, didn't she? When it ended, she came back. I thought the marriage was fine.

BETH. It works, I guess, but without the benefit of illusions, as she puts it.

CAL. You know, I really thought Nance would have forgiven him, wouldn't you?

BETH *(pausing in her cleaning).* No, I wouldn't. *(She picks up the stack of travel folders on the coffee table and throws them in a wastebasket.)*

CAL. Are you throwing those brochures out?

BETH. Con said he didn't want to go away for Christmas. Well, it's too late now anyway. *(*CAL *rises, walks over to her, and begins to put his arms around her from behind. She does not respond.)*

CAL. This is a very singular hug. *(He turns* BETH *around so they face one another.)* Can we do something to enhance the body contact here? *(He kisses* BETH, *but she still does not respond.)* Hey, if you want illusions, you have to work at it. I know a great one.

BETH *(drawing away from* CAL*).* I want to tell you something, Cal. You drink too much at parties.

CAL. Okay.

BETH. I heard what you told Marty Genthe about Conrad seeing that doctor in Evanston. She pumped you, and you let her do it. You let her draw that stuff out of you . . . and in front of Sue Keller, who was sitting right next to you and doesn't even know us.

CAL *(hoping to head off a fight).* My sentiments exactly. *(He gently brushes the hair back from* BETH'*s face.)*

BETH. Why did you tell her he was seeing a psychiatrist?

CAL. Look, some people consider that a status symbol—right up there with going to Europe.

BETH. I don't. And I thought your blurting it out like that was in the worst possible taste.

CAL. I'm sorry.

BETH. Not to mention a violation of privacy.

CAL. Whose privacy? *(He is angry.)* Whose privacy did I violate? *(There is cold silence.)*

BETH. I'm going to bed. *(She exits.* CAL *walks over to the bar and pours himself a drink. He sits down and stares ahead into the mist which is beginning to cloud his mind.)*

After a few moments, CONRAD *enters and looks at* CAL *thoughtfully.*

CONRAD. Hi. How was the party?

CAL. Fine, fine . . . Phil Murray managed his entire repertoire of crooked lawyer jokes.

CONRAD. I thought half the people there were lawyers.

CAL. Just about everybody but Phil. Truly this is a man who does not understand the meaning of the word "subtle." What'd you do?

CONRAD *(sitting down).* Studied. Got a history mid-term on Tuesday.

CAL. How's Lazenby? You see much of him?

CONRAD. Every morning on the way to school. At practice. On the way home.

CAL. Why don't you invite him over sometime?

CONRAD. I could.

CAL. He used to be around here a lot. *(He reconsiders, not wanting to push.)* I guess it takes time to get back into the swing of it again, huh?

CONRAD. This a mental health check?

CAL. Just a road test.

CONRAD. Truly this is a man who does not know the meaning of the word "subtle." *(Both laugh.)*

CAL. I miss Lazenby hanging around here. You used to play Liar's Poker, remember?

CONRAD. Buck was the one who could really play. He'd set up those weekend games. Once he ordered pizza for nine of us without telling Mom. I thought she was going to pass out when the delivery man handed her the bill. *(He is thoughtful.)* They were really all Buck's friends.

CAL. No. It just seems that way when you have an older brother. His friends become your friends. Your friends become his. You both had a lot of good friends. Who won that weekend?

CONRAD. Stillman, I think. Yeah, Stillman. He was obnoxious. We threw him in the Van Buren's swimming pool afterward, but he still couldn't stop bragging.

CAL. Stillman has a mouth, doesn't he? *(He finishes his drink and gets ready to stand up.)* I'm glad you're home, Con. I want things to go well. I told your mother you wanted to stay home for Christmas.

CONRAD. But if she really wants to go, I'll go.

CAL. No, it's all right. We'll stay home. Is there anything else I can do?

CONRAD. Stop worrying. That's all.

CAL *(standing).* I better get to bed. Good night.

CONRAD. Good night. *(*CAL *exits.* CONRAD *sits back in the chair, much as he did when the play opened. He stares straight ahead. The lights fade from normal yellow to the same blue, eerie color that was present in the beginning. He closes his eyes and begins to sleep, his breathing becoming slow and regular. His head rocks slightly as his breathing becomes faster, desperate. The blue light grows in intensity until he finally screams. He starts, awakens, opens his eyes, and stands up. He looks quickly around the room to see if anyone has seen him and tests.)* Dad? Mom? *(There is no response. Greatly relieved, he collapses into the chair. To himself.)* Don't scream out loud, damn it. Just don't scream out loud. *(As the lights begin to fade, he rises and walks to* BERGER'*s office.)*

A s the lights come up on BERGER'*s office,* CONRAD *walks to the chair behind* BERGER'*s desk and sits down.* BERGER *sits in one of the armchairs.* CONRAD *is tense, serious.* BERGER *listens carefully.*

CONRAD. The walls are polished gray, like the inside of a galvanized pail. It's lit, so I can see, but I can't see far because it turns. But every time I make the turn, the tunnel just goes on. No end in sight, only the dimensions have shrunk. The further I walk, the more it keeps shrinking, until I can reach out and touch the walls and the ceiling. They're cold and empty. No paint. No wires. Where does the light come from, I wonder? My legs ache so I kneel down to rest. But I can't get up. The tunnel's shrunk again. I'm on my hands and knees, moving forward, bumping my head. It gets darker, harder to see. I crawl on my stomach. I'm tired. I don't want to go on. I rest my head on the ground. It's sand. I close my eyes, but when I open them, it's black. No light. I want to back up, get out. But there's a wall there now. I can feel it with my feet. And my head bumps the ceiling and a wall in front of me. I can't move my hands to the side. It's a tomb, see, a metal tomb, and the more I move, the tighter it closes me in. And then, the air's gone! I can't breathe. I'm twisting and fighting to get out, but I can't breathe! And then I scream. I always scream out loud. And that wakes me up, see? And then it's over. *(He looks at* BERGER *as he waits for a response. There is no response.)* Well?

BERGER. I'm thinking.

CONRAD. So what does it mean?

BERGER. What do you think it means?

CONRAD. Hey, you're the doctor.

BERGER *(rising).* Let me put it this way. I don't hold much stock in dreams. In fact, I don't hold stock at all. Of any kind.

CONRAD *(annoyed).* What the hell sort of psychiatrist are you? They all believe in dreams.

BERGER. Do they? Damn, out of step again. Hey, do me a favor, will you? Lie down. There, on the floor. I want to try something.

CONRAD *(getting up, disgusted, then lying down where he's told).* You're nuts, you know that?

BERGER. I'm the doctor, remember? *(He lies down.)* Change of perspective. Steadies the blood.

CONRAD *(crossing his ankles, hands behind his head).* This is stupid. Besides, I lie down all the time. At home. It doesn't help. *(He sits up.)* I think I need some kind of tranquilizer.

BERGER. Tranquilizer.

CONRAD. Yeah. What d'you think?

BERGER. I think you came in here looking like something out of *The Bodysnatchers.* It is not my impression that you need a tranquilizer. *(A pause)* Maybe you've got too much to do. Maybe you ought to drop a course or two.

CONRAD. No.

BERGER. Why not?

CONRAD. Because. I'm behind already.

BERGER. Behind what? The Great Schedule in the Sky? The Golden Gradebook? What?

CONRAD *(lying back down).* You're preaching again. And your ceiling's dirty.

BERGER. So sue me. Listen, kiddo. I lied. I do believe in dreams. Only sometimes I want to hear about what happens to you when you're awake. Like right now. Something is making you very nervous. What is it?

CONRAD (*sitting up*). Okay. I don't want to swim anymore. I look horrible. My timing's all off. I hate all those guys. They're a bunch of boring jocks . . . I hate the coach! (*He loosens up and lets out some of the anger.*) He's a total idiot. You know what he says to me the other day? Says, "Jarrett, I got this friend . . . been in and out of mental hospitals for the last ten years." (*He laughs and shakes his head.*)

BERGER (*seriously*). Yeah . . . sometimes people say stupid things. They feel like they gotta say something, y'know?

CONRAD. Sometimes people say stupid things because they're stupid.

BERGER. So what's holding you back? Why don't you quit?

CONRAD. I can't. Look, I go to him and beg for one more chance. Then I swim for two months and quit again. Can't you see how dumb it looks?

BERGER. Forget how it looks. How does it feel?

CONRAD. No. That's what happened last year. Same damn thing.

BERGER. Forget last year. You think you're the same person you were last year? (*CONRAD shrugs and lies back down. He closes his eyes. BERGER rises, thoughtfully. He walks to an armchair and sits down.*) This problem, kiddo, it's real, you know. A good, healthy problem needs a good, healthy solution. Point of separation. Between the sicks and the wells. Real problems. Real solutions.

CONRAD (*rolling over on his stomach*). Sounds like a chapter heading to me.

BERGER (*smiling*). I hope to hell you're writing this stuff down.

CONRAD. I got it taped up over the back of the john. (*Both laugh. As the lights begin to dim on the office, STILLMAN's voice can be heard from the locker area. CONRAD and BERGER exit in the darkness.*)

The lights come up on LAZENBY and STILLMAN, *dressed in their swim trunks, standing in front of the lockers.*

STILLMAN. Lazenby, geez, why are you so nervous about making a commitment? Just yes or no!

LAZENBY. It costs money, that's why. For four bucks, I like to know what I'm seeing.

STILLMAN. It's a damn French sex film. What more do you have to know?

LAZENBY. Okay. How about if I ask Jarrett?

STILLMAN. You ever think of doing anything without Jarrett?

LAZENBY. What's that mean?

STILLMAN (*after a pause*). You know what happens when you hang around with flakes? You get flaky.

LAZENBY. Man, do you mind? (*He speaks mildly.*) He's a friend of mine.

STILLMAN. He's a flake. (*As he exits*) I'm gonna warm up.

LAZENBY. Get off his back, Stillman. The guy's got enough problems. (*He starts to follow STILLMAN off.*)

STILLMAN (*exiting*). He sure has! (*Both exit.*)

(*Downstage from the lockers, SALAN enters with CONRAD, in slacks and a shirt.*)

SALAN. Jarrett, you gotta be kidding me. I don't get it. I excuse you from practice twice a week so you can see some shrink. I work with you every damn night at your convenience . . . now what the hell more am I supposed to be doing for you?

CONRAD (*evenly, with control*). Nothing.

SALAN. A bright kid like you—with everything going for him—why do you want to keep messing up your life?

CONRAD. I don't think it will mess up my life if I stop swimming.

SALAN (*flatly*). Okay. This is it. You're a big kid now. I'm not taking you back again.

You remember that.

CONRAD. I won't ask you to, sir. (SALAN *turns and exits.* CONRAD *makes an offensive gesture behind* SALAN's *back as he leaves, then walks upstage to his locker, opens it, takes out a dufflebag, and begins to pack it.*)

(LAZENBY *enters, wet, with a towel wrapped around his shoulders.*)

LAZENBY. What happened? Salan says you quit.

CONRAD. Yeah.

LAZENBY. Why? (*The bell rings.*)

CONRAD. I felt like it. It was a bore.

LAZENBY. (*severely*). Some reason. (*He relents.*) Con, is something the matter?

CONRAD. What d'you mean?

LAZENBY (*worried, shrugging*). I don't know. You've been acting funny lately.

CONRAD (*hard, bitterly*). Laze, take my advice. You hang around with flakes, you get flaky.

LAZENBY (*angrily, bitterly*). I knew that was it! Well, hell, why are you mad at me?

CONRAD (*turning on* LAZENBY). I'm not mad at you! (*He slams his locker shut.*) I gotta get to choir.

LAZENBY. Wait a minute, will you? I talked to Salan and he says . . .

CONRAD. Quit talking to people! (*He walks upstage.*) Leave me alone. (*The light fades on* LAZENBY.)

LAZENBY. The hell with you, then. (*He exits.* CONRAD *walks downstage to the risers as the bell rings again. He stands waiting for a few moments as no one has arrived for practice.*)

(JEANNINE *enters with a large pile of music.*)

JEANNINE. I thought the swim team had practice this afternoon.

CONRAD. They do.

JEANNINE. I thought you were swimming.

(*She sits and begins to sort through the pile of music.*)

CONRAD. I was. I'm not anymore.

JEANNINE. (*looking at* CONRAD *for a moment, then deciding to try a neutral question*). Want to help me sort out these parts for the Bach piece?

CONRAD. Sure. (*He sits down next to* JEANNINE *and begins to help.*)

JEANNINE. So what happened?

CONRAD. What d'you mean?

JEANNINE. Why aren't you swimming?

CONRAD. Because I quit.

JEANNINE. Oh. (*Both continue to sort in silence for a moment.* CONRAD *turns to* JEANNINE.)

CONRAD (*abruptly*). Listen. You want to go out tonight?

JEANNINE. You mean with you? On a date?

CONRAD (*with a dry laugh*). Yeah, well . . . we don't have to call it a real date. We could just sort of fake it . . . see how it goes . . .

JEANNINE. I can't.

CONRAD. Oh. (*A silence*)

JEANNINE. We're having trouble getting started again. Why don't you get out your list?

CONRAD. I tore it up. Remember?

JEANNINE. Yeah. Well . . . can't you think of anything safe?

CONRAD. Sure. (*He turns to face* JEANNINE.) How come you can't go out with me tonight?

JEANNINE (*hesitating*). Because. I have to babysit my little brother. (*She speaks bitterly.*) Because my mother has a date.

CONRAD. Oh.

JEANNINE. With her boyfriend who flew in this morning from Akron.

CONRAD. I thought . . . you said your parents weren't divorced.

JEANNINE. They're not. This jerk from Ohio is trying to move things along. *(Near tears, she is embarrassed.)* I'm sorry. Geez, I hate this. I hate acting like this. *(She pulls herself together.)* Okay, my turn to choose a topic. How come you quit the swim team?

CONRAD *(seriously).* I don't know.

JEANNINE *(hesitating).* Did it . . . have anything to do with your brother?

CONRAD. *(looking at* JEANNINE, *surprised).* Who told you about that?

JEANNINE. Joe Lazenby. *(She speaks gently.)* I asked him, Connie.

CONRAD *(shrugging).* It's all right. Doesn't matter.

JEANNINE. He was a swimmer, too, wasn't he?

CONRAD. He was a great swimmer. *(A pause)* He was great at everything.

JEANNINE. Was he older than you?

CONRAD *(nodding).* A year.

JEANNINE. It must be hard on your parents . . . on everybody.

CONRAD *(with a bitter laugh).* Yeah, it's hard.

JEANNINE *(looking straight ahead).* I'm sorry.

CONRAD *(coolly).* I guess he told you all of it, then, huh? About me, I mean?

JEANNINE. *(softly).* Yes. There are worse things . . . people do worse things than that.

CONRAD *(looking away from* JEANNINE, *not convinced).* I guess so.

JEANNINE. *(after an uneasy silence).* I don't like this guy my mother is seeing. I don't like any guy who dates a married woman.

CONRAD. Do you know him? I mean, maybe he's not such a bad guy . . .

JEANNINE *(bitterly).* I know him. I hate him. I hate the way he looks . . . the way he smells . . . I hate it every time he walks into the house . . . I just hate him! Damn . . . I really believed that . . . I mean, I kept thinking that, sooner or later, my folks would get back together . . . and I kept hoping this other guy would just . . . disappear. And now I know it's never going to happen. They don't love each other anymore. They never will again. And that's that! *(She begins to cry in earnest and puts her face in her hands.* CONRAD *looks at* JEANNINE. *After a moment, he puts his arm around her shoulder to comfort her.)*

CONRAD. Hey . . . it's okay . . . it's okay.

JEANNINE *(shaking her head).* No, it's not. Oh, geez, I just don't get why these things have to happen.

CONRAD *(lightly, musing).* These questions I ask myself every day . . . and every day I answer myself. I say, "How the hell do I know?"

JEANNINE *(straightening slowly, composing herself, blowing her nose, but not looking at* CONRAD*).* You don't have to make jokes about everything, Connie. *(The lights slowly dim on the risers as she rises and exits.* CONRAD *continues to sit after she's gone.)*

CONRAD *(sighing wearily).* Wasn't a joke, Jeannine. *(He exits in the darkness.)*

The lights come up on the Jarrett living room. CAL *is decorating a Christmas tree, stringing popcorn and cranberries.* CONRAD *enters and begins to hang decorations on the tree.*

CAL. We'll need a ladder to finish decorating this, you know. I should have bought the stubby spruce. It would have been cheaper and easier.

CONRAD. That spruce had a hormone deficiency, Dad. It's gonna make some short family very happy. Not us. This is the tree for us.

CAL. I liked that tree.

CONRAD. You felt sorry for that tree. It's a good thing I went with you.

CAL. You won't think it's such a good idea when we're stringing this popcorn through the first of the year.

CONRAD. We gotta do this right. Nothing artificial this year.

CAL. You want Christmas-on-the-prairie, you got it! *(He sticks himself.)* Ouch! This needlework is very hard on my self-respect. *(He rises.)* I think I'll hang a few lights. *(He starts to hang the lights.)* How was your trig final?

CONRAD. You want the truth?

CAL. Sure.

CONRAD. I aced it.

CAL. Great. Terrific. That your first A this semester?

CONRAD *(smiling).* Yeah. I'm getting back in the swing of things, huh?

(BETH enters in an overcoat.)

BETH *(taking off the coat).* You started without me.

CAL. Couldn't wait. *(He kisses BETH.)* How was bridge?

BETH *(looking at the tree, her voice taut, controlled).* You went out and bought a tree.

CONRAD. It was my idea. I like the smell.

BETH *(examining the branches).* We've got a perfectly good artificial one in the basement. The needles will absolutely imbed themselves in that white shag, Cal.

CAL. Oh, it's probably flat and limp as hell, Beth. We haven't used it for five years. We're always on our way somewhere a week before Christmas.

BETH. I think I want a drink.

CAL. Sure. I'll make them. *(He walks over to the bar and makes each of them a drink.)*

CONRAD. We've got popcorn and cranberries to string. You want to help? *(BETH looks at*

him for a long moment, but does not reply.)

CAL. So who was high scorer?

BETH *(still looking at CONRAD).* Carole Lazenby. *(After a pause)* Carole had some interesting news.

CAL. Oh?

BETH *(not taking her eyes off CONRAD).* It's not my news. It's Conrad's. Maybe he should tell it.

CAL. Tell what?

BETH *(as CAL hands her a drink).* It was rather embarrassing. Carole thought I knew. After all, why wouldn't I know? It happened over a month ago.

CAL. What happened?

CONRAD. Dad, I quit the swim team.

CAL. Quit? Why? *(More concerned than angry)* Where have you been every night until six-thirty?

CONRAD. Nowhere. Around. The library.

CAL. I don't get it. Why didn't you tell us?

CONRAD. I was going to. I've been meaning to.

BETH. I'm sure you would have told us before the first meet. When is it, next Thursday?

CONRAD. I'm sure I would have told you if I thought you gave a damn!

CAL. What the hell does that mean?

BETH. Never mind. It's meant for me. Isn't it? I wish I knew, Conrad, why it is still so important for you to try to hurt me!

CONRAD. Hurt you? Me, hurt you? Listen, you're the one who's trying to hurt me!

BETH. And how did I do that? By making you look like a fool in front of a room full of people! Did you have to sit there getting those looks? Poor Beth, she has no idea what her son is up to. He lies and lies and she believes every word of it.

CONRAD. I didn't lie!

BETH. You did! You lied every night that you came into this house at six-thirty. *(She puts her hands to her head and presses them tightly.)* I can't stand this. If it's starting all over again—the lying, the disappearing for hours—I won't stand for it!

CONRAD. Don't, then! Go to Europe, why don't you? Go to hell!

CAL. Con!

CONRAD *(still to BETH).* Listen, the only reason you care, the only reason you give a damn about it, is because someone else knew about it first. You never wanted to know anything I was doing. You just wanted me to leave you alone!

CAL. Shut up, Con. Stop it!

CONRAD. Damn it! Tell her to stop! You never tell her a thing! Listen, I know why she never came to the hospital, not once. I know. Hell, she was going to Spain and Portugal. Why should she care if I was strapped by the brains to some damn voltage regulator?

CAL. That's enough! *(CONRAD gasps for air. On the verge of tears, he runs out of the room.)*

BETH *(still clutching her hands to her head).* I won't! I won't!

CAL *(going to BETH and putting his arms around her rigid body).* What the hell happened? Somebody better go after him.

BETH *(pulling away from CAL).* Go! That's the pattern, isn't it? Let him walk all over us, then go after him and apologize.

CAL. I'm not going to apologize.

BETH. Yes, you are! You always do!

CAL. I'm sorry. Let's not fight. Let's go find him.

BETH. No, you go. He wants somebody who's going to accept everything he does.

CAL. And you think that's what I do?

BETH. I know it is! Everything he does is all right. And everything I do is mixed up and wrong and could have been handled better.

CAL. That's not true! Beth, please, come with me. Please.

BETH. No! I will not be pushed! *(She walks away from CAL, sits down to calm herself, then speaks determinedly.)* I will not be manipulated. *(CAL searches for something to say. He looks confused, then finally turns away to follow CONRAD. The lights slowly dim on BETH as she sits staring ahead.)*

*T*he lights come up on BERGER's office. As CONRAD enters, BETH rises to watch him. He turns for a moment to look at her. She looks at him hard, resolute, then turns her back on him and walks away. CONRAD sits in one of the armchairs. BERGER sits in another.

BERGER. So why don't you talk to her, Con? Talk it out.

CONRAD. She and I do not connect. I told you that before.

BERGER. Does that bother you?

CONRAD. No. Why should it?

BERGER. I don't know. Some people it might bother, that's all.

CONRAD. My mother is a very private person. We don't ride the same bus. Who does? What do you have in common with your mother? Surface junk—brush your teeth, clean your room, get good grades. My mother . . . *(He gropes, not wanting to get worked up.)* . . . people have a right to be the way they are.

BERGER. They have a right to their feelings?

CONRAD. Yeah. They have a right to their feelings.

BERGER. And what about you, Con? Don't you have a right to your feelings? Why are you so afraid of letting go? What scares you, Con? Sadness? Anger? Any of the twenty-eight flavors?

CONRAD *(wincing as if his head hurt)*. What time is it?

BERGER. Lots of time. *(He rises, walks over to the desk, sits on top of it, and speaks gently.)* Hey, kiddo, you said you wanted more control. You see any connection here between control and this . . . this fear of feeling?

CONRAD *(leaning back in his chair, closing his eyes, feeling the pain of the conversation)*. I didn't say I was afraid.

BERGER. But you are, aren't you?

CONRAD. I don't know.

BERGER *(prodding* CONRAD*)*. Hey, come on. I'm doing all the work here. Don't play games.

CONRAD *(opening his eyes and becoming defensive)*. What games? *(He gets up and paces.)* I don't know what you want.

BERGER. Then I'll tell you. I want you to leave off the "I don't knows."

CONRAD. And what if I don't have an answer? You want me to make one up?

BERGER. Yeah, make one up. Tell me how you turned yourself inside out and you don't find any feelings in there. No feelings, nohow.

CONRAD *(angrily)*. I didn't say I don't have feelings! I have feelings.

BERGER. Now you have 'em, now you don't. Get it together, Jarrett.

CONRAD. Look, why're you hassling me? Why're you trying to make me mad?

BERGER. Are you mad?

CONRAD *(furiously)*. No!

BERGER. Like hell. You're mad. You got a right to be mad. I'm pushing you. That's a good, healthy reaction!

CONRAD. All right! I'm mad! So now what?

BERGER. So now that's better. A lot more direct. Only it's one thing to be mad at me and it's something else to be mad at your mother. *(A pause)* Isn't that right? (CONRAD *sits down on the floor and leans his back against* BERGER's *desk.* BERGER *sits in the armchair.)*

CONRAD *(with difficulty)*. I can't. It comes . . . too fast. There's always too much of it.

BERGER. It's a closet full of junk. You open the door and everything falls out.

CONRAD. No. There's a guy in the closet. I don't even know him, that's the problem.

BERGER. Only way you're ever gonna get to know him is to open the door.

CONRAD *(shaking his head)*. Takes too much energy.

BERGER. Kiddo, you got any idea how much energy it takes to hold that door closed? Now that's power!

CONRAD. When I let myself feel . . . all I feel is lousy.

BERGER. Maybe you gotta feel lousy sometime in order to feel better. *(A beat)* Listen, Connie. One of these days you and your mother have got to get down and deal.

CONRAD *(closing his eyes in pain)*. I can't . . . you don't know . . . I've pulled too much crap on her already.

BERGER. *(leaning forward in his chair)*. Yeah? Tell me about it. What crap have you pulled? (CONRAD *shakes his head, refusing to answer. He keeps his eyes closed.)* C'mon . . . did you forget to clean the oven or what? You oughta be able to come up with something.

CONRAD *(opening his eyes, his voice flat)*. All right. I tried to kill myself.

BERGER. That old turkey.

CONRAD *(explosively)*. It's not an old turkey! Don't you get it? It'll never be an old turkey. I locked myself in the bathroom to do it! *(The lights begin to turn a bluish color.)* I locked myself in the bathroom . . . and I sat down on the floor . . . it's cold. The tiles are so damn cold. I'm holding the blades. I brought the whole pack in with me. I don't know why . . . I take one out and I stare at it. I don't know how to do this. I touch my thumb to the edge of the blade . . . an accident, you know. I'm cut. Just like that. Then I sit and think about . . . things. Everything that hurts. *(He bows his head.)* And I cry. Inside, I'm burning up. Outside . . . all I can feel is the cold tile floor. And my chest feels so tight . . . it hurts . . . everything hurts . . . so I hold out my hand and close my eyes . . . and I slice, one quick cut, deep cut. And then I switch hands—can you believe that—right away I switch and pull the blade again. *(He breathes heavily and rocks slightly, back and forth, as he tries to compose himself enough to go on.)* And then I stop. And I open my eyes . . . and there it is . . . Oh, God, I'm thinking, this place is full of blood. It's everywhere, spilling all over her good towels and the walls, the floor, everywhere. I feel sick to my stomach all of a sudden . . . everything's going around . . . and I know they're downstairs in the den . . . watching television . . . they don't know anything. *(He hunches his shoulders and lowers his head as the lights begin to return to normal. He cries softly for a moment, then calms himself.)* I feel bad . . . that they don't know . . . that they're gonna come upstairs . . . and find this . . . this mess!

BERGER *(quietly).* Is that what happened?

CONRAD. Yeah. *(He sighs.)* She threw everything out. The rug, the bath mat, all the towels, everything. Chucked it. Hired a guy to come in and regrout the tile. *(He laughs.)* That's the way she is. *(He tips his head upward against the back of the desk and stares at the ceiling thoughtfully.)*

BERGER. And you think that's why she can't forgive you?

CONRAD *(laughing bitterly).* Geez, she fired a maid because she couldn't dust the living room right. If you think she's ever gonna let me off the hook . . .

BERGER. You're not her maid, Con. You're her son.

CONRAD. What's the difference? I screwed up! She can't . . . *(In a hard voice)* . . . She wasn't amused. She likes things to be . . . perfect!

BERGER *(gently).* And what about you?

CONRAD. Me? *(He thinks hard and it comes out slowly.)* I like things . . . to be perfect, too.

BERGER. Uh, huh. And she's not perfect, is she?

CONRAD *(after a beat).* No. *(He speaks sadly, painfully.)* She can't . . . she doesn't . . . know how to love me.

BERGER *(still very gently).* No, kiddo, that's not it. She can't love you enough. Not as much as you need her to, right now. She's who she is, you know? You gotta stop blaming her for not being the person you want her to be.

CONRAD *(slowly).* I get it. I figured it out.

BERGER. What?

CONRAD. Who it is who can't forgive who.

BERGER *(nodding).* That's part of it.

CONRAD *(looking around at BERGER).* What's the rest? Huh? What d'you mean?

BERGER. I mean first you forgive her. And then there's somebody else you gotta forgive. *(The lights fade to black and he and CONRAD exit.)*

ACT TWO

As the lights come up: BETH is packing away swimming trophies from the mantelpiece in the Jarrett living room. CAL enters with a tray of sandwiches.

CAL. Where's Con? He's supposed to be cleaning the ashes out of the fireplace. *(He sets the tray down on the bar.)* Maybe he doesn't think he should be working on his birthday. *(There is no response from BETH.)* I made a little lunch. Want something?

BETH *(concentrating on the trophies).* Ah, no. I'm going to the club in a few minutes.

CAL *(walking over to BETH).* What're you doing?

BETH. Just putting some of these trophies away. I've been thinking I should have put them away for a long time, but I couldn't. Now that Conrad's decided to stop swimming, I thought . . .

CAL *(looking at a trophy).* Most of these are Buck's. You remember this one? He won it his sophomore year.

BETH. We had a party that spring, for the whole team, right after the regional meet. He always insisted on a party—he manufactured excuses—a party for anything.

CAL. Buck knew how to enjoy himself.

BETH *(picking up a trophy and running her fingers over it).* When I packed away the things from his room after the accident, I found a snapshot from the Christmas party at the Lazenbys', remember that? Carole had the whole neighborhood over. After we ate, she tried to get us all to sing carols, but nobody would listen. Then I saw Buck walk over to the piano. He just sat down and began to play. Remember how we all gathered 'round? He kept us singing for two hours. *(After a beat, sadly, more to*

herself than CAL) He had such a good time, didn't he? Life was so much fun then. *(She turns to look at CAL.)* I want him back, Cal. *(CAL takes her in his arms and holds her. He guides her to the sofa and both sit. He holds his arms around BETH as they sit silently and thoughtfully for a few moments.)*

CAL. I have an idea, Beth.

BETH. Hmm?

CAL. How would you like to go to Texas?

BETH. Texas?

CAL. There's a golf tournament—the Lawyers' Invitational.

BETH. Just you and me?

CAL *(after thinking a moment).* Sure. Why not? Just the two of us.

BETH. When would we go?

CAL. Middle of March. The tournament starts on a Saturday and runs through Monday.

BETH. We could stay with my brother.

CAL. Sure. We haven't seen Ward and Audrey for a long time. It'd be fun.

BETH *(smiling).* Who knows? You might even win the tournament.

CAL *(laughing).* Right. All I need is for about a dozen guys to drop out! *(He speaks seriously.)* I know it isn't Europe, honey. But it's a chance to get away for a few days. Be together and talk. *(A pause)* I love you, Beth. *(He embraces BETH.)*

BETH. I love you, Cal.

CAL *(rising).* Okay, I'll make reservations today. You want to call Ward and Audrey? Let them know we're coming?

BETH. Let's call tonight. Together.

CAL. All right. And we can talk to your mother and dad, too. About them staying here while we're gone. You know, just to keep an eye on things. *(He moves to the telephone.)*

BETH (*after a beat*). You worry too much, Cal.

CAL. I do? About what?

BETH. About Conrad. Pleasing him. Making everything completely safe for him.

CAL (*smiling*). Well . . . I'm a man who believes in safety.

BETH. It's not always a virtue. He's eighteen years old now.

CAL (*still smiling*). Well, barely . . .

BETH. Let him go. (*There is silence as she and* CAL *look at each other.*)

CAL (*carefully*). I'm just . . . doing what I have to do, Beth.

BETH (*shaking her head*). You can do too much.

CAL. For who?

BETH (*vehemently*). For him. Who do you think? He's who we're talking about, isn't he? Who we're always talking about?

CAL. Maybe. (*He moves toward* BETH *on the sofa.*) What about you, Beth? Don't I do enough for you? (BETH *turns away slightly.*)

BETH. I don't know. We're not the same now, Cal. Something is not the same.

CAL (*standing in front of the sofa and taking* BETH'S *hands*). What are you saying?

BETH (*upset, almost tearful*). I'm saying I need you to love me the way you used to . . . please.

CAL (*stunned, gently*). I love you, Beth. (*He pulls* BETH *off the sofa, to her feet, and holds her.*) God, you know I love you!

(CONRAD *enters with a dust pan, small broom, and wastebasket.*)

BETH (*pulling away from* CAL). I'm due at the club. (*She sets the box of trophies aside so that it won't be in* CONRAD's *way.*) I'll see you for tennis later, Cal. Where should we go for dinner?

CAL. Anywhere the birthday boy says.

BETH (*to* CONRAD). Be careful with those ashes. Use the vacuum when you've finished, will you? (*She exits.*)

CONRAD. Sure. (*He stoops to scoop ashes.*) Hey, you know, you can't force a kid to be a chimney sweep against his will.

CAL (*getting two cans of beer*). Well, you just turned eighteen, so I *can* force you. Come on, how long does it take? An hour?

CONRAD. Forty-nine minutes when I could be eating cake, opening presents . . .

CAL. Finish up and then tell me your sad story. (CONRAD *finishes the sweeping and cleans himself with a wet towel. He goes over to the bar as* CAL *divides the sandwiches and hands* CONRAD *a beer and sandwich.*)

CONRAD. No mayonnaise on mine, okay?

CAL. Oh, hell!

CONRAD. All right, forget it. I'll eat it. (*He grins.*) What a birthday. (*Both sit down to eat.*)

CAL (*toasting* CONRAD). Happy birthday!

CONRAD. Thanks. (*Both drink.*)

CAL. I used to have to keep an eye on both of you whenever you did that job. Couldn't leave you alone for a minute. Especially Buck. He was a genius at goofing off.

CONRAD. Yeah, I remember.

CAL. In fact, the only time he worked his tail off was when we finished the rec room downstairs. Remember the plastering job we did down there? You guys wrote dirty words on the wall.

CONRAD. We wrote 'em in the fireplace, too.

CAL (*incredulously*). In my living room?

CONRAD. Sure, most of it's covered by soot, but underneath all that charcoal is a wall of graffiti.

CAL. You two did that?

CONRAD. Couldn't leave us alone for a minute, Dad. Good sandwich.

CAL. Thank you.

CONRAD. Next time, hold the mayo. *(Both eat for a moment.)*

CAL. Tell me something. You and this Doctor Berger, what do you guys talk about?

CONRAD *(surprised, shrugging).* Anything. I don't know. Why?

CAL. Just curious. What kinds of things?

CONRAD. Whatever we feel like. He's an easy guy to talk to.

CAL. What would you think if I were to go and talk with him?

CONRAD. What for? About me, you mean?

CAL. No. Just . . . I don't know. To get things straight in my own mind.

CONRAD *(setting his beer down with finality).* There's nothing wrong with you, Dad.

CAL *(smiling).* Thanks.

CONRAD *(after a beat).* See him, if you want. It's okay with me.

CAL *(rising).* Well, I have to run some errands for your mother. She has more work for me than Ray Hanley.

CONRAD. She's at the club a lot lately.

CAL. She's in charge of the big summer invitational. Two hundred golfers from all over the state.

CONRAD. She likes the club.

CAL. The club likes her. Carole Lazenby says they've never had a chairman like her. She's a very organized, competent lady, your mother. *(He looks at his watch.)* And very punctual. See you later. *(He exits.* CONRAD *clears the lunch tray from the bar, then walks to the mirror over the fireplace. He studies his hair, runs his fingers through it, and seems moderately pleased. He looks closely at his complexion. The blotches are gone and he looks happy. He turns over his hands and looks at his wrists, but his train of thought is broken by the doorbell.)*

*(*CONRAD *leaves the room and returns with* KAREN, *who looks a little nervous and shy.)*

CONRAD. Come in. What a surprise!

KAREN. My parents drove down for the day. My uncle lives only a mile or so from here. I thought I'd just say hi.

CONRAD. Sit down.

KAREN *(sitting down).* I can't stay long. I said I'd walk to my uncle's from here. I thought I should say hi.

CONRAD. I'm glad you came. It's my birthday. This is a great present.

KAREN *(still shy, hesitantly).* Oh, maybe I interrupted something.

CONRAD. No, no. I'm here all by myself. So, how's it going?

KAREN. Fine.

CONRAD. How was the . . . ah, play? What was it?

KAREN. *A Thousand Clowns.* Fine. We got through it okay.

CONRAD. It kept you busy?

KAREN. Yeah. I've been really busy. I think that's important. How's the swim team?

CONRAD *(not expecting the question and somewhat unsure how to answer).* Oh. I quit. *(He defends himself.)* I finally decided I didn't want to do it anymore.

KAREN. And you think it was a good thing to quit?

CONRAD. I guess so. *(He is more confident.)* Yeah. I'm glad I quit. I don't feel so much pressure.

KAREN *(a little unsure).* I suppose that's good.

CONRAD. What about you, Karen? You feeling the pressure?

KAREN. No, no. I just . . . try to keep busy, you know? The pressure's good for me. Keeps me from thinking too much. *(She* *smiles nervously at* CONRAD.) You can think too much about things, Conrad.

CONRAD. Yeah, I guess. Still . . . Berger says you don't have to feel like you need to prove yourself all the time . . .

KAREN. You're still seeing him, then? The doctor?

CONRAD (*a little ashamed*). Yeah. He's a good guy. (*A beat*) Hey, you want something to drink? You want a beer?

KAREN. No. No, thanks. I told them I'd only stay a few minutes.

CONRAD (*concerned*). You okay, Karen?

KAREN. What d'you mean?

CONRAD. I dunno . . . just . . . is everything okay with you?

KAREN (*firmly*). Yes. Sure. (*A beat*) I'm being careful. Not to get too high or too low. Those extremes . . . that's what kills you. (*She realizes what she's said and is upset.*) I don't mean literally kills you . . . you know what I mean.

CONRAD. Yeah . . . and you think that works? You feel good?

KAREN (*searching*). I feel . . . safe. Like I'm not ever going back to the hospital.

CONRAD (*searching, too*). And that's what you want. To feel safe.

KAREN (*rising*). Yes. Of course. Don't you?

CONRAD. I dunno . . . I guess I don't think safe is enough for me anymore. I need more than that. I need to feel good. (*He and* KAREN *look at each other in silence for a moment.*)

KAREN (*convincing herself*). Well . . . I feel good. I do.

CONRAD. Okay, yeah. I know you do. (*He and* KAREN *step toward each other and hold hands briefly. They break apart and both laugh nervously.*)

KAREN. I've got to go. They'll be wondering where I am.

CONRAD. Thanks for coming by. You take it easy, now.

KAREN. I will. You, too. And . . . be careful.

CONRAD. I'll be careful.

KAREN. Happy birthday!

CONRAD. Thanks. (KAREN *exits. The lights fade slowly to black as* CONRAD *stares thoughtfully after her. He exits in the darkness.*)

*T*he lights come up on CAL *sitting in an armchair in* BERGER's *office.* BERGER *stands at the coffee machine.*

BERGER. Coffee?

CAL. No, thanks. (BERGER *pours his cup and sits down in the other armchair. There is an uncomfortable silence.*) I don't really believe in psychiatrists.

BERGER (*with a twinkle in his eye*). Ah, maybe I oughta leave for this part of the session, then.

CAL. I meant that I don't believe in psychiatry as a blanket. A panacea for everybody, you know?

BERGER. Okay. Me, neither.

CAL. I'm not putting you down or what you've done for Conrad. He's better. I can see that.

BERGER. Well, he's working at it now.

CAL (*still groping, uncomfortable*). I knew something was wrong. Even before he did it. But he's very smart, you know. I just always thought intelligent people could work out their own problems. (*He pauses, searching.*) These books—are they all about treating people?

BERGER. No, not all.

CAL (*his discomfort peaking*). I wish I knew what the hell I was doing here.

BERGER. I could use an objective opinion on my coffee. Your son tells me it's lousy.

CAL. Yes, all right.

BERGER *(rising to get the coffee).* I get a feeling from you of heavy guilt. About missing the signals with Conrad. Am I right?

CAL. Yes. Sure. You don't have something like that happen and not feel the responsibility.

BERGER. Guilt.

CAL. Guilt. Yes. (BERGER *hands him the coffee.*) Well, I'm guilty and I'm lucky, too. I was there at the right time. I could have been at a meeting. We could have both been at meetings.

BERGER. So you think of yourself as a lucky man. *(He sits down.)*

CAL. No. Not anymore. I used to before . . . before the accident. Hell, all of life is accident . . . who you fall in love with, what grabs you and what you do with it.

BERGER. That sounds more like the philosophy of a drifter than an attorney.

CAL. Okay, I'm a drifter. I'm drifting now. I can see myself. I can see both of them drifting away from me while I stand there watching. And I don't know what to do about it.

BERGER. What do you want to do about it?

CAL. Nothing! I don't want to do anything but sit here on the fence. Until I fall off. On one side or the other.

BERGER. You see them on opposite sides of the fence, is that it?

CAL. Yes. No. I don't know. *(He gathers his thoughts.)* I see her not being able to forgive him.

BERGER. For what?

CAL. For surviving, maybe. No, that's not it. For being too much like her. Hell, I don't know. They're both so careful, so selective about what comes out and what stays inside. They want to do the right thing. All the time they're worried about what is the right thing. Buck wasn't like that. He didn't know how to worry. He made her relax. He made everybody relax. He was a charming kid; the kind of kid you want your friends to meet. She was very proud of him.

BERGER. She's not proud of Conrad?

CAL. Sure, I guess so. But it's not the same. Buck could get through to her. Con just can't.

BERGER. Con says he and his mother don't ride the same bus.

CAL. Hmmm. *(He smiles.)* Oh, I think they do. And I think sometimes they're riding so close to one another that it blinds them.

BERGER. I wonder if your wife has ever talked to anybody about Buck's death. Does she talk to you?

CAL. Yes. No. Not really. She talks about Buck, but not about the accident, not about death. Beth is like a watercolor. They're hard to look at, watercolors. You disappear in them sometimes. And after, you don't know where you've been or what's happened. We talk . . . but we don't talk about death. *(A beat)* God, I feel like such a lousy husband and father.

BERGER *(nodding).* Ah, maybe rotten sons deserve lousy fathers. Yours tells me Tuesdays and Fridays what a rotten kid he is.

CAL. He shouldn't. It isn't true.

BERGER. He comes by it honestly, though. *(He smiles at* CAL.*)*

CAL *(finally relaxing).* He used to call the hospital "the zoo." I asked him if coming to see you was like going to the zoo, but he said no. He said it was more like the circus.

BERGER (*laughing*). That's either a compliment or damned poor p.r.

CAL (*taking a deep breath*). I think I know why I came here. I think I really came to talk about myself.

BERGER. Sounds good. Why don't we do that? (*There is the sound of a locker door slamming and the lights fade to black on* BERGER's *office. He and* CAL *exit in the darkness.*)

T*he lights come up on the lockers.* JEANNINE *is standing with her back to the audience, rummaging around for something.* CONRAD *comes up behind her.*

CONRAD. I'm gonna make this real smooth and casual. Hey, chick, what're you doing tonight?

JEANNINE (*turning around and grinning slowly*). Knitting. (*Both laugh.*)

CONRAD. Great. What I always wanted to learn how to do.

JEANNINE (*looking* CONRAD *up and down*). It's not for the fainthearted, you know.

CONRAD. I'm up to it. I swear. (*He and* JEANNINE *walk forward and seat themselves on the choir risers.*)

JEANNINE. Conrad, I can't go out with you.

CONRAD. Look. Before you say no, I want to apologize for the other day.

JEANNINE. You don't need to . . .

CONRAD. Yeah, I do. I make a lot of jokes. Sometimes they're not funny.

JEANNINE. They're funny. It's just that they're not always . . . what a person needs.

CONRAD. I know. You're right.

JEANNINE. I like you, Connie. You have a great sense of humor and you're a great tenor . . .

CONRAD. Uh, oh. I feel it coming.

JEANNINE. What?

CONRAD. The old "thanks a lot, been nice knowing you, see you around" bit.

JEANNINE. (*shaking her head*). Not what I was going to say.

CONRAD. No?

JEANNINE. No. See, one of the things you do wrong is—

CONRAD (*interrupting*). Joke around when I should be serious. I know.

JEANNINE. Finish other people's sentences for them.

CONRAD. I do?

JEANNINE. Yes. You do.

CONRAD (*thoughtfully, standing up and moving away from the riser.*) I do do that, don't I? (*He turns back and snaps his finger.*) Okay. I won't do that anymore.

JEANNINE (*taken slightly aback*). Just like that?

CONRAD. Just like that. I make a decision and that's it. (*A beat*) So what did you want to finish saying?

JEANNINE (*bewildered, laughing*). I don't remember.

CONRAD. Hah! As I suspected! (*He sits down beside* JEANNINE *again.*) You need somebody to finish your sentences for you. And I need somebody to teach me how to knit. (*He is serious.*) So why won't you go out with me tonight?

JEANNINE. Because my father's in town. He wants to see me. (*She sighs.*) I don't want to do this, but I have to.

CONRAD. Why? Why don't you want to?

JEANNINE. It's a long story. Actually, I don't think my father likes me too much at the moment.

CONRAD. Ah, Jeannine, that can't be true.

JEANNINE (*matter-of-factly*). It's true. It's got a lot to do with my parents splitting up. I started doing some crazy things after it happened. Hanging around with . . . weird people. Getting into trouble. Taking pills, shoplifting, stuff like that. *(After a beat, she looks away from* CONRAD.*)* It's one of the reasons we moved here from Akron. My mother thought it was the town, but it wasn't. It was me. I guess I just wanted to hurt them the way I felt they had hurt me. *(*CONRAD *takes* JEANNINE's *hand and puts it on his knee. She is close to tears.)* I don't know . . . I just feel sick about it now . . . all those dumb things I did.

CONRAD *(gently).* Everybody does dumb things, Jeannine.

JEANNINE *(sighing).* I wish that was all of it. There's . . . a lot more.

CONRAD *(after a moment).* You want to tell me?

JEANNINE *(looking at* CONRAD, *searching).* I don't know.

CONRAD. I won't . . . say the wrong thing. I won't say anything, if you don't want me to.

JEANNINE *(near tears).* It's not what you'll say, Conrad, it's what you'll think.

CONRAD. Oh, geez, you don't mean that. What I'm gonna think? You don't ever need to worry about what I'm gonna think. *(He laughs.)* I don't make judgments about what people do anymore. I don't have room to make any. *(He looks at* JEANNINE.*)* And about you, I wouldn't anyway.

JEANNINE. Just don't be too nice to me, okay? It feels worse when you're so nice.

CONRAD. Right, okay. I'll be totally neutral. So tell me.

JEANNINE *(after a pause).* I . . . started seeing a lot of this one boy. I didn't even like him that much, but he was part of this gang I was hanging around with. I guess . . . I wanted to make my father mad . . . no, I wanted to punish him for letting my mother leave him. I don't know. It's so complicated . . .

CONRAD. I think . . . things get complicated when you try to keep it all inside your own head.

JEANNINE. Yes. Right. My father tried to talk to me about it. But I wouldn't listen to him. So, after a while, he just . . . left me alone. And then it was worse. Nobody seemed to care. *(She pauses, then goes on.)* One time this boy and I were in a department store . . . and we just started lifting things. Hiding them in our jacket pockets . . . it was crazy. I took lipsticks, scarves, a leather wallet, some earrings. Stuff I could've bought if I'd really wanted it. And then we walked out. And the store detective followed us. He'd been watching us the whole time. He called my parents and they had to come down . . . and, Con, the store manager knew my father. It was awful. My dad talked and pleaded with the guy not to prosecute, but the guy said he'd had it with shoplifters. *(She stops for a moment.)* And then . . . my dad broke down and cried. *(Her voice breaks.)* Geez, it was so terrible . . . I just wanted to fall in a hole and disappear. The guy finally gave in. He told us to get the hell out of his store and not come back.

CONRAD *(after a moment).* I know about falling into holes.

JEANNINE *(taking* CONRAD's *hand, turning his wrist up, and stroking it with her hand.)* Did it hurt?

CONRAD *(laughing softly).* I don't know. I don't remember.

JEANNINE. You don't like to talk about it?

CONRAD. I never talked about it to anybody but doctors.

JEANNINE (*thoughtfully*). Connie . . . you think people get punished for the things they do?

CONRAD. Punished? You mean by God?

JEANNINE. Uh, huh.

CONRAD (*after a moment*). I don't believe in God.

JEANNINE. Not at all?

CONRAD. It isn't a question of degree. Either you do or you don't.

JEANNINE. But did you before? Before the accident?

CONRAD (*laughing uncomfortably*). I guess. Whenever I thought about it.

JEANNINE (*firmly*). I believe in God.

CONRAD. I believe in wallpaper. I believe in . . . hiking boots. And I also believe in Philadelphia.

JEANNINE. What about Akron? Do you believe in Akron?

CONRAD. Yeah, I believe in Akron. (*He puts his arm around* JEANNINE *and kisses her.*) People from Akron. I believe in them, too.

JEANNINE (*kissing* CONRAD). You said you'd be totally neutral. I don't think this is being totally neutral.

CONRAD (*as he and* JEANNINE *kiss again*). No? (*He laughs.*) Guess I lied. (*The lights go down as he and* JEANNINE *sit together.* JEANNINE *exits in the darkness.*)

The lights come up on the living room as CONRAD *walks in. He sits down to read a magazine. There are suitcases by the door.* CAL, *in a light coat, enters.*

CAL. Okay, we're off. You've got the number at Audrey and Ward's?

CONRAD. Right next to the phone, Dad.

CAL. Have fun, huh?

CONRAD. I'll try.

CAL. Got plans?

CONRAD. Oh, I thought I'd cruise through town, run a few red lights, smoke some hash, get a few girls in trouble. Nothing special. Quit worrying.

CAL. I'm not. You want to drive up and see Karen? I'll give you some gas money.

CONRAD. You gave me enough money already.

(BETH *enters. She is dressed for traveling: very expensive, very neat, very beautiful.*)

BETH. You have the tickets, Cal? (*He nods and pats his pocket.*)

CONRAD (*rising, to* BETH). Goodbye.

BETH. Goodbye. Be nice to your grandmother.

CONRAD. I promise. You can check her for bruises when you get home.

BETH. That's not funny, Conrad.

CONRAD. Sorry.

BETH. The flight gets in Wednesday at four. You wait here at the house. We'll go out for dinner.

CONRAD. Okay. Give me the keys. I'll back the car out for you.

BETH (*handing the keys to* CONRAD). We'll bring the suitcases out the front door. (CONRAD *exits.*)

CAL (*as* BETH *walks over to the mirror to adjust her coat*). You look beautiful.

BETH. I can't wait to get away, Cal. I feel like I can't breathe lately.

CAL. The work at the country club?

BETH. It's been one thing after another . . . meetings, phone calls . . . I'm glad to have a break.

CAL. Me, too. (*Automatically*) I hope he'll be all right by himself.

BETH. (*turning around to look at* CAL). Do you

do that deliberately or is it a reflex action? I'm curious.

CAL. Do what?

BETH. Insert him into the conversation. Whenever we're talking about you and me.

CAL. I'm sorry. You just mentioned needing to get away and I wondered about Con being alone.

BETH. I'm surprised you haven't told him you'll call when we get there.

CAL. I said I'd give him a ring tomorrow.

BETH. It must be hard to grow up when your father is breathing down your neck all the time. I would hate it.

CAL. Come on, Beth. Not that old song and dance. I overprotect. I breathe down his neck.

BETH. You do.

CAL. It's a matter of opinion.

BETH. Right. We never agree. *(She stops a moment, then decides to pursue it.)* Why are you so obsessed? He controls you.

CAL. Oh, stop it. He isn't the problem.

BETH. Oh, no?

CAL. No! Let's talk about what's really bothering you.

BETH. Oh, no, let's talk about what's really bothering you. You're the one who's always worried, always depressed. As if it helped, being half-alive, dragging everyone down with you.

CAL. Damn it, Beth. Sure I was depressed. Sure I'm worried.

BETH. But you're not sick, Cal.

CAL. Of course I'm not sick. What does that mean?

BETH. It means you don't have to see a psychiatrist. It means you don't have to blame yourself.

CAL. You think I'm blaming myself?

BETH. No. No, that's not it. You know what I really think, Cal? I think you blame me.

CAL. You? For what?

BETH. For the whole thing. For the whole vicious thing. He did it to me!

CAL. He did it to himself, Beth. My God, can't you see anything except in terms of how it affects you?

BETH. No! Neither can you! Or anyone else.

CAL. He just wants to know that you don't hate him.

BETH. Hate him? I don't hate him. Mothers don't hate their sons. Is that what he told you?

(CONRAD enters.)

CONRAD *(noticing the tension but not sure what it is, handing the keys to BETH).* Car's ready.

BETH *(to CAL).* I don't know what you want from me, Cal. I don't know what anybody wants anymore. *(She exits. CAL hesitates for a moment, then follows BETH. The lights fade to black and CONRAD goes to the locker area.)*

The lights come up on CONRAD, *dressed in shirt and slacks, at his locker. He holds some books and appears to be waiting for someone.*

SALAN *(offstage, yelling).* It's the worst season I can remember. Hit the showers, all of you.

(SALAN walks in, passes CONRAD, looks at him briefly without a smile, and walks off.)

STILLMAN *(offstage).* Glad you can laugh about it, Lazenby.

(STILLMAN enters with LAZENBY behind him. both are wet, dressed in their swim trunks, and they towel down as they talk.)

LAZENBY. Oh, come on, we weren't that bad.

STILLMAN. We got waxed. *(He hasn't noticed CONRAD.)* You know, I can't stand that lecture about Buck Jarrett one more time . . . the all-time great swimmer of the world. (LAZENBY *notices* CONRAD.) God, when is Salan gonna quit kissing the guy's picture?

LAZENBY (*trying to cover for* STILLMAN). Hey, Con, we could have used you today.

CONRAD (*smiling uncomfortably*). Nah, I don't think so.

STILLMAN. How's it goin', Jarrett? Keepin' out of the water? (CONRAD *doesn't respond.* STILLMAN *moves toward the lockers.*) Hey, I hear you're goin' out with Pratt. How is it with her? Or aren't you makin' it with her yet? (*He flashes a provocative grin and turns to his locker.*)

CONRAD (*flatly*). Do me a favor, Stillman. Try not to be such a jerk. I know it'll be hard for you.

STILLMAN (*rising to it immediately*). Listen, you're the jerk. The way you walk around here acting like we all owe you something.

LAZENBY. Hey, you guys . . .

CONRAD. You don't owe me anything.

STILLMAN. No kiddin'! Hell, it ain't my fault you don't know how to sail. (CONRAD's *control snaps. He drops his books and moves toward* STILLMAN *in one forceful rush. He straight-arms* STILLMAN *and pushes him against the lockers.* STILLMAN *cries out in pain.*) You son of a—(CONRAD *punches him in the stomach and he doubles over.* LAZENBY *moves in to grab* CONRAD's *arms and pull him off.*)

LAZENBY. Cut it out! Connie, cut it out!

CONRAD (*pushing* LAZENBY *away*). Get lost! (STILLMAN *is up and goes after* CONRAD *as* LAZENBY *holds* CONRAD's *arms.* STILLMAN *lands a punch, then he and* CONRAD *grapple.* LAZENBY *is shoved aside.*)

LAZENBY. Damn it, cut it out! (*He manages to pull* CONRAD *forward, downstage. The lights go out on* STILLMAN.) Connie, geez, what's the matter with you?

CONRAD (*furious, turning on* LAZENBY). Beat it! Leave me alone!

LAZENBY (*just as furious*). No! I'm not leavin' you alone! I want to talk! Me! (*He points to himself.*) D'you hear me? (*Both stand and look at each other, breathing heavily.*)

CONRAD. I hear you.

LAZENBY. All right! First! The guy's a nothin'! A zero upstairs! You know that, Connie! Since fourth grade, you've known it!

CONRAD. So?

LAZENBY. So you just make yourself look stupid when you let him get to you like that.

CONRAD (*quietly*). So I look stupid. Is that the message?

LAZENBY. No. No, it isn't. What is it with you, man? I thought we were friends.

CONRAD. Laze . . . we are friends.

LAZENBY (*upset*). Are we? Why're you shutting me out, then? Why do you want to be alone in this? Don't you care how I feel?

CONRAD (*hearing this for the first time*). I care—

LAZENBY (*interrupting*). Listen! I loved him, too . . . and I'm still here! (*Both are stunned by* LAZENBY's *admission.* CONRAD *stares at him.* LAZENBY *puts his hand over his eyes.*)

CONRAD (*all his anger drained away*). I know . . . but it just . . . hurts too much to be around you. I can't help it.

LAZENBY (*wearily*). So what am I supposed to do? Huh?

CONRAD. I don't know. (*Both look at each other for a long moment, then* CONRAD *turns away.*) I gotta go.

LAZENBY (*walking away slowly*). Yeah, okay. I'll see you around.

(CONRAD *turns back and watches* LAZENBY *go. He remains for a moment. As the lights begin to dim, he walks into the living room. It's night, so the room is dark. He stands for a few moments and feels how alone he is. He walks slowly to the mirror, studies himself, then smashes his fists on the mantelpiece. He turns away from the mirror and leans against the mantel, his head in his hands. After a moment, he lifts his head, walks to the telephone, and dials.*)

CONRAD. Hullo, Mrs. Pratt? Is Jeannine there? Oh . . . d'you know when she'll be back? Uh, huh . . . no, no, that's okay. I just . . . no, it wasn't anything special. Yeah, thanks. 'Bye. (*He hangs up the telephone, then suddenly picks it up again and dials.*) Hullo . . . This is Conrad. Jarrett. Hullo, Mr. Aldrich. Is Karen around? . . . What? . . . No . . . No, I didn't see the paper. I didn't . . . When? . . . Oh, God . . . I didn't know . . . I didn't know . . . (*The lights fade to black and* CONRAD *exits in the darkness.*)

T he stage is black. There is a repeated, desperate sound of a fist pounding against a door. The lights come up slowly on BERGER *in his office. Dressed in a T-shirt, light jacket, and jeans, he is unshaven and his hair is uncombed. He is putting on a pot of coffee and turns toward the pounding.*

BERGER. All right! All right! Just a minute . . .
(BERGER *goes to the door and admits* CONRAD, *who is dressed as he was in the previous scene. He looks exhausted and frantic.*)

CONRAD. God, I didn't think you were here!

BERGER. I said I'd come . . . Here . . . take it easy. (*He guides* CONRAD *to a chair.* CONRAD *takes the one behind the desk and sits with his elbows on the desk, his head in his hands.*)

CONRAD. Oh, geez, I feel so awful . . . I feel like I'm gonna die.

BERGER. What happened? Connie, what happened?

CONRAD. Karen . . . she killed herself . . . it was in the paper . . . . I didn't even see it . . . (*He breaks off and drops his head lower on his arms.*)

BERGER. How? What'd she do?

CONRAD (*raising his head, dazed*). She . . . carbon monoxide . . . in the car . . . in the garage . . . (*He shakes his head.*) . . . I don't believe this . . . I don't believe it!

BERGER (*going to stand next to* CONRAD *and putting his hand on* CONRAD's *shoulder*). Let it out, Con . . . just let it out.

CONRAD (*tightly, between his teeth*). I can't! You . . . keep trying to make me do this . . . I tell you, I can't!

BERGER. Is that what you came over here to tell me?

(CONRAD *puts his head down and begins to cry.*)

CONRAD. It's all . . . hanging over my head. I can't get through this!

BERGER. What? What's hanging over your head? Tell me.

CONRAD (*lifting his head, the tears streaming*). Buck! It's Buck! I killed him!

BERGER. How? How did you kill him?

CONRAD. I let him drown!

BERGER. How did you do that? You said he was a better swimmer than you . . . he was stronger . . . he had more endurance . . . What could you have done to keep him from drowning?

CONRAD (*slamming his fists into the desktop*). I don't know! I just know it was my fault! Don't you see? It's gotta be someone's fault . . . or what was the point of it? (*He stands and paces the room. He sits in another chair, then stands again. He turns toward berger as the lights pale to blue.*) I keep seeing it . . . I can't make it stop. Everything black and wet . . . I can't breathe. It's blowing so hard, I can't breathe. (*He moves about the room, looking for a direction, as he tries to find what he wants to say.*) The sail keeps snapping . . . cracking like a rifle. He keeps yelling at me from the stern. "Get it down! Get the sail down!" I can't. (*He pleads with* BERGER.) I can't do it! And all of a sudden we're dismasted and we're rolling . . . we both roll under . . . Oh, God! (*He covers his head with his hands.*) And then we're back up again, both of us . . . and I can see him hanging on. "Take off your shoes," he says, so I do it. (*He looks pleadingly at* BERGER.) I did everything he told me to do!

BERGER. I know . . . I know you did.

CONRAD. It's blowing like a tornado out there . . . it won't stop. (*He half-laughs, half-cries.*) He's jokin' with me . . . He's laugh-ing . . . He says, "We screwed up this time, buddy . . . Dad's gonna go nuts over this one!" (*He stops again, looks off into empty space, then speaks calmly, hopelessly.*) It ain't so damn funny, Buck. (*He sits in the armchair.*) And then it stops. It's calm . . . and it's raining. No light. I don't know where the hell we are . . . or how long it's been . . . a long, long time. He keeps calling me from the other side of the bow. "Connie," he says, "don't let go." And then . . . he stops calling me. He's . . . gone. I can't look. I know he's gone! (*He looks off into space.*) Man . . . why'd you let go?

BERGER (*quietly*). Because I got tired.

CONRAD. The hell! You never get tired!

BERGER. I couldn't help it.

CONRAD (*jumping out of the chair*). Well, screw you, then! (*He turns away from* BERGER *and sobs. He wraps his arms around himself. His head is bent as if he is in pain.*)

BERGER (*after watching* CONRAD *in silence for a moment*). It hurts to be mad at him, doesn't it?

CONRAD (*crying softly*). Yeah . . . He was . . . always screwin' around. He just . . . wasn't careful. He never could see how a bad thing might happen.

BERGER. Sometimes bad things happen even when people are careful.

CONRAD. We should've gone in sooner . . . when things started to look bad. We stayed out there too long.

BERGER. Okay. You made a mistake. How long are you going to punish yourself for that? When are you going to quit?

CONRAD. Oh, geez, I'd like to quit . . .

BERGER. Why don't you?

CONRAD (*shaking his head*). Because! It's not that easy!

BERGER. You've been in pain over this for a year and a half. It's time to stop, Connie.

It's past time.

CONRAD (exhausted, drained). It isn't fair . . . you just do one thing wrong . . .

BERGER. No, it isn't fair. And what happened to Karen isn't fair, either.

CONRAD (crying again). I wish I'd've known . . . if I just would've known . . .

BERGER. Connie, you can't take that one on, too.

CONRAD (fiercely). I'm not! That's not what I mean! Dammit, I feel bad about this! Now, you just . . . let me feel bad about this!

BERGER. Okay. (He gets up and goes to CONRAD.) Listen, I feel bad about it, too.

CONRAD (rocking in the chair, crying). It wasn't my fault . . .

BERGER. No. It wasn't your fault.

CONRAD (stopping the rocking, sitting up, wiping his eyes, and sighing deeply). It wasn't my fault. (As the lights begin to dim on BERGER's office, JEANNINE and LAZENBY are heard in the living room. Once the lights are out, BERGER and CONRAD exit.)

LAZENBY (unseen). What a liar you are! You're a liar!

JEANNINE (unseen, laughing). You'll get over it.

The lights come up on the living room. JEANNINE and LAZENBY are sitting at a card table. LAZENBY is looking at the five cards in his hand. He slams them down on the table.

LAZENBY. I can't believe it! You lied to me! You told me three queens and two sevens! You just out-and-out lied to me!

JEANNINE. What's the name of the game? Liar's Poker. Get in the game, Joe.

LAZENBY. Yeah, but my mom always told me that girls never lie.

(CONRAD enters with three cans of soda. He tosses one to LAZENBY, sets the second in front of JEANNINE, and opens his own.)

CONRAD. Hah!

JEANNINE. Hah? What does that mean? (CONRAD climbs over the back of the third chair and sits between the others at the table.)

CONRAD. Means "tell me about it." (He turns to LAZENBY.) Means "how'd she get you over here today in the first place?"

LAZENBY (musing). How did she get me over here? Oh, yeah! Your mom needed some painting done while she was out of town.

CONRAD. Uh, huh. (He looks at JEANNINE.) She told me you wanted help on your calculus.

LAZENBY. And you believed that? Me needing help from you?

CONRAD (grinning). Sure. Why not? I taught you just about everything you know, didn't I? How to serve a tennis ball . . .

LAZENBY. What a joke! Give me a break! Who taught you how to hit a hook shot?

JEANNINE (standing). You know, I'm so glad I did this. You guys need each other. You deserve each other. (She rests a hand on each of their shoulders.) Bless you both.

CONRAD. Hey, where're you going?

JEANNINE. I gotta teach the girls in choir how to play Liar's Poker. (She rubs her fingers together and grins.) I need some dough.

CONRAD. Why don't you stick around? My parents are coming in from Texas. They're due any minute. I'd like you to meet them.

JEANNINE. Let's save that for another day, Con. How about Sunday? Are we still going to the movies?

CONRAD (snapping his fingers). Geez, I can't.

LAZENBY AND CONRAD (in unison). We're playing golf. (They look at each other and laugh.)

JEANNINE. Okay. I can see I'm gonna have to compete for your time. (She takes her sweater from the back of her chair and slips it *on.* LAZENBY *stands up.*)

LAZENBY. I oughta go, too. Got a bunch of errands to run. I'll see you Sunday. Pick you up around nine.

CONRAD. Yeah, okay. (*He stands and he and* LAZENBY *look at each other for a moment.* CONRAD *extends his hand.*) Good to see you, man. (LAZENBY *looks at the hand, starts to extend his, brushes* CONRAD's *aside, and gives him an awkward hug.* CONRAD *slaps* LAZENBY's *shoulder in an excess of emotion and they break the embrace, embarrassed.* JEANNINE *watches and steps in to kiss* CONRAD *when he and* LAZENBY *separate.*)

JEANNINE. Gotta go. Call me.

CONRAD. I will. (JEANNINE *and* LAZENBY *move toward the door as* CONRAD *picks up the soda cans.*)

LAZENBY. C'mon, cheater. I'll give you a ride home.

JEANNINE. I didn't cheat, Joe. I lied. There's a difference. (CONRAD *follows them out.*)

(CONRAD *returns without the soda cans and puts the cards away. He begins to fold up the card table as* CAL *enters with the suitcases.*)

CAL. Hi! Didn't think you'd be home from school yet.

CONRAD. Hey, welcome back! How was your vacation?

CAL. Fine. Fine. How was yours?

CONRAD. Good. Okay.

CAL. You get along all right with your grandmother?

CONRAD. Oh, yeah. (*A pause*) Actually, Dad, it was a rough week. But things are better. I got a feeling they're going to get a lot better from now on.

CAL (*going to the bar and pouring himself a drink*). You do, huh? Well, that's good. I'm glad to hear it.

CONRAD. Where's Mom?

CAL. She's upstairs. (*He sits on the couch and holds his drink with both hands as he stares ahead.* CONRAD *senses that something is wrong.*)

CONRAD. How are Uncle Ward and Aunt Audrey?

CAL. Oh, fine. Your uncle's put on some weight. Everything gets bigger when you move to Texas. (*He and* CONRAD *laugh.*) Aunt Audrey dyed her hair. She's a redhead now. That was a shock, even for your mother. (*He lapses into silence.* CONRAD *waits a moment before talking.*)

CONRAD. Lazenby was here.

CAL (*looking up*). Oh, yeah? When?

CONRAD. Just now. We played some Liar's Poker.

CAL (*trying to be social although it's an effort*). Poker? With two?

CONRAD (*laughing*). No . . . well . . . somebody else was here. A girl. (*He speaks shyly.*) Her name's Jeannine.

CAL. Jeannine, huh? (*He suddenly gets the picture.*) Hey. You got a girl?

CONRAD (*laughing, embarrassed*). Yeah, I guess.

CAL. Over the weekend?

CONRAD. No. No. I've had her . . . I mean, I've known her for a while. I just didn't know she was my girl.

CAL (*lapsing back into his own thoughts*). Well, that's good. I'm glad . . . I'm glad things are going better for you.

CONRAD. Yeah . . . well, I've been thinking a lot while you were gone.

CAL (*not paying attention*). Good.

CONRAD (*hesitating*). And I'm thinking that we should sit down . . . all of us . . . and talk about some things. (*He realizes that*

CAL *is lost in his own thoughts.)* Dad? You listening?

CAL *(looking up, somewhat startled).* I guess not. Sorry.

CONRAD. Something wrong? Dad? Did something happen in Texas?

CAL *(standing up and moving back to the bar).* No, not in Texas.

CONRAD *(looking to the doorway).* What's Mom doing upstairs?

CAL. She's packing.

CONRAD. Packing? What for? You two going away again?

CAL. Not us. Just her.

CONRAD. I don't get it. You just got back.

CAL. Your mother's not happy here. She's decided to go away for a while to think things over.

CONRAD. What things? What's going on?

(BETH enters, dressed for travel, with a suitcase. Her coat is over her arm.)

BETH *(to CAL).* I called a cab.

CAL. You didn't have to do that.

BETH. There's no point in you driving all the way back to the airport.

CONRAD. Mom, what's going on?

CAL. I don't understand this, Beth. I don't understand you.

BETH. Oh, please! No more of this! No more of you looking at me with that "poor Beth" expression on your face.

CAL. I am not looking at you like that. I'm not even thinking that. Not even close!

BETH. I heard what you said to Audrey. I heard you telling her I need help.

CAL. We all need help in this, Beth. We need help. What the hell is wrong with admitting that?

BETH *(walking to the window and looking out).* There's the cab.

CONRAD. Mom! No! Wait! We have to talk!

CAL. Let her go, Con. It isn't the right time . . .

CONRAD. But she's leaving! There is no other time! Mom, listen—

BETH *(turning on CONRAD).* Listen to what? Talk about what? What is it you want to talk about?

CONRAD. Everything! We have to talk about what we feel! About everything! About Bucky!

BETH *(quickly turning away, her arms about herself).* Don't say his name to me like that! *(There is silence. CAL sets his glass down and faces away from CONRAD.)*

CONRAD *(calmly, controlling his tears).* I'm not trying to hurt you. I swear to God! I'm not trying to hurt you.

BETH *(turning back to CONRAD).* That's just it. You are hurting me. It doesn't matter whether you mean to or not.

CAL. Beth. . . .

BETH *(raising her hand).* No, Cal. Let me say this. *(To CONRAD)* Conrad, I don't know what this need of yours is. I don't know why you feel you have to do this.

CONRAD. Mom, it isn't just for me . . .

BETH. No? Then who is it for? Have you thought it all through? Have you thought about whether you're ready for all of my feelings about it?

CONRAD *(seriously, looking straight at BETH).* I don't know. I'll try.

CAL. We can all try, Beth.

BETH *(shaking her head).* No. It's over. There's no point in talking about it any-more. *(Calm once again, she is in control.)* I'll write you when I get to Ward and Audrey's. I'll let you know where I'm going. *(She gathers her things and picks up her suitcase.)*

CONRAD *(straightly).* I love you, Mom. Please don't go.

BETH *(looking at* CONRAD *for a long moment).* I love you, too. *(A pause)* Don't you see? It's got nothing to do with love. *(She exits.* CAL *follows her out.* CONRAD *stands, looking after them.)*

(After several moments, CAL *returns and walks over to the bar. He appears lost in thought.* CONRAD *watches in silence.)*

CONRAD *(tentatively).* I'm sorry.

CAL *(neutrally).* I am, too.

CONRAD. It's all my fault.

CAL. It's not.

CONRAD *(near tears).* Yeah, it is! I shouldn't have pushed her. I shouldn't have made her feel . . .

CAL *(turning to* CONRAD).* Connie, stop it. You didn't make her do anything. You can't. You don't have that kind of power over her. Neither do I. *(He turns back to the bar.)* I wish I did. I sure as hell would have used it.

CONRAD *(desperately).* But she can't be gone . . . She can't be gone for good!

CAL *(turning back to* CONRAD).* No. No . . . she's not gone for good.

CONRAD *(sitting in a chair).* But you don't know that for a fact, do you?

CAL *(wearily).* No. I don't know that for a fact.

CONRAD *(looking intensely at* CAL).* So. What do we do now?

CAL *(with a hopeless laugh).* I don't know. You tell me.

CONRAD *(tentatively).* Hey. That ain't the way it's supposed to work.

CAL. No?

CONRAD *(shaking his head).* You're the father. You're supposed to have a handle on everything. *(CAL laughs.)* I mean it. You always have. I've always admired you for that.

CAL *(shaken, bitter).* Well, don't admire people too much. They tend to disappoint you.

CONRAD. Man, I'm not disappointed. I couldn't be disappointed. *(He moves to* CAL *and puts his arms around him.)*

CAL. I love you, son. *(The lights fade to black.)*

CURTAIN

Discussing and Interpreting
Ordinary People

Play Analysis

1. What do you think Conrad's prospects are for complete mental health? Explain your answer.
2. Discuss two static characters in the play, explaining why they are static.
3. In the novel, Beth leaves without telling Conrad. Why do you think the playwright chose to create a scene in which the two say goodbye?
4. Write a short description of Dr. Berger in terms of his appearance, habits, and way of speaking and moving.
5. **Thematic Connection: Family Matters** Do the Jarretts strike you as "ordinary people"? Why or why not?

Literary Skill: Adaptation

Making an adaptation is a lot like translation. Instead of working with foreign languages, however, writers who dramatize stories or novels translate them from one literary form to another. Often scenes from the original work must be deleted because they cannot be staged or because they impede the flow of the drama. At other times, the playwright feels a new scene must be created, taking care to retain the integrity of the original work.

Imagine that you as the playwright feel that an encounter between Beth Jarrett and Dr. Berger will help round out the play. Write the dialogue for such an encounter. Be sure to include stage directions for the actors.

Performance Element: Acting

With a partner, read aloud a scene between two of the characters in the play. Keep in mind your character's background, age, self-identity, and motivation, as well as the complexity of the relationship between these two characters. You might want to look back to page 159 for tips on creating a character.

The Veldt

short story and play adaptation by Ray Bradbury

Creating Context:
Science Fiction/Science Fact

In 1950, when Ray Bradbury's short story "The Veldt" was first published, the idea of a "virtual reality" had no place in the public consciousness. Yet Bradbury—soon to be recognized as the master of the intricately written science fiction tale—seized upon the idea of people in the future living in a home run entirely by machine (a

machine with a human presence) and having experiences conjured up for them in the form of a "Happylife Electrodynamic Playroom." Like all good science fiction writers, Bradbury saw the possibilities science held out for us and applied that science to a future world of his own making. For science fiction is almost universally based upon science fact—or at the very least the potential that science offers. Bradbury has said of the science fiction genre: "It's the most important fiction ever invented. But people haven't given it credit. Because it has to do with the history of ideas."

Isaac Asimov, one of literature's best known and most admired science fiction writers, defined the genre this way:

"A science fiction story must be set against a society significantly different from our own—usually, but not necessarily, because of some change in the level of science and technology—or it is not a science fiction story … the science fiction story destroys our own comfortable society. The science fiction story does not deal with the restoration of order, but with change and, ideally, with continuing change…we leave our society and never return to it."

As you read *The Veldt* think about what makes this play solid science fiction.

As a Reader: Analyzing Science Fiction

Ray Bradbury wrote both the play you are about to read and the story it is based on. The "nursery" he writes about in the short story and the "playroom" being installed in the play have capabilities far beyond any such rooms in our society. But then, the Hadley's entire house has features that put our technology to shame.

Compare the two excerpts below. Ask yourself these questions: Why did Bradbury begin the play with the installation of the playroom rather than in the middle of things as in the short story? What elements are included in both?

from Page • • • • • • to Stage

" George, I wish you'd look at the nursery."

"What's wrong with it?"

"I don't know."

"Well, then."

"I just want you to look at it, is all, or call a psychologist in to look at it."

"What would a psychologist want with a nursery?"

"You know very well what he'd want." His wife paused in the middle of the kitchen and watched the stove busy humming to itself, making supper for four.

"It's just that the nursery is different now than it was."

"All right, let's have a look."

They walked down the hall of their soundproofed, Happylife Home, which had cost them thirty thousand dollars installed, this house which clothed and fed and rocked them to sleep and played and sang and was good to them. Their approach sensitized a switch somewhere and the nursery light flicked on when they came within ten feet of it....

from "The Veldt" by Ray Bradbury

GEORGE. Lydia! Lydia, come here!

(She appears, a woman about thirty-two, very clean and fresh, dressed simply but expensively.)

GEORGE *(waving).* Come on! It's almost ready!

(She joins him at the door as the humming, squealing dies. The ELECTRICIAN *slams the trapdoor, rises, and comes toward them with his kit.)*

ELECTRICIAN. It's all yours, Mr. Hadley … There's your new—how does the advertisement read?—Happylife Electrodynamic Playroom! And what a room!

LYDIA *(ruefully).* It ought to be. It cost thirty thousand dollars.

GEORGE *(taking her arm).* You'll forget the cost when you see what the room can do.

ELECTRICIAN. You sure you know how to work it?

GEORGE. You taught me well!

ELECTRICIAN. I'll run on, then. Wear it in health! *(exits)*

GEORGE. Good-bye, Tom.

(GEORGE turns to find LYDIA staring into the room.)

GEORGE. Well!

LYDIA. Well…

GEORGE. Let me call the children!

from The Veldt by Ray Bradbury

As a Technical Director: Creating the Future

Staging a science fiction play calls for different technical elements than a play by Shakespeare or a contemporary light comedy. The technical director must work to set the proper atmosphere using light, sound, and other technical resources. As you read *The Veldt*, think about lighting, sounds, and other technical elements you would use to enhance the play.

The Veldt

Time
The future

The Characters
GEORGE HADLEY
LYDIA HADLEY
A married couple

PETER and WENDY
Their children

DAVID MACLEAN
A psychiatrist

AN ELECTRICIAN

SECRETARY'S VOICE
WEATHER VOICE

Setting
A large empty playroom and living quarters

*T*he curtain rises to find a completely empty room with no furniture of any kind in it. This room encompasses the entire front half of the stage. Its walls are scrim which appear when lighted from the front, vanish when lighted from the rear. In the center of the room is a door which leads to the living quarters of a house circa 1991. The living quarters dominate the entire rear half of the stage. There we see armchairs, lamps, a dining table and chairs, some abstract paintings. When the characters in the play are moving about the living area, the lights in the "empty" room, the playroom, will be out, and we will be able to see through into the back quarters of the house. Similarly, when the characters enter the empty playroom, the lights will vanish in the living room and come on, in varying degrees, as commanded, in the play area

At rise of curtain, the playroom is dimly lit. An ELECTRICIAN, *bent to the floor, is working by flashlight, fingering and testing electrical equipment set under a trapdoor. From above and all around come ultrahigh-frequency hummings and squealings, as volume and tone are adjusted.*

GEORGE HADLEY, *about thirty-six, enters and moves through the living area to look through the playroom door. He is fascinated, delighted in fact, by the sounds and the flicker of shadows in the playroom. He looks out through the fourth wall,[1] as he will do often in the play, and treats the audience area, on all sides, as if it were the larger part of the playroom. Much lighting, and vast quantities of sound, will come from the sides and back of the theater itself. At last, excited, GEORGE turns and calls.*

GEORGE. Lydia! Lydia, come here!

(She appears, a woman about thirty-two, very clean and fresh, dressed simply but expensively for a housewife.)

GEORGE *(waving).* Come on! It's almost ready!

(She joins him at the door as the humming and squealing dies. THE ELECTRICIAN *slams the trapdoor, rises, and comes toward them with his kit.)*

ELECTRICIAN. It's all yours, Mr. Hadley.

GEORGE. Thanks, Tom.

*(*THE ELECTRICIAN *turns to point a screwdriver into the room.)*

ELECTRICIAN. There's your new—how does the advertisement read?—Happylife Electrodynamic Playroom! And *what* a room!

LYDIA *(ruefully).* It ought to be. It cost thirty thousand dollars.

GEORGE *(taking her arm).* You'll forget the cost when you see what the room can do.

ELECTRICIAN. You sure you know how to work it?

GEORGE. You taught me well!

ELECTRICIAN. I'll run on, then. Wear it in

health! *(Exits)*

GEORGE. Good-bye, Tom. (GEORGE *turns to find* LYDIA *staring into the room.)* Well!

LYDIA. Well …

GEORGE. Let me call the children! *(He steps back to call down a hall.)* Peter! Wendy! *(Winks at his wife)* They wouldn't want to miss this.

(The BOY *and the* GIRL, *twelve and thirteen, respectively, appear after a moment. Both are rather pale and look as if they slept poorly.* PETER *is engrossed in putting a point to his sister as they enter.)*

PETER. Sure, I know, I know, you don't like fish. OK. But fish is one thing and fishing is something else! *(Turning)* Dad and I'll catch whoppers, won't we, Dad?

GEORGE *(blinking).* What, what?

PETER *(apprehensively).* Fishing. Loon Lake. You remember … today … you promised …

GEORGE. Of course. Yes.

(A buzzer and bell cut in. A TV screen, built into one wall at an angle so we cannot see it, flashes on and off. GEORGE *jabs a button. We see the flickering shadows on his face as the screen glows.)*

GEORGE. Yes?

SECRETARY'S RADIO VOICE. Mr. Hadley …

GEORGE *(aware of his son's eyes).* Yes? yes …

SECRETARY'S VOICE. A special board meeting is called for eleven. A helicopter is on its way to pick you up.

GEORGE. I … thanks. (GEORGE *snaps the screen off, but cannot turn to face his son.)* I'm sorry Peter. They own me, don't they?

*(*PETER *nods mutely.)*

LYDIA *(helpfully).* Well, now, it isn't all bad. Here's the new playroom finished and ready.

GEORGE *(hearing).* Sure, sure … you children don't know how lucky you are.

---

1. fourth wall, an imaginary wall between the stage and the audience

(The CHILDREN *stare silently into the room, as* GEORGE *opens the door very wide so we get a good view.*)

WENDY. Is that all there is to it?

PETER. But—it's *empty*.

GEORGE. It only *looks* empty. It's a machine, but more than a machine! (*He has fallen into the salesman's cadence as he tries to lead the* CHILDREN *through the door. They will not move. Perturbed, he reaches in past them and touches a switch. Immediately the room begins to hum. Slowly,* GEORGE HADLEY *steps gingerly into the room.*) Here, now. Watch me. If you please. (GEORGE *has addressed this last to the ceiling, in a pompous tone. The humming becomes louder. The* CHILDREN *wait, unimpressed.* GEORGE *glances at them and then says, quickly:*) Let there be light. (*The dull ceiling dissolves into very bright light as if the sun had come from a cloud! Electronic music begins to build edifices[2] of sound. The* CHILDREN, *startled, shield their eyes, looking in at their father.*) Paris. The blue hour of twilight. The gold hour of sunset. An Eiffel Tower, please, of bronze! An Arc de Triomphe of shining brass! Let fountains toss forth fiery lava. Let the Seine be a torrent of gold! (*The light becomes golden within the room, bathing him.*) Egypt now! Shape pyramids of white-hot stone. Carve Sphinx from ancient sand! There! There! Do you see, children? Come in! Don't stand out there! (*The* CHILDREN, *standing on either side of the door, do not move.* GEORGE *pretends not to notice.*) Enough! Begone! (*The lights go out, leaving only a dim light spotted on* GEORGE's *face. The electronic music dies.*) There! What do you think, eh?

WENDY. It's great.

GEORGE. Great? It's a miracle, that's what it is. There's a giant's eye, a giant's ear, a giant's brain in each of those walls, that remembers every city, town, hill, mountain, ocean, every birdsong, every language, all the music of the world. In three dimensions, by God. Name anything. The room will hear and obey.

PETER (*looking steadily at him*). You sound like a salesman.

GEORGE (*off balance*). Do I? Well, no harm. We all have some melodrama in us needs bleeding out on occasion. Tones the system. Go in, kids, go on. (WENDY *creeps in a toe.* PETER *does not move.*) Peter, you heard me! (*Helicopter thunder floods the house. All look up. Huge shadows flutter in a side window.* GEORGE, *relieved, breaks, moves from the room.*) There's my helicopter. Lydia, will you see me to the door?

LYDIA (*hesitating*). George … ?

GEORGE (*still moving*). Have fun, kids! (*Stops, suddenly, thinking*) Peter? Wendy? Not even "Thanks"?

WENDY (*calmly*). Thanks a lot, Dad. (*She nudges* PETER, *who does not even look at his father.*)

PETER (*quietly*). Thanks …

(*The* CHILDREN, *left behind, turn slowly to face the door of the playroom.* WENDY *puts one hand into the room. The room hums, strangely, now, at her approach. It is a different sound from the one we heard when* GEORGE *entered the place. The hum now has an atonal quality.*)

(WENDY *moves out into the empty space, turns, and waits for* PETER *to follow, reluctantly. The humming grows.*)

WENDY. I don't know what to ask it for. You. Go ahead. Please. Ask it to show us something.

(PETER *relents, shuts his eyes, thinks, then whispers.*)

WENDY. What? I didn't hear you.

PETER. The room did. Look.

(*He nods. Shadows stir on the walls, colors dilate.*

---

2. edifices, walls or buildings, in this case, imaginary

The CHILDREN *look about, obviously fascinated at what is only suggested to the audience.)*

WENDY. That's a lake. *Loon* Lake!

PETER. Yes.

WENDY. Oh, it's so blue! It's like the sky turned upside down. And there's a boat, white as snow, on the water! It's moving toward us. *(We hear the sound of water lapping, the sound of oars at a distance.)* Someone's rowing the boat.

PETER. A boy.

WENDY. Someone's behind the boy.

PETER. A man.

WENDY. Why, it's you, and Dad!

PETER. Is it? Yes. Now we've stopped, the lines are out, fishing. *(Suddenly excited)* There. I've caught a big one! A big one! *(We hear a distant splash of water.)*

WENDY. It's beautiful. It's all silver coins!

PETER. It's a beaut, all right. Boy! Boy!

WENDY. Oh, it slipped off the line! It's gone!

PETER. That isn't—

WENDY *(disappointed)*. The boat … it's going away. The fog's coming up. I can hardly see the boat … or you or Dad.

PETER. Neither can I …

WENDY *(forlorn)*. The boat's gone. Bring it back, Peter.

PETER. Come back! *(An echo, way off, repeats his words. The playroom grows dimmer.)* It's no use. The room's broken.

WENDY. You're not trying. Come back! Come back!

PETER. Come back!

*(*LYDIA *enters on this last, slightly concerned.)*

LYDIA. Peter, Wendy? Is everything all right?

PETER. Sure, swell …

LYDIA *(checks her watch)*. Have you tried Mexico yet? The instructions book said the most wonderful things about the Aztec ruins there. Well! I'll be downtown at 10:45, at Mrs. Morgan's at 11:30, at Mrs. Harrison's at noon, if you should want me. The automatic lunch timer will go off at 12:15; eat, both of you! At one o'clock do your musical tapes with the violin and piano. I've written the schedule on the electric board—

PETER. Sure, Mom, sure—

LYDIA. Have fun, and don't forget Bombay, India, while you're at it!

(She exits and is hardly gone when: a thunderous roar ensues. PETER, *throwing out one hand, pointing at the walls, has given a shout.)*

PETER. All right! Now! Now! Now!

(An unseen avalanche thunders down a vast mountain in torrents of destruction. WENDY *seizes* PETER's *arm.)*

WENDY. Peter!

PETER. Now! More! More!

WENDY. Peter, stop it!

(The avalanche filters away to dust and silence.)

WENDY. What are you doing? What was that?

PETER *(looks at her strangely)*. Why, an avalanche, of course. I made an avalanche come down a mountain, a hundred thousand tons of stone and rocks. An avalanche.

WENDY *(looking about)*. You filled the lake. It's gone. The boat's gone. You and Dad are gone.

PETER. Did I? Is it? Are they? *(Awed)* Yeah … sure … that's right. Hey, this is … *fun* … *(He accents this last word oddly.)* You try something now, Wendy.

WENDY. I—London Bridge. Let me see— London Bridge. *(The shadows spin slowly.* PETER *and* WENDY *stand, watching.)*

PETER. You're stupid. That's no fun. Think, girl, think! Now! Let's see. *(A beat)* Let there be darkness! Let there be—night!

(Blackout)

(The lights come up. We hear a helicopter come down, fly away. GEORGE *enters, stage left.)*

GEORGE. Hi! I'm home!

(In a small alcove, which represents only a section of the kitchen, far stage right, LYDIA *is seated staring at a machine that is mixing something for her.* GEORGE *advances across the stage.)* Hi! How goes it?

LYDIA *(looking up).* Oh, hello. Fine.

GEORGE. Perfect, you mean. Flying home just now I thought, Good Lord, what a house! We've lived in it since the kids were born, never lacked for a thing. A great life. Incredible.

LYDIA. It's incredible, all right, but—

GEORGE. But what?

LYDIA. This kitchen. I don't know. It's—selfish. Sometimes I think it'd be happy if I just stayed out, stayed away completely, and let it work. *(She tries to smile.)* Aren't I silly?

GEORGE. You are indeed. All these time-saving devices; no one on the block has half as many.

LYDIA *(unconvinced).* You're right, of course. *(She pauses.)* George … I want you to look at the playroom.

GEORGE. Look at it? Is it broken? Good Lord, we've only had it eight weeks.

LYDIA. No, not broken, exactly. Well, see it first, then you tell *me. (She starts leading him across the stage.)*

GEORGE. Fair enough. Lead on, Macduff.

LYDIA. I first noticed this "thing" I'm going to show you about four weeks ago. Then it kept reoccurring. I didn't want to worry you, but now, with the thing happening all the time—well—*here. (She opens the playroom door.* GEORGE *steps in and looks as across a great distance, silently.)*

GEORGE. Lord, but it's quiet.

LYDIA. Too quiet, yes.

GEORGE. Don't tell me. I know right off. This is—Africa.

LYDIA. Africa.

GEORGE. Good Lord, is there a child in the world hasn't wanted to go to Africa? Is there one exists who can't close his eyes and paint the whole thing on his inner lids? High blue deep warm sky. Horizons a billion miles off in the dust that smells like pulverized honeybees and old manuscripts and cloves and cinnamons. Boma-trees, veldtland. And a lush smell. Smell it?

LYDIA. Yes.

GEORGE. That must mean a water hole near-by, bwana. *(Laughs)* Oh, Lydia, it's perfect, perfect! But—the sun—damn hot. Look, a perfect necklace of sweat right off the brow! *(Shows her)* But I've lost the point. You brought me here because you were worried. Well—I see nothing to worry about.

LYDIA. Wait a moment. Let it sink in.

GEORGE. Let *what* sink in? I—

(Shadows flick over their faces. He looks quizzically up. She does, too, with distaste. We hear a dry rustling leathery sound from above; distant strange bird cries.)

LYDIA. Filthy things.

GEORGE *(looking up, following the circling birds).* What? Vultures? Yes, God made his ugliest kites on the day he sent those things sailing. Is *that* what worries you?

LYDIA. That's only part of it. Look around.

(GEORGE turns slowly. There is a heavy, rich purring rumble from off to the right. GEORGE blinks and smiles.)

GEORGE. It couldn't be—the lions?

LYDIA. I think so, yes. I don't like—having lions in the house.

GEORGE *(amused).* Well, they're not exactly in the house, dear. There! Look at that big male. Face like a blast furnace at high noon, and a mane like a field of wheat. Burns your eyes to look at him. There's another—a female—*and* another, a whole pride—isn't that a fine word? A pride—a regular tapestry of lions woven of gold thread and sunlight. *(An afterthought)* What are they up to? *(He turns to* LYDIA, *who is watching the unseen beasts, disquieted.)*

LYDIA. I think they're—feeding.

GEORGE. On what? *(Squints)* Zebra or baby giraffe, I imagine.

LYDIA. Are you certain?

GEORGE *(shielding his eyes)*. Well, it's a bit late to be certain of anything. They've been lunching quite some time. No—lunch is over. There they go toward the water hole! *(He follows with his eyes.)*

LYDIA. George? On our way down the hall just now … did you … hear a scream from in here?

GEORGE *(glances at her)*. A scream? No. For God's sake—

LYDIA. All right. Forget it. It's just, the lions won't go away.

GEORGE. What do you mean? Won't go?

LYDIA. Nor will Africa, either. George, the fact is the room has stayed that way for thirty-one days. Every day that same yellow sun in the sky. Every day the lions with teeth like daggers dusting their pelts out there, killing, slavering on the red-hot meat, printing their bloody tracks through the trees, killing, gorging, over and over, no day different, no hour any change. Doesn't it strike you as odd that the children never ask for a different locale?

GEORGE. No! They must love Africa as all kids do. The smell of violence. Life stark, raw, visceral.[3] Here, you, hey! Hey! *(He snaps his fingers, points, snaps his fingers again. He turns smiling to* LYDIA.) You see, they come to pay their respects.

LYDIA *(nervously; gasps)*. Oh, George, not so close!

(The rumbling of the lions is very loud now; to the right, we feel the approach of the beasts. The light from the right side of the room becomes more brightly yellow.)

GEORGE. Lydia, you're not afraid?

LYDIA. No, no, it's just—don't you *feel* it? It's almost as if they can see us!

GEORGE. Yes, the illusion is three-dimensional. Pure fire, isn't he? There. There. *(Holds out his hands)* You can warm yourself at a hearth like that. Listen to him breath, it's like a beehive swarming with yellow. *(He stretches one hand further out.)* You feel you could just—reach—and run your hands over the bronze, the gold—

LYDIA *(screams)*. Look out!

(There is a fearful snarling roar. The shadows race in the room. LYDIA *falls back, runs;* GEORGE, *startled, cannot stop her, so follows. She slams the door and falls against it. He is laughing. She is almost in tears.)*

GEORGE. Lydia, dear Lydia!

LYDIA. George, they almost—

GEORGE. Almost what? It's machinery, electronics, sonics, visuals!

LYDIA. No, *more*! Much more! Now listen to me, I insist, I insist, do you hear, that you warn the children this playing in Africa must cease!

GEORGE *(comforting, kissing her)*. OK, I'll talk to them.

LYDIA. Talk to them, no; lay down the law. Every day for a month I've tried to get their attention. But they just stroll off under that damned hot African sky! Do you remember that night three weeks ago when you switched the whole room off for twenty-four hours to punish the children?

GEORGE *(laughing quietly)*. Oh, how they hated me for that. It's a great threat. If they misbehave, I'll shut it off again.

---

3. visceral, instinctive

LYDIA. And they'll hate you again.

GEORGE. Let them. It's perfectly natural to hate your father when he punishes you.

LYDIA. Yes, but they don't say a word. They just look at you. And day by day, the playroom gets hotter, the veldtland wider and more desolate, and the lions grow big as the sun.

(There is an awkward moment. Then a buzzer rings, loudly. GEORGE *presses a panel in the wall. A loudspeaker bell sounds, there is a faint crackle and:)*

PETER'S VOICE. Mom, we won't be home for supper.

WENDY'S VOICE. We're at the automation show across town, OK?

GEORGE. I think that—

PETER'S VOICE. Swell!

WENDY'S VOICE. Keen! *(Buzz ding! Silence.* LYDIA *stares at the ceiling from which the voices came.)*

LYDIA. No hellos, no good-byes, no pleases, no thank-yous.

*(*GEORGE *takes her hand.)*

GEORGE. Lydia, you've been working too hard.

LYDIA. Have I really? Then why is something wrong with the room, and the house and the four people who live in the house? *(She touches the playroom door.)* Feel? It trembles as if a huge bake oven were breathing against it. *(She takes her hands off, burnt.)* The lions—they can't come out, can they? They can't?

*(*GEORGE *smiles, shakes his head. She hurries off.)*

GEORGE. Where are you going?

(She pauses near the door.)

LYDIA. Just to press the button … that will make us our dinner. *(She touches the wall panel. The lights go out. End of scene.)*

I n the dark, music. As the light comes up dimly again we find GEORGE in his easy chair, smoking his pipe, glancing at his watch, listening to the hi-fi system. After a moment, impatiently, he gets up and switches off the music. He moves next to the radio, switches it on, listens to a moment of news.

WEATHER VOICE. Weather in the city tomorrow will be 66 in the morning, 70 in the afternoon, with some chance of rain.

(He cuts this off, too, checking his watch. Next he switches on a TV screen to one side, its face away from us. For a moment, the ghostly pallor of the screen fills the room. He winces, shuts it off. He lights his pipe. There is a bell sound.)

LYDIA'S VOICE. George, are you in the living room?

GEORGE. I couldn't sleep.

LYDIA. The children *are* home, aren't they?

GEORGE. I waited up for them—*(Finishes lamely)* Not yet.

LYDIA. But it's midnight! I'll be down in a minute—

GEORGE. Don't bother—

(But the bell has rung. LYDIA *has cut off.* GEORGE *paces the floor, taps out his pipe, starts to reload it, looks at the playroom door, decides against it, looks again, and finally approaches it. He turns the knob and lets it drift open.)*

(Inside the room it is darker. GEORGE *is surprised.)*

GEORGE. Hello, what? Is the veldt gone? Wait—no. The sun's gone down. The vultures have flown into the trees far over there. Twilight. Bird cries. Stars coming out. There's the crescent moon. But where—? So you're *still* there, are you? *(There is a faint purring.)* What are you waiting for, eh? Why don't you want to go away? Paris, Cairo, Stockholm, London, they and all their millions of people swarmed out of this room when told to leave. So why not you? *(Snaps his fingers)* Go! *(The purring* *continues.*) A new scene, new place, new animals, people! Let's have Ali Baba and the Forty Thieves! The Leaning Tower of Pisa! I demand it, room! *Now!* (*A jackal laughs off in the darkness.*) Shut up, shut up, shut up! Change, change, now! (*His voice fades.*) … now …

(*The lions rumble. Monkeys gibber from distant trees. An elephant trumpets in the dusk.* GEORGE *backs off out the door. Slowly he shuts the door, as* LYDIA *enters stage left.*)

GEORGE. You're right … the fool room's out of order. It won't obey.

LYDIA. Won't or *can't?* (*She lights a candle on a table to one side.*)

GEORGE. Turn on the light. Why do you fuss with candles like that?

(*She looks at the flame as she lights a second and a third candle.*)

LYDIA. I rather like candles. There's always the chance they will blow out and then I can light them again. Gives me something to do. Anything else in the house goes wrong, electronic doors don't slide or the garbage disposal clogs, I'm helpless and must call an engineer or a photoelectric brain surgeon to put it right. So, as I think I said, I like candles.

(GEORGE *has seated himself.* LYDIA *turns to come to him now.*)

LYDIA. George, is it possible that since the children have thought and thought about Africa and lions and those terrible vultures day after day, the room has developed a psychological "set"?

GEORGE. I'll call a repair man in the morning.

LYDIA. No. Call our psychiatrist.

(GEORGE *looks at her in amazement.*)

GEORGE. David Maclean?

(*The front door springs open,* PETER *and* WENDY *run in laughing.*)

PETER. Last one there's an old maid in a clock factory!

WENDY. Not me, not me!

GEORGE. Children! (*The children freeze.*) Do you know what time it is?

PETER. Why, it's midnight, of course.

GEORGE. Of course? Are you in the habit of coming in this late?

PETER. Sometimes, yes. Just last month, remember, you had some friends over, drinking, and we came in and you didn't kick up a fuss, so—

GEORGE. Enough of that! We'll go into this late hour business again. Right now I want to talk about Africa! The playroom …

(*The children blink.*)

PETER. The playroom … ?

(LYDIA *tries to do this lightly.*)

LYDIA. Your father and I were just traveling through African veldtland; lions, grass, water holes, vultures, all that.

PETER. I don't remember any Africa in the playroom. Do you, Wendy?

WENDY. No …

(*They look at each other earnestly.*)

PETER. Run see and come tell.

(WENDY *bolts.* GEORGE *thrusts out his hand.*)

GEORGE. Wendy!

(*But she is gone through the door of the playroom.* GEORGE *leaps up.* PETER *faces him calmly.*)

PETER. It's all right, George. She'll look and give us a report.

GEORGE. I don't want a report. I've seen! And stop calling me George!

PETER (*serenely*). All right—Father.

GEORGE. Now get out of the way! Wendy!

(WENDY *runs back out.*)

WENDY. It's not Africa at *all!*

(GEORGE *stares, astonished at her nerve.*)

GEORGE. We'll see about that!

(He thrusts the playroom door wide and steps through, startled. Lush green garden colors surround him in the playroom. Robins, orioles, bluebirds sing in choirs, tree shadows blow on a bright wind over shimmering banks of flower colors. Butterfly shadows tatter the air about GEORGE's face which, surprised, grows dark as he turns to the smiling children; they stop smiling.)

GEORGE. You—

LYDIA. George!

GEORGE. She changed it from Africa to this!

(He jerks his hand at the tranquil, beautiful scene.)

WENDY. Father, it's only Apple Valley in April—

GEORGE. Don't lie to me! You changed it! Go to bed!

(PETER takes WENDY's hand and backs out of the room. Their parents watch them go, then turn to be surrounded again by green leaf colors, butterfly shadows, and the singing of the birds.)

LYDIA. George, are you sure you didn't change the scene yourself, accidentally?

GEORGE. It wouldn't change for me or you. The children have spent so much time here, it only obeys them.

LYDIA. Oh, God, I'm sorry, sorry, sorry you had this room built!

(He gazes around at the green shadows, the lovely flecks of spring light.)

GEORGE. No. No, I see now, that in the long run, it may help us in a roundabout way, to see our children clearly. I'll call our psychiatrist first thing tomorrow.

LYDIA (relieved). Good, oh good … (They start to move from the room. LYDIA stops and bends to pick something from the floor.) Wait a moment.

GEORGE. What is it?

LYDIA. I don't know. What does it look like, to you?

GEORGE (touches it). Leather. Why, it must be—my old wallet!

LYDIA. What's happened to it?

GEORGE. Looks like it's been run through a machine.

LYDIA. Or else—it's been chewed. Look, all the teethmarks!

GEORGE. Teethmarks, hell! The marks of cogs and wheels.

LYDIA. And this?

(They turn the wallet between them.)

GEORGE. The dark stuff? Chocolate, I think.

LYDIA. Do you?

GEORGE (He sniffs the leather, touches it, sniffs again.) Blood.

(The room is green spring around and behind them. The birds sing louder now, in the silence that follows the one word he has pronounced. GEORGE and LYDIA look around at the innocent colors, at the simple and lovely view. Far away, after a moment, we hear the faint trailing off of one scream, or perhaps two. We are not quite certain. GEORGE quickens.)

LYDIA. There! You heard it! This time, you *did!*

GEORGE. No.

LYDIA. You did. I know you did!

GEORGE. I heard nothing, nothing at all! Good Lord, it's late, let's get to bed! (He throws the wallet down, and hurries out.)

(After he is gone, LYDIA picks up the shapeless wallet, turns it in her hands, and looks through the door of the playroom. There the birds sing, the green-yellow shadows stir in leaf patterns everywhere, softly whispering. She describes it to herself.)

LYDIA.… flowering apple tree … peach blossoms … so white …

(Behind her, in the living room, GEORGE blows out one candle.) … so lovely …

(He blows out the other candle. Darkness. The scene is ended.)

(After a moment of silence and darkness, we hear a helicopter thunder down outside the house. A door opens. When it shuts, the lights come on, and

GEORGE *is leading* DAVID MACLEAN *on.*)

GEORGE. Awfully nice of you to come by so early, David.

DAVID. No bother, really, if you'll give me my breakfast.

GEORGE. I'll fix it myself—or—rather—almost fix it myself. The room's there. I'm sure you'll want to examine it alone, anyway.

DAVID. I would.

GEORGE. It's nothing, of course. In the light of day, I see that. But—go ahead. I'll be right back.

(GEORGE *exits.* MACLEAN, *who is carrying what looks like a medical kit, puts it down and takes out some tools. Small, delicate tools of the sort used to repair TV sets, unorthodox equipment for a psychiatrist. He opens a panel in the wall. We see intricate film spools, lights, lenses there, revealed for the first time.* MACLEAN *is checking it when the playroom door opens and* PETER *comes out. The boy stops when he sees* MACLEAN.)

PETER. Hello, who are you?

DAVID. David Maclean.

PETER. Electronics repair?

DAVID. Not exactly.

PETER. David Maclean. I know. You read the bumps on people's heads.

DAVID. I wish it were that simple. Right now I've come to see what you and your sister have written on the walls of this room.

PETER. We haven't written—oh, I see what you mean. Are you always this honest?

DAVID. People know when you lie.

PETER. But they don't! And you know why? They're not listening. They're turned to themselves. So you might as well lie, since, in the end, you're the only one awake.

DAVID. Do you really believe that?

PETER (*truly amazed*). I thought everyone did! (*He grabs the playroom door as if to go back in.*)

DAVID. Please.

PETER. I must clean the room.

(DAVID *steps between him and the door.*)

DAVID. If you don't mind, I'd *prefer* it untidy.

(PETER *hesitates. They stare each other down.*)

PETER. All right. It doesn't matter. Go ahead.

(PETER *walks off, circling once, then runs, gone.*)

(MACLEAN *looks after the boy, then turns to the door of the playroom, and slowly opens it. From the color of the light inside the room we can sense that it is Africa again. We hear faint lion sounds, far off, and the distant leather flapping of wings.* MACLEAN *looks around for only a moment, then kneels on the floor of the room where he opens a trapdoor and looks down at intricate flickering machineries where firefly lights wink and glow and where there is oiled secretive motion. He touches this button, that switch, that bit of film, this sprocket, that dial. In obedience to this, the light within the room gets fierce, oven-white, blinding as an atomic explosion, the screams get a bit louder, the roaring of the lions louder.* MACLEAN *touches into the paneling again. The roars get very loud, the screams very high and shrill, over and over, over and over, as if repeated on a broken phonograph record.* MACLEAN *stands riven. There is a tremendous rustling of wings. The lion rumble fades. And as silence falls, the color of the walls of the room is stained by crimson flowing red until all is redness within the room, all is bleeding sunset light upon which, slowly, slowly, with grim thoughtfulness,* DAVID MACLEAN *closes the trapdoor and backs out into the living room area.*)

(LYDIA *enters with a tray on which is breakfast coffee and toast. When she sees that* MACLEAN *is deep in thought, she says nothing, puts down the tray, pours coffee for three, at which point* GEORGE *enters and frowns when he sees* MACLEAN'S *deep concern. The husband and wife look at each other, and wait.* MACLEAN *at last comes over, picks up his coffee, sips it thoughtfully, and at last speaks.*)

MACLEAN. George ... Lydia ... (*He hesitates a*

moment, drinks more coffee, prepares himself.) When I gave my approval of your building that playroom it was because the record in the past with such playrooms has been exceptionally good. They not only provide imaginative atmospheres wherein children can implement their desires and dreams, they also give us, if we wish, as parents, teachers, psychiatrists, the opportunity to study the patterns left on the walls by the children's minds. Road maps, as it were, which we can look at in our leisure time to see where our children are going and how we can help them on their way. We humans are mostly inarticulate; there is so much we wish to say we cannot say, so the rooms, and the walls of such rooms, offered a way of speaking out with the silent tongue of the mind. In ninety-nine cases out of hundred, it works. Children use the rooms, parents observe the blueprints marked on the walls of the rooms, and everyone is happy. But in this case—*(He stops.)*

LYDIA. This case?

MACLEAN. I'm afraid the room has become a channel *toward* destructive thoughts rather than a release away from them. George … Lydia … why do your children hate you so much?

LYDIA *(surprised).* Hate us? They don't hate us!

GEORGE. We're their parents!

MACLEAN. Are you really? Let's see.

(MACLEAN paces the room, pointing out this door, indicating that machine panel, or another here or there.)

MACLEAN. What kind of life do you lead? Machines make your bed, shine your shoes, blow your noses for you. Machines listen for you, learn for you, speak for you. Machines ventilate your house, drive you down the street at ninety miles an hour, or lift you straight up into the sky, always away and away from your home. I call on

the phone and another machine answers, pre-recorded, and says you're not here. How long has it been since you got out of your car and walked with your children to find your *own* air, which means air no one else has breathed, outside of town? How long since you flew a kite or picked do-it-yourself wild strawberries? How long? How long? How long? *(MACLEAN sits. The parents are silent. Unnoticed, PETER and WENDY have come into the door at the far side of the room. MACLEAN drinks his coffee and finishes, as quietly as possible, thus:)* You haven't been around. And since you haven't been around, this house and its machines, that playroom has become the only available garden where your children can take root. But when you force-grow flowers in a mechanical greenhouse, don't be surprised if you wind up with exotic orchids, strange tiger lilies or Venus's flytraps.

GEORGE. What must we do?

MACLEAN. Now, very late, after playing an idiot Father Christmas for years, I'm going to ask you to play what will seem like Ebenezer Scrooge to your children.

(GEORGE rises up and turns toward the playroom door.)

GEORGE. You want me to switch off the room?

MACLEAN. The room, the house, the damned "sprinklers" in the lawn! Get out, stay out, get away; send the kids to me for treatment, but better yet, treat them yourselves. Look at them with your eyes, show them your faces, talk to them not on the intercom, but let them feel your warm breath in their ears, comb their hair with your fingers, wash their backs with your hands, sing to them, run with them a little way before they run so far ahead they run out of your lives.

(GEORGE moves toward the door.)

GEORGE. But if I switch off the room, the shock—

MACLEAN. Better a clean, hard shock now than letting the kids get any further from reality.

GEORGE. Yes … yes … (*He opens the door of the room. Crimson light pours out. The walls inside bleed with running color. Reacting to this,* GEORGE *kneels to the panel in the floor and tears at it.*)

(*Suddenly,* PETER *stands out from the door.*)

PETER. George! No!

(MACLEAN *and* LYDIA *are on their feet at this.*)

MACLEAN. Hold on, George. Not with the children here.

(GEORGE *whips the panel open.* PETER *leaps forward and slams it shut.*)

PETER. No, George, no, no!

MACLEAN. Listen to me—wait!

GEORGE. Get out of the way.

PETER. George!

GEORGE (*evenly*). Don't call me George.

(*He thrusts the boy aside, gets the panel open, but the boy is scrabbling now. Screams well out from the walls of the scarlet room in a tidal blast.* MACLEAN *and* LYDIA *freeze as the boy and* GEORGE *fight over the switches. Heat shimmers, animal heartbeats ricochet from walls, avalanches of zebras panic away with okapi, gazelle, and wildebeest, thundering, shrieking.* GEORGE *knocks* PETER's *hands off, twists and shoves him, and hits all the switches at once. There are great elephant trumpetings, a final cry from many creatures now struck by electronic death, dying … The sounds run down like a phonograph record. In a flush of red light, all the colors of the room dissolve like oil down the walls into the floor as blood might be let from a flask. Silence. The room shadows into darkness.* GEORGE *slams the trap and locks it with his key and stands on it. The only sound is* PETER's *sobbing and crying, slumped by* GEORGE.)

PETER. You! You!

GEORGE (*to himself*). Yes … me … me!

PETER (*rising*). You killed them! You killed them! I hate you! I wish you were dead! I wish you were dead!

(GEORGE *slaps his face.* PETER *holds his cheek, startled, then jumps and runs from the room.* WENDY, *bewildered, at the door, follows.* GEORGE *holds out a key to no one in particular.*)

GEORGE (*barely audible*). Lock the door. (LYDIA *does so.* GEORGE *holds out other keys.*) Now … turn off the stoves, the voice clocks, the talking books, the TVs, the telephones, the body scrubbers, the bedmakers—turn off everything!

(LYDIA *takes the keys, looks at* GEORGE's *face, and hurries away.* MACLEAN *looks after her.*)

MACLEAN. No, George. That was badly handled. Brutal … brutal! (MACLEAN *hurries off after* LYDIA.)

(GEORGE, *alone, rests his head against the playroom door, listening, eyes closed.*)

GEORGE (*to himself*). Brutal? Yes, but dead! Are you dead in there?! Good. (*Tiredly*) Good … (*He moves away across the room, exhausted, and at the door turns to look back at the door.*) I wonder, does the room hate me, too? Yes … it must. Nothing ever likes to die. Even a machine. (*He exits. Blackout.*)

Music in darkness. A small bedlight comes slowly up after half a minute. We see LYDIA *in bed at the front of the stage. A dark scrim has come down between the bed and the set in back, so we do this scene in-one.* LYDIA *rouses.*

LYDIA. George? (*She sees him to stage left now, back turned, in his dressing robe, looking out an imaginary window, smoking.*) Can't sleep?

GEORGE. Who can?

LYDIA. Not me, anyway.

GEORGE. It's after midnight.

LYDIA. Yes. Listen. the house is so still. (*She sits up, listening.*) It used to hum all the time, under its breath … I never quite guessed the tune … though I listened for years and tried to hum the same way, I never learned… .

GEORGE. Thank God for small favors. Good Lord, it was strange, walking around, shutting off all the heaters and scrubbers and polishers and washers. For an hour there, the house felt like a cemetery, and me its keeper. That's past now. I'm adjusting.

LYDIA. The children will, too. They cried themselves to sleep, but they will forgive us. (*She sits up listening as if she had heard something.*)

LYDIA. There's no way for them to—tamper—with the room, is there?

GEORGE. Tamper?

LYDIA. I just don't want them doing anything down there, messing about, rearranging things—they couldn't do anything to the room, could they?

GEORGE. *To* the room? What would they want to do *to* the room? Anyway, there's a lot of electricity in those walls with all the machinery. They know better than to mess, and get a nasty shock.

LYDIA (*She listens again, and breaks up her own mood by trying to be jocular.*) Oh, I'm glad we're leaving tomorrow, mountains, fishing, everything out in the open again after years.

GEORGE. Dave said he'd bring his helicopter round after breakfast and take us to the lake himself. Good old Dave! (GEORGE *comes back to sit on the edge of his wife's bed.*) Lydia?

LYDIA. Yes?

(*He takes her hand. He kisses her on the cheek. She jerks away suddenly.*)

GEORGE. What is it?

LYDIA. Oh, listen, listen!

(*Far away, the sound of running antelope, the roar of lions.*)

WENDY AND PETER (*very remote*). Help! Mother! Father! Help! Help!

LYDIA. The children!

GEORGE. The playroom! They must have broken into it!

PETER AND WENDY (*remote*). Mother! Father, help, oh, help!

LYDIA. Peter! Wendy!

GEORGE. Kids! Kids! We're coming! We're coming!

(*The parents rush off into darkness, as the lights go off over the bed. In the dark the voices continue.*)

PETER. Father, father, quick! Quick!

GEORGE. Peter, Wendy!

LYDIA. Children, where are you?

WENDY. Here, oh, here!

(*The lights flash on;* GEORGE *and* LYDIA *rush in through the playroom door.*)

GEORGE. They're in the playroom!

LYDIA. Peter! Wendy!

(*Once inside the door they peer around.*)

LYDIA. That's strange …

GEORGE. I'd have sworn—

(*They look about to left and right and straight ahead through the fourth wall, at the audience.*)

LYDIA. George, it's—Africa again, the sun, the veldt, the vultures …

(*She backs off,* GEORGE *half turns and as he does so, the door slams shut behind them.* GEORGE *leaps toward it.*)

GEORGE. Damn door. A draft must have— (*Locks click outside.* GEORGE *tries the lock, beats at the door.*) It's locked!

LYDIA. It can't be! There's no way for it to lock itself!

GEORGE (*thinking*). No… no … Peter? Wendy?

LYDIA. George, over there, under the trees …

GEORGE. Kids, open up … I know you're out there.

LYDIA. The lions … they're walking out into the sun …

GEORGE (*shaking the door*). Peter, Wendy, now don't be ridiculous. Unlock this door!

(*The light is getting brighter in the room; the sun is blazing from above. The sound of the rustling vulture wings grows louder. Shadows flash across the faces of* GEORGE *and* LYDIA. *The rumbling of the lions is nearer.*)

LYDIA. George, the lions, they're running toward us!

(GEORGE *looks out through the fourth wall, grows uneasy, somewhat panicky, and bangs at the door.*)

GEORGE. It's all right, Lydia. Children, damn you, you're frightening your mother, open up! You hear?

LYDIA. Running! Running! Near! Near!

GEORGE. Peter!

LYDIA. Oh, George, the screams, the screams. I know now what I never said … the screams were familiar … the voices … because the voices, the screams were us, you and me, George, you and me …

GEORGE. No! Kids! Hear me! (*He bangs the door, turns, freezes, horrified.*)

LYDIA. George, stop them running, stop them, stop, stop! (*She throws up her hands to guard her face, sinks to her knees.*) They're going to jump! Stop, stop!

GEORGE. No, they can't, they can't! No! No!

(*The light blazes, the lions roar! A great shadow rushes from the audience, as if the lions, in a solid pack, were engulfing the stage in darkness! Swallowing blackness takes all light away. In the* darkness, LYDIA *and* GEORGE *scream and scream. Then abrupt silence, the roar, the bumbling purr of the yellow beasts fading away. After a long while of silence, a helicopter lands nearby. We hear* DAVID MACLEAN *calling in the darkness.*)

MACLEAN (*easily*). George! Lydia! I'm here! George? Lydia?

(*The lights come slowly up. We are still inside the playroom. Seated facing the audience on two corduroy pillows are* PETER *and* WENDY, *their faces impassive, as if they had gone through all that life might ever do to them and were beyond hearing, seeing, feeling. On a pillow between them are small cups and saucers, a sugar and creamer set, and a porcelain pot.* WENDY *holds one cup and saucer in her frozen hands, as does* PETER. *The door to the playroom opens.* MACLEAN *peers in, does not see the children immediately.*)

MACLEAN. George—

(*He stops, peering off into the distance, as across a veldt. We hear the faint roar of lions. He hears the flap of vulture wings sailing down the sky, and looks up into the burning sun, protecting his eyes. Then at last he looks over at the children, sees them, and in his face is the beginning of realization, of horror, of insight into what they have done.*)

MACLEAN (*slowly*). Peter? … Wendy … ?

(PETER *turns his head slowly to look beyond the man.*)

PETER. Mr. Maclean.

(WENDY *turns more slowly, in shock, to hold out before her the small cup, her eyes blind to any sight, her voice toneless.*)

WENDY. A cup of tea?

(*Blackout*)

THE END

Discussing and Interpreting

The Veldt

Play Analysis

1. Do you think there are elements in your life that mirror the Hadley's way of living?
2. What does Lydia mean when she calls the kitchen "selfish"?
3. What technical elements would you use to create a sense of the African veldt on stage?
4. Write a short retelling of the story from the viewpoint of David Maclean.
5. **Thematic Connection: Family Matters** What mistakes do you think the parents in the play made? Explain your answer.

Literary Skill: Compare Genres

Below is the ending of the short story "The Veldt." Compare this ending to that of the play. Which ending gives you more of a jolt? Which do you think is more effective and why? (Note that the spelling of McClean's name was changed in the play.)

> He stared at the two children seated in the center of the open glade eating a little picnic lunch. ...He began to perspire. "Where are your father and mother?"
>
> The children looked up and smiled. "Oh, they'll be here directly."
>
> "Good, we must get going." At a distance Mr. McClean saw the lions fighting and clawing and then quieting down to feed in silence under the shady trees. He squinted at the lions with his hand up to his eyes.
>
> Now the lions were done feeding. They moved to the water hole to drink.
>
> A shadow flicked over Mr. McClean's hot face. Many shadows flickered. The vultures were dropping down the blazing sky.
>
> "A cup of tea?" asked Wendy in the silence.

Performance Element: Production

Analyze the script and work up a design that shows the visual environment for the entire play. Determine how you would light and use color in the opening and closing scenes and indicate this in your design.

Sir Gawain and the Green Knight

from the Middle English legend
adapted for the stage by Dennis Scott

Creating Context:
Knights of the Round Table

Legend has it that in 516 A.D. a small lad named Arthur became King of England after he alone was able to pull the great sword Excalibur from its secure place in a stone. From that day forward, King Arthur began to gather around him a

society of brave and noble knights at Camelot, his palace and court. Arthur and his knights became the living symbols of valor, honor, and courtly conduct.

Robert Wace first described the legend of King Arthur and his Round Table in 1155. Wace asserted that Arthur created the table in this shape so as to establish equality among the knights. Because each was as brave and true as the next, they had to be assembled so that no one would be at the head. In the later 1400s, Sir Thomas Malory, a knight himself, gathered information about Arthur's exploits and those of his knights and wove a unified narrative. Full of nostalgia for a way of life then ending—a life based on a code of chivalry whose virtues included chastity, courtesy, courage, and loyalty—Malory's account, published after his death by William Claxton, was given the title

Le Morte d'Arthur (*The Passing of Arthur*).

Sir Gawain is but one of the many legendary knights of Camelot. He was knighted at Arthur's wedding to Guinevere, and such other stalwart fellows as Galahad, Tristram, Gareth, Percivale, Geraint, and Lancelot served alongside him. Indeed, it is told that Sir Gawain and Sir Lancelot became avowed enemies, and it was Gawain's revenge against Lancelot that helped bring about Camelot's downfall. He was struck a mortal blow by Lancelot, but repented his hatred as he lay dying. Gawain is said to be buried in Dover Castle in England.

The story of Sir Gawain and his encounter with the Green Knight is considered by many one of the earliest and finest written accounts of the Middle English period (about 1066 to 1485). No one knows the real name of the original author of *Sir Gawain and the Green Knight*, but he is called the "Pearl Poet" because of his poem *The Pearl*. As you read the play, be aware of the poetry and the imagery used by playwright Dennis Scott to tell the heroic story.

As a Reader: Understanding Imagery

Imagery uses concrete words or details to appeal to our senses of sight, sound, touch, smell, and taste. Read the excerpts from the legend (left) and the play (right) and compare the images. Which do you find most vivid? Note that the CONTEUR is a kind of narrator.

from Page · · · · · · to Stage

"In faith," quoth the good knight, "Gawain am I, who give thee this buffet, let what may come of it; and at this time twelvemonth will I take another at thine hand with whatsoever weapon thou wilt, and none other."

Then the Green Knight swiftly made him ready; he bowed down his head, and laid his long locks on the crown that his bare neck might be seen. Gawain gripped his axe and raised it on high; the left foot he set forward on the floor, and let the blow fall lightly on the bare neck. The sharp edge sundered the bones, smote through the neck, and clave it in two, so that the edge of the steel bit on the ground, and the head rolled even to the horse's feet. The blood spurted forth, and glistened on the green raiment, but the knight neither faltered nor fell; he started forward with outstretched hand, and caught the head, and lifted it up...

from *Sir Gawain and the Green Knight* translated by Jessie L. Weston

GAWAIN. Before these lords, and you, I hereby swear to meet you, to receive a blow again, next year!

GREEN. Gawain! This is indeed a pleasure! I've heard so much about you. Now, show me your measure.

GAWAIN. Where shall I find you in a year, Sir Green?

GREEN. Oh, here and there—after you've swung my axe, I'll tell you where.

(GAWAIN *beheads the* GREEN KNIGHT.)

CONTEUR. The axe whirrs through. The neck is ringed with red!

COMPANY. The clear blade cleaved skin.

Flesh. Bone.

The great neck split.

The green head slammed the stone.

The red blood rushed like rain to the grey floor.

The wind sighed in on a silence through the door.

The head rolled round. The bright green man stood dead.

ARTHUR. Well done!

GUINEVERE. Gawain, well done!

GREEN. Give me my head.... .

from *Sir Gawain and the Green Knight* adapted by Dennis Scott

As an Interpreter of Text: Going Beyond the Spoken Word

The National Theatre of the Deaf was commissioned to create this play in 1977. Most of the actors in the company are deaf. They use American Sign Language, and created a new theatrical form based on this visual language. As you read the play, be aware of ways text could be conveyed through gesture and visual imagery.

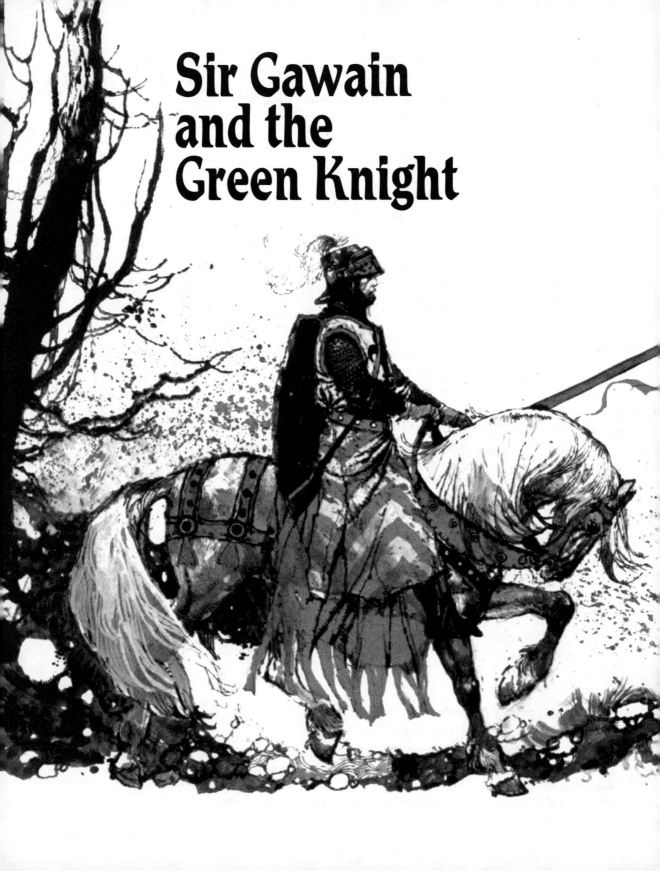

Sir Gawain and the Green Knight

Time

Medieval England

The Characters

CONTEUR / KING ARTHUR
SIR GAWAIN
BERCILAK / GREEN KNIGHT
ALISON / BIRD / GUINEVERE
GRINGOLET / DEER / BOAR / FOX
GUEST AT CAMELOT / SERVANT AT BERCILAK'S
GUEST AT CAMELOT / SQUIRE
DEER / BOAR / FOX

Setting

The Plains of Northern England
Camelot
Bercilak's Castle

GAWAIN *and* GRINGOLET *are fighting the wind, mist in their eyes: falling, getting up again.* CONTEUR *watches them, from far away.*

GAWAIN. In the name of God, is someone there?

(ALISON, *the bird, swoops and soars over. Watches them.*)

CONTEUR. Only a red bird, battling the wind, melts into mist. Be calm, Gawain. Help is coming. Oh, the cold!

(*Bird flies away, on a curved path, enters* BERCILAK's *castle, alights. Turns three times. Becomes a woman.*)

BERCILAK. Is he close?

ALISON. He's here.

BERCILAK. Now, then. Light the candles. Let the castle blaze like a diamond in Gawain's dark. He will come to us across the snowfield.

(*They light candles, torches, lamps. Set them in windows.*)

CONTEUR. That's right, make yourself small, by that tree. He's come a long, long way, this brave wanderer. Look, on the high hill a huge castle, every light burning. If the wind blows the mist clear for a moment, he will see it, and find safety! (*He blows a gust of wind toward* GAWAIN.) There.

GAWAIN. Gringolet! Look! A fine castle! You'll spend Christmas in warm straw, after all!

(*Man and horse begin to move against the wind towards the lights of the castle.*)

CONTEUR. Let nothing surprise you in this legend. There are knights, and magic, and lovely ladies, and adventure. Gawain will keep a promise, break a bond, and learn a lesson. For like all good stories, this marvellous adventure has—a moral!

Now he stands at the moat … Can you see the turrets and towers? The drawbridge is up. The walls are high, hewn from hard stone, smooth as glass. And the windows are shining like tall candles on the glittering white oak trees.

GAWAIN. I pray you shelter! I come in peace!

BERCILAK. Who goes? Friend or foe?

GAWAIN. Sir Gawain, knight of King Arthur's court! Sick from the cold, I seek your fire!

BERCILAK. I bid you come in joy! My name is Bercilak.

ALISON. Alison joins her Lord in welcome!

BERCILAK. Sound the trumpets! A noble knight is here, in need of friendship.

CONTEUR. And suddenly the windows and battlements of that great house were filled with lords and ladies, calling their greetings—"A Christmas guest! A Christmas guest! A guest at the gate! Welcome!" They dropped the drawbridge—it thundered down to the other side, and the great gates swung open.

GAWAIN. He walked in front of his weary horse like a prince, across the bridge to the castle, and servants ran out to stable his steed.

BERCILAK. Off with his armour! Attend my Lord!

(*A rug is spread.* GAWAIN *steps on it. He is divested of sword, gloves, helmet, breastplate unlaced, thigh armour unstrapped, steel shoes unbuckled, and a great cloak thrown round him.*)

ALISON. They took his sword and his shield.

BERCILAK. … and led him into the great warm hall; the torches were shining on his golden helmet, and on the shield he had carried with the perfect star. Each sharp point of that endless figure showed his perfection—

ALISON. Prepare him a place close to the fire.

SERVANT. And under the holly branches in the hall, Bercilak, his gracious host, hailed him.

CONTEUR. They led him to a table, and

washed his hands. The white cloth that seven ladies had sewn, embroidering it for seven winters, fell like snow on the fine wood. They set out silver spoons, and a dish of salt. And men hastened to make that table heavy with hot baked meats and fresh sweet breads.

BERCILAK. My apologies to you—we have eaten already, and this is all we have. Ah, but tomorrow we will feed you fairly!

(ALISON *serves wine, tastes it, presents it to* GAWAIN.)

GAWAIN. Your servant, Ma'am.

ALISON. Ah, what elegance, what grace!

BERCILAK. Sir, the ladies of my house will be delighted that you honour us with your presence.

ALISON. You will break every maiden's heart, Sir Gawain—we have heard of your gallantry!

GAWAIN. Ma'am, I'm a soldier, I break heads, not hearts!

BERCILAK. Well said! My Lady Alison, more wine!

CONTEUR. In the great hall under the tapestries shining with old tales of victory and death, the other courtiers danced the night away. Oh, what giving of gifts, what taking of favours! What fair women, what stealing of kisses—what music! What honest mirth! You couldn't hear the wind outside, howling like lost souls in the lonely dark. The stones echoed with laughter. And wrapped in their fine furs, spoke Gawain the gentle knight, and Alison, and my Lord Bercilak.

BERCILAK. Of course, you'll stay the winter?

GAWAIN. I cannot, sir.

ALISON. Where do you go?

GAWAIN. I travel north.

BERCILAK. Still further north? This is the edge of the world—go further and you come by places that the wise man does not wish to pass! The Magic Hills—

ALISON. Only the wolves go there, and they tremble for fear.

BERCILAK. Did your King, Arthur, send you?

GAWAIN. No, sir. It is a game that brings me here. I cannot stay.

ALISON. A game? So far from home, at Christmas tide?

CONTEUR. Listen! The dancers laughing, like silver blessings!

BERCILAK. Dance with my Lord. I'll leave you to my Lady.

(BERCILAK *exits.* GAWAIN *and* ALISON *dance.*)

CONTEUR. A maiden's heart grows weary,
A-watching by the fire,
To see the young men stride away
A-seeking their desire.
For the winter rocks are cruel sharp
And the blood is on the snow—
Oh, won't you stay at home with me,
And watch the heroes go?

GAWAIN. My Lady, you go light as a bird.

ALISON. Ah, Sir Gawain, you are a flatterer!

GAWAIN. A gay red bird! One followed me north all December.

ALISON. But birds fly south in winter! It was magic, I'm sure. You should have killed it. Those things are dangerous!

GAWAIN. It was a living thing, and kept me company in my adventures! I gave it food when there was food to give.

ALISON. How sad the music is …

GAWAIN. I wish to live! But I must keep my honour, and be bold.

CONTEUR. And here now is the tale that Gawain told …

GAWAIN. Christmas at Camelot. Fifteen days' feasting.
What a coming and going, what to-ing and fro-ing!
Dancing at night—joy at its height,
Wooing and fighting, ladies delighting in fashion and passion,
Chapel bells ringing, minstrels singing.

Dandies decked out in the latest attire—
No time for sorrow, no time for tears!
Young and old laughing their lives away
Through days of gold
And at the very center of that gorgeous
ring—
Queen Guinevere, and that most grave
and gracious ruler of the court, Arthur
the King!

ARTHUR. Sit down to dinner, my Lords and
Ladies. Give thanks to our savior for love-
liness and life; and make you merry!

GUINEVERE. Eat, drink and be warm.
Sit you down, friends, and feast!
Camelot greets you.
Come from the west or east–
Merriment meets you!
Drink to the fair and bold,
Drink to the young and old,
Camelot's call–
Welcome to all!

GAWAIN. God save the King!

(Enter GREEN KNIGHT*)*

GUINEVERE. You should have heard the
silence fall, like a fox-fur on the winter
fields …

GREEN. He was green, all over. From the
smallest hair to the ends of his fingers.
Like grass. (GREEN KNIGHT *moves slowly
round, peering into faces.)*

CONTEUR. And on one hip he had an axe of
pale green steel, hammered fine as a razor,
four feet wide. Green. Like spring, and
bound with vines like a young tree. Green.

GREEN. His beard was like moss.

GUINEVERE. And the Green Man wore no
shoes on his bright green feet, but his
tunic blazed with birds, and butterflies,
and jewels like leaves. Green.

CONTEUR. Only his eyes shone like two
flowers of fire. *(Pause)*

GREEN. Where is the King? Where is the
lord of this lovely company?

ARTHUR. I wear that crown, sir. I am Arthur.
Welcome. Feast with us till the day goes
down, sir.

GREEN. I have no wish to stay. I've come to
play. Some little, dangerous game. Some
little sport. I've heard so much about this
valiant court.

ARTHUR. A challenge! Excellent! Choose
your opponent, valour is our delight, sir!
Every man here is ready to fight, sir!

GUEST. The truth is, not a man had stirred.

GREEN *(laughs).* If I wanted to fight, I'd harvest out this gathering before night! No,
no. Fighting is not my reason. I come to
entertain you at this Christmas season.
Here's my axe. And here I stand. Wanted:
A man to chop me once with this. Just one
blow. I won't resist!

GUINEVERE. What?

ARTHUR. Quiet!

GREEN. One eager warrior is all I ask, to give
his best. After he's swung, I'll give him
back one blow. A fair exchange. A
Christmas jest! *(Pause)*

GUEST. Silence … Well, what would *you* do?

GUINEVERE. You'll give him back one blow?

GREEN. Not right away. Say, in a year. In one
year's time, today. *(Silence)* King Arthur's
Court. What a surprise! All these brave
warriors! Will no one rise?

GUEST. Each famous fighter sits still as a
mouse.

ARTHUR. This is folly. I won't be made a fool
of in my house! Come play!

GUINEVERE. My Lord!

GAWAIN. My Lord!

GREEN. My Lord!

ARTHUR. Stay where you are!

GAWAIN. My King! I am the least of all, in
deeds, in name. This foolish business fits
my station, not your fame! I pray you, let
me play the Green Man's game! *(Pause)*

COMPANY. Take care …

ARTHUR. Now do exactly what he said. That way you'll save our reputation, and your head!

GREEN. Before you strike, tell me, who cuts me down?

GAWAIN. Gawain.

GUINEVERE. A knight of great renown!

GREEN. So. Speak your bond.[1]

GAWAIN. Before these lords, and you, I hereby swear to meet you, to receive a blow again, next year!

GREEN. Gawain! This is indeed a pleasure! I've heard so much about you … Now, show me your measure.

GAWAIN. Where shall I find you in a year, Sir Green?

GREEN. Oh, here and there—after you've swung my axe, I'll tell you where.

(GAWAIN *beheads the* GREEN KNIGHT.)

CONTEUR. The axe whirrs through. The neck is ringed with red!

COMPANY. The clear blade cleaved skin. Flesh. Bone.
The great neck split.
The green head slammed the stone.
The red blood rushed like rain to the grey floor.
The wind sighed in on a silence through the door.
The head rolled round. The bright green man stood dead.

ARTHUR. Well done!

GUINEVERE. Gawain, well done!

GREEN. Give me my head. (GAWAIN *strides forward, picks it up.*) My axe. (*Takes it.*) My lords. I take my leave. There is a chapel in the north, a place most fair and green as trees; a green that will not fade. Follow, and take the bargain of my blade. I look to welcome you at the New Year! Seek me till I am found. All heard you swear! (*He goes.*)

CONTEUR. And that is Gawain's story, that is what moves him to ride so far from Camelot …
In Bercilak's house the Christmas guests are gay. Gawain, hear what the fire and the dancers say:

ALISON AND BERCILAK. There's magic in the mountains,
There's danger on the hill,
And those who seek adventure
Fall down, and soon are still.
The daring go away to dark,
It brings the bravest low—

ALISON. Oh, won't you stay at home with us
And let the young men go?
Good Gawain, stay with us!

GAWAIN. My Lady, if only I could. But I must come on the Green Chapel within three days, or break my bond.

ALISON. You're close. Too close. By horse, you'll come on it against the mountain not more than seven miles away.

CONTEUR. Surely that place has nothing holy housed there.

ALISON. It is a place to pass by, not to stay.

GAWAIN. That is its name? Green Chapel?

ALISON. So men say.

GAWAIN. Then it is settled. I have sworn.

ALISON. How sad the music sounds …
(*Pause*)

GAWAIN. Lady, let me sleep. The road was long.

ALISON. My dear, brave knight!

CONTEUR. What a charming hostess!

BERCILAK. Stay with us, here, till you must travel to keep your tryst.

CONTEUR. Observe her smile …

BERCILAK. This house is yours to take your ease in, till the year goes out.

CONTEUR. Look at her languid eyes …

GAWAIN. You are too kind.

---

1. bond, promise

ALISON. Three days, then go.

CONTEUR. Mark how the man's heart melts.

GAWAIN. So beautiful.

ALISON. So brave.

BERCILAK. She flutters like a bird …

CONTEUR. Gawain, beware!

BERCILAK. Our friend is sad!

ALISON. Then cheer him with a game!

BERCILAK. Well, I go hunting every day from now till season's end. Each evening I will give whatever I have gained to you.

CONTEUR. Observe his smile.

BERCILAK. —but you must give me what you get that day!

CONTEUR. Is not that an amusing game to play?

BERCILAK. A courtly game, to pass the time away!

GAWAIN (laughs). My witty host! How can a man be sad when all around delight to make him glad?

CONTEUR. Settled! The bird is in the net.

ALISON. To bed!

CONTEUR. A second bond is made. The rules are set. Gawain may have to give more than he'll get!

(BERCILAK summons a page. There are good night salutations. GAWAIN is led to his room with a lamp.)

COMPANY. Now may the Savior's mercy send sleep
Calm and deep.
Bring my soul bright
Clear into morning light.
May no harm fall
To any here at all.
Amen!

(GAWAIN sleeps.)

CONTEUR. Hear now about the first day's hunting of the heart. In the dim dawn he was dreaming …

DEER. Outside the hounds and the hunters came through the cold air. The great bucks flashed dew from their horns listening to the hue and cry; then broke from cover and outran the wind down the wild valley.

GAWAIN. Sure, someone is at the door! What bird rustles into my room? (ALISON enters.) What does she want? What shall I do?

CONTEUR. Back to bed. Close your eyes, Gawain!

DEER. The shy deer waits motionless in the cold morning, scenting danger.

GAWAIN. Who's there? (Pulls the covers up over himself)

ALISON. I've caught you, warrior!

GAWAIN. My Lady Alison! Fair morning to you!

ALISON. My dear prisoner!

DEER. The dogs are near.

GAWAIN. I surrender!

ALISON. No, no! I surrender! Take me! I can't resist!

DEER. Now the deer turns, head lifted.

GAWAIN. I had to think fast, of course. How to say no?

ALISON. I lay all night beside my Lord, wanting to come to you. I'm yours!

GAWAIN. Alison, dear Lady, I don't deserve you!

DEER. The deer's breath makes plumes of frost on the sharp air.

CONTEUR. She takes his hand. Her heart flutters like a bird.

ALISON. How many women are praying to be in my place!

DEER. Over the crags, slipping between the trees, the hooves are rattattatting over the snow. Echoes. Echoes! Run …

ALISON. The castle is buzzing with talk of your beauty.

GAWAIN. Thank God you chose a husband so much better than me. There must be a way out!

ALISON. Why do you hide your face from me?

GAWAIN. I am humbled by the honour you have paid me. May the Lord repay you, Lady.

ALISON. And is that all, my love?

DEER. The deer is tired now. The chase is almost over.

GAWAIN. I shall remember this moment on New Year's Day, as I go to my death.

CONTEUR. Well done, Gawain!

ALISON. Forgive my selfishness. You so near death—no wonder you have no heart for love!

GAWAIN (*sighs*). Ah, my Lady.

ALISON. I shall force myself on you no more. (*Rises*) I have shamed myself. (*Sobs*)

DEER. Somewhere, there must be safety!

ALISON. Gawain … ? Kiss me, then I'll go.

GAWAIN. I obey as a good knight should, when his love instructs him. (*Clutches the covers round him*)

ALISON. Come then.

DEER. The deer is in the open. Close behind, Bercilak bursts through the trees, smelling the blood already. The arrow notches in the bowstring. The deer stands still. Nowhere to go now.

(ALISON *tries to kiss* GAWAIN *on the mouth. At the last moment he bows his head, and she kisses him on the forehead. He sinks to one knee.*)

The arrow speeds on a following wind to the wild deer's forehead.

BERCILAK (*enters with a deer*). Gawain, Gawain! Here's a full day's harvest! I've dragged home a deer.

GAWAIN. Welcome, my Lord!

BERCILAK. Now you must give me what you got today!

GAWAIN. Here is what I received! (*Kisses him on the forehead*)

BERCILAK. No more?

GAWAIN. No more, my Lord.

BERCILAK. Now tell me true, where did your skill win such a gentle trophy? Whisper to me her name!

GAWAIN. God save, good friend, under our bargain, that's not yours to claim!

BERCILAK. You're right, of course. I wish you'd tell me; yet I must admit, you've fully paid your debt.
Behold, my lords and ladies fair, a faithful knight before us here!
Give Gawain praise, for he is pure—
What nobleman could ask for more?
He gives me that,
I grant him this—a deer is surely worth a kiss!
Fetch wine! Bring food! We'll laugh the night away!

CONTEUR. And so another night of feast and jest, a good night prayer, and then once more to rest. Darkness. The hunting of the second day.

(GAWAIN *paces restlessly.*)

BOAR. Sounds in the darkness. Dogs. Beware the boar.

CONTEUR. Moments ago, he woke to hear the dogs. The warriors are gone. The rest of the castle sleeps. Except—

GAWAIN. Someone. Outside my room again.

CONTEUR. Quick, into bed!

BOAR. I'm away, I'm away, running easy, by the marshes, by the pools in the forest. A black, hot shadow in the black of morning.

(ALISON *enters. Sits on the bed.*)

ALISON. Good morrow, Gawain. Awake so soon?

GAWAIN. I wish you a day of delight, my Lady.

ALISON. No! No!

GAWAIN. Forgive me, Alison. Good morrow, love!

ALISON. You've forgotten the lesson in love I provided. All you seem to think about is goodness and holiness. Politeness escapes you!

GAWAIN. What did I learn, sweet Alison?

ALISON. Kissing, of course.

BOAR. At the foot of the cliff, among the rocks, the boar pauses.

ALISON. When a lady looks for it, you must offer it.

BOAR. Trapped? Do they dare to think I'll wait for them to come dealing me death? The sky grows blood. Away.

GAWAIN. I, I couldn't dare to ask!

ALISON. The brave Sir Gawain!

GAWAIN. If you denied me, I should die of grief!

ALISON. How could any woman deny you anything? —and you're so strong!

GAWAIN. Indeed, I woke this morning with a pain in my leg. Cramp, perhaps; all that dancing last night. I'm no match for anyone today.

ALISON. Oh, my poor pupil. Here, let me massage it.

GAWAIN. No, please! Oh. Oh.

(She massages his thigh and calf.)

BOAR. Quick, through the woods. The sunlight slants down through the trees. I know where I'm going. There's a rocky hole over the river. Home.

ALISON. What powerful muscles. I'm sure whatever you wanted you could take from a poor defenseless maiden.

GAWAIN. But threats and force are very bad manners between friends.

ALISON. Ah, but between friends, there's no need! One need only ask!

(The massage is proving, apparently, very pleasant.)

GAWAIN. Well then, between friends, ask.

BOAR. He waits now down by the river, sharpening his tusks. Under the cliff.

CONTEUR. The hunters are reining their horses. They're afraid!

(ALISON nibbles GAWAIN's ear. He likes it, but controls himself. He crosses away from the bed.)

ALISON. How can you have me here twice, and never a word of love?

BOAR. From his bright scabbard, Bercilak brings out a sword. No closer. I will kill.

ALISON. I know what it is. You think me unworthy.

BOAR. The river stands between us. It flings back the day in a hundred glittering knives of sunlight.

ALISON. You think me stupid.

BOAR. The red scarves of the hunters drift like blood in the still river air. The sun is up! The horses shiver in fear.

GAWAIN. Sweet Alison, you are as beautiful as Guinevere. Were I your lover, I would never roam.

ALISON. Then teach me love, till Bercilak comes home!

BOAR. Bercilak is going into the river. Battle then! Blood.

GAWAIN. You flatter me. But how can I teach you? All I can do is serve you.

ALISON. Come then. Serve.

(GAWAIN crosses to her, strokes her hand, kisses it.)

CONTEUR. The great boar rushes into the water. It foams white.

BOAR. Die, man!

(ALISON kisses his cheek, and exits sinuously.)

CONTEUR. The sword cuts through.

(GAWAIN runs to the door. She is gone.)

GAWAIN. Virgin Mother, Guard from sin Without the castle, and within …

(BERCILAK enters.)

BERCILAK. I have brought back a boar. Complete your bond. (GAWAIN kisses him on the cheek.) And is that all?

GAWAIN. One more. (GAWAIN kisses him on the ear.)

BERCILAK. The prizes grow more precious! I thank you.

COMPANY. The season of merriment swings to its close,

Fragile as beauty, sweet as the rose.

Eat, drink, rejoice. Man's life is brief,

Falls like the flower, light as a leaf.

Lord keep us pure within this place.

Let all here sleep and wake within His grace.

CONTEUR. Frost, and a huge red sun. The third day rises. (GAWAIN *sleeps restlessly.*) White clouds. Under the clouds, white trees. Sunlight. Moving more swiftly than the clouds, the dogs are running—

FOX. D'you think it's me they're hunting for? Sniff. Sniff. Low and sleek, the fox is slipping through the winter snow.

(ALISON *enters, kisses the sleeping* GAWAIN *on the lips.*)

ALISON. How can you sleep, when the morning is so clear?

GAWAIN. How sweet to wake, and find a face so fair!

FOX. The trail is found! Sighted!

CONTEUR. Gawain, beware!

ALISON. This is your last day here. Come, I am sad, for you will leave. Flatter me, make me laugh, or I shall grieve. Come, read my palm. Tell me what lies ahead. No, do not rise. Be kind to me, in bed!

FOX. Doubling through bushes, thorns. Over a fence.

CONTEUR. Sunlight. Dogs and a fox, the woods are dense.

ALISON. Come, flatter me! Make me smile! What do you like the least about me? This? This? This? Oh, I am shivering. Let me be warm. (*Starts to get into bed*)

GAWAIN. Lady, it's most improper!

ALISON (*giggling*). No one will know. (*She lies down. He is at the edge of the bed, sitting.*) There's a lover you long for. Tell me! I must know!

GAWAIN. I have no lover. Nor will I ever, and the axe tomorrow will marry me only to dark and sorrow. (ALISON *kisses* GAWAIN's *cheek. She leaves the bed.*) My love. (*Strokes her hair*) How soft your hair is! Like a red bird's down.

FOX. The moss drifts back from the trees as the fox passes.

ALISON. Though you have given me nothing, take this from me.

CONTEUR. Red gold as the rising sun, a ring.

GAWAIN. I cannot. It is too rich a gift!

ALISON. Then take this: a poor, simple thing. (*Takes off her belt. He refuses.*) The belt is magic! No blade can harm the one who wears it! It is protection. Since my mother's mother, this house has owned it. Please …

GAWAIN. I … I cannot …

FOX. The dogs are coming from both sides!

ALISON. Sweet Gawain, save yourself! (GAWAIN *takes the belt.*) Swear not to tell my husband.

FOX. The dogs are there! Bercilak's blade is out!

GAWAIN. Lady, I swear.

(ALISON *turns to leave,* GAWAIN *runs to her, kneels.* ALISON *kisses her hand and touches* GAWAIN *lightly on the nape of his neck and goes.* BERCILAK *enters, carrying the* FOX.)

BERCILAK. I have found you a fox! My friend, what did you find today?

GAWAIN. My Lord, I have not fared as well as you.

BERCILAK. Well, here's my side of the bargain. A poor, simple thing.

GAWAIN. I offer these in fair exchange for what you bring. (GAWAIN *kisses* BERCILAK *on the lips.*)

BERCILAK. A good day's hunting! (GAWAIN *kisses* BERCILAK *on the cheek.*) Ah, friendship. From the same source?

(GAWAIN *touches the nape of* BERCILAK's *neck.*)

BERCILAK. A curious gift … (*Pause*) Is that all? (*Pause*)

GAWAIN. Yes.

BERCILAK. I grow tired of this game. Tomorrow we'll make a bargain of another kind.

GAWAIN. My Lord and friend. Tomorrow I must leave. (Pause)

BERCILAK. I had forgotten. We shall miss you, Gawain. Shall we not, Alison?

GAWAIN. I owe you more than I can say.

(*Pause.* BERCILAK *smiles.*)

GAWAIN. How strange that I discover
No joy on earth will stay!
The friends you found last evening
Are fading by today!
I give you thanks for all your fire
The warmth you bade me share,
For in the morning I must go
Like the ever greening year.

ALISON. A bed is by the fire
(The ice is cold and deep)
I do not know what waits you,
But even in my sleep
I hear the winter cries of men
Asleep beneath the snow.
Oh, won't you stay at home with me,
And watch the young men go?

BERCILAK. Joy and jest are passing;
Nothing lingers long.
You go to keep a promise—
I pray your heart be strong!

GAWAIN. I give you thanks for all your fire.
And the warmth you bade me share,
But in the morning I must die
Like the ever dying year … (*Pause*)

GAWAIN. My gracious Lady! I go early.
Goodbyes will grieve me so …

BERCILAK. We understand. You sir (*to* SERVANT), attend Lord Gawain in the morning. Set his feet towards the Green Chapel.

Then farewell, my friend. God go with you, until we meet.

(*They take formal leave of each other.* BERCILAK *and* ALISON *leave.*)

GAWAIN. All night Gawain watched by the dying fire; fingered the green belt under his shirt, and thought of home.

CONTEUR. Outside, the wind sang songs of death and weariness. The snow settled like white glass. The small animals scratched the fields with their feet. The world was motionless, and waiting. And in the morning, while the castle was asleep—

GAWAIN (*to* SQUIRE). Come, fellow!

CONTEUR. You will hear adventure call,
You will say that you are strong;
Yet be humble, or you fall—
Pride can lead you into wrong!
In the mist, in the snow,
Every man himself must know!

COMPANY. They put on his armour, and saddled his horse, and let down the drawbridge, and the three of them walked quietly out through the pale dawn. North again.

ALISON. And overhead, a red bird followed, the colour of a fox, or a deer's blood, or a boar's red eye. North.

SQUIRE. My Lord? We are close now. (*Pause*)

GAWAIN. Good.

SQUIRE. My Lord, let us turn back.

GAWAIN. Turn back?

SQUIRE. I say this as someone who loves you, sir. A fierce creature lives there, at the Green Chapel. No one rides by but he beats them to death with one blow of his axe. You'll lose your head! Hear what I've said.

GAWAIN. And what do you suggest?

SQUIRE. Sir, I swear to tell no one if you turn aside. (*Silence*) I had a brother, sir, he got himself a strong magic charm, and went hunting there. But the Green Man killed him just the same. We found him later in little pieces. Hear me, sir!

GAWAIN. I thank you.

SQUIRE. Take that path there, turn south, and make a safer ride.

GAWAIN. I cannot. I have sworn.

SQUIRE. Well, I'll go no further sir, I'm not as pure as you, I'm a wise coward. Keep your head about you—that's my rule!

GAWAIN. Which way, then?

SQUIRE. Go straight ahead. When the light grows dim because the trees thicken, and the cave mouths grow green and grim, there's the devil! I'll leave you to him.

GAWAIN. Farewell, then. God go with you.

SQUIRE. I'll say this much: it's a fine day to die. *(Pause)* I'm honoured to have met you, sir. Goodbye! *(He exits.)*

GAWAIN. Small red bird, where do you go, my friend? Does everything desert you at the end? Uphill now. My faithful Gringolet. I set you free. I'll die alone. Go home. Don't wait for me. How sweet the air is!

CONTEUR. The crags are scraping a white sky. But what's that? Round the next bend, on the banks of a brook, a queer kind of hill, like a honeycomb. And one large cave, green with moss. At the back of it, a huge green figure, whirring an axe, whetting it sharp as a winter wind, and singing, singing.

(The GREEN KNIGHT sharpens his axe.)

GREEN. The fairest Lord in all the land
Is come to fall beneath my hand.
I welcome you—you keep your pledge!
I offer you my axe's edge.
Bow down and dream—
The world will seem
A gentler place when I am done.
I offer peace
And sweet release—
All things that live must leave the sun
Some day!

GAWAIN. What a grinding and grating!

CONTEUR. What a rushing and ringing! What a terrible singing!

GAWAIN. I have come.

GREEN. Welcome, my Lord. I have waited for you one whole year.

GAWAIN. I am ready.

GREEN. Then hold yourself still, as I did a year ago.

GAWAIN. I commend myself now to the Lord of all,
Who watches over every weak bird's fall.
Amen. *(GREEN swings the blade down. GAWAIN flinches a little.)*

GREEN. You moved, you moved! I never moved an inch! Are you really Gawain? That man wouldn't flinch!

GAWAIN. Are you trying to shame me? Haven't I come here alone? And on time?
Get it over! I'll stay like stone! All this talk! Are you ready? I'm ready for anything! Shut up and do your work now. Swing!

(GREEN swings down again, halts the blade just short of GAWAIN. GAWAIN is steadfast.)

GREEN. Ah, that's better. I see you're finally ready. This time I swing for good. Good luck! Hold steady! *(A third time, and he barely touches the neck. GAWAIN swings away, grabs his sword.)*

CONTEUR. He's nicked his neck! Just a splash of blood on the snow!

GAWAIN. And that's the last time I'll stand for your blow!

GREEN *(laughing).* Gawain, my friend, the very finest knight—may you be blessed for giving me such delight!

CONTEUR. And there's a red bird falling from that tree, touching earth lightly. What can it be?

(ALISON alights in front of GAWAIN, courtsies to THE GREEN KNIGHT, who transforms into BERCILAK.)

ALISON (to GAWAIN). My Lord, I come to claim a trifle that I lack. Gawain, now that it's served its purpose, give it back!

GAWAIN. You're Alison. And Bercilak! And Not! Now God defend me from this witch's plot!

BERCILAK. My wondrous courtier![2] Finest of men!

GAWAIN. I am dishonoured forever. Here, take the belt!

BERCILAK. I have found you a fox!

GAWAIN. That's right, make fun of me!

ALISON. No, no! What other man could have been as faithful as you were?

BERCILAK. Or kept his promise so well?

GAWAIN. I cheated! How could you do this to me?

BERCILAK (sternly). Gawain! Life is precious! You are right to cherish it.

(SQUIRE enters with GRINGOLET.)

SQUIRE. My Lord, here's your horse.

GAWAIN. And you too, I suppose, my kind squire—part of the trick to make me turn back!

SQUIRE. But you didn't, did you? In spite of everything.

BERCILAK. He passed the test, almost without fault. Only on the third evening, you kept something back, for love of life. And so I wounded you, a very little.

GAWAIN. Here, take your belt.

BERCILAK. Keep it. And wear it well.

ALISON. Bind your wound with it. And wear it always to remind you that no man is perfect.

GAWAIN. Forgive me. (Kneels) I have been proud. And you have humbled me.

ALISON. You were a rough stone. I have smoothed you.

BERCILAK. You were a dull axe. I have sharpened you.

CONTEUR. You were a lost man. I have placed you on the road.

COMPANY. Go south. And south. And south. Away from winter. Ride down into spring. And suddenly, where Bercilak had stood, there was instead a great tree, with a bright axe held in one thick branch. And the squire vanished, as though he had never been, and a red bird soared up into its branches, laughing.

CONTEUR. And Gawain was alone with Gringolet. So Gawain rode south. And spring came again, slowly, a long way home. Flowers the color of his blood, skies the calm white of his heart, leaves the soft green of the baldric[3] around his neck. So the promise was kept. And the bond was broken. And the lesson was learnt.

GAWAIN. Lord, keep us safe and sure as the days leave us. May we journey from our separate winters into life and love. Amen.

---

2. courtier, a royal court attendant

3. baldric, an ornamental belt worn over one shoulder to support a sword or bugle

Sir Gawain and the Green Knight

Play Analysis

1. Were you surprised by the Green Knight's identity? Look back at his behavior throughout the play, and discuss any clues you find to his identity.
2. Gawain is truly a chivalrous knight. How does his conduct toward Alison illustrate this?
3. In what ways might this play be particularly appropriate for the hearing impaired?
4. Find and jot down images that appeal to each of the five senses.
5. **Thematic Connection: To Be a Hero** Who is the hero of this play? When does he or she show the greatest courage?

Literary Skill: Interpret a Spoof

Read the comic song lyrics below about the knights of Camelot. Do they relate in any way to what you have learned about knighthood and chivalry? See if you can adapt this song into a play.

We're Knights of the Round Table.
We dance when e'er we're able.
We do routines
And chorus scenes
With footwork impeccable.
We dine well here in Camelot.
We eat ham and jam and Spam a lot!

We're Knights of the Round Table.
Our shows are formidable.
But many times
We're given rhymes

That are quite unsingable.
We're opera-mad in Camelot.
We sing from the dia-phragm a lot!

In war, we're tough and able,
Quite indefati-gable.
Between our quests
We sequin vests
And impersonate Clark Gable.
It's a busy life in Camelot.
I have to push the pram a lot.

From *Knights of the Round Table* by Neil Innes

Performance Element: Problem Solving

Imagine that tonight's audience will be made up primarily of the hearing impaired. With your classmates, interpret a portion of the play using sound, sign language, dance, and any other elements you feel would be appropriate.

The Red Badge of Courage

from the novel by Stephen Crane
adapted for the stage by Kathryn Schultz Miller

Creating Context:
Boys of the Civil War

Everyone thought the Civil War would be short and glorious. *The New York Times* predicted that it wouldn't last over thirty days. No one, North or South, could have imagined how many young men would eventually die in this fearsome war that engulfed America beginning in 1861. One of the main issues was slavery. Southerners feared that as western territories became states, free states would outnumber slave states, making them a minority in the national government. The balance was broken when Abraham Lincoln, who opposed slavery, was elected President and Southern states refused to accept the outcome. Seven states seceded from the Union, declaring themselves a Confederacy. In April of 1861 the Confederacy attacked Fort Sumter in North Carolina, and full-scale fighting began.

It has been called "The Boy's War" because so many of the soldiers on both sides were so young. Farm boys, students, young merchants, blacksmiths, and clerks were the backbone of the armies. Three million of them wore either the

Civil War
drummer boys

blue of the North or the gray of the South and, according to one count, the average age on either side was twenty-one. Three hundred Union soldiers were thirteen or under. The youngest soldier on record was nine years old.

Many boys slipped into the fighting as musicians. Tales of buglers so small they couldn't climb onto a horse without help are common, as well as stories about little drummer boys no older than eleven. One account tells of a band of schoolboys between the ages of fourteen and eighteen from the Virginia Military Institute Cadet Corps who joined the Battle of New Market in the Shenandoah Valley. They marched off the campus and by May 15, 1864, had joined the fighting. They were 215 strong and they marched behind a twenty-four-year-old lieutenant colonel. A witness who watched them in battle said, "They came ... up the slope....Their line was as perfectly preserved as if on dress parade.... It would have been impossible to eject from six guns more missiles than those boys faced in their wild charge up that hill." The corps lost eight cadets and forty-four others were wounded.

As you read the play, keep in mind that the main character, Henry Fleming, is a very young man.

As a Reader: Understanding Protagonist and Antagonist

The main character in literature or drama is called the **protagonist**. Anything or anyone that opposes this chief character is called the **antagonist**. In the excerpts below, the protagonist, Henry, must watch his friend die. As you read the play, try to identify the antagonist.

from Page • • •  • • • to Stage

There was a silence.
Finally, the chest of the doomed soldier began to heave with a strained motion. It increased in violence until it was as if an animal was within and was kicking and tumbling furiously to be free.

The spectacle of gradual strangulation made the youth writhe, and once as his friend rolled his eyes, he saw something in them that make him sink wailing to the ground. He raised his voice in a last supreme call.

"Jim—Jim—Jim—"

The tall soldier opened his lips and spoke. He made a gesture. "Leave me be—don't tech me—leave me be— ….He was invaded by a creeping strangeness that slowly enveloped him. For a moment the tremor of his legs caused him to dance a sort of hideous hornpipe. His arms beat wildly… His tall figure stretched itself to its full height. There was a slight rending sound. Then it began to swing forward, slow and straight, in the manner of a falling tree. A swift muscular contortion made the left shoulder strike the ground first.

The body seemed to bounce a little way from the earth. "God!" said the tattered soldier.

from *The Red Badge of Courage* by Stephen Crane

NARRATOR. The tall soldier turned, and lurching dangerously, went on.

HENRY. Jim!

NARRATOR. And the youth followed.

JIM. Leave me be for a minute. Leave me be…

NARRATOR. At last, Henry saw him stop and stand motionless.

HENRY. Jim, what's the matter with you, Jim?

NARATOR. There was a silence.

JIM. Leave me be…

NARRATOR. Finally, the chest of the doomed soldier began to heave. For a moment the tremor of his legs caused him to dance a hideous sort of jig. His arms beat wildly about his head. The tall soldier stretched to his full height, then fell to the ground.

(JIM *stands, staggers downstage moving back into scene and falls into* HENRY's *arms.*)

HENRY (*sobs*). JIM! Oh, Gawd, oh Gawd, oh Gawd!!

from *The Red Badge of Courage* adapted by Kathryn Schultz Miller

As a Casting Director: Assessing Gender Roles

The Red Badge of Courage is a story about soldiers during the Civil War. As such, most of the characters are young white men. As you look at the list of characters in this play, think about how you might be inventive in your casting.

The Red Badge of Courage

Time

1861, during the American Civil War

The Characters

NARRATOR	HENRY
MOTHER	JIM CONKLIN
SOLDIER 1	SOLDIER 2
SOLDIER 3	WILSON
GENERAL	TATTERED SOLDIER

CHEERFUL SOLDIER

Setting

The homefront and the battlefield

AT RISE: (MUSIC CUE #1—"The Battle Cry of Freedom.") We hear rolling drums, softly at first, then building in intensity. SOLDIERS 1 and 2 enter marching, from opposite sides and carrying flags. They meet center, then march to either side of the stage and solemnly place flags in stands. NARRATOR enters. HENRY runs in as we hear "The Battle Cry of Freedom." He reveres each flag with boyish awe.

MUSIC

Yes, we'll rally round the flag, boys,
We'll rally once again,
Shouting the battle cry of freedom,

NARRATOR (over following music). In the troubled times of the American Civil War there was a youthful private who had dreamed of battles all his life.

MUSIC

We will rally from the hillside,
We'll gather from the plain,
Shouting the battle cry of freedom.

(During following music, SOLDIER 1 marches onto higher level. HENRY watches him put on jacket and cap. SOLDIER 2 ceremoniously hands him jacket, hat, then rifle. SOLDIER 1 stands at attention. HENRY is thrilled.)

MUSIC

We are springing to the call,
of the loyal, true and brave,
Shouting the battle cry of freedom,
And our battle cry shall be,
"Not one man shall be a slave!"
Shouting the battle cry of freedom.

(*During following music,* SOLDIER 1 *begins marching in place on the cubes.* HENRY, *filled with childish enthusiasm, begins to mimic the soldier's movements, marching awkwardly by his side.* HENRY *marches down center, then turns up, facing* SOLDIER 1.)

MUSIC

Our country forever,
Hurrah, boys, hurrah!
Down with the traitor,
Up with the star!

NARRATOR (*over following music*). He dreamed of vague and bloody conflicts which had thrilled him with their sweep and fire. In visions he had seen himself in many struggles.

(MOTHER *enters. Stands watching* HENRY.)

MUSIC

While we rally round the flag, boys,
Let's rally once again,
Shouting the battle cry of freedom.

HENRY (*turning out, on pause in music*). Ma, I'm going to enlist!

MOTHER (*putting on shawl*). Don't be a fool, Henry! (*Turns away.*)

(HENRY's *high spirits are not to be dampened. During following verse,* SOLDIER 1 *begins to march out,* SOLDIER 2 *in line behind him.* HENRY *ceremoniously dons his jacket and cap, awkwardly following* SOLDIERS *offstage.*)

MUSIC

Our country forever!
Hurrah, boys, hurrah!
Down with the traitor,
Up with the star!
While we rally round the flag, boys,
Let's rally once again,
Shouting the battle cry of freedom!

(*Drum rolls, slowly fading.* MOTHER *watches men march off, waving. She picks up bowl of potatoes and sits.*)

HENRY (*entering after drums, frightened but firm*). Ma, I did it. I enlisted.

MOTHER (*shocked, prays, accepts*). The Lord's will be done, Henry. Now, you watch out in this here fighting business—you watch out and take good care of yourself. Don't go a-thinking you can lick the whole rebel army at the start because you can't.

HENRY (*anxious and excited*). I know, I know.

MOTHER. You are just one little fellow amongst a whole lot of others, and you've got to keep quiet and do what they tell. I know how you are, Henry.

HENRY. Aw, Ma . . .

MOTHER. Now I've knit you eight pairs of socks, Henry, and I've put in all your shirts, because I want my boy to be just as warm and comfortable as any in the army.

HENRY. It's getting late . . .

MOTHER. And always be careful and choose your company. There's lots of bad men in the army, Henry. Now, I don't want you to ever do anything, Henry, that you would be ashamed to let me know about. Just think as if I was watching you. If you keep that in your mind always, I guess you'll come out about right. (*Turning away as if done, then remembers*) You must remember your father too, child, and remember he never drunk a drop of liquor in his life and seldom swore a cross oath.

HENRY. Ma, I gotta go . . .

(MUSIC CUE #2—"*Tenting Tonight*")

MOTHER (*Sudden tears, trying to hold them back*). I don't know what else to tell you, Henry, except that you should never do no shirking on my account. If so be a time comes when you have to be kilt . . . (*Tears*) or do a mean thing, why, Henry, don't think of anything except what's right.

HENRY (*finally taking notice of her pain*). I won't, Ma.

MOTHER *(picking herself up, recovering).* Now, I've put a cup of blackberry jam with your bundle . . . *(Smiles as she hands this to him)* because I know you love it above all things.*(MOTHER pulls HENRY to her and holds him in her embrace firmly, then pulls away.)*

MOTHER. Good-bye, Henry. Watch out and be a good boy.

(HENRY turns, starts to go. NARRATOR enters.)

NARRATOR. When the youth looked back from the gate he could see his mother's brown face, upraised and stained with tears. He bowed his head and went on, feeling suddenly ashamed of his purposes.

(HENRY exits as music swells. MOTHER exits. SOLDIER 3 enters—sets set pieces for camp scene. Other SOLDIERS and WILSON saunter in one by one. JIM CONKLIN enters and sits down center.)

The cold passed reluctantly from the earth and the retiring fogs revealed an army out on the hills, resting. Slowly Henry's regiment awakened and began to tremble with the eagerness of rumors.

JIM *(as HENRY enters).* We're going to move tomorrow, sure! We're going way up the river, cut across, and around behind them.

HENRY *(good-naturedly).* Aw, that's a lie.

JIM. I tell you, the army's going to move.

SOLDIER 3. Well, you don't know everything in the world, do you?

JIM. Didn't say I knew everything in the world.

HENRY. Aw, what are you talking about; how do you know this?

JIM *(cocky).* I heard it from a very reliable friend.

NARRATOR *(smiling).* Who had heard it from a cavalryman, who had heard it from his brother, who had heard it from an orderly at division headquarters.

JIM. You can believe it or not, just as you like. I don't care a hang.

SOLDIER 1. It's a lie! I don't believe this old army's ever going to move.

SOLDIER 2. I've got ready to move eight times in the last two weeks and we ain't moved yet.

JIM *(superior).* All you got to do is sit down and wait as quiet as you can. Then pretty soon you'll find out I was right.

HENRY. Good Lord!

NARRATOR. So they were going to move at last.

HENRY *(in a quiet fear).* Thunder!

SOLDIER 2. Like as not this story will turn out just like the others did.

(SOLDIERS move away, talk silently holding coffee tin cups.)

JIM *(dead serious).* Not much it won't. Not much it won't.

HENRY. Shucks.

JIM *(almost cheerful).* Oh, you'll see fighting this time, my boy, what'll be regular out and out fighting. They're saying everybody's taking off for Richmond and they're leaving us here to fight all the Johnnies. They're raising blazes all over the camp.

HENRY *(panic).* Jim!

JIM. What?

HENRY *(trying to hide his panic).* How do you think the regiment will do?

JIM *(cocky).* Oh, they'll fight all right, I guess, after they once get used to it.

NARRATOR *(smiling).* He made fine use of the third person.

JIM. There's been heaps of fun poked at them because they're new, of course. Hardly any of them done real fighting before, like me. Most of them younger than me. *(Friendly)* But most of 'em are like you. *(Assuring)* They'll fight all right, I guess.

HENRY. Think any of the boys will run?

JIM *(playing experienced).* Oh, there may be a few of 'em run, but there's them kind in every regiment, especially when they first goes under fire. They call the regiment "fresh fish" and "mule drivers," but the boys come from good stock and most of 'em will fight like fun after they once get shootin'.

WILSON. Oh, you think you know everything!

JIM (*standing for confrontation*). You know, I don't give a good hoot what you think . . .

(JIM *moves to fight,* WILSON *taunts,* "Yeah? Yeah?")

HENRY (*holding him back*). Hey, Jim . . .

JIM. Never said I know everything.

HENRY. No, you never did.

JIM. Did I, Henry?

HENRY. No, sir.

JIM. You hear me say I know everything?

HENRY. Sit down, Jim.

JIM. So why's this lunk-head saying it?

HENRY (*calming*). Jim . . .

(WILSON *backs off, goes back to other soldiers.*)

JIM (*cooling*). That's what I'd like to know.

HENRY. Jim. Did you ever think you might run yourself, Jim?

JIM (*laughs to show how ludicrous it would be*). Me? Run?

(JIM *thinks, looks around, then confides, speaking quietly and honestly to* HENRY, *who appreciates his candor.*)

Well, I've thought it might get too hot for Jim Conklin, some of them scrimmages, and if a whole lot of boys started to run, why, I suppose I'd start and run.

HENRY. No . . .

JIM. Yes, yes, I would.

HENRY (*poking him in the arm*). Oh, come on . . .

JIM. And I'll tell you, if I once started to run, I'd run like the devil and make no mistake.

HENRY. You mean it?

JIM. Sure shootin'.

NARRATOR. The youth felt the gratitude for these words from his friend.

JIM (*looks around, as if to set the record straight, boasts loud so all can hear*). But if everyone was standing and a-fighting, why, I'd stand and fight. By jiminey, I would.

(SOLDIERS *move away,* JIM *trails behind, nudges* HENRY *goodnight, exits.* MUSIC CUE #3— "Henry's Theme.")

NARRATOR. Henry had a serious problem. He lay in his bunk pondering upon it. He tried to mathematically prove to himself that he would not run from battle. A little panic-fear grew in his mind.

HENRY (*to himself*). Good Lord! What's the matter with me?

(WILSON *and* SOLDIERS 2 *and* 3 *are huddled over a game of dice.*)

NARRATOR. He told himself that he was not formed for a soldier. That he was different from the rest. He heard his friend, Wilson, bragging and boasting.

SOLDIER 1 (*breaking from huddle, accusing* WILSON). Oh, you're going to do great things, I suppose, Wilson!

WILSON. I s'pose I'll do like the rest. I'm going to try like thunder.

SOLDIER 2. How do you know you won't run when the time comes?

WILSON. Run? *Run?* The man that bets on my running will lose his money, that's all!

SOLDIER 3. Oh, shucks! You ain't the bravest man in the world, are you?

WILSON. I said I was going to do my share of the fighting—that's what I said. Who are you anyhow? You talk as if you thought you was Napoleon Bonaparte.

HENRY. What's the matter with me?

NARRATOR. As he sweated in the pain of these thoughts, he could hear the men in the next tent, betting on the outcome of the battle.

(Lonely, sad music; and with the music we hear the sounds of men betting.)

SOLDIER 2. "I'll bid five."

SOLDIER 3. "Make it six."

WILSON. "Seven."

SOLDIER 2. "Seven goes."

(All sounds fade.)

NARRATOR (rushing forward). The next morning, Jim woke Henry up.

JIM (rushing in). Come on, Henry.

HENRY. What? What's going on?

JIM. You'll see soon enough. (Exits)

NARRATOR. Before he was entirely awake, he found himself running down the road to a battlefield.

(Loud, triumphant brass sounds, a call to war. Then the sounds of guns firing. These sounds build. JIM moves cubes downstage to form bunkers. HENRY runs off, returning with guns. Other SOLDIERS enter.)

HENRY (running). You hear that firing, Jim?

NARRATOR. Henry was frightened. As he ran with his comrades he tried to think.

HENRY (speaking his thoughts). I didn't want to do this! The government forced me to come here! They're taking us out to be slaughtered. This is a trap. They don't know what they're doing. The generals are stupid!

NARRATOR. Shrill and passionate words came to his lips. But he gripped his outcry at his throat.

HENRY (stops running). It's no use. Even if the men were more scared than me they would just laugh at my warning.

NARRATOR. The brigade was halted in the fringe of a grove. The men crouched among the trees and pointed their restless guns. (JIM, HENRY, and SOLDIERS do as described.) A shell like the devil went over the heads of the reserves.

JIM. Here they come! HERE THEY COME!!

SOLDIERS 1, 2, AND 3. Here they come! Here they come!

(Sounds of galloping horses, louder firing of approaching enemy, cries of battle from men. Music expressing excitement and fury. GENERAL enters.)

NARRATOR. The enemy ran forward, giving shrill yells, stooping and swinging their rifles! A hatless general shook his fist and shouted . . .

GENERAL (stands on high level away from them). You've got to hold them back! You've got to hold them back!

JIM. Oh, we're in for it now! Oh, we're in for it now!

GENERAL. Reserve your fire, boys! Don't shoot till I tell you! Wait till they get close up! Don't be fools! (On tape we hear excited cries, "Fire! Fire!") FIRE! FIRE!

NARRATOR. Henry suddenly lost concern for himself. A burning roar filled his ears. He became consumed by a red rage. (HENRY is furiously loading his gun and shooting.)

JIM (in a kind of daze). Well, why don't they support us? Why don't they send us supports? What do they think?

(Fighting continues for several seconds.)

NARRATOR. At last an exultant yell went along the quivering line!

HENRY (in disbelief). Well, we've held them back. We've held them back!

JIM (amazed). Darned if we didn't!

HENRY (laughing with delight). We've held them back!

(JIM and HENRY whoop with joy. Then they sit down to rest. They become calm, then look out at the solemn battlefield.)

HENRY (seeing death for the first time). Gee! Ain't it hot, hey?

JIM (also affected). You bet! I never seen such a dumb hotness.

NARRATOR. But all of a sudden cries of amazement broke up along the ranks.

(*Sounds of galloping horses, hollers, men calling "Here they come again! Here they come again!" SOLDIERS run past crying, "Here they come again!"*)

HENRY (*stricken*). Oh, my God.

JIM. Oh, say, this is too much of a good thing!

HENRY. I didn't come here to fight the whole rebel army!

JIM. We can't stand a second banging! We can't stand it!

NARRATOR. The youth stared. Surely, he thought, this impossible thing was not about to happen.

JIM. Why can't somebody send us supports?

HENRY. They must be machines made of steel. (*Screams from the men, charge music*) This is a mistake. This can't happen!

NARRATOR. Henry saw some of the men throw down their rifles and run away.

(*SOLDIERS throw down rifles, run off. JIM follows.*)

There was no shame in their faces. They ran like rabbits.

(*Louder sounds of charging and chaos. HENRY begins to run. Wild and furious music.*)

The youth began to speed toward the rear. He ran like a mad man.

(*NARRATOR exits, running. HENRY falls, gulping for air, jumps up again.*)

HENRY. I've got to get away. Methodical idiots! Fools! Run! Run! Look at those gunners! Don't you see? You'll all be dead! DEAD! (*HENRY runs for several seconds, then indicates a hill.*) At the top of this hill I can see. (*Stands on higher level, stops, panting, horrified*) They're going like sheep to slaughter! What kind of men are they, any- how? How can they keep fighting? Fools! Don't you understand?

(GENERAL *enters wearing hat, waving his sword importantly.* HENRY *points.*)

There! There's the general. He doesn't understand how impossible this is, that's all. If I stay here a while maybe he'll call on me to tell him. I could tell him! Any fool can see that if they don't retreat while they have the chance . . .

GENERAL. Yes! Yes, by heavens, they have! (*Almost unbelieving*) Yes, by heavens, they've held them back!

HENRY. What?

GENERAL. They've held them now! We've got them sure! (*Laughs gleefully*)

HENRY. Held them? But . . . but . . . that's impossible.

GENERAL. They've held them back, by heavens!

(GENERAL *exits laughing as* HENRY *steps off cubes, disbelieving.* SOLDIERS 1 *and* 2 *and* WILSON *enter, whooping and shouting.*)

WILSON. By thunder, we did it!

(HENRY *"sees" this out front.* SOLDIERS *set stage for chapel scene. They exit with guns and ram- rods. MUSIC CUE #4—"Henry's Theme."*)

HENRY (*quietly, to himself*). By heavens, they won after all! How could they do that to me? (*He walks, thinking.*) I ran, yes I did, by thunder, I ran. Of course I ran. I had to save myself, didn't I? Well, didn't I? (*We hear gunshots in the background mixed with the music. Throwing his hands to his ears*) Stop! Stop! Stop that infernal firing! (*Gunshots continues softly, then fade.*) I'm a little part of this army and I saved myself for the army. Yes, I did. The others . . . why, they were just fools. Anybody could see that. (*Sees something*) Look! A squirrel! (*Perks up, looks around, finds a rock, throws it at squirrel, laughs merrily*) Now, don't you see? That there's a sign. That squirrel didn't stay to be hit, did he? No, he didn't! He took off running as fast as his legs could carry him, just like me. It's only natural for a man to run when he knows he's going to be hit! *(Looks up)* The sun. Strange that it still shines as if nothing is wrong.

(SOLDIERS 1 and 2 enter with guns in "chapel" position. They move slowly and hold guns high as if they were precious objects. We hear beautiful music, indicating a feeling of purity and innocence.)

NARRATOR. The youth went into the deep thickets.

HENRY. It's peaceful here.

NARRATOR. At length he reached a place where the arching boughs made a kind of chapel.

(SOLDIERS cross guns as if they were doors.)

He softly pushed aside the green doors and entered.

(HENRY pushes through guns. SOLDIERS turn.)

There was a religious half-light.

(Pause as HENRY takes joy in lovely scene, then a deep boom.)

He was being looked at by a dead man.

(HENRY "sees" dead man downstage. A jarring, intense chord. HENRY screams.)

The man was seated with his back against a tree, the eyes, staring at the youth. Over the gray skin of the face ran little ants.

(Another jarring chord, SOLDIERS cross guns, trapping HENRY.)

Henry burst into a run. He imagined that the dead man was screaming after him, from his chapel of green.

(HENRY frantically pushes through "boughs." On the tape we hear a voice calling, "Henry! Henry!" HENRY escapes, running. SOLDIERS exit with guns. As HENRY catches his breath we hear the song "Tramp, Tramp, Tramp," along with sounds of an army marching, horses, and groans from the wounded men.)

Finally Henry came to a road from which he could see a column of bloodstained, wounded men, marching.

(TATTERED SOLDIER enters using gun as a crutch.)

NARRATOR. The suffering men were cursing, groaning, and wailing with pain.

(TATTERED SOLDIER sings as he trudges in the march. There are bloody bandages around his body.)

TATTERED SOLDIER *(singing to the tune of "Sing a Song of Sixpence")*.

Sing a song of vic'try,

A pocket full of bullets,

Five and twenty dead men,

Baked in a pie.

NARRATOR. The youth joined the crowd and marched along with it.

(HENRY moves to join the line.)

There was a tattered man covered with dust and blood. The youth wished that he too had a wound, a red badge of courage. *(NARRATOR exits.)*

TATTERED MAN. Was a pretty good fight, wasn't it?

HENRY *(not wanting to talk)*. What?

TATTERED MAN. Was a pretty good fight, wasn't it?

HENRY. Yes. *(HENRY tries to move away from TATTERED MAN.)*

TATTERED MAN. Darn if I ever see fellers fight so. Law, how they did fight! I knowed it'd turn out this way. You can't lick them, boys. No sir! They's fighters, they be. They didn't run did they? No sir! They fought and fought and fought. *(Friendly, looks HENRY over)* Where you hit, old boy?

HENRY *(struck)*. What?

TATTERED MAN. Where you hit?

HENRY. Hit? Well, I'm not hit.

TATTERED MAN. Not hit?

HENRY. I . . . I guess I'm just lucky, that's all.

TATTERED MAN. You're lucky, all right.

(JIM *enters, near death.*)

NARRATOR (*entering*). One of the men had the gray seal of death upon him. His hands were bloody from where he had pressed them upon his wound.

(HENRY *moves in front of* JIM. JIM *puts his hand on* HENRY. HENRY *jumps as if he had been touched by a ghost.* HENRY *turns to the man, sees it is* JIM.)

HENRY. Gawd! Jim Conklin!

JIM. Hello, Henry. (*A vacant stare, ahead*)

HENRY (*horrified, gulping back tears*). Oh, Jim . . . oh, Jim . . . oh, Jim . . .

JIM (*eyes fixed ahead, dazed*). Where you been, Henry? I thought maybe you got keeled over. There's been thunder to pay today.

HENRY. Oh, Jim . . . oh, Jim . . . oh, Jim . . .

JIM. You know, I was out there. And Lord, what a circus! And by jiminey, I got shot. (*Leans to speak confidentially to* HENRY) I tell you what I'm afraid of, Henry, I'll tell you what I'm afraid of. I'm afraid I'll fall down and then, you know, them dumb artillery wagons—they like as not'll run over me. That's what I'm afraid of.

HENRY (*hysterical*). I'll take care of you, Jim! I'll take care of you. I swear to God I will.

JIM. Will you, Henry?

HENRY. Yes! Yes! I tell you . . . I'll take care of you, Jim.

JIM. Just pull me out of the road. I'd do it for you, wouldn't I, Henry?

HENRY (*awkwardly wiping tears away with his sleeve*). Lean on me, Jim, just lean on me.

JIM (*pushes him away*). No . . . no . . . no, leave me be, leave me be . . .

HENRY. I better take you out of the road, Jim. There's a battery coming. (JIM *is vacant.*) Gawd, Jim, how can you keep walking like this? (JIM *keeps walking doggedly.* HENRY *is exasperated.*) JIM! JIM!

JIM (*thinking he understands*). Oh! In the fields! Oh!

HENRY. Gawd! Don't run, Jim! (HENRY *grasps* JIM, *crying.*) Jim, what makes you do this way? You're hurt bad, Jim!

(MUSIC CUE #5—"Jim's Death")

JIM. No, no, no, don't touch me, leave me be, leave me be . . .

(JIM *pushes* HENRY *away and falls onto cube.* NARRATOR *enters. She and* HENRY *quickly move downstage "following"* JIM. HENRY *and* NARRATOR *play the scene as if seeing* JIM *out front.* JIM *remains on cube.*)

NARRATOR. Turning his head swiftly, the youth saw his friend running in a staggering and stumbling way toward a little clump of bushes.

HENRY. Where you going, Jim? What are you thinking about? Where you going? Tell me, won't you, Jim?

NARRATOR. The tall soldier turned, and lurching dangerously, went on.

HENRY. JIM!

NARRATOR. The youth followed.

JIM. Leave me be for a minute. Leave me be . . .

NARRATOR. At last, Henry saw him stop and stand motionless.

HENRY. Jim, what's the matter with you, Jim?

NARRATOR. There was a silence.

JIM. Leave me be . . .

NARRATOR. Finally, the chest of the doomed soldier began to heave. For a moment the tremor of his legs caused him to dance a hideous sort of jig. His arms beat wildly about his head. The tall soldier stretched to his full height, then fell to the ground.

(JIM *stands, staggers downstage moving back into scene and falls into* HENRY's *arms.*)

HENRY (sobs). JIM!! Oh, Gawd, oh Gawd, oh Gawd!!

NARRATOR. As the flap of the blue jacket fell away from the body, Henry could see that his side looked as if it had been chewed by wolves. (Pause) The youth turned toward the battlefield.

HENRY (raising his fist, furious). DAMNATION!!

(Dramatic drumming, then a flute picking up a part of the tune, "When Johnny Comes Marching Home." HENRY folds JIM's arms across his chest, puts hat over JIM's hands and crawls away sobbing. NARRATOR moves in front of them, JIM stands and exits. HENRY moves up, back to audience. Suddenly, frantic sounds of men and horses, running.)

NARRATOR. Suddenly the youth saw dark waves of blue men sweeping down upon him. (Exits)

(Loud galloping sounds and terrible panic and confusion, fight sounds, gunfire and cannon fire, loud and continuing. SOLDIERS 1, 2, and 3 come charging and wailing all around him, causing complete confusion and chaos.)

HENRY. Why, why what's . . . what's the matter?

SOLDIER 1 (hysterical, grabs him). Say, where's the plank road? Where's the plank road?!!

(SOLDIERS 2 and 3 echo this line.)

HENRY (calling). But what's the matter? Is the war lost? (Grabs SOLDIER 2) Tell me! What's the matter? What's going on?

SOLDIER 2 (screaming). Let me go! Let me go!

HENRY. Tell me why . . . ?!

SOLDIER 2. Let me go!! Let me go!!

(HENRY will not release him.)

SOLDIER 2. Well then . . . !

(SOLDIER 2 brings his rifle down to a crushing blow on HENRY's head.)

HENRY (screaming). AHHHH!! (HENRY falls to the ground, grasping his head. Dramatic sounds continue. SOLDIERS exit, running.)

HENRY writhes in pain, groaning and trying to stand. He touches the wound and brings back blood on his hand. He calls out. Shouts and gunfire fade. We hear "Sometimes I Feel Like a Motherless Child." CHEERFUL SOLDIER enters.)

CHEERFUL SOLDIER. You seem in a pretty bad way, boy.

(HENRY groans, but does not look up. He never sees the face of the CHEERFUL SOLDIER.)

HENRY. Uhhh!

CHEERFUL SOLDIER. Well, I'm going your way. The whole gang is going your way. I guess I can give you a lift. (CHEERFUL SOLDIER helps HENRY walk.) What regiment you belong to, eh? (HENRY grunts.) What's that? The 304th New York? Oh, you're a far way off then. Come on. This was the most mixed up fighting I ever did see. Men scattered all over the place. It'll be a miracle if half of 'em find their regiments tonight.

(CHEERFUL SOLDIER and HENRY trudge along, CHEERFUL SOLDIER stops him downstage center and looks out past audience. HENRY hangs on.)

CHEERFUL SOLDIER. Ho! There they go with an officer, I guess. Look at his hand a-draggin'. He's got all the war he wants, I bet. He won't be talking about his reputation and all when they go sawin' off his arm. (Still cheerful as possible, speaks as if he accepts that this is the way war has to be.) You know, there was a boy killed in my company today that I thought the world of. Jack was a nice feller. By ginger, it hurt like thunder to see old Jack get knocked flat. (Shakes head)

(We hear the swelling music of "Sometimes I Feel Like a Motherless Child" as they trudge upstage left. WILSON enters and begins to set up camp. Other SOLDIERS may enter and set up camp upstage.)

CHEERFUL SOLDIER. Oh! Ah, there you are! See that fire?

HENRY (*stupidly*). Uh-huh.

CHEERFUL SOLDIER. See that fire? Right over there. (*Points*) That's where your regiment is. Good-bye old boy. Good luck to you.

(HENRY *trudges toward* WILSON *as* CHEERFUL SOLDIER *exits.* HENRY *groans.*)

WILSON (*surprised*). Who goes there? Who is that?

HENRY (*speaks as he groans*). It's me, Wilson. Henry.

WILSON. Henry?! Henry Fleming?! Well, well, old boy! By ginger, I'm glad to see you! I give you up for a goner. I thought you was dead for sure!

HENRY (*obviously making it up as he goes along*). Yes, yes. I've . . . I've had an awful time. I've been all over. Way over on the right. Terrible fighting over there. I had an awful time. I got separated from the regiment. Over on the right I got shot.

WILSON. What? Got shot?!

HENRY. Just grazed a little in the head.

WILSON. Well, why didn't you say so? Poor old boy! We'll fix you up.

(WILSON *gets bandage, ad libs while wrapping* HENRY's *head.*)

HENRY (*tired*). I never seen such fighting. Awful time. I don't see how I could a' got separated from the regiment. I got shot, too.

WILSON. Here, take my blanket. (*He wraps* HENRY *in blanket.*) We'll see how you feel in the morning.

(MUSIC CUE #6. HENRY *falls into an uneasy sleep.* WILSON *watches over him and eventually falls asleep as well. Music should make a lingering bridge to next action, indicating the passing of night. Morning comes with the sound of birds.* HENRY *sits up, remembers his head, and groans.*)

HENRY. Ahhh! (*Touches head*) Thunder!

WILSON. Well, Henry, old man, how do you feel this morning?

HENRY. Oh, Lord, I feel pretty bad.

WILSON. Shoot! I hoped you'd feel all right this morning. Let's see the bandage. I guess it slipped. (*Works with dressing*)

HENRY. Gosh-darnit! Why in thunderation can't you be more easy? I'd rather you'd stand off and throws guns at it! (WILSON *fiddles with bandage.*) Ow! Now go slow and don't act like you was nailing down a carpet!

WILSON. Quit your belly-aching! You sound like an old woman! (*Forgetting* HENRY's *wound,* WILSON *gently smacks his head.* HENRY *howls in pain.*) Oh! Sorry, old boy. Come on, now. Have a drink. You'll feel better. (*He offers canteen.* HENRY *drinks.*) Well, Henry, what do you think the chances are? You think we'll wallop them?

HENRY. Day before yesterday you woulda bet you could lick the whole kit-and-kaboodle all by yourself.

WILSON. Would I? (*Smiles, humble*) Well, I guess I would. I guess I was a pretty big fool in those days. (*Cheers up*) All the officers say we got the rebs in a pretty tight box.

(MUSIC CUE #7—"Motherless Child")

HENRY. From where I was, it looked as if we was getting a pretty good pounding yesterday. (*Remembers*) Oh! Jim Conklin's dead.

WILSON. Jim Conklin?

HENRY. Shot in the side.

WILSON. You don't say so. Jim Conklin . . . poor cuss!

(NARRATOR *enters.*)

NARRATOR. The youth saw that he would suffer no reproach from his friend. He had performed his mistakes in the dark. No one had actually seen him run. So he was still a man. (*We hear soft phrases of "Motherless Child."*) The youth's regiment was marched to relieve a command that had lain long in some wet trenches.

(NARRATOR *exits.* HENRY *and* WILSON *begin to pack up "camp."*)

HENRY. By jiminey, we're generaled by a lot of lunk-heads.

WILSON. Maybe it's not their fault—not altogether. They're doing the best they know how. It's just bad luck, that's all.

HENRY. Well, don't we fight like the devil? Don't we do all that men can? No man dare say we don't fight like the devil. NO man will ever say it!!

WILSON (*good naturedly*). Henry, do you think you fought the whole battle yesterday, all by yourself?

HENRY (*suddenly ashamed*). Why, no. I don't think I fought the whole battle yesterday.

GENERAL (*backstage*). Ten-hut!

WILSON. Shh! The general.

(GENERAL *enters.* HENRY *and* WILSON *stand at attention,* SOLDIERS *fall in beside them.*)

GENERAL. You boys shut right up. You've been jawing like a lot of hens. All you got to do is to fight and you'll get plenty of that in about ten minutes.

(GENERAL *exits.* MEN *relax.* MUSIC CUE #8—"Battle." We hear a shell drop and loud, defiant brass sounds that announce impending battle. Loud shots and cannon fire. SOLDIERS shoot upstage. HENRY and WILSON take their places and fire shot after shot like machines. Sounds of whooping men and yells of the wounded. They fight furiously until we hear the GENERAL yell.*)

GENERAL. Cease fire! Cease fire!

(WILSON *stops and wipes his neck with a handkerchief.* HENRY *continues firing furiously, never breaking his pace.*)

WILSON. Henry? Henry?

(HENRY *continues.* WILSON *looks around, as if to say, "What's the matter?"* HENRY *takes no notice. He is in a trance, firing. They struggle for gun.*)

WILSON. Henry! You infernal fool, don't you know enough to quit when there ain't nothing to shoot at? Good Gawd!

HENRY (*finally*). Oh.

WILSON. You all right? There ain't nothing the matter with you is there?

HENRY. No.

(NARRATOR *enters.*)

NARRATOR. He saw that his comrades now looked upon him as a war devil. He was now a hero. And he had not been aware of the process. He had slept and, awakening, found himself a knight.

(*Very victorious, magnificent version of "When Johnny Comes Marching" to emphasize "a knight." The mood is changed with a softer version of the same.*)

HENRY (*standing to attention*). Request permission to go for water, sir.

WILSON. Wait, I'll go with you.

(*As* SOLDIERS *move quietly offstage,* HENRY *and* WILSON *mime going through the overgrown forest, pushing away branches.*)

Shucks, no water here. I thought there was a stream . . .

HENRY (*waving*). Shhh! (*Points to an empty point on stage*)

WILSON. The general.

HENRY. Shhh!

(GENERAL *enters opposite side, speaking out toward audience.*)

GENERAL. The enemy is forming on the right . . . Let's be ready when they charge . . . Now, up there's old General Waterside . . . They think they'll break through . . .

WILSON. What? What's he saying?

HENRY. They're going to charge.

GENERAL. What troops can you spare? . . . The 304th . . . Yes, yes, they'll do, maybe . . .

HENRY. He says he's going to put us on it. Our regiment!

WILSON. You don't say!

HENRY. Shhh!

GENERAL. They fight like a bunch of mule drivers!

HENRY (amazed). He says we fight like a bunch of mule drivers.

(Both are amazed and can hardly think what to do next.)

WILSON. So we're going to charge.

HENRY. That's what he says.

(They stare in disbelief at each other.)

WILSON (in quiet fear). Henry! We'll get swallowed!

(The tape plays loud brass charging music. We hear voices of officers. "Charge!" "Come on you fools, come on!" "Come on!" "Charge!" HENRY and WILSON run to the battlefield.)

WILSON. Come on, Henry. We got to do it!

HENRY. We'll all get killed if we stay here!

WILSON. This way! We've got to get across that lot!

(WILSON and HENRY move cubes and freeze upstage.)

NARRATOR. Over the field went the scurrying mass of soldiers. (NARRATOR brings Union flag downstage.) In the mad scramble they saw that the color sergeant flinched suddenly. They lunged for the flag. The color sergeant was dead. The corpse would not relinquish its trust. There was a grim struggle.

(NARRATOR steps away and HENRY and WILSON break freeze and struggle against each other for the flag.)

WILSON. Give it to me!

HENRY. No, let me keep it! (Pushes WILSON away.) I'll have it, I say!

(HENRY finally gets the flag and moves downstage, waving it during following speech.)

NARRATOR. The youth walked into the battle, into the mob of men. The fast and angry firings went back and forth. But the youth continued to the front holding the flag. At last the enemy began to weaken. Henry's regiment gazed about with looks of uplifted pride. They had proven the general wrong. (Exits. Battle sounds fade.)

WILSON (rushing to HENRY). Henry! Henry, did you hear? Lieutenant says the general's mad as blazes!

HENRY. What in thunderation for?

WILSON. General says if we'd have gone another hundred feet farther we'd a'made a pretty success of it!

HENRY. What? Well, we went as far as we could! I wonder what he does want! He must think we went out there and played marbles!

WILSON. I should say we did have awful luck. But, Henry, that's not all. I heard the colonel talking, you know the one way down the way at the 27th. (Delighted with his news) Oooh! Henry, you just oughta heard!

HENRY. Heard what?

WILSON. Well, he was talking to a lieutenant right by me and it was the darndest thing. (Imitating) "Ahem! Ahem!" He says, "Mr. Hasrouk!" he says, "by the way, who was that lad that carried the flag?" he says. "Well, that there was Henry Fleming," he says, "and he's a jimhickey," he says. Those were his very words! And he says, "Ahem! Ahem! Well, now I saw him and that feller Wilson keeping that flag way out in front," he says. "Well, well," says the colonel, "they deserve to be major generals, they do, major generals." What do you think of that?

(MUSIC CUE #9—"Battle")

HENRY (delighted). Aw, go to blazes!

WILSON. It's the gosh darn truth, Henry!

(NARRATOR enters.)

NARRATOR. The young men exchanged a secret glance of joy and congratulations. The youth, still the bearer of the colors, became deeply absorbed as a spectator. Standing on a hill above the battle, he could see the desperate rushes of men.

(SOLDIERS *rush to the corners of the stage, anxiously calling out their lines. With each new line all* SOLDIERS *change position, running to a new corner.*)

NARRATOR. To and fro they swelled.

SOLDIER 1. They screamed and yelled like maniacs.

NARRATOR. The men burst out in a barbaric cry of rage and pain.

SOLDIER 2. The regiment bled extravagantly.

NARRATOR. The colonel came running along the back of the line.

SOLDIER 3. "We must charge 'em! We must charge 'em!"

NARRATOR. The youth sprang to action!

SOLDIER 1. He kept the bright colors to the front.

SOLDIER 3. He felt the daring spirit of a savage!

(SOLDIERS *freeze.*)

WILSON. Henry, Henry! We're going to have to pull back. That band on the right, they're just not moving!

NARRATOR. The youth centered the gaze of his soul upon that other flag. Its possession would be high pride!

HENRY. AAAAHHHH!! THE FLAG!!!

(*Intense drumming to underscore scene. A stylized fight scene:* HENRY *is furiously breaking through enemy line, engaging in hand-to-hand combat with each* SOLDIER *as they throw* HENRY *off. Moving upstage and freezing, they stand with backs to audience, ending with* HENRY *downstage on his knees.* SOLDIERS *turn slowly, aiming their guns at him and preparing to fire. All freeze. Then we hear a gentle, simple version of "Henry's*

Theme." The tune takes on a kind of dreamy, eerie quality during the following lines. There should be a feeling of a dream, flashback or remembrance as HENRY *speaks his lines with a hint of the earlier emotion of the reading. Lines should follow each other closely, almost overlapping at the ends. One* SOLDIER *moves his gun slowly down on each line that is not* HENRY's. MOTHER, JIM, TATTERED SOLDIER, *etc., enter on their lines.*)

HENRY. Ma, I'm going to enlist!

MOTHER (*entering*). Don't be a fool, Henry!

HENRY. Think any of the boys will run, Jim?

JIM (*entering*). The man that bets on my running will lose his money, that's all.

HENRY. What's the matter with me?

TATTERED SOLDIER. Sing a song of vic'try, A pocketful of bullets . . .

HENRY. I'll take care of you, Jim!

CHEERFUL SOLDIER. Five and twenty dead men, Baked in a pie . . .

HENRY. I'll take care of you! I swear to God I will!

WILSON. Well, don't we fight like the devil?

HENRY. Jim?

GENERAL. They fight like a bunch of MULE DRIVERS!

HENRY. Mule drivers?

WILSON. Don't we do all that men can?

HENRY. Mule drivers?

(*All now chant the words "They fight like a bunch of mule drivers" in a kind of round that lets us hear only a jumbled version as their delivery and taped music swells.*)

ALL. Mule drivers . . . like a bunch . . . they fight . . . they fight like a bunch of MULE DRIVERS . . . mule drivers . . . like a bunch . . . mule drivers . . . mule drivers . . . (*They continue.*)

HENRY (*lunging for the flag*). AAAHHH!!! THE FLAG!!!!

(HENRY *grabs the flag. The minute his hand touches it, there is a tremendous sound of joyful cheering. As the cheers continue,* HENRY *takes the flag in slow motion and hurls it high so that the colors dance above his head. He twirls it around in victory.* HENRY *crosses downstage, waving flag.*)

NARRATOR. THEY WERE *NOT* MULE DRIVERS!!! *(Pause)* He had been to where there was red blood and black of night. He had been to touch the great death . . . and found that, after all, it was but a great death. *He was a man.*

(*All freeze,* NARRATOR *is up right,* WILSON *and* HENRY *remove their hats in unison. They look around them as they did after their first battle together. Slowly, one by one, characters of* MOTHER *and* JIM *exit silently.* GENERAL *is last to leave.* HENRY *and* WILSON *wipe their brows. During the following lines they subtly notice that it is beginning to rain.*)

WILSON. Well, it's all over.

HENRY. By God, it is.

(They both sit.)

NARRATOR *(quietly).* Within a little while the regiment received the order to retrace its way.

GENERAL. C'mon, boys, we're headin' back. *(Exits)*

(NARRATOR *exits.*)

WILSON *(standing).* Oh, Lord.

HENRY. Here we go again. It's getting cloudy, Wilson.

(They walk, trudging slowly, exhausted.)

Well, we both did good. I'd like to see the fool what'd say we both didn't do good.

WILSON *(smiling).* We deserve to be major generals.

HENRY *(smiling back).* Aw, go to blazes with your major generals.

WILSON *(imitating).* "Ahem! Ahem! Say, lieutenant, who was that feller keeping that flag out to the front? Who could that feller be?"

HENRY *(laughing).* That's a big lie, Wilson.

WILSON. "Why, that there's Henry Fleming. He's a jimhickey, a jimhickey! And he and that Wilson feller—that *Wilson* feller—why they deserve to be *major generals.*" *(They laugh, then* WILSON *repeats quietly.)* Major generals.

(*They walk together upstage with arms on each other's shoulders. They stop and freeze in this position, backs to audience, as* NARRATOR *enters.*)

NARRATOR. It rained. The procession of weary soldiers became a bedraggled train of despondent men marching through the mud under a low wretched sky. Yet the youth smiled. He had rid himself of the red sickness of battle. The nightmare was in the past.

(*MUSIC CUE #10—"Ending."* WILSON *and* HENRY *move to the flags introduced in the beginning.*)

Through the hosts of leaden rain clouds, came a golden ray of sun.

(WILSON *and* HENRY *flourish their flags and hold them high as if they symbolize the rising sun. We hear "The Battle Cry of Freedom" as the men march away. The sound fades to quiet drumming, then fades to silence.*)

END

Discussing and Interpreting
The Red Badge of Courage

Play Analysis

1. Who do you think is the antagonist in *The Red Badge of Courage*? Why?
2. Explain the significance of the title of the play.
3. Throughout the play, hope and faith turn into despair and disbelief, then back again. Which do you believe predominates, and why?
4. Which of Henry's experiences in the Civil War do you think would be the same in a war in the twenty-first century?
5. **Thematic Connection: To Be a Hero** Just because Henry Fleming is the protagonist, or main character, of this play doesn't necessarily make him a hero. Do you think Henry is heroic? Why or why not?

Literary Skill: Write Interesting Dialogue

Imagine that one of the people below is a spy trying to get a message to the North or the South during the Civil War. The other person is aware of the spy's activities and intends to thwart them, but doesn't want to let on. Decide who is the antagonist and who is the protagonist, and then write their dialogue. Avoid stereotypes and traditional assumptions regarding gender.

Performance Element: Play Against Type

Having read *The Red Badge of Courage*, discuss with your classmates the kind of actors who would normally be cast in the roles of Henry, Jim, Wilson, Mother, and Narrator. Brainstorm ways that the parts could be adapted to include less traditional actors. Discuss whether this might detract from or enhance the production.

Black Elk Speaks

from the biography by John G. Neihardt
adapted for the stage by Christopher Sergel

Creating Context:
The Sioux Nation

Black Elk was an Oglala Sioux holy man who told the story of his life as well as his role in American history to John Neihardt in the early 1930s. At the age of nine, Black Elk had a vision that convinced him he must try to help his people "do the work of the Grandfathers." According to historian Vine Deloria, Jr., Black Elk "shared his visions with Neihardt because he wished to pass along to future generations some of the reality of Oglala life and…to share the burden of visions that remained unfulfilled." The biography that resulted, as well as the play based upon it, tells the story of the important events in Sioux history.

> "They made us many promises, more than I can remember, but they never kept but one; they promised to take our land, and they took it."
>
> Red Cloud (Mah'piua Luta) of the Oglala

During their golden age, the Sioux roamed freely and peacefully throughout the northern plains as hunters and gatherers. As land grew scarce, they turned into warriors, battling with white men and other tribes for territory. Most Sioux now live in South Dakota. They call themselves *Oceti Sakowin*, or *Seven Council Fires*, signifying that they are sub-divided into seven independent bands. These seven bands are:

Oglala (*They Scatter Their Own* or *Dust Scatterers*). Red Cloud and Crazy Horse were Oglala Sioux.

Sicangu or **Brulé** (*Burnt Thighs*). Spotted Tail was a Brulé chief.

Hunkpapa (*Camps at the Edge*). Sitting Bull was a Hunkpapa.

Minneconjou (*Plants by the Water*). Big Foot was a chief of the Minneconjou. The tribal name may be spelled other ways: *Minniconjou, Miniconjou, Mnikoju* or *Mnikowoju*, among others.

Itazipco or **Sans Arc** (*Without Bow*). *Itazipcola* is the full way of saying this name. The *la* is dropped during speech, as it is "understood." *Sans Arc*, which is a French word, means *No Bow, Without Bow,* or *Plain Bow*.

Sihasapa or **Black Foot** (*Black Feet*). Also spelled *Siha Sapa*.

Oohenupa (*Two Kettle* or *Two Boilings*). Also spelled *Oo'henumpa*.

As a Reader: Reading Historical Texts Critically

When reading historical accounts, one must be careful to remember that most human events can be described from more than one point of view. Soldiers who fought with General Custer might tell a different story about the Battle of the Little

Big Horn, or the Greasy Grass, than either of the accounts below. Notice how descriptions from the biography become stage directions in the play.

from Page • • • • • • to Stage

Then another cry went up out in the dust: "Crazy Horse is coming! Crazy Horse is coming!" Off toward the west and north they were yelling "Hoka hey!" like a big wind roaring, and making the tremolo;* and you could hear eagle bone whistles screaming.

The valley went darker with dust and smoke, and there were only shadows and a big noise of many cries and hoofs and guns. On the left of where I was I could hear the shod hoofs of the soldiers' horses going back into the brush and there was shooting everywhere. ...

Many of our warriors were following the soldiers up a hill on the other side of the river. ...

I will sing you some of the kill-songs that our people made up and sang that night:

"Long Hair has never returned,
So his woman is crying, crying.
Looking over here, she cries . ...."
"Long Hair, where he lies nobody knows.
Crying, they seek him. He lies over here."
"Let go your holy irons (guns).
You are not men enough to do any harm.
Let go your holy irons!"

from *Black Elk Speaks* by John G. Neihardt

* a rapidly vibrating musical tone.

VOICES *(crying as part of the great wind).* Crazy horse is coming! Crazy horse is coming! C-r-a-z-y H-o-r-s-e! (INDIAN GIRLS *make the tremolo).* Reno is still held—Custer tries to get to the river where he's checked— He's driven back to the high ridge by Sitting Bull—by some of the Cheyenne— He's up there—the Wolf of Washita.... George Armstrong Custer! *(The sounds climax, leading to BLACK ELK's vocal climax)* Suddenly! All at once! Like bees swarming out of a hive! Like a hurricane! A battle cry. D-a-k-o-t-a-s! *(the climax.)* There—never— was —a—better—day—to—die!

(With this cry, INDIAN WARRIORS *suddenly appear on all levels from behind, as though storming the top of a high ridge. They hold* CUSTER *and his* MEN. ALL *come up at the same moment.)*

WARRIORS *(their weapons aloft, with a great shout).* Hoka hey! *(Blackout.)....*

BLACK ELK *(quietly, respectfully).* Crazy Horse? (CRAZY HORSE *looks over to him.)* I'm told it was Santee who killed Custer.

CRAZY HORSE *(quietly).* Yes.

BLACK ELK. Someone said it was White Bull of the Minneconjous.

CRAZY HORSE. Yes.

BLACK ELK *(puzzled, smiling).* I thought probably you killed him.

CRAZY HORSE *(quietly).* Yes, I killed him, too. He was killed by the Indian people.

from *Black Elk Speaks* adapted by Christopher Sergel

As a Set Designer: Re-creating Events

In a historical play, the set designer must balance the actual with the suggestive. Nothing should appear out of its time period. On the other hand, a designer must be free to interpret the events artistically and symbolically. As you read the play, think about sets that capture the spirit of the play.

Black Elk Speaks

Time
Early 1930s

The Characters

BLACK ELK	YELLOW WOMAN
OLD WOMAN	BLACK KETTLE
CHIEF TECUMSEH	WILLIAM BENT
INDIAN/COLUMBUS	MAJOR WYNKOOP
INDIAN GIRL	COLONEL CHIVINGTON
ANDREW JACKSON	LIEUTENANT CRAMER
MANUELITO	CRAZY HORSE
YOUNG NAVAHO	RED CLOUD
GENERAL CARLETON	COMMISSIONER TAYLOR
INDIAN WOMAN	COLONEL CARRINGTON
A. B. NORTON	GENERAL SHERMAN
LITTLE CROW	MAGPIE
SHAKOPEE	GENERAL CUSTER
THOMAS GALBRAITH	GENERAL SHERIDAN
WOWINAPA	CHIEF TOSAWI
LONG TRADER SIBLEY	JOHN FINERTY

PET-SAN-WASTE-WIN

VARIOUS INDIANS,

SOLDIERS and VOICES

Setting
Pine Ridge Reservation, South Dakota

ACT ONE

As the houselights dim, a deep drumbeat begins accompanied by an Indian flute. Women begin to sing softly, joining the drum and the flute. In the darkness, there is the brief flash of a fire being struck at a high level upstage. A spot of light comes up on this high place revealing BLACK ELK *in prayer. Before him on a large stone are some small bags of onion and sage that send up a little smoke and a sweet smell. Below, more women enter to join the others in the song. Some are with children, who laugh and play as their mothers try to restrain them.* BLACK ELK *rises to pray and, as he does, those below pause, looking up to him.*

BLACK ELK. Grandfather. Great Mysterious One. You have been always. You are older than all need, older than all pain and prayer. Look upon your children with children in their arms! That they may face the winds and walk the Good Road to the Day of Quiet. Teach us to walk on the soft earth, a relative to all that live. Help us, for without you we are nothing.

OLD WOMAN *(speaking as the others sing under).* During The-Moon-When-Ponies-Shed, which is the month of May, following The-Winter-When-They-Issued-Out-Blankets, which is the year 1931, Black Elk tries to save the story of the People.

(Other INDIANS *enter and join softly in the song.)*

OLD WOMAN. With these friends to help, Black Elk will speak of this . . . because people without history are no more than wind on the buffalo grass. *(She considers the area.)* This is a place of the spirit . . . where our old men come to pray and to wait. *(She calls to* BLACK ELK.*)* What do you wait for, old man?

BLACK ELK *(with wry humor).* I wait for yesterday. But all that will come again is what an old man can remember. *(He starts down.)* If this were only my life, I would not speak of it. What is one man that he should make much of his winters? It is the story of all life that is holy and good to tell and of us two-leggeds sharing in it with the four-leggeds and the wings of the air and all green things; for these are the children of one mother which is the earth and their father which is the sky. *(He indicates the singers.)* Words to a song in a foreign tongue can sound a little peculiar. *(He speaks gently.)* But of course we were not singing in a foreign tongue. The only foreign language here . . . is English. *(The song is concluding.)* Let me be courteous and translate. *(He does so.)* The old men say "The Earth only endures." You spoke truly. You are right. *(With finality)* And we are no more than names whispered by a wind rustling through a field of corn on a summer night . . . people who lived in happiness and sorrow to become grass on these hills, and a few names on the map. Sioux City, Pontiac, Miami, Lake Huron, Omaha. *(He speaks lightly.)* Before the roadsigns were erected to our memory, these were people. See them with me.

*(*INDIANS *enter on various levels as* BLACK ELK *continues. All are proud and magnificently dressed. Some are evidently on horseback.)*

BLACK ELK. See the great horse nations of the Sioux ride out across the unfenced prairie . . . free men with weapons in their hands, eagle feather bonnets in the wind. Bone whistles pierce the air! Women send the tremolo![1] *(An* INDIAN *picks up a mask of a great chief of an earlier time,* TECUMSEH, *and holds it above his head.)* And hear the ghost of Chief Tecumseh cry out a warning that still haunts us.

TECUMSEH. Sleep no longer, O my brothers! Think not you can remain passive to the

---

1. tremolo, the repetition of musical tones to create a trembling, or vibrato, effect

common danger and escape the common fate . . . or we will vanish before the avarice and oppression of the white man as snow before the summer sun. *(Others come forward in support.)* Shall we let the white man cut down our trees to build fences around us? Shall we give up our homes, our country bequeathed to us by the Great Spirit, the graves of our dead and everything that is clear and sacred to us? *(His voice reaches a climax.)* I know you will cry with me . . . never!

ALL *(an explosion). Never! (The light on them dims as they disperse, muttering "Never.")*

BLACK ELK. I saw *never* come to an end a few days after Christmas in 1890, right over there at Pine Ridge, South Dakota . . . along a ravine, and beside a stream called Wounded Knee. I did not know then how much was ending. When I look back now from this high hill of my old age, I can still see the butchered women and children heaped and scattered all along the crooked gulch as plain as when I saw them with eyes still young. And I can see that something else died there. Lean to hear my voice. What I've seen is for you. You must see what else died in the bloody snow and was buried in the blizzard . . . I was not born till The-Moon-of-Popping-Trees in The-Winter-When-Four-Crows-Were-Killed. December 1863. I'm a Medicine Man of the Oglala. Like my father and his father, my name is Black Elk. When I was young and could still hope, I was given a vision. During The-Summer-Moon-When-Cherries-Turn-Black, I heard a Voice call to me. *(A drumbeat begins.)* The Voice said, "All over the universe, they've finished a day of happiness."

(Others appear, moving in a ritual rhythm to the drum.)

BLACK ELK. The Voice was so beautiful that nothing anywhere could keep from dancing. The Voice said, "Behold this day, for it is yours to make. You shall stand upon the center of the world." *(He starts up the highest level.)* I asked where that might be, and the Voice said, "Anywhere is the center of the world." It seemed I reached the highest mountain in the Black Hills, and from the rocks color flashed upward to become a rainbow in flame. As I stood there, I saw more than I can tell, and I understood more than I saw, for I was seeing in a sacred manner. (BLACK ELK *now becomes the holy man; the drum and the dance of the others an accompaniment to what he says.)* I saw that the sacred hoop of my people was one of the many hoops that made one circle, and being endless, it was holy . . . with all powers becoming one power in the People without end. I was offered a wooden cup full of water and in the water was the sky. "Take this," the Voice said. "It's the power to make live, and it's yours." I was given a mission in the form of a bright red stick that by my power I must bring to life. I was to place it at the living center of the nation's hoop. I was to make it grow into a shielding tree that would bloom . . . a mighty flowering tree to shelter the children: a tree to protect the People, to save us from the winds! *(He takes a breath.)* Soon I shall be under the grass and the vision lost, unless . . . you were sent to save it. Hear our story, so the terrible isolation of our lives can break. We will show you in simple ways . . . like picture drawings. Some of us will put on hats and try to look like the white settlers or the bluecoat soldiers. Consider what we do in this place an Indian pictograph in which you finally see what else was killed at Wounded Knee.

(An INDIAN *enters on a raised level.)*

BLACK ELK. If you're to understand the ending in the blizzard, you should know the beginning in the warm ocean off a tropical island of the people that Christopher Columbus was about to name for the Saviour. *(He calls to the* INDIAN.*)* Arrange your blanket like a Columbus robe. *(He speaks critically.)* Like Columbus! His crew had mutinied. They were about to turn back, leave us alone a little longer. Then the lookout saw something in the water, something that made them decide to sail on for a few more hours. *(He is incredulous at the irony.)* A branch from a tree in flower.

VOICE. *Terra! Terra firma!*

(Warm lights come up. INDIANS *enter. Some are curious and friendly, others are cautious and half-hidden.)*

INDIAN *(becoming* COLUMBUS, *humorously).* Look at all the redskins! *(All laugh.)*

BLACK ELK. No, no. You're a great chief. *(To the audience)* Within your heart, you must see him as though real.

COLUMBUS *(changing, with a graceful gesture).* I ask you to forgive their nakedness, which is only from ignorance. These gentle *Indios* are a people without fraud or malice, to be delivered to our faith by love. *(He is amused.)* They believe that we come from the sky.

INDIAN GIRL *(gently correcting* COLUMBUS*).* At first we thought they'd come from the sky. We thought they'd come like the light of dawn.

COLUMBUS *(regretfully).* Unfortunately these are not a practical people . . . existing simply as you see, gathering wild fruit and mollusks. *(He speaks firmly.)* Such people must be made to work, clear land, and do all that is necessary. This is part of the natural order.

INDIAN GIRL *(with finality).* We were wrong about the dawn. They came like the night . . . and we began to die.

COLUMBUS. Not before you'd been baptized!

We gave you hope for heaven. *(To the audience)* Redskinned people are not mentioned in the Bible . . . which raises a serious question as to whether or not they are actually human beings. *(He speaks graciously.)* Personally, I'm convinced they are human beings . . . and generous with what they have to such a degree as no one would believe but he who has seen it. Let me show you. Truly I think they would give their hearts. *(He calls to an* INDIAN GIRL, *using gestures to indicate his meaning.)* Child . . . I admire that ornament on your arm. *(Trying to understand, she follows his gestures, then touches her bracelet.)* Yes . . . that's it. *(He nods, smiling. The* INDIAN GIRL *takes off her bracelet and hands it up to* COLUMBUS.*)* Thank you, child.

INDIAN GIRL. At the time, it seemed such a trifle.

COLUMBUS *(inspecting the bracelet, low key).* Quite malleable . . . no alloys. *(He smiles down at the* INDIAN GIRL.*)* Charming . . . thank you.

INDIAN GIRL *(perceiving tragedy).* If there was any hope for us . . . this is the moment in which it was lost.

COLUMBUS *(as the light goes out on him, softly).* Oro!²

INDIAN GIRL *(to* BLACK ELK*).* Why weren't you prepared on the mainland? Surely some cry from the islands reached the mainland? *(She speaks bitterly.)* If you hadn't let them come ashore! If you hadn't met them with gifts!

BLACK ELK *(gently).* If you hadn't been wearing gold. *(The* INDIAN GIRL *has no reply and rejoins the others.)* The storm that gathered in the islands began blowing out across the land of the people. On our prairies we see the approach of pitiful survivors from the proud tribes where the sun

---

2. *oro (Spanish),* gold

rises, driven like dead leaves before the wind. We discover that a prominent Indian fighter has been elected your president . . . the man you call Andrew Jackson.

(*A tall, distinguished* INDIAN *wearing a suggestion of colonial attire enters L.*)

BLACK ELK. The man we call Sharp Knife.

JACKSON. To prevent racial incidents between citizens of Georgia and the Cherokee, I suggest the propriety of removing the Indians to an area west of the Mississippi where they'll have the protection of a permanent Indian frontier, which I promise . . . for as long as grass grows or water runs.

BLACK ELK (*after* JACKSON, *who starts off*). It won't be the grass or water that forgets. (JACKSON *stops, irked.*) You made us so many promises, more than we can remember. But you never kept but one. You promised to take our land, and you took it.

JACKSON (*prodded by anger into frankness*). It is vain to charge us with results that grow out of the inevitable march of human events. We're the superior race. It's our destiny to possess this land.

BLACK ELK. Is it because of the yellow metal that drives you crazy?

JACKSON (*amused*). What would Indians do with gold?

BLACK ELK. Make ornaments.

JACKSON (*finding it hard to contain his amusement*). There—you see?

BLACK ELK. I don't see . . . except your special way with words. When you steal land, you call it Manifest Destiny. If an Indian tries to defend himself, you call him a hostile. Even after destroying us with guns, whiskey, and smallpox, you find your word to describe what happened. You say we've vanished. (JACKSON *exits as song begins offstage.*) To the south, from where the summer comes, the winds are already blowing

dust stirred up by soldiers. Our cousins, the Navaho, elect a new chief . . . Manuelito.

(MANUELITO *enters UR, revealed by light.*)

BLACK ELK. He's a man so prosperous with his livestock, he was not thought a hostile. A man of big enthusiasms, and large appetites . . . and a hostile! Pay attention. Some things will not vanish. (*He exits.*)

MANUELITO (*picking up the song*). In a sacred manner I live. My horses are many. (*With great good humor*) My wives are also numerous, and my mules . . . more than you could count! Men call me Manuelito of the Navaho, and we capture mules from the Mexicans. This began because the Mexicans capture children from us to sell as slaves. And when we go to recapture the children, we gather up all the livestock in sight. This is so logical! Then the Americans came and they complicated everything. They named our land New Mexico, and the Mexicans became American citizens. This doesn't stop them from stealing Navaho children, but now when we retaliate, soldiers chase after us because we did not become citizens, because we're Indians. Do you follow that? I don't follow that! When soldiers shot some of our livestock, I assembled a great force, and just before dawn we attacked their fort. (*With enthusiasm*) We burned some buildings and got them so confused, they started shooting each other. At daylight we pulled back into our hills. A magnificent demonstration! (*Incredulously*) You can't imagine how seriously this was taken by the United States Army. They sent companies of cavalry to scour the Chuska Mountains for the hostiles. When they tried to corner us in our own mountains, they only accomplished one thing . . . they exhausted their horses. (*With an amused shrug*) Finally they made peace.

(INDIANS *and* SOLDIERS, *Indians in soldiers' coats, enter behind* MANUELITO *in animated discussion, and with music appropriate to the place and period.*)

MANUELITO. Now when we come to the fort, it's to trade . . . and for horse races.

SOLDIERS AND INDIANS (*alternately, in a festive swirl*). Bet ya a dollar agin two blankets . . . We've got a bet . . . No Navaho pony kin beat a quarter horse . . . Quarter horses don't last . . . A jug of Tizwin against your pipe tobacco . . . I bet on the Chief . . . Name your wager, and no beads . . . Your pick from my ponies, my pick from your ponies.

MANUELITO (*talking over the swirl behind*). We have a big contest today. Their best horse will be ridden by Lieutenant Ortiz. And our best horse will be ridden by me! Manuelito! So there are many large bets. (*A big bell clangs sharply. All face front watching a horse race. There is the sound of horses galloping made by a drum.* MANUELITO *pantomimes riding. With excitement.*) The horses are off at a gallop, and already I know . . . my pony is much faster than his overfed quarter horse. (*The watchers shout with excitement.*) I'm getting ready to talk to my pony . . . talk to him with my knees . . . as soon as we get around the turn, I'll say . . . time to move, little one . . . time to show the speed of a Navaho pony! Hi-ya! I'm unable to turn—I have no reins—the reins come apart in my hands . . . my pony is running off the track! (*The watchers, apparently seeing this out over the audience, are divided. The* INDIANS *are stunned, incredulous. The* SOLDIERS *are derisive.*)[3]

SOLDIERS. We win! We win! Whipped him good! Can't even handle his pony! Collect the bets! We won!

MANUELITO (*after bringing the remnants of a leather strap from behind his back, half sad,* half amused). Probably some soldier bet more than he could afford. Probably that's why he slashed my bridle.

(*A* YOUNG NAVAHO *comes up to* MANUELITO, *incredulously taking the cut reins from him and inspecting them.*)

SOLDIERS (*meanwhile*). Indians can't stand competition—just come apart—got no grit, none of 'em! Come on . . . back to the fort.

YOUNG NAVAHO (*shouting at the* SOLDIERS, *holding up the reins*). Wait! The bridle was cut. See for yourself!

SOLDIERS (*hard*). We already seen . . . (*He jerks the blanket from the* YOUNG NAVAHO's *shoulder.*) . . . and you lost.

YOUNG NAVAHO. You cheated! Give back my blanket!

MANUELITO. It doesn't matter. Let him take it!

SOLDIER (*contemptuously*). Was you thinking he might stop me? Ya thieving Navahos kin always steal somethin' else to bet. (*As he exits*) Ladrone![4]

YOUNG NAVAHO (*calling after the* SOLDIERS *as they go off*). Run the race over! Come back and run an honest race! Cowards! (*Racing after the* SOLDIERS) Bluecoat dogs! (*All watch anxiously. As his cry fades off L, there is a tense pause, then a shot. For a moment, all are frozen with horror.*)

MANUELITO (*breaking into this, urgently*). Get the children, get on your ponies—get out! Quickly! Get mounted! Get to the hills! (*As he speaks, there are whimpers of fear and cries of fright. Women search frantically for children. More shots are fired and the* INDIANS *scatter, running, trying to collect each other and get out.*) Get away! (*He takes hold of two confused* INDIAN GIRLS *and hurries them off.*) This way—go! (*During the above*

---

3. derisive, expressing scorn or ridicule
4. *ladrone* (Spanish), thief

and after, there are sounds from offstage; sounds of shouted orders, shots, horses galloping, cries and shouts. The character of the light has shifted. Only MANUELITO *remains. The sound diminishes.)* After this we had some unexpected good luck . . . the white soldiers started killing each other. *(Regretfully)* Like many nice things, it didn't last. The graycoats were driven away, but more and more bluecoats kept coming . . . an army of bluecoats under General Carleton. Naturally, he began looking around for someone to kill.

(GENERAL CARLETON *enters L.)*

CARLETON. As commanding general, I'm concerned with the future of this great pastoral region, this princely realm.

MANUELITO *(calling across to* CARLETON *graciously).* Thank you.

CARLETON *(with distaste).* Unfortunately, this valuable tract is infested with Indians. The Navaho are wolves that run through these mountains.

MANUELITO. It was beginning to dawn on me just who he was deciding to kill.

CARLETON. The Navaho must be removed and confined on lands set aside—the Bosque Redondo.

MANUELITO. Why the wretched Bosque Redondo? What's the purpose in forcing people onto land so arid it won't grow beans or feed sheep?

CARLETON *(the answer is obvious).* To open this land for American citizens.

MANUELITO. What about the human beings who already live here?

CARLETON *(replying to a foolish question).* You're not citizens.

MANUELITO. For more generations than anyone can count, the Navaho has lived in the Chuska Mountains.

CARLETON. But now you have to be moved.

MANUELITO. Why must we be confined hundreds of miles from our homes? *(Still no reply. A threat.)* If you cage the badger, he'll fight to break free. Chain the eagle, and he'll struggle with fury to regain the sky which is his home.

CARLETON. I'm sending out the following order, effective immediately. There is to be no council held with the Indians. Unless they go to the Bosque Redondo, the men are to be slain wherever found.

MANUELITO. There didn't seem much room for negotiation. The skirmishing had an enjoyable side . . . it always does. But General Carleton had no humor. He ordered his soldiers to destroy our fields. *(Incredulously)* Can you understand this? Destroying the earth with its pastures, corn, peach trees? *(Helplessly)* We can't hide a crop of grain or a pumpkin patch. They began burning the food for children! *(Conceding)* I've raided, too. Who hasn't? Against the Mexicans, which is only natural. But we never took so much as to ruin a man. And it's stupid to kill—also bad business. After all, a dead Mexican can't raise more cattle. But these raids . . . their purpose was starvation.

CARLETON *(implacably).* Go to the Bosque Redondo or we'll destroy you. We will not make peace on any other terms. If you don't go, the war will be pursued . . . *(He is hard.)* . . . until you cease to exist.

MANUELITO. We choose to stay on our land—on the burned-out remains of our land.

CARLETON. Then suffer the consequences.

MANUELITO. Then we suffer the consequences. *(Unhappily)* The very old and the very young suffer them especially. Our children are eating palmilia root. We're almost naked . . . freezing. *(He speaks with hushed fury.)* But we have not ceased to exist! *(A rat-a-tat-tat begins on a drum.)*

CARLETON. I'm informing Washington that I require an additional regiment of cavalry.

MANUELITO. To fight a few starving Navaho?

CARLETON. Additional troops for my command are essential. (*The rat-a-tat-tat grows louder.*)

MANUELITO (*bitterly*). Now hear the perfect argument for getting more troops.

CARLETON (*as he exits*). We need them to protect people going to and from mine fields. Providence has indeed blessed us—precious metals lie here at our feet, to be had for the mere picking up. Precious metals. (*The military drums now seem to be coming from all sides.*)

MANUELITO. Fresh troops kept coming—like water down a stream bed after a cloudburst.

(*An* INDIAN WOMAN, *a refugee, crosses in front of* MANUELITO.)

MANUELITO (*speaking over the climaxing military drums*). But we shall not be washed away. My God lives here and I shall not leave. I shall not submit. I was born in the Chuska Mountains and I shall remain. I shall never—(*The drums stop and he interrupts himself.*)

(*An* INDIAN WOMAN *enters and* MANUELITO *looks over to her.*)

MANUELITO (*quietly*). Where do you go?

INDIAN WOMAN. To turn ourselves in. To be sent to the Bosque Redondo.

MANUELITO. Do you *know* about the Bosque?

INDIAN WOMAN. The soldiers run you through a pen gate like sheep so you can be counted. There are no implements, so to get firewood you have to dig out mesquite roots with your hands. For shelter, you clear out a burrow in the ground where you live like an animal.

MANUELITO. Could any fate be worse?

INDIAN WOMAN. Watching my children starve to death. (MANUELITO *looks at her for a moment, then turns away. Half plea, half accusation.*) Can you protect your women? Can you feed your children? (MANUELITO *can only stand mute and frustrated.*) Then come with us to the Bosque.

MANUELITO (*defeated, but unable to surrender*). I will not move from our mountains.

INDIAN WOMAN (*as she goes up to the higher level to follow the others across*). I leave you as if your grave were already made.

(*Other* INDIANS, *perhaps seen in silhouette, join the slow walk across the high level, and this continues.*)

MANUELITO (*as the* INDIANS *cross behind him*). It's The-Moon-of-the-Strong-Cold as they start their four-hundred-mile walk to the Bosque. Soldiers harass them. Children are snatched from their mothers by slavers. The food is flour with which we are not familiar. My people mix the flour with water and try to eat the cold paste. (*With passion*) And they walk, people with empty eyes . . . and as they walk, they think about their home in the mountains . . . watching flocks feed in valley pastures, riding where they can smell sage or the piñon smoke from their campfires, watching an eagle sweep across the sky. (*Bitterly*) And they start to die.

(CARLETON *enters.*)

MANUELITO. Even the New Mexicans are beginning to criticize the brutal insanity of General Carleton. (*He starts across to* CARLETON.) But you're too busy to listen—busy deploying your vast forces against what still survives of Navaho resistance—less than twenty men against a regiment . . . ragged, starving . . .

CARLETON (*giving the final description*). Hostiles!

MANUELITO (*with angry agreement*). Hostiles!

CARLETON. Throw down your weapons.

MANUELITO. Weapons? If we still had weapons, we could not go to the Bosque. (*He goes up after the others.*) If we still had weapons, we'd use them! (*As he starts across after the others,* CARLETON *watches.*)

CARLETON. The exodus of this whole people from the land of their fathers is not only an interesting but a touching sight. They fought us gallantly; they defended their mountains with heroism of which any people might be proud . . . until they found it was their destiny, as it had been the destiny of their brethren, tribe after tribe, away back toward the rising of the sun, to give way to the insatiable[5] progress of our race! (*He insists.*) I made them give way! (*He is shaken as he crosses L. He pauses, bewildered.*) Eighteen days after I forced the surrender of the hostiles—for what reason I can't imagine—I've been removed from this command. (*He turns to go off.* MANUELITO *pauses R.*) For what reason? I'd opened this land for you—for your claims and settlement—this princely realm! (*He exits.*)

(MANUELITO *looks back as a civilian,* A. B. NORTON, *enters.*)

MANUELITO (*looking toward* NORTON). There should be a special page in your history called, "The time when three right things were done." The first—removing an oppressive general. The second—appointing a humane man superintendent of an Indian reservation. Let his name be noted—it was Norton.

NORTON. Why would any sensible man select a spot for a reservation where the water is scarcely bearable, where the soil is poor and cold, and where the mesquite roots twelve miles distant are the only wood for the Indians to use? If they remain on this reservation, they must always be held by force and not from choice. (*Impassioned*) Oh, let them go back—back to where they can have good cool water to drink, wood plenty to keep them from freezing to death, and where the soil will produce something for them to eat! (*He stands with clenched fists, unable to continue, then turns and goes off R.*)

MANUELITO. Now we come to the third miracle. Someone heard this man! (*He goes DR.*) It was to take time. Officials came from what we call "The Place Where Everything Is Disputed." Others call it Washington.

(INDIANS *enter R, carrying blankets, bundles, belongings.*)

MANUELITO. These people held many councils with us. We agreed four times to a new treaty—we said yes four times—if we could go home. (*He walks over a few steps and stands a little to the right of the* INDIANS.) The nights and days were long before we could start. (*Hushed with excitement*) Then it was time to load the wagons. (*He shouts.*) Time to move out! Now! (*Cries explode from the waiting* INDIANS.) Move the wagons! Get the mules pulling! Hi-ya! Faster! (*The* INDIANS *struggle with their bundles, laboring to keep the pace.*) We drove the mules! We were in such a hurry, I'm ashamed how we drove those mules! (*Apologetically*) We couldn't stop ourselves. (*He shouts.*) Faster! (*All look at a point out over the audience now, looking with intense, but uncertain hope.*) We continued to press, and we reached Albuquerque, and we saw the top of a mountain, and we wondered if it was our mountain. (*Softly, joyously*) And it was—it was our mountain. (*The look of uncertain hope changes to joy.*) Some of the old men and women cried, they were so happy. (*The light on them dims off. Softly.*) We felt like talking to the earth, we loved it so much.

---

5. insatiable, unable to be satisfied; unstoppable

The light is off the NAVAHO. BLACK ELK *enters.*

BLACK ELK. The Navaho had returned to a tiny, burned-out remnant of their land, but they'd make it live. There's something you might have learned from this; something about the connection between people and the earth, and how you could take most of what they have, but still let them live. (*He considers this for an instant before turning slight L.*) To the east, where the light comes from, something was happening from which we should have learned. The winds that will finally pile up the snow over the crooked gulch in South Dakota are blowing across the eastern frontier of the People. This is where the grassland starts out of the Minnesota forests . . . and where our cousins, the Santee, guard the land on the east. We're unaware that they've already been confined to a narrow reservation along a river. The young men of the Santee blame their chief.

VOICE (*taunting, from offstage*). Ta-oya-te-duta is a coward!

BLACK ELK. Ta-oya-te-duta is the name of their chief, who is also called Little Crow.

VOICE (*more provocatively, from offstage*). Ta-oya-te-duta is a coward!

BLACK ELK. And he's called coward. But he's not a coward. However, he has a quality often mistaken for cowardice—realism.

(*Light is coming up.* LITTLE CROW *enters, carrying a jacket with brass buttons.*)

BLACK ELK. The worst reality for Little Crow is that he touched the pen to the treaties that deceived his people. He starts searching desperately for some way to deal with these powerful, avaricious[6] men who always tell lies. Little Crow hopes it will help if he can appear more like them.

LITTLE CROW (*putting on the jacket, to* BLACK ELK). Our training doesn't apply anymore.

Instead of learning to live with nature, we should become clever lawyers. (BLACK ELK *exits.*) I started wearing the white man jacket, built a house, joined the Episcopal Church. Then I journeyed to Washington to seek assistance from Great White Father—which is how Indians are expected to address President Buchanan.

(INDIANS *enter.*)

LITTLE CROW. Achieving what? My people are starving. (*Dryly*) Perhaps we're supposed to starve.

SHAKOPEE. There's no game on the reservation. I'm sending a hunting party to our hunting grounds.

LITTLE CROW. You will not. We must observe the treaty.

WOMAN. We can't eat the treaty.

LITTLE CROW. The treaty provides for payments.

SHAKOPEE. What payments? I've seen no payments.

LITTLE CROW. The payments are called annuities, and, when they come, we'll exchange them for food.

SHAKOPEE. Let's take the food now, and they can keep the annuities.

LITTLE CROW. That's not the way it's done. You're very ignorant of these things.

SHAKOPEE. My stomach is especially ignorant. (*There's a general murmur of agreement. He points L.*) The agency warehouse is filled with provisions and we could—

LITTLE CROW (*sharply*). We must observe the treaty!

VOICE (*calling from offstage R.*). Ta-oya-te-duta is a coward!

LITTLE CROW (*hard, ignoring the voice*). Observe the treaty or elect another to speak for you.

---

6. avaricious, greedy

SHAKOPEE. It's under discussion.

LITTLE CROW *(with sarcasm).* When I no longer have the responsibility, I'll enjoy discussion too. I look forward to uncomplicated discussions of how great heroes should deal with our problems.

SHAKOPEE *(stung).* What we discuss is electing Traveling Hail to speak for us.

LITTLE CROW. Traveling Hail would be an excellent spokesman.

(THOMAS GALBRAITH, head of the Indian agency, enters DL. He stops there as he sees the INDIANS.)

SHAKOPEE. Meanwhile, you have the responsibility. What will you do about your responsibility?

LITTLE CROW *(pausing, frankly).* What I can. *(As he turns to continue L, he sees* GALBRAITH. *In spite of himself, he hopes.)* Have you come to pay the annuities?

GALBRAITH. What made you think of annuities?

LITTLE CROW. I saw you talking with the post trader. I thought perhaps he smelled a little money.

GALBRAITH. The money hasn't come. *(There is a stir of anger.)*

LITTLE CROW. Annuities were pledged by the treaties and we must have them to exchange for food.

GALBRAITH *(importantly).* The Great Council in Washington—

LITTLE CROW *(interjecting).* The Congress.

GALBRAITH *(irked).* The Great Congress in Washington has many more important—

LITTLE CROW *(interrupting).* Then give back our hunting grounds and we'll say no more about it. *(*GALBRAITH *is amused and laughs.)*

GALBRAITH. Listen to the Indian!

LITTLE CROW *(furiously).* Listen to the Indian—listen to him say something simple. The money is ours, but we can't get it.

We have no food—but here are warehouses filled with food. We ask that you, the agent, make some arrangement by which we can get something to eat from these warehouses.

GALBRAITH *(flatly).* I have no intention of issuing food before the arrival of the funds.

LITTLE CROW. Then we may have to take our own way to keep ourselves from starving. When men are hungry—

GALBRAITH. The correct procedure is to wait. *(He turns to go.)* That's all I have to say to you.

LITTLE CROW *(goes after* GALBRAITH, *frantic with frustration).* What are my people to eat while we wait?

GALBRAITH *(as he exits).* As far as I'm concerned—eat grass! *(There is a moment of stunned silence after his exit. Then rage and frustration explode from the INDIANS.)*

INDIANS *(simultaneously).* Grass! Are we now sheep? Break into the warehouses! Take the food! It's our food! Take our food and burn their buildings!

SHAKOPEE *(in a climaxing outburst).* War!

LITTLE CROW. Wait!

WOMAN. Now!

SHAKOPEE. The bluecoats are still fighting the graycoats.

WOMAN. He's right!

LITTLE CROW *(a cry).* He is not right! Stop such foolish talk. *(A tense pause)*

SHAKOPEE. It's also foolish to starve to death.

LITTLE CROW *(anxiously).* You don't realize their power. You have no idea. To fight a war against such power as they—

SHAKOPEE. Is this all you can say?

LITTLE CROW. I say—no war!

SHAKOPEE *(outraged).* We need someone else to speak for us. *(The INDIANS begin to push past him and start off R.)*

LITTLE CROW (*trying to reason with the* INDIANS). I've been to their land in the east—seen their giant forces, their terrible guns . . .

SHAKOPEE (*as he walks past, speaking into* LITTLE CROW'S *face*). Someone else! (*All are gone.* LITTLE CROW *is alone, rejected.*)

LITTLE CROW (*unhappily*). It would have been so easy for the agent to have given us a little food—with which I might have kept a little control. (*An absurdity*) What always defeats you is stupidity. If it isn't your own stupidity, it's the stupidity of someone else. I was quiet. I waited in the quiet hoping it would stay quiet.

(*The lights begin to dim slowly. A young teenage Indian boy,* WOWINAPA, *comes on, bringing a blanket and lighted kerosene lantern.*)

LITTLE CROW. I made a special point of attending church, listening closely to the sermon, shaking hands with everybody. (LITTLE CROW *walks up to a raised level where* WOWINAPA *has completed rolling out the blanket and has put the lantern near it.*) Then I returned to my house.

WOWINAPA. I've heard sounds of unusual activity tonight, Father.

LITTLE CROW (*seating himself on the blanket*). Activity is not presently our concern, my son. (WOWINAPA *would like to continue, but* LITTLE CROW *stops him gently.*) Please . . . go to bed. (WOWINAPA *goes off.* LITTLE CROW *turns down the lamp.*) My son had good hearing. Perhaps he heard the first sounds of what was to come.

(*In the dim light below,* SHAKOPEE *hurries on, followed by other braves. They are disturbed, and talking in low, anxious voices.*)

LITTLE CROW. I started hearing sounds, too . . . the sounds that run with trouble. People are coming into my house. (*Worried voices are heard as he gets up.*) I doubted very much that they were coming to wake

me with good news. (*He turns up his lantern and holds it out to see* SHAKOPEE *and the other* BRAVES.) Why are you here?

SHAKOPEE (*defensively*). Some young men of my band were hungry. We crossed the river to hunt in the Big Woods—because we were very hungry.

LITTLE CROW. Go on.

SHAKOPEE (*grimly*). Something happened.

BRAVE. We came to a settler's fence and I found a hen's nest with some eggs.

SHAKOPEE. I warned him—don't take the eggs. They belong to a white man and we may get into trouble. This made him so angry he called me a coward.

LITTLE CROW (*resigned to the worst*). What did you do to prove you're not a coward?

SHAKOPEE. I asked if he was brave enough to go up to the house with me while I shot the white man.

BRAVE (*angrily*). I said we'd see who is braver.

LITTLE CROW (*apprehensively*). The others with you—they decided to be brave too?

BRAVE (*proudly*). We all went after them. We killed three men and two women.

LITTLE CROW (*hushed as the news is even worse then he expected*). And two women?

BRAVE (*nodding*). Then we hitched up a wagon we found there and drove back to camp . . . to tell what we had done. (LITTLE CROW *looks down at the* BRAVES, *utterly horrified. It is a moment before he can even speak.*)

LITTLE CROW (*with difficulty*). It must have been a very big wagon.

SHAKOPEE (*puzzled*). Why a big wagon?

LITTLE CROW (*bitterly*). To carry all the punishment, suffering, and death you've brought back to the Santees.

SHAKOPEE (*defensively*). It became a question of manhood.

LITTLE CROW. So you killed two women. My congratulations. But why tell your heroic exploits to me? Go talk to Traveling Hail.

BRAVE *(subdued).* We need your experience. No Santee's life will be safe.

SHAKOPEE *(also subdued, as* LITTLE CROW *looks to him).* You're our chief.

LITTLE CROW *(calling R as light comes up).* My son—take the blanket and lantern. It's dawn.

*(*WOWINAPA *enters R.)*

LITTLE CROW *(to the* BRAVES*).* We should start appreciating every new dawn we see. *(*WOWINAPA *takes the blanket and lantern and goes off R.)*

SHAKOPEE. Instead of waiting for the soldiers to come kill us, let's strike first!

BRAVE. Now! While they're fighting among themselves to the south.

LITTLE CROW. No.

SHAKOPEE. With women killed, they'll take a dreadful vengeance.

LITTLE CROW. You're right.

SHAKOPEE. We have no choice.

LITTLE CROW. We do. We can accept their vengeance.

SHAKOPEE *(stunned).* In place of fighting?

LITTLE CROW *(sharply).* In place of extermination.

BRAVE *(the voice we've heard before, but now a direct taunt).* Ta-oya-te-duta is a coward! *(There is a hushed pause at this challenge.* LITTLE CROW *looks down at the* BRAVES.*)*

BRAVE *(shouting up at* LITTLE CROW*).* Coward!

*(*WOWINAPA *enters, stands on the platform and watches.)*

LITTLE CROW *(softly, sadly).* This terrible word—coward. Is this word worth the lives of all the young men who die for it? *(The* BRAVES *hesitate.)* Is it? *(The* BRAVES *hesitate*

again. LITTLE CROW *is contemptuous.)* You're like little dogs in the Hot Moon when they run mad and snap at their own shadows.

SHAKOPEE *(contritely).* What do we do?

LITTLE CROW. First you open your eyes and try to see. The white men are like the snow when the sky is a blizzard. You may kill one-two-ten; yes, as many as the leaves in the forest yonder, and their brothers will not miss them. Kill one-two-ten, and ten times ten will come to kill you. Count your fingers all day long and white men with guns in their hands will come faster than you can count.

SHAKOPEE. We'll fight so bravely . . .

LITTLE CROW. Go talk about your bravery into the mouth of a cannon. You're fools. You can't see the face of your chief, your eyes are full of smoke. You can't hear his voice, your ears are full of roaring waters. You will die like the rabbits when the hungry wolves hunt them in the Hard Moon of January.

SHAKOPEE *(in despair).* What should we do?

LITTLE CROW *(considering the* BRAVES *a moment, then speaking brokenheartedly).* Evidently there's only one thing you can do—go clean your guns. Go . . .

SHAKOPEE *(as the* BRAVES *hesitate).* What will you do?

LITTLE CROW. *(seeing their inevitable fate).* Perhaps Ta-oya-te-duta is also a fool. Ta-oya-te-duta will die with you. *(*WOWINAPA *watches the sober* BRAVES *follow* LITTLE CROW *off R. The lights dim except for a pin spot on* WOWINAPA.*)*

WOWINAPA. My father did not die so easily. *(A red glow begins in the sky.)* Early next morning, I could see red in the sky toward the agency, and I knew my father had attacked! One of the first killed was the trader who told us to eat grass. It's not wise to taunt people who are starving.

Someone stuffed his mouth with grass. My father won some battles, but there was no victory.

(LONG TRADER SIBLEY, *in military uniform, enters DR.*)

SIBLEY. How could there be a victory? No one who fights white people ever becomes rich or remains two days in one place—but is always fleeing and starving.

WOWINAPA. We were already starving. You gave us many lies, but we couldn't eat them.

SIBLEY. You have a tongue like your father.

WOWINAPA. Long Trader Sibley, who cheated the Santee out of most of our treaty money, then he led the Minnesota Regiment against us.

(BLACK ELK, *carrying the jacket with the brass buttons, enters DL.*)

SIBLEY. Little Crow is holding white women prisoners. He is trying to use the white women for bargaining.

BLACK ELK. What else can he use? You have all the cannons.

SIBLEY. He was doing pretty well without cannons. Of course, the savage has no stomach for protracted[7] war.

BLACK ELK (*in dry agreement*). We have some lack.

WOWINAPA. Is that my father's coat? Where is my father?

BLACK ELK. Doing what he can—without his white man coat. He goes to rouse the prairie Sioux. (*He tosses the coat to* WOWINAPA.) Take his coat. Go with him. Go carry his bundles. (WOWINAPA *exits.*)

SIBLEY (*demanding*). What about the captives? What about the white women?

BLACK ELK. Safe in the sacred custody of those who never joined the fighting, people anxious to return the captives, anxious to receive the protection of your gratitude.

SIBLEY (*coming forward, clenching his fists*). The moment we recovered the white women, the moment they were actually within our lines, I put a ring of artillery around that camp! I started rounding up every male Santee we could still find in Minnesota!

BLACK ELK. Those still in Minnesota were innocent.

SIBLEY. They're Indians! (*He controls himself.*) I formed a military court . . . the civilized way to proceed. (*A funeral drum begins a slow beat.*) Three hundred and three were sentenced to the gallows. It was to be the greatest mass hanging in our history! We built a special gallows. (*Bitterly*) Then we were betrayed! Abraham Lincoln assigned hair-splitting, Indian-loving lawyers to review the convictions—which they reviewed down to just thirty-nine!

(*An Indian chant begins offstage, and some* INDIANS *appear on a high level carrying black hoods.*)

SIBLEY. The citizens of Minnesota were outraged!

BLACK ELK. What's wrong in this decision of the Great Father—which I call him with respect?

SIBLEY (*Can't* BLACK ELK *see?*) They raped white women! (*The* INDIANS *on the "gallows" have put the hoods over their heads. They are calling out names. The drum beats faster.*) Look at them—on the gallows—trying to get their hands free—not the slightest sign of human dignity—shouting their names as though they're proud to be there! Let them pay for their crimes—*now!* (*There is the sudden sound of the gallows' drop, and compete silence. All have snapped their heads to the side. He collects himself with an effort, then forces himself to speak casually.*) The military part of the program was carried out in the best tradition. Every

---

7. protracted, drawn-out; lengthy

detachment knew its appointed place. We have never seen a finer military display in the state. *(He turns away.)*

BLACK ELK *(quietly).* They were trying to get their hands free—free enough to grasp some other's hand there beside them. They were calling out their names and the names of their friends to say they were together at this moment. Together. Together! Each was saying to the other, "I'm with you! I'm here." *(He turns away.)*

(WOWINAPA enters quietly.)

WOWINAPA. Word of the hanging reached us in the Dakota country, but still my father could not convince the prairie Sioux. They couldn't believe there wasn't land enough for everyone. My father decided to go back home. We reached our land during the Moon-of-the-Red-Blooming-Lilies.

SIBLEY *(looking over at WOWINAPA, muttering).* The arrogance of the Indian! Thinking he could walk back into Minnesota!

WOWINAPA. We didn't know the state of Minnesota was paying a scalp-bounty of twenty-five dollars. We were sighted by a farmer and his son who immediately opened fire.

SIBLEY *(as he exits).* As they should!

WOWINAPA *(quietly).* My father was hit twice. I gave him water, and then he died. *(He "sees" LITTLE CROW lying there.)* Before I ran, I covered his body.

BLACK ELK. Go! Get away!

WOWINAPA *(still "seeing" LITTLE CROW).* He'd come back, still trying to do what he could.

BLACK ELK. Please, hurry!

WOWINAPA *(still "seeing" LITTLE CROW, but starting off, softly).* Ta-oya-te-duta was not a coward!

BLACK ELK *(quietly).* All that was left of the Santees in Minnesota was the skull and scalp of Little Crow, which was preserved and put on exhibition in St. Paul. As for those who killed him, the Minnesota legislature appropriated an extra bounty of five hundred dollars. *(He is incredulous.)* From all this, we still learned nothing. From all this, the great tribes of the prairie would do nothing—nothing! Somehow we still couldn't accept what had happened . . . that the people of the east had been destroyed, that there was now no one guarding our frontier, and that we ourselves were in deadly peril!

An impressive Indian woman, YELLOW WOMAN, *enters DR.*

BLACK ELK. Each still thought himself an Arapaho, or Kiowa, or Crow—or some sub-tribe of the Sioux such as the Teton, which is further subdivided into Brule, Blackfoot, Oglala, Hunkpapa—and so forth, endlessly splintered. Much more was needed to make us start thinking ourselves one People. *(He speaks grimly.)* Soldiers and politicians were about to provide *much more.* They were about to send a message no one could mistake screaming across the prairie!

YELLOW WOMAN *(calling up to BLACK ELK).* But why the Cheyenne? Why attack the Cheyenne?

BLACK ELK *(ironically).* Because they're such an easy target.

YELLOW WOMAN. I don't understand that reasoning.

BLACK ELK *(starting off R).* You're closer to the whites, so I thought you might. *(He goes off R.)*

YELLOW WOMAN *(after turning to the audience).* I'm known as Yellow Woman, and my blood is pure Cheyenne. My husband, however, is white. The blood of our children, of course, is half-his, half-Cheyenne. The name of my husband is Little White Man, but he is also called . . . *(She pro-*

nounces it carefully so you will understand.) William Bent. A man of importance. There are three sons; all with unusual names— Robert, George, and Charles. *(She speaks with great pride.)* We live on what is called a ranch.

(BLACK KETTLE, an old, but active, axe-faced Indian, enters R on the platform. He carries a large American flag of the period, which he seems to be planting in the ground. YELLOW WOMAN notices his entrance above her.)

YELLOW WOMAN. Black Kettle is a chief of the Southern Cheyenne. He tries every way to avoid the slightest provocation! We know what happened to the Santees, so he's especially careful to keep the young men busy all the time and out of trouble. If trouble comes anyway, we can depend on two things to protect us. *(She indicates.)* Colonel Greenwood gave this magical flag to Black Kettle and explained that as long as we display it, no soldier will ever fire on us. (BLACK KETTLE, *having planted the flag, hurries down the steps from the platform to* YELLOW WOMAN.*)* The Cheyenne also depend on my husband—the Little White Man.

BLACK KETTLE. Where can a messenger find him?

YELLOW WOMAN. He could be on the trail from Fort Lyon. Is it trouble?

BLACK KETTLE. Lean Bear brought it on himself. Some soldiers were approaching and he rode out to greet them. *(Concerned about the implications)* The soldiers must be under new orders. They opened fire without warning. They shot Lean Bear out of his horse. *(He starts off R, speaking anxiously.)* Find Little White Man. Tell him we do not know what the shooting was about. I need to talk with him. *(He pauses R, then speaks with utter conviction, half to himself.)* We are not able to fight the whites. If we are to exist, we must have peace. (YELLOW

WOMAN *looks after* BLACK KETTLE *as he goes off R.)*

(WILLIAM BENT enters L on the platform.)

YELLOW WOMAN. This talk does not appeal to young leaders—strong young leaders.

WILLIAM BENT. Hear me, Yellow Woman. The strong young leaders better untie their horses' tails and stay very quiet. *(He is concerned.)* Where are my sons?

YELLOW WOMAN. Hunting on the Smokey Hill.

WILLIAM BENT. Good, I hope they stay there. *(He is disturbed.)* Colonel Chivington gave orders for his soldiers to kill Cheyenne wherever found. I ruined my horse getting to Chivington to explain that Black Kettle desires only to be friendly. He replied that he was not authorized to make peace and that he is on the warpath! What kind of talk is this?

YELLOW WOMAN *(anxiously).* Our sons must stay out of danger.

WILLIAM BENT. There is no out-of-danger. There's madness in these men!

YELLOW WOMAN. Not all of them. The officer commanding Fort Lyon might help— Tall Chief Wynkoop.

WILLIAM BENT. Major Wynkoop is a decent man. *(Deciding, he hurries down the steps and crosses to* YELLOW WOMAN.*)* I'd better talk with Wynkoop right away. *(He embraces* YELLOW WOMAN.*)* Stay close to the ranch and avoid all white men.

YELLOW WOMAN. *(amused, touching* BENT's *face with affection).* That's not entirely possible.

WILLIAM BENT *(exiting, pleased).* Be careful!

YELLOW WOMAN *(looking after* BENT *with love).* The Little White Man is very unusual. *(To the audience)* This is why the Cheyenne can depend on him . . . and his family can depend on him.

(BLACK KETTLE *enters R on the platform, going toward the flag.*)

YELLOW WOMAN. There was a daring new idea to get the soldiers to stop the killing.

(MAJOR WYNKOOP *enters DL.*)

YELLOW WOMAN. Tall Chief Wynkoop explained he did not have authority. But he would escort Black Kettle to Denver so he could talk face to face with the big chief—and tell him face to face we want peace.

WYNKOOP. We should be going.

BLACK KETTLE. I'll catch up. I want to bring the flag.

WYNKOOP. Good idea. Bring the flag.

YELLOW WOMAN. The first problem . . . the Big Chief had no intention of seeing them. (WYNKOOP *considers the situation.*)

WYNKOOP (*calling back to* BLACK KETTLE). Forward march. (*He and* BLACK KETTLE *begin across with the flag.*)

YELLOW WOMAN. Tall Chief responded by making them hard to ignore. He led a procession through the streets of Denver with Black Kettle waving his flag.

(WYNKOOP *and* BLACK KETTLE *march across with the flag to where* CHIVINGTON *enters.*)

YELLOW WOMAN. They were met by Colonel Chivington.

WYNKOOP (*to* CHIVINGTON, *respectfully*). Thank you, sir, for granting this meeting.

CHIVINGTON. We didn't have much choice. Say what you want to say and go back to Fort Lyon. I won't have anything to do with Indians.

WYNKOOP. All the Indians want to do is to discover how they can have peace.

CHIVINGTON. They should discover a little powder and lead.

WYNKOOP. Sir?

CHIVINGTON. The department commander telegraphed his opinion this morning and I quote directly: "I want no peace till the Indians suffer more." And he's right. They have to be taught a lesson.

WYNKOOP. Chief Black Kettle is ready to comply with absolutely every requirement you—

CHIVINGTON. If I make peace, what shall I do with the Third Colorado Regiment? This is very complicated.

WYNKOOP. Let them fight the Confederates.

CHIVINGTON (*sharply*). That isn't their purpose. The Third Regiment has been raised to kill Indians and must kill Indians!

WYNKOOP. Unresisting Indians?

CHIVINGTON. You're damned impertinent.[8] How dare you bring that Indian to Denver?

WYNKOOP (*a bit harder*). That Indian came four hundred miles to discuss peace. (*He resumes his respectful manner.*) I apologize for my error in judgment, sir. In my written report, I'll explain why you do not wish to discuss peace with the Indian. (CHIVINGTON *looks at him with half-suppressed fury at the position into which he has been thrust. Seeing no alternative, he gestures to* BLACK KETTLE.)

CHIVINGTON. Speak up. What do you want to say? (BLACK KETTLE *looks nervously to* WYNKOOP *who nods encouragement.*)

YELLOW WOMAN (*turning away, heartsick*). I don't like to remember these words—pleading words from a Cheyenne Chief!

BLACK KETTLE (*humbly*). All we ask is that we may have peace with the whites. We want to hold you by the hand. You are our father. We have been traveling through a cloud. The sky is dark ever since the fighting began. We want to take good tidings home to our people—that they may sleep in peace. (*He holds out a hand. A plea.*) I want to be able to go home and tell my

---

8. impertinent, bold; disrespectful

people that I have taken your hand. (CHIVINGTON *considers the outstretched hand. His hand comes out too, but to point a finger at* BLACK KETTLE.)

CHIVINGTON. I accuse you of going into a war alliance against us with the Sioux!

BLACK KETTLE (*stunned*). Alliance? What alliance? We have no alliance!

CHIVINGTON. What are the Sioux going to do next?

WYNKOOP (*outraged*). How could the Southern Cheyenne know what the Dakota—

CHIVINGTON (*sharply*). Major!

BLACK KETTLE. Tall Chief Wynkoop knows the truth, and I want you to know the truth! We have no alliances. We are separate tribes, entirely separate, and at whatever cost—we must have peace!

CHIVINGTON (*considering the situation, then speaking coldly*). Since you have such confidence in Major Wynkoop, bring your people over to be under his protection at Fort Lyon.

BLACK KETTLE (*eager to oblige*). The protection of Tall Chief—Fort Lyon—yes, we'll do that!

CHIVINGTON. The sooner the better.

BLACK KETTLE (*ready to go*). As quickly as we can—we'll report to Tall Chief at Fort Lyon. As fast as we . . . (*He starts R, hoping that he is moving fast enough.*) Immediately, thank you. The sooner the—yes, thank you . . . (*He crosses R with his "immediately, thank you" assurances, carrying the flag. He goes up the steps and replants the flag where it was before, then comes down and recrosses L. Meanwhile,* CHIVINGTON *confronts* WYNKOOP, *who salutes.* WYNKOOP *turns and goes off.*)

YELLOW WOMAN. Black Kettle was eager to comply. Frantic, he hurried the Cheyenne night and day to a camp on Sand Creek which was only forty miles from Fort Lyon. Meanwhile, my husband was hearing bad things. Tall Chief Wynkoop was no longer at Fort Lyon. (*She turns toward* BLACK KETTLE.) Black Kettle went to the fort to try to discover what was happening. (BLACK KETTLE's *cross back to DL brings him here at this moment.*)

BLACK KETTLE. Where is Tall Chief?

CHIVINGTON. I've taken command.

BLACK KETTLE (*His shock is turning to concern.*) I . . . see. Tall Chief is no longer . . .

YELLOW WOMAN. The Cheyenne were beginning to see.

BLACK KETTLE (*interrupting himself*). I've been thinking I should move our camp to the south of the Arkansas—well to the south.

CHIVINGTON. You'll be safe at Sand Creek.

BLACK KETTLE. But only forty miles from Fort Lyon . . .

CHIVINGTON. You'll remain at Sand Creek under our protection.

BLACK KETTLE (*nervously sorting this over*). Under the protection . . . the protection of . . .

CHIVINGTON (*reassuringly*). As evidence of my good will, you have permission to send your young men east toward Smokey Hill to hunt buffalo.

YELLOW WOMAN (*hushed, calling*). Black Kettle . . .

BLACK KETTLE (*considering the good side to this*). The young men could get us meat— plenty for the winter.

YELLOW WOMAN (*This is heartbreaking.*) He's telling you to send away your warriors! (BLACK KETTLE *is in another time and place, and he does not hear.*)

BLACK KETTLE (*relaxing*). The words of Colonel Chivington are good to hear, and they make us feel safe at Sand Creek. (*He starts to withdraw.*) Thank you. (*As he goes*)

We'll winter at Sand Creek. *(Pleasantly)* Under your protection and also the protection of the great flag given us by . . . (CHIVINGTON *isn't responding.* BLACK KETTLE *feels he should hurry along.*) Yes . . . and we're very grateful . . . Thank you very much. *(The lights begin a slow dim and shift to red. The sound of a wind blowing begins to be heard.* CHIVINGTON *continues to stare impassively after* BLACK KETTLE.)

YELLOW WOMAN *(as* BLACK KETTLE *crosses).* They sent Grey Blanket Smith to Sand Creek to trade for hides. Who could worry with a post trader in camp? Then Chivington disbanded a small Arapaho camp near the fort. Perhaps he was under the foolish impression the Indians had learned enough to start joining together.

CHIVINGTON *(turning, calling sharply off L).* Lieutenant Cramer! *(He takes a paper from his tunic.)*

(LIEUTENANT CRAMER *hurries on L and stands at attention.*)

YELLOW WOMAN *(unhappily).* Now our young men are gone, our neighbors disbanded, our people dealing with the post trader.

LIEUTENANT CRAMER. Sir?

CHIVINGTON *(handing the paper to* CRAMER*).* Telegraph this dispatch.

LIEUTENANT CRAMER. Yes, sir. I'll . . . *(He stops as he looks at the paper.)* Sir, I don't understand this message.

CHIVINGTON. It should read: "There is a band of hostile Indians within forty miles of the post and I urgently require reinforcements."

LIEUTENANT CRAMER. Yes, sir. I don't understand it.

CHIVINGTON. The message is correct, secret, and urgent. (LIEUTENANT CRAMER *hesitates.*) Lieutenant! (LIEUTENANT CRAMER *goes off. The lights continue to shift. The sound of the wind is increasing.*)

YELLOW WOMAN *(as* LIEUTENANT CRAMER *exits).* The Army moves with incredible speed. Seven hundred men under Colonel Chivington threw pickets around Fort Lyon so no one could leave. Two of our sons were already with the Cheyenne on Sand Creek . . . but we did not yet realize their peril. (CHIVINGTON, *dusting his uniform, goes DL.* YELLOW WOMAN *continues through the action, moving to DRC.*) We were to hear that Colonel Chivington greeted his soldiers with talk of "wading in gore." How could a human being speak in this way about our bodies? The colonel said his men couldn't wait to pitch into the Indians.

(LIEUTENANT CRAMER *enters L and stands at attention.*)

YELLOW WOMAN. The colonel was wrong. Not every man felt that way.

LIEUTENANT CRAMER *(flatly).* I refuse to participate in the attack on Black Kettle's peaceful camp.

CHIVINGTON *(shocked).* You refuse?

LIEUTENANT CRAMER. I also speak for Captain Soule and Lieutenant Connor.

CHIVINGTON. On what basis do you propose to disobey lawful orders from a superior officer?

LIEUTENANT CRAMER. The orders are not lawful. They violate the pledged safety the United States has given the Indians.

CHIVINGTON. I'm not responsible for Wynkoop's coddling of the—

LIEUTENANT CRAMER. You also pledged safety.

CHIVINGTON. The Indians at Sand Creek are hostile!

LIEUTENANT CRAMER *(hard in reply).* The Indians at Sand Creek are there at our request and, if we attack, I say we dishonor this uniform.

CHIVINGTON. And I say—damn you! Damn any man who sympathizes with Indians! I've come to kill Indians, and I believe it is right and honorable to use any means under God's heaven to kill Indians!

LIEUTENANT CRAMER. "Any means under God's heaven?" I don't understand that remark, sir.

CHIVINGTON. Then understand this. Get your men mounted, or turn them over to the next in command, and report to the guard house under arrest.

LIEUTENANT CRAMER (unflinchingly). I assume the inquiry will come later.

CHIVINGTON (snorting). Inquiry into what?

LIEUTENANT CRAMER. Murder. (He turns and goes off L.)

CHIVINGTON (to himself, as he goes off). I want to be moving out by nine o'clock tonight . . . before one of them sneaks a warning to the hostiles. (The light on the stage is wan, except for that on YELLOW WOMAN at DRC.)

YELLOW WOMAN (speaking factually). My oldest son, Robert, was also to be at Sand Creek. All three sons would see what happened at Sand Creek. (A drummer makes the sound of distant horses' hooves.) The foolish Cheyenne were so confident, they had no sentries.[9] Just before sunrise, there was the sound of hooves. It was a few moments before anyone realized they were shod hooves—soldier horses. (The sound of the horses' hooves gets louder.)

(A WOMAN comes on UR and crosses L.)

WOMAN (concerned but not frightened). Buffalo. Lots of buffalo coming into camp. (She strains to see better.) No . . . it's the pony herd. They've been frightened . . . (With growing concern) Men on horses. (She suddenly realizes.) Soldiers!

(There are cries of fear as INDIANS, not knowing which way to run, scurry this way and that in the dim light. The drumming of the hooves is now very loud. BLACK KETTLE enters and goes to the flag on the raised level. With the cry of "Soldiers!" he steps forward to the edge.)

BLACK KETTLE. Everyone —hear me! Come this way—up by the flag. Do not be afraid! The soldiers will not hurt you! But you must come here by the flag! You'll be safe up here—hurry! (From both sides, INDIANS begin to collect on the platform, huddling together around the base of the flagstaff.) Here is your protection! The flag is your protection! Trust me! Do not provoke the soldiers! Do not fight! Do not make war! Stand here and you'll be safe! Listen to me—Black Kettle—and you'll be safe! (At this, there is a volley of rifle fire.) Soldiers! (He points frantically at the flag.) The flag! We were promised! We were given the flag! No soldiers will ever fire—(Another volley cuts him off. The light on the platform dims off quickly. He is shocked.) The promise . . . as long as the flag . . . you will not shoot—(Another volley. The only light now is on YELLOW WOMAN. There are distant cries and shots; their sounds mingling with that of the wind which is blowing hard.)

YELLOW WOMAN (her voice now hollow, beyond horror, almost beyond all emotion). I don't know if there was such a high wind blowing or if the screaming was only in my mind. Seven hundred soldiers attacked. There were only thirty-five braves to face them—the rest were away, as they'd been sent, hunting buffalo. The soldiers had been drinking whiskey during the night ride which might explain why they shot so poorly and why a few Cheyenne escaped . . . including my sons. (She has to swallow before she can continue.) We might have been more prepared for what was to happen if we'd known what Colonel

_____

9. sentries, guards; lookouts

Chivington had been saying.

(WILLIAM BENT *enters R and stands.*)

YELLOW WOMAN. He urged the killing and scalping of Indian children as well—because "nits make lice!" Nits make lice! If you don't kill the Indian children, they might grow up!

WILLIAM BENT (*calling to* YELLOW WOMAN). Yellow woman! Yellow Woman! (*He crosses to* YELLOW WOMAN.) Our sons are safe.

YELLOW WOMAN (*without emotion*). I know that, Little White Man.

WILLIAM BENT. But there's such a strangeness. They don't want to talk.

YELLOW WOMAN. They've talked to me. (*Her voice, as before, is beyond emotion.*) As soon as the firing began, the warriors put the families together trying to protect them, but there were so few young men and soon they'd been killed. The women didn't know what to do. A few of them ran out to let the soldiers see they were women. They exposed themselves and they begged for mercy. (*There are sharp raps on the drum.*) Their bodies were mutilated in such a manner—I can't say the words. (*She takes a breath.*) Some of the others tried to hide in a ravine, but they saw the soldiers coming toward them. They were so terrified they tied a bit of white on a stick—then they sent a six-year-old girl to walk toward the soldiers waving the white flag. (*She turns to* BENT.) Can you measure the terror now? The terror that would make women send out a child—a bewildered child walking toward the soldiers waving her flag? (*She "sees" it. Hushed.*) No . . . No . . . (*A sharp rap on the drum and she screams.*) Iiiieeee!

WILLIAM BENT (*going to* YELLOW WOMAN, *desperately concerned*). Yellow Woman . . .

YELLOW WOMAN (*verging on insanity, clutching* BENT). They won't let us live! We can't stay here—we can't go there—they want our farm land—our hunting land. We don't have enough to give them. They still want more—they want us dead! There's nothing left but to fight!

WILLIAM BENT (*grabbing* YELLOW WOMAN's *wrists*). Listen to me! Wife!

YELLOW WOMAN (*breaking from* BENT, *no longer sane, hushed*). We have to fight . . . (*She points at* BENT.) Fight all of them.

WILLIAM BENT. I'm your husband.

YELLOW WOMAN. You're one of them!

WILLIAM BENT. I'm your husband.

YELLOW WOMAN. You're a white man! I'm starting north with my sons.

WILLIAM BENT. They have my blood, too! My sons, too!

YELLOW WOMAN. We are no part of any white man. We're Cheyenne. We go north to look for warriors! Warriors to save our bodies from desecration![10] (*She goes off. The heartbroken* WILLIAM BENT *turns and goes. War drums begin.*)

(BLACK ELK *enters R on the high level as the lights come up.*)

BLACK ELK (*an urgent prayer*). Grandfather, Great Spirit, we rub earth on ourselves to show that we are nothing without you. There is nothing upon which we can depend except you. Give us strength to defend the helpless ones!

(*A strong Indian chant begins.* INDIANS, *wearing bright warpaint, enter and begin a war dance.*)

BLACK ELK. Within a few minutes after dawn over Sand Creek, the soldiers achieved what no Indian statesman had been able to contrive in generations—they made us start uniting.

(*Another group of* INDIANS, *differently costumed and painted, but also doing a war dance, comes*

---

10. desecration, violation; abuse

into another area of the stage. The drumming is louder and from more directions, as is the singing.)

BLACK ELK. No more Cheyenne, Arapaho, Kiowa, Sioux! We're a people! The Indian people!

A thunder being nation we are, we have said it.

A thunder being nation we are, we have said it.

We shall live!

We shall live!

We shall live!

(The INDIANS are becoming one group in one war dance.)

Others were horrified, too. Shocked men in Washington are demanding a full inquiry. But we no longer care about your after-death inquiries! You sent an emissary to see if it was still possible to avoid trouble with the Indians! *(The drums and the chant now come from every direction.)* It was no longer possible to avoid trouble with the Indian! *(The dance, the drum and the chant build toward the climax. His voice, over the sounds, is a heartbroken cry.)* When your emissary reached us, we asked if the soldiers wanted to come back and finish killing our families. He told us the soldiers were in disfavor and we should make peace. He said we'd have to make peace anyway because we are not enough to fight the whites. We told him we know we are not enough, but what is there to live for? The white man has taken our country, killed our game; and not satisfied with that, killed our wives and children, too. Now, no peace! We want to meet our families in the spirit land! *(He holds up a tomahawk. A cry.)* We raise the battle axe until death! *(He stands thus as the drums beat violently. Blackout.)*

ACT TWO

The lights dim off and, in the darkness, an Indian flute begins playing softly. A pinpoint of light comes up on the face of BLACK ELK. *"Sunrise Song" begins softly offstage.*

BLACK ELK. Grandfather, Great Spirit, I send a voice for the People, forgetting nothing you have made, the stars of the universe and the grasses of the earth. You came to me when I was young. You took me to the center of the world and showed the goodness and the beauty and the strangeness of the greening earth. At the center of this sacred hoop you said I should make a shielding tree and that it should bloom. Great Spirit, my Grandfather, I must say now that the tree has never bloomed. Hear me that the People may still save the sacred hoop of our nation and that the tree will flourish and shield us from the winds. O make my people live! *(Lights come up as offstage voices pick up the melody of the flute singing softly: "The Song Of The Prophet.")*

VOICES.

Ho-co-ka wan

Ci-cu gon yu-

Ton-kal nun-

We he-e ai yu

Ee ai yu hi e ya ee

Ee ai yu hi e ya ee

Ee ai yo he yu. *(The light reveals* BLACK ELK *standing DC.)*

BLACK ELK *(over the voices).* The Indian camp is arranged in a circle as if all nature—the circle of the prairie horizon, of the unbitten moon, of the flow of life from seed to flower to the seed again. In time of war, the holy man establishes his round tepee in the center of the camp around which the warriors wait in a circle. The holy man has his visions, then comes forth singing to the warriors of what he's seen. "Within this circle," he sings, "hear me." *(The singing stops.* BLACK ELK *holds out his arm as though to encompass the audience.)* Within this circle, hear me. *(He drops his arms.)* We show you what remains of our Indian pictograph. The winds of expansion continue to blow on us as it began. But we're beginning to change. Watching you make and break nearly four hundred treaties is teaching a little skepticism. *(A pulsating, yodel-like sound, the "tremolo," is begun softly offstage by girl voices. It increases in volume just enough to be heard and remembered by the audience.)* The sound of the tremolo made by Indian women to communicate with men in battle. The tremolo carries a long distance. It reminds warriors of the helpless ones who depend on them or face death and mutilation. The tremolo is their battlefield connection. It cheers warriors to fight with special fury! *(Hard)* Soldiers will hear the tremolo! George Armstrong Custer will hear the tremolo! *(The sounds stop.)* The logistics against the Indians are staggering. Breech-loading Springfields against—bullrushes. It may help you to appreciate our battle cry—"It's a good day to die!" Then we shout "Hoka hey!" which means, "I'm ready!" What we needed was a gun factory. What we had were men called "braves." As the chief, Red Cloud, fights back, we discover the most formidable weapon ever created by the Indian people—the strange young brave to whom I'm distantly related, Tashunco Utico.

(As BLACK ELK *says this, a slender young Indian,* CRAZY HORSE, *comes up onto a high level from behind. He has half-hooded his head with a cloth. An effect of steam is rising in front of him, and he kneels beside it, capturing it in his extended hood.* BLACK ELK *continues through this.)*

BLACK ELK. He cares nothing for possessions, not even ponies. If game is scarce and people are hungry, he won't eat at all. He's usually so preoccupied he doesn't see or hear others. Yet within his slender body there's something that spreads around him in battle like wind blowing fire through grass. And he has what we need much more than courage—a genius for military tactics! *(He looks up to* CRAZY HORSE.*)* He purifies himself in preparation and seeks strength from the world of his vision. His name is Crazy Horse.

CRAZY HORSE *(after putting back the hood, with soft intensity).* The world men live in is only a shadow of the real world, which is the world of the spirit. In the real world, which is the world behind this one, everything floats and dances because it is made of the spirit; nothing is material. *(He starts off.)* I'm on my horse in the real world, and we dance through trees and rocks. *(He exits.)*

BLACK ELK. Yellow metal is found in Montana, and they tell us a trail blazed by John Bozeman must become a road. They tell us they want only a little land, as much as a wagon would take between wheels. *(He is amused.)* Look about you now and you can see what it was they wanted. General Patrick Connor leads the invasion, with the usual orders, "Attack and kill every male Indian over twelve years of age." But Indians no longer think they can remain passive. Connor is harassed by Sitting Bull, by Roman Nose, and by Red Cloud. Connor's expedition to kill Indians is later figured to have cost about a million dollars per Indian. This makes a very bad impression on Washington. They decide negotiation might be more profitable.

(A SOLDIER *enters and sets up a small campaign table and a high-backed chair DL. A tall Indian,* RED CLOUD, *appears on one of the levels.)*

BLACK ELK (*as he exits*). Red Cloud and the other leaders agree to meet with the treaty commission. Since they've stopped General Connor, he hopes this may prove an unusual negotiation—one in which there's something for the Indian. The meeting is soon and Red Cloud prays. His prayers concern what we want most from your government; something so rare we can only pray for it. (*He goes off.*)

RED CLOUD (*looking up*). We pray that what is spoken here be the truth.

(COMMISSIONER TAYLOR *enters as* RED CLOUD *prays. He sits at the table, taking papers from a leather case and arranging them. At the same time, a small group of* INDIAN LEADERS *in ceremonial dress enter DR.*)

TAYLOR (*looking up to* RED CLOUD, *rising*). Chief Red Cloud, my name is Mr. Taylor, president of the treaty commission. We are anxious to reach an agreement about opening the Bozeman Road.

RED CLOUD (*starting down as he speaks*). I hope you are anxious to reach other agreements. There are white people all around us. We have but a small spot of land left. The Great Spirit told us to keep it.

TAYLOR. We're greatly concerned because we expect heavy travel on the Bozeman Road in the spring.

RED CLOUD. Impossible. It would violate our treaty prohibiting such travel. If soldiers come into our country, we'll fight them.

TAYLOR. Why all this talk of fighting? Why not talk of our friendship for our red brothers, and of the train we have loaded ready to bring presents?

(As TAYLOR *continues, an army officer,* COLONEL CARRINGTON, *enters L and crosses to* TAYLOR.)

TAYLOR. I have a manifest of this rich cargo which I would like to read to you in detail. (*He finds the paper.*) The generosity of the Great Father—his consideration for your welfare—the bales of fine blankets—the tins of prime tobacco—

RED CLOUD (*to* TAYLOR). This officer was met some distance from here—and asked where he and his men were going. (*To* CARRINGTON) You keep your regiment at a distance, Colonel.

CARRINGTON. To avoid any chance of trouble, I halted my regiment four miles east of the post.

RED CLOUD. That's very tactful. And from there, Colonel?

CARRINGTON. Sir?

RED CLOUD. You are now four miles east of this post. Do you intend to turn north into our territory?

TAYLOR. You have no right to interrogate an officer of the—

RED CLOUD. We've made special prayers—prayers that you tell us the truth!

TAYLOR (*stung*). The truth is that we intend to open the Bozeman Road.

RED CLOUD. Congratulations.

TAYLOR (*startled*). For opening the road?

RED CLOUD. For telling the truth.

TAYLOR (*seething*). How dare you speak to me in this outrageous—

RED CLOUD (*with cool disgust*). Why do you try to treat Indians in this childish way?

TAYLOR. Why do I? I was . . . all I was trying to—(RED CLOUD's *anger is controlled, but growing through this exchange. He cuts in again.*)

RED CLOUD. Why do you pretend to negotiate for a country while preparing to take it with your soldiers?

TAYLOR. It's a matter of a road and a few forts, and because of the seasonal requirements . . . (*He is frantic to make his point.*) The Great Father sends presents!

RED CLOUD. While this soldier goes to steal the road before the Indians say yes or no.

(He regards TAYLOR.*)* This earth is my mother. For what presents should I sell my mother?

TAYLOR. You don't speak for all Indians. Perhaps others would like to hear about the annuities,[11] about the wealth of supplies—

RED CLOUD *(his anger reaching a climax).* Any Indian wishing to sell the home of the People—stay here and negotiate. *(He turns abruptly and goes. With equal abruptness, the other* INDIANS *follow him off.)*

TAYLOR *(after the* INDIANS*).* You haven't even heard the offer! *(The* INDIANS *are gone. He is furious.)* Savage! *(To* CARRINGTON*)* Does he think we're going to leave this valuable land as a camping ground for . . . nomads! *(He and* CARRINGTON *start off L as he continues to* CARRINGTON.*)* In any case, I don't expect he'll give you much trouble.

CARRINGTON *(noncommittally).* Is that your opinion, sir?

*(*RED CLOUD *enters R on a higher level, holding a lance and looking after* TAYLOR *and* CARRINGTON *as they exit.)*

RED CLOUD. It's very easy to give trouble, but this is not my concern. We've been invaded—treaties broken—we're at war. *(Emphatically)* My concern is to win the war! *(He walks across the level.)* For several weeks, we watch Colonel Carrington's wagon train moving north along the Bozeman Road. There are two hundred loaded wagons! *(He smiles.)* We deduce they are not planning a short visit. I watch, I plan, I look for vulnerability. *(There are offstage shouts and the sound of galloping.)* We make our first counter-stroke. At dawn we stampede their horses. Soldiers come riding in pursuit. *(The sound of distant guns)* The soldiers are strung out in a chase, and we commence hostilities. *(He paces along the edge of the platform as he evidently directs operations. He walks, excitedly.)* Our strategy

is proving effective. However, it's getting harder to find bluecoats outside their powerful forts.

*(*CRAZY HORSE, *now dressed for battle, enters on the platform at R.)*

RED CLOUD. Then we start discovering our special weapon—the genius of Crazy Horse!

CRAZY HORSE *(to* RED CLOUD*).* Decoys! They can't resist if they think we're fleeing or impudent. If they see an Indian make an insulting gesture, they get hot and make mistakes. With Yellow Eagle I discovered this is so. I dismounted and showed myself in front of some young cavalry officers. They came charging after me and as soon as I had them strung out behind, Yellow Eagle hit them from the side killing a lieutenant, a sergeant, and wounding several more.

RED CLOUD *(pleased, but casual).* A useful skirmish.

CRAZY HORSE *(pressing his point).* The same tactics could entice a large number of troops into a useful battle!

*(*RED CLOUD *takes a breath to dispute this, but then thinks better of the idea. He nods.)*

RED CLOUD. You discovered this is so. *(He considers.)* A useful battle . . . *(Deciding to move on it, he starts off L.)* This will take organization. *(He exits.)*

CRAZY HORSE *(looking front).* We prepare in our camp a few miles from Fort Kearney in the little valley of Peno Creek. *(He tenses.)* I'm to lead the decoys, and this war party has an unusual composition—Cheyenne, Arapaho, and the rest Oglala, Minneconjou, and Brule. When Chief Red Cloud has our main party in position, we make our first move—a feint by several warriors toward some woodcutters. This

---

11. annuities, compensation; payment

draws shooting which brings a rescue company galloping from the fort. We're after a large force, but at least they're beginning to commit themselves. As the rescue party gallops out of sight, the decoys move in till they're close to the fort itself. Then we make our next move! *(With this, he shouts for attention, and makes a great leap from a level onto the stage. As he leaps, he shouts.)* Hoka hey! *(He waves a red blanket in a dramatic swirl, then faces front again, half-crouched in a challenging position. There is the heavy thump of a howitzer[12] firing.* CRAZY HORSE *appears terrified. He runs this way and that as though confused. He stops, faces front, and makes an insulting gesture. As he turns and races back up onto the platform, there is an outburst of shooting, yells, and galloping. On the platform, he turns to watch, with almost clinical interest.)*

*(*RED CLOUD *enters behind* CRAZY HORSE.*)*

RED CLOUD *(also clinical).* They committed a major force.

CRAZY HORSE *(incredulously[13]).* Because an Indian is impudent! *(As he exits)* I'll keep them coming. *(During this, the sound of shouts, shooting, and galloping increases.)*

RED CLOUD *(watching with cool interest).* The force from the fort is commanded by Captain Fetterman, who is under explicit orders not to pursue beyond Lodge Trail Ridge. But Crazy Horse rides along that ridge, taunting the soldiers. As he said, they get hot and make mistakes. The soldiers hesitate again at the top, but then they see Crazy Horse dismount. He makes insulting gestures and then turns to examine his pony's hooves. Every move he makes is precisely correct. The soldiers go wild. They must catch this Indian! They charge down into the little valley of Peno Creek. *(He turns to look offstage, at a distance behind the platform.)* I watch for the signal that the soldiers are within the trap. *(He sees the signal.)* The decoys swing back to the road. That's the signal! *(He raises his lance and gives a shout. There is a wild outburst of Indian yells in reply coming from both off R and off L. The sound is extremely loud. There is an explosion of cries, then utter silence. He slowly turns back to the front and speaks quietly.)* It was over quickly. Captain Fetterman, who foolishly got himself and all his men killed, had a fort named in his honor. Colonel Carrington, whose sensible orders were disobeyed, was recalled from command. I began to hope we might win this war.

*(*COMMISSIONER TAYLOR *and* GENERAL SHERMAN *enter L and start toward the table and chair.)*

RED CLOUD *(as* TAYLOR *and* SHERMAN *enter).* They asked me to come in and talk peace. The commissioner returned bringing Great Warrior General Sherman. This time, they were not quite so offensive.

SHERMAN. If, on examination, we find the road hurts you, we will give it up or pay for it. *(To* RED CLOUD*)* We sent a supply of tobacco.

RED CLOUD. And I'll smoke it. And I'll come to Laramie as soon as the soldiers leave my country.

SHERMAN *(to* TAYLOR*).* This is an embarrassment and a humiliation, but I don't see alternatives.

TAYLOR *(in an undertone).* The only way to deal with these . . .

SHERMAN. The only way is to end it. It's too expensive. The War Department wants an immediate treaty. Tell Red Cloud—

RED CLOUD *(calling down to* TAYLOR *and* SHERMAN*).* We are on the mountains looking down on the soldiers and the forts. When we see the soldiers moving away

---

12. howitzer, a short cannon

13. incredulously, in disbelief or amazement

and the forts abandoned, then I will come down to talk. (SHERMAN *looks up at him a moment, then crosses to the table and picks up his leather case.*)

SHERMAN *(to TAYLOR).* Abandon the forts north of the Platte.

TAYLOR. Sir?

SHERMAN *(acidly).* My special competence is military reality. Red Cloud has given us a beating. Abandon the forts! *(He walks out, leaving TAYLOR aghast.)*

RED CLOUD *(softly).* We watched from the hills as they packed their gear and the great wagon trains started south. We waited to be sure, waited till we could wait no longer . . . *(With strength)* Then we rode in and burned their forts. *(He starts down and walks across to face TAYLOR at the table.)* What does the treaty say about the home of the People?

TAYLOR *(reading).* No white person shall be permitted to settle upon or occupy any portion of the Black Hills or, without the consent of the Indians, to pass through the same.

RED CLOUD. Present the pen. *(TAYLOR holds a pen out upright with its point resting on the treaty. RED CLOUD comes up to it.)* The Indians desire peace, and I pledge my honor to maintain it.

As RED CLOUD *reaches out and touches the tip of the pen, the light dims out, leaving only a spot on* BLACK ELK *who stands on a high level.*

BLACK ELK. My judgments about this time are not so sensible because I was so much a part of it. I'm angry with our chief, Red Cloud, because from the moment he touched the pen to the treaty renouncing war, he never fought again. *(Self-critically)* Angry because he's a man of honor! *(There is a distant train whistle.)* Some hot-heads

among the Southern Cheyenne are about to give your army an excuse to once more achieve a new glory—by once more attacking an old man! *(The train whistle blows again.)* Railroad tracks are being laid toward the Smokey Hill, and the Iron Horse[14] is an irresistible challenge. *(The train whistle blows louder and there are off-stage whoops of excitement. General light comes up quickly.)* The young hot-heads derail a train, break in and drink whiskey, then tie ends of cloth bolts they find in the baggage to their pony tails and race out across the prairie.

As BLACK ELK *speaks, whooping young* INDIANS *with long colored cloths streaming behind them zigzag wildly across the stage and go off.*

BLACK ELK. The forces assembling to deal with this and other threats to civilization included the glory hunter George Armstrong Custer. In your recent Civil War, he commanded a division. At twenty-three, he became a brigadier general. Then raised in rank again. Your youngest, most dashing major-general. When he finishes here, his trail turns north to a collision with our youngest—Crazy Horse! They're almost exactly the same age. They are both given high command. They each have a strangeness. But there's a difference. *(He smiles wryly.)* One of them is a savage! *(This is so absurd.)* Custer's soldiers try to pretend the Civil War is not over, and that they're preparing for well-armed Confederates. All they find below the Arkansas are some frightened Cheyenne trying to keep away from the hot-heads and be safe with Black Kettle.

(MAGPIE enters.)

---

14. Iron Horse, locomotive; train

MAGPIE. Because Black Kettle is well known to be for peace. Because he does everything to keep the young men from foolishness—which is also well known.

BLACK ELK *(seeing more than* MAGPIE *does as he goes off R.)* I would like to think it was not so well known.

MAGPIE *(faintly perplexed).* What does that mean? *(She shrugs and smiles.)* My name is Magpie, and I am related to Chief Black Kettle. His niece. I am also about to be related to the son of Yellow Woman, George Bent. George and his brother, Charles, fought because Charles said everyone should join Roman Nose and make trouble. Then soldiers killed Roman Nose. So what good was the trouble?

(BLACK KETTLE enters DR.)

MAGPIE. In spite of Sand Creek, more of the Cheyenne now realize they'll be safer here. *(She smiles.)* Soon things will be calm again. We'll be happy again. We'll have a great ceremony for my marriage to George Bent. *(To* BLACK KETTLE*)* More and more they come back to you.

BLACK KETTLE *(with frankness rather than self-pity).* They look on me as old, discredited, and defeated—and they're right. They only come because there's nowhere else to go—and perhaps they'll be safer south of the Arkansas. *(He smiles.)* We've already been massacred! *(The word turns his thoughts to his fear.)* But I hear of bad talk around the fort.

MAGPIE *(concerned for* BLACK KETTLE*).* You keep upsetting yourself. You start having your nightmare again.

BLACK KETTLE. Where is George Bent?

MAGPIE. With the Kiowa, trading for buffalo robes.

BLACK KETTLE. Go ask him to take you north to visit his father.

MAGPIE *(in spite of herself).* This is just the nightmare creeping into the daylight.

BLACK KETTLE. Today! *(He makes a small but sharp gesture.* MAGPIE *bows her head and hurries off R. He watches her go, then looks back to the audience, his sternness giving way to uncertainty.)* The girl could be right. My mind is sometimes feeble and does not always produce order. Sometimes the nightmare of Sand Creek comes into my mind, and it's so real I think it's happening again—and I cry out, which disturbs people. However, there is bad talk about Custer and his pony soldiers, and this is real and not a matter of my mind. The best hope for safety is to move our lodges so close to the fort our peaceful intentions are displayed for all. *(He is bothered.)* I'm told we are not allowed to do this. *(This is ominous.)* I'm told we'll be safe by the Washita River—that we must stay by the Washita River! *(He is frightened.)* Something is beginning to run loose in my mind. Am I looking at the Washita River, or am I seeing Sand Creek? *(He turns and hurries up onto the level. The light begins to dim. The wind sound heard at Sand Creek starts again. It rises as* BLACK KETTLE *speaks.)* If we're attacked, the snow is too deep for escape. *(It gets darker and the wind rises. He looks up at the sound.)* I won't know if it's such a high wind blowing or if the screaming is only in my mind.

(A WOMAN *enters UR and crosses L.)*

WOMAN *(concerned, but not frightened).* Buffalo. Lots of buffalo coming into camp. *(She sees better, but speaks as before.)* No—it's the pony herd.

BLACK KETTLE. I've heard this before. *(He is relieved.)* It's just the nightmare again . . . that's all it is.

WOMAN *(frightened, pointing).* Men on horses—coming from every direction. *(She finally realizes.)* Soldiers!

BLACK KETTLE *(shouting to the* WOMAN*)*. Woman—calm yourself!

WOMAN *(repeating)*. Soldiers!

BLACK KETTLE. You've had a bad dream.

WOMAN. Pony soldiers! They're coming!

BLACK KETTLE. If they were really coming, we'd hear the drumming of hooves!

WOMAN. We can't hear them!

BLACK KETTLE. Because it's a bad dream!

WOMAN *(frantically)*. Because of the snow!

BLACK KETTLE. *(hit by what the* WOMAN *has said)*. Because of the snow—*(Bugles blow furiously.* BLACK KETTLE *speaks with growing terror.)* Bugles! There were no bugles! *(Shots are being fired, and* BLACK KETTLE *rejoins reality. He snatches up a gun and fires it in the air, then shouts.)* We're under attack! Get mounted! Scatter! Escape! *(As the lights dim out completely: a cry of despair.)* C-h-e-y-e-n-n-e! *(Blackout)*

(A tiny spot of light comes up on the platform at far L, revealing TALL CHIEF EDWARD WYNKOOP*.)*

WYNKOOP *(with quiet force)*. I protest the deceit and brutality inflicted on peaceful Cheyenne by George Custer. *(The sound of a military band a short distance away comes up as do the lights generally. The band gets closer, playing the rousing "Garry Owen.")* They killed one hundred and three Cheyenne of which only eleven were warriors. *(He speaks with increasing passion.)* Black Kettle was betrayed! He met his death at the hands of men in whom he had fatally trusted! I, Edward Wynkoop, hereby resign my commission in the army. *(The band music gets louder and there is the sound of men cheering. There are shouts of "Custer! Custer!")*

(CUSTER, as much like the classic image as possible, triumphantly enters DL, followed by cavalry officers and other men. Those directly behind CUSTER carry wands like fishing poles from which dangle many bits of hair. They also carry

their Seventh Cavalry guidons.[15] *The band music is now very loud, as is the sound of cheering.* CUSTER *acknowledges the acclaim with waves. He doffs his hat to the audience.* CUSTER's *men doff their hats. He makes a victorious cross R, where a beaming* GENERAL SHERIDAN *enters and receives* CUSTER's *salute. It becomes quiet.)*

WYNKOOP *(bitterly)*. Custer was first called "Hard Backsides" because he rode such long hours after the Indians. Then they called him "Long Hair." After his recent butchery, admiring newspaper correspondents called him "The Wolf of Washita." The Indians found a better name. They call him "Squaw Killer."

(In the quiet, a worried Indian leader, TOSAWI, *enters L and crosses to where* SHERIDAN *and* CUSTER *have just finished congratulating each other.)*

WYNKOOP. Not everyone had been cheering, and General Sheridan decided to set up a few showplace camps for friendly Indians. He sent runners to nearby tribes telling them to report to these friendly camps or they'd be killed. *(He points to* TOSAWI.*)* Chief Tosawi brought in his little band of frightened Commanche, giving Sheridan the opportunity to say something immortal.

TOSAWI. Great Chief, my name is Tosawi. Tosawi good Indian.

SHERIDAN. The only good Indians I ever saw were dead. *(The band picks up the "Garry Owen" again, and the exultant* CUSTER *dances off followed by the others.)*

WYNKOOP. To the north in their holy land of the Black Hills, there were still proud, free Indians. *(Unhappily)* But on the southern plains, soon all that would be left were "good Indians."

(Light comes up again as JOHN FINERTY, *a newspaper reporter enters DR.)*

---

15. guidons, military flags

FINERTY. My name is John Finerty, of the *Chicago Times,* accompanying the Big Horn expedition which is to involve the most renown generals of the Civil War—Sheridan, Crook, Custer—Custer, himself! I'm to cover the final destruction of the savage. These barbarous descendants of Cain presently occupy the magnificent territory of the Black Hills and the Big Horn. *(He talks about his hero.)* With great dash, and bravery, Custer pacified the plains. Then he made a daring foray into the Black Hills—as our readers well know—and he confirmed all rumors. From the grass roots down . . . Gold! How this news fires the Caucasian heart with the spirit of adventure to which the attendant danger adds additional zest. Our government made every reasonable effort to purchase this property, receiving nothing but insolence in reply. *(He speaks with pride.)* Our government has decided to act. *(A military drum beat begins in the distance.)* A sophisticated attack is designed to surround and destroy. My wish is to go with Custer, who will attack from the east, but I'm assigned to General Crook, who will march up simultaneously from the south. *(The lights dim.)* Scouts report a Sioux village ahead on the Rosebud River. We'll crash through here, then drive on to the Big Horn, where we meet the others!

(Battle sounds are heard in the distance. CRAZY HORSE *appears on the level at L. He holds a mirror with which he flashes signals.)*

FINERTY *(watching* CRAZY HORSE *with astonishment).* The battle is not going well. The savages are not fighting in the manner expected. The Indian on the ridge is flashing signals and his fighters perform in a manner more effective than thought possible. General Crook is increasingly concerned. The man with the mirror he tells me is Crazy Horse. He seems to be causing great difficulty for the United States Army. I assume this is because the savages greatly outnumber us. *(The battle sounds grow.)* I find this is not the case. They do not outnumber us. *(With horror at the realization)* And our weapons are superior! I ask General Crook—I demand of General Crook—when will he break through? He speaks with unaccustomed rudeness, suggesting I put the question to Crazy Horse. *(A bugle blows.)* When I hear this, I think, at last. *(He pauses, undone at what he sees.)* I thought bugles signalled men to charge forward. *(He looks up to* CRAZY HORSE.*)* Why does he fight like this? He could have sold the land for a great deal of money. *(He goes off.)*

CRAZY HORSE *(from the high level, softly but with intense conviction).* One does not sell the earth upon which the People walk. *(With hushed intensity)* When I'm in the world of men and things, I watch soldiers—their soldiers, ours, and the ways of fighting. Then I dream myself into the real world, which is of the spirit, and seek visions to protect the people. My vision tells me their soldiers will fight in the old way, but we must not fight in our old way. *(With increasing urgency)* We must not charge into massed firepower hoping to perform brave foolish deeds for the retelling. Or stop to count coups[16] or takes scalps or capture horses. We do not get tired or hungry and decide to break off. We are Dakota, we fight for our nation. *(A cry)* Dakota! *(He is in battle.)* We surprise General Crook by attacking his skirmish lines from the flanks. We break the big battle into many little battles. We find openings—we get in among them—we create confusion, frustration. By the time the sun is on top of the sky, he can no longer fight

16. count coups (kü), take stock of the number you have killed in battle

an orderly battle, and he's making terrible mistakes. By the time the sun is going down, General Crook is pulling back. *(He paces the platform.)* With daybreak star, we're out along the ridges and we see the bluecoats. They're moving south—in retreat . . . They are leaving the land of the People! *(He is concerned.)* But inside my head something is whispering a message about the bluecoats. These soldiers are not alone. I want to know where is Custer. I leave a few warriors to show themselves to Crook—start grass fires—shoot into his camp at night—keep him moving south. *(Softly)* My vision whispers again. *(Urgently)* We turn and race for the Little Big Horn. *(Underplayed)* Hoka hey! *(He jumps out of sight.)*

(BLACK ELK enters DR.)

BLACK ELK. The east and west of the planned assault have joined forces and started south expecting to crush us between them and General Crook. They are unaware of his defeat by Crazy Horse, who rides like the wind to join us. The main attack is about to begin. Out in front is the elite Seventh Cavalry, led by the Wolf of Washita. When he sights evidence of our large settlement ahead, he waves his hat in the air and shouts "Hurray! Custer's luck!"

(An Indian Girl, PET-SAN-WASTE-WIN, enters DL.)

PET. I was digging turnips and I could see many men on horses—six to eight miles distant. I could see the flashing of their weapons—and that they were many!

BLACK ELK. I was thirteen years old—swimming in the Little Big Horn. The sun was straight up when we first heard the cry— "The charges are coming! They are coming!" I could hear the cry going from camp on to the camp of the Santee. *(Others*

repeat this cry, "They are coming," as though from a distance offstage.)

PET. Women race to catch ponies for the warriors to mount. When we look up, the soldiers are always closer. We try not to think of bad times, of bad things done by Custer. We just catch ponies!

(During this, various INDIANS rush across the stage in different directions in half-panic and half-preparation. The wind rises with this. Bugles sound in the distance. There is the sound of galloping and distant shouts.)

BLACK ELK. Custer has divided his force. His second-in-command, Reno, hits the south end of the camp. I can see great swirls of dust going up in that direction, because there's panic! Reno's first charge catches women and children in the open and the bullets wipe out families! It makes our hearts bad! *(The sound of the bugles and the galloping now mingles with gunfire.)* Our fury turns Reno away, forces him into the woods, then isolates him on some bluffs. Now we can divert warriors . . . Sitting Bull can turn to attack Custer. *(Bugles blare, shots and shouts. The noise level is much higher, and the wind begins to roar. BLACK ELK speaks with great excitement.)* Then a great cry goes up out in the dust—eagle bone whistles screaming—and the cry like a great wind!

VOICES *(crying as part of the great wind).* Crazy Horse is coming! Crazy Horse is coming! C-r-a-z-y H-o-r-s-e! *(INDIAN girls make the tremolo.)* Reno is still held— Custer tries to get to the river where he's checked—He's driven back to the high ridge by Sitting Bull—by some of the Cheyenne—He's up there—the Wolf of Washita, Hard Backsides, Long Hair, Squaw Killer, George Armstrong Custer! *(The sounds climax, leading to BLACK ELK's vocal climax.)* Suddenly! All at once! Like bees swarming out of a hive! Like a hurricane! *(A battle cry)* D-a-k-o-t-a! *(The climax)* There—never—was—a—better—day—to—die!

(With this cry, INDIAN WARRIORS *suddenly appear on all levels from behind, as though storming the top of the high ridge. They hold* CUSTER *and his men. All come up at the same moment.)*

WARRIORS *(their weapons aloft, with a great shout).* Hoka hey!

(Blackout. The sounds are gone.) (A light slowly comes up on CRAZY HORSE, *who stands alone and quietly on the platform at L. Another light comes up on* BLACK ELK, *who still stands DR.)*

BLACK ELK *(quietly, respectfully).* Crazy Horse? *(*CRAZY HORSE *looks over to him.)* I'm told it was a Santee who killed Custer.

CRAZY HORSE *(quietly).* Yes.

BLACK ELK Someone else said it was White Bull of the Minneconjou.

CRAZY HORSE. Yes.

BLACK ELK *(puzzled, smiling).* I thought probably you killed him.

CRAZY HORSE *(quietly).* Yes, I killed him, too. He was killed by the Indian people.

(An Indian song is begun again, either played on an instrument, such as a flute, or sung offstage. In either case, it is done softly. The lights on CRAZY HORSE *dim, leaving him a shadow silhouette figure on the platform. A pin spot remains on the face of* BLACK ELK *at DR. During this, the silhouette figure of* CRAZY HORSE *on the platform raises his arms to the sky in prayer.)*

BLACK ELK *(with a wry smile).* The particular day of this battle is to speed our destruction. It's June 25, 1876—but it takes a little longer for the news to travel. The supply steamboat was waiting at the mouth of the Big Horn, and it makes a record passage south. When they reach Bismark, the telegraph operator spends twenty-two hours tapping out the dispatches. Now it's July 4, 1876. America thrills to their centennial. A celebration—from which they wake the next morning to the news smeared across their newspapers . . . *(A drumbeat begins. The silhouette figure of* CRAZY HORSE *begins a dance movement to the beat of the drum. The movement suggests a man trying to move this way and then that way, but always stopped, always forced in other directions.* BLACK ELK *continues without a pause.)* Savages have destroyed their hero! They go insane. Wherever we try to go now, they follow with overwhelming force. No treaty, no rule applies anymore. It doesn't matter that it was Custer's forces charging through our village that began the battle. We try to reason. We send messages—"What have we done that the white people want us to stop?" There's no answer. We have to keep running, running. *(The drumbeat is faster, as are* CRAZY HORSE's *silhouette movements on the platform.)* We're tired. We get tired of running—except Crazy Horse. He's off in the snow dodging armies. Crazy Horse still outmaneuvers the soldiers! Tactical brilliance! He's defeated two of your greatest Civil War generals, but now he has nothing left with which to fight. The cold and the hunger are becoming unbearable. The only hope for his people now is to negotiate and ride his bony horse into Fort Robinson.

CRAZY HORSE. I come for peace. Now let the people eat.

BLACK ELK *(shaking his head).* They do not negotiate. *(*CRAZY HORSE *dances a pantomime of the described action.)* He's made prisoner. They decide to lock him in a guard house. As they lead him out of the daylight into a stifling cell, he sees windows barred with iron; men with chains. He turns for the door and charges the world! One man holds him and another . . . the other runs a bayonet through his body. (*The drum stops. He has to take a breath before he can continue. He is heartbroken.*) All he ever wanted was to help the People . . . and he only fought when the soldiers came to kill us. They couldn't defeat him. They could only kill him in this way they have. He's dying. (CRAZY HORSE *lies on the level.* BLACK ELK *reaches to him.*)

CRAZY HORSE. Father, I want to see you. Mother, I want to see you. Come to me. (*He gasps for breath.*) Tell the People . . . tell them they can no longer depend on me. Tell the People they must find someone else—(*He suppresses a cry of pain as the light on him goes out.*)

BLACK ELK. All that lasts is the earth. (*He comes down.*) His father and mother were given his body. They took it away on a pony drag and buried it in a private place—close by here. It doesn't matter where . . . his body is grass. (*He goes down front.*) We had nothing left. We turned to visions and to a dance. A Paiute holy man told us the Great Spirit had sent his son to the white people a long time ago who nailed him to a tree where he died. But now he was coming back, this time as an Indian, and there would be a new earth. All we had to do was dance—dance and it would bring back our dead—dance the dance of the ghosts, and once more we'd all be alive and together. We held hands— like the Indians on the gallows in Minnesota—to be touching another—to say "I'm here! I'm here!"

(*As* BLACK ELK *speaks, a line of* INDIANS, *holding hands, comes on, doing a slow rhythmic movement to the drumbeat and flute. The line becomes a circle.* BLACK ELK, *in front of them, continues to speak through this action. Lights suggesting the hallucination resulting from prolonged dance come into this.*)

BLACK ELK. The Messiah promises that in the next springtime with the new grass appearing another world is coming: coming like a cloud; coming like a whirlwind out of the west! And all the Indians that ever lived will be alive again; and all the bison and all the other animals . . . if we dance the dance of the ghosts. Our Messiah—his hair long and hanging loose—with light like a rainbow spreading 'round him—he'll come to us . . . where only the Indians will live. (*Hand in hand, the dancers continue, as does the drum. The effects are dazzling.*) At Pine Ridge, Big Foot's band of Minneconjou began the dance; widows, broken families. They kept dancing till they fainted because they wanted so much to bring back those that had been killed. But you won't even let us dance! There's outrage everywhere! At Pine Ridge, the agent telegraphs Washington, "Indians are dancing in the snow. We need protection." Protection against dancing! Forces are assembling— serious forces to stop our dancing—military forces! (*Now* BLACK ELK *begins to dance as he faces the audience and, perhaps, hallucinates.*) We can't contain any more brutality! We escape into our visions. We continue to dance the dance of the ghosts. (*He raises his arms, in a vision.*) We float . . . We see our beautiful land—green grass—fat horses—singing hunters. We're in a great sacred circle . . . the hoop of our Indian nation . . . and at the center is the sacred tree . . . and the tree is in bloom! (*His hands drop. The* INDIANS *behind him continue to dance and have their vision, but it is no longer possible for* BLACK ELK. *His voice is hard.*) Our dance is to be stopped. Soldiers are out arresting us. (*The dance freezes on the word* stopped.) Big Foot has started his people from Pine Ridge. Perhaps Red Cloud can protect them. Big Foot has pneumonia and lies on a wagon. When the cavalry gallops up, Big Foot shows a white flag. Major Whiteside of the cavalry tells Big Foot to move to a camp over on Wounded Knee Creek. The Indian families huddle there along the frozen stream. Before dark, the soldiers post Hotchkiss guns[17] on top of a rise overlooking this miserable camp. The soldiers belong to the Seventh Cavalry. In the action about to take place, twenty-six soldiers will win the Medal of Honor! *(There's a moment of silence. Then, a bugle blows.)* At dawn, they start taking away the weapons of these sick and freezing people—knives, a few rifles! There's a scuffle when a young Indian doesn't want to give up his rifle— and it goes off. *(He takes a breath, then speaks quietly.)* Then they destroy us. *(With drums effecting the guns, the* INDIANS *are massacred. Then silence with a cold light coming up. The* INDIANS *sprawl about the stage in the grotesque frozen positions of death. There is an effect of blowing snow.)* The winds have reached us, and they're blowing themselves out—blowing the snow over us to make one long grave for the People—who had never done any harm and were only trying to run away. *(He has to take a breath.)* I did not know then how much was ending. When I look back now from this high hill of my old age, I can still see the butchered women and children lying heaped and scattered all along the crooked gulch as plain as when I saw them with eyes still young. And I can see that something else died here in the bloody snow and was buried in the blizzard. *(He looks to the audience.)* It was a people's dream—a beautiful dream, as you must know . . . Because it was your dream, too! There is no center any longer. The nation's hoop is broken and scattered, and the sacred tree is dead. It may be that some small root of the sacred tree still lives—a root that could be nourished. *(He reaches out to the audience, his hands cupped together. The light dims.)* We offer the wooden cup filled with water. It's the power to make live, and it's yours. *(He speaks quietly.)* We have spoken.

DIM OUT

---

17. Hotchkiss guns, small cannons that fire 3.2-inch shells

Discussing and Interpreting

Black Elk Speaks

Play Analysis

1. How important do you think it is that historical events and characters be portrayed accurately in a work of art. Why?
2. Were Black Elk's visions "unfulfilled?" Explain your answer.
3. From beginning to end, many characters in this play lie, steal, and kill. Pick two ideologically opposed characters and discuss how they explain these actions.
4. Do you think this play gives a fair account of the United States' representatives and soldiers who opposed the Indians? Why or why not?
5. **Thematic Connection: To Be a Hero** Who would you say are the heroes in this play? What makes them heroes?

Literary Skills: Comparing Perspectives

Following is an excerpt from an account of the Battle of the Little Big Horn made by a white reporter. Having read *Black Elk Speaks*, what do you make of this writer's assumptions?

> After the battle, the Indians came through and stripped the bodies and mutilated all the uniformed soldiers, believing that the soul of a mutilated body would be forced to walk the earth for all eternity and could not ascend to heaven. Inexplicably, they stripped Custer's body and cleaned it, but did not scalp or mutilate it. He had been wearing buckskins instead of a blue uniform, and some believe that the Indians thought he was not a soldier and so, thinking he was an innocent, left him alone.

from "The Battle of the Little Bighorn, 1876,"
EyeWitness - history through the eyes of those who lived it, www.ibiscom.com (1997).

Performance Element: Researching History

John Neihardt sought to understand early American Indian history by talking to Black Elk and his friends—people who could give first-hand reports. Much of the book *Black Elk Speaks* contains direct quotations from these Native Americans. The play, however, is presented in a very different way. Historical figures, such as Crazy Horse, Custer, and Andrew Jackson become players in the drama. Make a list of the ways you might research actual historical events in order to fairly present them in play form, then research someone who played a role in American Indian history and write a monologue for that person. Perform your monologue for the class.

Setting the Stage for

Twain by the Tale

from the humorous writings of Mark Twain
adapted for the stage by Dennis Snee

> *"I came in 1835 with Halley's Comet... and I expect to go out with it. It'll be the great disappointment of my life if I don't. The Almighty has said, no doubt, 'Now here are two indefinable freaks. They came in together. They must go out together.'"*
>
> Mark Twain

Creating Context: The Life of Mark Twain

In his lifetime, Mark Twain wrote over 30 books filled with memorable characters such as Huckleberry Finn and Tom Sawyer. Twain was a man bristling with ideas and opinions, and he was a thrilling storyteller and speaker. He told his stories with an inventiveness, authenticity, and wry humor unlike any writer before or since.

Born Samuel Langhorne Clemens on November 30, 1835, he grew up in Missouri. He was a sickly child, and like Tom Sawyer's Aunt Polly, his mother treated him often with various medicines. As a very young man he worked in Hannibal, Missouri, at his brother Orion's print shop. In 1857, he was apprenticed to a riverboat pilot and journeyed on the Mississippi. There he heard the call "by the mark, twain," meaning two fathoms, or twelve feet, deep—enough for safe passage. The name Mark Twain was born. In 1866, when he was employed by *The Sacramento Union*, he contributed a series of letters from the Sandwich Islands that were very popular with readers. Thereafter he was invited to lecture up and down the West Coast. In 1867 he took a tour of the Orient for five months, during which time he contributed regularly to the *Alta-California* and wrote several letters for the *New York Tribune*. His writing created a new kind of travel literature—one in which honesty and sincerity ruled. When he returned home, Twain was a celebrity. His letters were compiled into book form, and in 1869 the popular *Innocents Abroad* was published.

Twain met the gentle and refined Olivia Langdon in 1869, and in 1870 they were married. Their first child, Langdon, died at a year and a half, but three girls, Suzy, Clara, and Jean, followed. In 1884, Twain went on the lecture circuit to promote the forthcoming *Adventures of Huckleberry Finn*. Tragedy struck in 1897, when Suzy died at the age of 23. Then Olivia's health began to deteriorate, and she went into seclusion. She was taken to Italy's warm climate to recover, but died six months later, in 1902. In 1909 Twain's youngest daughter, Jean, died. Twain then wrote his last piece of writing, "The Death of Jean." He died on April 21, 1910 at age 74. Halley's Comet was again visible in the night sky, as it had been on the day he was born.

As a Reader: Understanding Satire

When an author uses humor to ridicule a subject (usually a social institution or a human shortcoming), he is using **satire**. Often satire is intended to inspire reform. Mark Twain was a master of the technique. Compare the excerpts below. Are they equally satirical?

from Page · · · · · · to Stage

I said I supposed he would wish me to act as his second* and he said, "Of course." I said I must be allowed to act under a French name, so that I might be shielded from obloquy [ill repute] in my country, in case of fatal results. He winced here, probably at the suggestion that dueling was not regarded with respect in America. However, he agreed to my requirement …

First, we drew up my principal's will. I insisted upon this, and stuck to my point. I said I had never heard of a man in his right mind going out to fight a duel without first making his will. He said he had never heard of a man in his right mind doing anything of the kind. When he had finished the will, he wished to proceed to a choice of his "last words." He wanted to know how the following words, as a dying exclamation, struck me:

"I die for my God, for my country, for freedom of speech, for progress, and the universal brotherhood of man!"

I objected that this would require too lingering a death…

from *The Complete Humorous Sketches and Tales of Mark Twain* by Mark Twain

*to support or assist in a fight

AMERICAN. Gambetta, you must allow me to act as your second.

GAMBETTA (*touched*). You are a true and good friend. But you have no experience in these matters.

AMERICAN. I will learn, my friend; I will learn quickly…But, come, let us attend to the matters at hand.

GAMBETTA. Yes, yes.

AMERICAN. First things first.

GAMBETTA. Yes, of course.

AMERICAN. We shall draw up your will.

GAMBETTA (*alarmed*). What! My will?? (*Crossing to* AMERICAN) My friend, you are delirious. Please sit down.

AMERICAN. But Gambetta, I never heard of a man in his right mind fighting a duel without making his will.

GAMBETTA. Now listen to me closely. What we must determine immediately are my last words.

AMERICAN. Your last words?

GAMBETTA. What do you think of this: "I die for my God, for my country, for freedom of speech, for progress, and the universal brotherhood of man."…Well?

AMERICAN. Well, if you were dying of a lingering disease, perhaps…

from *Twain by the Tale* adapted by Dennis Snee

As a Director: Helping Actors Use Comic Timing

As you read *Twain by the Tale*, try to determine how a director might help the actors respond quickly, vary the pace, and change tone in order to convey humor.

Twain by the Tale

Time
The era of Mark Twain

The Characters
SIX MEN

FIVE WOMEN

Setting
Bare stage with pieces

ACT ONE
MISSISSIPPI BREAKS

❖

Music is heard in the darkness. A brisk rag-time number begins. After a moment the lights come up full on ACTOR ONE, ACTRESS ONE, ACTOR TWO, ACTRESS TWO, ACTOR THREE, and ACTRESS THREE. If possible, all or any of the actors can accompany the music on banjo, guitar, harmonica, wash-tub bass, kazoo, etc. If the actors do not play instruments along with the music, they can be seated on two benches with their backs to the audience, and turn front to deliver their lines at the appropriate breaks.

ACTRESS ONE (Music break No. 1). There are several good protections against temptation, but the surest is cowardice. (Music; out)

ACTOR ONE (Music break No. 2). "Classic." A book which people praise, and don't read. (Music; out)

ACTRESS TWO (Music break No. 3). It takes your enemy and your friend, working together, to hurt you to the heart; the one to slander you, and the other to get the news to you. (Music; out)

ACTOR TWO (Music break No. 4). Few things are harder to put up with than the annoyance of a good example. (Music; out)

ACTRESS THREE (*Music break No. 5*). If you hope to succeed in any endeavor, first get all the fools in town on your side. That's a big enough majority in any town. (*Music; out*).

ACTOR THREE (*Music break No. 6*). Good breeding consists in concealing how much we think of ourselves and how little we think of the other person. (*Music; out*)

ACTOR ONE (*Music break No. 7*). Put all your eggs in the one basket, and watch that basket! (*Music; out*)

ACTRESS ONE (*Music break No. 8*). Be good and you will be lonesome. (*Music; out*)

ACTOR TWO (*Music break No. 9*). If you pick up a starving dog and make him prosperous, he will not bite you. This is the principal difference between a dog and a man. (*Music; out*)

ACTRESS TWO (*Music break No. 10*). Familiarity breeds contempt. And children. (*Music; out*)

ACTOR THREE (*Music break No. 11*). The holy passion of friendship is of so steady, and loyal, and enduring a nature that it will last a whole lifetime, if not asked to lend money. (*Music; out*)

ACTRESS THREE (*Music break No. 12*). Soap and education are not as sudden as a massacre, but they are more deadly in the long run. (*Music; out*)

ACTOR ONE (*Music break No. 13*). When angry, count to four; when very angry, swear. (*Final music out. Blackout. Twain theme up on blackout.*)

NOTICE

Twain theme fades as lights come up. Spot up on ACTRESS FOUR, D.C. *The benches have been removed.*

ACTRESS FOUR. At this time, we would like to read a letter to the audience from the author under consideration this evening,

Mr. Mark Twain. We would like to. Unfortunately, we were unable to find such a letter. What we were able to find, understandably perhaps, considering the brevity to which Mark Twain was given, is the following postcard to the audience, which we hope will suffice. (*She takes a postcard from her pocket; reading.*) "Dear Audience, Persons attempting to find a motive in this presentation will be prosecuted. Persons attempting to find a moral in it will be banished. Persons attempting to find a plot in it will be shot. Cordially, Mark Twain."

(*Blackout. Interlude music up.*)

NOAH AND THE BUREAUCRACY

The lights come up full on ACTOR FOUR, D.L., *and* ACTRESS FIVE, D.R.

ACTOR FOUR. And in the beginning, God created man. Not at the very beginning, but near the beginning.

ACTRESS FIVE. And from the beginning, man differed from the rest of the animals because man had the ability to think; the ability to question.

ACTOR FOUR. One of the questions that has burdened man since his creation is why he was created. Many answers have been proposed, including that of Mark Twain, who said, "I believe our Heavenly Father invented man because He was disappointed in the monkey."

ACTRESS FIVE. Aside from his ability to think, man has always possessed other distinguishing characteristics. Twain: "Man is the only animal that blushes. (*Pauses*) Or needs to."

ACTOR FOUR. At the time of his creation, man was God's crowning achievement, created in God's own image and likeness. But gradually, man turned away from his benevolent[1] creator, and finally rejected God completely.

ACTRESS FIVE. This transgression so aroused the wrath of the Almighty that he decided to destroy man. That is, all men except one. (NOAH—ACTOR FIVE—*enters and crosses to U.C. He wears a loose fitting Biblical type garment and sandals. He carries a wooden box with some simple tools; he puts the tools down and takes a wooden hammer or mallet and starts to pantomime working on the hull of the Ark.*)

ACTOR FOUR. Noah, a good man, and his family were to be saved by the construction of an ark that would carry them safely over the waters of the great flood. And in this way the race of man was given a second chance, and increased its numbers and flourished.

ACTRESS FIVE. But eventually, mankind produced an atheist and God wondered if He had made a mistake. "Later," said Twain, "the race produced an insurance salesman, and He was certain that He had."

ACTOR FOUR. Some would say that Noah was responsible for the events that resulted from his successful voyage, but Noah was only concerned with building the Ark. If he were to undertake that project today, however, he would be faced with many other concerns.

ACTRESS FIVE. For civilization has learned the importance of being more particular in the great art of shipbuilding, of being more careful of human life. And so civilization created a bureaucrat, which in time created a bureaucracy, which was charged with insuring that certain standards and guidelines were complied with. (BUREAUCRAT—ACTOR SIX—*enters and comes center to NOAH. ACTOR FOUR and ACTRESS FIVE exit. BUREAUCRAT wears a white inspector's jacket and a hard hat, and carries a clipboard. He takes a long look at the Ark.*)

BUREAUCRAT. Interesting ship.

NOAH. It's an Ark.

BUREAUCRAT. An "Ark," you say?

NOAH. Yes. (BUREAUCRAT *flips to the right form on his clipboard.*)

BUREAUCRAT. Well, in that case we'll need a form 621—Government Safety Compliance and Nautical Regulation Checklist for Arks. Now, what is her length?

NOAH. Six hundred feet.

BUREAUCRAT. Depth?

NOAH. Sixty-five.

INSPECTOR. Beam?

NOAH. Fifty or sixty.

INSPECTOR. Constructed of—

NOAH. Wood.

INSPECTOR. What kind?

NOAH. Buoyant, hopefully.

INSPECTOR. Passengers?

NOAH. Eight.

INSPECTOR. Sex?

NOAH. Half male, the others female.

INSPECTOR. Ages?

NOAH. From a hundred years up.

INSPECTOR. Up to where?

NOAH. Six hundred.

INSPECTOR. Ah—going to Florida; good idea, too. Doctor's name?

NOAH. We have no doctor.

INSPECTOR. You must provide a doctor. Also an undertaker—particularly an undertaker. Crew?

NOAH. The same eight.

INSPECTOR. The same eight?

NOAH. Yes, sir.

INSPECTOR. And half of them women?

NOAH. Yes, sir.

---

1. benevolent, kind; merciful

INSPECTOR. Have they ever served as sea-men before?

NOAH. No, sir.

INSPECTOR. Have the men?

NOAH. No, sir.

INSPECTOR. Have any of you ever been to sea?

NOAH. No, sir.

BUREAUCRAT. Where were you raised?

NOAH. On a farm. All of us.

BUREAUCRAT *(looks at* NOAH *a moment).* This vessel will require a crew of eight hundred men. She must have four mates and nine cooks. Who is the captain?

NOAH. I am.

BUREAUCRAT. You must get a captain. Also sick nurses. Cargo?

NOAH Animals.

BUREAUCRAT. How many?

NOAH. Big ones, seven thousand; big and lit-tle together, ninety-eight thousand.

BUREAUCRAT. Very well. You must provide twelve hundred keepers. Now, what is your motive power?

NOAH. What is my which?

BUREAUCRAT. Motive power. What power do you use in driving the ship?

NOAH. None.

BUREAUCRAT. You must provide either sails or steam. How long do you expect your voyage to last?

NOAH. Eleven or twelve months.

BUREAUCRAT. Eleven or twelve months! Pretty slow. May I ask what the animals are for?

NOAH. Just to breed others from.

BUREAUCRAT. Others? You mean you don't have enough?

NOAH. For the present needs of civilization, yes. But the rest are going to be drowned in a flood, and these are to renew the sup-ply.

BUREAUCRAT. A flood?

NOAH. Yes, sir.

BUREAUCRAT. Are you sure of that?

NOAH. Perfectly sure. It's going to rain forty days and forty nights.

BUREAUCRAT. I guess we can use some rain.

NOAH. Not this kind of rain. This is going to cover the mountaintops, and the earth will pass from sight.

BUREAUCRAT. In that case, I'll have to with-draw the option I gave you as to sails or steam. You must use steam. You'll have to have condensed water for the animals' water supply.

NOAH. But I'm going to dip water from out-side the ship with buckets.

BUREAUCRAT. No, no, no. Before the flood reaches the mountain tops, the fresh waters will have joined the salt seas, and it will all be salt. You must have steam, and condense your water. *(He takes the form from his clipboard and hands it to* NOAH.*)* Well, if you can correct this handful of minor discrepancies, you should be ship-shape and ready to sail. (NOAH *opens the form up; it folds down, reaching to the floor.)*

NOAH. I have to do all this before I can sail? This could take months.

BUREAUCRAT *(shrugs).* Work weekends.

NOAH. It's against my religion to work weekends.

BUREAUCRAT (*Music in, loud; continues as dia-logue trails off.*) Well, you should have told me you were a bureaucrat! Let me see if I can't alleviate some of this red tape … (BUREAUCRAT *begins tearing up the form.)* You know, my brother-in-law works for the Coast Guard.

NOAH. That's very interesting …

(Lights dim to black; interlude music softens.)

A PAGE FROM A CALIFORNIAN ALMANAC

The lights come up full; music fades out. There is a chair D.C. ACTRESS *is D.R.*

ACTRESS. Mark Twain, whose real name was Samuel Clemens, began his career as a journalist. In California during the 1860's Twain wrote for several newspapers, and he also sent reports to other newspapers back East concerning conditions in the new territory. Concerning the quality of medical treatment, he reported, "Doctors are about as successful here, both in killing and curing, as they are anywhere." Some goods and services were in short supply. Hotels, for example. Twain said that good hotels in California were "as rare, perhaps, as lawyers in heaven." But the most common questions put to Twain at the time concerned California's climate. "What about earthquakes," people asked. "Are they really as frequent and as terrible as people say?" (THE REPORTER, *a young* MARK TWAIN, *enters from the left and crosses to the chair D.C. He is writing on a pad as he walks, engrossed. He sits in the chair and continues writing.*) Realizing the need for a scientifically accurate report on the subject, Twain rose to the journalistic challenge (REPORTER *stands, finishing his notes.*) by writing—

REPORTER (*finished writing; triumphantly*). A page from a Californian Almanac. (*Reads from the pad*)

October 17th—Weather hazy; atmosphere murky and dense. An expression of profound melancholy will be observable on most countenances.

October 18th—Slight earthquake. Countenances grow more melancholy.

October 19th—Look out for rain. It would be absurd to look in for it. The general depression of spirits increases.

October 20th—More weather.

October 21st—Same.

October 22nd—Light winds, perhaps; if they blow, it will be from the "east'ard," or the "nor'ard," or the "west'ard," or the "suth'ard," or from some general direction approximating more or less to these points.

October 23rd—Mild, balmy earthquakes.

October 24th—Shaky.

October 25th—Occasional shakes, followed by light showers of bricks and plastering.

October 26th—Considerable phenomenal atmospheric foolishness.

October 27th—Universal despondency, indicative of approaching disaster. Abstain from smiling or indulgence in humorous conversation.

October 28th—Misery, dismal forebodings, and despair. Beware of all light discourse— a joke uttered at this time would produce a popular outbreak.

October 29th—Beware!

October 30th—Keep dark!

October 31st—Go slow!

November 1st—Terrific earthquake. This is the great earthquake month. More stars fall and more worlds are slathered around carelessly and destroyed in November than in any other month of the twelve.

November 2nd—Spasmodic but exhilarating earthquakes, accompanied by occasional showers of rain and churches and things.

November 3rd—Make your will.

November 4th—Sell out.

November 5th—Select your last words.

November 6th—Prepare to shed this mortal coil.[2]

---

2. mortal coil, everyday cares and worries

November 7th—Shed!

November 8th—The sun will rise as usual, perhaps; but if he does, he will doubtless be staggered some to find nothing but a large round hole eight thousand miles in diameter in the place where he saw this world serenely spinning the day before. *(Considering the page)* Not too dramatic, maybe—but accurate.

(EDITOR—ACTOR SIX—enters at right and watches THE REPORTER exit.)

EDITOR. I spent thirty-two years as a newspaper editor and I never knew another reporter like young Sam Clemens. Once I attempted to impart some of my editorial wisdom upon his young mind. I cautioned him, "Never report anything as fact unless you can verify it from personal knowledge." That night he covered an important society event, and the next day he filed this story: *(Takes a newspaper clipping from his vest pocket)* "A woman giving the name of Mrs. James Jones, who is reported to be one of the society leaders of the city, is said to have given what purported to be a party yesterday to a number of alleged ladies. The hostess claims to be the wife of a reputed attorney." *(He folds up the clipping.)* It was the last advice I ever gave to young Sam Clemens. *(THE NEWSPAPERMAN— TWAIN in middle age; white jacket, string tie, carrying a cigar—enters on the tail end of this and listens to THE EDITOR. THE EDITOR exits at the end of his dialogue; NEWSPAPERMAN watches him, then turns front.)*

NEWSPAPERMAN. Once when Bill Swanson and I were poor young cub reporters, a frightful financial shortage occurred. We had to have three dollars that very day. Swanson maintained with simple confidence, "The Lord will provide." *(He goes to the chair and sits, continuing.)* Believing the Lord helps those who help themselves, I wandered into a hotel lobby, trying to think of some way to get the money. Presently, a handsome dog came along and rested his jaw on my knee. General Miles passed by and stopped to pet him. "He's a beautiful dog. Would you sell him?" I was greatly moved; it was marvelous the way Swanson's prediction had come true. "Yes," I said. "His price is three dollars." The general was surprised. "Only three dollars? Why, I wouldn't take $100 for him. You must reconsider." "No, three dollars," I said firmly. The general acquiesced and led the dog away. In a few minutes a sad-faced man came along, looking anxiously about. "Are you looking for a dog?" His face lit up. "Yes I am. Have you seen him?" "Yes, and I think I could find him for you." I have seldom seen a person look so grateful. I said I hoped he would not mind paying me three dollars for my trouble. "Dear me!" he said. "That is nothing! I will pay you ten dollars willingly." I said, "No, three is the price," and started off. Swanson had said that that was the amount the Lord would provide; it would have been sacrilege to ask more. I went up to the general's room and explained I was sorry but I had to take the dog again; that I had only sold him in the spirit of accommodation. I gave him back his three dollars and returned the dog to his owner. I went away then with a good conscience, because I had acted honorably. I never could have used the three that I had sold the dog for; it was not rightly my own. But the three I got for restoring him was properly mine. That man might never have gotten that dog back at all if it hadn't been for me. *(Blackout)*

(Twain theme music up until spot opens for THE LEGEND OF SAGENFELD)

THE LEGEND OF SAGENFELD

*S*pot opens on ACTRESS FOUR at D.R. Music *changes to a quaint fanfare, then continues under the dialogue, as a dainty minuet.*

ACTRESS FOUR. Once upon a time there was a kingdom, a tiny kingdom, known as Sagenfeld, in Germany. It existed in a dreamlike tranquility, far removed from the strife and jealousy of everyday life. There was no malice, no envy, no ambition, and consequently no heartburn. Now in the course of time the old king died, and his young son, Hubert, came to the throne. *(HUBERT enters at left. He waves to his admiring subjects as he comes to D.L. He is followed by ACTRESS ONE, who lugs his travelling throne, waiting to be told where to put it.)* Hubert was well-loved by all his subjects; he was good, and pure, and noble— *(HUBERT has indicated the spot he wants his throne; ACTRESS ONE puts it down. She bows and starts off but HUBERT motions her back. He takes a coin from his pocket and tips her. She smiles gratefully.)* and generous. *(ACTRESS ONE looks front after looking at the coin; it's not the tip she was hoping for. She moves her hand to indicate "so-so." HUBERT sits; ACTRESS ONE exits.)* Now on the day that Hubert was born, the kingdom soothsayer *(SOOTHSAYER enters at left),* who had predicted many startling and wondrous things, looked to the stars and issued the following prediction:

SOOTHSAYER. In Hubert's fourteenth year, a monumental event shall happen. The animal whose singing shall sound sweetest in Hubert's ear shall save Hubert's life. So long as the king and the people honor this animal's race for this good deed, the nation shall not know war, nor poverty, nor pestilence. But beware an erring choice! *(Music STING)*

ACTRESS FOUR. This prophecy caused great consternation throughout the kingdom, for if young King Hubert were to choose incorrectly, the nation would be in dire straights. Therefore, on the eve of the king's fourteenth year, he was approached by the two most trusted members of his cabinet *(MINISTER OF STATE enters at left and goes to the king on the throne, with THE SOOTHSAYER.)*—his minister of state, and the very venerable soothsayer.

MINISTER. Your highness, we must consider the prophecy.

SOOTHSAYER. Yes, sire. If you are in agreement, tomorrow, all the singing creatures of the kingdom will be brought before you.

MINISTER. And you shall choose that animal whose singing sounds sweetest in your ear.

SOOTHSAYER. Is it agreed then, your highness? *(HUBERT isn't too sure. Looking at each of them with uncertainty.)*

HUBERT. Ah … Ah … *(Finally; what the heck)* Well, if you can't trust your cabinet, who can you trust? *(Music STING)*

(Lights come up full; subjects begin entering with their singing creatures; ACTRESS TWO with ACTOR THREE, and ACTRESS THREE with ACTOR TWO. These two songbirds are THE THRUSH and THE LINNET. As HUBERT and his cabinet confer, the songsters warm up vocally with their owners.)

ACTRESS FOUR. And so the edict went forth; all subjects in the kingdom who owned singing creatures would bring them to the great hall of the great palace and the ultimately important animal would be chosen. And so on the following day, the judgment began.

MINISTER *(to the subjects and songsters).* Attention, your attention please. You all know the ground rules. Please keep your selections brief, and if possible, somewhat snappy. Any questions? Very well, let us begin. *(ACTRESS TWO steps before HUBERT* *with her thrush*—ACTOR THREE.) Your majesty, the first animal for consideration.

ACTRESS TWO. Your highness, it gives me great, great pleasure to present the sweetest songbird within my possession—my thrush. (ACTRESS TWO *hums a note on a pitch pipe;* THRUSH *sings the word "thrush" to several bars of "Way Down Upon the Swanee River," finishes with her arms open, waiting for applause.*)

HUBERT (*He applauds politely.*) Thank you very much. That was very nice. We'll get in touch with you. Thank you. Next?

MINISTER (ACTOR THREE *steps forward with his linnet*—ACTRESS THREE.) Your highness, the second animal for consideration.

ACTOR THREE. With your royal permission, your majesty, my most celebrated songbird, the linnet. (LINNET *hums her opening note;* ACTOR THREE *corrects her, humming a slightly higher note; they tune thusly a few moments, then* THE LINNET *is ready. She sings "linnet" in a high falsetto to the tune of "Greensleeves." After several bars, she pauses.*)

HUBERT. Ah, thank you, that'll be fine. (THE LINNET, *however, is caught up in the spirit of the competition, and continues merrily along.*)

SOOTHSAYER. His highness has heard enough! (THE MINISTER *and* SOOTHSAYER *both look impatiently at the owner of the bird, who tries to put his hand over* THE LINNET's *mouth to shut her up; she evades him once; he finally silences her;* HUBERT *breathes a sigh of relief.*)

HUBERT. Thank you. Next? (*Other combinations of owners and songbirds now approach* HUBERT *and mime their auditions as* ACTRESS FOUR *continues.*)

ACTRESS FOUR. And so King Hubert continued in this way, listening to one songbird, and then another, and then another. The precious minutes slipped by; among so many bewitching songsters he found it impossible to choose—and all the more difficult because the promised penalty for error was so terrible. (SOOTHSAYER *and* MINISTER *move discreetly D.R. of the throne.*) Indeed, there was speculation throughout the kingdom that Hubert would choose incorrectly, and the minister and soothsayer conferred privately:

SOOTHSAYER. I fear our young king may be losing his courage.

MINISTER. I believe his cool head is gone.

SOOTHSAYER. I regret that his dynasty and people may be doomed.

MINISTER. And I shudder to think—that includes us! (*They return to the throne, where the judging continues.*)

ACTRESS FOUR. And so the hours waned, spirits drooped. The young king looked nervous, and a deep melancholy was beginning to descend over the palace. Fear quickly spread throughout the kingdom that Hubert would be unable to choose, and distress settled upon all the subjects in the land. And as it was becoming finally clear that all was surely lost, from the remotest parts of the palace was heard: (HUBERT *and entourage look up, their faces alive with hope at the sound—from offstage—of a lovely soprano singing a few melodic bars.*) The nightingale! And a light spread over the king's face, and as he began to raise his scepter to indicate that the sacred bird had been found—(THE PEASANT MAID *has entered at right with her* DONKEY.)

DONKEY. Waw-he … Waw-HE, Waw-He, Waw-HEEEE!!

ACTRESS FOUR. —there was a hideous interruption at the door. (PEASANT MAID *timidly leads* THE DONKEY *to* HUBERT *at the throne.*)

PEASANT MAID. My lord, the king, I pray you pardon me, for I meant no wrong. I have no father and no mother, but I do have a goat, and a donkey, and they are all in all to me. My goat gives the sweetest milk, and when my dear good donkey brays it seems to me there is no music like to it. So when my lord the king's jester said the sweetest singer among all the animals should save the crown and nation, and moved me to bring him here, well … (THE MINISTER *and* SOOTHSAYER *begin chuckling at the thought. The king begins to smile also, and they are suddenly roaring with derisive[3] laughter. Humiliated,* THE PEASANT MAID *quickly leads* THE DONKEY *off, she is almost in tears.)*

ACTRESS FOUR. And with the poor peasant maid humiliated and her disastrous donkey led away, the king at last began to proclaim his choice.

HUBERT *(standing).* Up! Let the bells proclaim that the choice has been made, and the king, people, and dynasty are saved. From henceforth let the nightingale be honored throughout the land. And publish it among the people that whosoever shall injure a nightingale, or insult it, shall suffer death. Up! The king has spoken!! *(Much rejoicing; people applaud;* HUBERT *accepts the adulation of the remaining subject and songbird;* SOOTHSAYER *and* MINISTER *surreptitiously wipe a bead of sweat from their brow.)*

ACTRESS FOUR. Yes, and all that little kingdom was drunk with joy. And the bells pealed, and the celebration continued, and from that day forward the nightingale was a sacred bird. And so all was well in the kingdom and many months passed, and at last summer came. Now it happened that the young king was very fond of the chase, and so on the first golden day of summer he said:

HUBERT *(breathing deeply).* Unbelievable! A perfect day for the chase.

SOOTHSAYER. A perfect day for the chase … *(He and* THE MINISTER *look at each with feigned enthusiasm.)*

MINISTER. A perfect day for the chase …

HUBERT. Wonderful. It's unanimous. Bring on the horses, the hounds; let us begin. *(Stick horses are brought to the three; they begin riding around the stage.* ACTRESS FOUR *moves D.L.)*

ACTRESS FOUR. And in the brilliant company of his nobles, the king rode forth. Over hill, through dale, around trees; onward they rode, savoring the day and enjoying the chase, until by and by they came to a great forest. *(Lights dim to indicate forest; the group begins riding more slowly.* ACTRESS ONE, *in a shoulderless peasant blouse and long wig, enters at right.)* And there the king had the great misfortune to become separated from his nobles. *(ACTRESS ONE, *beckoning to* THE MINISTER *and* SOOTHSAYER*)*

ACTRESS ONE. Yoo-Hoo! Boys! *(MINISTER *and* SOOTHSAYER *elbow each other and follow her off in hot pursuit.)*

ACTRESS FOUR. On and on the young king rode, taking what he thought to be a shortcut, but alas—he was mistaken. Twilight came and his spirits began to sink. *(Lights dim a little more to indicate twilight.)* He plunged ahead through the unknown land until finally he forced his horse over a steep and rocky declivity.[4] *(HUBERT *teeters on the brink of an imaginary cliff, then topples forward, landing on his back with both legs in the air.)*

HUBERT. Curses!

ACTRESS FOUR. When horse and rider reached the bottom of the cliff, one had a broken neck, and the other a broken leg. *(HUBERT *bends one of his legs at the knee and moans.)* The poor little king lay there suffering agonies of pain, and each hour seemed an eternity. He listened for sounds

---

3. derisive, scornful; taunting
4. declivity, slope; decline

of aid, but none came; he waited in hope of rescue, but all for naught. Finally, when his hope was all but gone, across the still wastes of night—he heard … (NIGHTIN-GALE *sings a scale from offstage.)*

HUBERT. Can it be true?? (NIGHTINGALE *sings again.)* It is the sacred bird; the prophecy is fulfilled! Now, I will be saved!

ACTRESS FOUR. And so the little king wait-ed, and the nightingale sang; and the king waited, and the nightingale sang; and the king waited—all through the night, and into the next day the nightingale sang, yet still no help came.

HUBERT. I have failed. I have chosen incor-rectly, and all … is lost.

ACTRESS FOUR. Another day passed, and another. The king grew feeble and weak, and as he came to what he knew must be his last moments, a final prayer came from his heart:

HUBERT. Oh, but once more that I could see my family … my subjects … my home. *(To the heavens)* Please … !

ACTRESS FOUR. And at that moment, he heard the sweetest song that ever entered his ears:

DONKEY (*entering at left).* Waw-he! Waw-he!! Waw-HE!!!

HUBERT. Oh! That song! Sweeter by far than the nightingale! Now is the oracle ful-filled—my house; my people—saved! (DONKEY *goes to* HUBERT.)

DONKEY. Waw-he… .

HUBERT. Hello, noble beast! We will let bygones be bygones? (DONKEY *gestures, "Don't mention it."* HUBERT *crawls onto the* DONKEY's *back; lights up full as they meander to the palace—U.C.)*

ACTRESS FOUR. And the donkey came to the little king, and with the king on his back,

they returned to the palace where there was great rejoicing. *(Subjects entering see the* DONKEY *with* HUBERT; *they beckon to others; all rush to the scene. Much rejoicing.)* And when the king had been returned to his beloved people, and his strength was partly restored, he made proclamations concern-ing the incredible turn of events.

HUBERT (*surrounded by the crowd).* My loyal subjects; officials of the crown. From this day forward let it be known throughout the land that the ass shall be sacred, and invaluable. Secondly, this particular ass shall be made chief minister of the king-dom. (DONKEY *tries to look humble as crowd congratulates him.)* And thirdly, when the good and fair owner (PEASANT MAID *steps forward.)* of this animal, the lovely peasant maid whose beauty we observe today, reaches her fifteenth birthday, she shall become my queen. The king has spoken! *(Great rejoicing; a medal is hung on* THE DONKEY; HUBERT *exits, followed by the crowd. As the lights dim, one spot remains full on* ACTRESS FOUR, *D.L.)*

ACTRESS FOUR. And such is the legend of the kingdom of Sagenfeld. And through the legend we are informed as to why, during many centuries, an ass was always the chief minister in the royal cabinet. Just as it is still the case in most cabinets to this day.

(ACTRESS FOUR *exits, spot dims, Twain theme music in until* ACTOR ONE *speaks. Spot comes up full on* ACTOR ONE, TWAIN *in middle years, D.R.)*

ACTOR ONE. Author's note: The Legend of Sagenfeld is what is commonly referred to as a fairy tale. This puts it under the same general heading as fables, legends, and political speeches.

(Blackout)

SOME CURES FOR WARTS

Spot light up on ACTRESS ONE, *D.R. After a moment, she begins reading from a book—*The Adventures of Tom Sawyer.

ACTRESS ONE. The juvenile pariah of the village of St. Petersburg was Huckleberry Finn, son of the town drunkard. Huckleberry came and went, at his own free will. He slept on doorsteps in fine weather and in empty barrels in wet; he did not have to go to school or to church; or call any being master or obey anybody; he could go fishing or swimming when and where he chose, and stay as long as it suited him. He never had to wash, nor put on clean clothes; he could swear wonderfully. Huckleberry was warmly hated and dreaded by all the mothers of the town (HUCKLEBERRY *enters from U.L. Stage lights up about half;* HUCKLEBERRY *wears a motley ensemble of cast-off men's clothes, the trousers supported by a lone suspender.* HUCK *comes to center stage carrying a stuffed cat by the tail, and seats himself by a road sign that reads* CITY LIMITS—ST. PETERSBURG, MO. POP. 241), because he was idle and lawless and vulgar—and because all their children admired him so. Tom Sawyer (TOM *enters, from U.R. He wears a straw hat, rolled up blue jeans with two suspenders, and is missing a front tooth—it is blackened out—which he carries in a piece of paper in his pocket. Stage lights up full now.* TOM *walks leisurely, thumbs in his suspenders, finally meandering to the spot where* HUCK *sits.)* was like the rest of the respectable boys, in that he envied Huckleberry his gaudy outcast condition and was under strict orders not to play with Huckleberry. So—he played with him every time he got a chance.

(Spot out on ACTRESS ONE; *she exits.* TOM *hails* HUCK.)

TOM. Hello, Huckleberry!

HUCK. Hello yourself, and see how you like it.

TOM *(eyeing the cat).* What's that you got?

HUCK. Dead cat.

TOM. Lemme see him, Huck. (HUCK *hands the cat to him.* TOM *inspects it.)* My, he's pretty stiff. What is dead cats good for, Huck?

HUCK. Good for? Cure warts with.

TOM. No! Is that so? I know something that's better.

HUCK. I bet you don't. What is it?

TOM. Why, spunk water.

HUCK. Spunk water! I wouldn't give a dern for spunk water.

TOM. You wouldn't, wouldn't you? D'you ever try it?

HUCK. No, I hain't. But Bob Tanner did.

TOM. You tell me how Bob Tanner done it, Huck.

HUCK. Why, he took and dipped his hand in a rotten stump where the rain water was.

TOM. In the daytime?

HUCK. Certainly.

TOM. With his face to the stump?

HUCK. Yes. Least I reckon so.

TOM. Did he say anything?

HUCK. I don't reckon he did. I don't know.

TOM. Aha! Talk about trying to cure warts with spunk water such a blame-fool way as that! Why, that ain't a-going to do any good. You got to go all by yourself, to the middle of the woods, where you know there's a spunk-water stump, and just as it's midnight you back up against the stump and jam your hand in and say: "Barley corn, barley corn, Injun-meal shorts; Spunk water, spunk water, swaller these warts." Then you walk away quick, eleven steps, with your eyes shut, and then turn around three times and walk home without speaking to anybody. Because if you speak, the charm's busted.

HUCK. Well, that sounds like a good way, but that ain't the way Bob Tanner done.

TOM. No, sir, you can bet he didn't, becuz he's the wartiest boy in this town; and he wouldn't have a wart on him if he'd knowed how to work spunk water. I've took off thousands of warts off my hands that way, Huck. I play with frogs so much that I've always got considerable many warts. Sometimes I take 'em off with a bean.

HUCK. Yes, bean's good. I've done that.

TOM. Have you? What's your way?

HUCK. You take and split the bean, and cut the wart so as to get some blood, and then you put the blood on one piece of the bean and take and dig a hole and bury it 'bout midnight at the crossroads in the dark of the moon, and then you burn up the rest of the bean. You see, that piece that's got the blood on it will keep drawing and drawing, trying to fetch the other piece to it, and so that helps the blood to draw the wart, and pretty soon off she comes.

TOM. Yes, that's it, Huck—that's it; though when you're burying it if you say "Down bean; off wart: come no more to bother me!" it's better. But say—how do you cure 'em with dead cats?

HUCK. Why, you take your cat and go and get in the graveyard 'long about midnight when somebody that was wicked has been buried; and when it's midnight a devil will come, or maybe two or three, but you can't see 'em, you can only hear something like the wind, or maybe hear 'em talk; and when they're taking that corpse away, you heave your cat after 'em and say, "Devil follow corpse, cat follow devil, warts follow cat, I'm done with Ye!" That'll fetch any wart.

TOM. Sounds right. D'you ever try it, Huck?

HUCK. No, but old Mother Hopkins told me.

TOM. Well, I reckon it's so, then. Becuz they say she's a witch.

HUCK. Say! Why, Tom, I know she is. She witched Pap. Pap says so his own self. He come along one day, and he see she was a-witching him, so he took up a rock, and if she hadn't dodged, he'd a' got her. Well, that very night he rolled off'n a shed wher' he was a-layin' drunk, and broke his arm.

TOM. Why, that's awful. How did he know she was a-witching him?

HUCK. Lord, Pap can tell, easy. Pap says when they keep looking at you right stiddy, they're a-witching you. 'Specially if they mumble. Becuz when they mumble they're saying the Lord's Prayer backards.

TOM. Say, Hucky, when you going to try the cat?

HUCK. Tonight. I reckon they'll come after old Hoss Williams tonight.

TOM. But they buried him Saturday. Didn't they get him Saturday night?

HUCK. Why, how you talk! How could their charms work till midnight? And then it's Sunday. Devils don't slosh around much of a Sunday, I don't reckon.

TOM. I never thought of that. That's so. Lemme go with you?

HUCK. Of course—if you ain't afeard.

TOM. Afeard! 'Tain't likely. Will you meow?

HUCK. Yes—and you meow back, if you get a chance. Last time, you kep' me a-meowing around till old Hays went to throwing rocks at me and says "Dern that cat!" and so I hove a brick through his window—but don't you tell.

TOM. I won't. I couldn't meow that night becuz auntie was watching me, but I'll meow this time. (HUCK *has now taken a matchbox from his pocket and is looking inside it.*) Say—what's that?

HUCK. Nothing but a tick.

TOM. Where'd you get him?

HUCK. Out in the woods.

TOM (*considering the prize*). What'll you take for him?

HUCK. I don't know. I don't want to sell him.

TOM (*looking in the box now*). All right. It's a mighty small tick, anyway.

HUCK. Oh, anybody can run a tick down that don't belong to them. I'm satisfied with it. It's a good enough tick for me.

TOM. Sho, there's ticks a-plenty. I could have a thousand of 'em if I wanted to.

HUCK. Well, why don't you? Becuz you know mighty well you can't. This is a pretty early tick, I reckon. It's the first one I've seen this year.

TOM (*considers it*). Say, Huck—I'll give you my tooth for him.

HUCK. Le's see it. (*TOM gets a bit of paper from his pocket and carefully unrolls it. HUCK views the tooth wistfully. The temptation is strong.*) Is it genuwyne? (*TOM lifts his lip, showing the vacancy.*) Well, all right. It's a trade. (*TOM takes the matchbox with the tick; HUCK eagerly accepts the tooth. They each eye their new acquisition, contentedly. After a moment, they shake on the deal, happily. Fade to black.*)

END OF ACT ONE

ACT TWO
ANSWERS TO CORRESPONDENCE

Music begins in the darkness. Two spots come up full; one D.C. and one D.L. In the D.C. spot are two chairs; ACTOR ONE, Twain in later years, sits in one; the other is empty. Between the chairs is a table with an ash-tray and a large dictionary. In the D.L. spot stands ACTOR THREE, a disappointed suitor. ACTOR ONE, Twain, and the other correspondents, all speak directly ahead through this. Play-on music out.

ACTOR THREE. Dear Mark Twain. My life is a failure. I have adored, wildly, madly; and she whom I love has turned coldly from me and shed her affections on another. What would you advise me to do?

ACTOR ONE. Dear Discarded Lover. You should set your affections on another also—or on several, if there are enough to go around. There is an absurd idea disseminated in novels that the happier a girl is with another man, the happier it makes the old lover she has blighted. Don't allow yourself to believe any such nonsense as that. The more cause that girl finds to regret that she did not marry you, the more comfortable you will feel over it. It isn't poetical, but it is mighty sound doctrine. (*Music up. Spot comes up full D.R. as spot dims at D.L. ACTOR THREE exits. In the D.R. spot stands ACTRESS ONE, lovingly holding an infant in swaddling clothes.*)

ACTRESS ONE (*music out*). Dear Mark Twain. Why do you speak so disparagingly of babies? I have a baby myself, and I can assure you that a baby is a thing of beauty and a joy forever.

ACTOR ONE. Dear Young Mother. You are doubtless referring to my statement that a baby is an inestimable[5] blessing and bother. But you think a baby is a thing of

---

5. inestimable, unable to be counted or described

beauty and a joy forever. Well, the idea is pleasing, but not very original. Every cow thinks the same of its own calf. I honor the cow for it. We all honor this touching maternal instinct wherever we find it. But really, madam, when I come to examine the matter in all its bearings, I find that your assertion does not assert itself in all cases. A soiled baby, with a neglected nose, cannot be conscientiously regarded as a thing of beauty; and inasmuch as baby-hood spans but three short years, no baby is competent to be a joy "forever." Aside from that, I agree with you. *(Music up. Spot up full D.L.; spot dims D.R.* ACTRESS ONE *exits as* ACTRESS TWO *enters at left. She is a dowager-type; stuffy and proper.)*

ACTRESS TWO *(music out).* Dear Mr. Twain. Again last week you publicly endorsed the filthy habit of smoking. Just as you have similarly endorsed drinking coffee, and other stimulants, and the playing of games of chance. Please take note of the following statistics: *(She reads from a piece of paper.)* One. A man who reaches the age of sixty-five and smokes throughout his life wastes hundreds of dollars of earnings, damages his health, and risks his mental stability. Two. Drinking coffee, or its equally perni-cious[6] counterpart—liquor—leads thou-sands of unsuspecting persons to infamy, disgrace, and violent crimes every year. And three. Games of chance are Lucifer[7]'s chil-dren. At least one half of one percent of the nation's wealth is annually diverted into these nefarious[8] channels, never to be used for honorable purposes again. And you support this? It gives me great pleasure to stand up and be counted as one individual eternally opposed to these vices.

ACTOR ONE. Dear Moral Statistician. I don't want any of your statistics. I shall take the whole batch and light my next cigar with them. Your kind of people are always ciphering out how much a man's health is injured, and how much his intellect is impaired, and how many pitiful dollars and cents he wastes in the course of ninety-two years, indulgence in the fatal practice of smoking; and in the equally fatal practice of drinking coffee; and in playing billiards occasionally; and in taking a glass of wine at dinner, etc., etc., etc. You are blind to the fact that most old men in America smoke and drink coffee, although, according to your theory, they ought to have died young. And of course you can save money by denying yourself all those little vicious enjoyments for fifty years; but then what can you do with it? It won't do for you to say that you can put it to better use in buy-ing a good table, and in charities, and in supporting book societies, because you know yourself that you people who have no petty vices are never known to give away a cent. You never dare to laugh in the daytime for fear some poor wretch, seeing you in a good humor, will try to borrow a dollar of you; and you never give the rev-enue officers a full statement of your income. So what is the use of your saving money that is so utterly worthless to you? Now I don't approve of dissipation[9], and I don't indulge in it, either. But I don't have a particle of confidence in a man who has no redeeming petty vices, and so I don't want to hear from you any more. I think you are the very same person who read me a long lecture last week about the degrading vice of smoking cigars, and then came back, in my absence, with your reprehensible fire-proof gloves on, and carried off my beauti-ful new parlor stove. *(He puffs a few puffs on his cigar;* ACTRESS TWO *exits.* ACTRESS SIX *enters as she exits. Lights up full.)*

---

6. pernicious, wicked; harmful

7. Lucifer, the devil

8. nefarious, evil; wretched

9. dissipation, scattering of one's money; wasteful spending

ADVICE TO LITTLE GIRLS

ACTRESS SIX *comes to D.L. She wears a baby-doll dress and carries a stuffed Raggedy Ann doll.*

ACTRESS SIX *(music out).* Advice to little girls. *(She curtsies.)* Good little girls ought not to make faces at their teacher for every trifling offense. This retaliation should only be resorted to under peculiarly aggravated circumstances. Also, if you have nothing but a rag doll stuffed with sawdust while one of your more fortunate little playmates has a costly china one, you should treat her with a show of kindness nevertheless. And you ought not to attempt to make a forcible swap unless your conscience would justify you in it, and unless you know you are able to do it. Also, you ought never to take your little brother's chewing gum away from him by main force. It is better to rope him in with the promise of the first two and a half dollars you find floating down the river on a grindstone. This eminently plausible fiction has repeatedly led the unsuspecting infant to financial ruin and disaster. And, if at any time you find it necessary to correct your brother, do not correct him with mud—mud will spoil his clothes. It is better to scald him a little, for then you secure his immediate attention, and your hot water will have the tendency to remove impurities from his person, and possibly the skin, in spots. Furthermore, if your mother tells you to do something, it is wrong to reply that you won't. It is better to intimate that you will, and then afterward act according to the dictates of your own best judgment. And finally, good little girls always show marked deference[10] for the aged. You ought never to sass old people, unless they sass you first. *(Music STING. She smiles and curtsies. Blackout.)*

WHEN THE BUFFALO CLIMBED THE TREE

Lights dim on TWAIN *while a full spot comes up D.R. on* ACTRESS ONE. TWAIN *moves to D.L. where a campfire—some wood surrounding a flashlight covered with red cellophane—is brought onstage.* TWAIN *sits by campfire.* ACTRESS ONE *begins as soon as spot is up on her.)*

ACTRESS ONE. During his life and career, Mark Twain traveled around the globe more than once. But his first extended trip away from his home state of Missouri came when his brother, Orion, was appointed secretary of the Nevada Territory, and Twain accompanied him on his trip west. They traveled by stage coach, mud wagon, and horseback across the western wilderness ... *(Spot out on* ACTRESS ONE; *she exits.* TWAIN *is joined by* ACTOR TWO, *his brother* ORION, *at the campfire.* TWAIN *writes on a pad with a pencil, reading aloud what he's writing.* ORION *chews a piece of beef jerky. Lights are up full.)*

TWAIN. About five hundred and fifty miles from St. Joseph, our mud wagon broke down. We faced a delay of five or six hours, and so we took horses, by invitation, and joined a party of people who were just starting on a buffalo hunt. It was noble sport, galloping over the plain in the freshness of the morning, but our part of the hunt ended in disaster and disgrace when a wounded buffalo bull chased our fellow passenger, Bemis, nearly two miles. Then Bemis forsook his horse and took to a lone tree. It made him afterwards an object of ridicule and derision. He was very sullen about the matter for almost twenty-four hours. *(*BEMIS *enters at this, seating himself between* TWAIN *and* ORION *at the campfire.*

---

10. deference, respect

BEMIS's *feelings are still a bit tender.*) But the following night he began to soften, little by little, and finally he said …

BEMIS (*To* TWAIN *and* ORION; TWAIN *stops writing now.*) Well, it wasn't funny, and there was no sense in those loafers making themselves so facetious[11] over it, and laughing at my misfortune. I should have shot that gangly lubber they called Hank, if I could have done it without crippling six or seven other people—but of course I couldn't. I wish that Hank had been up in that tree; he wouldn't have wanted to laugh so much. And if only I had had a horse worth a cent—but no, the minute he saw that buffalo turn on him and give a bellow, he raised straight up in the air and stood on his heels. Then the saddle began to slip, and he gave it a lift with his heels that sent it more than four hundred yards up in the air, I wish I may die in a minute if he didn't. I fell at the foot of the only solitary tree there was in nine counties adjacent, and the next second I had hold of the bark with four sets of nails and my teeth, and the next second after that I was astraddle of the main limb. I had the buffalo, now—if he did not think of one thing. But that one thing I dreaded. There was a possibility that the buffalo might not think of it, but there were greater chances that he would. I made up my mind what I would do in case he did. It was a little over forty feet to the ground from where I sat. I cautiously unwound the lariat from the pommel of my saddle—

ORION. Your saddle?? Did you take your saddle up in the tree with you?

BEMIS. Take it up in the tree with me? Why, how you talk. Of course I didn't. No man could do that. It fell in the tree when it came down.

ORION. Oh. Of course.

BEMIS. Certainly. I unwound the lariat, and fastened one end of it to the limb. I made a slip-noose in the other end, and then hung it down to see the length. It reached down twenty-two feet—halfway to the ground. I then loaded every barrel of my revolver with a double charge. I felt satisfied. I said to myself, if he never thinks of that one thing I dread, all right. But if he does—all right anyhow—I am ready for him. But don't you know that the very thing a man dreads is the thing that always happens? Indeed it is so. I watched the buffalo now, and presently a thought came into his eye. I knew it! Said I—if my nerve fails now, I am lost. Sure enough, it was just as I had dreaded, he started to climb the tree.

ORION. What??

TWAIN. The buffalo?

BEMIS. Of course. Who else?

ORION. But a buffalo can't climb a tree.

BEMIS. He can't, can't he? Since you know so much about it, did you ever see a buffalo try?

ORION. I never dreamed of such a thing.

BEMIS. Well, then, what is the use of your talking that way, then? Because you never saw a thing done, is that any reason why it can't be done?

TWAIN. All right—go on.

ORION. What did you do?

BEMIS. The buffalo started up, and got along well for about ten feet, then slipped and slid back. I breathed easier. He tried it again—got up a little higher—slipped again. But he came at it once more, and this time he was careful. He got gradually higher and higher, and my spirits went down more and more. Up he came—an inch at a time—with his eyes hot, and his

---

11. making themselves so facetious, joking about

tongue hanging out. He looked up at me, as much as to say, "You are my meat, friend." He was within ten feet of me! I took a long breath—and then I said, "It is now or never." I had the coil of the lariat all ready; I paid it out slowly, till it hung right over his head; all of a sudden I let go of the slack, and the slip-noose fell fairly around his neck! Quicker than lightning I out with my revolver and let him have it in the face. It was an awful roar. When the smoke cleared away, there he was, dangling in the air, twenty foot from the ground, and going out of one convulsion and into another faster than you could count! I didn't stop to count, anyhow—I shinnied down the tree and shot for home. (TWAIN *and* ORION *look at* BEMIS *a moment, then at each other; then back at* BEMIS.)

ORION. Bemis … Bemis, is all that true, just as you have stated it?

BEMIS. I wish I may rot in my tracks and die the death of a dog if it isn't.

TWAIN. Well, we can't refuse to believe it …

ORION. And we don't. But if there were some proof—

BEMIS. Proof! Did I bring back my lariat?

TWAIN. No.

BEMIS. Did I bring back my horse?

ORION. … No.

BEMIS. Did you ever see that buffalo again?

TWAIN. Well …

BEMIS. What more do you want? (*He stands.*) I never saw anybody as particular as you two about a little thing like that. (*Exits. After a moment.*)

ORION. If that man is not a liar—

TWAIN. He only missed it by the skin of his teeth. (TWAIN *goes back to writing. Lights fade. Twain theme music up until spot opens for* THE GREAT FRENCH DUEL.)

THE GREAT FRENCH DUEL

*S*pot up on D.L. *and* ACTRESS FOUR. *Interlude music out.*

ACTRESS FOUR. The year, 1880. The place, France. During this period men of honor with disputes of a serious nature meet on the battlefield to take part in that glorious but terrible tradition, the French duel. In this typical year over two hundred such duels have already taken place. Curiously, there have been no recorded fatalities. Or casualties. Or injuries. This has led certain cynical people to observe that the principal danger of dueling lies in the fact that since the duels are always fought in the open air, the combatants are nearly certain to catch cold. Others have referred to the French duel as "The most health-giving of recreations." These are serious charges, particularly since France is a nation of honor. (*Lights up on D.R. and* GAMBETTA; *he wears a jacket and shirt with a ruffled front; carries a silk handkerchief.*) In order to moderate this talk, therefore, we invite you to observe the following events, faithfully recorded by an impartial observer whose only interest was to preserve the truth … (ACTRESS FOUR *exits, left;* GAMBETTA *begins pacing. He mutters to himself, occasionally exclaiming "Mon Dieu!" and biting the back of his hand, then repeating the cycle. After a moment,* THE AMERICAN *enters from the left; he crosses to* GAMBETTA *who doesn't notice him.*)

AMERICAN. My friend!

GAMBETTA. (*Turning, with happy relief*). Mon ami! (*He embraces* THE AMERICAN.) But— what brings you here? I thought you had returned to America.

AMERICAN. Did you think I could return to America after learning of your duel? (GAMBETTA *crosses away.*)

GAMBETTA. Ah, the duel …

AMERICAN. Gambetta, you must allow me to act as your second.

GAMBETTA *(touched).* You are a true and good friend. But you have no experience in these matters.

AMERICAN. I will learn, my friend; I will learn quickly. *(He takes a quill from his jacket, looking about for something to write on.)* But come, let us attend to the matters at hand.

GAMBETTA. Yes, yes.

AMERICAN. First things first.

GAMBETTA. Yes, of course.

AMERICAN. We shall draw up your will.

GAMBETTA *(alarmed).* What!! My will?? *(Crossing to* AMERICAN*)* My friend, you are delirious. Please, sit down.

AMERICAN. But Gambetta, I never heard of a man in his right mind fighting a duel without making his will.

GAMBETTA *(puts his hand to* AMERICAN*'s forehead).* I thought as much; you're beginning a fever. Now listen to me closely. What we must determine immediately are my last words.

AMERICAN. Your last words?

GAMBETTA. What do you think of this: "I die for my God, for my country, for freedom of speech, for progress, and the universal brotherhood of man." *(Looks for a reaction)* Well?

AMERICAN. Well, if you were dying of a lingering disease, perhaps. But on the field of honor, shouldn't your last words be brief?

GAMBETTA. Brief? *(Considers it)* Brief. *(Crosses, thinking; an idea)* I die that France may live. That's it! I die that France may live.

AMERICAN. But I fail to see the relevance, my friend.

GAMBETTA. Ah, in dying words, relevance is of no importance. Thrill is what you want. I must memorize them … *(Turning away)* I

die that France may live … I die that France may live …

AMERICAN. Gambetta, excuse me, but what about weapons? Has the choice of weapons been made?

GAMBETTA *(another unpleasant thought).* Weapons? *(Bites the back of his hand)* I am exhausted. *(Crosses to bench, D.R., sits)* I will leave the details to you and the other second. You are now authorized to act in my behalf. Good luck—and God be with you. *(He looks shaken, turning over the idea of the duel in his mind. From the left,* DUBOIS *enters and comes to D. C.* AMERICAN *crosses and meets him. Each bows slightly.)*

DUBOIS. Permit me to introduce myself. I am the designated second for Monsieur Fourtou.

AMERICAN. I will be acting in a like capacity for Monsieur Gambetta. *(They shake hands.)*

DUBOIS. Very well.

AMERICAN. As such, I am authorized to make the following proposals: Plessis-Piquet as the place of meeting; tomorrow morning at daybreak as the time; and axes as the weapons.

DUBOIS *(horrified).* Axes!?

AMERICAN. Yes.

DUBOIS. Have you considered, sir, what would be the inevitable result of such a meeting as this?

AMERICAN. Well, what would it be?

DUBOIS. Bloodshed!

AMERICAN. Well if it is a fair question, what was your side proposing to shed? *(DUBOIS now tries to laugh it away.)*

DUBOIS. Of course; of course; I am speaking only in jest. My principal and I would enjoy axes. In fact, we would prefer them. However, the French code does not permit axes as weapons. You must alter your proposal.

AMERICAN. The French code?

DUBOIS. Yes.

AMERICAN. Hmm. *(Thinks a moment)* How about Gatling guns at fifteen paces?

DUBOIS. Quite impossible.

AMERICAN *(thinks).* Rifles?

DUBOIS. Not permitted.

AMERICAN. Shotguns?

DUBOIS. Out of the question.

AMERICAN *(stumped).* Hmmm. How about empty milk bottles at three quarters of a mile?

DUBOIS. Excellent idea! Ah, but no; it is a good idea, except for the danger to disinterested parties passing in between.

AMERICAN. Of course.

DUBOIS. Now, if you prefer, I suppose it would be possible that I, that I could—

AMERICAN. Suggest a weapon?

DUBOIS. It will be my pleasure! *(Feeling his pockets)* Now … what could I have done with those? *(Finally, he finds it.)* Ah!

(He produces a small box containing two miniature pistols. He opens the box and offers it toward THE AMERICAN. AMERICAN *is struck by the daintiness of the guns. He peers into the box, takes out one tiny gun, and holds it up to the light, squinting to see it.)*

AMERICAN. I must congratulate you on carrying two instruments of such bulk without assistance.

DUBOIS. Wait—the cartridges. *(He takes a smaller box from a pocket, opens it, holds it toward* AMERICAN.*)*

AMERICAN *(peers inside, then).* Two cartridges?

DUBOIS. Correct.

AMERICAN. Does this mean that each participant is to be allowed but one shot apiece?

DUBOIS. The French code allows no more. *(*AMERICAN *regards him, then takes a*

cartridge—barely visible to the human eye—and DUBOIS *puts the boxes away.)*

AMERICAN. I am afraid my mind is growing confused under this strain. If you would be so good as to recommend a distance, perhaps we can conclude this business.

DUBOIS. Certainly. Considering the nature of the confrontation … the elements of danger both external and internal … I would recommend sixty-five yards.

AMERICAN. Sixty-five yards? With these instruments? Squirt guns would be deadlier at fifty. My friend, let us keep in mind that we are banded together to destroy life, not make it eternal.

DUBOIS *(torn).* Yes, yes, but I cannot abide the thought of such bloodshed!

AMERICAN. I assure you, with these instruments, at that distance, the danger is eyestrain, not bloodshed. *(*DUBOIS *deliberates a moment.)*

DUBOIS. Very well. I will make a final concession of thirty-five yards—but let the massacre be on your head. Good day, sir. *(*DUBOIS *exits U.L.* AMERICAN *watches him; looks at the pistol and cartridge again; crosses right to* GAMBETTA.*)* My friend, I have—

GAMBETTA. You have made the fatal arrangements—I see it in your eyes!

AMERICAN. Yes, the arrangements have been made.

GAMBETTA *(draws a breath).* The weapon; quickly. What is the weapon?

AMERICAN *(holds it up).* This. *(*GAMBETTA *looks at; swoons.* AMERICAN *catches him; trying to bring him around.)* Gambetta … my friend … are you alright? *(*GAMBETTA *groggily comes to.)*

GAMBETTA. Ah … *(Blinking a few times)* I am afraid that the appearance of outward calm which I have forced myself to exhibit has taken its toll. *(Another breath; new determination)* But away with weakness! I will confront my fate like a man and a

Frenchman. *(Macho)* Behold, I am ready. I am calm. Reveal to me the distance.

AMERICAN. Thirty-five yards, my friend. *(GAMBETTA swoons again; AMERICAN catches him.)* My friend … my friend, can you hear me … ?

GAMBETTA *(coming around).* Thirty-five yards? Without a rest? But why ask? *(Moves right)* Since murder was that man's intention, why should he concern himself with small details? *(Turning)* But remember this—in my fall the world shall see how the chivalry of France meets death.

AMERICAN. But if the arrangements are not acceptable to you—

GAMBETTA. No. The wheels are in motion. *(Military drum sounds and continues under dialogue.)* The massacre now is unavoidable. The hour. What is the hour fixed for the collision?

AMERICAN. Dawn. Tomorrow.

GAMBETTA. What! That is ridiculous! Absurd! No one is up at such an hour.

AMERICAN. You don't mean to say you wish an audience?

GAMBETTA. This is no time to bandy words.[12] I am astonished that Fourtou would agree to such a thing. Go at once and request a later hour.

AMERICAN. Of course, my friend. *(GAMBETTA again stares blankly into space; AMERICAN starts for D.C., where he intercepts DUBOIS.)*

DUBOIS. I have the honor, sir, to bid you a good day.

AMERICAN. And a good day to you, sir.

DUBOIS. I wish to relay the news that my principal strenuously objects to the hour chosen.

AMERICAN. Oh … ?

DUBOIS. We ask that you will consent to changing the hour to half-past nine.

AMERICAN. Ah … Not at all! Any courtesy within our power is at your service. We agree to the proposed change.

DUBOIS. I have the honor to beg you to accept the thanks of my client. Now, I will meet you tomorrow morning shortly before the designated hour to make the final arrangements. I have already provided for the chief surgeon, the consulting surgeons, the poet-orators, the newspapermen, the coroner, the police, the head undertaker, and the hearse. *(Looks up)* If the weather holds, I believe we will have a very nice crowd. I bid you good day, sir. *(Music in. DUBOIS turns and exits; AMERICAN watches him, then returns to GAMBETTA.)*

GAMBETTA. Well, *mon ami*, I presume the matter has been settled in a satisfactory manner.

AMERICAN. It has, my friend.

GAMBETTA. Very well. At what hour is the engagement to begin?

AMERICAN. Half-past nine.

GAMBETTA. Excellent. Then there is no more to be done.

AMERICAN. Gambetta, perhaps you should retire, my friend, and rest.

GAMBETTA. Rest? Rest?? *(Soft, heroic theme music enters, continues under dialogue.)* Rest is for women! For children! A man, with his life in the balance, he does not rest. He waits; he watches; he thinks. *(Pause)* Well, perhaps a short nap—but wake me early for I wish to contemplate my fate. *(GAMBETTA goes to the D.R. platform and sits; sleeps with his head in his hands; with GAMBETTA now asleep, AMERICAN talks aloud to himself.)*

AMERICAN. A remarkable phenomena, this French duel. True, it is the first I've been associated with and I am perhaps understandably upset. But Gambetta is also upset, and he's been a participant in more than twenty of these contests. Perhaps I

---

12. bandy words, discuss trivial things

should advise him of what his physician told me, that if he continues dueling in this way for another fifteen years he could possibly endanger his health. But this isn't the time for that. My duty now is to remain with him until the night is passed. Yes, until the night is passed … (*Music swells. As he stands in his vigil, the lights dim to about half; after a few moments they come back full; he turns and goes to* GAMBETTA. *Music out.*) Gambetta. Gambetta, my friend. It is morning … Gambetta—(*He touches* GAMBETTA *on the shoulder and he shoots off the bench with a yell; wild-eyed, he looks around.*)

GAMBETTA. What's wrong?

AMERICAN. It's time. (GAMBETTA *gathers his composure; as* AMERICAN *leads him to U.C., he rehearses his dying words.*)

GAMBETTA. I die that France may live … I die that France may live. (*Procession music up. As they move toward U.C., a procession enters for the same spot from U.L. A* DOCTOR *with a black bag, a* POLICEMAN, THE LOADER, *and several observers. Finally comes* DUBOIS *followed by* FOURTOU, *who looks as unnerved as* GAMBETTA. *They meet at center; the seconds bow to each other. Music out, except for drum pattern, which continues under dialogue.*)

DUBOIS. I trust you spent a comfortable night.

AMERICAN. Very comfortable. And you?

DUBOIS (*not to be out-done*). Extremely comfortable; no—exceedingly comfortable!

AMERICAN. Excellent. After all, it could prove to have been someone's last night—if the results of the duel are fatal. (GAMBETTA *and* FOURTOU *choke in unison at the word.*)

DUBOIS. Allow me to suggest that the weapons be loaded.

AMERICAN. Allow me to endorse your suggestion. (LOADER *steps forward and the seconds hand him their pistols and cartridges; he* loads each and hands them back.)

LOADER. The weapons are duly loaded. (LOADER *steps back.*)

DUBOIS. I suggest the distance be paced.

AMERICAN. I support your suggestion. (*Each second takes his principal, both of whom have been standing by in stupors, and walks him to the appropriate U.L. and D.R. corner. To* GAMBETTA *as they walk:*) Gambetta, are you well? (*No answer*) My friend? (*They reach the spot, still no reply.*) My friend, can you hear me?

GAMBETTA. No, I would not like a cigarette.

AMERICAN. But I didn't offer you a cigarette.

GAMBETTA. Of course not. I don't smoke. (*Eyes his opponent*) I die that France may live … I die that France may live … (THE POLICEMAN, *after considering the circumstances, steps forward.*)

POLICEMAN (*holding up his hand*). Attention! Attention! (*Drummer stops cadence.*) By virtue of the authority vested in me by the government of France, and in the interest of the safety of these observers, I order all witnesses here to remove themselves from this unsafe position and take up places directly behind the duelists. (*The entourage of doctors and witnesses quickly disperses and moves to spot behind* GAMBETTA *and* FOURTOU; AMERICAN *tries to encourage* GAMBETTA *who is mumbling again to himself.*)

AMERICAN. Gambetta, take heart, my friend. Considering the nature of the weapons, the limited number of shots allowed, and the distance involved, there is a considerable likelihood that both of you will survive. Cheer up, my friend!

GAMBETTA. I am myself again. Give me the weapon. (*Hands it to him;* FOURTOU *also snaps out of it.*)

FOURTOU. (*to* DUBOIS). *Mon ami*—my weapon! (DRUMMER *begins roll;* LOADER, *the only person remaining U.C.*)

LOADER. Ready on the right?

AMERICAN. Yes.

LOADER. Ready on the left?

DUBOIS. Yes.

GAMBETTA (getting nervous once more; to AMERICAN). My friend, stand at my back. Do not desert me at this solemn hour. (Moves back-to-back with him)

AMERICAN. I am here, Gambetta; you have my word.

LOADER. Ready. (The duelists raise their pistols straight up.) Aim. (They cover their eyes with their free hands and wave the pistols in the general vicinity of each other.)

GAMBETTA (shaking). It is not death that I fear, but mutilation! (Drum roll crescendo. Stops.)

LOADER. Fire! (FOURTOU and GAMBETTA fire; each then uncovers his eyes to make sure his pistol has discharged—they have; GAMBETTA swoons, falling backwards on top of AMERI-CAN; FOURTOU begins staggering about feeling himself for the fatal wound—there is none; observers encircle each duelist; a DOCTOR goes to GAMBETTA, helps him to his feet, checks him quickly for injury; then:)

DOCTOR (to GAMBETTA). A miracle! You have not been hit—you are well! (Music in and continues under dialogue. FOURTOU and GAMBETTA now look at each other, long lost friends.)

GAMBETTA. Fourtou!

FOURTOU. Gambetta! (They cross and embrace; observers applaud and buzz with approval; crowd follows them off, U.L.; DUBOIS has gone to help AMERICAN up; enthused.)

DUBOIS. Mon ami! Congratulations! (AMERI-CAN gets up slowly, a little sore.) Congratulations! You are the first person to be injured in a French duel in over forty years. It is likely you will receive the French medal of honor—of course, that is

a distinction that few escape. (He helps AMERICAN as they move U.L.)

AMERICAN (surveying the scene of the great duel). You know, my friend, I think from this day forward I will never be afraid to stand before a French duelist.

DUBOIS. Ah, such courage, mon ami! (Music out.)

AMERICAN. But as long as I am in my right mind, I will never, never, never consent to stand behind one. (Twain theme enters softly. AMERICAN and DUBOIS continue off, exit U.L. as the lights dim except for one full spot, D.R., on ACTOR ONE—again Twain in later years. He stands in his white suit, smoking a cigar.)

ACTOR ONE (Twain theme out). This is the end of the performance, and I have been asked to bring the festivities to a close with any random observations that may have registered in the course of the proceedings. First, I have never witnessed a theatrical presentation of this nature, that is, a the-atrical tribute to one man and his work, that was more ably produced, or richly deserved. The decision to honor so worthy and magnificent a subject reflects not only on the excellence of the source material, but on the great humility of the author as well. Many years ago I was approached by a young man who had studied my work over a lengthy period of time; a fact veri-fied by his sleepy and disoriented look. He asked me what single quality a writer most needed in order to become successful. I was gratified to be able to answer prompt-ly, and I did. I said I didn't know. The remainder of my personal philosophy can be summed up in this: Always do right. This will gratify some people and astonish the rest. Good night. (Twain theme up.)

CURTAIN

Discussing and Interpreting

Twain by the Tale

Play Analysis

1. The "Legend of Sagenfeld" is called, in turn, a fairy tale, a fable, a legend, and a political speech. In what ways is it all of these things?
2. Tom Sawyer and Huck Finn are icons of the American novel. Based on the adaptation you read, why do you think they have remained popular?
3. Pretend you are Mark Twain and write a humorous response to one of the letters he receives in "Answers to Correspondence."
4. Imagine that you are assigned the part of Gambetta in "The Great French Duel." Write a character sketch describing his looks, mannerisms, way of speaking and moving, and any other of his personality traits.
5. **Thematic Connection: What's So Funny?** Which of the vignettes did you find the most amusing? Why?

Literary Skill: Adapt a Humorous Extract

Mark Twain once said, "Man is the only animal that blushes. Or needs to." Below is an excerpt from his book *Extract's from Adam's Diary*. With a partner, write this excerpt as a two-person dialogue between Adam and Eve.

Monday This new creature with the long hair is a good deal in the way. It is always hanging around and following me about. I don't like this; I am not used to company. I wish it would stay with the other animals. Cloudy today, wind in the east; think we shall have rain.... We? Where did I get that word? I remember now—the new creature uses it.

Tuesday Been examining the great waterfall. It is the finest thing on the estate, I think. The new creature calls it Niagara Falls—why, I am sure I do not know. Says it looks like Niagara Falls. That is not a reason; it is mere waywardness and imbecility. I get no chance to name anything myself. The new creature names everything that comes along, before I can get in a protest. And always that same pretext is offered—it looks like the thing. There is the dodo, for instance. Says the moment one looks at it one sees at a glance that it "looks like a dodo." Dodo! It looks no more like a dodo than I do.

Wednesday Built me a shelter against the rain, but could not have it to myself in peace. The new creature intruded. When I tried to put it out it shed water out of the holes it looks with.... I wish it would not talk; it is always talking....

Performance Element: Listening and Reacting

The interaction between actors holds the play together. They must be good listeners as well as good speakers. With a partner, read the scenes between Noah and the Bureaucrat. Then put your books away and re-enact the scene from memory, just by speaking and listening.

Setting the Stage for

Two Chekhov Stories

"The Audition" and "A Defenseless Creature"

written for the stage by Neil Simon
based on short stories by Anton Chekhov

Creating Context:
The Life and Work of Anton Chekhov

Anton Pavlovic Chekhov was born in 1860 in Taganrog, Russia, during the time when Czars still ruled the Russian empire. His grandfather had been a serf, bound to the soil and subject to the will of a Russian lord, and his father, a grocer, was determined that his son should have the best education possible. Chekhov was pulled in two directions. Early on he felt a call to practice medicine, but he was also drawn to literature. He wrote much of his early work—broad, funny sketches published under an assumed name—in order to support himself and his family while he attended medical school. His hard work caused him to contract tuberculosis, a disease of the lungs, which plagued him the rest of his life.

Anton Chekhov
and Maxim Gorky

Chekhov is reputed to have been an excellent physician, especially sympathetic to his female patients. He once observed that family and friends "were always condescending toward my writing and constantly advised me in a friendly way not to give up real work (his medical practice) for scribbling." His first collection of stories, published in 1886, brought critical acclaim, and he immediately followed this with collections in 1887 and 1888. He soon established a literary reputation not only for his stories but also for such plays as *The Seagull* (1898), *Uncle Vanya* (1899), *Three Sisters* (1901), and *The Cherry Orchard* (1904), all of which are considered classics of the stage.

Much of Chekhov's more humorous writing concerns human folly—the triviality, banality, social maneuvering, and class prejudices of his time. And while his characters may often appear silly or misguided, they are always presented with compassion and understanding. They are realistic people whose lives unfold in a precise, simple style. In giving writing advice to his friend Maxim Gorky, Chekhov once wrote, "... cross out as many adjectives and adverbs as you can." Anton Chekhov died at 44 at a health spa in Germany.

As a Reader: Understanding Humor

Humor may be hard to define but it is easy to appreciate. Anton Chekhov's writing abounds in humor—some of it dry and sweet and some of it broad and outrageous. Compare the humor in Chekhov's original, on the left, to that in Neil Simon's play, on the right. Try to imagine where pauses would be appropriate in the play, or where you might speed up the dialogue to enhance the humor.

from Page · · ·  · · · to Stage

The petitioner was blinking, and dived into her mantle for her handkerchief. Kistunov took her petition from her and began reading it.

"Excuse me, what's this?" he asked, shrugging his shoulders. "I can make nothing of it. Evidently you have come to the wrong place, madame. Your petition has nothing to do with us at all. You will have to apply to the department in which your husband was employed."

"Why, my dear sir, I have been to five places already, and they would not even take the petition anywhere," said Madame Shtchukin. "I'd quite lost my head.... Help me, your Excellency!"

"We can do nothing for you, Madame Shtchukin. You must understand: your husband served in the Army Medical Department, and our establishment is a purely private commercial undertaking, a bank. Surely you must understand!"

from "A Defenceless (sic) Woman"
by Anton Chekhov

KISTUNOV. … madame, I don't wish to be unkind, but I'm afraid you've come to the wrong place. Your petition, no matter how justified, has nothing to do with us. You'll have to go to the agency where your husband was employed.

WOMAN. What do you mean? I've been to five agencies already and none of them will even listen to my petition. I'm about to lose my mind. The hair is coming out of my head. *(She pulls out a handful.)* Look at my hair. By the fistful. *(She throws a fistful on his desk.)* Don't tell me to go to another agency!

KISTUNOV *(Delicately and disgustedly, he picks up her fistful of hair and hands it back to her. She sticks it back in her hair.)* Please, madame, keep your hair in its proper place. Now listen to me carefully. This-is-a-bank. A bank! We're in the banking business. We bank money. Funds that are brought here are banked by us. Do you understand what I'm saying?

WOMAN. What are you saying?

from "A Defenseless Woman"
from *The Good Doctor* by Neil Simon

As a Lighting Designer: Lighting the Stage

The two plays you are about to read occur in different places—the stage of a theatre and a bank office. These two locations call for very different kinds of lighting. As you read, try to imagine how you would light each play.

The Audition

Time
The late 1890s

The Characters
VOICE   A writer
GIRL   A young actress

Place
A theatre in Moscow, Russia

VOICE. Next actress, please! Next actress, please!

(*A* YOUNG GIRL *enters and walks to the center of the stage. She is quite nervous and clutches her purse for security. She doesn't know where to look or how to behave. This is obviously her first audition. She tries valiantly to smile and give a good impression. She has a handkerchief in her hand and constantly wipes her warm brow.*)

VOICE. Name.

GIRL (*doesn't understand the question*). What?

VOICE. Your name.

GIRL. Oh … Nina.

VOICE. Nina? Is that it? Just Nina?

GIRL. Yes, sir … No, sir … Nina Mikhailovna Zarechnaya.

VOICE. Age.

GIRL. My age?

VOICE. Yes, please … That means "How old are you?"

GIRL *(thinks).* How old are you looking for?

VOICE. Couldn't you answer the question simply, please?

GIRL. Yes, but I just wanted you to know, I can be any age you want—sixteen, thirty … In school I played a seventy-eight-year-old woman with rheumatism, and everyone said it was very believable. A seventy-nine-year-old rheumatic woman told me so herself.

VOICE. Yes, but I'm not looking for a seventy-eight-year-old rheumatic woman. I'm looking for a twenty-two-year-old girl … Now, how old are you?

GIRL. Twenty-two, sir.

VOICE. Really? I would have guessed twenty-seven or twenty-eight.

GIRL. I have a bad head cold, sir. It makes me look older. Last year when I had influenza, the doctor thought I was thirty-nine. I promise I can look twenty-two when you need it, sir. *(She wipes her forehead.)*

VOICE. Do you have a temperature?

GIRL. Yes, sir … a hundred and three.

VOICE. Good God, what are you doing walking around in the dead of winter with a hundred and three temperature? Go home, child. Go to bed. You can come back some other time.

GIRL. Oh, no please, sir. I've waited six months to get this audition. I waited three months just to get on the six-month waiting list. If they put me on the end of that list again, I'll have to wait another six months and by then I'll be twenty-three and it'll be too late to be twenty-two. Please let me read, sir. I'm really feeling much better. *(Feels her forehead)* I think I'm down to a hundred and one now.

VOICE. I can see you have your heart set on being an actress.

GIRL. My heart, my soul, my very breath, the bones in my body, the blood in my veins—

VOICE. Yes, yes, we've had enough of your medical history … But what practical experience have you had?

GIRL. As what?

VOICE. Well, for example, the thing we're discussing. Acting. How much acting experience have you had?

GIRL. You mean on a stage?

VOICE. That's as good a place as any.

GIRL. Well, I studied acting for three years under Madame Zoblienska.

VOICE. She teaches here in Moscow?

GIRL. No. In my high school … in Odessa … But she was a very great actress herself.

VOICE. Here in Moscow?

GIRL. No. In Odessa …

VOICE. You are then, strictly speaking, an amateur.

GIRL. Yes, sir … In Moscow. In Odessa, I'm a professional.

VOICE. Yes, that's all very well, but you see, we need a twenty-two-year-old professional actress in Moscow. Odessa—although, I grant you, a lovely city—theatrically speaking, is not Moscow. I would advise you to get more experience and take some aspirin …

GIRL *(starts off; stops).* I've traveled four days to get here, sir. Won't you just hear me read?

VOICE. My dear child, I find this very embarrassing …

GIRL. Even if you did not employ me, just to read for you would be a memory I would cherish for all of my life … If I may be so bold, sir, I think you are one of the greatest living authors in all of Russia.

VOICE. Really? That's very kind of you …

Perhaps we do have a *few* minutes—

GIRL. I've read almost everything you've written … The articles, the stories. *(She laughs.)* I loved the one about—*(She laughs harder.)*—the one about—*(She is hysterical.)*—oh, dear God, every time I think of it, I can't control myself …

VOICE *(laughs, too)*. Really? Really? Which story is that?

GIRL *(still laughing)*. The "Death of a Government Clerk." Oh, God, I laughed for days.

VOICE. "Death of a Govern—" I don't remember that … What was that about?

GIRL. Cherdyakov? The sneeze … The sneezing splatterer?

VOICE. Oh, yes. You found that funny, did you? … Strange, I meant it to be sad.

GIRL. Oh, it *was* sad. I cried for days … It was tragically funny …

VOICE. Was it, really? … And of everything you've read, what was your favorite?

GIRL. My *very* favorite?

VOICE. Yes, what was it?

GIRL. Tolstoy's *War and Peace.*

VOICE. I didn't write that.

GIRL. I know, sir. But you asked me what my favorite was.

VOICE. Well, you're an honest little thing, aren't you? It's refreshing … Irritating, but refreshing. Very well, what are you going to read for me?

GIRL. I should like to read from *The Three Sisters.*

VOICE. Indeed? Which sister?

GIRL. All of them … if you have the time.

VOICE. *All* of them? Good heavens, why don't you read the entire play while you're at it.

GIRL. Oh, thank you, sir. I know it all. Act One … *(She looks up.)* "A drawing room in the Prozorovs' house. It is midday; a bright sun is shining through the large French doors—"

VOICE. *That's not necessary!* An excerpt will do nicely, thank you.

GIRL. Yes, sir. I would like to do the last moment of the play.

VOICE. Good. Good. That shouldn't take too long. Whenever you're ready.

GIRL. I've been ready for six months … Not counting the three months I waited to get on the six-month waiting list.

VOICE. PLEASE, begin!

GIRL. Yes, sir. Thank you, sir. *(She clears her throat; then just as she's about to begin:)* Oh, sir, could you please say, "Ta-ra-ra boom-de-ay, sit on the curb I may"?

VOICE. Certainly not. Why would I say such an idiotic thing?

GIRL. I don't know, sir. You wrote it. Chebutykin says it at the end of the play. It would help me greatly if you could read just that one line. I've waited six months, sir. I walked all the way from Odessa …

VOICE. All right, all right. Very well, then. Ready?

GIRL. Yes, sir.

VOICE. "Ta-ra-ra boom-de-ay, sit on the curb I may—"

GIRL. And Masha says, "Oh, listen to that music! They are leaving us, one has gone for good, forever; we are left alone to begin our life over again. We must live … We must live …" And Irina says, "A time will come when everyone will know what all this is for … *(She is reading with more feeling and compassion than we expected.)* … why there is all this suffering, and there will be no mysteries; but meanwhile, we must live … we must work, only work! Tomorrow I shall go alone, and I shall teach in the school, and give my whole life to those who need it. Now it is autumn, soon winter will come and cover everything with snow, and I shall go on working, working ..." Shall I finish?

VOICE *(softly).* Please.

GIRL. And Olga says, "The music plays so gaily, so valiantly, one wants to live! Oh, my God! Time will pass, and we shall be gone forever; we'll be forgotten, our faces will be forgotten, our voices, and how many there were of us, but our sufferings will turn into joy for those who live after us; happiness and peace will come to this earth, and then they will remember kindly and bless those who are living now. Oh, my dear sisters ... it seems as if just a little more and we shall know why we live, why we suffer ... If only we knew, if only we knew ..." *(It is still.)* Thank you, sir. That's all I wanted ... You've made me very happy ... God bless you, sir.

(She walks off the stage ... The stage is empty.)

VOICE *(softly).* Will someone go get her before she walks all the way back to Odessa ... ?

DIM OUT

A Defenseless Creature

Time

The late 1890s

The Characters

KISTUNOV   A bank manager
ASSISTANT   Pochatkin
WOMAN

Place

A bank in Russia

The lights come up on the office of a bank official, KISTUNOV. *He enters on a crutch; his right foot is heavily encased in bandages, swelling it to three times its normal size. He suffers from the gout and is very careful of any mishap, which would only intensify his pain. He makes it to his desk and sits. An* ASSISTANT, *rather harried, enters.*

ASSISTANT *(with volume).* Good morning, Mr. Kistunov!

KISTUNOV. Shhh! Please ... Please lower your voice.

ASSISTANT *(whispers).* I'm sorry, sir.

KISTUNOV. It's just that my gout is acting up again and my nerves are like little firecrackers. The least little friction can set them off.

ASSISTANT. It must be very painful, sir.

KISTUNOV. Combing my hair this morning was agony.

ASSISTANT. Mr. Kistunov ...

KISTUNOV. What is it, Pochatkin?

ASSISTANT. There's a woman who insists on seeing you. We can't make head or tail out of her story, but she insists on seeing the directing manager. Perhaps if you're not well—

KISTUNOV. No, no. The business of the bank comes before my minor physical ailments. Show her in, please … quietly. *(The ASSISTANT tiptoes out. A WOMAN enters. She is in her late forties, poorly dressed. She is of the working class. She crosses to the desk, a forlorn look on her face. She twists her bag nervously.)* Good morning, madame. Forgive me for not standing, but I am somewhat incapacitated. Please sit down.

WOMAN. Thank you. *(She sits.)*

KISTUNOV. Now, what can I do for you?

WOMAN. You can help me, sir. I pray to God you can help. No one else in this world seems to care … *(And she begins to cry, which in turn becomes a wail—the kind of wail that melts the spine of strong men. KISTUNOV winces and grits his teeth in pain as he grips the arms of his chair.)*

KISTUNOV. Calm yourself, madame. I *beg* of you. Please calm yourself.

WOMAN. I'm sorry. *(She tries to calm down.)*

KISTUNOV. I'm sure we can sort it all out if we approach the problem sensibly and quietly … Now, what exactly is the trouble?

WOMAN. Well, sir … It's my husband. Collegiate Assessor Schukin. He's been sick for five months … Five agonizing months.

KISTUNOV. I know the horrors of illness and can sympathize with you, madame. What's the nature of his illness?

WOMAN. It's a nervous disorder. Everything grates on his nerves. If you so much as touch him he'll scream out—*(And without warning, she screams a loud bloodcurdling scream that sends KISTUNOV almost out of his*

seat.) How or why he got it, nobody knows.

KISTUNOV *(trying to regain his composure).* I have an inkling … Please go on, a little less descriptively, if possible.

WOMAN. Well, while the poor man was lying in bed—

KISTUNOV *(braces himself).* You're not going to scream again, are you?

WOMAN. Not that I don't have cause … While he was lying in bed these five months, recuperating, he was dismissed from his job—for no reason at all.

KISTUNOV. That's a pity, certainly, but I don't quite see the connection with our bank, madame.

WOMAN. You don't know how I suffered during his illness. I nursed him from morning till night. Doctored him from night till morning. Besides cleaning my house, taking care of my children, feeding our dog, our cat, our goat, my sister's bird, who was sick …

KISTUNOV. The bird was sick?

WOMAN. My *sister!* She gets dizzy spells. She's been dizzy a month now. And she's getting dizzier every day …

KISTUNOV. Extraordinary. However—

WOMAN. I had to take care of *her* children and *her* house and *her* cat and *her* goat, and then her bird bit one of my children and so our cat bit her bird, so my oldest daughter, the one with the broken arm, drowned my sister's cat, and now my sister wants my goat in exchange, or else she says she'll either drown my cat or break my oldest daughter's other arm—

KISTUNOV. Yes, well, you've certainly had your pack of troubles, haven't you? But I don't quite see—

WOMAN. And then, when I went to get my husband's pay, they deducted twenty-four rubles and thirty-six kopecks. For what? I asked. Because, they said, he borrowed it from the employees' fund. But that's impossible. He could never borrow without my approval. I'd break his arm … Not while he was sick, of course … I don't have the strength. I'm not well myself, sir. I have this racking cough that's a terrible thing to hear—(*She coughs rackingly—so rackingly that* KISTUNOV *is about to crack.*)

KISTUNOV. I can well understand why your husband took five months to recuperate … But what is it you want from me, madame?

WOMAN. What rightfully belongs to my husband—his twenty-four rubles and thirty-six kopecks. They won't give it to me because I'm a woman, weak and defenseless. Some of them have laughed in my face, sir … *Laughed!* (*She laughs loud and painfully.* KISTUNOV *clenches everything.*) Where's the humor, I wonder, in a poor, defenseless creature like myself? (*She sobs.*)

KISTUNOV. None … I see none at all. However, madame, I don't wish to be unkind, but I'm afraid you've come to the wrong place. Your petition, no matter how justified, has nothing to do with us. You'll have to go to the agency where your husband was employed.

WOMAN. *What do you mean?* I've been to *five* agencies already and none of them will even *listen* to my petition. I'm about to lose my mind. The hair is coming out of my head. (*She pulls out a handful.*) Look at my hair. By the fistful. (*She throws a fistful on his desk.*) Don't tell me to go to another agency!

KISTUNOV (*Delicately and disgustedly, he picks up her fistful of hair and hands it back to her. She sticks it back in her hair.*) Please, madame, keep your hair in its proper place. Now listen to me carefully. This-is-a-bank. A bank! We're in the banking business. We bank money. Funds that are brought here are banked by us. Do you

understand what I'm saying?

WOMAN. What are you saying?

KISTUNOV. I'm saying that I can't help you.

WOMAN. Are you saying you can't help me?

KISTUNOV (*sighs deeply*). I'm trying. I don't think I'm making headway.

WOMAN. Are you saying you won't believe my husband is sick? Here! Here is a doctor's certificate. (*She puts it on the desk and pounds it.*) There's the proof. Do you still doubt that my husband is suffering from a nervous disorder?

KISTUNOV. Not only do I not doubt it, I would *swear* to it.

WOMAN. *Look at it!* You didn't look at it!

KISTUNOV. It's really not necessary. I know *full well* how your husband must be suffering.

WOMAN. *What's the point in a doctor's certificate if you don't look at it?!* LOOK AT IT!

KISTUNOV (*frightened, quickly looks at it*). Oh, yes … I see your husband is sick. It's right here on the doctor's certificate. Well, you certainly have a good case, madame, but I'm afraid *you've still come to the wrong place.* (*Getting perplexed*) I'm getting excited.

WOMAN (*stares at him*). You lied to me. I took you as a man of your word and you lied to me.

KISTUNOV. I? LIE? WHEN?

WOMAN (*snatches the certificate*). When you said you read the doctor's certificate. You couldn't have. You couldn't have read the description of my husband's illness without seeing he was fired unjustly. (*She puts the certificate back on the desk.*) Don't take advantage of me just because I'm a weak, defenseless woman. Do me the simple courtesy of reading the doctor's certificate. That's all I ask. Read it, and then I'll go.

KISTUNOV. But I *read it!* What's the point in reading something twice when I've already *read it once?*

WOMAN. You didn't read it carefully.

KISTUNOV. I read it *in detail!*

WOMAN. Then you read it too fast. Read it slower.

KISTUNOV. *I don't have to read it slower. I'm a fast reader.*

WOMAN. Maybe you didn't absorb it. Let it sink in this time.

KISTUNOV (almost apoplectic[1]). I *absorbed* it! It *sank* in! I could pass a *test* on what's written here, *but it doesn't make any difference because it has nothing to do with our bank!*

WOMAN (She throws herself on him from behind.) Did you read the part where it says he has a nervous disorder? Read that part again and see if I'm wrong.

KISTUNOV. THAT PART? OH, YES! I SEE YOUR HUSBAND HAS A NERVOUS DISORDER. MY, MY, HOW TERRIBLE! ONLY I CAN'T HELP YOU! NOW PLEASE GO! (He falls back into his chair, exhausted.)

WOMAN (crosses to where his foot is resting). I'm sorry, Excellency. I hope I haven't caused you any pain.

KISTUNOV (trying to stop her). Please, don't kiss my foot. (He is too late—she has given his foot a most ardent embrace. He screams in pain.) Aggghhh! Can't you get this into your balding head? If you would just realize that to come to us with this kind of claim is as strange as your trying to get a haircut in a butcher shop.

WOMAN. You can't get a haircut in a butcher shop. Why would anyone go to a butcher shop for a haircut? Are you laughing at me?

KISTUNOV. *Laughing!* I'm lucky I'm breathing … Pochatkin!

WOMAN. Did I tell you I'm fasting? I haven't eaten in three days. I want to eat, but nothing stays down. I had the same cup of coffee three times today.

KISTUNOV (with his last burst of energy, screams). POCHATKIN!

WOMAN. I'm skin and bones. I faint at the least provocation … Watch. (She swoons to the floor.) Did you see? You saw how I just fainted? Eight times a day that happens.

(The ASSISTANT *finally rushes in.*)

ASSISTANT. What is it, Mr. Kistunov? What's wrong?

KISTUNOV (screams). GET HER OUT OF HERE! Who let her in my office?

ASSISTANT. You did, sir. I asked you and you said, "Show her in."

KISTUNOV. I thought you meant a human being, not a lunatic with a doctor's certificate.

WOMAN (to POCHATKIN). He wouldn't even read it. I gave it to him, he threw it back in my face … You look like a kind person. Have pity on me. You read it and see if my husband is sick or not. (She forces the certificate on POCHATKIN.)

ASSISTANT. I *read* it, madame. Twice!

KISTUNOV. Me too. I had to read it twice too.

ASSISTANT. You just showed it to me outside. You showed it to *every*one. We *all* read it. Even the doorman.

WOMAN. You just looked at it. You didn't read it.

KISTUNOV. Don't argue. Read it, Pochatkin. For God's sakes, read it so we can get her out of here.

ASSISTANT (quickly scans it). Oh, yes. It says your husband is sick. (He looks up; gives it back to her.) Now will you please leave, madame, or I will have to get someone to remove you.

KISTUNOV. Yes! Yes! Good! Remove her! Get the doorman and two of the guards. Be careful, she's strong as an ox.

---

1. apoplectic, showing symptoms of a stroke

WOMAN (*to* KISTUNOV). If you touch me, I'll scream so loud they'll hear it all over the city. You'll lose all your depositors. No one will come to a bank where they beat weak, defenseless women … I think I'm going to faint again …

KISTUNOV (*rising*). WEAK? DEFENSELESS? You are as defenseless as a charging rhinoceros! You are as weak as the king of the jungle! You are a plague, madame! A plague that wipes out all that crosses your path! You are a raging river that washes out bridges and stately homes! You are a wind that blows villages over mountains! It is women like you who drive men like me to the condition of husbands like yours!

WOMAN. Are you saying you're not going to help me?

KISTUNOV. Hit her, Pochatkin! Strike her! I give you permission to knock her down. Beat some sense into her!

WOMAN (*to* POCHATKIN). You hear? You hear how I'm abused? He would have you hit an orphaned mother. Did you hear me cough? Listen to this cough. (*She "racks" up another coughing spell.*)

ASSISTANT. Madame, if we can discuss this in my office—(*He takes her arm.*)

WOMAN. Get your hands off me … Help! Help! I'm being beaten! Oh, merciful God, they're beating me!

ASSISTANT. I am not beating you. I am just holding your arm.

KISTUNOV. Beat her, you fool. Kick her while you've got the chance. We'll never get her out of here. Knock her senseless! (*He tries to kick her, misses, and falls to the floor.*)

WOMAN (*Pointing an evil finger at* KISTUNOV, *she jumps on the desk and punctuates each sentence by stepping on his desk bell.*) A

curse! A curse on your bank! I put a curse on you and your depositors! May the money in your vaults turn to potatoes! May the gold in your cellars turn to onions! May your rubles turn to radishes, and your kopecks to pickles …

KISTUNOV. STOP! Stop it, I beg of you! … Pochatkin, give her the money. Give her what she wants. Give her anything—only get her out of here!

WOMAN (*to* POCHATKIN). Twenty-four rubles and thirty-six kopecks … Not a penny more. That's all that's due me and that's all I want.

ASSISTANT. Come with me, I'll get you your money.

WOMAN. And another ruble to get me home. I'd walk but I have very weak ankles.

KISTUNOV. Give her enough for a taxi, anything, only get her out.

WOMAN. God bless you, sir. You're a kind man. I remove the curse. (*With a gesture*) Curse be gone! Onions to money, potatoes to gold—

KISTUNOV (*pulls on his hair*). REMOVE HERRRR! Oh, God, my hair is falling out! (*He pulls some hair out.*)

WOMAN. Oh, there's one other thing, sir. I'll need a letter of recommendation so my husband can get another job. Don't bother yourself about it today. I'll be back in the morning. God bless you, sir … (*She leaves.*)

KISTUNOV. She's coming back … She's coming back … (*He slowly begins to go mad and takes his cane and begins to beat his bandaged leg.*) She's coming back … She's coming back …

DIM OUT

Discussing and Interpreting
Two Chekhov Stories

Play Analysis

1. Which of the characters in the two plays would you like to portray, and why?
2. The Voice in the play "The Audition" is supposedly that of the author, Anton Chekhov. As an actor, how would you go about playing the Voice?
3. If you were Kistunov, what would you do to prepare for the next visit from the woman? Use the text to support your answer.
4. Discuss how you would light the scene in the theatre and the scene in Kistunov's office.
5. **Thematic Connection: What's So Funny?** Compare the different styles used in "The Audition" and "A Defenseless Creature." Which did you find funnier? Why?

Literary Skill: Critique the Critic

Below is an excerpt from a letter that Chekhov wrote to the writer Maxim Gorky in 1899 about Gorky's writing. Read the letter, bearing in mind the plays based on Chekhov's short stories that you just read. Write a short critique of Chekhov's letter discussing whether you believe he was true to his own advice.

> When you read proof cross out as many adjectives and adverbs as you can. You have so many modifiers that the reader has trouble understanding and gets worn out. It is comprehensible when I write: "The man sat on the grass," because it is clear and does not detain one's attention. On the other hand, it is difficult to figure out and hard on the brain if I write: "The tall, narrow-chested man of medium height and with a red beard sat down on the green grass that had already been trampled down by the pedestrians, sat down silently, looking around timidly and fearfully." The brain can't grasp all that at once, and art must be grasped at once, instantaneously.
>
> —Anton Chekhov to Maxim Gorky, September 3, 1899

Performance Element: Write and Perform a Humorous Sketch

Now that you have had a taste of the humor of both Anton Chekhov and Neil Simon, try your hand at writing a short, humorous sketch about an everyday event. Feel free to collaborate with a friend. When you are ready, share your sketch with the class.

Sweat

from the short story by Zora Neale Hurston
adapted for the stage by George C. Wolfe

Creating Context: Zora Neale Hurston

Born in 1891, Zora Neale Hurston grew up in Eatonville, Florida, a town that has the historical distinction of being the first owned and run entirely by blacks. In 1925, Hurston went to New York to study anthropology at Columbia University. She then returned to Eatonville to collect folklore. The 1930s and early 1940s marked the peak of Hurston's literary career. She completed graduate work at Columbia, published four novels and an autobiography, and was awarded a Guggenheim Fellowship. Her anthropological research brought her to Haiti, Jamaica, and Bermuda, where she became interested in the practice of voodoo. She incorporated some of these elements into her novels and stories. Between 1938 and 1939 Hurston also wrote a collection of articles on the folklore of African Americans living in Florida.

Hurston once wrote, "There is no agony like bearing an untold story inside you." The play you are about to read reflects the lives of people Hurston knew and cared about deeply. Her use of black Southern dialect has not always been appreciated by literary scholars or understood by the reading public. Like Mark Twain before her, however, Hurston had an ear for the speech patterns and rhythms of the people she wrote about—and she was compelled to let them speak. Her serious study of black culture and language, at a time when these were not popular areas of study, influenced the Harlem Renaissance writers of the time.

Zora Neale Hurston

By the1950s, Hurston had returned to Florida. She experienced health problems as she grew older, died impoverished in 1960, and was buried in an unmarked grave. Not until the 1970s was her writing rediscovered.

As a Reader: Understanding Dialect

The language in the play *Sweat,* like that of the short story it is adapted from, is written in dialect—just as the people would say it. Dialect has its own particular pronunciations and meanings. Zora Neale Hurston believed that to tell a people's story you had to let the people tell it their way. Writers and playwrights use dialect so that we can hear real people speaking honestly to us. It creates a sense of realism, and it draws us to the characters.

Compare the two excerpts below, and read a bit of each out loud. Think about the rhythm and sound of the words. Then discuss why Joe Clarke's monologue is interrupted in the play.

from Page · · · · · · · to Stage

Clarke spoke for the first time. "Taint no law on earth dat kin make a man be decent if it aint in 'im. There's plenty men dat takes a wife lak dey do a joint uh sugar-cane. It's round, juicy an' sweet when dey gets it. But dey squeeze an' grind, squeeze an' grind an' wring tell dey wring every drop uh pleasure dat's in 'em out. When dey's satisfied dat dey is wrung dry, dey treats 'em jes lak dey do a cane-chew. Dey thows 'em away. Dey knows whut dey is doin' while dey is at it, an' hates theirselves fuh it but they keeps on hangin' after huh tell she's empty...."

from "Sweat" by Zora Neale Hurston

GUITAR MAN. Joe Clarke spoke for the first time. (*Music underscore.*)

BLUES SPEAK WOMAN (*The voice of* JOE CLARKE). Taint no law on earth dat kin make a man be decent if it ain't in 'im.

MAN ONE/TWO (*Ad lib*). Speak the truth Joe. Tell it! Tell it!

BLUES SPEAK WOMAN (*As* JOE CLARKE). Now-now-now, there's plenty men dat takes a wife lak dey a joint uh sugar cane. It's round, juicy an' sweet when dey gits it. But dey squeeze an' grind, squeeze an' grind an' wring tell dey wrings every drop uh pleasure dat's in 'em out. When dey's satisfied dat dey is wrung dry...

MAN ONE. What dey do Joe?

BLUES SPEAK WOMAN (*As* JOE CLARKE). Dey treats 'em jes' lak dey do a cane-chew. Throws em away! Now-now-now now, dey knows whut dey's doin' while dey's at it, an' hates theirselves fur it. But they keeps on hangin' after huh tell she's empty....

from *Sweat* adapted by George C. Wolfe

As an Actor: Working with Dialect

As you read *Sweat*, be aware that the dialect is written phonetically—you say the words just as you read them. The word *scare* is written *skeer*, and spoken just as it is spelled. Keep a chart of these words to help you with your reading and dramatic presentation. Stop on occasion to read the play aloud and listen to the voices.

Sweat

Time
"Round about long 'go"

The Characters
BLUES SPEAK WOMAN
GUITAR MAN
SYKES
DELIA

Setting
"O, way down nearby"

Lights reveal DELIA *posed over a washtub and surrounded by mounds of white clothes. Music underscore.)*

BLUES SPEAK WOMAN. It was eleven o'clock of a spring night in Florida. It was Sunday. Any other night Delia Jones would have been in bed …

DELIA *(presenting herself).* But she was a washwoman.

BLUES SPEAK WOMAN. And Monday morning meant a great deal to her.
So she collected the soiled clothes on Saturday, when she returned the clean things. Sunday night after church, she

would put the white things to soak.
She squatted …
She squatted …
on the kitchen floor beside the great pile of clothes, sorting them into small heaps, and humming humming a song in a joyful key …

DELIA. But wondering through it all where her husband, Sykes, had gone with her horse and buckboard.

(Lights reveal SYKES, *posed at the periphery of the playing arena, a bullwhip in his hand. As he creeps toward* DELIA. . .

BLUES SPEAK WOMAN. Just then …

GUITAR MAN (*taking up the chant*). Sykes ... Sykes ... (*Etc.*)

BLUES SPEAK WOMAN. Something long, round, limp and black fell upon her shoulders and slithered to the floor beside her.

DELIA. A great terror took hold of her!

BLUES SPEAK WOMAN. And then she saw, it was the big bullwhip her husband liked to carry when he drove.

DELIA. Sykes!

(*Music underscore ends. As the scene between* DELIA *and* SYKES *is played,* BLUES SPEAK WOMAN *and* GUITAR MAN *look on.*)

DELIA. Why you throw dat whip on me like dat? You know it would skeer me—looks just like a snake, an' you know how skeered Ah is of snakes.

SYKES (*laughing*). Course Ah knowd it! That's how come Ah done it.

DELIA. You ain't got no business doing it.

SYKES. If you such a big fool dat you got to have a fit over a earthworm or a string, Ah don't keer how bad Ah skeer you.

DELIA (*simultaneously*). Gawd knows it's a sin. Some day Ah'm gointuh drop dead from some of yo' foolishness. And another thing!

SYKES (*mocking*). " 'Nother thing."

DELIA. Where you been wid mah rig? Ah feed dat pony. He ain't fuh you to be drivin' wid no bullwhip.

SYKES. You sho' is one aggravatin' n----- woman!

DELIA (*to the audience*). She resumed her work and did not answer him. (*Humming, she resumes sorting the clothes.*)

SYKES. Ah tole you time and again to keep them white folks' clothes outa dis house.

DELIA. Ah ain't for no fuss t'night, Sykes. Ah just come from taking sacrament at the church house.

SYKES. Yeah, you just come from de church house on Sunday night. But heah you is gone to work on them white folks' clothes. You ain't nothing but a hypocrite. One of them amen-corner Christians. Sing, whoop, and shout ... (*Dancing on the clothes*) Oh, Jesus! Have mercy! Help me, Jesus! Help me!

DELIA. Sykes, quit grindin' dirt into these clothes! How can Ah git through by Sat'day if Ah don't start on Sunday?

SYKES. Ah don't keer if you never git through. Anyhow Ah done promised Gawd and a couple of other men, Ah ain't gointer have it in mah house.

(DELIA *is about to speak.*)

SYKES. Don't gimme no lip either ...

DELIA. Looka heah Sykes, you done gone too fur.

SYKES (*overlapping*). ... else Ah'll throw 'em out and put mah fist up side yo' head to boot.

(DELIA *finds herself caught in* SYKES*'s grip.*)

DELIA. Ah been married to you fur fifteen years, and Ah been takin' in washin' fur fifteen years. Sweat, sweat, sweat! Work and sweat, cry and sweat, and pray and sweat.

SYKES. What's that got to do with me?

DELIA. What's it got to do with you, Sykes? (*She breaks free of him.*) Mah tub of suds is filled yo' belly with vittles more times than yo' hands is filled it. Mah sweat is done paid for this house and Ah reckon Ah kin keep on sweatin' in it. (*To the audience*) She seized the iron skillet from the stove and struck a defensive pose.

And that ole snaggle-toothed yella woman you runnin' with ain't comin' heah to pile up on mah sweat and blood. You ain't paid for nothin' on this place, and Ah'm gointer stay right heah till Ah'm toted out foot foremost.

(*Musical underscore.* DELIA *maintains her ground, skillet in hand.*)

SYKES. Well, you better quit gettin' me riled up, else they'll be totin' you out sooner than you expect. Ah'm so tired of you Ah don't know whut to do. *(To the audience)* Gawd! How Ah hates skinny wimmen.

(He exits.)

BLUES SPEAK WOMAN. A little awed by this new Delia, he sidled out of the door and slammed the back gate after him. He did not say where he had gone, but she knew too well. She knew very well that he would not return until nearly daybreak. Her work over, she went on to bed …

DELIA. But not to sleep at once. *(She envelops herself in a sheet, which becomes her bed.)*

BLUES SPEAK WOMAN. She lay awake, gazing upon the debris that cluttered their matrimonial trail. Not an image left standing along the way.

DELIA. Anything like flowers had long ago been drowned in the salty stream that had been pressed from her heart.

BLUES SPEAK WOMAN. Pressed from her heart..

DELIA. Her tears …

BLUES SPEAK WOMAN *(echoing).* Tears.

DELIA. Her sweat …

BLUES SPEAK WOMAN. Sweat.

DELIA. Her blood …

BLUES SPEAK WOMAN. Her blood.

DELIA. She had brought love to the union…

BLUES SPEAK WOMAN. And he had brought a longing after the flesh.

DELIA. Two months after the wedding, he had given her the first brutal beating.

BLUES SPEAK WOMAN. She was young and soft then. So young … so soft ….

DELIA *(overlapping).* But now she thought of her knotty, muscled limbs, her harsh knuckly hands, and drew herself up into an unhappy little ball...

BLUES SPEAK WOMAN. In the middle of the big feather bed
Too late for hope,
Too late for love,
Too late now to hope for love,
Too late now for everything.

DELIA. Except her little home. She had built it for her old days, and planted one by one the trees and flowers there.

BLUES SPEAK WOMAN. It was lovely to her.

DELIA. Lovely.

BLUES SPEAK WOMAN. Lovely. Somehow before sleep came, she found herself saying aloud—

DELIA. Oh well, whatever goes over the Devil's back, is got to come under his belly. Sometime or ruther, Sykes, like everybody else, is gonna reap his sowing.

BLUES SPEAK WOMAN. Amen! She went to sleep and slept …

(Music underscore ends.)

BLUES SPEAK WOMAN. Until he announced his presence in bed.

(SYKES enters.)

DELIA. By kicking her feet and rudely snatching the covers away.

(As he grabs the sheet, blackout. Lights isolate GUITAR MAN. *Music underscore.)*

GUITAR MAN. People git ready for Joe Clarke's Porch. Cane chewin'! People watchin'! Nuthin' but good times, on Joe Clarke's Porch.

(Lights reveal THE MEN ON THE PORCH, MAN ONE *and* TWO. *Sitting between them, a life-size puppet,* JOE CLARKE. *The* MEN ON THE PORCH *scan the horizon, their movements staccato[1] and stylized. Upon seeing an imaginary woman walk past …)*

---

1. staccato, abrupt; disjointed

MEN ON PORCH. Aww sookie! Sookie! Sookie! (*Ad lib*) Come here gal! Git on back here! Woman wait!

(*The "woman" continues on her way as the morning heat settles in.*)

MAN TWO. It was a hot, hot day … near the end of July.

MAN ONE. The village men on Joe Clarke's porch even chewed cane … listlessly.

MAN TWO. What do ya say we … naw!

MAN ONE. How's about we … naw!

MAN TWO. Even conversation …

MAN ONE. Had collapsed under the heat.

(*Music underscore ends.*)

MAN TWO. "Heah come Delia Jones," Jim Merchant said, as the shaggy pony came 'round the bend of the road toward them.

MAN ONE. The rusty buckboard heaped with baskets of crisp, clean laundry.

MAN ONE/TWO. Yep.

MAN ONE. Hot or col', rain or shine, jes'ez reg'lar ez de weeks roll roun', Delia carries 'em an' fetches 'em on Sat'day.

MAN TWO. She better if she wanter eat. Sykes Jones ain't wuth de shot an' powder it would tek tuh kill 'em. Not to huh he ain't.

MAN ONE. He sho' ain't. It's too bad, too, cause she wuz a right pretty li'l trick when he got huh. Ah'd uh mah'ied huh mahself if he hadnter beat me to it.

(JOE CLARKE *scoffs at* MAN ONE's *claim.*)

MAN ONE. That's the truth, Joe.

BLUES SPEAK WOMAN. Delia nodded briefly at the men as she drove past.

(*The men tip their hats and bow.*)

MAN ONE/TWO. How ya do, Delia.

MAN TWO. Too much knockin' will ruin any 'oman. He done beat huh 'nough tuh kill three women, let 'lone change they looks. How Sykes kin stommuck dat big, fat, greasy Mogul he's layin' roun' wid, gets me.

What's hur name? Bertha?

MAN ONE. She's fat, thass how come. He's allus been crazy 'bout fat women. He'd a' been tied up wid one long time ago if he could a' found one tuh have him. Did Ah tell yuh 'bout him sidlin' roun' mah wife— bringin' her a basket uh pecans outa his yard fuh a present?

MAN TWO. There oughter be a law about him. He ain't fit tuh carry guts tuh a bear.

GUITAR MAN. Joe Clarke spoke for the first time.

(*Music underscore*)

BLUES SPEAK WOMAN (*the voice of* JOE CLARKE). Tain't no law on earth dat kin make a man be decent if it ain't in 'im

MAN ONE/TWO (*Ad lib*). Speak the truth, Joe. Tell it! Tell it!

BLUES SPEAK WOMAN (*as* JOE CLARKE). Now-now-now, there's plenty men dat takes a wife lak dey a joint uh sugar cane. It's round, juicy an' sweet when dey gits it. But dey squeeze an' grind, squeeze an' grind an' wring tell dey wrings every drop uh pleasure dat's in 'em out. When dey's satisfied dat dey is wrung dry …

MAN ONE. What dey do, Joe?

BLUES SPEAK WOMAN (*as* JOE CLARKE). Dey treats 'em jes' lak dey do a cane-chew. Throws 'em away! Now-now-now-now, dey knows whut dey's doin' while dey's at it, an' hates theirselves fur it. But they keeps on hangin' after huh tell she's empty. Den dey hates huh fuh bein' a cane-chew an' in de way.

MAN ONE. We oughter take Sykes an' dat stray 'oman uh his'n down in Lake Howell swamp an' lay on de rawhide till they cain't say Lawd a' mussy.

MAN TWO. We oughter kill 'em!

MAN ONE. A grunt of approval went around the porch.

MEN. Umhmm, umhmm, umhmm.

MAN TWO. But the heat was melting their civic virtue.

MAN ONE. Elijah Mosley began to bait Joe Clarke. Come on Joe, git a melon outa dere an' slice it up for yo' customers. We'se all sufferin' wid de heat. De bear's done got me!

BLUES SPEAK WOMAN (*as* JOE CLARKE). Yaw gimme twenty cents and slice away.

MAN ONE/TWO (*ad lib*). Twenty cents! I give you a nickel. Git it on out here Joe. (*Etc.*)

BLUES SPEAK WOMAN. The money was all quickly subscribed and the huge melon brought forth. At that moment …

SYKES. Sykes and Bertha arrived …

(BLUES SPEAK WOMAN *dons a hand-held mask and becomes* BERTHA.)

MAN ONE. A determined silence fell on the porch.

MAN TWO. And the melon was put away.

BLUES SPEAK WOMAN (*lifting the* BERTHA *mask*). Just then …

(DELIA *enters*.)

DELIA. Delia drove past on her way home, as Sykes …

SYKES. Was ordering magnificently for Bertha. (*He kisses* BERTHA's *hand. She squeals.*)

SYKES. It pleased him for Delia to see this. Git whutsoever yo' heart desires, Honey. Give huh two bottles uh strawberry soda-water. (BERTHA *squeals*.)

SYKES. Uh quart uh parched ground-peas … (BERTHA *squeals*.)

SYKES. An' a block uh chewin' gum.

DELIA. With all this they left the store.

SYKES. Sykes reminding Bertha that this was his town …

(MAN ONE *makes a move to go after* SYKES. JOE CLARKE *restrains him.*)

SYKES. And she could have it if she wanted it.

(*Music underscore ends. As* SYKES *and* BERTHA *exit.*)

MAN ONE. Where did Sykes Jones git dat stray 'oman from nohow?

MAN TWO. Ovah Apopka. Guess dey musta been cleanin' out de town when she lef'. She don't look lak a thing but a hunk uh liver wid hair on it.

MAN ONE (*laughing*). Well, she sho' kin squall. When she gits ready tuh laff, she jes' opens huh mouf an' latches it back tuh de las' notch. No ole granpa alligator down in Lake Bell ain't got nothin' on huh.

(*Music underscore. In isolated pools of light, the men on the porch,* DELIA, *and* SYKES.)

GUITAR MAN. Sweat … Sweat …

BLUES SPEAK WOMAN. Bertha had been in town three months now.

MAN TWO. Sykes was still paying her room-rent at Della Lewis's.

MAN ONE. Naw!

MAN TWO. The only house in town that would have taken hcr in.

MAN ONE. Delia avoided the villagers and meeting places in her efforts to be blind and deaf.

MAN TWO. But Bertha nullified this to a degree, by coming to Delia's house to call Sykes out to hcr at the gate!

(DELIA *is seen listening as* SYKES *talks to the audience as if they were* BERTHA.)

SYKES. Sho' you kin have dat li'l ole house soon's Ah git dat 'oman outa dere. Everything b'longs tuh me an' you sho' kin have it. You kin git anything you wants. Dis is mah town an' you sho' kin have it.

BLUES SPEAK WOMAN. The sun had
Burned July to August.
The heat streamed down
Like a million hot arrows
Smiting all things living upon the earth.
Grass withered! Leaves browned! Snakes went blind in shedding! And men and dogs went mad. (*Eyeing* SYKES) Dog days.

GUITAR MAN. Sykes … Sykes …

(SYKES *surreptitiously places a wire-covered soap box, and covers it with the mound of clothes.*)

BLUES SPEAK WOMAN. Delia came home one day and found Sykes there before her. She noticed a soap box beside the steps, but paid no particular attention to it.

SYKES. Look in de box dere Delia; Ah done brung yuh somethin'.

BLUES SPEAK WOMAN. When she saw what it held …

(DELIA *crosses to the box and lifts the lid. Lights*

reveal the men on the porch. With rattlers in hand, they produce the sound of a snake's rattle.)

DELIA. Sykes! Sykes, mah Gawd! You take dat rattlesnake 'way from heah! You gottuh. Oh, Jesus, have mussy!

SYKES. Ah ain't got tuh do nuthin' uh de kin'—fact is Ah ain't got tuh do nuthin' but die.

(Sound of the snake's rattle)

DELIA. Naw, now Sykes, don't keep dat thing 'round tryin' tuh skeer me tuh death. You knows Ah'm even feared uh earthworms.

SYKES. Tain't no use uh you puttin' on airs makin' out lak you skeered uh dat snake. He wouldn't risk breakin' out his fangs 'gin yo' skinny laigs nohow. He's gointer stay right heah tell he die. Now he wouldn't bite me cause Ah knows how to handle 'im.

DELIA. Kill 'im Sykes, please.

SYKES *(staring transfixed into the box).* Naw, Ah ain't gonna kill it. Ah think uh damn sight mo' uh him dan you! Dat's a nice snake.

(SYKES turns to find DELIA standing over him ready to strike him. He lifts the lid to the snake box—she backs away.)

SYKES. An anybody doan lak it, kin jes' hit de grit.

BLUES SPEAK WOMAN. The snake stayed on.

MAN ONE. The snake stayed on.

MAN TWO. The snake stayed on.

(As DELIA continues to speak, SYKES stalks the playing arena, waiting for her to "break.")

DELIA. His box remained by the kitchen door. It rattled at every movement in the kitchen or the yard.

BLUES SPEAK WOMAN. One day Delia came down the kitchen steps. She saw his chalky-white fangs curved like scimitars[2] hung in the wire meshes. This time she did not run away with averted eyes as usual. She stood for a long time in the doorway …

DELIA. In a red fury that grew bloodier for every second that she regarded the crea-ture that was her torment.

BLUES SPEAK WOMAN. That night she broached the subject as soon as Sykes sat down to the table.

DELIA. Sykes !

(Music underscore ends. As the scene between DELIA and SYKES is played, BLUES SPEAK WOMAN and GUITAR MAN look on.)

DELIA. Ah wants you tuh take dat snake 'way fum heah. You done starved me an' Ah put up widcher. You done beat me an Ah took dat. But you done kilt all mah insides bringin' dat varmint heah.

SYKES *(to the audience).* Sykes poured out a saucer full of coffee and drank it deliberately before he answered.

A whole lot Ah keer 'bout how you feels inside uh out. Dat snake ain't goin' no damn wheah till Ah gets ready fuh 'im tuh go. So fur as beatin' is concerned, yuh ain't took near all dat you gointer take if yuh stay 'round me.

DELIA. Delia pushed back her plate and got up from the table.

Ah hates you, Sykes. Ah hates you tuh de same degree dat Ah useter love yuh. Ah done took an' took till mah belly is full up tuh mah neck. Dat's de reason Ah got mah letter fum de church an' moved mah membership tuh Woodbridge—so Ah don't haf-tuh take no sacrament wid yuh. Ah don't wantuh see yuh 'round me atall. Lay 'round wid dat 'oman all yuh wants tuh, but gwan 'way fum me an' mah house. Ah hates yuh lak uh suck-egg dog!

SYKES. Well, Ah'm glad you does hate me. Ah'm sho' tiahed uh you hangin' ontuh me. Ah don't want yuh. Look at yuh stringy ole neck! Yo' rawbony laigs an' arms is enough tuh cut uh man tuh death. You look jes' lak de devvul's doll-baby tuh me.

---

2. scimitars, sabers with curved blades

You cain't hate me no worse dan Ah hates you. Ah been hatin' you fuh years.

DELIA. Yo' ole black hide don't look lak nothin' tuh me, but uh passle uh wrinkled up rubber, wid yo' big ole yeahs flappin' on each side lak uh paih uh buzzard wings. Don't think Ah'm gointuh be run 'way fum mah house neither. Ah'm goin' tuh de white folks 'bout you, mah young man, de very nex' time you lay yo' han's on me. (*She pushes him. He grabs her. She breaks free.*)

DELIA. Mah cup is done run ovah!

Sykes departed from the house!

(SYKES *abruptly turns to exit, but his rage takes hold and he comes charging back, ready to hit her.*)

SYKES (*smiling*). He threatened her, but he made not the slightest move to carry out any of them. (*He exits.*)

BLUES SPEAK WOMAN. That night he did not return at all. And the next day being Sunday …

(*Music underscore. Lights reveal the* MEN ON THE PORCH, *swaying to the gospel beat.*)

DELIA. Delia was glad she did not have to quarrel before she hitched up her pony and drove the four miles to Woodbridge.

BLUES SPEAK WOMAN. She stayed to the night service which was very warm and full of spirit. As she drove homeward she sang.

DELIA. Jurden water

BLUES SPEAK WOMAN/MEN ON PORCH. Jurden water

DELIA. Black n' cold

WOMAN/MEN. Black n' cold

DELIA. Chills the body

WOMAN/MEN. Chills the body

DELIA. But not the soul

WOMAN/MEN. Not the soul

DELIA. Said I wanna cross Jurden

WOMAN/MEN. Cross over Jurden

DELIA. In a calm …

WOMAN/MEN. Calm time, Calm time, Calm time,

DELIA. Time …

(MEN ON PORCH *repeat the "calm time" refrain as the action continues.*)

BLUES SPEAK WOMAN. She came from the barn to the kitchen door and stopped and addressed the snake's box.

DELIA. Whut's de mattah, ol' Satan, you ain't kickin' up yo' racket. (*She kicks the snake box.*)

BLUES SPEAK WOMAN. Complete silence.

DELIA. Perhaps her threat to go to the white folks had frightened Sykes. Perhaps he was sorry.

BLUES SPEAK WOMAN. She decided she need not bring the hamper out of the bedroom; she would go in there and do the sorting. So she picked up the pot-bellied lamp and went in.

DELIA. The room was small and the hamper stood hard by the foot of the white iron bed.

BLUES SPEAK WOMAN (*a gospel riff*). Said I wantah cross Jurden

(MEN ON PORCH/GUITAR MAN *add in.*)

WOMAN/MEN/GUITAR. In calm …

(DELIA *screams.*)

DELIA. There lay the snake in the basket!

BLUES SPEAK WOMAN. She saw him pouring his awful beauty from the basket upon the bed. The wind from the open door blew out the light. She sped to the darkness of the yard, slamming the door after her before she thought to set down the lamp. She did not feel safe even on the ground. So she climbed up into the hay barn.

DELIA (*sitting atop a ladder*). Finally she grew quiet. And with this stalked through her a cold, bloody rage. She went to sleep … a twitchy sleep … and woke to a faint gray sky.

BLUES SPEAK WOMAN. There was a loud, hollow sound below. She peered out …

DELIA/BLUES SPEAK WOMAN Sykes!

(SYKES *abruptly appears.*)

SYKES. Was at the wood-pile, demolishing a wire-covered box. He hurried to the kitchen door, but hung outside there some minutes before he entered and stood some minutes more inside before he closed it after him.

No mo' skinny women! No mo' white folks' clothes. This is my house! My house!

DELIA. Delia descended without fear now …

BLUES SPEAK WOMAN. And crouched beneath the low bedroom window. The drawn shade shut out the dawn, shut in the night, but the thin walls …

MAN ONE. Held …

MAN TWO. Back …

DELIA. No …

BLUES SPEAK WOMAN. Sound. Inside, Sykes heard nothing until he—

SYKES. Knocked a pot lid off the stove.

DELIA. Trying to reach the match safe in the dark.

(*Music underscore.* MEN ON PORCH *create sound of the snake rattle.* SYKES *stops dead in his tracks.*)

SYKES (*leaping onto a chair*). Sykes made a quick leap into the bedroom.

BLUES SPEAK WOMAN. The rattling ceased for a moment as he stood …

SYKES. Paralyzed. He waited.

BLUES SPEAK WOMAN (*sardonically*). It seemed that the snake waited also.

(*With regained composure,* SYKES *gets down from the chair and cautiously moves about.*)

SYKES. Where you at? Humm. Wherever that is, stay there while I …

DELIA. Sykes was muttering to himself …

BLUES SPEAK WOMAN. When the whirr began again.

(*Sound of snake's rattle and music underscore*)

SYKES. Closer, right underfoot this time. He leaped—onto the bed.

(*In isolated light, the actor playing* SYKES *becomes both* SYKES *and the snake.*)

DELIA. Outside Delia heard a cry.

(SYKES *cries out in pain.*)

MAN ONE. A tremendous stir inside!

MAN TWO. Another series of animal screams!

(SYKES *cries out.*)

MAN ONE. A huge brown hand seizing the window stick!

MAN TWO. Great dull blows upon the wooden floor!

MAN ONE. Punctuating the gibberish of sound long after the rattle of the snake …

MAN TWO. Had abruptly subsided.

(*Music underscore ends.*)

BLUES SPEAK WOMAN. All this Delia could see and hear from her place beneath the window. And it made her ill. She crept over to the four-o'clocks[3] and stretched herself on the cool earth to recover.

(*Music underscore. As* BLUES SPEAK WOMAN *talks/sings,* SYKES *crawls toward* DELIA. *Meanwhile, the* MEN ON THE PORCH *scan the horizon, signaling the beginning of a new day.*)

BLUES SPEAK WOMAN. She lay there. She could hear Sykes … calling in a most despairing tone, as one who expected no answer.

The sun crept on up …

And he called. Delia could not move. She never moved.

He called and the sun kept on risin'

"Mah Gawd!" she heard him moan. "Mah Gawd fum hebben."

She heard him stumbling about and got up from her flower bed.

The sun was growing warm.

(*The music ends.*)

---

3. four o'clocks, flowers with blooms that open in afternoon

SYKES. Delia, is dat you Ah heah?

BLUES SPEAK WOMAN. She saw him on his hands and knees. His horribly swollen neck, his one eye open, shining with …

SYKES. Hope.

(SYKES *extends his hand toward* DELIA. *The weight and desperation of his grip pulls her to the ground. She is about to console him, but instead, scurries away.*)

DELIA. A surge of pity too strong to support bore her away from that eye …

BLUES SPEAK WOMAN. That must, could not, fail to see the lamp.

DELIA. Orlando with its doctors …

BLUES SPEAK WOMAN. Oh, it's too far!

(SYKES *tries to grab the hem of her dress.* DELIA *calmly steps beyond his reach.*)

DELIA. She could scarcely reach the china-berry tree, where she waited … in the growing heat …

BLUES SPEAK WOMAN. While inside she knew, the cold river was creeping up … creeping up to extinguish that eye which must know by now that she knew.

(*Music underscore.* DELIA *looks on as* SYKES *recoils into a fetal position and dies. The sound of the snake's rattle as she looks at the audience.*)

DELIA. Sweat!

Blackout

Discussing and Interpreting

Sweat

Play Analysis

1. What will Delia's life be like now that Sykes is dead?
2. What purpose do Blues Speak Woman and Guitar Man serve in the play?
3. Do you think the play would be substantially different if dialect were not used? Why or why not?
4. Write a description of Delia's movement as compared to Sykes in the play.
5. **Thematic Connection: And Justice for All** Do you think that Sykes received the justice he deserved? Why or why not?

Literary Skill: Dramatization

Below is an excerpt written by Zora Neale Hurston. Rewrite this passage as a play script. Be sure to retain the dialect. Indicate in parentheses any important information regarding the set, costumes, or characters.

> A giant of a brown skinned man sauntered up the one street of the village and out into the palmetto thickets with a small pretty woman clinging lovingly to his arm.
>
> "Looka theah, folkses!" cried Elijah Mosley, slapping his leg gleefully, "Theah they go, big as life an' brassy as tacks."
>
> All the loungers in the store tried to walk to the door with an air of nonchalance but with small success.
>
> "Now pee-eople!" Walter Thomas gasped. "Will you look at 'em!"
>
> "But that's one thing Ah likes about Spunk Banks—he ain't skeered of nothin'on God's green foot-stool—nothin'! He rides that log down at saw-mill jus' like he struts 'round wid another man's wife—jus' don't give a kitty. When Tes' Miller got cut to giblets on that circle-saw, Spunk steps right up and starts ridin'...."
>
> A round-shouldered figure in overalls much too large, came nervously in the door and the talking ceased....
>
> "Gimme some soda-water. Sass'prilla Ah reckon," the newcomer ordered, and stood far down the counter....
>
> Elijah nudged Walter and turned with mock gravity to the new-comer. "Say, Joe, how's everything up yo' way? How's yo' wife?"
>
> Joe started and all but dropped the bottle he held in his hands....
>
> "She jus' passed heah a few minutes ago goin' thata way," with a wave of his hand in the direction of the woods.
>
> from "Spunk" by Zora Neale Hurston

Performance Element: Publicity

One of the basic tenets of the theatre business is that before the public can see the play, they have to know it exists and WANT to see it. That is where publicity comes in. Think about how you would let your community know about your school's production of *Sweat*, then write out or draw your ideas.

Setting the Stage for

The Scarlet Letter

from the novel by Nathaniel Hawthorne
adapted for the stage by James F. De Maiolo

Creating Context:
Puritan Beliefs

The Puritans came to the New World in the early 1600s to find a place where they could worship as they pleased. Indeed, they were called Puritans because of their attempts to "purify" the Church of England. For this, the powers of the English church persecuted them and drove them out of the country. They settled in Holland for a time, and from there sailed to the New World, where they hoped to worship God in their own way. This they did—with a vengeance.

The young people in the picture at the left are a romanticized depiction of good Puritans. They are neatly dressed, modest, and probably thrifty, hardworking, and honest. That would be expected of them. It would be assumed, also, that their daily lives would revolve around God—praying, worshipping, and reading the Bible. A belief in "good works" was paramount in Puritan theology, as was the conviction that God punishes sinners and rewards the chosen with eternal life. This young couple would be expected to ascribe to those beliefs.

But what of those who questioned Puritan theology? Dissenters were simply not tolerated. Anne Hutchison, who believed that "He who has God's grace in his heart cannot go astray," was jailed and then cast out of Boston by the governor for her dissenting ways. Others were branded with an *H* for heretic, had their tongues lacerated with a hot iron, or had an ear nailed to a board and then chopped off.

When Nathaniel Hawthorne wrote *The Scarlet Letter* years later, he had an intimate understanding of these cruel laws. He descended from a long line of Puritan ancestors, including a judge who presided over the Salem witch trials.

As you read *The Scarlet Letter*, be aware of the characters' words and actions.

As a Reader: Understanding Theme

The theme of any work is the important idea the author tries to convey to readers.

Compare the two excerpts below. What do we learn about Chillingworth and Hester? What might the play's theme be?

from Page · · · · · · to Stage

At his arrival in the market place, and some time before she saw him, the stranger had bent his eyes on Hester Prynne. It was carelessly, at first. Very soon, however, his look became keen and penetrative. A writhing horror twisted itself across his features, like a snake gliding swiftly over them...After a brief space the convulsion grew almost imperceptible, and he found the eyes of Hester Prynne fastened on his own ... touching the shoulder of a townsman who stood next to him, he addressed him in a formal and courteous manner.

"I pray you, good Sir," said he, "who is this woman?—and wherefore is she here set up to public shame?

... "Hester Prynne . . . . She hath raised a great scandal, I promise you, in godly Master Dimmesdale's church .... they have doomed Mistress Prynne to stand only a space of three hours on the platform of the pillory, and then and thereafter, for the remainder of her natural life, to wear a mark of shame upon her bosom."

"A wise sentence!" remarked the stranger, gravely bowing his head. "Thus she will be a living sermon against sin, until the ignominious letter be engraved upon her tombstone. It irks me, nevertheless, that the partner of her iniquity should not, at least, stand on the scaffold by her side. But he will be known!...

from *The Scarlet Letter* by Nathaniel Hawthorne

(HESTER *ascends the stairs, to stand shoulder height above the crowd.* HESTER *stands silently for all to see.* LIGHTS *change. Everyone moves in slow motion gesturing to her, the baby, and the Scarlet Letter... As she fingers the Scarlet Letter, she sees, in the back of the crowd, an older man. Seeing* CHILLINGWORTH *causes* HESTER *to squeeze the child, who cries again...*)

CHILLINGWORTH (*to the men around him*). I pray you, good Sir," said he, "who is this woman and why is she here set up to public shame?

MAN #2. Mistress Hester Prynne, ... She hath raised a great scandal, I promise you, in godly Master Dimmesdale's church.

CHILLINGWORTH. Will it please you, therefore, to tell me of Hester Prynne's —have I her name rightly?—of this woman's offences?

MAN # 2. Madame Hester absolutely refuseth to speak, and the magistrates have laid their heads together in vain ... they have doomed Mistress Prynne to stand as you see on the platform of the pillory, and then and thereafter, for the remainder of her natural life, to wear a mark of shame upon her bosom.

CHILLINGWORTH. A wise sentence! Thus she will be a living sermon against sin, until the ignominious letter be engraved upon her tombstone. It irks me, nevertheless, that the partner of her iniquity should not, at least, stand on the scaffold by her side. But he will be known!...

from *The Scarlet Letter* adapted by James F. De Maiolo

As a Cast Member: Movement That Supports the Theme

How an actor moves tells us a lot about the character. In turn, each character has something to tell us about the play's meaning. Be aware of how movement can convey the emotions that reflect the theme of *The Scarlet Letter*.

The Scarlet Letter

Time

Mid 1600s

The Characters

HESTER PRYNNE   A young, fallen woman

ARTHUR DIMMESDALE   A young reverend, head of the congregation

ROGER CHILLINGWORTH   An old doctor, husband of Hester Prynne

PEARL   Eight- or nine-year-old child of Hester Prynne and Arthur Dimmesdale

REVEREND JOHN WILSON   Elder reverend of the Massachusetts Colony

GOVERNOR BELLINGHAM   The governor during Act 1

MISTRESS HIBBINS   The sister of Governor Bellingham, a suspected witch

DAME OF FIFTY

TOWN BEADLE

MASTER BRACKET

RESPECTABLE WOMEN (#1 / #2 / #3)

YOUNG WOMAN

MEN (#1 SERF / NEW GOVERNOR / #2 DYING MAN / #3)

SAILORS

CAPTAIN

THE CROWD

Setting

Boston, Massachusetts

ACT ONE   SCENE 1

The suggestion of a street. One end is a door with a small window with bars—the jailhouse door. There are no walls. On the other end of the street is a scaffolding approximately one and a half stories high. Right behind the scaffolding is a raised platform like the balcony of a building representing the GOVERNOR'S house. Between is the suggestion of a marketplace: carts and people with baskets of ware.

It is summer.

At rise: *It is early morning and a* CROWD *is gathered at the door to the jail. The* TOWN BEADLE[1] *is at the oaken jail door unlocking it. The* CROWD *is very quiet, the men with steeple-crowned hats, women with hoods and farthingales.[2] The* CROWD *is quiet and respectful, yet self-righteous and stoic[3] in their beliefs and interpretation of God's and man's laws.*

DAME OF FIFTY. Goodwives, I'll tell ye a piece of my mind. It would greatly for the pubic behoof, if we women, being of mature age and church members in good repute, should have the handling of such malefactresses as this Hester Prynne. What think ye, gossips?

RESPECTABLE WOMAN #1. If the hussy stood up for judgment before us five, would she come off with such a sentence as the worshipful magistrates have awarded?

DAME OF FIFTY. Marry, I doubt not!

RESPECTABLE WOMAN #2. People say that the Reverend Master Dimmesdale, her godly pastor, takes it very grievously to heart that such a scandal should have come upon his congregation.

RESPECTABLE WOMAN #3. The magistrates are God-fearing gentlemen, but over merciful, that is a truth.

RESPECTABLE WOMAN #1. At the very least they should have put the brand of a hot iron on Hester Prynne's forehead. Madam Hester would have winced at that, I warrant you.

RESPECTABLE WOMAN #3. But she, the naughty baggage, little will she care what they put upon the bodice of her gown! Why, look you, she may cover it with a brooch, or suchlike heathenish adornment, and walk the streets as brave as ever!

YOUNG WOMAN. Ah, but let her cover the mark as she will, the pang of it will be always in her heart.

DAME OF FIFTY. What do we talk of marks and brands, whether on the bodice of her gown, or the flesh of her forehead?

RESPECTABLE WOMAN #1. Truth, this woman has brought shame upon us all, and ought to die. Is there no law for it?

DAME OF FIFTY. Truly there is, both in the Scripture and the statute-book.

RESPECTABLE WOMAN #2. Then let the magistrates, who have made it of no effect, thank themselves if their own wives and daughters go astray!

MAN #1. Mercy on us, goodwife, is there no virtue in woman, save what springs from a wholesome fear of the gallows?

(From out of nowhere, MISTRESS HIBBINS, *an old crone[4] and the sister to the* GOVERNOR, *is at the elbow of this group of people. The group of people pulls back from her as if touched by evil.)*

MISTRESS HIBBINS. Death would be the easy way for this sinner! Suffering and shame shall be most beneficial to her and to us all!

MAN #1 *(A lock is heard.)* Hush now, gossips! Here comes Mistress Prynne herself.

(The TOWN BEADLE, *the church officer, steps from the jail door with his staff and sword. He raises the staff and puts his hand on the shoulder of* HESTER PRYNNE *to bring her into the street from the jail. She shakes off his hand and boldly enters into view of the town of Boston. In her arms is a four-month-old baby. At first,* HESTER *wants to hide what is on her bosom by bringing the baby up to her breast, but one shame cannot cover another.* HESTER *is tall and elegant with black hair and beautiful dark eyes. She radiates beauty. Embroidered on her bosom is the letter "A" in fine red cloth with elaborate embroidery and gold thread.)*

---

1. beadle, court official; bailiff
2. farthingales, supports worn beneath skirts to expand the hipline
3. stoic, indifferent to pleasure or pain; serious
4. crone, withered old woman; witch

RESPECTABLE WOMAN #2. She hath good skill at her needle, that's certain.

RESPECTABLE WOMAN #1. But did ever a woman, before this brazen hussy, contrive such a way of showing it! Why gossips, what is it but to laugh in the faces of our godly magistrates, and make a pride out of what the worthy gentlemen meant for a punishment?

DAME OF FIFTY. It were well if we stripped Madam Hester's rich gown off her dainty shoulders; and as for the red letter, which she hath stitched so curiously, I'll bestow a rag of mine own rheumatic flannel, to make a fitter one!

YOUNG WOMAN (whispering). O, peace neighbors, peace! Do not let her hear you! Not a stitch in that embroidered letter, but she has felt it in her heart.

TOWN BEADLE (gesturing and leading the way). Make way, good people, make way, in the King's name! Open a passage and I promise ye, Mistress Prynne shall be set where man, woman, and child may have a fair sight of her brave apparel. A blessing on the righteous Colony of the Massachusetts, where iniquity[5] is dragged out into the sunshine! Come Mistress Hester, show your scarlet letter in the marketplace!

(A lane is opened for HESTER. The CROWD is looking at her, at the baby, and at the scarlet letter. HESTER walks to the scaffolding, situated below the cross of Boston's earliest church.)

TOWN BEADLE. Mistress Hester is sentenced to wear the emblem upon her bosom for all her life and to stand on this scaffold of the pillory[6] for all to see her shame till the sun is high in the sky and spend one more night in yonder prison to be released at first light on the morrow.

(HESTER ascends the stairs, to stand shoulder height above the CROWD. HESTER stands silently for all to see.

Lights change. Everyone moves in slow motion gesturing to her, the baby, and the scarlet letter. HESTER gathers the wrapped baby within her arms, and the child cries out. As she fingers the scarlet letter, she sees, in the back of the crowd, an older man with one shoulder higher than the other, small in stature, with a mix of clothing—both Puritan and Indian. Seeing CHILLINGWORTH causes HESTER to squeeze the child, who cries again. CHILLINGWORTH makes a gesture of silence as they stare at each other.

Lights change. The CROWD moves again at normal speed.)

CHILLINGWORTH (to the men around him). I pray you, good Sir, who is this woman and why is she here set up to public shame?

MAN #2. You must needs be a stranger in this region, friend, else you surely would have heard of Mistress Hester Prynne, and her evil doings. She hath raised a great scandal, I promise you, in godly Master Dimmesdale's church.

CHILLINGWORTH. You say truly, I am a stranger, and have been a wanderer, sorely against my will. I have met with grievous mishaps by sea and land, and have been long among heathen folk to the southward. Will it please you, therefore, to tell me of Hester Prynne's—have I her name rightly—of this woman's offences?

MAN #2. Truly, friend, and methinks it must gladden your heart after your troubles and sojourn in the wilderness to find yourself in a land where iniquity is searched out, and punished in the sight of rulers and people; as here in our godly New England.

MAN #3. Yonder woman, Sir, was the wife of a certain learned man, English by birth, but

---

5. iniquity, sin; wickedness

6. pillory, a device for publicly punishing offenders, consisting of a wooden frame with holes in which the head and hands can be locked

who had long dwelt in Amsterdam, whence, some good time agone, he decided to cross over and cast in his lot with us of Massachusetts. To this purpose he sent his wife before him, remaining himself to look after some necessary affairs.

MAN #2. Marry, good Sir, in some two years, or less, that the woman has been a dweller here in Boston, no tidings have come of this learned gentleman; and his young wife, has been left to her own misguidance.

CHILLINGWORTH. So learned a man as you speak of, should have learned this too in his books. And who, by your favor, Sir, may be the father of yonder babe—it is some three or four months old, I should judge—which Mistress Prynne is holding in her arms?

MAN #1. Truth, friend, that matter remaineth a riddle; and the one who shall expound it has yet spoken.

MAN #2. Madame Hester absolutely refuseth to speak, and the magistrates have laid their heads together in vain.

MAN #1. The guilty one stands looking on at this sad spectacle, unknown of man, and forgetting that God sees him.

CHILLINGWORTH. The learned man should come himself, to look into the mystery.

MAN #3. It behooves him well, if he be still in life. Now, good Sir, our Massachusetts magistrates, bethinking themselves that this woman is youthful and fair, and doubtless was strongly tempted to her fall …

MAN #1. As it is likely, her husband may be at the bottom of the sea—they have not been bold to put in force the extremity of our righteous law against her.

MAN #2. The penalty thereof is death. But in their great mercy and tenderness of heart, they have doomed Mistress Prynne to stand as you see on the platform of the pillory, and then and thereafter, for the remainder of her natural life, to wear a mark of shame upon her bosom.

CHILLINGWORTH. A wise sentence! Thus she will be a living sermon against sin, until the ignominious[7] letter be engraved upon her tombstone. It irks me, nevertheless, that the partner of her iniquity should not, at least, stand on the scaffold by her side. But he will be known! He will be known! (*Bowing to the townspeople,* CHILLINGWORTH *moves past the scaffolding, never taking his eyes from* HESTER.)

(HESTER *never removes her eyes from* CHILLINGWORTH *as he passes, but there is a defiance in her eyes.*)

REVEREND WILSON. Hearken unto me, Hester Prynne!

(HESTER, *becoming aware that she has been spoken to now turns her face to the platform, where sit* REVEREND WILSON, GOVERNOR BELLINGHAM, *and* REVEREND MASTER DIMMESDALE.)

REVEREND WILSON. Hester Prynne, (*Placing a hand on* MASTER DIMMESDALE) I have sought to persuade this godly youth that he should deal with you, here in the face of Heaven, and in hearing of all the people as touching the vileness and blackness of your sin. Knowing your natural temper better than I, he may better judge what arguments to use, to reveal the name of him who tempted you to this grievous fall.

GOVERNOR BELLINGHAM. Good Master Dimmesdale, the responsibility of this woman's soul lies greatly with you. It behooves you, therefore, to exhort her to repentance and to confession, as a proof and consequence thereof.

REVEREND WILSON (*to* DIMMESDALE). Must it be thou, or I, that shall deal with this poor sinner's soul?

---

7. ignominious, shameful; disgraceful

(Murmurs are heard around the balcony and throughout the CROWD. *The* CROWD *looks at* DIMMESDALE *who continues to hesitate.)*

REVEREND WILSON. Speak to the woman, my brother. Exhort her to confess the truth!

(Saying a silent prayer with head bent, DIMMESDALE *moves forward to speak to* HESTER PRYNNE.*)*

DIMMESDALE. Hester Prynne, thou hearest what this good man says, and seest the accountability under which I labor. For thy soul's peace, and that thy earthly punishment will thereby be made more effectual to salvation, I charge thee to speak out the name of thy fellow-sinner!

(Silence)

DIMMESDALE *(stronger).* Be not silent from any mistaken pity and tenderness for him; for, believe me Hester, though he were to step down from a high place, and stand there beside thee on thy pedestal of shame, yet better were it so, than to hide a guilty heart through life.

(Silence. The CROWD *does not move.* HESTER *stands perfectly still, even the child has not made a sound.)*

REVEREND WILSON. Defy us not, Hester Prynne! Pity for thy plight has kept this sentence light—push us not!

DIMMESDALE. What can thy silence do for him? Heaven hath granted thee an open ignominy, that thereby thou mayest work out an open triumph over the evil within thee, and the sorrow without. Take heed how thou deniest to him—who, perchance, hath not the courage to grasp it for himself—the bitter, but wholesome, cup that is now presented to thy lips!

(The crowd is becoming impatient and restless. HESTER *looks at* DIMMESDALE. *Crying sounds are heard.* HESTER *shakes her head.)*

REVEREND WILSON *(harshly).* Woman, transgress not beyond the limits of Heaven's mercy! *(Pause)* That little babe hath been gifted with a voice to second and confirm the counsel which thou hast heard. Speak out the name! That, and thy repentance, may avail to take the scarlet letter off thy breast.

HESTER. Never! *(Looking at* WILSON, *not at* DIMMESDALE) It is too deeply branded. Ye cannot take it off. And would that I might endure his agony, as well as mine!

CHILLINGWORTH. Speak woman! Speak; and give your child a father!

HESTER. I will not speak! *(Responding to his voice,* HESTER *stares at him.)* And my child must seek a Heavenly Father; she shall never know an earthly one!

MISTRESS HIBBINS *(Stands off to the side watching* CHILLINGWORTH *and* HESTER PRYNNE. *She is the only one that notices the scene. To herself.)* There is darkness here, I can see within them both! These two will strengthen our ranks in the deep forest on dark nights!

DIMMESDALE *(murmuring to himself).* Wondrous strength and generosity of a woman's heart! She will not speak!

REVEREND WILSON. Sinner! God hath sent down his demands that we must follow for redemption …

(As the REVEREND WILSON *talks the lights slowly change to scarlet. The* CROWD *and* REVEREND WILSON *move in slow motion in the fading light to continue on his discourse of sin.* HESTER *stands with the same hard demeanor; the baby has started wailing and screaming.* HESTER *mechanically tries to hush the screaming.*

Lights fade to normal. HESTER *is led back to prison and vanishes inside the portal. The scarlet light is seen inside the dark of the jail.)*

SCENE 2

Inside the prison. A cot and a trundle bed or small crib. A small table with a water pitcher and basin. No walls, just the door to the jail and lights indicating bars.

In blackout, HESTER *and the child are under extreme duress and cannot stop moaning and wailing. Lights up on* MASTER BRACKET, *the jailer, watching* HESTER *as she ignores the child's cries and throws herself with force against the door and onto the bed. The baby is heard crying and wailing.*

MASTER BRACKET. Mistress Hester! Continue not this. Has Satan gotten to thee for all time? Peace, prithee. This canst continue!

(He waits and she continues. He exits and returns with CHILLINGWORTH. HESTER, *seeing him, becomes quiet. The baby is heard whimpering.)*

MASTER BRACKET *(surprised by the quiet).* Mistress Hester, this good doctor has come. Roger Chillingworth. Wouldst thou allow his help for thee and thine child?

HESTER *(through quiet tears).* I will not let … I cannot … Prithee be gone!

CHILLINGWORTH. Prithee, friend, leave me alone with my patients. Trust me, good jailer, you shall briefly have peace in your house; and, I promise you, Mistress Prynne shall hereafter be more amenable[8] to just authority than you may have found her before.

MASTER BRACKET. Verily, the woman hath been like a possessed one; nay, if your worship can accomplish that I shall own you for a man of skill indeed! If not, I should take in hand to drive Satan out of her with stripes.

*(*MASTER BRACKET *gives one look around and exits—leaving* CHILLINGWORTH *and* HESTER *alone with the crying child.* CHILLINGWORTH *moves first to the child in the crib. He examines her and unclasps a leather bag from under his clothes. He mixes some powder with water.)*

CHILLINGWORTH. My old studies in alchemy and my sojourn, for above a year past, among a people well versed in the kindly properties of herbs, have made a better physician of me than many that claim the medical degree. Here, woman! The child is yours—she is not of mine. Neither will she recognize my voice or aspect as a father's. Administer this draught, therefore, with thine own hand.

HESTER *(not taking the medicine).* Wouldst thou avenge thyself on the innocent babe?

CHILLINGWORTH. Foolish woman! *(Coldly)* What should ail me, to harm this misbegotten and miserable babe? The medicine is potent for good; and were it my child—yea, mine own, as well as thine—I could do no better for it.

*(*HESTER *hesitates.* CHILLINGWORTH *takes the child and administers the medicine himself. The moans subside after a few moments. He sets her in the crib and with a calm and businesslike manner attends* HESTER. HESTER *never stops staring into his eyes.)*

CHILLINGWORTH *(mingles another cure).* I have learned many new secrets in the wilderness, and here is one of them. *(Holding the drink to* HESTER*)* Drink it! It may be less soothing than a sinless conscience. That I cannot give thee. But it will calm the swell and heaving of thy passion, like oil thrown on the waves of a tempestuous sea.

HESTER *(takes the cup and looks at her child.)* I have thought of death, have wished for it, would even have prayed for it, were it fit that such as I should pray for anything. Yet, if death be in this cup, I bid thee think again, before thou beholdest me drink it. See! It is even now at my lips.

CHILLINGWORTH. Drink, then. Dost thou know me so little, Hester Prynne? Even if I imagine a scheme of vengeance, what could I do better for my object than to let thee live so that this burning shame may *(Touching the scarlet letter)* still blaze upon thy bosom?

---

8. amenable, obedient to; accepting of

(HESTER *pulls back from his touch.* CHILLING-WORTH *smiles.*)

CHILLINGWORTH. Live, therefore, and bear thy doom with thee, in the eyes of men and women—in the eyes of yonder child! And, that thou may live, take of this draught.

(HESTER *drains the cup. She watches him.*)

CHILLINGWORTH. Hester, I ask not wherefore, nor how, thou hast ascended to the pedestal of infamy on which I found thee. The reason is not far to seek. It was my folly, and thy weakness. I—a man of thought, the bookworm of great libraries—a man already in decay, having given my best years to feed the hungry dream of knowledge—what had I to do with youth and beauty like thine own! Misshapen from my birth-hour, how could I delude myself with the idea that intellectual gifts might call me wise. Nay, from the moment when we came down the old church steps together, a married pair, I might have beheld the bale-fire of that scarlet letter blazing at the end of our path!

HESTER. Thou knowest—thou knowest that I was frank with thee. I felt no love, nor feigned any.

CHILLINGWORTH. True, it was my folly! I have said it. But up to that epoch of my life, I had lived in vain. The world had been so cheerless! My heart was a lonely and chill habitation without a household fire. I drew thee into my heart, into its innermost chamber, and sought to warm thee by the warmth which thy presence made there!

HESTER. I have greatly wronged thee.

CHILLINGWORTH. We have wronged each other. Mine was the first wrong, when I betrayed thy budding youth into a false and unnatural relation with my decay. Therefore, I seek no vengeance, plot no evils against thee. Between thee and me,

the scale hangs fairly balanced. But Hester, the man lives who has wronged us both! Who is he?

HESTER (*staring him down*). That thou shalt never know!

CHILLINGWORTH. Never, sayest thou? (*Smiling wickedly*) Never know him! Believe me, Hester, there are few things—whether in the outward world, or in the invisible sphere of thought—few things hidden from the man who devotes himself earnestly to the solution of a mystery. Thou mayest cover up thy secret from the prying multitude. Thou mayest conceal it from the ministers and magistrates. (HESTER *grasps at her heart.* CHILLINGWORTH *is fired up with confidence*). I shall seek this man as I have sought truth in books, as I have sought gold in alchemy. I shall see him tremble. Sooner or later, he must needs be mine! He bears no letter of infamy wrought into his garment, as thou dost; but I shall read it on his heart. Yet fear not for him! Think not that I shall interfere with Heaven's own method of retribution, or, to my own loss, betray him to the grip of human law. Neither do thou imagine that I shall not contrive against his life; no, nor against his fame, if as I judge, he be a man of fair repute. Let him live! Let him hide himself. He shall be mine!

HESTER (*bewildered*). Thy acts are like mercy, but thy words interpret thee as a terror!

CHILLINGWORTH. One thing, thou that was my wife, I would enjoin upon thee as thou hast kept the secret of thy paramour, keep, likewise, mine! Breathe not, to any human soul, that thou didst ever call me husband! No matter whether of love or hate; no matter whether of right or wrong! Thou and thine, Hester Prynne, belong to me. My home is where thou art, and where he is. But betray me not!

HESTER. Why dost thou desire it? Why not

announce thyself openly, and cast me off at once?

CHILLINGWORTH. It may be because I will not encounter the dishonor that besmirches the husband of a faithless woman. It may be for other reasons. It is my purpose to live and die unknown. Let, therefore, thy husband be to the world as one already dead.

HESTER. I will keep thy secret, as I have his.

CHILLINGWORTH. Recognize me not, by word, by sign, by look! Breathe not the secret, above all, to the man thou keep unknown. Shouldst thou fail me in this, beware! His fame, his position, his life— will be in my hands. Beware! Swear it!

HESTER. I swear it upon God and him whose name I have sworn never to utter.

(CHILLINGWORTH *smiles.*)

HESTER. Why dost thou smile so at me? Art thou like the devil, the Black Man that haunts the forest round about us? Hast thou enticed me into a bond that will prove the ruin of my soul?

CHILLINGWORTH. Not thy soul. *(Smiling)* No, not thine!

(Light fades.)

SCENE 3

The same as Scene 1. *The scene takes place chronologically over time. Each new scene is a tableau that represents a new year in the life of* HESTER, PEARL, DIMMESDALE, *and* CHILLINGWORTH. DIMMESDALE *becomes more and more weak,* CHILLINGWORTH *more and more focused on his one task.*

The first scene is the following day as her sentence is completed. The jailhouse door is thrown open. HESTER *with the child in her arms steps out into the day. Unlike the last time she walked from the jail—no one is there.* HESTER *hesitates, then walks across the stage. Years pass with each step.*

She walks from one spot light to another and at each light another change has occurred and the only constant is her somber dress and the brilliance of the scarlet letter.

By the final tableau she is by the shore, the jail has become her small thatched cottage and her daughter is now a young girl of seven years of age. The sound of the ocean is heard. Birds, wind and rustling leaves can be heard.

These scenes alternate with scenes of CHILLINGWORTH *and* DIMMESDALE.

✄ *FIRST HESTER TABLEAU: A small crib sits by* HESTER'S *feet. She is seated doing needlework.* DAME OF FIFTY *steps into the light.*

HESTER. I have done as you requested. The gloves for thy husband's funeral dress. I am sorry for thy loss.

DAME OF FIFTY *(looking at the scarlet letter).* Prithee, I do not want your sorrow.

(She holds out payment, HESTER *hands the gloves over and takes the payment.* DAME OF FIFTY *flinches at the nearness.* HESTER *begins to cover the scarlet letter, then lets her hand drop. Lights fade.)*

✄ *FIRST CHILLINGWORTH/DIMMESDALE TABLEAU: The sound of the ocean is heard.* CHILLINGWORTH *is carrying a basket of herbs, weeds, and flowers.* DIMMESDALE *enters the light.)*

DIMMESDALE. Good day, Sir. Art thou the physician many speak of that has studied in England and Europe?

CHILLINGWORTH. I think I must be he, Roger Chillingworth, and I knowest thee to be the Master Dimmesdale. I have heard much good of thee.

DIMMESDALE. This unworthy one wouldst never claim goodness. I am set forth to teach the Holy Writ so that men's souls can be with God and, perchance, this ungodly soul can make its home not with Satan.

CHILLINGWORTH. I have heard similar

words from many holy men, but none with more sadness, truth, or conviction! Mayest I walk with thee? I enjoy thy words and do wish to know thee better.

(They move out of the light together as the light fades.)

🎣 *SECOND HESTER TABLEAU: Light up.* HESTER *is on her knee with her arms out as if to a small child.* HESTER *hugs the imagined child. The hug breaks.* HESTER *grabs at the imagined child's hand as it reaches for the scarlet letter and we hear a child giggling and running off.)*

HESTER. Oh, Father in Heaven—thy gift of yonder child has made clear mine own path I am to lead, but prithee, what shall I make of this gift, this child, which I have brought into the world! No other children have whims more strange and magical as my Pearl. I love her so, yet is this mine punishment for my sins? That she scare me so? *(Standing straighter)* Then I shall bear my sin as I do this scarlet letter. She shall know thy name and thy laws. And I shalt love her with all my being.

(Lights fade.)

🎣 *SECOND CHILLINGWORTH/DIMMESDALE TABLEAU: A gravestone is visible.* DIMMESDALE *and* CHILLINGWORTH *are talking.*

CHILLINGWORTH. I thank thee for asking the Widow Johnson to let me a room down the hall from thee. Happily, near a new friend and in this neighboring grave-yard there are many unusual plants that I may study for medicinal uses.

DIMMESDALE. It is to help Widow Johnson that I extended the invitation, but I am glad that thou will find it to your satisfaction.

CHILLINGWORTH. Prithee, if I am down the hall, may I help thee in thy sickness?

DIMMESDALE. I am not sickly. *(Grabbing his heart)* I need not your medicines.

CHILLINGWORTH. If thou change your mind, I am here for thee.

(DIMMESDALE looks away as the light fades.)

🎣 *THIRD HESTER TABLEAU:* YOUNG WOMAN *is laughing and cooing over* MAN #1. *As* HESTER *walks into the light,* YOUNG WOMAN *sees* HESTER, *then sees the scarlet letter and drops her head in shame, breaks with* MAN #1 *and moves quickly away.* MAN #1 *turns to see* HESTER *and moves off in the opposite direction of* YOUNG WOMAN.

HESTER. What evil thing is at hand? Behold, Hester, there goes a companion! Have I begun an evil? That all young women will fall in this pit? Is not the scarlet letter enough to teach them?

(Light fades.)

🎣 *THIRD CHILLINGWORTH/DIMMESDALE TABLEAU: Night, the woods.* CHILLINGWORTH *has a basket with him. Out of nowhere steps* MISTRESS HIBBINS *into the light.*

MISTRESS HIBBINS. The Black Man knows thy name! Thou must have signed his book in thy blood.

CHILLINGWORTH. I have signed my name many a time. What dost thou want Mistress Crone?

MISTRESS HIBBINS. Speak not thus to me! I have the Black Man's attention! And I knowest the black spot in thy soul. It is vengeance!

CHILLINGWORTH. Ay, vengeance is in my soul and my heart. Yet it is mine, not thine, and not the Black Man's. Now let me pass!

(MISTRESS HIBBINS steps aside and vanishes, only her cackle is heard as the light fades.)

🎣 *FOURTH HESTER TABLEAU: Light up.* HESTER *walks into it looking all around her.* CHILDREN *are heard laughing and tormenting* HESTER *and the unseen* PEARL.

VOICE OF CHILD #1. Behold, verily, there is the woman of the scarlet letter.

VOICE #2. And there is the likeness of the scarlet letter running along by her side!

VOICE #3. Come, and let us fling mud at them!

VOICES OF CHILDREN. Yea, let us fling mud and stones at them. Let them suffer for their sins!

(*The noise of the* CHILDREN *rises. A shriek is heard from* PEARL. *We hear the* CHILDREN *scream and scatter. We hear a little girl's voice shout with a terrific volume.*)

HESTER (*distressed*). Pearl. Prithee stop! Come hither!

(*Light fades.*)

⚓ *FOURTH CHILLINGWORTH/DIMMESDALE TABLEAU: A table is covered in plants and bottles, and a candle burns as* CHILLINGWORTH *uses a mortar and pestle.* DIMMESDALE *is there.*)

CHILLINGWORTH. Thou look worse each passing day, Master Dimmesdale. I am mixing a draught to help thee in thy quest for good health. But I canst do thee much good if thou wilt not tell me thy ill.

DIMMESDALE. I will not speak to thee of my ills. It is I who must listen to the ills of others. I am merely fatigued, I need not your medicines.

CHILLINGWORTH. Confession is as helpful for thy physical well-being as thy spiritual one. Tell me what is thy pain?

DIMMESDALE. Good night, Mr. Chillingworth. I hope to see thee at the sermon on the morrow. Thou canst hear me speak on confession and the soul then.

(*The light fades as* DIMMESDALE *moves away.*)

⚓ *FIFTH HESTER TABLEAU: Light up. A couple passes* HESTER *as* PEARL, *laughing, is running around* HESTER. *The couple are whispering.*

RESPECTABLE WOMAN #1. Hast thou beheld the strangeness of yonder child?

MAN #1. Learning sinful ways from her mother. How canst she be naught but strange?

RESPECTABLE WOMAN #1. The child should be delivered into the hands of God where her soul can be saved.

(HESTER *hears these words and holds fast to*

"PEARL" *in her arms. Boldly she faces her accusers.*)

HESTER. God bless thee on this morning good Sir and kind Gentlewoman.

(*The* RESPECTABLE WOMAN *and* MAN *rush off embarrassed. Lights fade.*)

⚓ *FIFTH AND FINAL CHILLINGWORTH/ DIMMESDALE TABLEAU: Lights up.* DIMMESDALE *is in a straight-back chair. He is studying the Bible on his lap. Each time he begins quoting a passage, he strikes himself with the Bible.*

DIMMESDALE (*repeating*). "I will bear the indignation of the Lord, because I have sinned against him, until he plead my cause, and execute judgment for me; he will bring me forth to the light, and I shall behold his righteousness."

(*Unknown to him,* CHILLINGWORTH *is behind him with a smile on his face. The light fades on* DIMMESDALE *first, then on the face of* CHILLINGWORTH.)

⚓ *SIXTH AND FINAL HESTER TABLEAU: Lights up first as a spot on* HESTER, *as the sound of the waves crashing against a shore is heard, the lights come up on a cottage door, set pieces of* HESTER's *and* PEARL's *home near the shore.* PEARL— *this is the first time we actually see* PEARL—*a child of seven, is gathering flowers near the cottage.*

HESTER *sits on a rock, doing her needlework.* PEARL *comes up and throws the gathered flowers at the scarlet letter on* HESTER's *bosom as in a game of darts.*

HESTER. Child, what art thou?

PEARL. Oh, I am your little Pearl. (*She starts laughing and impishly dancing up and down.*)

HESTER. Art thou my child, in very truth?

PEARL (*continuing her antics*). Yes; I am little Pearl!

HESTER (*half playfully*). Thou art not my child! Thou art no Pearl of mine! (*Suffering*)

Tell me, then, what thou art, and who sent thee hither?

PEARL. Tell me, Mother! *(Seriously, moving to her mother's knees)* Do thou tell me!

HESTER *(hesitantly).* Thy Heavenly Father sent thee.

PEARL *(hearing the pause, touches the scarlet letter).* He did not send me! *(Positively)* I have no Heavenly Father!

HESTER. Hush, Pearl, hush. Thou must not talk so! He sent us all into this world. He sent even me, thy mother. Then, much more, thee. Or, if not, thou strange and elfin child, whence didst thou come?

PEARL. Tell me! Tell me! *(Laughing)* It is thou that must tell me!

(HESTER does not answer. HESTER looks at her daughter with a mixture of fear and concern. Lights fade.)

SCENE 4

Acemetery represented by a gravestone and strange-looking plants. An open window frame represents the home, adjoining the cemetery, that DIMMESDALE and CHILLINGWORTH share. A straight-back chair stands behind the window, with a book-laden table beside it.

DIMMESDALE is kneeling near the chair in prayer. He looks weak and thin. A knock is heard. Silence. Another knock.

DIMMESDALE. Prithee hold. *(DIMMESDALE getting up)* I beseech thee to enter.

(REVEREND WILSON, the TOWN BEADLE, GOVERNOR BELLINGHAM, and CHILLINGWORTH are at the door.)

REVEREND WILSON. Master Dimmesdale. We fear for thee. Thou hast been fasting much and we have seen thy late vigils through yonder window.

DIMMESDALE. I study much, I wish to answer all concerns of the congregation through God's Holy Writ.

GOVERNOR. Thy congregation most admires thy heavenly knowledge. Yet they do not want to see thee sickly for their souls.

REVEREND WILSON. Is it not each man to whom God will question? Thou canst save them, only teach them.

TOWN BEADLE. At thy podium, the town sees thou art thin and pale and weak. This doth worry them.

DIMMESDALE. I must keep these vigils and fasts to prevent the grossness of this earthly state from obscuring my humblest mission here on earth.

CHILLINGWORTH. You have not but taken some water and bread in four days now. This cannot be good for your weakened condition.

GOVERNOR. All of us; the elders, the deacons, motherly dames, young and fair maidens, have asked Mr. Chillingworth to be thy physician.

DIMMESDALE. I need no medicine.

REVEREND WILSON. Providence hath provided this good doctor to our land. It is a sin to reject this aid. He even shares this home—it is no less than Manifest Providence.

DIMMESDALE. Were it God's will; I could be well content, that my labors, and my sorrows, and my sins, should shortly end with me, and what is earthly of them be buried in my grave, and the spiritual go with me to my eternal state, rather than you put your skill to the proof in my behalf.

CHILLINGWORTH. Youthful men, not having taken a deep root, give up their hold of life so easily! And saintly men, who walk with God on earth, would fain be away, to walk with him on the golden pavements of New Jerusalem.

DIMMESDALE. Nay *(Holding his heart)*, were I

worthier to walk there. I couldst be better content to toil here.

REVEREND WILSON. Good men ever interpret themselves too meanly. We leave thee in Mr. Chillingworth's hands to gain thy strength, so that thy wisdom remain with us till God's call is heard. Good day!

(*All exit, leaving* CHILLINGWORTH *and* DIMMESDALE *regarding each other. Lights fade.*)

SCENE 5

GOVERNOR BELLINGHAM's *home. A heavy curtain and a garden beyond is all that is seen.* HESTER, *with* PEARL, *is talking with a* SERVANT. *She is carrying a pair of embroidered gloves for the governor.*

HESTER. Is the worshipful Governor Bellingham within?

SERVANT (*staring at the scarlet letter*). His honorable worship is within. He hath a godly minister or two with him and likewise a leech.[9]

HESTER. I will wait. (*The* SERVANT *exits.*) Come along, Pearl. (*Pulling her*) Come and look into this fair garden. It may be we shall see flowers there; more beautiful ones than we find in the woods.

(PEARL *happily runs to the heavy curtains and looks at all the garden.*)

PEARL. Verily, I think that I shall have a rose!

HESTER. Nay, daughter, those are not for you.

PEARL. Prithee let me have a rose.

HESTER. Hush, child, I say thee nay.

(PEARL *begins to cry and will not be pacified.*)

HESTER. Hush! Do not cry, dear little Pearl! I hear voices in the garden. The Governor is coming.

(PEARL *does not listen to her mother and screams at the top of her lungs, then is immediately quiet as men move toward the entrance. From the garden* GOVERNOR BELLINGHAM, REVEREND WILSON, REVEREND DIMMESDALE, *and* CHILLINGWORTH *enter.* GOVERNOR *flings aside the draperies revealing* PEARL; *the curtain half obscures* HESTER.)

GOVERNOR (*surprised*). What have we here? There used to be these small apparitions, in holiday time; and we called them children of the Lord of Misrule. But how got such a guest into my hall?

REVEREND WILSON. Ay indeed! What little bird of scarlet plumage may this be! Prithee, young one, who art thou, and what has ailed thy mother to denizen thee in this strange fashion? Art thou a Christian child—ha? Dost thou know thy catechism?

PEARL. I am Mother's child and my name is Pearl!

REVEREND WILSON. Pearl? Ruby, rather—or Coral or Red Rose, judging from thy hue! (*Trying to pat* PEARL *on the head*) But where is this mother of thine? Ah! I see. (*To the* GOVERNOR) This is the selfsame child of whom we have held speech together; and behold here the unhappy woman.

GOVERNOR. But she comes at a good time; and we will look into this matter forthwith.

REVEREND WILSON. Hester Prynne, the point hath been weightily discussed, whether we, that are of the authority and influence, so might discharge our consciences by trusting an immortal soul, such as there is in yonder child, to the guidance of one who hath stumbled and fallen amid the pitfalls of this world.

GOVERNOR. Were it not best for thy little one's temporal and eternal welfare, that she be taken out of thy charge, and clad soberly, and disciplined strictly, and instructed in the truths of heaven and earth? What canst thou do for the child, in this kind?

---

9. leech, old term for physician, derived from the practice of using leeches to bleed patients; in this case, Chillingworth

HESTER. I can teach my little Pearl what I have learned from this! (*Touching her breast and the scarlet letter*)

GOVERNOR. Woman, it is thy badge of shame! It is because of that stain which that letter indicates that we would transfer thy child to other hands.

HESTER. Nevertheless, (*Calmly—yet pale*) this badge hath taught me—it daily teaches me—it is teaching me at this moment—lessons whereof my child may be the wiser and better, albeit they can profit nothing to myself.

(REVEREND WILSON *kneels and tries to coax* PEARL *to sit on his knee. She slides past him to stand just in the garden.*)

REVEREND WILSON. Pearl, canst thou tell me, my child, who made thee?

PEARL. Why I was not made at all. My mother plucked me off the wild rose bush that grew at the prison door.

GOVERNOR. Blasphemy! Here is a child of seven years old and she cannot tell who made her. Without question, she is equally in the dark as to her soul, its present depravity, and future destiny! Methinks, gentlemen, we need inquire no further.

(HESTER *catches hold of* PEARL *and draws her into her arms with a fierce expression.*)

HESTER. God gave me the child! He gave her in requital of all things else, which ye had taken from me. She is my happiness—she is my torture, none the less! See ye not, she is the scarlet letter, only capable of being loved, and so endowed with a millionfold the power of retribution for my sin? Ye shall not take her! I will die first!

REVEREND WILSON (*kindly*). My poor woman, the child shall be well cared for—far better than thou canst do it.

HESTER (*Raising her voice. Turning to* DIMMESDALE.) Speak thou for me! God gave her into my keeping. I will not give her up! Thou knowest—for thou hast sympathies which these men lack—thou knowest what is in my heart, and what are a mother's rights and how much the stronger they are when that mother has but her child and the scarlet letter! Look thou to it! I will not lose the child.

(DIMMESDALE, *looking even weaker than before, steps forward with his hand over his heart.*)

DIMMESDALE. Is there not a quality of awful sacredness in the relation between this mother and this child? …

GOVERNOR. … Ay! How is that, good Master Dimmesdale? Make it plain, I pray you.

DIMMESDALE. This child of its father's guilt and its mother's shame hath come from the hand of God, to work in many ways upon her heart, who pleads so earnestly and with such bitterness of spirit, the right to keep her.

REVEREND WILSON. It is meant doubtless, for a retribution too.

DIMMESDALE. A torture to be felt; a pang, a sting, and ever-recurring agony, in the midst of a troubled joy! Hath she not expressed this thought in the garb of the poor child, so forcibly reminding us of that red symbol which sears her bosom?

REVEREND WILSON. Well said again.

DIMMESDALE. This boon was meant, above all things else, to keep the mother's soul alive, and to preserve her from blacker depths of sin into which Satan might else have sought to plunge her!

GOVERNOR. Dost thou think this then good?

DIMMESDALE. The child reminds her, at every moment, of her fall, and teaches her of the Creator's sacred pledge that if she bring the child to heaven, the child also will bring its parent thither! Herein is the sinful mother happier than the sinful father. For Hester Prynne's sake, then, and no less for the poor child's sake, let us leave them as Providence hath seen fit to place them.

CHILLINGWORTH (*smiling*). You speak, my friend, with a strange earnestness.

REVEREND WILSON. And there is a weighty import in what my young brother hath spoken. Care must be had, nevertheless, to put the child to due and stated examination in the catechism, at thy hands or Master Dimmesdale's.

(*During this last speech,* PEARL *sneaks to* DIMMESDALE *who has stepped back into the shadow of the curtain, and takes his hand and caresses it gently against her cheek.*)

HESTER (*to herself*). Is that my Pearl?

(DIMMESDALE *looks around and places his hand upon her head—hesitates and kisses her brow.* PEARL *laughs and cavorts in the hallway toward the exit with* HESTER.)

CHILLINGWORTH. A strange child. It is easy to see the mother's part in her. Would it be beyond a philosopher's research, think ye, gentlemen, to analyze that child's nature, and from its make and mold, to give a shrewd guess at the father?

REVEREND WILSON. Nay; it would be sinful, in such a question, to follow the clue of profane philosophy. Better it may be to leave the mystery as we find it, unless Providence reveal it of its own accord. Thereby, every good Christian man hath a title to show a father's kindness toward the poor deserted babe.

(*The* MEN *exit.* HESTER *and* PEARL *move to leave. As they step out,* MISTRESS HIBBINS *appears as if from nowhere.*)

MISTRESS HIBBINS. Wilt thou go with us tonight? There will be a merry company in the forest; and I well-nigh promised the Black Man that comely Hester Prynne should be with us.

HESTER (*frightened yet triumphant*). Had they taken her from me, I would willingly have gone with thee into the forest, and signed my name in the Black Man's book too, and that with mine own blood!

(MISTRESS HIBBINS *vanishes. Lights fade.*)

SCENE 6

Same as Scene 4. DIMMESDALE *sits in the window overlooking the graveyard.* CHILLINGWORTH *is in the graveyard picking plants.*

CHILLINGWORTH. I found these herbs growing on a grave which bore no tombstone, nor other memorial of the dead man, save these ugly weeds. They typify, it may be, some hideous secret that was buried with him, and which he had done better to confess during his lifetime.

DIMMESDALE. Perchance he earnestly desired it, but could not.

CHILLINGWORTH. And wherefore not; since all the powers of nature call so earnestly for the confession of sin, that these black weeds have sprung up out of a buried heart to make manifest an unspoken crime.

DIMMESDALE. There can be no power, short of the Divine mercy, to disclose the secrets that may be buried with a human heart. The heart, making itself guilty of such secrets, must hold them, until the day when all hidden things shall be revealed, not with reluctance, but with a joy unutterable at the last day.

CHILLINGWORTH. Then why not reveal them here? Why should not the guilty ones sooner avail themselves of this unutterable solace?[10]

DIMMESDALE. What a relief have I witnessed in those sinful brethren! Even as in one who at last draws free air, after long stifling with his own polluted breath. Why should

---

10. solace, consolation; comfort

a wretched man, guilty, we will say, of murder, prefer to keep the dead corpse buried in his own heart, rather than fling it forth at once, and let the universe take care of it!

CHILLINGWORTH (*moving to* DIMMESDALE). Yet some men bury their secrets thus.

DIMMESDALE (*turning away*). Guilty as they may be, they shrink from displaying themselves black and filthy in the view of men; because, thenceforward, no good can be achieved by them; no evil of the past be redeemed by better service. So, to their own unutterable torment, they go about among their fellow creatures looking pure as new-fallen snow; while their hearts are all speckled and spotted with iniquity of which they cannot rid themselves.

CHILLINGWORTH. These men deceive themselves. They fear to take up the shame that rightfully belongs to them. If they seek to glorify God, let them not lift heavenward their unclean hands! Wouldst thou have me to believe, Oh wise and pious friend, that a false show can be better than God's own truth? Trust me.

(*Laughing from offstage,* PEARL *enters running from grave to grave; dancing on the graves.* HESTER *enters walking. They do not notice* CHILLINGWORTH *or* DIMMESDALE *watching them from the house.*)

HESTER. Pearl, I beseech you to act in godly fashion! Cease this and continue on the path!

(PEARL, *still laughing, gathers nettles and runs back to* HESTER *and decorates the scarlet letter with the prickly weeds.* HESTER *does not remove them, but tries to continue on her way.*)

CHILLINGWORTH. There is no law, nor reverence for authority, right or wrong, mixed up with that child's composition. What, in Heaven's name, is she? Hath she affections? Hath she any principles?

DIMMESDALE. None—save the freedom of a broken law. Whether capable of good, I know not.

(PEARL *hears the voices and smiles wickedly and throws a burr at* DIMMESDALE. DIMMESDALE *shrinks back.* PEARL *claps her hands wildly.* HESTER *looks up. All four regard each other till* PEARL *laughs again.*)

PEARL. Come away, Mother! Come away, or yonder Black Man will catch you! He hath got hold of the minister already. Come away, Mother, or he will catch you! But he cannot catch little Pearl!

(PEARL *grabs her* MOTHER's *hand and pulls her along, still dancing upon the graves, laughing and skipping.*)

CHILLINGWORTH. There goes a woman who, be her demerits what they may, hath none of that mystery of hidden sinfulness which you deem so grievous to be borne. Is Hester Prynne the less miserable, think you, for that scarlet letter on her breast?

DIMMESDALE. There was a look of pain in her face which I would gladly have been spared the sight of. But still, methinks, it must needs be better for the sufferer to be free to show his pain, as this poor woman Hester is, than to cover it all up in his heart. (*Pause*)

CHILLINGWORTH. He to whom only the outward and physical evil is laid open, knoweth, oftentimes, but half the evil which he is called upon to cure. A bodily disease, which we look upon as whole and entire within itself, may after all, be but a symptom of some ailment in the spiritual part.

DIMMESDALE. You deal not, I take it, in medicine for the soul!

CHILLINGWORTH (*with the same tone*). How may your physician heal the bodily evil unless you first lay open to him the wound in your soul?

DIMMESDALE (*passionately*). No—not to thee! Not to an earthly physician! (*Turning to* CHILLINGWORTH *with a fierceness*) If it be the soul's disease, then do I commit myself to the one Physician of the soul! He, if it stand with his good pleasure, can cure; or He can kill! But who art thou, that meddles in this matter?—that darest thrust himself between the sufferer and his God? (*With a frantic gesture—he turns to leave.*)

CHILLINGWORTH (*to himself*). But see, now how passion takes hold upon this man. He hath done a wild thing ere now, this pious Master Dimmesdale, in the hot passion of his heart! (CHILLINGWORTH *moves toward the window, smiling.*)

(*Lights fade.*)

SCENE 7

The inside of DIMMESDALE's *room expands to more of the stage, less of the cemetery is seen. It is midday.*

DIMMESDALE *has fallen asleep with a large volume on his lap. The chair is facing directly to the audience.* CHILLINGWORTH *enters quietly.*

DIMMESDALE *has fallen into a deep slumber—very deep. Being very cautious,* CHILLINGWORTH *steps directly in front of* DIMMESDALE. *His back is to the audience. He lays a hand on* DIMMESDALE's *bosom and moves aside his vestments. A scarlet glow emanates from* DIMMESDALE's *chest.* DIMMESDALE *shudders and stirs, but does not awaken. There is a pause.*

CHILLINGWORTH *turns around quickly. The scarlet color is reflected in his face. He looks ugly and evil.* CHILLINGWORTH *throw his hands into the air and stomps his feet. A look of triumph is seen by all. The red glow grows and expands across* CHILLINGWORTH's *face and onto the entire set.*

Lights fade.

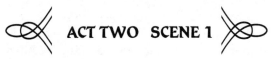

ACT TWO SCENE 1

DIMMESDALE'S ROOM. *A tight spotlight on* DIMMESDALE *standing at the table. Darkness surrounds him.* DIMMESDALE *stands at his table as if in front of a congregation at sermon time. A voiceover is heard.*

VOICE OF DIMMESDALE (*sermonizing*). I, whom you behold in these black garments of the priesthood—I, who ascend the sacred desk and turn my pale face heavenward, taking upon myself to hold communion, in your behalf, with the Most High Omniscience—I, in whose daily life you discern the sanctity of Enoch[11]—I whose footsteps, as you suppose, leave a gleam along my earthly track, whereby the pilgrim that shall come after me may be guided to the region of the blest—I, who have breathed the parting prayer over your dying friends, to whom the Amen sounded faintly from a world which they had quitted—I, your pastor, whom you so reverence and trust, am utterly a pollution and a lie!

DIMMESDALE (*horrified*). Spoken? Have I spoken? Have I let my vile nature be known to all?

(*The* CROWD *is in shadow all around* DIMMESDALE.)

VOICES OF THE CONGREGATION. The godly youth! The saint on earth! If he discern such sinfulness in his own white soul … What horrid spectacle would he behold in thine or mine!

(*The* CONGREGATION *fades as the lights come up to reveal* DIMMESDALE *in his room. He turns his back to the audience. He drops his vestments to reveal red welts on his shoulders and back. He pulls out a bloody scourge and proceeds to beat*

---

11. Enoch, an Old Testament patriarch and father of Methuselah

himself about the shoulders. He begins to laugh. Lights fade.

Lights return to normal as DIMMESDALE *starts from his chair, grabs his coat, and exits.)*

SCENE 2

Same as Act I Scene 1. The street, late night/early morning. The same market area where the jail can be seen as well as the scaffolding and the cross above it.

DIMMESDALE *moves slowly as if in a trance, slowly walking the route that* HESTER *took on that fateful day seven years ago.* DIMMESDALE *walks up the stairs of the scaffolding. It is a cloudy night. The town is asleep. At the top he grabs at his breast and screams.*

DIMMESDALE. AHHHHHH!! *(Pause)* It is done! The whole town will awake, and hurry forth, and find me here!

(There is silence. Nothing moves. MISTRESS HIBBINS *appears coming from the forest with a lantern. She looks around, but does not see* DIMMESDALE *and hastily exits.* DIMMESDALE *visibly relaxes. Another light is seen moving toward him on the street. It is* REVEREND WILSON. REVEREND WILSON *passes the scaffolding with his light.)*

VOICE OF DIMMESDALE. A good evening to you venerable Father Wilson! Come hither, I pray you, and pass a pleasant hour with me! *(Fear comes over his face.)*

DIMMESDALE *(spoken softly and aloud).* Good heavens. Have I spoken thus? *(He watches* REVEREND WILSON.*)*

*(THE REVEREND *continues on his way with no stop in his step.* DIMMESDALE *sees another light moving toward him.* PEARL *is laughing and giggling lightly.)*

DIMMESDALE *(aloud).* Pearl! Little Pearl! Hester! Hester Prynne! Are you there?

HESTER. Yes, it is Hester Prynne! *(With sur-*

prise) It is I and my little Pearl.

DIMMESDALE. Whence come you, Hester? What sent you hither?

HESTER. I have been watching at a deathbed, and have taken measure for a robe.

DIMMESDALE. Come up hither, Hester, thou and little Pearl. Ye have both been here before, but I was not with you. Come up hither once again, and we will stand all three together!

*(HESTER *and* PEARL *silently climb the stairs. At the top,* HESTER *has* PEARL's *hand and* DIMMESDALE *grabs for the other hand.)*

PEARL. Minister *(Whispering)*, wilt thou stand here with Mother and me, tomorrow noontide?

DIMMESDALE *(with renewed strength after grabbing* PEARL's *hand).* Nay; not so, little Pearl. *(Almost joyful)* Not so, my child. I shall, indeed, stand with thy mother and thee one other day, but not tomorrow.

*(PEARL *laughs and tries to pull away from* DIMMESDALE; *he holds on.)*

DIMMESDALE. A moment longer, my child!

PEARL. But wilt thou promise to take my hand, and Mother's hand, tomorrow noontide?

DIMMESDALE. Not then, Pearl, but another time.

PEARL. What other time?

DIMMESDALE. At the great judgment day. Then and there before the judgment seat, thy mother, and thou, and I must stand together. But the daylight of this world shall not see our meeting!

*(PEARL *laughs.* CHILLINGWORTH *enters below them.*

A momentary flash of light. DIMMESDALE, HESTER, *and* PEARL *are caught in tableau:* DIMMESDALE *with his hand on his heart,* HESTER *touching the glowing scarlet letter,* PEARL *devilishly smiling, and* CHILLINGWORTH *is below the scaffolding looking up at the three of them.*

PEARL *spots* CHILLINGWORTH *looking up at them on the scaffolding. She pulls her hand free of* DIMMESDALE *yet still is holding his glove.* PEARL *drops it and points at* CHILLINGWORTH *as* DIMMESDALE *is looking at the sky clutching his heart.* CHILLINGWORTH'S *face reveals his hatred. The light is gone.*)

DIMMESDALE. Who is that man, Hester? I shiver at him! Dost thou know the man? I hate him, Hester!

(HESTER *is silent.*)

PEARL. Minister, I can tell thee who he is!

DIMMESDALE. Quickly, then, child! *(Bending toward* PEARL*)* Quickly—and as low as thou canst whisper!

PEARL *(whispering to* DIMMESDALE*).* The Black Man, Reverend. He looks for you. He knows where you live. He wants to know why thou clutch at thy breast!

DIMMESDALE. Dost thou mock me now?

PEARL *(angry and defensive).* Thou wast not bold! Thou wast not true! Thou wouldst not promise to take my hand, and Mother's hand, tomorrow noontide!

CHILLINGWORTH *(from the foot of the steps).* Worthy Sir. Pious Master Dimmesdale, can this be you? Well, dost thou walk in thy sleep? Come, good Sir, and my dear friend, I pray you, let me lead you home!

DIMMESDALE *(fearfully).* How knowest thou that I was here?

CHILLINGWORTH. Verily, I knew nothing of the matter. I spent the better part of the night at the bedside of the worshipful Governor Winthrop, doing what my poor skill might to give him ease. He is going home to a better world. I likewise, was on my way homeward, when this strange light shone out. Come with me.

DIMMESDALE. No I will not!

CHILLINGWORTH. I beseech you, Reverend

Sir; else you will be poorly able to do Sabbath duty tomorrow.

DIMMESDALE. Sabbath? The morrow? Art thou sure of tomorrow? I have much to study—I must keep holy God's day. I needs write my sermon. Truth, I am weary and weak. For this, I will go home with you.

(CHILLINGWORTH *leads* DIMMESDALE *away.*)

HESTER. My heart doth ache to see Arthur so weak and struggling. I have sat by as he fell into the hands of an enemy. I wouldst help others, can I turn my face to him?

(*Lights fade on* HESTER *and* PEARL *on the scaffolding, crouching in a darkened corner.*)

SCENE 4

🕭 *A series of short scenes in spotlight. FIRST HESTER SCENE:* HESTER *at a bedside caring for a* DYING MAN.

RESPECTABLE WOMAN #1. Sister of Mercy, he hath suffered little since thy care.

HESTER. Wouldst I could have done more to ease thy pain. I do as God has asked of me.

DYING MAN. All that mine eyes see is the "A" upon thy breast, does it not mean "Angel"?

RESPECTABLE WOMAN #1. How canst I ever repay thy kindness?

HESTER. I ask for nothing. God bless thee and thine.

(*Light fades.*)

🕭 *FIRST DIMMESDALE/CHILLINGWORTH SCENE:* TOWN BEADLE, CHILLINGWORTH, *and* DIMMESDALE *on the street.*

TOWN BEADLE. Thy congregation is most concerned regarding our godly Reverend. Is he well, Doctor?

CHILLINGWORTH. It is most curious, I try all I know, but still he weakens.

DIMMESDALE. Good sirs, I am as God wantest me. I am well enough.

(*Light fades.*)

꧁ *SECOND HESTER SCENE:* HESTER's *darkened room.* HESTER *sits with the Bible on her lap and holds a hand on her bosom.*

PEARL. ... "If thine enemy hunger, feed him; Love your enemies, do good to them that hate you." Matthew: 5, 44. *(Pause)* Mother, shall I love the Black Man, for he is mine enemy, as I love my Heavenly Father?

HESTER *(hesitantly).* What art thou child, to ask such a question? Love must be in thine heart at all times. Follow what thy Heavenly Father has asked of ye and follow not the Black Man.

(Light fades.)

꧁ *SECOND DIMMESDALE/CHILLINGWORTH SCENE: Street scene.* DAME OF FIFTY *and* RESPECTABLE WOMEN *from town.*

DAME OF FIFTY. It is as if God hath taken our leaders away. First, good Governor Winthrop and now I worry for Master Dimmesdale.

RESPECTABLE WOMAN #1. It is whispered that Satan hath his hands on our goodly reverend.

RESPECTABLE WOMAN #2. A battle is being fought for the very soul of our own Master Dimmesdale.

DAME OF FIFTY. God save him!

(Light fades.)

꧁ *THIRD HESTER SCENE: A group of citizens talking in the marketplace.*

MAN #1. Reverend Wilson and Master Bracket and others discuss Hester Prynne and the scarlet letter. They mayest let her part with the emblem!

RESPECTABLE WOMAN #1. Hester hadst sat and sat by Governor Winthrop's bed and hath been a comfort for the whole family, as with many other infirm and dying. Maybe it wouldst be for the best to let it fly from her bosom.

MAN #1. Master Dimmesdale places her as example to all and is in favor of the parting. Yet, she tends not to Master Dimmesdale as she doth for others. Truth, Doctor Chillingworth never leaves his side and perchance she feels that others need her more.

RESPECTABLE WOMAN #2. What strength she hath! 'Tis the emblem that provides that strength. I hear tell that an Indian arrow didst stop with broken shaft upon the letter and our Hester is forever safe from all harm. Wouldst be wise to take it from her?

(Light fades.)

꧁ *THIRD DIMMESDALE/CHILLINGWORTH SCENE:* DIMMESDALE's *darkened room.* DIMMESDALE *is sitting facing the audience in his hard wooden chair, trying to read.* CHILLINGWORTH *is standing in the shadows of his room staring at him.*

DIMMESDALE. I know not what thou want of me. I take thy medicines; I talk with thee at length, but never is it enough! *(Pause)* Starest at something else—someone else! I understand thee not! Leave me to my peace.

CHILLINGWORTH. As thou wish.

(He moves as if to leave. DIMMESDALE *listens and we hear a door close.* DIMMESDALE *is visibly relieved,* CHILLINGWORTH *still appears in the shadows—watching and listening.)*

DIMMESDALE. Heavenly Father, is he a test? Or is this Satan in disguise! I must know before I go mad with not knowing!

*(CHILLINGWORTH *smiling—exits.* DIMMESDALE *turns around quickly, but* CHILLINGWORTH *is gone. Light fades.)*

꧁ *FOURTH HESTER SCENE: Outside* HESTER's *home.*

(As HESTER *watches* PEARL *playing nearby,* DIMMESDALE *and* CHILLINGWORTH *are walking by.* CHILLINGWORTH *is supporting* DIMMESDALE, *who moves slowing as if in pain.)*

HESTER (*contemplatingly*). Was I wrong to keep this dark truth, a secret borne of fear? Had I but known its power and were I not prepared to the evil that has befallen the delicate Mr. Dimmesdale I might not have acquiesced[12] in Roger Chillingworth's scheme of disguise. I must hereby make amends. Of both wrongs, I must a right make. Roger Chillingworth has revenged and stooped too far. (*Calling for* PEARL) Come! Come child, I must walk.

(PEARL *runs to her* MOTHER'S *waiting hand. Cross fade.*)

SCENE 5

As the lights change, HESTER *and* PEARL *are walking along the beach.* CHILLINGWORTH *is gathering roots and herbs for his medicines. He is carrying a basket and has a staff in one hand.*

HESTER (*upon seeing* CHILLINGWORTH). Pearl, run and play. I must talk with Mr. Chillingworth.

(HESTER *stares at* CHILLINGWORTH, *who appears changed; smaller in stature, older, more crippled.*

The scarlet letter glows on HESTER'S *bosom.*

PEARL *runs off to play upon the shore. She is in the background—moving on and offstage.*)

CHILLINGWORTH. Why, Mistress, I hear good tidings of you, on all hands! On my life, Hester, I made my own entreaty to the worshipful magistrate that yonder scarlet letter might be taken off your bosom.

HESTER. It lies not in the pleasure of the magistrates to take off this badge. Were I worthy to be quit of it, it would fall away of its own nature, or be transformed into something that should speak a different purport. (*Stares at* CHILLINGWORTH.)

CHILLINGWORTH. Nay, then wear it, if it suit you better. A woman must needs follow her own fancy, touching the adornment of her person. (*Pause*) What see you in my face that you look at it so earnestly?

HESTER. Something that would make me weep, if there were any tears bitter enough for it. But let it pass! It is of yonder miserable man that I would speak.

CHILLINGWORTH. And what of him? My thoughts happen just now to be busy with the gentleman.

HESTER. Some years ago it was your pleasure to extort a promise of secrecy, as touching yourself and me. It was not without heavy misgivings that I thus bound myself; for, there remained a duty toward him; and something whispered me that I was betraying it. Since that day, you tread behind his every footstep. You are beside him, sleeping and waking. You burrow and rankle in his heart! Your clutch is on his life, and you cause him to die daily a living death; and still he knows you not. In permitting this, I have surely acted a false part by the only man to whom the power was left me to be true!

CHILLINGWORTH. What choice had you? My finger, pointed at this man, would have hurled him from his pulpit into a dungeon—thence to the gallows!

HESTER. It had been better so!

CHILLINGWORTH. What evil have I done the man? But for my aid, his life would have burned away in torments within the first two years after the perpetration of his crime and thine. For, Hester, his spirit lacked the strength that could have borne up, as thine has, beneath a burden like thy scarlet letter.

HESTER. Better he had died at once!

CHILLINGWORTH. Yea, woman, thou sayest truly! Never did mortal suffer what this man has suffered. And all, all in the sight of his worst enemy! With the superstition

---

12. acquiesced, taken part; agreed to

common to his brotherhood, he fancied himself given over to a fiend, to be tortured with frightful dreams, as a foretaste of what awaits him beyond the grave. He did not err! There was a fiend at his elbow! A mortal man, with once a human heart, a fiend for his especial torment!

HESTER. Hast thou not tortured him enough? Has he not paid thee all?

CHILLINGWORTH. No—no! He has but increased the debt! *(Becoming fierce)* Dost thou remember me, Hester? My life had been made up of earnest, studious, thoughtful, quiet years, bestowed faithfully for the increase of mine own knowledge, and faithfully, too, for the advancement of human welfare. Was I not, though you might deem me cold, nevertheless a man thoughtful for others, craving little for himself—kind, true, just, and of constant if not warm affections? Was I not all this?

HESTER. All this, and more.

CHILLINGWORTH. And what am I now? *(Demanding)* I have already told thee what I am! A fiend! Who made me so?

HESTER *(shuddering).* It was myself! It was I, not less than he. Why hast thou not avenged thyself on me?

CHILLINGWORTH. I have left thee to the scarlet letter. If that have not avenged me, I can do no more! *(Touching the letter and smiling)*

HESTER. It has avenged thee!

CHILLINGWORTH. I judged no less and now, what wouldst thou with me regarding this man?

HESTER. I must reveal our secret. He must discern thee in thy true character. What may be the result, I know not. But this long debt due from me to him, shall at length be paid. I do not perceive such advantages in his living any longer a life of ghastly emptiness, that I shall stoop to implore thy mercy. Do with him as thou wilt! There is no good for him—no good for little Pearl! There is no path to guide us out of this dismal maze!

CHILLINGWORTH. Woman, I could well-nigh pity thee! Thou hadst great elements. Hadst thou met earlier with a better love than mine, this evil had not been. I pity thee, for the good that has been wasted in thy nature!

HESTER. And I thee, for the hatred that has transformed a wise and just man to a fiend! Wilt thou yet purge it out of thee, and be once more human? If not for his sake, then doubly for thine own! Forgive, and leave his further retribution to the Power that claims it!

CHILLINGWORTH. Peace, Hester, peace! It is not granted me to pardon. By thy first step awry, thou didst plant the germ of evil; but since that moment, it has all been a dark necessity. Ye that have wronged me are not sinful, save in a kind of illusion; neither am I fiendlike. It is our fate. Let the black flower blossom as it may. Go now.

*(*CHILLINGWORTH *turns away from her and continues to gather herbs and roots.* HESTER *stares after him as he gathers and exits slowly offstage.)*

HESTER. Be it sin or no, I hate the man! Yes, I hate the man! He betrayed me! He has done me worse wrong than I did him! Pearl! Little Pearl! Where are you?

*(*PEARL *enters dressed in seaweed, coral, seashells and on her chest is a letter "A" in green.* PEARL *runs to* HESTER*—dancing and laughing.)*

HESTER. My little Pearl! *(Silence as she sees the letter.)* The green letter, and on thy childish bosom, has no purport. But dost thou know, my child, what this letter means which thy mother is doomed to wear?

PEARL. Yes, Mother. It is the great letter "A." Thou has taught me in the lesson book.

HESTER *(staring at her daughter).* Dost thou know, child, wherefore thy mother wears this letter?

PEARL. Truly do I! It is for the same reason that the minister keeps his hand over his heart!

HESTER. And what reason is that? *(Half smiling, then going pale)* What has the letter to do with any heart, save mine?

PEARL. Nay, Mother, I have told all I know. Ask yonder old man whom thou hast been talking with! It may be he can tell. Mother dear, what does this scarlet letter mean? And why does the minister keep his hand over his heart?

(PEARL takes her MOTHER's hands and looks at her with so much sincerity and with love that HESTER is taken aback. PEARL repeats these questions again and again.)

HESTER. What know I of the minister's heart? And as for the scarlet letter, I wear it for the sake of its gold thread.

(They start toward home.)

PEARL. Mother, what does the scarlet letter mean?

(Lights fade.)

SCENE 6

Midday the next day, in the woods. HESTER and PEARL are walking on a narrow footpath.

PEARL. Mother, the sunshine does not love you. It runs away and hides itself, because it is afraid of something on your bosom. Now see! There it is playing a good way off. Stand you here, and let me run and catch it. I am but a child. It will not flee from me; for I wear nothing on my bosom yet!

(Lights play a game with PEARL. The lights follow her. HESTER remains in "dark" spots of the woods.)

HESTER. Nor ever will, my child, I hope.

PEARL. And why not, Mother? *(Stopping)* Will not it come of its own accord, when I am a woman grown?

HESTER. Run away, child, and catch the sunshine! It will soon be gone.

(PEARL runs around as HESTER looks on smiling at her child. The light plays on and about PEARL as a playmate playing tag. HESTER gets near.)

HESTER. See! Now I can stretch out my hand, and grasp some of it.

(As she reaches for the light it vanishes. The light sticks to PEARL. PEARL is glowing with her impish grin.)

HESTER. Come, my child. We will sit down a little way within the wood, and rest ourselves.

PEARL. I am not aweary, Mother. But you may sit down, if you will tell me a story meanwhile.

HESTER. A story, child! And about what?

PEARL. Oh, a story about the Black Man. *(Grabbing hold of HESTER's gown and grinning up at her.)* How he haunts this forest, and carries a book with him—a big, heavy book, with iron clasps; and how this ugly Black Man offers his book and an iron pen to everybody that meets him here among the trees; and they are to write their names with their own blood. And then he sets his mark on their bosoms! Didst thou ever meet the Black Man, Mother?

HESTER. And who told you this story, Pearl?

PEARL. It was the old dame in the chimney-corner, at the house where you watched last night. And Mother, the old dame said that this scarlet letter was the Black Man's mark on thee, and that it glows like a red flame when thou meetest him at midnight, here in the dark wood. Is it true, Mother? And dost thou go to meet him in the nighttime?

HESTER. Didst thou ever wake and find your mother gone?

PEARL. Not that I remember. If thou fearest to leave me in our cottage, thou mightest take me along with thee. I would very gladly go! But, Mother, tell me now! Is there such a Black Man? And didst thou ever meet him? And is this his mark?

HESTER. Wilt thou let me be at peace, if I once tell thee?

PEARL. Yes, if thou tellest me all.

HESTER. Once in my life I met the Black Man! This scarlet letter is his mark!

PEARL. Oh brook! Oh foolish and tiresome brook! Why art thou so sad? (*Listening to the brook*) What does this sad little brook say, Mother?

HESTER. If thou hadst a sorrow of thine own, the brook might tell thee of it even as it is telling me of mine! (*Footfalls and branches are heard.*) But now, Pearl, I hear a footstep along the path. I would have thee betake thyself to play, and leave me to speak with him that comes yonder.

PEARL. Yes, Mother, but if it be the Black Man, wilt thou not let me stay a moment and look at him, with his big book under his arm?

HESTER. Go silly child! (*Impatiently*) It is no Black Man! (*Pointing*) It is the minister.

PEARL. And Mother, he has his hand over his heart! Is it because, when the minister wrote his name in the book, the Black Man set his mark in that place? But why does he not wear it outside his bosom, as thou dost, Mother?

HESTER. Go now child. But keep where thou canst hear the babble of the brook.

(PEARL *runs off singing and laughing to gather violets and wood anemones and scarlet seaweed.*

HESTER *takes a step or two toward the oncoming* DIMMESDALE. *He looks haggard and feeble. Listlessness is in his gait, his hand over his heart.*)

HESTER (*softly*). Arthur Dimmesdale! (*Louder*) Arthur Dimmesdale!

DIMMESDALE. Who speaks?

(DIMMESDALE *straightens and looks around.* HESTER *is in the shadows. As he takes a step*

toward the figure, the scarlet letter glows.)

DIMMESDALE. Hester! Hester Prynne. Is it thou? Art thou in life?

HESTER. Even so. In such life as has been mine. And thou, Arthur Dimmesdale, dost thou yet live?

(DIMMESDALE *and* HESTER *reach out in fear and touch as if they each are ghosts. They grasp hands and move to sit.* PEARL *gathering wildflowers moves in and out of sight.*)

DIMMESDALE. Hester, hast thou found peace?

HESTER (*smiling, looking at her bosom*). Hast thou?

DIMMESDALE. None! Nothing but despair. What else could I look for being what I am, and leading such a life as mine? Hester, I am most miserable!

HESTER. The people reverence thee and surely thou workest good among them! Doth this bring thee no comfort?

DIMMESDALE. More misery, Hester. What can a ruined soul like mine effect toward their purification? And as for the people's reverence, would that it were turned to scorn and hatred!

HESTER (*gently*). You wrong yourself in this. Your present life is no less holy, in very truth, than it seems in people's eyes. Is there no reality in the penitence[13] thus sealed and witnessed by good works? And wherefore should it not bring you peace?

DIMMESDALE. Happy are you, Hester, that wear the scarlet letter openly upon your bosom! Mine burns in secret! Thou little knowest what a relief it is, after the torment of a seven years' cheat, to look into an eye that recognizes me for what I am! Had I one friend—or were it my worst enemy—to whom, when sickened with the praises of all other men, I could daily betake myself and be known as the vilest

---

13. penitence, repentance; making up for one's sins

of all sinners, methinks my soul might keep itself alive thereby. Even thus much of truth would save me! But now, it is all falsehood!—all emptiness!—all death!

HESTER (*Looking into his face. Fearfully.*) Such a friend as thou hast even now wished for, with whom to weep over thy sin, thou hast in me, the partner of it. (*Hesitating*) Thou hast long had such an enemy, and dwellest with him, under the same roof.

DIMMESDALE. Ha! What sayest thou! An enemy! And under mine own roof! What mean you?

HESTER. Oh Arthur! Forgive me! In all things else I have striven to be true. Truth was the one virtue which I might have held fast, and did hold fast, through all extremity; save when thy good—thy life—thy fame— were put in question. Then I consented to a deception. But a lie is never good, even though death threaten on the other side! Dost thou not see what I would say? That old man! The physician, he whom they call Roger Chillingworth—he is my husband!

DIMMESDALE. I did know it! Was not the secret told me, in the natural recoil of my heart, at the first sight of him, and as often as I have seen him since? Why did I not understand? Oh Hester Prynne, thou knowest little all the horror of this! And the shame—the indecency—the horrible ugliness of this exposure of a sick and guilty heart to the very eye that would gloat over it! Woman, woman, I cannot forgive thee!

HESTER. Thou shalt forgive me! (*Flinging herself to the leaves beside him*) Let God punish! Thou shalt forgive!

(HESTER *throws her arms around* DIMMESDALE *and presses his head against the scarlet letter. He tries to break free, but in vain.*)

HESTER (*repeating*). Wilt thou forgive me? Wilt thou forgive me? Wilt thou not frown? Wilt thou forgive me?

DIMMESDALE (*Deeply sad. Pause.*) May God forgive us both! We are not, Hester, the worst sinners in the world. There is one worse than even the polluted priest! That old man's revenge has been blacker than my sin. He has violated in cold blood, the sanctity of a human heart. Thou and I, Hester, never did so!

HESTER. Never, never! What we did had a consecration[14] of its own. We felt it so! We said so to each other. Hast thou forgotten it?

DIMMESDALE. Hush, Hester. I have not forgotten! (*They sit hand in hand.*)

DIMMESDALE. And I, how am I to live longer, breathing the same air with this deadly enemy? (*Grabbing his heart*) Think for me, Hester! Thou art strong. Resolve for me!

HESTER. Thou must dwell no longer with this man. Thy heart must be no longer under his evil eye.

DIMMESDALE. It were far worse then death! But how avoid it? What choice remains to me? Shall I lie down here and die at once?

HESTER. Is the world, then, so narrow? Doth the universe lie within the compass of yonder town, which only a little time ago was but a leaf-strewn desert, as lonely as this around us? Whither leads yonder forest track? Backwards to the settlement, thou sayest! Yes; but onward, too! Deeper it goes, and deeper, into wilderness, less plainly to be seen at every step until, some few miles hence, the yellow leaves will show no vestige of the white man's tread. There thou art free! Is there not shade enough in all this boundless forest to hide thy heart from the gaze of Roger Chillingworth?

DIMMESDALE. Yes, Hester; but only under the fallen leaves.

HESTER. Then there is the broad pathway of the sea! It brought thee hither. If thou so

_____

14. consecration, sacredness

choose, it will bear thee back again. In our native land, whether in some remote rural village or in vast London—thou wouldst be beyond his power and knowledge!

DIMMESDALE. I am powerless to go. Wretched and sinful as I am, I have had no other thought than to drag on my earthly existence in the sphere where Providence hath placed me. Lost as my own soul is, I would still do what I may for other human sentinels, whose sure reward is death and dishonor, when his dreary watch shall come to an end!

HESTER. This weight of misery, thou shalt leave it all behind thee! There is good to be done. Exchange this false life of thine for a true one. Let thy spirit summon thee to such a mission, the teacher and apostle of the red men. Or as is more thy nature, be a scholar and a sage among the wisest and the most renowned of the cultivated world. Preach! Write! Act! Do anything, save to lie down and die! Give up this name of Arthur Dimmesdale and make thyself another, such as thou canst wear without fear or shame. Up and away!

DIMMESDALE. Oh Hester! Thou tellest of running a race to a man whose knees are tottering beneath him. I must die here! There is not the strength or courage left me to venture into the wide, strange, difficult world alone! *(Pause)* Alone, Hester.

HESTER *(whispering).* Thou shalt not go alone!

(DIMMESDALE gazes at HESTER with hope and joy. They look at each other and both smile.)

DIMMESDALE. Do I feel joy again! Oh Hester, thou art my better angel! I seem to have flung myself—sick, sin-stained, and sorrow-blackened—down upon these forest leaves, and to have risen up all made anew, and with new powers to glorify Him that hath been merciful. This is already the better life! Why did we not find it sooner?

HESTER. Let us not look back. The past is gone. Wherefore should we linger upon it now? See! With this symbol, I undo it all, and make it as it had never been!

(HESTER unclasps the scarlet letter and throws it into the woods. It glitters like a lost jewel near the babbling brook. HESTER sighs.)

HESTER. Oh exquisite relief!

(HESTER, feeling the freedom, removes her formal cap and her hair falls upon her shoulders. A smile plays across her lips and the sunshine bursts through on HESTER and DIMMESDALE.)

HESTER. Thou must know Pearl! Our little Pearl! She is a strange child! I hardly comprehend her. But thou wilt love her dearly, as I do, and wilt advise me how to deal with her.

DIMMESDALE. Dost thou think the child will be glad to know me?

HESTER. But she will love thee dearly. She is not far off. Pearl! Pearl!

(PEARL is standing in a stream of sunshine on the other side of the brook. PEARL approaches her MOTHER slowly. Again, PEARL had adorned herself in violets and twigs and looks like a nymph child.)

HESTER *(cont'd.)* And thou wilst love her dearly. Dost thou not think her beautiful? And see with what natural skill she has made those simple flowers adorn her! Had she gathered pearls, and diamonds, and rubies, in the wood, they could not have become her better. She is a splendid child. But I know whose brow she has!

DIMMESDALE. Dost thou know, Hester, that this dear child, tripping about always at thy side, hath caused me many an alarm? That my own features were partly repeated in her face, and so strikingly that the world might see them! But she is mostly thine.

(Pause)

HESTER *(They both watch the advancing PEARL.)* Let her see nothing strange—no passion nor eagerness—in thy way of accosting her. Our Pearl is a fitful and fantastic little elf sometimes. Especially, she is seldom tolerant of emotion when she does not fully comprehend the why and wherefore. But the child hath strong affections! She loves me, and will love thee!

DIMMESDALE. Thou canst not think how my heart dreads this interview, and yearns for it!

(PEARL *stops on the other side of the brook at a pool of water and looks at her* MOTHER *and* THE REVEREND.)

DIMMESDALE. I have a strange fancy that this brook is the boundary between two worlds. Is she an elfish spirit, who, as the legends of our childhood taught us, is forbidden to cross a running stream? Pray hasten her; for this delay has already imparted a tremor to my nerves.

HESTER. Come dearest child! How slow thou art! When hast thou been so sluggish before now? Here is a friend of mine, who must be thy friend also. Thou wilt have twice as much love, henceforward as thy mother alone could give thee! Leap across the brook and come to us. Thou canst leap like a young deer!

(PEARL *stays where she is.* PEARL *looks at one then the other and then at them both.* DIMMESDALE *shudders at* PEARL*'s eyes upon him and places his hand over his heart.* PEARL *lifts her hand at the same time and points at her* MOTHER*'s bosom.*)

HESTER. Thou strange child, why dost thou not come to me?

(PEARL *looks at her* MOTHER *and still pointing stomps her foot.*)

HESTER. Hasten, Pearl, or I shall be angry with thee! Leap across the brook, naughty child, and run hither! Else I must come to thee.

(PEARL *doesn't listen to her* MOTHER *and then starts shrieking and gesticulating violently— pointing at* HESTER*'s bosom.*)

HESTER (*whispering*). I see what ails the child. Children will not abide the slightest change in the accustomed aspect of things that are daily before their eyes. Pearl misses something which she has always seen me wear! (*Blushing*) Pearl, look down at thy feet! There—before thee! On the hither side of the brook!

(PEARL *looks where her* MOTHER *points and the scarlet letter is gleaming in the light on the other side of the brook.*)

HESTER. Bring it hither!

PEARL. Come thou and take it up!

HESTER. Was ever such a child! Oh, I have much to tell thee about her! But in very truth, she is right as regards this hateful token. I must bear its torture yet a little longer—only a few days longer—until we shall have left this region and look back hither as to a land which we have dreamed of. The forest cannot hide it! The mid-ocean shall take it from my hand and swallow it up forever.

(HESTER *moves toward the letter and places it back upon her bosom. She gathers her hair up into her cap. The sunlight on* HESTER *is gone.* HESTER *extends her hand to* PEARL.)

HESTER. Dost thou know thy mother now, child? Wilt thou come across the brook and own thy mother, now that she has her shame upon her—now that she is sad?

PEARL. Yes; now I will! (*Jumps across the brook*) Now thou art my mother indeed! And I am thy little Pearl.

(PEARL *pulls her* MOTHER *down to her and kisses her brow and both cheeks, then kisses the scarlet letter.*)

PEARL (*Cont'd.*) Why doth the minister sit yonder?

HESTER. He waits to welcome thee. Come

thou, and entreat his blessing. He loves thee, my little Pearl, and loves thy mother too. Come! He longs to greet thee!

PEARL. Doth he love us? Will he go back with us, hand in hand, we three together, into the town?

HESTER. Not now, dear child, but in days to come he will walk hand in hand with us. We will have a home and fireside of our own; and thou shalt sit upon his knee; and he will love thee dearly. Thou wilt love him; wilt thou not?

PEARL. And will he always keep his hand over his heart?

HESTER. Foolish child, what a question is that! Come and ask his blessing.

(PEARL *is reluctant to move toward* DIMMESDALE *and* HESTER *physically moves her in front of him.* PEARL *grimaces.* DIMMESDALE *bends forward and places a kiss upon her brow.* PEARL *breaks free and runs back to the brook and washes her face vigorously. She then stands apart from them as they look at her. Lights fade.*)

SCENE 7

The minister's room. DIMMESDALE *sits at his writing desk with an unfinished sermon and the Bible opened to the Scriptures. Half-eaten dinner is on the table beside his work. A knock is heard at the door.* DIMMESDALE *reluctantly listens to the knock.*

DIMMESDALE (*pause*). Come in.

(CHILLINGWORTH *enters.* DIMMESDALE *puts one hand on the Bible, the other over his heart.*)

CHILLINGWORTH. Welcome home, reverend Sir. You look pale; as if the travel through the wilderness had been too sore for you. Let my aid put you in heart and strength to preach your election sermon.

DIMMESDALE. Nay, I think not so. My journey and the free air which I have breathed, have done me good, after so long confine-

ment in my study. I think to need no more of your drugs, my kind physician, good though they be, and administered by friendly hand.

(CHILLINGWORTH *takes the time to look* THE REVEREND *over and realizes that there is a change in* DIMMESDALE.)

CHILLINGWORTH. I joy to hear it. It may be that my remedies, so long administered in vain, begin now to take due effect. Happy man were I, and well deserving of New England's' gratitude, could I achieve this cure!

DIMMESDALE. I thank you from my heart, most watchful friend. I thank you, and can but repay your good deeds with my prayers.

(CHILLINGWORTH *exits.* DIMMESDALE *ravenously eats and frantically writes. Lights fade.*)

SCENE 8

The Marketplace. The morning of the election of the new Governor. All sorts of people are in attendance, those that were in attendance at HESTER PRYNNE's *sentence.* HESTER *and* PEARL *are together. The* CROWD *stares at them.*

HESTER (*to herself*). Look your last on the scarlet letter and its wearer! Yet a little while, and she will be beyond your reach. A few hours longer, and the deep, mysterious ocean will quench and hide forever the symbol which ye have caused to burn upon her bosom!

(PEARL *is dressed airily, bright and sunny. She flits around her* MOTHER, *sometimes breaking into unrecognizable music and song.*)

PEARL. Mother, wherefore have all the people left their work today? Is it a playday for the whole world? See, there is the blacksmith! He has washed his sooty face and put on his Sabbath day clothes and looks as if he would gladly be merry. But see, Mother, how many strange faces. And sailors! What have they all come to do here in the marketplace?

HESTER. They wait to see the procession pass for the new Governor. The magistrates are to go by, and the ministers, and all the great and good people, with the music and the soldiers marching before them.

PEARL. And will the minister be there? Will he hold out both his hands to me, as when thou ledst me to him from the brookside?

HESTER. He will be there, child, but he will not greet thee today; nor must thou greet him.

(CHILLINGWORTH *enters in deep conversation with the captain of the ship from the Spanish Main. The* CAPTAIN *is dressed in ribbons, gold lace, a hat with a feather, and a sword at his side.*)

PEARL. What a strange, sad man is he! In the dark nighttime he calls us to him, and holds thy hand and mine, as when we stood with him on the scaffold yonder! And in the deep forest, where only the old trees can hear and the strip of sky see it, he talks with thee. He kisses my forehead, too, so that the little brook would hardly wash it off! But here, in the sunny day, and among all the people, he knows us not; nor must we know him! A strange, sad man is he, with his hand always over his heart.

HESTER. Be quiet, Pearl! Think not now of the minister, but look about thee, and see how cheery is everybody's face today. For today a new man is beginning to rule over them: they make merry and rejoice; as if a good and golden year were at length to pass over the poor old world!

(*The Puritans celebrate more so at this one event than all others. Compared to most peoples, they would still look stiff and grave. People are smiling and enjoying the festivities. There are no theatrical events, but sports events take place around the marketplace. A display of quarterstaffs[15] and wrestling can be seen in the street.*)

CAPTAIN (*moving to* HESTER). So, Mistress, I bid the steward make ready one more berth than you bargained for. No fear of scurvy or ship-fever, this voyage! What with the ship's surgeon and this other doctor, our only danger will be from drug or pill; more by token, as there is a lot of apothecary's stuff aboard, which I traded for with a Spanish vessel.

HESTER. What mean you? (*Startled*) Have you another passenger?

CAPTAIN. Why know you not that this physician here—Chillingworth, he calls himself— is minded to try my cabin fare with you? Ay, ay, you must have known it; for he tells me he is of your party, and a close friend of the gentleman you spoke of—he that is in peril from these sour old Puritan rulers!

HESTER (*calm*). They know each other well indeed. They have long dwelt together.

(HESTER *looks up and sees* CHILLINGWORTH *smiling at her. Pause. Military music is heard and the procession of magistrates and citizens marches toward the meeting house. The music is from drums and clarion—not professional sounding at all.* PEARL *starts to clap to the swells of the music and then stops and laughs when she sees the weapons that the honorary escort of the procession carry. The men who follow are dressed as public men and are followed by* DIMMESDALE *and* REVEREND WILSON. DIMMESDALE *moves with energy and strength.*

HESTER *gazes at* DIMMESDALE *as he passes.* DIMMESDALE *does not see her. Her spirit falls.* PEARL *jumps up and down beside her.*)

PEARL. Mother, was that the same minister that kissed me by the brook?

HESTER. Hold thy peace, dear little Pearl! We must not talk in the marketplace of what happens to us in the forest.

PEARL. I could not be sure that it was he; so

---

15. quarterstaffs, a type of sporting event in which participants joust with long, stout staffs

strange he looked. Else I would have run to him, and bid him kiss me, before all the people; even as he did yonder among the dark old trees. What would the minister have said, Mother? Would he have clapped his hand over his heart, and scowled at me, and bid me begone?

HESTER. What should he say, Pearl, save that it was no time to kiss, and that kisses are not to be given in the marketplace?

(MISTRESS HIBBINS, *dressed very richly for a Puritan, moves toward* HESTER. *As she approaches a wide circle is made around the three.*)

MISTRESS HIBBINS. Now, what mortal imagination could conceive it! Yonder divine man. That saint on earth, as the people uphold him to be, and as—I must needs say—he really looks! Who, now, that saw him pass in the procession, would think how little while it is since he went forth out of his study—to take an airing in the forest! Aha, we know what that means, Hester Prynne! Couldst thou surely tell, Hester, whether he was the same man that encountered thee on the forest path?

HESTER. Madam, I know not of what you speak. It is not for me to talk lightly of a learned and pious minister of the Word, like the Reverend Mr. Dimmesdale.

MISTRESS HIBBINS. Fie, woman, fie! (*Shaking her finger at* HESTER) Dost thou think I have been to the forest so many times, and have yet no skill to judge who else has been there? Yea; though no leaf of the wild garlands, which they wore while they danced, be left in their hair! I know thee, Hester; for I behold the token. We may all see it in the sunshine; and it glows like a red flame in the dark. Thou wearest it openly; so there need be no question about that. But this minister! Let me tell thee, in thine ear! When the Black Man sees one of his own servants, signed and sealed, so shy of owning to the bond as is the Reverend

Dimmesdale, he hath a way of ordering matters so that the mark shall be disclosed in open daylight to the eyes of all the world!

PEARL. What is it good Mistress Hibbins? (*Eagerly*) Hast thou seen it?

MISTRESS HIBBINS (*reverently*). Thou thyself wilt see it, one time or another. They say child, thou art of the lineage of the Prince of Air. Wilt thou ride with me, some fine night, to see thy father? (*She laughs.*)

(DIMMESDALE *is on a platform to give the election sermon and begins. The scene happens around and over the actual election speech. It is spoken under the following scenes.* MISTRESS HIBBINS *moves away from* HESTER *and* PEARL.)

DIMMESDALE (*under the action*). ... to do justly, to love mercy, to walk humbly with our God. For this end, he must help knit together this work as one man. We must entertain each other in brotherly affection. He must be willing to abridge us of our superfluities, for the supply of other's necessities. He must uphold a familiar commerce together with us in all meekness, gentleness, patience and liberality ...

(*While* DIMMESDALE *delivers his speech,* HESTER *intently listens to the sermon.* PEARL *begins playing around the marketplace, beyond her* MOTHER'S *supervision.*)

DIMMESDALE (*under the action*). ... He must aid us in delighting in each other, make other's conditions his own, rejoice with us, mourn with us, labor and suffer with us always having before his eyes and ours our commission and community in the work. So shall he help us keep the spirit in the bond of peace. The Lord will be our God and he our Governor, and both will delight to dwell among us as his own people, and will command a blessing upon us in all our ways, so that we shall see much more of God's wisdom, power, goodness, and truth.

(*The sermon is still being given.* CAPTAIN *takes off*

a gold chain and throws it to PEARL. *She catches it and places it around her neck and waist.*)

CAPTAIN. Thy mother is yonder woman with the scarlet letter. Wilt thou carry her a message from me?

PEARL. If thou message please me, I will.

CAPTAIN. Then tell her that I spake again with the black-a-visaged, hump-shouldered, old doctor; and he engages to bring his friend, the gentleman she spoke of, aboard with him. So let thy mother take no thought, save for herself and thee. Wilt thou tell her this, thou witch-baby?

PEARL. Mistress Hibbins says my father is the Prince of the Air. (*Smiling wickedly*) If thou callest me that ill name, I shall tell him of thee, and he will chase thy ship with a tempest!

(PEARL *takes off zigzagging around* THE CROWD *and returns to her* MOTHER *and tells her the news.* HESTER *is visibly shaken by the news.*)

DIMMESDALE (*under the action*). We shall find that the God of Israel is among us, when ten of us shall be able to resist a thousand of our enemies; when God shall make us a praise and glory that men shall say of succeeding colonies, "The Lord make it like that of New England."

(*The sermon ends; the people murmur their praise.* DIMMESDALE *bows on the pulpit as* HESTER *stands next to the scaffolding with the scarlet letter blazing. Military music is heard again.*

The procession goes in reverse and we see that DIMMESDALE *is again completely weak and pale looking.* REVEREND WILSON *runs to support the weakened* DIMMESDALE. *They move toward the scaffold, where* HESTER *is holding* PEARL's *hand.* MASTER BRACKET *rushes forward, but the look on* DIMMESDALE *face stops him short.* DIMMESDALE *is staring at the scarlet letter and the scaffolding above.*)

DIMMESDALE. Hester, come hither. Come, my little Pearl!

(PEARL *runs to him and clasps his knees.* HESTER *hesitates, but moves toward him.* CHILLINGWORTH *rushes up and grabs* DIMMESDALE's *arm.*)

CHILLINGWORTH (*whispering*). Madman, hold! What is thy purpose? Wave back that woman! Cast off this child! All shall be well! Do not blacken your fame, and perish in dishonor! I can yet save you! Would you bring infamy on your sacred profession?

DIMMESDALE. Ha, tempter, methinks thou art too late! Thy power is not what it was! With God's help, I shall escape thee now. (*He extends his hand to* HESTER.) Hester Prynne, in the name of Him, so terrible and so merciful, who gives me grace, at this last moment, to do what—for my own heavy sin and miserable agony—I withheld myself from doing seven years ago, come hither now, and twine thy strength about me! Thy strength, Hester; but let it be guided by the will which God hath granted me! This wretched and wronged old man is opposing it with all his might, and the fiend's! Come Hester, come. Support me up yonder scaffold!

(HESTER *moves to support* DIMMESDALE *with her shoulder as they head toward the scaffolding. Holding* PEARL's *hand, they ascend the steps. All music stops. Everyone turns to see them.* CHILLINGWORTH *follows them up the steps.*)

CHILLINGWORTH. Hadst thou sought the whole earth over there was no one place so secret—no high place nor lowly place where thou couldst have escaped me— save on this very scaffold!

DIMMESDALE. Thanks be to Him who hath led me hither! (*Trembling, he turns to* HESTER *and feebly smiles.*) Is it not better than what we dreamed of in the forest?

HESTER. I know not! I know not! Better? Yea; so we may both die and little Pearl die with us!

DIMMESDALE. For thee and Pearl, be it as

God shall order and God is merciful! Let me now do the will which he hath made plain before my sight. For, Hester, I am a dying man. So let me make haste to take my shame upon me!

(DIMMESDALE *turns to the crowd, with the support of* HESTER *and* PEARL. *The sun shines down upon him.*)

DIMMESDALE. People of New England! Ye, that have loved me!—ye, that have deemed me holy!—behold me here, the one sinner of the world! At last, at last, I stand upon the spot where, seven years since, I should have stood; here with this woman, whose arm, more than the little strength wherewith I have crept hitherward, sustains me, at this dreadful moment. Lo, the scarlet letter which Hester wears! Ye have all shuddered at it! Wherever her walk hath been—wherever, so miserably burdened, she may have hoped to find repose it hath cast a lurid gleam of awe and horrible repugnance round about her. But there stood one in the midst of you, at whose brand of sin and infamy ye have not shuddered!

(DIMMESDALE *throws off the help of* HESTER *and* PEARL *and stands alone.*)

DIMMESDALE (*cont'd.*) It was on him! God's eye beheld it! The angels were forever pointing at it! The Devil knew it well, and fretted it continually with the touch of his burning finger! But he hid it cunningly from men, and walked among you with the mien of a spirit, mournful, because so pure in a sinful world! Now, at the death-hour, he stands up before you! He bids you look again at Hester's scarlet letter! He tells you that, with all its mysterious horror, it is but the shadow of what he bears on his own breast, and that even this, his own red stigma, is no more than the type of what has

seared his inmost heart! Stand any here that question God's judgment on a sinner? Behold! Behold a dreadful witness of it!

(DIMMESDALE *rips open his vestments to reveal his chest.* THE CROWD *gasps. There is a scarlet letter "A."* DIMMESDALE *falls in a heap upon the scaffolding.* HESTER *supports his head.* CHILLINGWORTH *kneels beside him.*)

CHILLINGWORTH. Thou hast escaped me! Thou hast escaped me!

DIMMESDALE. May God forgive thee. Thou, too, hast deeply sinned! (*He turns to look at* PEARL *and* HESTER.) My little Pearl, (*Smiling weakly*) dear little Pearl, wilt thou kiss me now? Thou wouldst not, yonder, in the forest! But now thou wilt!

(PEARL *kisses him on the lips and begins to cry.*)

DIMMESDALE. Hester.

HESTER. Shall we not meet again? Shall we not spend our immortal life together? Surely, surely, we have ransomed one another, with all this woe? Thou lookest far into eternity, with those bright dying eye! Then tell me what thou seest?

DIMMESDALE. Hush, Hester, hush! The law we broke—the sin here so awfully revealed. I fear! I fear, it may be, that when we forgot our God—when we violated our reverence, each for the other's soul—it was thenceforth vain to hope that we could meet hereafter, in an everlasting and pure reunion. God knows; and he is merciful! He hath proved his mercy, most of all, in my afflictions. By giving me this burning torture to bear upon my breast! By sending yonder dark and terrible man to deep the torture always at red heat! By bringing me to die this death of triumphant ignominy before the people! Had either of these agonies been wanting, I had been lost forever! Praised be His name! His will be done. Farewell!

(THE CROWD is stunned silent, then a strange deep moaning rolls across the people. Blackout.)

SCENE 9

On the Prow of the ship. PEARL *and* HESTER *stand looking forward. A couple of months have passed and* PEARL *is a quiet and respectful child—unlike what she was.*

CAPTAIN. Wilt thou be needing anything else, Mistress Prynne?

HESTER. I think not, Captain. Thank you for your kindness. We wouldst still be in Boston hadst thou not offered us reasonable fare to England.

CAPTAIN. When I heard that Doctor Chillingworth passed and having seen that young Reverend fall on that election day, I thought it best that you and Pearl get away from those Puritanical zealots.

HESTER. I fear that thou speakest the truth. Old Mistress Hibbins has been put to death for witchery this past month and I feared for Pearl and myself.

PEARL. Mother, now is it time? I fear it is best that you get inside. The wind is cool this fall evening. I wouldst not want you sick here with no doctor aboard to heal thee.

HESTER. Thank you, sweet child. It is time— and I am starting to feel cold.

(With that, HESTER *takes the scarlet letter off her bodice and holds it—looking down at it in her hand. She then without warning throws it out to sea. Turning to* PEARL *smiling—* PEARL *smiles beautifully back at her mother.)*

HESTER. It is done. You have been the happiness of my life these past few years. I am glad that you, perchance, will have a life ahead of you in England.

CAPTAIN. She is most beautiful, like her mother, and many an honest man will find her so. Thou and thy daughter art starting anew. Have no fear Mistress Prynne.

HESTER. Fear. I know not fear, only sadness *(Hugging* PEARL*)* and love.

(Lights fade.)

THE END

The Scarlet Letter

Play Analysis

1. Dimmesdale acquires "his own red stigma," and finally shows it to the towns-people. How do you think he acquired it?
2. Why does little Pearl finally kiss Dimmesdale just before he dies?
3. What do you see as the theme of *The Scarlet Letter?* Support your answer with lines from the play.
4. In Hawthorne's account of Hester Prynne, she remains in New England and never abandons the scarlet letter, which is finally "looked upon with awe, yet with reverence too." Do you think De Maiolo's ending is more effective? Why or why not?
5. **Thematic Connection: And Justice for All** Do you believe that Hester and Dimmsdale's suffering was just? Bear in mind the beliefs of the time.

Literary Skill: Adapt a Passage

The following exchange between Mistress Hibbins and Reverend Dimmesdale appears in Hawthorne's book, but not in the play. Write the scene in script form, paying particular attention to stage directions such as movement and emotion.

...Mistress Hibbins, the reputed witch-lady, is said to have been passing by. She made a very grand appearance; having on a high headdress, a rich gown of velvet, and a ruff done up with a famous yellow starch .... Whether [she] had read the minister's thoughts or no, she came to a full stop, looked shrewdly into his face, smiled craftily, and—though little given to converse with clergymen—began a conversation.

...“So, reverend Sir, you have made a visit into the forest,” observed the witch-lady, nodding her high headdress at him. “The next time, I pray you to allow me only a fair warning, and I shall be proud to bear you company. Without taking overmuch upon myself, my good word will go far towards gaining any strange gentleman a fair reception from yonder potentate you wot of!”

“I profess, Madam,” answered the clergyman, with a grave obeisance, such as the lady's rank demanded and his own good breeding made imperative—“I profess, on my conscience and character, that I am utterly bewildered as touching the purport of your words!—I went not into the forest to seek a potentate... .”

...“Ha, ha, ha!” cackled the old witch-lady, still nodding her high headdress at the minister. “Well, well, we must needs talk thus in the daytime! You carry it off like an old hand! But at midnight, and in the forest, we shall have other talk together!”

...She passed on with her aged stateliness, but often turning back her head and smiling at him, like one willing to recognize a secret intimacy of connection.

Performance Element: Analyze the Text

Exchange the script you wrote with a classmate. Read the script, then get together and talk about the scripts you each have. Choose one of the two scripts and ana-lyze the two parts, paying attention to stage directions, tone, and character.

The Devil and Daniel Webster

short story and stage adaptation by Stephen Vincent Benét

Creating Context:
The Devil in All His Guises

Call him Satan. Call him Beelzebub, Lucifer, Mephistopheles, Beliel, or the Prince of Darkness. Or, if you're in a down-home frame of mind, you might call him Old Nick, Old Harry, Old Ned, or Old Scratch. He is also known as the Old Serpent because the Bible suggests he was the snake that tempted Eve to eat the Apple of Knowledge

"Those are the seven deadly sins. You may choose any two of them."

(which caused Adam and Eve to be expelled from the Garden of Eden). He is the Devil—and many a question-able deed has been laid at his cloven feet. The Devil is often depicted as half man, half goat, with hooves, horns, and an overall red cast about him (reflections from hell, perhaps). He looks much like the Roman god Pan, who was popular at the time the early Christians were trying to establish their religion. It has been suggested that in order to draw people away from Pan's pagan followers, the Christians demonized Pan by creating the Devil in his image. For whatever reason, the Devil's image has become one of the most famous in history—the subject of countless paintings, poems, stories, songs, sermons, and even cartoons.

John Milton, in his epic poem *Paradise Lost,* called him the "infernal Serpent …whose guile stirred up with Envy and Revenge, deceiv'd The Mother of Mankind. …" Cast out of heaven as a rebel angel who sought glory, set himself above the other angels, and declared war on God, his image inspires everything from hatred and fear to envy and humor. He is depicted, in turn, as cunning, smooth, wicked, enticing, clever, amusing, and—as you can see in the cartoon above—a very good salesman.

The concept of a person selling his soul to the devil is a very old one. Christopher Marlowe's play *The Tragical History of Doctor Faustus,* written in the late 1500s, tells the story of a scholar who sells himself to the devil Mephisto in order to have twenty-four years of absolute knowledge and power. More modern tales find people selling their souls to gain love, money, power, and even a chance to help the Washington Senators beat the Yankees and win the pennant.

In the play you are about to read, a young man made a bargain with Mr. Scratch in order to gain property and wealth. When the hour arrives to pay his debt, the man turns to a national hero, Daniel Webster, to save his soul.

As a Reader: Being Willing to Suspend Disbelief

Samuel Taylor Coleridge called it the "willing suspension of disbelief," and it is what we must do when we encounter art that seems fantastic or beyond the realm of possibility. Reading *The Devil and Daniel Webster* requires that we do as Coleridge advises. Look at the two passages below and compare their styles. Both the original short story, at left, and the play, at right, allude to a rock appearing on the landscape out of nowhere. Think about what this might mean as you read the play.

from Page · · ·  · · · **to Stage**

He'd been plowing that morning and he'd just broke the plowshare on a rock that he could have sworn hadn't been there yesterday. And, as he stood looking at the plowshare, the old horse began to cough — that ropy kind of cough that means sickness and horse doctors. There were two children down with the measles, his wife was ailing, and he had a whitlow* on his thumb. It was about the last straw for Jabez Stone. "I vow," he said, and he looked around him kind of desperate—"I vow it's enough to make a man want to sell his soul to the devil! And I would, too, for two cents!" Then he felt a kind of queerness come over him at having said what he'd said; though, naturally, being a New Hampshireman, he wouldn't take it back. And, sure enough, next day, about suppertime, a soft-spoken, dark-dressed stranger drove up in a handsome buggy and asked for Jabez Stone.

from "The Devil and Daniel Webster" by Stephen Vincent Benét

*deep inflammation of the finger

MARY. Oh, Jabez—why didn't you tell me?

JABEZ. It happened before I could. Just an average day—you know—just an average day. But there was a mean east wind and a mean small rain. Well, I was plowing, and the share broke clean off on a rock where there hadn't been any rock the day before. I didn't have money for a new one—I didn't have money to get it mended. So I said it and I said loud, "I'll sell my soul for about two cents," I said. *(He stops. MARY stares at him.)* Well, that's all there is to it, I guess. He came along that afternoon—that fellow from Boston—and the dog looked at him and ran away. Well, I had to make it more than two cents, but he was agreeable to that.

from *The Devil and Daniel Webster*
by Stephen Vincent Benét

As a Stage Designer: Creating an Illusion

Much of what you are about to read occurs in a time long ago in an unknown place filled with people who could not really be there. All that being said, it is a play with powerful ideas and up-to-the-minute issues. While reading, be aware of how a serious yet unearthly atmosphere might be created on the stage.

The Devil and Daniel Webster

Time
1841

The Characters
JABEZ STONE
MARY STONE
DANIEL WEBSTER
MR. SCRATCH
THE FIDDLER
JUSTICE HATHORNE
JUSTICE HATHORNE'S CLERK
KING PHILIP
TEACH
WALTER BUTLER
SIMON GIRTY
DALE
MEN AND WOMEN of Cross Corners, New Hampshire

Setting
New Hampshire

JABEZ STONE's *Farmhouse, a big comfortable room that hasn't yet developed the stuffiness of a front-parlor. A door, right, leads to the kitchen—a door, left, to the outside. There is a fireplace, right. Windows, in center, show a glimpse of summer landscape. Most of the furniture has been cleared away for the dance which follows the wedding of* JABEZ *and* MARY STONE, *but there is a settle or bench by the fireplace, a table, left, with some wedding presents upon it, at least three chairs by the table, and a cider barrel on which* THE FIDDLER *sits, in front of the table. Near the table, against the side-wall, there is a cupboard where there are glasses and a jug. There is a clock.*

A country wedding has been in progress—the wedding of JABEZ *and* MARY STONE. *He is a husky young farmer, around twenty-eight or thirty. The bride is in her early twenties. He is dressed in stiff, store clothes but not ridiculously—they are of good quality and he looks important. The bride is in a simple white or cream wedding dress and may carry a small, stiff bouquet of country flowers.*

Now the wedding is over and the guests are dancing. THE FIDDLER *is perched on the cider barrel. He plays and calls square-dance figures. The guests include the recognizable types of a small New England town, doctor, lawyer, storekeeper, old maid, schoolteacher, farmer, etc. There is an air of prosperity and hearty country mirth about the whole affair.*

At rise, JABEZ *and* MARY *are up left center, receiving the congratulations of a few last guests who talk to them and pass on to the dance. The others are dancing. There is a buzz of conversation that follows the tune of the dance music.*

FIRST WOMAN. Right nice wedding.

FIRST MAN. Handsome couple.

SECOND WOMAN (*passing through crowd with dish of oyster stew*). Oysters for supper!

SECOND MAN (*passing cake*). And layer-cake—layer-cake—

AN OLD MAN (*hobbling toward cider barrel*). Makes me feel young again! Oh, by jingo!

AN OLD WOMAN (*pursuing him*). Henry, Henry, you've been drinking cider!

FIDDLER. Set to your partners! Dosy-do!

WOMAN. Mary and Jabez.

MEN. Jabez and Mary.

A WOMAN. Where's the State Senator?

A MAN. Where's the lucky bride?

(*With cries of "Mary—Jabez—strike it up, fiddler—make room for the bride and groom," the crowd drags* MARY *and* JABEZ, *pleased but embarrassed, into the center of the room and* MARY *and* JABEZ *do a little solo dance, while* THE CROWD

claps, applauds, and makes various remarks.)

A MAN. Handsome steppers!

A WOMAN. She's pretty as a picture.

A SECOND MAN. Cut your pigeon-wing,[1] Jabez!

THE OLD MAN. Young again, young again, that's the way I feel! (*He tries to cut a pigeon-wing himself.*)

THE OLD WOMAN. Henry, Henry, careful of your rheumatiz!

A THIRD WOMAN. Makes me feel all teary—seeing them so happy. (*The solo dance ends, the music stops for a moment.*)

THE OLD MAN (*gossiping to a neighbor*). Wonder where he got it all—Stones was always poor.

HIS NEIGHBOR. Ain't poor now—makes you wonder just a mite.

A THIRD MAN. Don't begrudge it to him—but I wonder where he got it.

THE OLD MAN (*starting to whisper*). Let me tell you something—

THE OLD WOMAN (*quickly*). Henry, Henry, don't you start to gossip. (*She drags him away.*)

FIDDLER (*cutting in*). Set to your partners! Scratch for corn! (*The dance resumes, but as it does so,* THE CROWD *chants back and forth.*)

WOMEN. Gossip's got a sharp tooth.

MEN. Gossip's got a mean tooth.

WOMEN. She's a lucky woman. They're a lucky pair.

MEN. That's true as gospel. But I wonder where he got it.

WOMEN. Money, land, and riches.

MEN. Just came out of nowhere.

WOMEN AND MEN (*together*). Wonder where he got it all— But that's his business.

FIDDLER. Left and right—grand chain!

---

1. pigeon-wing, a fancy dance step done by jumping and striking the legs together

(The dance rises to a pitch of ecstasy with the final figure—the fiddle squeaks and stops. The dancers mop their brows.)

FIRST MAN. Whew! Ain't danced like that since I was knee-high to a grasshopper!

SECOND MAN. Play us "The Portland Fancy," fiddler!

THIRD MAN. No, wait a minute, neighbor. Let's hear from the happy pair! Hey, Jabez!

FOURTH MAN. Let's hear from the State Senator! *(They crowd around* JABEZ *and push him up on the settle.)*

OLD MAN. Might as well. It's the last time he'll have the last word!

OLD WOMAN. Now, Henry Banks, you ought to be ashamed of yourself!

OLD MAN. Told you so, Jabez!

THE CROWD. Speech!

JABEZ *(embarrassed).* Neighbors—friends—I'm not much of a speaker—spite of your 'lecting me to State Senate—

THE CROWD. That's the ticket, Jabez. Smart man, Jabez. I voted for ye. Go ahead, Senator, you're doing fine.

JABEZ. But we're certainly glad to have you here—me and Mary. And we want to thank you for coming and—

A VOICE. Vote the Whig ticket!

ANOTHER VOICE. Hooray for Daniel Webster!

JABEZ. And I'm glad Hi Foster said that, for those are my sentiments, too. Mr. Webster has promised to honor us with his presence here tonight.

THE CROWD. Hurray for Dan'l! Hurray for the greatest man in the U.S.!

JABEZ. And when he comes, I know we'll give him a real New Hampshire welcome.

THE CROWD. Sure we will—Webster forever—and to hell with Henry Clay!

JABEZ. And meanwhile—well, there's Mary and me *(Takes her hand)*—and, if you folks don't have a good time, well, we won't feel right about getting married at all. Because I know I've been lucky—and I hope she feels that way, too. And, well, we're going to be happy or bust a trace![2] *(He wipes his brow to terrific applause. He and* MARY *look at each other.)*

A WOMAN *(in kitchen doorway).* Come and get the cider, folks!

*(*THE CROWD *begins to drift away—a few to the kitchen—a few toward the door that leads to the outside. They furnish a shifting background to the next little scene, where* MARY *and* JABEZ *are left alone by the fireplace.)*

JABEZ. Mary.

MARY. Mr. Stone.

JABEZ. Mary.

MARY. My husband.

JABEZ. That's a big word, husband.

MARY. It's a good word.

JABEZ. Are you happy, Mary?

MARY. Yes. So happy, I'm afraid.

JABEZ. Afraid?

MARY. I suppose it happens to every girl—just for a minute. It's like spring turning into summer. You want it to be summer. But the spring was sweet. *(Dismissing the mood)* I'm sorry. Forgive me. It just came and went, like something cold. As if we'd been too lucky.

JABEZ. We can't be too lucky, Mary. Not you and me.

MARY *(rather mischievously).* If you say so, Mr. Stone. But you don't even know what sort of housekeeper I am. And Aunt Hepsy says—

JABEZ. Bother your Aunt Hepsy! There's just you and me, and that's all that matters in the world.

MARY. And you don't know something else—

---

2. bust a trace, try so hard one wears oneself out

JABEZ. What's that?

MARY. How proud I am of you. Ever since I was a little girl. Ever since you carried my books. Oh, I'm sorry for women who can't be proud of their men. It must be a lonely feeling.

JABEZ (*uncomfortably*). A man can't always be proud of everything, Mary. There's some things a man does, or might do—when he has to make his way.

MARY (*laughing*). I know—terrible things—like being the best farmer in the county and the best State Senator—

JABEZ (*quietly*). And a few things, besides. But you remember one thing, Mary, whatever happens. It was all for you. And nothing's going to happen. Because he hasn't come yet—and he would have come if it was wrong.

MARY. But it's wonderful to have Mr. Webster come to us.

JABEZ. I wasn't thinking about Mr. Webster. (*He takes both her hands.*) Mary, I've got something to tell you. I should have told you before, but I couldn't seem to bear it. Only, now that it's all right, I can. Ten years ago—

A VOICE (*from offstage*). Dan'l! Dan'l Webster!

(JABEZ *drops* MARY's *hands and looks around.* THE CROWD *begins to mill and gather toward the door. Others rush in from the kitchen.*)

ANOTHER VOICE. Black Dan'l! He's come!

ANOTHER VOICE. Three cheers for the greatest man in the U.S.!

ANOTHER VOICE. Three cheers for Daniel Webster!

(*And, to the cheering and applause of the crowd,* DANIEL WEBSTER *enters and stands for a moment upstage, his head thrown back, his attitude leonine[3]. He stops the cheering of* THE CROWD *with a gesture.*)

WEBSTER. Neighbors—old friends—it does me good to hear you. But don't cheer me—I'm not running for President this summer. (*A laugh from the crowd*) I'm here on a better errand—to pay my humble respects to a most charming lady and her very fortunate spouse. (*There is the twang of a fiddle string breaking.*)

FIDDLER. 'Tarnation! Busted a string!

A VOICE. He's always bustin' strings.

(WEBSTER *blinks at the interruption but goes on.*)

WEBSTER. We're proud of State Senator Stone in these parts—we know what he's done. Ten years ago he started out with a patch of land that was mostly rocks and mortgages and now—well, you've only to look around you. I don't know that I've ever seen a likelier farm, not even at Marshfield—and I hope, before I die, I'll have the privilege of shaking his hand as Governor of this State. I don't know how he's done it—I couldn't have done it myself. But I know this—Jabez Stone wears no man's collar. (*At this statement there is a discordant squeak from the fiddle and* JABEZ *looks embarrassed.* WEBSTER *knits his brows.*) And what's more, if I know Jabez, he never will. But I didn't come here to talk politics—I came to kiss the bride. (*He does so among great applause. He shakes hands with* JABEZ.) Congratulations, Stone—you're a lucky man. And now, if our friend in the corner will give us a tune on his fiddle—

(THE CROWD *presses forward to meet the great man. He shakes hands with several.*)

A MAN. Remember me, Mr. Webster? Saw ye up at the State House at Concord.

ANOTHER MAN. Glad to see ye, Mr. Webster. I voted for ye ten times.

(WEBSTER *receives their homage politely, but his mind is still on the music.*)

---

3. leonine, regal; kingly

WEBSTER *(a trifle irritated).* I said, if our friend in the corner would give us a tune on his fiddle—

FIDDLER *(passionately, flinging the fiddle down).* Hell's delight—excuse me, Mr. Webster. But the very devil's got into that fiddle of mine. She was doing all right up to just a minute ago. But now I've tuned her and tuned her and she won't play a note I want.

(And, at this point, MR. SCRATCH *makes his appearance. He has entered, unobserved, and mixed with the crowd while all eyes were upon* DANIEL WEBSTER. *He is, of course, the devil—a New England devil, dressed like a rather shabby attorney but with something just a little wrong in clothes and appearance. For one thing, he wears black gloves on his hands. He carries a large black tin box, like a botanist's collecting-box, under one arm. Now he slips through* THE CROWD *and taps* THE FIDDLER *on the shoulder.)*

SCRATCH *(insinuatingly).*[4] Maybe you need some rosin on your bow, fiddler?

FIDDLER. Maybe I do and maybe I don't. *(Turns and confronts the stranger)* But who are you? I don't remember seeing you before.

SCRATCH. Oh, I'm just a friend—a humble friend of the bridegroom's. *(He walks toward* JABEZ. *Apologetically.)* I'm afraid I came in the wrong way, Mr. Stone. You've improved the place so much since I last saw it that I hardly knew the front door. But, I assure you, I came as fast as I could.

JABEZ *(obviously shocked).* It—it doesn't matter. *(With a great effort)* Mary—Mr. Webster—this is a—a friend of mine from Boston—a legal friend. I didn't expect him today but—

SCRATCH. Oh, my dear Mr. Stone—an occasion like this—I wouldn't miss it for the world. *(He bows.)* Charmed, Mrs. Stone. Delighted, Mr. Webster. But—don't let me break up the merriment of the meeting.

(He turns back toward the table and THE FIDDLER.*)*

FIDDLER *(with a grudge, to* SCRATCH*).* Boston lawyer, eh?

SCRATCH. You might call me that.

FIDDLER *(tapping the tin box with his bow).* And what have you got in that big tin box of yours? Law papers?

SCRATCH. Oh—curiosities for the most part. I'm a collector, too.

FIDDLER. Don't hold much with Boston curiosities, myself. And you know about fiddling too, do you? Know all about it?

SCRATCH. Oh— *(A deprecatory shrug)*

FIDDLER. Don't shrug your shoulders at me—I ain't no Frenchman. Telling me I needed more rosin!

MARY *(trying to stop the quarrel).* Isaac—please—

FIDDLER. Sorry, Mary—Mrs. Stone. But I have been playing the fiddle at Cross Corners weddings for twenty-five years. And now here comes a stranger from Boston and tells me I need more rosin!

SCRATCH. But, my good friend—

FIDDLER. Rosin indeed! Here—play it yourself then and see what you can make of it!

(He thrusts the fiddle at SCRATCH. *The latter stiffens, slowly lays his black collecting-box on the table, and takes the fiddle.)*

SCRATCH *(with feigned embarrassment).* But really, I—*(He bows toward* JABEZ.*)* Shall I— Mr. Senator? *(*JABEZ *makes a helpless gesture of assent.)*

MARY *(to* JABEZ*).* Mr. Stone—Mr. Stone—are you ill?

JABEZ. No—no—but I feel—it's hot—

WEBSTER *(chuckling).* Don't you fret, Mrs. Stone. I've got the right medicine for him. *(He pulls a flask from his pocket.)* Ten-year-old Medford, Stone—I buy it by the keg

---

4. insinuatingly, in an accusing manner

down at Marshfield. Here—(*He tries to give some of the rum to* JABEZ.)

JABEZ. No—(*He turns.*)—Mary—Mr. Webster—(*But he cannot explain. With a burst.*) Oh, let him play—let him play! Don't you see he's bound to? Don't you see there's nothing we can do?

(*A rustle of discomfort among the guests.* SCRATCH *draws the bow across the fiddle in a horrible discord.*)

FIDDLER (*triumphantly*). I told you so, stranger. The devil's in that fiddle!

SCRATCH. I'm afraid it needs special tuning. (*Draws the bow in a second discord*) There— that's better. (*Grinning*) And now for this happy—this very happy occasion—in tribute to the bride and groom—I'll play something appropriate—a song of young love—

MARY. Oh, Jabez—Mr. Webster—stop him! Do you see his hands? He's playing with gloves on his hands.

(WEBSTER *starts forward, but, even as he does so,* SCRATCH *begins to play and all freeze as* SCRATCH *goes on with the extremely inappropriate song that follows. At first his manner is oily and mocking— it is not till he reaches the line "The devil took the words away" that he really becomes terrifying and the crowd starts to be afraid.*)

SCRATCH (*accompanying himself fantastically*).
Young William was a thriving boy.
(Listen to my doleful tale.)

Young Mary Clark was all his joy.
(Listen to my doleful tale.)

He swore he'd love her all his life.
She swore she'd be his loving wife.

But William found a gambler's den
And drank with livery-stable men.

He played the cards, he played the dice.
He would not listen to advice.

And when in church he tried to pray,
The devil took the words away.

(SCRATCH, *still playing, starts to march across the stage.*)

The devil got him by the toe
And so, alas, he had to go.

"Young Mary Clark, young Mary Clark,
I now must go into the dark."

(*These last two verses have been directed at* JABEZ. SCRATCH *continues, now turning on* MARY.)

Young Mary lay upon her bed.
"Alas my Will-i-am is dead."

He came to her a bleeding ghost—

(*He rushes at* MARY *but* WEBSTER *stands between them.*)

WEBSTER. Stop! Stop! You miserable wretch—can't you see that you're frightening Mrs. Stone? (*He wrenches the fiddle out of* SCRATCH's *hands and tosses it aside.*) And now, sir—out of this house!

SCRATCH (*facing him*). You're a bold man, Mr. Webster. Too bold for your own good, perhaps. And anyhow, it wasn't my fiddle. It belonged to—(*He wheels and sees* THE FIDDLER *tampering with the collecting-box that has been left on the table.*) Idiot! What are you doing with my collecting-box? (*He rushes for* THE FIDDLER *and chases him round the table, but* THE FIDDLER *is just one jump ahead.*)

FIDDLER. Boston lawyer, eh? Well, I don't think so. I think you've got something in that box of yours you're afraid to show. And, by jingo—(*He throws open the lid of the box. The lights wink and there is a clap of thunder. All eyes stare upward. Something has flown out of the box. But what?* FIDDLER, *with relief:*) Why, 'tain't nothing but a moth.

MARY. A white moth—a flying thing.

WEBSTER. A common moth—*telea polyphemus*—

THE CROWD. A moth—just a moth—a moth—

FIDDLER (terrified). But it ain't. It ain't no common moth! I seen it! And it's got a death's-head on it! (He strikes at the invisible object with his bow to drive it away.)

VOICE OF THE MOTH. Help me, neighbors! Help me!

WEBSTER. What's that? It wails like a lost soul.

MARY. A lost soul.

THE CROWD. A lost soul—lost—in darkness—in the darkness.

VOICE OF THE MOTH. Help me, neighbors!

FIDDLER. It sounds like Miser Stevens!

JABEZ. Miser Stevens!

THE CROWD. The Miser—Miser Stevens—a lost soul—lost.

FIDDLER (frantically). It sounds like Miser Stevens—and you had him in your box. But it can't be. He ain't dead.

JABEZ. He ain't dead—I tell you he ain't dead! He was just as spry and mean as a woodchuck Tuesday.

THE CROWD. Miser Stevens—soul of Miser Stevens—but he ain't dead.

SCRATCH (dominating them). Listen! (A bell offstage begins to toll a knell,[5] slowly, solemnly.)

MARY. The bell—the church bell—the bell that rang at my wedding.

WEBSTER. The church bell—the passing bell.

JABEZ. The funeral bell.

THE CROWD. The bell—the passing bell—Miser Stevens—dead.

VOICE OF THE MOTH. Help me, neighbors, help me! I sold my soul to the devil. But I'm not the first or the last. Help me. Help Jabez Stone!

SCRATCH. Ah, would you!

(He catches THE MOTH in his red bandanna, stuffs it back into his collecting-box, and shuts the lid with a snap.)

VOICE OF THE MOTH (fading). Lost—lost forever, forever. Lost, like Jabez Stone. (The crowd turns on JABEZ. They read his secret in his face.)

THE CROWD. Jabez Stone—Jabez Stone—answer us—answer us.

MARY. Tell them, dear—answer them—you are good—you are brave—you are innocent. (But THE CROWD is all pointing hands and horrified eyes.)

THE CROWD. Jabez Stone—Jabez Stone. Who's your friend in black, Jabez Stone? (They point to SCRATCH.)

WEBSTER. Answer them, Mr. State Senator.

THE CROWD. Jabez Stone—Jabez Stone. Where did you get your money, Jabez Stone? (SCRATCH grins and taps his collecting-box. JABEZ cannot speak.)

JABEZ. I—I—(He stops.)

THE CROWD. Jabez Stone—Jabez Stone. What was the price you paid for it, Jabez Stone?

JABEZ (looking around wildly). Help me, neighbors! Help me! (This cracks the built-up tension and sends the crowd over the edge into fanaticism.)

A WOMAN'S VOICE (high and hysterical). He's sold his soul to the devil! (She points to JABEZ.)

OTHER VOICES. To the devil!

THE CROWD. He's sold his soul to the devil! The devil himself! The devil's playing the fiddle! The devil's come for his own!

JABEZ (appealing). But, neighbors—I didn't know—I didn't mean—oh, help me!

THE CROWD (inexorably).[6] He's sold his soul to the devil!

SCRATCH (grinning). To the devil!

THE CROWD. He's sold his soul to the devil! There's no help left for him, neighbors! Run, hide, hurry, before we're caught! He's

---

5. knell, a stroke or sound of a bell indicating a death, funeral, or disaster

6. inexorably, without pity; unrelenting

a lost soul—Jabez Stone—he's the devil's own! Run, hide, hasten!

(They stream across the stage like a flurry of bats, the cannier picking up the wedding-presents they have given to take along with them. MR. SCRATCH *drives them out into the night, fiddle in hand, and follows them.* JABEZ *and* MARY *are left with* WEBSTER. JABEZ *has sunk into a chair, beaten, with his head in his hands.* MARY *is trying to comfort him.* WEBSTER *looks at them for a moment and shakes his head, sadly. As he crosses to exit to the porch, his hand drops for a moment on* JABEZ's *shoulder, but* JABEZ *makes no sign.* WEBSTER *exits.* JABEZ *lifts his head.)*

MARY *(comforting him).* My dear—my dear—

JABEZ. I—it's all true, Mary. All true. You must hurry.

MARY. Hurry?

JABEZ. Hurry after them—back to the village—back to your folks. Mr. Webster will take you—you'll be safe with Mr. Webster. You see, it's all true, and he'll be back in a minute. *(With a shudder)* The other one. *(He groans.)* I've got until twelve o'clock. That's the contract. But there isn't much time.

MARY. Are you telling me to run away from you, Mr. Stone?

JABEZ. You don't understand, Mary. It's true.

MARY. We made some promises to each other. Maybe you've forgotten them. But I haven't. I said, it's for better or worse. It's for better or worse. I said, in sickness or in health. Well, that covers the ground, Mr. Stone.

JABEZ. But, Mary, you must—I command you.

MARY. "For thy people shall be my people and thy God my God." *(Quietly)* That was Ruth, in the Book. I always liked the name of Ruth—always liked the thought of her. I always thought—I'll call a child Ruth, some time. I guess that was just a girl's

notion. *(She breaks.)* But, oh, Jabez—why?

JABEZ. It started years ago, Mary. I guess I was a youngster then—I guess I must have been. A youngster with a lot of ambitions and no way in the world to get there. I wanted city clothes and a big white house—I wanted to be State Senator and have people look up to me. But all I got on the farm was a crop of stones. You could work all day and all night but that was all you got.

MARY *(softly).* It was pretty—that hill-farm, Jabez. You could look all the way across the valley.

JABEZ. Pretty? It was fever and ague[7]—it was stones and blight. If I had a horse, he got colic—if I planted garden-truck, the wood-chucks ate it. I'd lie awake nights and try to figure out a way to get somewhere—but there wasn't any way. And all the time you were growing up, in the town. I couldn't ask you to marry me and take you to a place like that.

MARY. Do you think it's the place makes the difference to a woman? I'd—I'd have kept your house. I'd have stroked the cat and fed the chickens and seen you wiped your shoes on the mat. I wouldn't have asked for more. Oh, Jabez—why didn't you tell me?

JABEZ. It happened before I could. Just an average day—you know—just an average day. But there was a mean east wind and a mean small rain. Well, I was plowing, and the share broke clean off on a rock where there hadn't been any rock the day before. I didn't have money for a new one—I didn't have money to get it mended. So I said it and I said loud, "I'll sell my soul for about two cents," I said. *(He stops.* MARY *stares at him.)* Well, that's all there is to it, I guess. He came along that afternoon—that fellow from Boston—and the dog looked at him

---

7. ague, shivering; chills

and ran away. Well, I had to make it more than two cents, but he was agreeable to that. So I pricked my thumb with a pin and signed the paper. It felt hot when you touched it, that paper. I keep remembering that. *(He pauses.)* And it's all come true, and he's kept his part of the bargain. I got the riches and I've married you. And, oh, God Almighty, what shall I do?

MARY. Let us run away! Let us creep and hide!

JABEZ. You can't run away from the devil— I've seen his horses. Miser Stevens tried to run away.

MARY. Let us pray—let us pray to the God of Mercy that He redeem us.

JABEZ. I can't pray, Mary. The words just burn in my heart.

MARY. I won't let you go! I won't! There must be someone who could help us. I'll get the judge and the squire—

JABEZ. Who'll take a case against old Scratch? Who'll face the devil himself and do him brown? There isn't a lawyer in the world who'd dare do that. *(WEBSTER appears in the doorway.)*

WEBSTER. Good evening, neighbors. Did you say something about lawyers—

MARY. Mr. Webster!

JABEZ. Dan'l Webster! But I thought—

WEBSTER. You'll excuse me for leaving you for a moment. I was just taking a stroll on the porch, in the cool of the evening. Fine summer evening, too.

JABEZ. Well, it might be, I guess, but that kind of depends on the circumstances.

WEBSTER. H'm. Yes. I happened to overhear a little of your conversation. I gather you're in trouble, Neighbor Stone.

JABEZ. Sore trouble.

WEBSTER *(delicately).* Sort of law case, I understand.

JABEZ. You might call it that, Mr. Webster. Kind of a mortgage case, in a way.

MARY. Oh, Jabez!

WEBSTER. Mortgage case. Well, I don't generally plead now, except before the Supreme Court, but this case of yours presents some very unusual features and I never deserted a neighbor in trouble yet. So, if I can be of any assistance—

MARY. Oh, Mr. Webster, will you help him?

JABEZ. It's a terrible lot to ask you. But— well, you see, there's Mary. And, if you could see your way to it—

WEBSTER. I will.

MARY *(weeping with relief).* Oh, Mr. Webster!

WEBSTER. There, there, Mrs. Stone. After all, if two New Hampshire men aren't a match for the devil, we might as well give the country back to the Indians. When is he coming, Jabez?

JABEZ. Twelve o'clock. The time's getting late.

WEBSTER. Then I'd better refresh my memory. The—er—mortgage was for a definite term of years?

JABEZ. Ten years.

WEBSTER. And it falls due—?

JABEZ. Tonight. Oh, I can't see how I came to be such a fool!

WEBSTER. No use crying over spilt milk, Stone. We've got to get you out of it, now. But tell me one thing. Did you sign this precious document of your own free will?

JABEZ. Yes, it was my own free will. I can't deny that.

WEBSTER. H'm, that's a trifle unfortunate. But we'll see.

MARY. Oh, Mr. Webster, can you save him? Can you?

WEBSTER. I shall do my best, madam. That's all you can ever say till you see what the jury looks like.

MARY. But even you, Mr. Webster—oh, I know you're Secretary of State—I know you're a great man—I know you've done wonderful things. But it's different—fighting the devil!

WEBSTER *(towering).* I've fought John C. Calhoun, madam. And I've fought Henry Clay. And, by the great shade of Andrew Jackson, I'd fight ten thousand devils to save a New Hampshire man!

JABEZ. You hear, Mary?

MARY. Yes. And I trust Mr. Webster. But—oh, there must be some way that I can help!

WEBSTER. There is one, madam, and a hard one. As Mr. Stone's counsel, I must formally request your withdrawal.

MARY. No.

WEBSTER. Madam, think for a moment. You cannot help Mr. Stone—since you are his wife, your testimony would be prejudiced. And frankly, madam, in a very few moments this is going to be no place for a lady.

MARY. But I can't—I can't leave him—I can't bear it!

JABEZ. You must go, Mary. You must.

WEBSTER. Pray, madam—you can help us with your prayers. Are the prayers of the innocent unavailing?

MARY. Oh, I'll pray—I'll pray. But a woman's more than a praying machine, whatever men think. And how do I know?

WEBSTER. Trust me, Mrs. Stone.

(MARY turns to go, and, with one hand on JABEZ's shoulder, as she moves to the door, says the following prayer:)

MARY.

Now may there be a blessing and a light betwixt thee and me, forever.

For, as Ruth unto Naomi, so do I cleave unto thee.

Set me as a seal upon thy heart, as a seal upon thine arm, for love is strong as death.

Many waters cannot quench love, neither can the floods drown it.

As Ruth unto Naomi, so do I cleave unto thee.

The Lord watch between thee and me when we are absent, one from the other.

Amen. Amen. *(She goes out.)*

WEBSTER. Amen.

JABEZ. Thank you, Mr. Webster. She ought to go. But I couldn't have made her do it.

WEBSTER. Well, Stone—I know ladies—and I wouldn't be surprised if she's still got her ear to the keyhole. But she's best out of this night's business. How long have we got to wait?

JABEZ *(beginning to be terrified again).* Not long—not long.

WEBSTER. Then I'll just get out the jug, with your permission, Stone. Somehow or other, waiting's wonderfully shorter with a jug. *(He crosses to the cupboard, gets out jug and glasses, pours himself a drink.)* Ten-year-old Medford. There's nothing like it. I saw an inchworm take a drop of it once and he stood right up on his hind legs and bit a bee. Come—try a nip.

JABEZ. There's no joy in it for me.

WEBSTER. Oh, come, man, come! Just because you've sold your soul to the devil, that needn't make you a teetotaller. *(He laughs and passes the jug to JABEZ who tries to pour from it. But at that moment the clock whirs and begins to strike the three-quarters, and JABEZ spills the liquor.)*

JABEZ. Oh, God!

WEBSTER. Never mind—it's a nervous feeling, waiting for a trial to begin. I remember my first case—

JABEZ. 'Taint that. *(He turns to WEBSTER.)* Mr. Webster—Mr. Webster—for God's sake harness your horses and get away from this place as fast as you can!

WEBSTER *(placidly).* You've brought me a

long way, neighbor, to tell me you don't like my company.

JABEZ. I've brought you the devil's own way. I can see it all, now. He's after both of us—him and his damn collecting-box! Well, he can have me, if he likes—I don't say I relish it but I made the bargain. But you're the whole United States! He can't get you, Mr. Webster—he mustn't get you!

WEBSTER. I'm obliged to you, Neighbor Stone. It's kindly thought of. But there's a jug on the table and a case in hand. And I never left a jug or a case half-finished in my life. *(There is a knock at the door.* JABEZ *gives a cry.)* Ah, I thought your clock was a trifle slow, Neighbor Stone. Come in! (SCRATCH *enters from the night.)*

SCRATCH. Mr. Webster! This *is* a pleasure!

WEBSTER. Attorney of record for Jabez Stone. Might I ask your name?

SCRATCH. I've gone by a good many. Perhaps Scratch will do for the evening. I'm often called that in these regions. May I? *(He sits at the table and pours a drink from the jug. The liquor steams as it pours into the glass while* JABEZ *watches, terrified.* SCRATCH *grins, toasting* WEBSTER *and* JABEZ *silently in the liquor. Then he becomes businesslike. To* WEBSTER.) And now I call upon you, as a law-abiding citizen, to assist me in taking possession of my property.

WEBSTER. Not so fast, Mr. Scratch. Produce your evidence, if you have it. (SCRATCH *takes out a black pocketbook and examines papers.)*

SCRATCH. Slattery—Stanley—Stone. *(Takes out a deed)* There, Mr. Webster. All open and aboveboard and in due and legal form. Our firm has its reputation to consider—we deal only in the one way.

WEBSTER *(taking deed and looking it over).* H'm. This appears—I say, it appears—to be properly drawn. But, of course, we contest the signature. *(Tosses it back, contemptuously)*

SCRATCH *(suddenly turning on* JABEZ *and shoot-*

ing a finger at him). Is that your signature?

JABEZ *(wearily).* You know damn well it is.

WEBSTER *(angrily).* Keep quiet, Stone. *(To* SCRATCH) But that is a minor matter. This precious document isn't worth the paper it's written on. The law permits no traffic in human flesh.

SCRATCH. Oh, my dear Mr. Webster! Courts in every state in the Union have held that human flesh is property and recoverable. Read your Fugitive Slave Act. Or, shall I cite Brander versus McRae?

WEBSTER. But, in the case of the State of Maryland versus Four Barrels of Bourbon—

SCRATCH. That was overruled, as you know, sir. North Carolina versus Jenkins and Co.

WEBSTER *(unwillingly).* You seem to have an excellent acquaintance with the law, sir.

SCRATCH. Sir, that is no fault of mine. Where I come from, we have always gotten the pick of the Bar.

WEBSTER *(changing his note, heartily).* Well, come now, sir. There's no need to make hay and oats of a trifling matter when we're both sensible men. Surely we can settle this little difficulty out of court. My client is quite prepared to offer a compromise. (SCRATCH *smiles.)* A very substantial compromise. (SCRATCH *smiles more broadly, slowly shaking his head.)* Hang it, man, we offer ten thousand dollars! (SCRATCH *signs "No.")* Twenty thousand —thirty—name your figure! I'll raise it if I have to mortgage Marshfield!

SCRATCH. Quite useless, Mr. Webster. There is only one thing I want from you—the execution of my contract.

WEBSTER. But this is absurd. Mr. Stone is now a State Senator. The property has greatly increased in value!

SCRATCH. The principle of *caveat emptor*[8] still

---

8. *caveat emptor* *(Latin)*, a principle of commerce meaning, "Let the buyer beware," or, the buyer takes the risk of quality upon him- or herself

holds, Mr. Webster. *(He yawns and looks at the clock.)* And now, if you have no further arguments to adduce—I'm rather pressed for time—*(He rises briskly as if to take* JABEZ *into custody.)*

WEBSTER *(thundering).* Pressed or not, you shall not have this man. Mr. Stone is an American citizen and no American citizen may be forced into the service of a foreign prince. We fought England for that, in '12, and we'll fight all hell for it again!

SCRATCH. Foreign? And who calls me a foreigner?

WEBSTER. Well, I never yet heard of the dev—of your claiming American citizenship!

SCRATCH. And who with better right? When the first wrong was done to the first Indian, I was there. When the first slaver put out for the Congo, I stood on her deck. Am I not in your books and stories and beliefs, from the first settlements on? Am I not spoken of, still, in every church in New England? 'Tis true, the North claims me for a Southerner and the South for a Northerner, but I am neither. I am merely an honest American like yourself—and of the best descent—for, to tell the truth, Mr. Webster, though I don't like to boast of it, my name is older in the country than yours.

WEBSTER. Aha! Then I stand on the Constitution! I demand a trial for my client!

SCRATCH. The case is hardly one for an ordinary jury—and indeed, the lateness of hour—

WEBSTER. Let it be any court you choose, so it is an American judge and an American jury. Let it be the quick or the dead, I'll abide the issue.

SCRATCH. The quick or the dead! You have said it!

(He points his finger at the place where THE JURY *is to appear. There is a clap of thunder and a flash of light. The stage blacks out completely. All that can be seen is the face of* SCRATCH, *lit with a ghastly green light as he recites the invocation that summons* THE JURY. *As, one by one, the important jurymen are mentioned, they appear.)*

I summon the jury Mr. Webster demands.
From churchyard mould and gallows grave,
Brimstone pit and burning gulf,
I summon them!
Dastard, liar, scoundrel, knave,
I summon them! Appear!
There's Simon Girty, the renegade,
The haunter of the forest glade
Who joined with Indian and wolf
To hunt the pioneer.
The stains upon his hunting-shirt
Are not the blood of the deer.
There's Walter Butler, the loyalist,
Who carried a firebrand in his fist
Of massacre and shame.
King Philip's eye is wild and bright.
They slew him in the great Swamp Fight,
But still, with terror and affright,
The land recalls his name.
Blackbeard Teach, the pirate fell,
Smeet the strangler, hot from hell,
Dale, who broke men on the wheel,
Morton, of the tarnished steel,
I summon them, I summon them
From their tormented flame!
Quick or dead, quick or dead,
Broken heart and bitter head,
True Americans, each one,
Traitor and disloyal son,
Cankered earth and twisted tree,
Outcasts of eternity,
Twelve great sinners, tried and true,
For the work they are to do!
I summon them, I summon them!
Appear, appear, appear!

(The jury has now taken its place in the box—
WALTER BUTLER *in the place of foreman. They are eerily lit and so made up as to suggest the unearthly. They sit stiffly in their box. At first, when one moves, all move, in stylized gestures. It is not till the end of* WEBSTER's *speech that they begin to show any trace of humanity. They speak rhythmically, and, at first, in low, eerie voices.)*

JABEZ *(seeing them, horrified).* A jury of the dead!

JURY. Of the dead!

JABEZ. A jury of the damned!

JURY. Of the damned!

SCRATCH. Are you content with the jury, Mr. Webster?

WEBSTER. Quite content. Though I miss General Arnold from the company.

SCRATCH. Benedict Arnold is engaged upon other business. Ah, you asked for a justice, I believe. *(He points his finger and* JUSTICE HATHORNE, *a tall, lean, terrifying Puritan, appears, followed by his* CLERK.) Justice Hathorne is a jurist of experience. He presided at the Salem witch trials. There were others who repented of the business later. But not he, not he!

HATHORNE. Repent of such notable wonders and undertakings? Nay, hang them, hang them all! *(He takes his place on the bench.* THE CLERK, *an ominous little man with claw-like hands, takes his place. The room has now been transformed into a courtroom.)*

CLERK *(in a gabble of ritual).* Oyes, oyes, oyes. All ye who have business with this honorable court of special session this night, step forward!

HATHORNE *(with gavel).* Call the first case.

CLERK. The World, the Flesh, and the Devil versus Jabez Stone.

HATHORNE. Who appears for the plaintiff?

SCRATCH. I, Your Honor.

HATHORNE. And for the defendant?

WEBSTER. I.

JURY. The case—the case—he'll have little luck with this case.

HATHORNE. The case will proceed.

WEBSTER. Your Honor, I move to dismiss this case on the grounds of improper jurisdiction.

HATHORNE. Motion denied.

WEBSTER. On the grounds of insufficient evidence.

HATHORNE. Motion denied.

JURY. Motion denied—denied. Motion denied.

WEBSTER. I will take an exception.

HATHORNE. There are no exceptions in his court.

JURY. No exceptions—no exceptions in this court. It's a bad case, Daniel Webster—a losing case.

WEBSTER. Your Honor—

HATHORNE. The prosecution will proceed—

SCRATCH. Your Honor—gentlemen of the jury. This is a plain, straightforward case. It need not detain us long.

JURY. Detain us long—it will not detain us long.

SCRATCH. It concerns one thing alone—the transference, barter, and sale of a certain piece of property, to wit, his soul, by Jabez Stone, farmer, of Cross Corners, New Hampshire. That transference, barter, or sale is attested by a deed. I offer that deed in evidence and mark it Exhibit A.

WEBSTER. I object.

HATHORNE. Objection denied. Mark it Exhibit A.

(SCRATCH hands the deed—an ominous and impressive document—to THE CLERK, who hands it to HATHORNE. HATHORNE hands it back to THE CLERK, who stamps it. All very fast and with mechanical gestures.)

JURY. Exhibit A—mark it Exhibit A. *(SCRATCH takes the deed from THE CLERK and offers it to THE JURY, who pass it rapidly among them,* *hardly looking at it, and hand it back to* SCRATCH.) We know the deed—the deed —it burns in our fingers—we do not have to see the deed. It's a losing case.

SCRATCH. It offers incontestable evidence of the truth of the prosecution's claim. I shall now call Jabez Stone to the witness stand.

JURY *(hungrily).* Jabez Stone to the witness stand, Jabez Stone. He's a fine, fat fellow, Jabez Stone. He'll fry like a batter-cake, once we get him where we want him.

WEBSTER. Your Honor, I move that this jury be discharged for flagrant and open bias!

HATHORNE. Motion denied.

WEBSTER. Exception.

HATHORNE. Exception denied.

JURY. His motion's always denied. He thinks himself smart and clever—lawyer Webster. But his motion's always denied.

WEBSTER. Your Honor! *(He chokes with anger.)*

CLERK *(advancing).* Jabez Stone to the witness stand!

JURY. Jabez Stone—Jabez Stone.

(WEBSTER gives JABEZ an encouraging pat on the back, and JABEZ takes his place in the witness stand, very scared.)

CLERK *(offering a black book).* Do you solemnly swear—testify—so help you—and it's no good for we don't care what you testify?

JABEZ. I do.

SCRATCH. What's your name?

JABEZ. Jabez Stone.

SCRATCH. Occupation?

JABEZ. Farmer.

SCRATCH. Residence?

JABEZ. Cross Corners, New Hampshire.

(These three questions are very fast and mechanical on the part of SCRATCH. He is absolutely sure of victory and just going through a form.)

JURY. A farmer—he'll farm in hell—we'll see that he farms in hell.

SCRATCH. Now, Jabez Stone, answer me. You'd better, you know. You haven't got a chance and there'll be a cooler place by the fire for you.

WEBSTER. I protest! This is intimidation! This mocks all justice!

HATHORNE. The protest is irrelevant, incompetent, and immaterial. We have our own justice. The protest is denied.

JURY. Irrelevant, incompetent, and immaterial—we have our own justice—oh, ho, Daniel Webster! *(The jury's eyes fix upon* WEBSTER *for an instant, hungrily.)*

SCRATCH. Did you or did you not sign this document?

JABEZ. Oh, I signed it! You know I signed it. And, if I have to go to hell for it, I'll go! *(A sigh sweeps over the jury.)*

JURY. One of us—one of us now—we'll save a place by the fire for you, Jabez Stone.

SCRATCH. The prosecution rests.

HATHORNE. Remove the prisoner.

WEBSTER. But I wish to cross-examine—I wish to prove—

HATHORNE. There will be no cross-examination. We have our own justice. You may speak, if you like. But be brief.

JURY. Brief—be very brief—we're weary of earth—incompetent, irrelevant, and immaterial—they say he's a smart man, Webster, but he's lost his case tonight—be very brief—we have our own justice here.

(WEBSTER stares around him like a baited bull. Can't find words.)

MARY'S VOICE *(from offstage).* Set me as a seal upon thy heart, as a seal upon thine arm, for love is strong as death—

JURY *(loudly).* A seal!—ha, ha—a burning seal!

MARY'S VOICE. Love is strong—

JURY *(drowning her out).* Death is stronger than love. Set the seal upon Daniel Webster—the burning seal of the lost. Make him one of us—one of the damned—one with Jabez Stone!

(THE JURY's *eyes all fix upon* WEBSTER. THE CLERK *advances as if to take him into custody. But* WEBSTER *silences them all with a great gesture.*)

WEBSTER. Be still!

I was going to thunder and roar. I shall not do that.

I was going to denounce and defy. I shall not do that.

You have judged this man already with your abominable justice. See that you defend it.

For I shall not speak of this man.

You are demons now, but once you were men. I shall speak to every one of you.

Of common things I speak, of small things and common.

The freshness of morning to the young, the taste of food to the hungry, the day's toil, the rest by the fire, the quiet sleep.

These are good things.

But without freedom they sicken, without freedom they are nothing.

Freedom is the bread and the morning and the risen sun.

It was for freedom we came in the boats and the ships. It was for freedom we came.

It has been a long journey, a hard one, a bitter one.

But, out of the wrong and the right, the sufferings and the starvations, there is a new thing, a free thing.

The traitors in their treachery, the wise in their wisdom, the valiant in their courage—all, all have played a part.

It may not be denied in hell nor shall hell prevail against it.

Have you forgotten this? (*He turns to* THE JURY.) Have you forgotten the forest?

GIRTY (*as in a dream*). The forest, the rustle of the forest, the free forest.

WEBSTER (*to* KING PHILIP). Have you forgotten your lost nation?

KING PHILIP. My lost nation—my fires in the wood—my warriors.

WEBSTER (*to* TEACH). Have you forgotten the sea and the way of ships?

TEACH. The sea—and the swift ships sailing—the blue sea.

JURY. Forgotten—remembered—forgotten yet remembered.

WEBSTER. You were men once. Have you forgotten?

JURY. We were men once. We have not thought of it nor remembered. But we were men.

WEBSTER.

Now here is this man with good and evil in his heart.

Do you know him? He is your brother. Will you take the law of the oppressor and bind him down?

It is not for him that I speak. It is for all of you.

There is sadness in being a man but it is a proud thing, too.

There is failure and despair on the journey—the endless journey of mankind.

We are tricked and trapped—we stumble into the pit—but, out of the pit, we rise again.

No demon that was ever foaled can know the inwardness of that—only men—bewildered men.

They have broken freedom with their hands and cast her out from the nations—yet shall she live while man lives.

She shall live in the blood and the heart—she shall live in the earth of this country—she shall not be broken.

When the whips of the oppressors are broken and their names forgotten and destroyed,

I see you, mighty, shining, liberty, liberty! I see free men walking and talking under a free star.

God save the United States and the men who have made her free.

The defense rests.

JURY (*exultantly*). We were men—we were free—we were men—we have not forgotten—our children—our children shall follow and be free.

HATHORNE (*rapping with gavel*). The jury will retire to consider its verdict.

BUTLER (*rising*). There is no need. The jury has heard Mr. Webster. We find for the defendant, Jabez Stone!

JURY. Not guilty!

SCRATCH (*in a screech, rushing forward*). But, Your Honor—

(*But, even as he does so, there is a flash and a thunderclap, the stage blacks out again, and when the lights come on,* JUDGE *and* JURY *are gone. The yellow light of dawn lights the windows.*)

JABEZ. They're gone and it's morning—Mary, Mary!

MARY (*in doorway*). My love—my dear.

(*She rushes to him. Meanwhile* SCRATCH *has been collecting his papers and trying to sneak out. But* WEBSTER *catches him.*)

WEBSTER. Just a minute, Mr. Scratch. I'll have that paper first, if you please. (*He takes the deed and tears it.*) And, now, sir, I'll have *you!*

SCRATCH. Come, come, Mr. Webster. This sort of thing is ridic—ouch—is ridiculous. If you're worried about the costs of the case, naturally, I'd be glad to pay.

WEBSTER. And so you shall! First of all, you'll promise and covenant[9] never to bother Jabez Stone or any other New Hampshire man from now till doomsday. For any hell we want to raise in this state, we can raise ourselves, without any help from you.

SCRATCH. Ouch! Well, they never did run very big to the barrel but—ouch—I agree!

WEBSTER. See you keep to the bargain! And then—well, I've got a ram named Goliath.

He can butt through an iron door. I'd like to turn you loose in his field and see what he could do to you. (SCRATCH *trembles.*) But that would be hard on the ram. So we'll just call in the neighbors and give you a shivaree.[10]

SCRATCH. Mr. Webster—please—oh—

WEBSTER. Neighbors! Neighbors! Come in and see what a long-barrelled, slab-sided, lantern-jawed, fortune-telling note-shaver I've got by the scruff of the neck! Bring on your kettles and your pans! (*A noise and murmur outside*) Bring on your muskets and your flails!

JABEZ. We'll drive him out of New Hampshire!

MARY. We'll drive old Scratch away!

(THE CROWD *rushes in, with muskets, flails, brooms, etc. They pursue* SCRATCH *around the stage, chanting.*)

THE CROWD.
We'll drive him out of New Hampshire!
We'll drive old Scratch away!
Forever and a day, boys,
Forever and a day!

(*They finally catch* SCRATCH *between two of them and fling him out of the door.*)

A MAN. Three cheers for Dan'l Webster!

ANOTHER MAN. Three cheers for Daniel Webster! He's licked the devil!

WEBSTER (*moving to center stage, and joining* JABEZ'*s hands and* MARY'*s*). And whom God hath joined let no man put asunder. (*He kisses* MARY *and turns, dusting his hands.*) Well, that job's done. I hope there's pie for breakfast, neighbor Stone. (*And, as some of the women, dancing, bring in pies from the kitchen*)

THE CURTAIN FALLS

---

9. covenant, pledge
10. shivaree, a noisy, mock serenade

Discussing and Interpreting

The Devil and Daniel Webster

Play Analysis

1. In the original story, Jabez Stone is a married man with two children. Why do you think he is presented as a newlywed in the play?
2. Compare the language in *The Devil and Daniel Webster* to a more contemporary play, such as *Stand and Deliver*. How are they different? Are they alike in any way?
3. What does Scratch mean when he says, " ... the North claims me for a Southerner and the South for a Northerner..."?
4. Describe how you would create the presence of the moth in the play.
5. **Thematic Connection: And Justice for All** Which of Daniel Webster's courtroom arguments seems the most persuasive to you? Why?

Literary Skill: Create a Character

"You are demons now, but once you were men." So says Daniel Webster to Jabez Stone's jury of the dead. In Christopher Marlowe's play *The Tragical History of Doctor Faustus,* the scholar Faustus also faces demons who represent the worst in men: the Seven Deadly Sins. They are Pride, Covetousness (or Greed), Wrath (or Anger), Envy, Gluttony, Sloth, and Lechery. They appear "in their proper shapes," and give short, bawdy descriptions of themselves in the language and style of the sixteenth century. Like the jury in *The Devil and Daniel Webster,* the Deadly Sins are very colorful characters.

Create your own persona for one of the Seven Deadly Sins. Choose any one and write a short monologue. Offer personal information—where you were born, what you enjoy, plans for the future—the more imaginative the better. Think in terms of how this Deadly Sin would speak, move, gesture, and dress. Then read your monologue to the class.

Performance Element: Design-Team Collaboration

Get together with two classmates and take the roles of sound, lighting, and design engineers. Choose one of your "Seven Deadly Sins" monologues and discuss ideas for accompanying music or sound effects, lighting, and sets or props needed. Write up your plans for the scene and present it to the class.

Setting the Stage for

Animal Farm

from the novel by George Orwell
adapted for the stage by Nelson Bond

Creating Context:
George Orwell and His Politics

George Orwell was an English citizen born in the Bengal region of eastern India, in 1903. His real name was Eric Blair. As a youngster, Orwell attended boarding school in England. Before his twentieth birthday, he enlisted in the Indian Imperial Police and served in Burma for five years. In 1936, Orwell fought with the Republicans in the Spanish Civil War. Here he saw propaganda and the distortion of facts used by both Left and Right as instruments of war. Orwell believed that reinventing historical facts would create a worse situation for mankind than any ideological war could.

Like Orwell's other famous novel, *Nineteen Eighty-Four*, the story of intrusive government control over individuals, *Animal Farm* tells a very political story. It has long been considered an attack on Communism in general and Stalinism in particular. In the 1940s, when Orwell wrote *Animal Farm*, western sympathy was with Stalin's Soviet Union due to the Soviet Army's heroic stand against the Nazis of Germany. During World War II, the Red Army courageously fought Germany to a standstill. It was difficult, therefore, for anyone to write critically about the Soviet Union, despite Stalin's brutal purges and the inhumanity of the Soviet police state. Orwell, however, was convinced that the destruction of "the Soviet myth" was essential. He wrote *Animal Farm* in 1943, during the height of the war, in an attempt to enlighten people to the realities of the Communist state.

George Orwell   Publishers at first rejected *Animal Farm*, in which the two main characters, Napoleon and Snowball, are large pigs who represent Stalin and his second in command, Leon Trotsky. The book was not published until well after the end of the war. In America in 1946, the book sold 600,000 copies. It has never gone out of print.

Animal Farm has been called a modern fable "with a sting." As you read the play, try to identify the aspects that make it a fable.

As a Reader: Understanding the Fable

Traditionally, fables have been stories in which a lesson—moral, social, or political—is taught. The true fable aims at the improvement of human conduct, and often does so by giving speech and emotion to animals. *Animal Farm* is written in the form of a fable, with farm animals facing life-and-death issues. The characters in Orwell's fable, however, are more complex than those in a traditional fable. Compare Orwell's narration at the left to the adaptation by Nelson Bond. In terms of characterization, what does the play script do that the novel does not?

from Page · · · · · · **to Stage**

With some difficulty (for it was not easy for a pig to balance himself on a ladder) Snowball climbed up and set to work, with Squealer a few rungs below him holding the paint-pot. The Commandments were written on the tarred wall in great white letters that could be read thirty yards away. They ran thus:

THE SEVEN COMMANDMENTS

Whatever goes upon two legs is an enemy.
Whatever goes upon four legs, or has wings, is a friend.
No animal shall wear clothes.
No animal shall sleep in a bed.
No animal shall drink alcohol.
No animal shall kill another animal.
All animals are equal.

It was very neatly written, and except that "friend" was written "freind" and one of the "S's" was the wrong way round, the spelling was correct all the way through. Snowball read it aloud for the benefit of all the others.

from Animal Farm *by George Orwell*

SNOWBALL. With some difficulty (for it is not easy for a pig to balance himself on a ladder) Snowball climbed up and set to work. The Commandments were written on the wall in great white letters.

CLOVER. Whatever goes upon two legs is an enemy.

BOXER. Whatever goes upon four legs, or has wings, is a friend.

NAPOLEON. No animal shall wear clothes.

MURIEL. No animal shall sleep in a bed.

CAT. No animal shall drink alcohol.

SNOWBALL. No animal shall kill any other animal.

SQUEALER. All animals are equal.

NARRATOR. It was all very neatly written… except that one of the S's was the wrong way round. Snowball read it aloud. All the animals nodded in complete agreement, and the cleverer ones at once began to learn the Commandments by heart.

from Animal Farm *adapted by Nelson Bond*

As a Director: Character Interpretation

The play *Animal Farm* is presented as Readers Theatre, with actors sitting on stools and reading from scripts. It is the director's responsibility to make sure that the actors understand their roles. There is very little in the way of sets or costuming to help them establish character. As you read, think about how a director might help the actors express their characters through words alone.

Animal Farm

A Fable in Two Acts

Time

The present

The Characters

Stool No. 1   PRINCIPAL NARRATOR /   JONES, a farmer

Stool No. 2   SNOWBALL, a pig / BENJAMIN, a donkey

Stool No. 3   SQUEALER, a pig / MOSES, a raven /   FREDERICK, a farmer

Stool No. 4   CLOVER, a horse / CAT

Stool No. 5   BOXER, a horse / PILKINGTON, a farmer

Stool No. 6   MAJOR, a boar / NAPOLEON, a pig

Stool No. 7   MOLLIE, a horse / MURIEL, a goat

Setting

A farm in England

Note: In addition to their assigned roles above, readers may also serve as NARRATOR, thus aiding the PRINCIPAL NARRATOR (Stool No. 1).

ACT 1

As the house lights lower, Music Cue No. 1 begins. After the music has established, the curtains part on an empty stage, dimly illuminated by the holding lights on the reading stands. The six readers occupying STOOLS 2 through 7 enter and seat themselves. When they are seated, the PRINCIPAL NARRATOR (Stool 1) enters, moves swiftly to his stool and turns on his reading light. As the music ends, he begins reading. (Numbers in front of character names are the stool numbers.)

1 JONES. Mr. Jones, of the Manor Farm, was drunk! He lurched across the yard, kicked off his boots at the back door, drew himself a last glass of beer from the barrel in the scullery, and made his way up to bed.

4 NARRATOR. As soon as the light went out there was a stirring and a fluttering all through the farm buildings.

6 MAJOR. Word had gone round that old Major, the prize boar, had had a strange dream, and wished to communicate it to the other animals as soon as Mr. Jones was safely out of the way.

5 NARRATOR. Old Major was so highly regarded that everyone was quite ready to lose an hour's sleep in order to hear what he had to say.

2 NARRATOR. First came the dogs, then the

pigs, who settled down in the straw immediately in front of the platform.

7 NARRATOR. The hens perched themselves on the windowsills, the pigeons fluttered up to the rafters, the sheep and cows lay down behind the pigs and began to chew the cud.

3 NARRATOR. The two cart-horses, Boxer and Clover, came in together, setting down their vast, hairy hoofs with great care, lest there should be some small animal concealed in the straw.

4 CLOVER. Clover was a stout, motherly mare who had never quite got back her figure after her fourth foal.

5 BOXER. Boxer was an enormous beast nearly eighteen hands high, as strong as any two ordinary horses put together. He was not of first-rate intelligence, but he was universally respected for his steadiness of character and tremendous powers of work.

4 NARRATOR. After the horses came Muriel, the goat, and Benjamin, the donkey. Benjamin was the oldest animal on the farm … and the worst tempered. He seldom talked, and when he did it was usually to make some cynical remark, such as:

2 BENJAMIN. God gave me a tail to keep the flies off. But I'd rather have had no tail … and no flies!

7 MOLLIE. At the last moment, Mollie, the foolish, pretty white mare who drew Mr. Jones's trap, came mincing daintily in, flirting her mane to draw attention to the red ribbons it was plaited with.

1 NARRATOR. All the animals now being present, Major cleared his throat and began:

6 MAJOR. Comrades, you have heard about the strange dream I had last night. But I have something else to tell you about first.

I do not think, comrades, I shall be with you very much longer …

ALL. Oh, no, Major! No!

6 MAJOR (*over them*). And before I die, I feel it my duty to pass on to you such wisdom as I have acquired. I have had a long life, and think I understand the nature of life on this earth as well as any animal now living. It is about this I wish to speak to you. Now, comrades, what is the nature of this life of ours? Let us face it … our lives are miserable, laborious, and short. We are given just so much food as will keep the breath in our bodies, are forced to work to the last atom of our strength … and the moment our usefulness has come to an end, we are slaughtered with hideous cruelty.

2 BENJAMIN. Isn't this simply part of the order of nature?

4 CLOVER. Isn't it because this land is so poor?

6 MAJOR. No, comrades! A thousand times, no! This farm of ours would support a dozen horses, twenty cows, hundreds of sheep, in a comfort and dignity almost beyond our imagining!

3 SQUEALER. Then why do we continue in this miserable condition?

6 MAJOR. Because the produce of our labor is stolen from us. Comrades, the answer to all of our problems lies in a single word … Man! Man is the only creature that consumes without producing.

7 MURIEL. True! He does not give milk …

4 CLOVER. He does not lay eggs …

5 BOXER. He is too weak to pull a plough …

6 MAJOR. Yet he is the lord of all the animals. He sets us to work, gives back the bare minimum that will keep us from starving … and keeps the rest for himself.

5 BOXER. *Our* labor tills the soil.

2 BENJAMIN. *Our* dung fertilizes it.

7 MOLLIE. Yet there is not one of us that owns more than his own skin!

6 MAJOR. Even the miserable lives we lead are not allowed to reach their natural span. No animal escapes the cruel knife in the end. You young porkers sitting in front of me … within a year, every one of you will scream your lives out at the block. To that horror we must all come … cows, pigs, hens, everyone!

ALL. No! No! Oh, no!

5 BOXER. Even the horses?

6 MAJOR. You, Boxer … the day those great muscles of yours lose their power, Jones will sell you to the knacker,[1] who will cut your throat and boil you down into glue.

4 CLOVER. What, then, must we do?

6 MAJOR. Why, work, night and day, body and soul, for the overthrow of the human race! That is my message to you, comrades. Rebellion!

ALL *(firmly)*. Rebellion! *(Uncertainly)* Rebellion?

6 MAJOR. Rebellion! Fix your eyes on that, comrades. Never listen when they tell you Man and the animals have a common interest. Man serves the interest of no creature except himself. Whatever goes on two legs is an enemy. Whatever goes on four legs, or has wings, is a friend.

ALL. All animals are friends! Down with Humanity!

6 MAJOR. And remember that in fighting Man we must not come to resemble him. No animal must ever live in a house, or sleep in a bed, or wear clothes, or drink alcohol, or smoke tobacco, or engage in trade. Above all, no animal must ever tyrannize over his own kind. Weak or strong, clever or simple, we are all brothers. No animal must ever kill any other animal. All animals are equal!

ALL. All animals are equal! All animals are brothers!

6 MAJOR. And now, comrades, I will tell you about my dream. It was a dream of the earth as it will be when Man has vanished. Many years ago, when I was a little pig, my mother used to sing an old song. Last night in my dream the words of that song came back … words sung by the animals of long ago, and lost to memory for generations. I will sing that song now, comrades. I am old, and my voice is hoarse. But when I have taught you the tune you can sing it better for yourselves. It is called …"Beasts of England."

(Music Cue No. 2. Sings.)

Beasts of England, beasts of Ireland,
Beasts of every land and clime,
Hearken to my joyful tidings
Of the golden future time.

1 AND 7 *(join in).*

Soon or late the day is coming
Tyrant Man shall be o'erthrown,
And the fruitful fields of England
Shall be trod by beasts alone.

4 AND 5 *(join in).*

Rings shall vanish from our noses,
And the harness from our back,
Bit and spur shall rust forever,
Cruel whips no more shall crack.

2 AND 3 *(join in).*

Bright will shine the fields of England,
Purer shall its waters be,
Sweeter yet shall blow the breezes
On the day that sets us free.

ALL.

Beasts of England, beasts of Ireland,
Beasts of every land and clime,
Hearken well and spread my tidings
Of the golden future time.

(all continue to hum softly under:)

---

1. knacker *(British)*, one who buys worn-out domestic animals for use as food, fertilizer, etc.

1 NARRATOR. Before Major had reached the end, even the stupidest of them had picked up the tune. The whole farm burst into "Beasts of England" in tremendous unison. The cows lowed it, the dogs whined it, the ducks quacked it. They were so delighted with the song that they might have continued singing all night. Unfortunately the uproar woke Mr. Jones, who sprang out of bed, seized the gun which stood in the corner of his bedroom, and let fly a charge of Number 6 shot into the darkness. The meeting broke up hurriedly!

(The music breaks off abruptly. After a pause we hear Music Cue No. 3, which fades under:)

7 NARRATOR. Old Major died early in March. During the next three months there was much secret activity. Major's speech had given the animals a completely new outlook on life. They did not know *when* the predicted Rebellion would take place, but they saw it was their duty to prepare for it.

1 NARRATOR. The work of organizing fell naturally on the pigs, who were generally recognized as being the cleverest of the animals. Pre-eminent among the pigs were two named Snowball and Napoleon.

6 NAPOLEON. Napoleon was a large, fierce-looking Berkshire pig with a reputation for getting his own way.

2 SNOWBALL. Snowball was a more vivacious pig, quicker in speech and more inventive …

6 NAPOLEON. … but not considered to have the same depth of character!

3 SQUEALER. All the other male pigs on the farm were porkers. The best known among them was a small, fat pig named Squealer … a brilliant talker, and very persuasive.

1 NARRATOR. These three elaborated old Major's teachings into a complete system of thought to which they gave the name Animalism. Several nights a week they held secret meetings in the barn and expounded the principles of Animalism to the others. At the beginning, they met with much stupidity and apathy.[2]

7 MOLLIE. We should be loyal to Mr. Jones. He's our Master!

4 CLOVER. Besides, he feeds us. If he were gone, wouldn't we starve to death?

2 BENJAMIN. Why should we care what happens after we're dead?

4 BOXER. If this Rebellion is going to happen anyway, what difference whether we work for it or not?

1 NARRATOR. The stupidest questions of all were asked by Mollie, the white mare.

7 MOLLIE *(to* NAPOLEON*)*. Will there still be sugar after the Rebellion?

6 NAPOLEON. You do not need sugar. You will have all the hay and oats you want.

7 MOLLIE. And shall I still be allowed to wear ribbons in my hair?

6 NAPOLEON. Comrade, those ribbons you are so devoted to are the badge of slavery. Can't you understand that liberty is worth more than ribbons?

1 NARRATOR. Mollie agreed, but she did not sound very convinced. The pigs had an even harder time attempting to counteract the lies put out by Moses, the raven. Moses, who was Mr. Jones's special pet, claimed to know of the existence of a mysterious country called …

3 MOSES *(raptly)*. Sugarcandy Mountain! Oh, Sugarcandy Mountain, brethren … that wondrous land to which all good animals go when they depart this vale of tears! It lies 'way up there in the sky, dearly beloved, a little distance beyond the clouds. On Sugarcandy Mountain clover is in season all year round … lump sugar and

---

2. apathy, disinterest; unconcern

linseed cake grow on the hedges. Oh, hallelujah, brethren … be joyous for the day when we shall all see Sugarcandy Mountain!

1 NARRATOR. The animals hated Moses because he did no work. But most of them believed in Sugarcandy Mountain, and the pigs had to argue very hard to persuade them there was no such place.

7 NARRATOR. The most faithful disciples were the two horses, Boxer and Clover. These two had great difficulty in thinking anything out for themselves. But once having accepted the pigs as their teachers, they absorbed everything they were told, and led the singing of "Beasts of England" with which the meetings always ended.

4 AND 5. All together, now! *(Sing)* Beasts of England, beasts of Ireland, beasts of every land and clime …

1 NARRATOR. Now, as it turned out, the Rebellion came about much earlier then anyone had expected. On Midsummer's Eve, Mr. Jones got so drunk that he went to sleep on the drawing-room sofa with a newspaper over his face. When evening came, the animals were still unfed.

4 CAT. At last they could stand it no longer. One of the cows broke in the door of the store shed, and all the animals began to help themselves from the bins.

1 JONES. Just then Mr. Jones woke up. The next moment, he and four of his men were in the store shed with whips, lashing out in all directions.

2 BENJAMIN. This was more than the hungry animals could bear. Though nothing of the kind had been planned, they flung themselves upon their tormentors.

1 JONES. Jones and his men suddenly found themselves being butted and kicked from all sides. This sudden uprising of creatures they were used to thrashing and maltreating frightened them almost out of their wits. They took to their heels. A minute later all five of them were in full flight down the road, with the animals crying after them:

ALL *(shout).* Get out! And *stay* out!

7 NARRATOR. And so, almost before the animals knew what was happening, the Rebellion had been successfully carried through. Jones was expelled, and the Manor Farm was theirs.

3 NARRATOR. Their first act was to wipe out the last traces of Jones's hated reign. The harness room was broken open. The bits, the nose rings, the cruel knives Mr. Jones had used to castrate the pigs and lambs, all were flung down the well.

6 NARRATOR. The reins, the halters, the blinkers, and the degrading nosebags were thrown on the rubbish fire. So were the whips.

1 NARRATOR. Snowball also threw onto the fire the ribbons with which the horses' manes and tails had been decorated on market days, explaining:

2 SNOWBALL. Ribbons should be considered as clothes, which are a mark of the human being. All animals should go naked.

5 BOXER. When Boxer heard this, he fetched the small straw hat he wore in summer to keep the flies out of his ears, and flung it on the fire with the rest.

7 NARRATOR. In a very little while the animals had destroyed everything that reminded them of Mr. Jones. Then they filed back to the farmhouse and halted outside the door.

2 SNOWBALL. After a moment, Snowball and Napoleon butted the door open and the animals entered. They tiptoed from room to room, gazing with a kind of awe at the unbelievable luxury … at the beds with their feather mattresses, the looking-glasses, the sofa made of horsehair, the

Brussels carpet, the lithograph of Queen Victoria over the drawing-room mantel piece.

7 MOLLIE. As they were coming down the stairs, Mollie was discovered to be missing. Going back, the others found her in the best bedroom. She had taken a piece of blue ribbon from Mrs. Jones's dressing table, and was holding it against her shoulder, admiring herself in the glass.

1 NARRATOR. The others reproached her sharply and went outside. Some hams hanging in the kitchen were taken out for burial. A unanimous resolution was passed on the spot that the farmhouse should be preserved as a museum. All agreed that no animal must ever live there.

7 NARRATOR. The next day Snowball and Napoleon called them all together again and revealed that during the past three months the pigs had taught themselves to read and write.

6 NAPOLEON. Napoleon sent for pots of paint, and led the way to the gate that gave onto the main road.

2 SNOWBALL. Snowball painted out the name *Manor Farm* from the top bar of the gate, and in its place painted *Animal Farm.*

7 NARRATOR. After this, they went back to the farm buildings, where Snowball and Napoleon set a ladder against the end wall of the big barn. They explained that the pigs had succeeded in reducing the principles of Animalism to Seven Commandments. These would now be inscribed on the wall, and would form an unalterable law by which all the animals on Animal Farm must live forever after.

2 SNOWBALL. With some difficulty (for it is not easy for a pig to balance himself on a ladder) Snowball climbed up and set to work. The Commandments were written on the wall in great white letters.

4 CLOVER. Whatever goes upon two legs is an enemy.

5 BOXER. Whatever goes upon four legs, or has wings, is a friend.

6 NAPOLEON. No animal shall wear clothes.

7 MURIEL. No animal shall sleep in a bed.

4 CAT. No animal shall drink alcohol.

2 SNOWBALL. No animal shall kill any other animal.

3 SQUEALER. All animals are equal.

7 NARRATOR. It was all very neatly written … except that one of the *S*'s was the wrong way round. Snowball read it aloud. All the animals nodded in complete agreement, and the cleverer ones at once began to learn the Commandments by heart.

1 NARRATOR. But at this moment the three cows set up a loud lowing. They had not been milked for hours, and their udders were bursting. The pigs sent for buckets, and milked the cows fairly successfully. Soon there were five buckets of frothing, creamy milk, at which many of the animals looked with considerable interest.

4 CAT. What's going to happen to all that milk?

5 BOXER. Jones used to mix some of it in our mash.

6 NAPOLEON. Never mind the milk, comrades. The harvest is more important. Comrade Snowball will lead the way. I shall follow in a few minutes. Forward, comrades! The hay is waiting!

1 NARRATOR. So the animals trooped down to the hayfield to begin the harvest. And when they came back in the evening, it was noticed that the milk had disappeared.

(Music Cue No. 4)

7 NARRATOR. How they toiled and sweated to get the hay in! But their efforts were rewarded, for the harvest was an even bigger success than they had hoped.

6 NAPOLEON. The work was hard. The implements had been designed for human beings, and no animal was able to use any tool that involved standing on his hind legs. But the pigs were so clever that they could think of a way around every difficulty.

4 CLOVER. The pigs did not actually work, but supervised the others. Boxer and Clover would harness themselves to the cutter or horse-rake (no bits or reins were needed, of course), and tramp steadily around and around the field with a pig walking beside and calling out:

3 SQUEALER. Gee there, comrade! Whooa there, comrade!

7 NARRATOR. Every animal down to the humblest worked. Even the ducks and hens toiled to and fro carrying tiny wisps of hay in their beaks. In the end, they finished the harvest in two days less time than it had usually taken Jones and his men. Moreover, it was the biggest harvest the farm had ever seen.

1 NARRATOR. All that summer the work of the farm went like clockwork. The animals were happy as they had never conceived it possible to be. Every mouthful of food was a positive pleasure now that it was truly their own food, produced by themselves and for themselves.

5 BOXER. Boxer was the admiration of everybody. From morning to night he was always at the spot where the work was hardest. He had made arrangements with one of the cockerels to call him in the mornings half an hour earlier than anyone else, and would labor at whatever seemed most needed before the regular day's work began. His personal motto was, "I will work harder!"

7 MOLLIE. Nobody shirked … or almost nobody. Mollie would vanish for hours, then reappear at mealtimes. But she always had such excellent excuses that it was impossible not to believe in her good intentions.

1 NARRATOR. Only old Benjamin, the donkey, seemed quite unchanged. He did his work in the same slow, obstinate way as in Jones's time, never shirking, and never volunteering for extra work, either. About the Rebellion he would express no opinion. When asked whether he was not happier now that Jones was gone, he would only say cryptically:

2 BENJAMIN. Nobody's ever seen a dead donkey!

7 NARRATOR. On Sundays all the animals trooped into the big barn for a general assembly. Here the work of the coming week was planned, and resolutions were debated. It was always the pigs who put forward the resolutions. The other animals could not think of any. Snowball and Napoleon were by far the most active in the debates. But it was noticed that whatever suggestion either of them made, the other could be counted on to oppose it.

2 SNOWBALL. Snowball busied himself organizing committees. He formed the Egg Production Committee for the hens, the Clean Tails Committee for the cows, and the Wild Comrades Re-education Committee. The object of this last was to tame the rats and rabbits, but the project broke down almost immediately.

4 CAT. The cat joined the Re-education Committee, and was very active in it … for a while. She was seen one day sitting on a roof and talking to some sparrows who were just out of her reach. She was telling them that all animals were now comrades, and that any sparrow who chose could come and perch on her paw. But the sparrows kept their distance.

1 NARRATOR. By autumn, almost every animal on the farm was literate to some degree. The pigs could read and write perfectly. The dogs learned to read fairly well. Muriel, the goat, could read somewhat better than the dogs. Benjamin could read as well as any pig, but never exercised his faculty. He said:

2 BENJAMIN. Far as I can see, there's nothing worth reading!

4 CLOVER. Clover learned the whole alphabet, but she could never put words together.

5 BOXER. Boxer couldn't get beyond the letter *D*. He would trace out *A, B, C, D* in the dust with his hoof, then stand staring at the letters, trying with all his might to remember what came next. On several occasions he did learn *E, F, G, H*. But by the time he knew them, he had forgotten *A, B, C* and *D*.

7 MOLLIE. Mollie refused to learn any but the letters which spelt her own name. She would form these very neatly out of pieces of twig, then decorate them with a flower or two and walk around them, admiring them.

1 NARRATOR. None of the other animals could get farther than the letter *A*. It was also found that the stupider animals, such as the sheep, hens, and ducks, were unable to learn the Seven Commandments by heart. After much thought, Snowball solved this problem.

2 SNOWBALL. Comrades, for your benefit I have reduced the Seven Commandments to a single maxim. Listen carefully. "Four legs good; two legs bad. Four legs good; two legs bad." Now, repeat after me. Four legs good …

ALL. Four legs good …

2 SNOWBALL. Two legs bad.

ALL. Two legs bad.

2 SNOWBALL. Excellent! Now, all together once more!

ALL. Four legs …

2 SNOWBALL (*prompting*). Good.

ALL. Good. Two legs …

2 SNOWBALL. Bad.

ALL. Two legs bad.

2 SNOWBALL. Now, once again.

ALL (*with increasing confidence*). Four legs, good; two legs, bad. Four legs, good; two legs, bad.

1 NARRATOR. This maxim was inscribed on the wall of the barn above the Seven Commandments. Once they had it by heart, the sheep developed a great liking for the maxim, and often as they lay in the field would all start bleating:

ALL. Four legs good; two legs bad. Four legs good; two legs baaad. Four legs good; two legs baaaaad!

1 NARRATOR (*up, over them*). And keep it up for hours on end!

6 NAPOLEON. Napoleon took no interest in Snowball's committees. He said education of the young was more important. Two farm dogs had whelped soon after the harvest, giving birth to nine sturdy puppies. As soon as they were weaned, Napoleon took them, saying he would make himself responsible for their education. He took them to a loft over the harness room, and there kept them in such seclusion that the rest of the animals quite forgot their existence.

1 NARRATOR. The mystery of where the milk went to was soon cleared up. It was mixed every day into the pigs' mash. The early apples were now ripening, and the orchard was littered with windfalls. The animals had assumed these would be shared equally. One day, however, the order went forth that all windfalls were to be brought to the harness-room for the use of the pigs. At this, some of the other animals murmured. Squealer was sent to make the necessary explanations.

3 SQUEALER. Comrades, surely you do not imagine we pigs are doing this in a spirit of selfishness or privilege? Many of us actually *dislike* milk and apples! Our sole object is to preserve our health. Milk and apples … this has been proven by Science, comrades! … contain substances absolutely necessary to the well-being of a pig. We pigs are brain workers. The whole management of this farm depends on us. It is for *your* sake we drink that milk and eat those apples. Do you know what would happen if we pigs failed in our duty? Jones would come back! Surely, comrades, there is no one among you who wants to see Jones come back?

7 NARRATOR. Now, if there was one thing the animals were completely certain of, it was that they did not want Jones back. When it was put to them in this light they had no more to say. So it was agreed that the milk and the windfall apples … and also the main crop of apples when they ripened … should be reserved for the pigs alone.

(Music Cue No. 5)

2 SNOWBALL. Every day Snowball and Napoleon sent out flights of pigeons to tell animals on neighboring farms the story of the Rebellion and teach them "Beasts of England."

1 JONES. Most of this time Mr. Jones spent sitting in the taproom of the Red Lion Inn, complaining to anyone who would listen of the monstrous injustice he had suffered. The other farmers didn't give him much help. Each was secretly wondering how he could turn Jones's misfortune to his own advantage.

5 PILKINGTON. The owners of the two farms which adjoined Animal Farm were on permanently bad terms. One of the farms, named Foxwood, was a large, neglected, old-fashioned place much overgrown by woodland. Its owner, Mr. Pilkington, was an easy-going gentleman farmer who spent most of his time fishing or hunting.

3 FREDERICK. The other farm, Pinchfield, was smaller and better kept. Its owner was a Mr. Frederick, a tough, shrewd man with a name for driving hard bargains.

1 NARRATOR. These two disliked each other so much that it was difficult for them to come to any agreement. But they were both thoroughly frightened by the rebellion on Animal Farm, and anxious to prevent their own animals from learning too much about it.

7 NARRATOR. At first they pretended to scorn the idea of animals managing a farm for themselves. The whole thing would be over in a fortnight, they said. They put it about that the animals were perpetually fighting amongst themselves, and were also rapidly starving to death. But as time passed, and the animals had evidently not starved to death, Frederick and Pilkington changed their tune and began to talk about the terrible wickedness that flourished on Animal Farm. It was given out that the animals there practised cannibalism, tortured one another with red-hot horseshoes … and had their females in common!

4 NARRATOR. However, these stories were never fully believed. Rumors of a wonderful farm where animals managed their own affairs continued to circulate, and a wave of rebelliousness ran through the countryside. Bulls which had always been tractable suddenly turned savage; sheep broke down hedges and devoured the clover; cows kicked over the pail. Above all, the words and tune of "Beasts of England" were known everywhere. The blackbirds whistled it in the hedges; the pigeons cooed it in the elms; it got into the din of the smithies and the chime of the church bells. And when the human beings listened to it, they secretly trembled, hearing in it a prophecy of their future doom.

1 JONES. Early in October a flight of pigeons came whirling through the air to alight in the yard of Animal Farm in the wildest excitement. Jones and his men were entering the gate! They were all carrying sticks, except Jones, who was marching ahead with a gun in his hands. Obviously they were going to attempt to recapture the farm.

2 SNOWBALL. Snowball, who had studied an old book of Julius Caesar's campaigns, gave orders quickly, and in a couple of minutes every animal was at his post. As the human beings approached the farm buildings, Snowball launched his first attack. All the pigeons flew over the men's heads and muted[3] on them from midair, and while the men were dealing with this, the geese rushed out and pecked viciously at their legs. However, the men easily drove the geese off with their sticks.

4 NARRATOR. Snowball now launched his second line of attack. Muriel, Benjamin, and all the sheep, with Snowball at their head, rushed forward and prodded and butted the men, while Benjamin turned round and lashed at them with his hoofs. But once again the men were too strong for them. Suddenly, at a squeal from Snowball, all the animals turned and fled through the gateway into the yard.

1 JONES. The men gave a shout of triumph. They saw, as they imagined, their enemies in flight, and rushed after them in disorder.

2 SNOWBALL. This was exactly what Snowball had intended. As soon as they were inside the yard, the horses, the cows, and the rest of the pigs, who had been lying in ambush in the cowshed, suddenly emerged in their rear. Snowball gave the signal for the charge. He himself dashed straight for Jones.

1 JONES. Jones raised his gun and fired. The pellets scored bloody streaks along Snowball's back … and a sheep dropped dead.

2 SNOWBALL. Snowball flung himself against Jones's legs. Jones was hurled into a pile of dung, and his gun flew out of his hands.

5 BOXER. The most terrifying spectacle was Boxer rearing up on his hind legs and striking out with his great iron-shod hoofs like a stallion. His very first blow took a stableboy on the skull and stretched him lifeless in the mud.

1 JONES. At this sight, several men dropped their attack and tried to run. Panic overtook them, and the next moment all the animals were chasing them round and round the yard. They were gored, kicked, bitten, trampled on. Within five minutes of the invasion they were in ignominious[4] retreat, with a flock of geese hissing after them.

6 NAPOLEON. The animals reassembled in wildest excitement, each recounting his own exploits in the battle at the top of his voice. An impromptu celebration of the victory was held immediately. "Beasts of England" was sung a number of times, and the sheep who had been killed was given a solemn funeral. Napoleon made a little speech, emphasizing the need of all animals to be ready to die for Animal Farm if need be.

1 NARRATOR. The animals decided unanimously to create a military decoration, Animal Hero First Class, consisting of a brass medal to be worn on Sundays and holidays. It was conferred then and there on Snowball and Boxer.

2 BENJAMIN. There was also Animal Hero Second Class, which was conferred posthumously on the dead sheep.

1 NARRATOR. There was much discussion as

---

3. muted, defecated
4. ignominious, shameful; disgraceful

to what the battle should be called. In the end, it was named the Battle of the Cowshed, since that was where the ambush had taken place. Mr. Jones's gun was set up at the foot of the flagstaff to be fired twice a year: once on the anniversary of the Battle of the Cowshed, and once on the anniversary of the Rebellion.

(*Music Cue No. 6*)

7 MOLLIE. As winter drew on, Mollie became more and more troublesome. She was late for work every morning, and complained of mysterious pains, though her appetite was excellent. One day Clover took her aside.

4 CLOVER. Mollie, I have something very serious to say to you. This morning I saw you looking over the hedge that divides Animal Farm from Foxwood. One of Mr. Pilkington's men was on the other side of the hedge, and you were allowing him to stroke your nose. What does this mean, Mollie?

7 MOLLIE. He didn't! I wasn't! It isn't true!

4 CLOVER. Mollie, look me in the face. Do you give me your word of honor that man was not stroking your nose?

7 MOLLIE. It isn't true!

1 NARRATOR. But she could not look Clover in the face, and the next moment she took to her heels and galloped away. For some weeks nothing was known of her whereabouts. Then some pigeons reported they had seen her between the shafts of a smart dog-cart standing outside a public house. A fat, red-faced man was stroking her nose and feeding her sugar. Her coat was newly clipped, and she wore a scarlet ribbon round her forelock. None of the animals ever mentioned Mollie again.

2 SNOWBALL. In January the earth was like iron, and nothing could be done in the fields. The pigs occupied themselves with planning the work of the coming season. It had come to be accepted that the pigs should decide all questions of farm policy … though their decisions had to be ratified by a majority vote. This arrangement would have worked out well had it not been for Snowball and Napoleon. These two disagreed at every point where disagreement was possible. Each had his own following, and there were some violent debates. At the meetings, Snowball often won over the majority by his brilliant speeches …

6 NAPOLEON. … but Napoleon was better at canvassing support for himself in between times. He was especially successful with the sheep. Snowball often had the greatest difficulty in finishing a speech.

2 SNOWBALL. Comrades, I have something to tell you… .

ALL. Four legs good; two legs baaad! Four legs good, two legs baaaad!

2 SNOWBALL (*up, over them*). Nevertheless, Snowball was full of plans for innovations and improvements.

6 NAPOLEON. Napoleon produced no schemes of his own, but said Snowball's would come to nothing, and seemed to be biding his time.

1 NARRATOR. Of all their controversies, none was so bitter as the one that took place over the windmill. In the long pasture was a small knoll, the highest point on the farm. Snowball declared this was just the place for a windmill, which could be made to operate a dynamo.

2 SNOWBALL. Snowball used as his study a shed which had a smooth wooden floor, suitable for drawing on. Gradually his plans grew into a complicated mass of cranks and cog-wheels covering more than half the floor, which the other animals found completely unintelligible, but very impressive. All of them came to look at

Snowball's drawings at least once a day.

6 NAPOLEON. Napoleon had declared himself against the windmill from the start. One day he arrived unexpectedly to examine the plans. He walked heavily around the shed, looked closely at every detail, stood for a while contemplating them out of the corner of his eye … then suddenly lifted his leg, urinated over the plans, and walked out without uttering a word!

1 NARRATOR. At last the question of whether or not to begin work on the windmill was to be up to the vote. When the animals were assembled, Snowball stood up and set forth his reasons in glowing terms:

2 SNOWBALL. A whole new life opens up to us, comrades! A life of ease and luxury. Electricity will operate thrashing machines, ploughs, harrows, reapers and binders, besides supplying every stall with its own electric light, hot and cold running water, and an electric heater!

1 NARRATOR. By the time he had finished speaking there was no doubt as to which way the vote would go. But at this moment Napoleon uttered a high-pitched whimper of a kind no one had ever heard before … (6 NAPOLEON, *high-pitched whimper*) At this there was a terrible baying … and nine enormous dogs came bounding into the barn. They dashed straight for Snowball, who sprang from his place barely in time to escape their snapping jaws.

7 NARRATOR. In a flash he was out of the door and they after him. Too amazed to speak, the animals crowded through the door to watch the chase.

2 SNOWBALL. Snowball was racing across the pasture, the dogs close on his heels. Once he slipped, and one of them all but closed his jaws on his tail. But Snowball whisked free just in time, put on an extra spurt, slipped through a hole in the hedge, and was seen no more.

1 NARRATOR. Silent and terrified, the animals crept back into the barn. In a moment the dogs came bounding back. At first no one could imagine where these creatures came from. But the problem was soon solved. They were the puppies Napoleon had taken away and reared privately. Though not yet full-grown, they were as fierce as wolves. They kept close to Napoleon and wagged their tails to him in the same way as the other dogs had been used to do to Mr. Jones. Napoleon now spoke.

6 NAPOLEON. Comrades, hear me! From now on all questions of farm management will be settled by a special committee of pigs over which I, Napoleon, will preside. You will still assemble on Sundays to salute the flag, sing "Beasts of England," and receive your orders of the week. But there will be no more debates.

2 BENJAMIN. Four young porkers in the front row uttered shrill squeals of disapproval, sprang to their feet and began speaking all at once. But the dogs let out deep, menacing growls, and the pigs fell silent.

7 NARRATOR. Afterwards, Squealer was sent around the farm to explain the new arrangement to the others.

3 SQUEALER. Comrades, I trust every animal appreciates the sacrifice Comrade Napoleon has made in taking on this extra labor to himself? No one believes more firmly than Comrade Napoleon that all animals are equal. He would be only too happy to let you make your decisions for yourselves. But suppose you made the wrong decisions, comrades? Then where should we be? Suppose you had decided to follow Snowball who, as we now know, was no better than a criminal?

4 CLOVER. He fought bravely at the Battle of the Cowshed.

3 SQUEALER. Bravery is not enough. Loyalty

and obedience are more important. As to the Battle of the Cowshed … Snowball's part in it was very much exaggerated. Discipline, comrades … iron discipline. That is the watchword. One false step and our enemies will be upon us. Surely, comrades, you do not want Jones back?

1 NARRATOR. Once again this argument was unanswerable. Certainly the animals did not want Jones back. If the holding of debates on Sunday mornings was liable to bring him back, then the debates must stop. Boxer voiced the general feeling.

5 BOXER. If Comrade Napoleon says it, it must be right.

1 NARRATOR. And from then on he adopted the second maxim, "Napoleon is always right," and added it to his private motto, "I will work harder."

7 NARRATOR. On the third Sunday after Snowball's expulsion, the animals were surprised to hear Napoleon announce that the windmill *was* to be built after all! That evening Squealer explained to the other animals that Napoleon had never really been opposed to the windmill.

3 SQUEALER. On the contrary, comrades … the plans Snowball drew on the floor of the shed were actually stolen from Napoleon. The windmill was, in fact, Napoleon's creation.

5 BOXER. Then why did he speak so strongly against it?

3 SQUEALER. Oh, comrade, that was Comrade Napoleon's cunning! He pretended to oppose the windmill to get rid of that dangerous character, Snowball. Now that Snowball is out of the way, the plan can go through. Strategy, comrades! That is called strategy!

1 NARRATOR. The animals were not certain what the word meant. But Squealer spoke with such assurance and the dogs with him growled so threateningly that they

accepted his explanation without further question.

(Music Cue No. 7)

1 NARRATOR. All that year the animals worked like slaves. Throughout the spring and summer they worked a sixty-hour week, and in August Napoleon announced there would be work on Sunday afternoons as well.

6 NAPOLEON. This work will be strictly voluntary, comrades. Strictly voluntary. But any comrade who fails to volunteer will have his rations reduced by half.

7 NARRATOR. The windmill presented unexpected difficulties. There was a good limestone quarry on the farm, but the problem was how to break up the stone without picks and crowbars … which no animal could use. Only after some weeks did the idea occur to somebody of utilizing the force of gravity. Huge boulders were lying all over the bed of the quarry. The animals lashed ropes round these, then dragged them up the slope to the top of the quarry, where they were toppled over the edge to shatter to pieces below. Frequently it took a whole day of exhausting labor to drag a single boulder to the top of the quarry.

5 BOXER. Nothing could have been achieved without Boxer. To see him toiling up the slope inch by inch, his breath coming fast, the tips of this hoofs clawing at the ground, and his great sides matted with sweat, filled everyone with admiration. Clover warned him not to overstrain himself but Boxer would not listen. He had made arrangements with the cockerel to call him three-quarters of an hour earlier in the mornings, instead of half an hour. In his spare moments he would go alone to the quarry, collect a load of broken stones, and drag it to the windmill unassisted.

7 NARRATOR, One Sunday morning Napoleon announced a new policy.

6 NAPOLEON. From now on, comrades, Animal Farm will engage in trade with the neighboring farms.

ALL. What?! But, Comrade Napoleon …

6 NAPOLEON. The needs of the windmill must override everything else. I am therefore making arrangements to sell a stack of hay and part of this year's wheat crop.

4 CLOVER. But, Comrade Napoleon, this means dealing with *humans!*

6 NAPOLEON. True, comrade. And I have taken care of that. There will be no need for any of you to come in contact with human beings. A Mr. Whymper has agreed to act as intermediary between Animal Farm and the outside world.

1 NARRATOR. Thus, every Monday, Mr. Whymper visited the farm. The animals avoided him as much as possible. Nevertheless, the sight of Napoleon on all fours delivering orders to a man who stood on two legs, roused their pride and partly reconciled them to the new arrangement.

7 NARRATOR. It was about this time the pigs suddenly moved into the farmhouse. The animals seemed to remember that a resolution against this had been passed in the early days. But again Squealer was able to convince them this was not the case.

3 SQUEALER. It is absolutely necessary, comrades, that we pigs should have a quiet place to work. It is also more suited to the dignity of Napoleon. Comrades, you would not want to see our noble leader living in a mere sty, would you?

1 NARRATOR. Nevertheless, some of the animals were disturbed when they heard that the pigs not only took their meals in the kitchen and used the drawing-room as a recreation room, but also slept in the beds. Boxer passed it off with:

5 BOXER. Napoleon is always right!

1 NARRATOR. But Clover went to the barn and tried to puzzle out the Seven Commandments inscribed there.

4 CLOVER. Muriel, read me the Fourth Commandment. Doesn't it say something about never sleeping in a bed?

1 NARRATOR. With some difficulty, Muriel spelled it out.

7 MURIEL. No, Clover. It says, No animal shall sleep in a bed … *with sheets.*

1 NARRATOR. Clover had not remembered that the Commandment mentioned sheets. But since it was written on the wall, it must be so. Squealer was able to put the whole matter in its proper perspective.

3 SQUEALER. You have heard, then, comrades, that we pigs now sleep in the beds at the farmhouse? And why not? A bed is merely a place to sleep in. The rule was against *sheets*, which are a human invention. We have removed the sheets from the beds and sleep between *blankets.* You would not want to rob us of our repose, would you, comrades? Surely none of you wants to see Jones back?

1 NARRATOR. No more was said about the pigs sleeping in the farmhouse beds. And when it was announced that from now on the pigs would get up an hour later in the mornings than the other animals, no complaint was made about that, either.

(Music Cue No. 8)

7 NARRATOR. All this while, no more had been seen of Snowball. He was rumored to be in hiding on one of the neighboring farms: Foxwood or Pinchfield. Now it happened that there was in the yard a pile of timber which both Mr. Pilkington and Mr. Frederick were anxious to buy. Napoleon was hesitating between the two. Whenever he seemed to favor making an agreement with Frederick, Snowball was declared to be hiding at Foxwood … while when he was inclined toward Pilkington, Snowball was said to be at Pinchfield.

2 SNOWBALL. Suddenly, early in spring, an alarming thing was reported. Snowball was secretly invading the farm by night! Every night, it was said, he came creeping in under cover of darkness to perform all kinds of mischief. He stole the corn, upset the milk pails, broke the eggs; he trampled the seed-beds; he gnawed the bark off the fruit trees.

6 NAPOLEON. Napoleon decreed a full inves-tigation. With his dogs, he made a careful tour of the farm buildings. In the evening, Squealer had serious news to report.

3 SQUEALER. Comrades, a most terrible thing has been discovered. Snowball has sold himself to Frederick of Pinchfield, who is plotting to attack us!

ALL. Oh, no! No!

3 SQUEALER. Yes! But there is worse than that. Snowball was in league with Jones from the very start! This has been proved by documents which we have just discov-ered. This explains a great deal, comrades. Did we not see for ourselves how he attempted to get us defeated at the Battle of the Cowshed?

1 NARRATOR. The animals were stupefied.[5] They all remembered … or thought they remembered … Snowball charging ahead of them at the Battle of the Cowshed. It was a little difficult to see how this fitted in with his being on Jones's side.

5 BOXER. I don't understand. Snowball fought bravely at the Battle of the Cowshed. Didn't we give him Animal Hero First Class immediately afterward?

3 SQUEALER. That was our mistake, comrade. We know now that in reality he was trying to lure us to our doom.

5 BOXER. But he was wounded! We all saw him running with blood.

3 SQUEALER. That was part of the plot. Jones's shot only grazed him. The plan was

for Snowball, at the critical moment, to give the signal for flight and leave the field to the enemy. And he very nearly succeeded. Comrade, he would have succeeded if it had not been for our heroic leader, Comrade Napoleon. Do you not remember how, just at the moment when Jones and his men had got inside the yard, Snowball suddenly turned and fled? And do you not remember, too, that just at that moment, when all seemed lost, Comrade Napoleon sprang for-ward with a cry of "Death to Humanity!" and sank his teeth in Jones's leg?

1 NARRATOR. Now that Squealer described the scene so graphically, it seemed to the animals that they *did* remember it. But Boxer was still uneasy.

5 BOXER. I don't believe Snowball was a trai-tor at the beginning. What he's done since is different. But I believe that at the Battle of the Cowshed he was a good comrade.

3 SQUEALER. Comrade Boxer! Our Leader, Comrade Napoleon, has stated categorically[6] … categorically, comrade! … that Snowball was Jones's agent from the very beginning!

5 BOXER. Ah, that's different. If Comrade Napoleon says so, it must be right.

3 SQUEALER. That is the true spirit, comrade. I warn every animal on this farm to keep his eyes wide open. We have good reason to suspect that at this very moment some of Snowball's secret agents are lurking amongst us.

7 NARRATOR. Four days later, Napoleon ordered all of the animals to assemble in the yard. When they were all gathered, Napoleon emerged from the farmhouse with his nine dogs frisking around him. He stood sternly surveying his audience for a moment. Then:

---

5. stupefied, shocked; bewildered
6. categorically, positively; conclusively

6 NAPOLEON (*stridently*). Seize them!

1 NARRATOR. Immediately the dogs seized four of the pigs by the ear and dragged them squealing with terror to Napoleon's feet. The pigs' ears were bleeding … the dogs had tasted blood … and for a few moments they appeared to go quite mad. To the amazement of everybody, three of them flung themselves upon Boxer!

5 BOXER. Boxer put out his great hoof, caught one dog in mid-air, and pinned him to the ground. The dog shrieked for mercy. Boxer looked at Napoleon to know whether he should crush the dog to death.

6 NAPOLEON (*grudgingly*). Let him go!

5 BOXER. Boxer lifted his hoof, and the dog slunk away. Presently the tumult died. The four pigs waited, trembling. They were the same four who had protested when Napoleon abolished the Sunday meetings.

6 NAPOLEON. Comrades, in the name of the Rebellion I now call upon you to confess your heinous crimes!

7 NARRATOR. Without further prompting the porkers confessed that they had been secretly in touch with Snowball ever since his expulsion, and had entered into an agreement with him to hand over the farm to Mr. Frederick. They added that Snowball had privately admitted to them that he had been Mr. Jones's secret agent for years. When they had finished their confessions, the dogs promptly tore their throats out.

6 NAPOLEON. Has any other animal anything to confess?

1 NARRATOR. Three hens now stated that Snowball had appeared to them in a dream and incited them to disobey Napoleon's orders. Then a goose confessed to having secreted six ears of corn and eaten them in the night. Then a sheep confessed to having urinated in the drinking pool … urged to do this by Snowball. They were all slain on the spot.

7 NARRATOR. So the tale of confessions and executions went on and on, until there was a pile of corpses lying before Napoleon's feet, and the air was heavy with the smell of blood. When it was all over, the animals crept away in a body, shaken and miserable. They made their way to the little knoll where the half-finished windmill stood. Boxer seemed bewildered by it all.

5 BOXER. I do not understand. I wouldn't have believed such things could happen on our farm. It must be some fault in ourselves. The solution, as I see it, is to work harder. From now on I will get up a whole hour earlier in the mornings.

1 NARRATOR. And Boxer made for the quarry. The other animals huddled about Clover, not speaking. The knoll where they were lying gave them a wide prospect across the countryside. Most of Animal Farm was within their view … the long pasture stretching down to the main road, the hayfield, the spinney[7], the drinking pool, the ploughed fields where the young wheat was thick and green, and the red roofs of the farm buildings with smoke curling from the chimneys. It was a clear spring evening. The grass and the bursting hedges were gilded by the level rays of the sun. Never had the farm appeared to the animals so desirable. As Clover looked down the hillside, her eyes filled with tears.

4 CLOVER. But surely this is not what we looked forward to on that night when old Major first stirred us to rebellion? He told of a society of animals set free from hunger and the whip … all equal, each working according to his capacity, the strong protecting the weak. What has happened to us? We have come to a time when no one dares speak his mind; when fierce, growling dogs roam everywhere; when you have

---

7. spinney (*British*), a small wood with undergrowth

to watch your comrades torn to pieces after confessing to shocking crimes. Oh, things are far better off than in the days of Jones. And before all else it is needful to prevent the return of the human beings. But still it was not for *this* that we have hoped and toiled. It was not for *this* we faced the bullets of Jones's gun.

1 NARRATOR. Such were Clover's thoughts, though she lacked the words to express them. At last, feeling it to be in some way a substitute for the words they were unable to find, the animals began singing "Beasts of England" …

ALL (*softly*).

Beasts of England, beasts of Ireland,

Beasts of every land and clime,

Hearken to my joyful tidings

Of the golden future time.

(*Sing until stopped by* SQUEALER.)

1 NARRATOR (*over them*). They sang it slowly and mournfully in a way they had never sung it before … until suddenly Squealer appeared.

3 SQUEALER. Stop! Comrades, hear me! Stop singing that song. "Beasts of England" has been abolished. From now on it is forbidden to sing it.

ALL. What?! But why?

3 SQUEALER. Because it is no longer needed. "Beasts of England" was the song of the Rebellion. But the Rebellion is now completed. The execution of the traitors this afternoon was the final act. In "Beasts of England" we expressed our longing for a better society to come. Now that society has been established. Clearly this song no longer has any purpose. We have a new song which I shall now teach you. (*Sings*)

Animal Farm, Animal Farm,

Never through me shalt thou come to harm …

7 NARRATOR. The new anthem was sung every Sunday morning after the hoisting of the flag. But somehow neither the words nor the tune ever seemed to the animals to come up to "Beasts of England."

(*Music Cue No. 9*)

THE CURTAIN FALLS

END OF ACT 1

ACT ll

T he readers return to their stools during the playing of Music Cue No. 10, which is faded out under:

1 NARRATOR. A few days later, when the terror caused by the executions had died down, some of the animals thought they remembered that the Sixth Commandment decreed no animal should kill any other animal. It was felt that the killings which had taken place did not square with this.

4 CLOVER. Clover asked Benjamin to read her the Sixth Commandment …

2 BENJAMIN. Not I! Nobody has ever seen a dead donkey.

4 CLOVER. … . and when Benjamin refused to meddle in such matters, she fetched Muriel to read the Commandment for her.

7 MURIEL. No animal shall kill any other animal … *without cause.*

1 NARRATOR. Somehow or other these last two words had slipped everyone's memory. But they saw now that the Commandment had not been violated, for clearly there was good reason for killing the traitors who had leagued themselves with Snowball.

5 BOXER. Throughout that year the animals worked even harder than the previous year. At times it seemed they worked longer hours and were fed no better than in Jones's day. But on Sunday mornings, Squealer would read them long, reassuring lists of figures.

3 SQUEALER. Production Report for the week just completed: Hay production, up 200 percent … grains, 300 percent … milk, 400 percent … eggs, 506.2 percent.

7 NARRATOR. The animals saw no reason to disbelieve these impressive figures. All the same, Benjamin expressed the general sentiment when he said:

2 BENJAMIN. I'd rather have less figures and more food!

6 NAPOLEON. All orders were now issued through Squealer. Napoleon himself was not seen in public once in a fortnight. Even in the farmhouse Napoleon inhabited separate apartments, took his meals alone, and always ate from the Crown Derby dinner service. It was also announced that the gun would be fired every year on Napoleon's birthday, as well as on the other two anniversaries.

1 NARRATOR. Napoleon was now always referred to in formal style as Our Leader, Comrade Napoleon, and the pigs liked to invent for him such titles as Father of All Animals, Protector of the Sheepfold, Ducklings' Friend, and the like. In his speeches, Squealer would talk with the tears running down his cheeks of Napoleon's wisdom, the goodness of his heart, and the deep love he bore to all animals everywhere. It had become customary to give Napoleon the credit for every successful achievement. You would often hear one hen remark to another:

4 NARRATOR. Under the guidance of Our Leader, Comrade Napoleon, I have laid five eggs in six days.

1 NARRATOR. Or two cows, drinking at a pool, would exclaim:

7 NARRATOR. Thanks to the leadership of Comrade Napoleon, how excellent this water tastes!

6 NAPOLEON. Meanwhile, Napoleon was engaged in complicated negotiations with Frederick and Pilkington. The pile of timber was still unsold. Frederick was the more anxious to get hold of it, but he would not offer a reasonable price. At the same time there were renewed rumors that Frederick and his men were plotting to attack Animal Farm and destroy the windmill.

3 SQUEALER. Frederick plots to bring against us twenty men, all armed with guns. And, comrades, have you heard about the terrible cruelties Frederick practises on his animals? He flogged an old horse to death … he starves his cows … he killed his dog by throwing it into the furnace … he amuses himself in the evenings by making cocks fight with splinters of razor blade tied to their spurs!

1 NARRATOR. The animals' blood boiled with rage when they heard of these things, and sometimes they clamored to be allowed to attack Pinchfield Farm and set the animals free.

6 NAPOLEON. Napoleon explained that he had never contemplated selling the timber to Frederick. The pigeons, who were still sent out to spread tidings of the Rebellion, were forbidden to set foot on Pinchfield, and were ordered to drop their former slogan of "Death to Humanity" in favor of "Death to Frederick."

2 SNOWBALL. In the late summer, yet another of Snowball's machinations was laid bare. The wheat crop was full of weeds, and it was discovered that on one of his nocturnal visits Snowball had mixed weed seeds with the seed corn. A gander who had been privy to the plot confessed his guilt, and immediately committed suicide by swallowing deadly nightshade berries.

4 CLOVER. The animals now also learned that Snowball had never received the order of Animal Hero First Class, as many of them had believed.

3 SQUEALER. This was merely a legend circulated by Snowball himself. Far from being decorated, he was actually censured for cowardice in the battle!

7 NARRATOR. By autumn the windmill was finished. Tired but proud, the animals walked round and round their masterpiece, which appeared beautiful in their eyes. When they thought of how they had labored, what discouragements they had overcome, and the enormous difference that would be made in their lives when the sails were turning and the dynamos running, their weariness forsook them and they gambolled round and round the windmill uttering cries of triumph. Napoleon himself came to inspect the completed work, congratulated the animals on their achievement, and dedicated the edifice.

6 NAPOLEON. I hereby name this structure … Napoleon Mill!

1 NARRATOR. Two days later the animals were struck dumb with surprise to learn that Napoleon had sold the pile of timber to Frederick. Throughout the whole of his seeming friendship with Pilkington, he had really been in secret agreement with Frederick!

7 NARRATOR. The pigs were in ecstasies over Napoleon's cunning. By seeming to be friendly with Pilkington, he had forced Frederick to raise his price by twelve pounds. Squealer gloated:

3 SQUEALER. Comrades, the superior quality of Napoleon's mind is shown in the fact that he trusted *nobody*. Frederick wanted to pay for the timber with something he called a cheque. But Our Leader was too clever for him. He demanded payment in real five pound notes, to be handed over before the timber is removed.

1 NARRATOR. Frederick removed the timber with amazing speed. But three days later there was a terrible hullabaloo. Whymper, his face deadly pale, came racing up the path on his bicycle and rushed straight to the farmhouse. The next moment the animals heard a choking roar of rage from Napoleon's apartment.

6 NAPOLEON (*outraged scream*). Death! Death to Frederick!

1 NARRATOR. News of what had happened spread around the farm like wildfire. The banknotes were forgeries! Frederick had got the timber for nothing!

7 NARRATOR. Napoleon called the animals together, and in a terrible voice pronounced judgment on Frederick.

6 NAPOLEON. When captured, he shall be boiled alive!

7 NARRATOR. At the same time, he warned them that after this treacherous deed, Frederick and his men might make their long-expected attack at any moment. Four pigeons were sent to Foxwood with a conciliatory message which it was hoped might re-establish good relations with Pilkington.

1 NARRATOR. The very next morning the attack came. The lookouts came racing in with the news that Frederick and his men had come through the gate. Boldly the animals sallied forth to meet them. But this time they did not have the easy victory they had had in the Battle of the Cowshed. There were fifteen men with half a dozen guns, and they opened fire as soon as they got within fifty yards.

7 NARRATOR. The animals took refuge in the farm buildings and peeped cautiously out from chinks and knotholes. The whole of the big pasture, including the windmill, was in the hands of the enemy.

6 NAPOLEON. Napoleon seemed at a loss. He paced up and down, casting wistful glances in the direction of Foxwood. If Pilkington and his men would help, the day might yet be won. But at this moment the pigeons returned bearing a scrap of paper.

3 SQUEALER. A message from Pilkington, Comrade Napoleon!

6 NAPOLEON. Quickly, what does it say?

4 CLOVER. Is he coming?

5 BOXER. Will he help us?

6 NAPOLEON. What does it say?

3 SQUEALER. It says … "Serves you right!"

1 NARRATOR. Frederick and his men halted at the windmill. Two of the men produced a crowbar and a sledge hammer. The animals watched them, and a murmur of dismay went round.

7 MURIEL. They are going to knock the windmill down!

6 NAPOLEON. Impossible! The walls are too thick. They could not knock it down in a week. Courage, comrades.

1 NARRATOR. But the men were drilling a hole in the base of the windmill. Slowly, and with an air almost of amusement, Benjamin nodded his long muzzle.

2 BENJAMIN. I thought so. Do you see what they're doing? They're packing blasting powder into that hole.

1 NARRATOR. In a few minutes there was as sudden deafening roar. All the animals flung themselves flat on their faces. When they got up again, a huge cloud of smoke was hanging where the windmill had been. Slowly the breeze drifted it away. (ALL *ad lib moans of distress.*) The windmill had ceased to exist. At this sight the animals' fear and despair were drowned in their rage against this vile, contemptible act. (ALL *ad lib roars of fury.*) A mighty cry of vengeance went up, and without waiting for orders from Napoleon, they charged forth in a body and made straight for the enemy. This time they did not heed the cruel pellets that swept over them like hail. It was a savage and bitter battle. A cow, three sheep, and two geese were killed, and nearly everyone was wounded … except Napoleon, who was directing operations from the rear.

7 NARRATOR. The men did not go unscathed, either. Two of them had their heads broken by blows from Boxer's hoofs; another was gored in the belly by a cow's horn. And when the nine dogs suddenly appeared on the men's flank, baying ferociously, the cowardly enemy turned and ran for dear life. The animals chased them right down to the bottom of the field and got in some last kicks at them as they forced their way through the thorn hedge.

5 BOXER. Weary and bleeding, the animals began to limp back to the farm. They halted in sorrowful silence at the place where the windmill had once stood. It was gone. Almost the last trace of their labor was gone. It was as though the windmill had never been.

3 SQUEALER. But as they approached the farm, Squealer, who had unaccountably been absent during the fight, came skipping towards them, beaming. From the direction of the farm buildings the animals heard the solemn firing of a gun.

2 BENJAMIN. What is that gun firing for?

3 SQUEALER. To celebrate our victory.

2 BENJAMIN. Victory! *What* victory?

3 SQUEALER. What victory, comrade? Have we not driven the enemy off the sacred soil of Animal Farm?

2 BENJAMIN. But they have destroyed the windmill!

3 SQUEALER. What matter? We will build *another* windmill. We'll build *six* windmills if we feel like it. You do not appreciate, comrade, the mighty thing we have done. The enemy was in occupation of the very ground we stand on. Now, thanks to the leadership of Comrade Napoleon, we have won back every inch of it.

2 BENJAMIN. Then we've won back what we had before.

3 SQUEALER. *That* is our victory!

5 BOXER. Boxer, who had suffered a split hoof, limped painfully back into the yard. He saw ahead of him the heavy labor of rebuilding the windmill from its foundations, and already in imagination braced himself for the task. But for the first time it occurred to him that he was eleven years old, and his great muscles were not what they once had been.

1 NARRATOR. But when the animals heard Napoleon's speech, congratulating them on their conduct, it *did* seem to them that, after all, they *had* won a great victory. The animals slain in the battle were given a solemn funeral. It was announced that the battle would be called the Battle of the Windmill.

2 BENJAMIN. And Napoleon created a new decoration, the Order of the Green Banner … which he conferred upon himself.

7 NARRATOR. A few days later, the pigs came upon a case of whisky in the cellar of the farmhouse, overlooked when the house was first occupied. That night there came from the farmhouse the sound of raucous singing. At about half past nine, Napoleon, wearing an old bowler hat of Mr. Jones's, was distinctly seen to emerge from the back door, gallop rapidly around the yard, and disappear indoors again.

1 NARRATOR. But in the morning a deep silence hung over the farmhouse. Not a pig appeared to be stirring. It was nearly nine o'clock before Squealer made his appearance, walking slowly and dejectedly, his eyes dull, with every appearance of being seriously ill. He called the animals together and told them he had terrible news to impart.

3 SQUEALER. Comrades … Comrade Napoleon is dying!

1 NARRATOR. A cry of lamentation went up. With tears in their eyes the animals asked one another what they should do if their leader were taken from them. A rumor went round that Snowball had contrived to *poison* Napoleon. At eleven o'clock Squealer came to make another announcement.

3 SQUEALER. As his last act on earth, Comrade Napoleon has pronounced a solemn decree … the drinking of alcohol is to be punished by death!

6 NAPOLEON. By evening, however, Napoleon appeared to be somewhat better. The following morning Squealer was able to tell them he was well on his way to recovery. And the next day it was learned that he had instructed Whymper to purchase some books on brewing and distilling. The small paddock beyond the orchard was to be ploughed up. Napoleon intended to sow it with barley.

1 NARRATOR. About this time occurred a strange incident. One night there was a loud crash in the yard, and the animals rushed out of their stalls. At the foot of the end wall of the big barn, where the Seven Commandments were written, lay a ladder broken in two. Squealer was sprawling beside it, and near at hand lay a lantern, a paint brush, and an overturned pot of white paint. None of the animals could form any idea what this meant, except old Benjamin, who nodded his muzzle with a knowing air and would say nothing.

7 MURIEL. But a few days later, Muriel, reading over the Seven Commandments to herself, noticed there was yet *another* of them which the animals had remembered wrong. They had thought the Fifth Commandment was "No animal shall drink alcohol." But there were two words they had forgotten. Actually the Commandment read, "No animal shall drink alcohol … *to excess!*"

(Music Cue No. 11)

5 BOXER. Boxer's split hoof was a long time healing. They had started rebuilding the windmill the day after the victory celebration. Boxer refused to take even a day off, and made it a point of honor not to let it be seen that he was in pain. Clover treated the hoof with poultices,[8] and both she and Benjamin urged Boxer to work less hard, but he would not listen. He had one burning ambition: to see the windmill completed before he reached the age for retirement.

1 NARRATOR. At the beginning, the retirement age had been fixed for horses and pigs at twelve, for cows at fourteen, for dogs at nine, sheep at seven, for hens and geese at five. So far no animal had actually retired. But now that the small field beyond the orchard had been planted in barley, it was rumored that a corner of the large pasture was to be turned into a grazing ground for super-annuated animals. Boxer's twelfth birthday was due in the summer of the next year.

7 NARRATOR. Meanwhile, life was hard. The winter was as cold as the last one, and food was even shorter. Once again all rations were reduced … except those of the pigs and the dogs. Squealer explained:

3 SQUEALER. We are not *really* short of food, comrades. In comparison with the days of Jones the improvement is tremendous. We have more oats, more hay, more turnips. We work shorter hours, our drinking water is of better quality, we live longer, have more straw in our stalls … and suffer less from fleas.

7 NARRATOR. The animals believed every word of it. Truth to tell, Jones and all that he stood for had almost faded out of their memories.

1 NARRATOR. In the autumn, the four sows all littered simultaneously, producing thirty-one young pigs. It was announced that a schoolroom would be built in the farmhouse garden. For the time being, the young pigs were to be given their instruction by Napoleon himself. They were discouraged from playing with the other young animals. It was laid down as a rule that when a pig and any other animal met on a path, the other animal must stand aside. Also, all pigs now enjoyed the privilege of wearing green ribbons in their tails on Sundays.

2 BENJAMIN. The farm was still short of money. There were bricks, sand, and lime for the schoolroom to be purchased, and it was also necessary to begin saving up again for machinery for the windmill. Rations, reduced in December, were reduced again in February. Lanterns in the stall were forbidden to save oil. But the pigs seemed comfortable enough and, in fact, were putting on weight, if anything. The news leaked out that every pig was now receiving a ration of a pint of beer daily, with half a gallon for Napoleon himself, which was always served to him in a Crown Derby tureen.

1 NARRATOR. But if there were hardships to be borne, they were partly offset by the fact that life nowadays had greater dignity than ever before. There were more songs, more speeches, more processions. So what with Squealer's lists of figures and the fluttering of the flag, the animals were able to forget … at least part of the time … that their bellies were empty.

7 NARRATOR. In April, Animal Farm was proclaimed a republic, and it became necessary to elect a President. There was only

---

8. poultices, warm, medicated cloths applied to sores or other lesions

one candidate, Napoleon. He was elected unanimously. On the same day it was given out that fresh documents had been discovered which revealed further details about Snowball's complicity with Jones. It now appeared that Snowball had not merely attempted to lose the Battle of the Cowshed, but had openly been fighting on Jones's side! In fact, he had actually been the *leader* of the human forces, charging into battle with the cry, "Long Live Humanity!" on his lips. The wounds on Snowball's back, which a few of the animals still remembered seeing, had been inflicted by Napoleon's teeth.

1 NARRATOR. In the middle of the summer, Moses the raven suddenly reappeared on the farm. He was quite unchanged, still did no work, and would still talk by the hour to anyone who would listen about:

3 MOSES. Sugarcandy Mountain, comrades! Oh, beautiful, glorious Sugarcandy Mountain … up there, up there, comrades, just on the other side of that dark and dismal cloud. That happy land where we poor animals shall rest forever from our labors. Oh, I've been there, brethren … I've seen it! The everlasting fields of clover … the linseed cake and lump sugar growing on the hedges. Oh, it's beautiful, comrades … beautiful!

1 NARRATOR. Many of the animals believed him. Was it not right and just that somewhere a better world should exist? A thing difficult to comprehend was the attitude of the pigs toward Moses. They declared contemptuously that his stories about Sugarcandy Mountain were lies … yet they allowed him to remain on the farm, not working, with an allowance of a gill of beer a day.

5 BOXER. After his hoof healed, Boxer worked harder than ever. Sometimes the long hours on insufficient food were hard to bear, but Boxer never faltered. In nothing he said or did was there any sign that his strength was not what it had been. It was only his appearance that was a little altered … his hide less shiny than it used to be, and his great haunches seemed to have shrunken. Sometimes on the slope leading to the top of the quarry, when he braced his great muscles against the weight of some vast boulder, it seemed that nothing kept him on his feet except the will to continue. Clover and Benjamin begged him to take care of his health, but Boxer paid no attention. Late one evening in summer, two pigeons came racing in with dreadful news.

2 NARRATOR. Boxer has fallen!

7 NARRATOR. He is lying on his side and can't get up!

1 NARRATOR. The animals rushed to the knoll where the windmill stood. There lay Boxer, his neck stretched out, unable even to raise his head. His eyes were glazed, his sides matted with sweat, and a thin stream of blood had trickled out of his mouth. Clover dropped to her knees beside him.

4 CLOVER. Boxer, what is it? What's wrong?

5 BOXER. It's … my lung. No matter. You will be able to finish the windmill without me. I had only a month to go, in any case. To tell you the truth, I have been looking forward to my retirement.

2 BENJAMIN. We must get help at once. Run, somebody, and tell Squealer what has happened!

1 NARRATOR. About a quarter of an hour later Squealer appeared, full of sympathy and concern.

3 SQUEALER. Comrade Napoleon has learned with the deepest distress of this misfortune to one of our most loyal workers. He has already made arrangements to send Boxer to the town hospital for treatment.

7 NARRATOR. The animals felt a little uneasy at this. They did not like to think of their sick comrade in the hands of human beings. However, Squealer convinced them that the veterinary surgeon could treat Boxer more satisfactorily than could be done on the farm. And about a half hour later, when Boxer had somewhat recovered, he managed to limp back to his stall.

5 BOXER. I'm not too sorry about what's happened. Why, if I make a good recovery I might expect to live another three years. I look forward to the peaceful days I will spend in the corner of the big pasture.

4 CLOVER. But, Boxer ... what will you ever do with your spare time?

5 BOXER. I have a plan. Something I've long wanted to do.

4 CLOVER. What is it, Boxer?

5 BOXER. I'm going to devote the rest of my life to learning the remaining 22 letters of the alphabet.

1 NARRATOR. In the middle of the day a van came to take him away. The animals were at work when Benjamin came galloping from the direction of the farm buildings, braying at the top of his voice. It was the first time they had ever seen Benjamin excited.

2 BENJAMIN. Quick! Quick! Come at once! They're taking Boxer away!

1 NARRATOR. The animals raced back to the farm buildings. Sure enough, there in the yard stood a large closed van with a sly looking man sitting on the driver's seat. The animals crowded round the van.

6 NARRATOR. There he is, inside!

7 NARRATOR. He's going away.

3 AND 4 NARRATORS (*fatuously*[9] *cheerful*). Goodbye, Boxer! Goodbye!

2 BENJAMIN. Fools! Fools! Don't you see what's written on the side of that van?

4 CLOVER (*slowly, with mounting horror*).

Alfred Simmonds ... Horse Slaughterer and Glue Boiler!

2 BENJAMIN. Don't you understand what that means? They're selling Boxer to the knacker!

(ALL *ad lib cries of horror and rejection*.)

4 CLOVER. Stop him, somebody! Stop him!

7 MURIEL. Come back here!

2 BENJAMIN. Boxer, get out! Get out, quickly! They're taking you to your death!

5 BOXER. They heard the sound of a tremendous drumming of hoofs from inside the van. But the van was already gathering speed. In another moment it disappeared down the road. Boxer was never seen again.

7 NARRATOR. Three days later it was announced that he had died in the hospital in spite of receiving every attention a horse could have. Squealer came to announce the news to the others.

3 SQUEALER. I was at his bedside at the very last. At the end, almost too weak to speak, he whispered in my ear that his sole sorrow was to have passed on before the windmill was finished. "Forward, comrades!" he whispered. "Forward in the name of the Rebellion! Long live Animal Farm! Long live Napoleon!" Those were his very last words, comrades.

7 NARRATOR. The animals were enormously impressed. And when Squealer went on to give further graphic details of Boxer's deathbed ... the admirable care he had received, and the expensive medicines for which Napoleon had paid without a thought as to the cost ... the sorrow they felt for their comrade's death was tempered by the thought that at least he had died happy.

1 NARRATOR. Napoleon himself appeared at the meeting the following Sunday morning

---

9. fatuously, foolishly

and pronounced a short oration in Boxer's honor.

6 NAPOLEON. We deeply regret that it was not possible to bring back our late lamented comrade's remains for interment on the farm. But in a few days the pigs intend to hold a memorial banquet in Boxer's honor. Meanwhile, let me remind you of his priceless heritage to us: two maxims which every animal would do well to adopt as his own. Remember forever, comrades, the wise words of our dear Boxer … "I will work harder!" … and "Comrade Napoleon is always right!"

1 NARRATOR. On the day appointed for the banquet, a grocer delivered a large wooden crate to the farmhouse. That night there was the sound of uproarious singing from within. No one stirred in the farmhouse until noon the following day. From somewhere or other the pigs had acquired the money to buy themselves another case of whisky.

(Music Cue No. 12)

7 NARRATOR. Years passed. A time came when there was no one who remembered the old days before the Rebellion except Clover, Benjamin, Moses, and a few of the pigs.

2 BENJAMIN. Muriel was dead. Jones had died in an inebriates' home in another part of the country. Snowball was forgotten. Boxer was forgotten … except by the few who had loved him. Clover was an old, stout mare now, two years past the retiring age … but in fact no animal had ever actually retired. Napoleon was now a mature boar of 24 stone.[10] Squealer was so fat that he could with difficulty see out of his eyes. Only old Benjamin was much the same as ever, except for being a little grayer about the muzzle and, since Boxer's death, more taciturn[11] than ever.

1 NARRATOR. Many animals had been born to whom the Rebellion was only a dim tra-

dition. The farm was more prosperous now, and better organized. The windmill had been successfully completed at last, and the farm possessed a threshing machine and a hay elevator, and various new buildings.

7 NARRATOR. The windmill had not, after all, been used for generating electrical power. It was used for milling corn, and brought in a handsome profit. But the luxuries of which Snowball had taught the animals to dream … the stalls with electric lights, and hot and cold running water … these were no longer talked about. Napoleon had denounced such ideas as being contrary to the spirit of Animalism. True happiness, he said, lay in working hard and living frugally.

2 BENJAMIN. Somehow it seemed the farm had grown richer without making the animals themselves any richer. Except, of course, for the pigs and the dogs. It wasn't that these creatures didn't work … after their fashion. There was, as Squealer never tired of explaining, endless work in the supervision and organization of the farm.

3 SQUEALER. We pigs have to expend enormous labor everyday on things called files, reports, and memoranda. These are large sheets of paper which have to be closely covered with writing … and as soon as they are so covered, must be burnt in the furnace. This is of the highest importance for the welfare of the farm!

2 BENJAMIN. As for the others, they were generally hungry; they slept on straw; they labored in the fields. In winter they were troubled by the cold, and in summer by the flies. Sometimes the older ones among them racked their dim memories and tried to determine whether in the early days of the Rebellion things had been better or

---

10. stone *(British)*, a measure of weight equal to 14 pounds.
11. taciturn, uncommunicative; silent

worse. But they could not remember. Squealer's lists of figures invariably demonstrated that everything was getting better and better. Only old Benjamin professed to know that things never had been, nor ever could be, much better or much worse. Hunger, hardship, and disappointment were, he said, the unalterable law of life.

4 CLOVER. Yet the animals never gave up hope. They were still the only farm in all England owned and operated by animals. And when they heard the gun booming, and saw the flag fluttering at the masthead, their hearts swelled with pride, and the talk would turn to the old, heroic days … the expulsion of Jones, the writing of the Seven Commandments, the great battles in which the human invaders had been defeated. None of the old dreams had been abandoned. The republic of animals which old Major had foretold was still believed in. If they went hungry, it was not from feeding tyrannical human beings. If they worked hard, at least they worked for themselves. No creature amongst them went on two legs. No creature called any other creature Master. All animals were equal!

3 SQUEALER. One day in early summer, Squealer ordered the sheep to follow him to a piece of waste ground at the other end of the farm. There they remained for a whole week, during which time Squealer was with them for the greater part of every day, teaching them to sing a new song.

4 CLOVER. It was just after the sheep had returned, on a pleasant evening when the animals had finished work and were making their way back to the farm buildings, that a terrified neighing sounded from the yard. It was Clover. She neighed again, and all the animals rushed into the yard. Then *they* saw what Clover had seen.

1 NARRATOR. It … it's Squealer!

4 CLOVER. He's walking!

2 BENJAMIN. On his hind legs!

3 SQUEALER. Yes, it was Squealer, walking on his hind legs. A little awkwardly, as though not quite used to supporting his considerable bulk in that position, but with perfect balance he was strolling across the yard. And a moment later, out from the farmhouse came a long file of pigs … all walking on their hind legs. One or two looked as though they would have liked the support of a stick. But every one of them made his way round the yard successfully.

6 NAPOLEON. Finally there was a tremendous baying of dogs and out came Napoleon himself, majestically upright, casting haughty glances from side to side, with his dogs gambolling about him. And in his trotter … he carried a whip!

1 NARRATOR. There was deadly silence. Amazed, terrified, the animals watched the long line of pigs march slowly round the yard. It was as though the world had turned upside down. Then came a moment when in spite of everything, in spite of their terror of the dogs, and of the habit developed through long years of never complaining, never criticising, they might have uttered some word of protest. but just at that moment … as though at a signal … all the sheep burst into a tremendous bleating:

ALL. Four legs good; two legs *better*! Four legs good; two legs *better*!

1 NARRATOR. It went on for five minutes without stopping. And by the time the sheep had quieted down, the pigs had marched back into the farmhouse.

2 BENJAMIN. Benjamin felt a nose nuzzling at his shoulder. It was Clover. She tugged gently at his mane and led him to the end of the big barn where the Seven Commandments were written.

4 CLOVER. My sight is failing. But it appears to me that the wall looks different. Are the Seven Commandments the same as they used to be, Benjamin?

1 NARRATOR. For once, Benjamin consented to break his rule, and he read out to her what was written on the wall. There was nothing there now except a single commandment. It read:

2 BENJAMIN. All animals are equal. But some animals are more equal than others.

1 NARRATOR. After that, it did not seem strange when next day the pigs all carried whips. It did not seem strange to learn the pigs had bought themselves a wireless set, were arranging to install a telephone, and had taken out subscriptions to the daily papers. It did not seem strange when Napoleon was seen strolling in the garden with a pipe in his mouth… . No, not even when the pigs took Mr. Jones's clothes out of the wardrobes and put them on.

7 NARRATOR. A week later, a deputation of neighboring farmers came to inspect the farm. They were shown all over, and expressed great admiration for everything they saw; especially the windmill. The animals worked diligently, hardly raising their faces from the ground, not knowing whether to be more frightened of the pigs or of the human visitors. That evening, loud laughter and bursts of song came from the farmhouse. At the sound of the mingled voices the animals were stricken with curiosity. What could be happening in there, now that for the first time animals and humans were meeting on terms of equality? They began to creep quietly into the farmhouse garden.

1 NARRATOR. They tiptoed up to the house and peered in the dining-room window. There, round the long table, sat half a dozen farmers and half a dozen of the more eminent pigs. Napoleon himself sat at the head of the table. A large jug was circulating, and the mugs were being refilled. Mr. Pilkington stood up.

5 PILKINGTON. Mr. Napoleon, ladies, gentleman … it is a great source of satisfaction to me to feel that a long period of distrust and misunderstanding has now come to an end. There was a time when the respected proprietors of Animal Farm were regarded with a certain amount of misgiving by their human neighbors. It used to be felt that the existence of a farm owned and operated by pigs might have an unsettling effect on the neighborhood. Too many of us assumed, I fear, that on such a farm a spirit of license would prevail. We were nervous about the effect on our own animals. But today we have inspected Animal Farm … and what did we find? Not only the most up-to-date methods, but a discipline which should be an example to all farmers everywhere. I believe I am right in saying that on this farm the lower animals do more work and receive less food than any animals in the country!

3 SQUEALER. Hear, hear!

5 PILKINGTON. Between pigs and human beings there is not, nor need ever be, any clash of interests whatever. Our problems are exactly the same. You have your lower animals to contend with … we have our lower classes. And so, gentlemen, I give you a toast! To the prosperity of Animal Farm! (ALL *ad lib applause.*)

3 SQUEALER. Thank you, Mr. Pilkington, for those kind remarks. And now our great leader, Napoleon, will say a few words.

6 NAPOLEON. Squealer, honored guests, fellow pigs … I, too, am happy that the period of misunderstanding has come to an end. For a long time there were rumors, circulated by a foul and malignant enemy, that there was something subversive … even revolutionary … in the outlook of myself and my colleagues. We have even been accused of attempting to stir up rebellion among the animals on neighboring farms. Gentlemen, nothing could be farther from the truth! Our sole wish now, as in the past, is to live at peace with everyone.

3 **SQUEALER.** Hear, hear!

6 **NAPOLEON.** I do not believe any of the old suspicions still linger. But certain changes recently effected should have the effect of promoting confidence still farther. For example, heretofore the animals on this farm have had the rather foolish custom of addressing each other as "comrade." This is to be discontinued immediately. Moreover, tonight it gives me great pleasure to announce another important change. The name Animal Farm has been abolished. Henceforth this farm is to be known by its correct and original name … the Manor Farm. (ALL *ad lib cheers.*) So, friends, I give you the same toast as before, but in a different form. Fill your glasses to the brim, gentlemen, here is my toast. To the prosperity of … the Manor Farm!

(ALL *ad lib cheers.*)

4 **CLOVER.** There was the same hearty cheering as before, and the mugs were emptied to the dregs. But as the animals outside gazed at the scene, it seemed to them that some strange thing was happening. What *was* it that had altered in the faces of the pigs? Clover's old dim eyes flitted from one face to another. Some of them had five chins, some had four, some three. But what was it that seemed to be melting and changing? The creatures outside looked from pig to man, and from man to pig, and from pig to man again. But already it was impossible to say which was which.

(*Music Cue No. 13 to crashing climax, then:*)

THE CURTAIN FALLS

Discussing and Interpreting
Animal Farm

Play Analysis

1. Communism has been described as "an idealist's dream, converted by realists into a nightmare." How does the action in *Animal Farm* parallel this description?

2. Orwell called *Animal Farm* "a fairy story." We have described it as a fable. Which is it? Can it be both? Use the play to support your answer.

3. Write a short newspaper account of the "Life of Snowball." Be sure to give your account a headline.

4. What is the significance of the song "Beasts of England," and why do the pigs finally have the song abolished?

5. **Thematic Connection: Decisions, Decisions** "Not to decide is to decide," goes the old saying. Discuss one major decision that an animal makes or doesn't make that proves to have unhappy consequences.

Literary Skill: Adapting a Fable

Below is a retelling of a familiar fable by Aesop. Read the fable, then write a script for a short play based upon the fable.

The Ants and the Grasshopper

The ants were busy one fine winter's day drying the grain they had collected during the summer. A grasshopper, his stomach rumbling in hunger, passed by and begged them for some food. The ants asked him, "Why didn't you store up food for yourself during the winter?" The grasshopper replied, "I did not have the time. I passed the days in singing." The ants then said scornfully, "If you were foolish enough to sing all summer, then you must dance dinnerless to bed in winter."

When you have finished your script, collaborate with a few classmates to refine it. Present your play as Readers Theatre.

Performance Element: An Authentic Voice

Most of the actors in *Animal Farm* play the part of animals. Chose one of these animals and practice saying his or her lines as authentically as possible. For example, CAT might speak her lines slowly and with a throaty purr on certain words, such as *Re-education Committee*. SQUEALER, as his name implies, might speak in a high-pitched, breathless way. As you practice, focus on using strong inflection and vocalizations that are true to the character. Be sure to project out rather than into your script.

The Summer People

from the short story by Shirley Jackson
adapted for the stage by Brainerd Duffield

Creating Context:
Shirley Jackson's Style

The play you are about to read, like the short story it is based upon, presents a seemingly ordinary country town with folks going about their business. The summer people, a couple who visit yearly from the city, chat with the locals, buy sundries from their stores, and feel a certain kinship with them. Life would appear to be easy and pleasant.

READER, BEWARE!! Make no assumptions. For this is a play based on a story by Shirley Jackson, master of the subtle build-up and the shattering finale. Her tone—so matter-of-fact and low key—may lull you into a false sense of security. False security is Jackson's forte.

Jackson is famous for her Gothic novels of suspense, such as *The Haunting of Hill House* and *We Have Always Lived in the Castle*. The former was twice made into an edge-of-the-seat suspense film, both titled *The Haunting*. Her classic short story "The Lottery" caused a sensation when it was first published in 1948, and many schools—as well as the government of South Africa—banned it for a time.

So, stay on your toes as you read *The Summer People*, and be aware of the ways in which the quiet, subtle tone belies the actual events in the play. Think about what the characters reveal about themselves and one another. Notice what words are used to tell us about them. Try to find the telling detail here and there that gives a hint about something brewing beneath the surface.

Shirley Jackson

As you progress in your reading, try to find a point where the tone alters. Ask yourself, "How does the tone shape the play?"

As a Reader: Understanding Tone

Tone is a very personal thing. It reveals the way an author feels about what he or she is writing, and it can influence how the reader feels about the subject also. It would be fairly easy to distinguish the writing of Mark Twain from that of Shirley Jackson based solely on their tone. Twain's important themes are fringed with humor while Jackson shrouds hers in mystery.

Compare the two excerpts below. How does the tone in the short story by Jackson carry over into the play by Brainerd Duffield? How would the director or actor interpret the character's words without the author's descriptions?

from Page · · · · · · to Stage

"Heard you was staying on," Mr. Charley Walpole said. His old fingers fumbled maddeningly with the thin sheets of newspaper, carefully trying to isolate only one sheet at a time, and he did not look up at Mrs. Allison as he went on, "Don't know about staying on up there to the lake. Not after Labor Day."

"Well, you know," Mrs. Allison said, quite as though he deserved an explanation, "it just seemed to us that we've been hurrying back to New York every year, and there just wasn't any need for it. You know what the city is like in the fall." And she smiled confidingly up at Mr. Charley Walpole.

Rhythmically he wound string around the package. He's giving me a piece long enough to save, Mrs. Allison thought, and she looked away quickly to avoid giving any sign of impatience.

"I feel sort of like we belong here, more," she said. "Staying on after everyone else has left." To prove this, she smiled brightly across the store at a woman with a familiar face. . . .

"Well," Mr. Charley Walpole said. . .

"Well," he said again. "Never been summer people before, at the lake after Labor Day."

from *The Summer People* by Shirley Jackson

WALPOLE. Yes, I heard a rumor you was stayin' on.

JANET (*almost gaily*). Nothing wrong with that, is there?

WALPOLE. Hard to say.

JANET (*brightly*). I mean, we've got a right to if we want to.

WALPOLE. Don't know about livin' at the lake when the season's ended. Never been done before.

JANET. Robert and I talked it all over, and we simply made up our minds not to hurry back this year. There just wasn't any need for it.

WALPOLE. I daresay. Well, what can I do for you this afternoon?…

JANET. I was looking at these glass baking dishes. They seem like a bargain.

WALPOLE. They are. I marked 'em down last week. Had 'em here all summer. Country people won't buy 'em …

JANET. All right, I'll buy them from you. I can get a lot of use out of these. (WALPOLE *starts to wrap the dishes individually in newspaper.*)

WALPOLE. I expect you will…I'll wrap 'em up good, and I'm givin' you extra string, so's you'll have a piece long enough to save.

JANET. Thank you, Mr. Walpole…People are so kind and thoughtful in this town. I feel sort of like we belong here more. Staying on after everyone else has left. (WALPOLE *shoves the package across the counter and accepts the money she offers him.*)

from *The Summer People* adapted by Brainerd Duffield

As a Set Designer: Reflecting the Author's Tone

As you read *The Summer People*, think of how you would use the descriptions and illusions in the play to create just the right set. Keep a list of your ideas gathered from the play directions and any important details found in the dialogue.

The Summer People

Time

September of the present year

The Characters

ROBERT ALLISON ⎫	
JANET ALLISON ⎭	The summer people
MR. BABCOCK	The grocer
MISS TILDA BABCOCK	The grocer's sister
MR. CHARLEY WALPOLE	Owner, hardware and general store
MRS. LARKIN	Newspaper and sandwich shop owner
MR. WITHERS	Kerosene and ice delivery

Setting

Rural New England

*T*he scene is a bare stage. During the first sequence it will represent the village. The lights come up gradually. MR. BABCOCK, assisted by TILDA, erects the grocery store DR. It consists of a counter: two chair backs with a plank between them. At the same time MR. CHARLEY WALPOLE sets up an identical structure DL where the counter will serve as his hardware and general store. Meanwhile, ULC, a third character, MRS. LARKIN, is repeating the same business for her newspaper and sandwich shop. She also places two stools in front of the counter. Presently, ROBERT and JANET ALLISON, walking shoulder to shoulder, enter from L, each carrying a chair, which they place side by side LC. This is presumed to be the front seat of their car. They sit down and ROBERT, on her left, pantomimes driving. The shopkeepers exit into the wings adjacent to their stores. ROBERT and JANET drive for a little while, jiggling gently up and down to show they are traveling on a bumpy country road. She is the first to speak, and in the ensuing conversation they seem to be trying to reassure one another. It is evidently a discussion they've been through before.*

JANET *(rather wistfully)*. Robert, when you think about it, there isn't really anything to take us back to the city.

ROBERT *(nodding)*. I agree with you. We might as well enjoy the country as long as possible.

JANET. Seventeen years we've been coming up here, and we've always felt we *had* to get back to New York by the first week in September.

ROBERT. Why should we, after all? We don't want to go. Especially when the weather's so fine.

JANET. And we're never as happy as when we're up here in New England.

ROBERT. Exactly what I've been saying right along.

JANET. It's not as though anybody needed us. Both the children outgrew the cottage years ago. They've gone on to families of their own. Margaret's in Los Angeles, and Jerry's in Chicago. (*She looks to* ROBERT *as if he might dispute her statement.*)

ROBERT (*nodding*). Our friends are either dead or settled down in year-round houses. (*Amused*) Nobody understands why we like to come up here.

JANET. It's our real home. We spend all winter in that New York apartment, waiting for summer, so we can get back to the country.

ROBERT. Well, Janet, like I say, there's nothing to prevent us staying on into October.

JANET (*smiling*). I'm glad we decided. I can't tell you how glad. (*She looks around to right and left.*) Here we are. Such a nice little town. Everybody's so pleasant. It's like an adventure, driving to the village every two weeks. Buying things we can't get delivered. (ROBERT *brakes and parks the car. They get out on opposite sides.*) You go to Mrs. Larkin's, have your soda and read the local paper. I'll take my grocery list over to Mr. Babcock's.

(ROBERT *goes* ULC, *pantomimes opening and closing a door, then sits on one of the stools.* MRS. LARKIN *enters from* UL *to wait on him.*)

MRS. LARKIN. How do, Mr. Allison?

ROBERT. Very well, thank you, Mrs. Larkin. Give me a copy of the *Messenger*, and I'll have my usual. Double chocolate soda.

MRS. LARKIN. That's right. I could've told without your askin' me. Double chocolate soda.

ROBERT. Janet and I are old enough not to be ashamed of regular habits. Though sometimes, of course, I like to have one of your fried egg and onion sandwiches.

MRS. LARKIN. That's my specialty.

ROBERT. Today I'll just have the soda.

MRS. LARKIN. Should taste good on a day like this. Right warm for September.

ROBERT. Yes, it is.

(MRS. LARKIN *has handed him an invisible paper which he unfolds and begins to scan. She pumps and mixes the soda, placing it on the counter. During this exchange,* JANET *has paused, carefully checking through her shopping list. Now she turns the knob and goes into the grocery store.* MR. BABCOCK *comes from the wings to greet her.*)

BABCOCK. Howdy do, Miz' Allison?

JANET. Never better. Here's my list, Mr. Babcock.

(TILDA *enters from* UR, *putting boxes on a shelf* R.)

JANET. Good morning, Tilda. (*Raises her voice.* TILDA *is a trifle deaf.*)

TILDA. Just fine. And you?

JANET. First rate, thanks. We came into town to pick up a few items.

TILDA. So I see. You'll be leavin' soon, I s'pose. (*It is a statement, not a question.*)

JANET (*with a smile*). Matter of fact, no. Robert and I decided to stay on as long as the weather lasts. Another week or two at least.

TILDA. Land's sake! You don't say so?

BABCOCK. Nobody ever stayed at the lake past Labor Day before. (*He is occupied with the list, putting articles on the counter.*) Nobody.

JANET. But the city ... it's so hot—you've really no idea.

BABCOCK. Can't say I do. Never havin' been there.

JANET. We're always sorry when we leave.

BABCOCK. That's how summer people are. Hate to leave. I'd hate to leave myself. But I never heard of anybody staying on at the lake after Labor Day.

TILDA. Me neither.

JANET. I realize there'll be problems. And it's a twenty-mile drive to the village. Still, we thought we'd give it a try.

BABCOCK. Never know till you try. Let's see now. Two pounds of sugar …

(BABCOCK *exits into the wings DR.* JANET *starts examining the items on the counter.* TILDA *has finished with shelving things for the moment. She goes out a rear door and crosses from URC to ULC where she has a brief, surreptitious chat with* MRS. LARKIN. ROBERT, *studying his newspaper, takes no notice.* TILDA *proceeds UL to L, where she taps on what is evidently a screen door.* CHARLEY WALPOLE *enters DL and they have a short whispered conversation, after which* TILDA *retraces her route via upstage back to her brother's store and starts rearranging shelves again.* WALPOLE, *expressionless, wipes off his counter, then exits DL. During this,* BABCOCK *has continued his fetching and carrying, enumerating items as he puts them down for* JANET'S *approval.*)

BABCOCK. Cornstarch … vinegar … coffee … sardines … Couldn't interest you in some nice red eatin' apples?

JANET. Oh, yes, please. I'll have a big bagful. What are they—McIntosh?

BABCOCK. Yes, ma'am. These are McIntosh. I got some Red Astrakhans, if you'd rather have 'em.

JANET. No, these will be fine. Perfume the whole kitchen.

BABCOCK. Yes, I like the *smell* of 'em myself.

JANET. This is our big trip into town, you know, every two weeks, so we more or less spend the day at it. We depend on you, Mr. Babcock, for deliveries—but I always seem to need odds and ends I forget to ask for on the phone. Then, of course, we like to get the local vegetables when we come in.

BABCOCK. Got some fresh packaged candy, too.

JANET. I'll take a box.

BABCOCK. Thought you would. Knowing Mr. Allison.

JANET. We've both got a sweet tooth. No doubt about it. I've been thinking I might be real extravagant and use those eating apples to bake a pie. (TILDA *has completed her circuit in time to hear this last remark.*)

TILDA. I declare. Well, I always say the short cut to a man's heart is through his gizzard.

BABCOCK. That's the whole list. (*He presents the bill and* JANET *pays him.*) Shall I carry 'em out to the car for you?

JANET. I'd be grateful. (BABCOCK *gathers up the bundles, comes around counter to the door, then crosses to LC and puts the purchases in the back seat of the car.*)

TILDA. Bye, bye, Miz' Allison.

JANET. Good-bye, Tilda. Expect I'll be seeing you next time we drive in.

TILDA. Hope you won't regret stayin' on. It can turn chilly overnight.

JANET. We're going to risk it—for once.

TILDA. Suit yourself and you'll live the longer. That's what my mother used to say. (JANET *goes out the door DRC and passes* BABCOCK, *who is on his way back. They beam at one another.*)

BABCOCK. Going to Johnson's?

JANET. What? Oh, yes, that's right.

BABCOCK. You take care now.

JANET. We will. Don't worry.

(BABCOCK *re-enters his store, exchanges a glance with* TILDA, *wags his head. Both exit off R.* ROBERT *looks up from his paper and waves at* JANET *through the window of the sandwich shop. She waves back, as she now crosses DL. As she enters the hardware store,* CHARLEY WALPOLE *comes to welcome her.*)

WALPOLE. Miz' Allison. Thought maybe you'd

be gone back to New York by this time.

JANET (*chuckling*). No, not yet, Mr. Walpole. Usually we go the first Tuesday after Labor Day—

WALPOLE. That's today.

JANET. Except this year, we're planning to linger a little while—maybe even till October.

WALPOLE. Yes, I heard a rumor you was stayin' on.

JANET (*almost gaily*). Nothing wrong with that, is there?

WALPOLE (*with a smile*). Hard to say.

JANET (*brightly*). I mean, we've got a right to if we want to.

WALPOLE. Don't know about livin' at the lake when the season's ended. Never been done before.

JANET. Robert and I talked it all over, and we simply made up our minds *not* to hurry back this year. There just wasn't any need for it.

WALPOLE. I daresay. Well, what can I do for you this afternoon?

JANET. For one thing, I'd like some colored thumbtacks. I'm going to put up new shelf edging in the kitchen.

WALPOLE. I got green ones and I got yella.

JANET. Green will do very nicely.

(WALPOLE *exits and returns to put the packet on the counter.*)

WALPOLE. Here you go.

JANET. I was looking at these glass baking dishes. They seem like a bargain.

WALPOLE. They are. I marked 'em down last week. Had 'em here all summer. Country people won't buy 'em. They won't trust anythin' that don't look permanent as rocks.

JANET (*laughing*). I'm sure that's the truth, if *you* say so.

WALPOLE. Yes, ma'am. Local folks started usin' aluminum now—but that's very recent.

JANET. All right, I'll buy them from you. I can get a lot of use out of these. (WALPOLE *starts to wrap the dishes individually in newspaper.*)

WALPOLE. I expect you will. You'll know how to handle 'em. I knew if I sold 'em it'd be to summer people. Showed 'em to my wife. She wouldn't have 'em in the house.

JANET (*amused*). You can tell her tonight that you found a customer.

WALPOLE. I'll wrap 'em up good, and I'm givin' you extra string, so's you'll have a piece long enough to save.

JANET. Thank you, Mr. Walpole.

WALPOLE. Might come in handy some day.

JANET. It's bound to. People are so kind and thoughtful in this town. I feel sort of like we belong here more. Staying on after everyone else has left. (WALPOLE *shoves the package across the counter and accepts the money she offers him.*)

WALPOLE. Out of five dollars… . (*He carefully counts out the change, which she puts in her purse.*) Well, I wish you luck, both of you— there's never been summer people before, at the lake after Labor Day.

JANET (*cheerfully*). I'll be seeing you, Mr. Walpole.

WALPOLE. Hope so. (*As she goes out the door to DLC, he frowns, scratches behind his ear, then exits into wings DL.* JANET *puts her parcel in the back seat of the car, then crosses ULC to fetch her husband. She opens the door and enters the sandwich shop.*)

MRS. LARKIN. Miz' Allison—I imagine you'll want a cool drink.

JANET (*perching on stool*). Same as I always have.

MRS. LARKIN. Small raspberry phosphate with a squeeze of lemon.

JANET. That's right. I'm very partial to your raspberry phosphates. (*She gives her husband a little wink, as* MRS. LARKIN *briskly prepares and serves the drink.*)

ROBERT. Buy lots of things we don't need but can't get along without?

JANET. You know *me*. We won't starve for a day or two, you can be sure of that. Did Robert tell you about our change of schedule, Mrs. Larkin?

MRS. LARKIN. No, he didn't. Mr. Allison's had his nose in the newspaper ever since he came in here. But I did hear as how you're stayin' on.

JANET *(agreeably)*. News travels fast around here.

ROBERT. We thought we'd take advantage of the lovely weather.

MRS. LARKIN. That's what they told me. Must say I was startled to hear it. *(But she doesn't sound startled.)*

JANET. It seemed a shame to go so soon.

MRS. LARKIN. I don't guess anyone's ever stayed out there so long before. They usually leave Labor Day.

JANET *(finishing drink)*. That was very tasty. (ROBERT *puts money on the counter.*)

ROBERT. We'd better be starting back … if we want to see the sunset on the lake.

JANET. Yes, we really should. Good-bye, Mrs. Larkin, and thanks.

MRS. LARKIN. You're entirely welcome.

ROBERT. Thank you again.

MRS. LARKIN. Entirely welcome.

(MRS. LARKIN *stands and watches* THE ALLISONS *as they go out the door and return to their car LC. The lights are dimming gradually, and the various shopkeepers can be seen dismantling their counters and disappearing into the wings. An overhead Pinspot holds on* JANET *and* ROBERT, *seated in the car to begin their homeward journey. They joggle and sway to show the movement of the car on the country road.)*

JANET *(after a pause)*. Anything of interest in the *Messenger?*

ROBERT. You know better than that. Less news than ever this time of year. But there's fair weather predicted.

JANET. I call that good news.

ROBERT. Cows and horses being auctioned off.

JANET *(smiling)*. We don't need any.

ROBERT. A barn dance at Plato Center on the far side of the mountain. The way my back's been acting, I couldn't get around the floor more than once.

JANET. Nor could I. We're getting to be a pair of rickety old fossils.

ROBERT. Happy ones, though. Did the villagers seem surprised when you broke the news?

JANET. They took it very calmly. Scarcely batted an eye. You know, they're wonderful. That old New England stock. Not much for deep thinking or reading books …

ROBERT. They can be a bit peculiar sometimes. It's generations of inbreeding. That and the bad land.

JANET. But they're great people. So solid and reasonable and so *honest.*

ROBERT *(nodding agreement)*. Makes you feel good, knowing there are still towns like this.

JANET. I bought some glass baking dishes from Charley Walpole. Back in New York, I might have paid a few cents less, but there wouldn't have been anything sort of personal in the transaction.

ROBERT. That sun's going down fast. When we get to the top of the next hill, we should be able to see the lake in the distance.

JANET. And our cottage.

ROBERT. Our home, you mean. *(Both peer ahead, anticipating.)*

JANET *(with a radiant smile)*. There it is—silhouetted against the water.

ROBERT. We've still got a long trip over that dirt road.

JANET. You just drive carefully and let me relax after my day of whirlwind shopping. (*She leans back in the seat.*)

ROBERT (*after a pause*). What are you thinking about, Janet?

JANET (*softly*). I'm thinking how good it'll be to get there.

ROBERT. It always is. We made a wise decision—to stay on.

JANET. Yes, didn't we?

(*The spotlight dims, leaving the stage in darkness.*)

THE FIRST DAY

When the lights come up again, the two straight chairs have been removed and two rocking chairs are now placed stage C to represent the porch of the cottage. The door to the cottage is LC behind the chairs and the kitchen is in the ULC area. The path to the cottage runs diagonally from UR to DC. A lawn is DLC and DL, and the lake is directly out front. THE ALLISONS *spend much of their time sitting in the rockers and gazing at the lake. Right now,* JANET *is in the kitchen, wearing an apron and drying dishes. Glancing out the window, she sees something that interests her. She comes out of the door and goes to DLC, where she crouches, as if trying to coax an animal out of the tall grass.*

JANET. Come here, kitty. I'm not going to hurt you. Here, kitty, kitty ... (*Seeing that it is useless, she straightens up, returns to the porch, sits and rocks gently back and forth.*)

(ROBERT *comes into view UR and walks down the path. He is noticeably out of breath from climbing the hill. He joins his wife and sits in the porch rocker beside her.*)

ROBERT. Taking it nice and easy?

JANET. Oh, I've been busy. Put a pie in the oven. Very wasteful of me, using eating apples to make a pie. Yesterday I told Tilda Babcock I was going to do just that. She looked scandalized.

ROBERT. I can imagine.

JANET. Then I washed the new baking dishes. There was a chip on the edge of one. I guess Mr. Walpole hadn't noticed.

ROBERT. You mean he put one over on you.

JANET. I hardly think so. Charley's much too innocent for that. (*She sees a printed brochure in her husband's hand.*) You mean to say that's all the mail we got?

ROBERT. Just a circular from Macy's. (*He hands it to her.*)

JANET. Better than no reading matter at all. We didn't even get the New York paper?

ROBERT. Well, you know how erratic that can be. Always late. Some days we get none, then three will arrive in the same mail.

JANET. It's hardly worth the effort going down the hill—a mile to the mailbox—and up again for a thing like this.

ROBERT. I expect the walk is good for me.

JANET. What do you suppose has happened to the children? We used to hear as regular as clockwork.

ROBERT. Margaret's too busy out in California, taking her kids to the beach or playing tennis. She never was famous for letter writing, anyhow.

JANET. But Jerry's been very good this summer, very dutiful about writing.

ROBERT. Oh, I could recite the news from Chicago, if you care to hear it. His letters always follow the same pattern.

JANET. That's true. Still, I never get tired of receiving them. Let's see what Macy's has to say to us.... (*Reading from the brochure*) "Our fringed white knit poncho crisscrossed with red and blue stripes. A great way to look while cheering the home team or snow-turtling[1] around your favorite resort."

---

1. snow-turtling, a form of sledding using a plastic disk

ROBERT (*thinking about it*). You can get along without one of those.

JANET. There's a sale of wool blankets. I'd better make a note to look at them when we get back to New York. It's hard to find good ones in pretty colors nowadays.

ROBERT. Did I pump you enough pails of water this morning?

JANET. I've got plenty for the time being. Tank's getting real low on kerosene, but Mr. Withers should be here tomorrow.

ROBERT. Yes, he's very dependable.

JANET. It's a wonder how we've managed down through the years, getting water from the backyard pump, cooking on a kerosene stove. All those houses across the lake put in plumbing and electricity ages ago.

ROBERT. I wouldn't want to change a thing about this place.

JANET. I'm not suggesting we should. Hardship is part of the charm. (*Looking off DL*) I noticed a stray cat out there in the grass a while ago, not much bigger than a kitten. Isn't it a crime the way some people will keep a pet all summer and then move back to the city and leave it to fend for itself?

ROBERT. It's downright heartless. Shouldn't be allowed to have animals at all, people like that.

JANET. I called to it, but it's gone sort of wild. I'm going to put out a saucer of food later and coax it to be friendly.

ROBERT. By the end of the week it'll be up here sitting in your lap and purring its head off. Say, I can smell that pie in the oven.

JANET. It ought to be a good one. I spared no expense.

ROBERT. When did you ever?

JANET (*rocking*). This is my favorite time of the afternoon, watching the lights and shadows on the lake going gray and blue as the clouds move over. (ROBERT *squints at the sky, farmer-style.*)

ROBERT (*with a Yankee twang*). Looks like we might have some rain.

JANET (*countrified accent*). Good for the crops. (*They laugh.*)

ROBERT. No, it's not going to rain. I'd call this the end of a perfect day, wouldn't you?

JANET. That's *exactly* what I'd call it.

(*Both rock slowly in their chairs, gazing out at the lake and the sky. Lights fade slowly to darkness.*)

THE SECOND DAY

JANET *is at the sink in the kitchen, peeling potatoes. A truck can be heard approaching, and a car door slams off R. The motor of the truck is left idling during the scene that follows.* JANET *wipes her hands on her apron and goes on the porch, as* MR. WITHERS *enters UR and comes down the path.*

JANET (*warmly*). Good morning, Mr. Withers. You're a sight for sore eyes.

WITHERS. Howdy, Miz' Allison. Passed your husband at the foot of the hill. On his way to get the mail, I guess.

JANET. That's right. I sure am glad to see you. We were getting pretty low on oil. (WITHERS *stares at her uncomfortably, as his truck motor throbs away in the background.*)

WITHERS. Thought you folks would be leavin'.

JANET (*optimistically*). We're staying on another month. The weather was so nice and it seemed like—

WITHERS. That's what they told me. Can't give you no oil, though.

JANET. What do you mean? We're just going to keep on with our regular … (*She raises her eyebrows.*)

WITHERS. After Labor Day. I don't get so much oil myself after Labor Day.

(*Striving to keep her temper,* JANET *gives him a brave smile.*)

JANET. But can't you get extra oil, at least while we stay?

WITHERS. I dunno … (*Scratching his chin*) You see … you see, I order this oil. I order it down from maybe fifty, fifty-five miles away. I order back in June, how much I'll need for the summer. Then I order again … oh, about November. Round about now, it's startin' to get pretty short. (*He makes a half-turn UR, as if about to go.*)

JANET. But, Mr. Withers, can't you give us *some?* Isn't there anyone else who sells it?

WITHERS (*after due consideration*). Don't know as you could get oil anywheres else right now. Might try Babcock's or Johnson's. *I* can't give you none. (*Turns to go*)

JANET. What did you drive up here for, Mr. Withers, if it wasn't to deliver oil?

WITHERS. I'm just goin' the rounds, haulin' garbage away from the city folks' houses. Country people don't need that service. Country people don't have garbage. (*He is now UR at the end of the path. He turns back to face her.*) Ice? I could let you have some ice. (*She takes a few desperate steps in his direction.*)

JANET. Mr. Withers … would you please *try* to get us some oil—for next week?

WITHERS. Don't see's I can. After Labor Day, it's harder. (*He exits. Car door slams off R. The truck is heard driving away.*)

(JANET *returns to the porch, sits in her rocker, moving back and forth in mild indignation. Presently* ROBERT *appears UR and approaches down the path. He is empty-handed and more out of breath than usual.*)

ROBERT (*sitting in his chair*). No mail. No newspaper. Nothing. (*Reacts to her expression*) What's ailing *you?*

JANET (*seething*). That man! Mr. Withers!

ROBERT. Didn't he fill the tank?

JANET. He did not. Next summer. Just let *him* try coming around next summer!

ROBERT. He didn't offer me a ride up the hill, either. I thought that was very impolite.

JANET. I kept my temper with him. I told myself that city manners are no good with country people. You can't boss them around.

ROBERT. Maybe we can get kerosene from Mr. Babcock.

JANET. That's what I'm hoping. I was going to call in a special order tomorrow.

ROBERT. Why not phone him now? (JANET *sighs.*)

JANET. I postpone using that telephone as long as possible. Last time, I had to turn the sidecrank half a dozen times before I even got the operator.

ROBERT. It's aggravating, I know. There can't be many communities left that still use those sidewinders.

JANET (*smiling in spite of herself*). It's a rarity, probably a valuable antique, but it taxes my patience.

ROBERT. I suppose Mr. Withers is holding back his oil supply for a high price during the winter. What worries me is Jerry and Margaret. What's happened to them, do you think?

JANET (*reassuring*). We'll be hearing soon. They won't forget us altogether.

ROBERT. Ought to realize how we wait for their letters. Thoughtless, selfish children. Ought to know better.

JANET. Well, dear, wishing won't bring the mail.

ROBERT (*muttering*). At least they could send a postcard. (*He rocks back and forth wearily.*) I'm going to rest up today and start mending the pier and patching up the rowboat tomorrow.

JANET. You do that. No real hurry about anything, is there? (*She rises abruptly, staring off DL.)* There! I saw it again … that kitten! *(She gets a saucer of food from the kitchen, emerges and carries the plate DL. She kneels and holds out the food.)* Here, little kitty. Here, kitty, come. Don't be scared of *me* … here, little baby …

ROBERT. It'll come to you. It takes time to win them over. Everything takes time.

JANET. Here, kitty. Here, kitty, come …

(Lights fade out.)

THE THIRD DAY

When the lights come up, JANET *is at the wall telephone in the kitchen, holding the receiver to her ear, and nervously fingering her apron with the other hand. A telephone bell is ringing off DR. It rings several times before* MR. BABCOCK *arrives in a pinspot at the DR proscenium to answer the call.*

BABCOCK. Store? *(He uses a rising, suspicious inflection, as though mistrustful of modern inventions.)*

JANET. This is Mrs. Allison, Mr. Babcock. I thought I'd give you my order a day early this week, because I wanted to be sure and get some—

BABCOCK. What say, Mrs. Allison?

(ROBERT comes down the path from UR, puffing as usual. When he hears what his wife is doing, he sits in his rocking chair and listens sympathetically.)

JANET *(raising her voice)*. I said, Mr. Babcock, I thought I'd call in my order early so you could send me—

BABCOCK. Mrs. Allison? You'll come and pick it up?

JANET. Pick it up? *(In her astonishment, JANET's voice has dropped back to its normal tone.)*

BABCOCK *(loudly)*. What's that, Mrs. Allison?

JANET. I thought I'd have you *send* it out, as usual.

BABCOCK. Well, Miz' Allison … *(Long pause)*

Miz' Allison, I'll tell you, boy's been working for me went back to school yestiddy. Now I got nobody to deliver. I only got a boy deliverin' summers, y' see.

JANET. I thought you *always* delivered.

BABCOCK. Not after Labor Day, Miz' Allison. *(Firmly)* You never been here after Labor Day before, so's you wouldn't know, of course.

JANET *(helplessly)*. Well … are you *sure?* Couldn't you just send an order out today, Mr. Babcock?

BABCOCK. Matter of fact, I guess I couldn't Miz' Allison. It wouldn't hardly pay, deliverin', with no one else out at the lake.

JANET *(now very anxious)*. What about Mr. Hall … those people that live three miles away from us out here? Mr. Hall could bring it out when he comes.

BABCOCK. Hall? John Hall? They've gone to visit her folks upstate, Miz' Allison.

JANET. But they bring all our butter and eggs …

BABCOCK. Left yestiddy. Prob'ly didn't think you folks'd stay on up there.

JANET *(plaintively)*. But I told Mr. Hall … *(She stops resignedly.)* All right. I'll send Mr. Allison later today.

BABCOCK *(satisfied)*. You got all you need till then. *(It is a confirmation, not a question. He hangs up and exits DR. His spotlight dims out.* JANET *goes slowly to the porch and sits beside her husband.)*

JANET. He won't deliver. You'll have to go in this afternoon. We've got just enough kerosene to last till you get back.

ROBERT. He should have told us sooner. Never mind. I've got a present for you. *(He produces a letter from his pocket.)*

JANET *(delighted)*. From Jerry! *(She takes the envelope and admires it.)* Look at that childish scrawl—and dirty fingerprints all around the edges. *(Hands it back)* You read it to me. (ROBERT *opens the letter.*)

ROBERT (*reading aloud*). "Dear Mother and Dad. Am glad this goes to the lake as usual, we always thought you came back too soon and ought to stay up there as long as you could. Alice says that now you're not as young as you used to be and have no demands on your time, fewer friends, et cetera, in the city, you ought to get what fun you can while you can. Since you two are both happy up there, it's a good idea for you to stay. Things are the same in Chicago. There are measles going around, but we figure if the kids get them now they'll be better off later. Alice is well, of course; me, too. Been playing a lot of bridge lately with some people you don't know, named Carruthers. Nice young couple about our age. Well, will close now as I guess it bores you to hear about things so far away. Tell Dad old Dickson in our Chicago office died. He used to ask about Dad a lot. Have a good time up at the lake, and don't bother about hurrying back. Love from all of us, Jerry." (*A rather long pause*)

JANET. Funny. It doesn't sound like Jerry. He never wrote anything like … (*She breaks off, without finishing.*)

ROBERT. Like what? Never wrote anything like what?

JANET (*quietly*). It sounds so funny … so final … As if they were glad to be rid of us … .

ROBERT. Fiddlesticks! You're imagining things.

JANET. Didn't enclose any snapshots of the baby?

ROBERT (*shaking envelope*). Nope. No snapshots.

JANET. What a pity … (*She shivers, stroking her elbows.*) I can feel winter coming. We're going to want hot water bottles tonight. Bed socks, too.

ROBERT. Janet, it's not going to be that cold.

JANET. You don't want to catch pneumonia, do you?

ROBERT. Certainly not, and I'm not going to. (*They keep on rocking for a while in silence.*)

JANET. Robert … you know, that little cat— it's getting real friendly. Came up on the porch a while ago, and let me pet her. She's a sweet little thing.

ROBERT. Misery loves company. (*JANET gives him a sheepish smile and nods.*)

JANET. That's what they say. It's the truth, Robert.

ROBERT. Well, I'll go warm up the old tin lizzie, if you'll get to work on your shopping list.

JANET. Shouldn't take me long. (*ROBERT disappears down the path and exits off UR. JANET gets up and crosses DR.*) Here, kitty, kitty, kitty. Here, kitty. Come on out, kitty. I'll give you another good meal. Here, kitty, kitty. Now where could that little cat go to? She was so tame and friendly yesterday and this morning she was rubbing against my leg purring away. I thought she'd be ready to move in with us by now. Here, kitty, kitty. Here, kitty. (*She walks back and forth near the edge of the stage looking for the cat. Suddenly she stops.*) Oh, there you are. Why don't you come over—(*She stoops down to coax the cat, putting her hand out to pet it.*) Come on, kitten, I won't hurt you— (*She jerks her hand back suddenly, exclaiming:*) Oh, no!

(JANET *reluctantly puts her hand out again and feels the off stage cat, then she returns to her chair, wiping her hands on her apron. When she is seated,* ROBERT *reappears. He is in a bad temper.*)

JANET. You almost ready to go? I got my list ready. (*She hands it to him. He crumples the list and tosses it aside. She stares at him in surprise.*)

ROBERT. Lot of good that list is going to do.

JANET. Robert! Why did you do that? Have you taken leave of your senses?

ROBERT (*at the end of his tether*). The damn car won't start.

JANET (*hesitates, then ventures a smile*). You're making a bad joke, aren't you?

ROBERT. It's no joke.

JANET. What's wrong with it? It was all right on Tuesday.

ROBERT (*between his teeth*). Well, it's not all right today.

JANET. Can't you fix it?

ROBERT. No, I cannot. I'll have to call someone.

JANET. Who?

ROBERT. Man that runs the filling station. He fixed it last summer. (*He goes purposefully into the kitchen, cranks the telephone vigorously, then waits for the operator.*) Three-five-one-double two. (*He waits again with growing irritation.*) Three-five-one-double two.... (*He waits longer.*) Well, ring it again.... (*This time he slams down the receiver. He returns to the porch, avoiding his wife's glance.*) No one there.

JANET (*placidly*). He's probably gone out for a minute. He's there alone, I imagine, so if he goes out, there's no one to answer the phone....

ROBERT (*with heavy irony*). That must be it.

JANET. Would you like some crackers and milk?

ROBERT. No, thanks.

JANET. Why don't you go down and see what the mailman had to bring, and then call again?

ROBERT (*impatient*). I've already been to the mailbox. We had a letter from Jerry, don't you remember?

JANET. Oh, dear. That's right. But—we haven't had a New York paper in over a week. How are we going to know what's going on in the world outside?

ROBERT. I seem to remember—when I put the order in, I told them not to bother sending it after the first week in September.

JANET. Well, that would explain it....

ROBERT. Something else. Something else I remembered, too. One time when I was in Mrs. Larkin's sandwich shop ... I recollect somebody saying that all mail deliveries at the lake were discontinued when the summer season was over.

JANET. That would be dreadful....You mean there won't be ...

ROBERT. Maybe not. It could be that letter from Jerry is the last one we're going to get.

(ROBERT *goes inside the cottage.* JANET *waits and watches until he reappears, carrying a small article by the handle. He sits again.*)

JANET. What are you up to?

ROBERT. See if I can't get some news on this portable radio.

JANET. We've hardly turned it on, since we bought it last June.

ROBERT. I'd like to hear some baseball scores. Or a little music to cheer us up.... (*He tinkers with the machine, shakes it, and then puts it down angrily on the deck of the porch.*)

JANET. Won't it work?

ROBERT. No, and it's my own damn fool fault. I meant to take it in to Charley Walpole, and ask him to check the battery. (JANET *is shaking with silent laughter.*)

JANET. Oh, dear, oh, my ...

ROBERT. What do you find so funny at a time like this?

JANET (*still laughing weakly*). I was thinking about those people in the village. Most of them call it Johnson's. I mean, Charley Walpole's hardware store. Because it used to be owned by a man named Johnson, when the place burned down fifty years ago. They don't like things to change, do they? (*A storm wind is heard, rising rapidly.*) Hear the wind, Robert—and look at the waves on the lake! (*General lighting dims perceptibly.*)

ROBERT. I noticed. Storm clouds, too. Flashes of lightning behind the mountain ...

JANET. No thunder yet. But it's getting so dark I may have to light the lamps at four o-clock. I hate to waste the oil.

ROBERT (*soberly*). Doesn't really matter. (*Smiles at her*) It's as plain as Pike's Peak. There's going to be some rain, and it'll come down hard. (*He gets up and goes back to the kitchen. He picks up the telephone receiver, twists the sidecrank. She asks no questions, but she listens. When he hangs up, she is still there in the porch rocker. He returns and announces briefly:*) The phone's dead.... (*She has no comment, but a moment later* JANET *says:*)

JANET. I'm not surprised.... I didn't tell you about the cat.

ROBERT. Has it disappeared?

JANET. No. It's dead.

ROBERT. Dead! What did it die of?

JANET. I don't know. Poor little creature. I'm glad she didn't know what was going to happen.

ROBERT. But we do ... now. I had a notion the night before last—when the lights weren't turned on at Mr. Hall's place ... (*A pause, while this sinks in*)

JANET. I wonder if we're supposed to *do* anything?

ROBERT. No, I don't think so. Just wait.

JANET. Poor little lost kitty ...

ROBERT. The car had been tampered with, you know. Even I could see that.

JANET. I suppose the phone wires had been cut?

ROBERT. Oh, yes. They'd been cut all right. Within the last few minutes.

JANET. Surely they don't meant to let us stay here—all alone—until we starve or freeze to death?

ROBERT. I'm afraid they intend to do just that.

JANET. But why, Robert ... why? What have we done to be treated like this? They were so polite and kind to us all summer long.

ROBERT. That's it, don't you see. We're summer people—outsiders. They don't want us here when the season's over. We have broken a taboo. We were supposed to go back home on Labor Day.

JANET. But this is our home.

ROBERT. They don't look at it that way. We're city people and we've overstayed our welcome.

JANET. Oh, dear ... oh, dear ... I still can't believe it.

ROBERT. It's true, though, and there's nothing we can do about it.

JANET. Well, if it's going to happen, I'd rather be right here with you—than anywhere else on earth. And we couldn't ask for prettier scenery.

ROBERT (*gazing off above the lake*). The storm's coming.

(*The wind starts up again, echoing from afar, then stirring through the nearby trees. Then: the first sudden crash of violent thunder. It rumbles away into silence. In the gathering gloom,* ROBERT *reaches out to clasp his wife's hand. The elderly couple sit side by side, as the stage lights fade gradually to blackness.*)

CURTAIN

The Summer People

Play Analysis

1. Why do you suppose Jackson wrote this story? What is she telling us?
2. Jerry's letter is disturbing to the Allisons. Do you think it was written by someone else? Why or why not?
3. In Jackson's story there is no kitten. Why do you think Duffield added these scenes?
4. The play ends with the Allisons holding hands and quietly accepting their fate. Write a paragraph describing what happens to them next.
5. **Thematic Connection: Decisions, Decisions** At what point in the play did you realize that the Allisons made the wrong decision in staying on? Explain your reasoning.

Literary Skill: Artistic License

Go back and reread the scenes in which Janet interacts with or discusses the kitten (pages 436, 439, 440, and 442). Brainerd Duffield had his artistic reasons for creating this new "character." Is it significant that we never actually see the kitten? What do you think the kitten's death might symbolize?

Performance Element: Scenery

Look at the list of set ideas you kept while reading the play. Reread any scenes that aren't clear in your mind. Think of ways in which you would make the scenery reflect the tone of the play using your ideas. Keeping in mind the set suggested by the playwright—simple store counters, chairs, stool, and rocking chairs—sketch a simple backdrop or similar structure that would suggest the scenery for the village and the Allisons' cottage.

Setting the Stage for

The Gift of the Magi

from the short story by O. Henry
adapted for the stage by Arthur L. Zapel

Creating Context: Who Were Those Three Men?

The play you are about to read begins by relating a very common belief about the Magi, also called "the three kings"—Caspar, Melchior, and Balthasar. We are told that they were "wise men (who) came from the East bearing valuable gifts for the baby Jesus, destined to be the Saviour."

The word *magi* is the plural of an old Persian word, *magus*, meaning "a priest." The Magi were, indeed, a priestly caste in ancient Persia (what we now know as Iran), but exactly who they later became, and how many appeared to pay their respects to the infant Jesus is still in question. In fact, there is no absolute agreement as to whether there were three of them, two of them, or fourteen of them. And it also appears that they were not kings at all. Many documents depict them as noble pilgrims seeking the way or learned astronomers following a beckoning star. In most accounts there does appear in Bethlehem men of a high class who come to pay homage to the newborn babe. It is also told that Herod, King of Judea (now Palestine), had been foretold about this child's birth and wanted him dead. So Herod told these men to bring him word of the child and its whereabouts. The Magi are said to have been warned in a dream of Herod's ill intent and did not return to him.

And as to the gifts—gold, frankincense, and myrrh—it is possible that these were not meant to be presents but a kind of test similar to one used to this day by Tibetan monks trying to find the new Dalai Lama. Three items are placed before the baby—if the infant takes the gold, this means he will be an earthly king; if he takes the frankincense (a kind of incense that was burned in rituals), it means he will be a divine king; and if he takes the myrrh (a kind of medicinal ointment), he will be a great healer. The great explorer Marco Polo brought back the account told in Persia describing how the Magi, so astounded by what they encountered in Bethlehem, gave *all* the gifts to the baby.

It probably doesn't matter what gifts were brought or why. The important thing to remember is that the story of the Magi is one of love and kindness. This is what the Magi's gifts symbolize. As you read the play, look for similar symbols of love and caring.

As a Reader: Understanding Symbolism

Symbolism in literature gives a person, place, or thing a meaning that suggests something beyond itself. A wedding ring, for example, is a lovely thing in and of itself, but it also symbolizes a commitment to marriage. Compare O. Henry's narration at the left to the adaptation at right. Think about what a present for Jim symbolizes for Della. How might an actor mime Della's feelings in the play?

from Page · · · · · · to Stage

Twenty dollars a week doesn't go far. Expenses had been greater than she had calculated. They always are. Only $1.87 to buy a present for Jim. Her Jim. Many a happy hour she had spent planning for something nice for him. Something fine and rare and sterling—something just a little bit near to being worthy of the honor of being owned by Jim.

There was a pier-glass between the windows of the room. Perhaps you have seen a pier-glass in an $8 flat. A very thin and very agile person may, by observing his reflection in a rapid sequence of longitudinal strips, obtain a fairly accurate conception of his looks. Della, being slender, had mastered the art.

Suddenly she whirled from the window and stood before the glass. Her eyes were shining brilliantly....

from "The Gift of the Magi" by O. Henry

READER 2. Twenty dollars a week doesn't go far. Expenses had been greater than she had calculated. They always are. Only one dollar and eighty-seven cents to buy a present for Jim. Her Jim. Many a happy hour she had spent planning for something nice for him. Something fine and rare and sterling–something just a little bit near to being worthy of the honour of being Jim's wife.

There was a pier-glass between the windows of the room. Perhaps you have seen a pier-glass in an eight dollar flat. A very thin and very agile person may, by observing his reflection in a rapid sequence of longitudinal strips, obtain a fairly accurate conception of oneself's looks. Della, being slender, had mastered the art.

(DELLA, *who has returned to look forlornly out the window, suddenly gets a flash idea. She whirls and steps across the room to the dresser, and she takes up her and mirror and a comb as she crosses to the table. She loosens her hair and it falls down along her back. Slowly she combs out the long strands of her hair as she studies her reflection in the hand mirror. Then she puts the hand mirror and comb down on the table and whirls again to look at her full image in the pier glass strips.*)

Suddenly she whirled from the window and stood before the glass. Her eyes were shining brilliantly, ...

from *The Gift of the Magi*
adapted by Arthur L. Zapel

As an Actor: Creating Dramatizations

The following play is a kind of Readers Theatre in which scenes are acted out as the Reader narrates. The Reader also recites some of the characters' dialogue. As you read, think about the action that corresponds to the Readers' narration.

The Gift of the Magi

Time
1915

Characters
READER 1

READER 2*

DELLA
A young woman of about 21 with long brown hair

JIM
A young man of about the same age

MADAME SOFRONIE
A middle-aged woman who deals in hair goods

Optional EXTRAS during shopping scene

Setting
A flat in New York

READER 1 *(from Stage Left apron).* Every year new Christmas stories are written. In the past one hundred years the total must be several thousand or more. Most were forgotten after the first reading, others enjoyed a brief flare of popularity for a few years and were lost to time. But a very few really exceptional stories have endured and very likely will continue to be with us for

---

*If Reader 1 is a male, Reader 2 should be a female and vice versa so that the viewpoints of both sexes are suggested by the READERS.

another hundred years or more—the Santa Claus story; Rudolph, the red-nosed reindeer; the legend about why the chimes rang, and several others. And, of course, the first story of Christmas—the story of the Nativity—the beautiful story of how Christ came to be born in a relatively small village in a faraway country over two thousand years ago. The story of how wise men came from the East bearing valuable gifts for the baby Jesus destined to be the Saviour. It was this part of the Nativity story that gave us the wonderful custom of exchanging gifts at Christmas, a custom we all enjoy because of the love giving and receiving expresses. It is just this thought that inspired the imagination of one of America's most popular short story writers at the turn of the century. He wrote hundreds of stories, most of which had surprise endings. He entertained people because he knew people—he knew how they really were and how they really acted and reacted. But even his many popular stories are forgotten today, almost all of them except, perhaps, one which seems to live on and on—"The Gift of the Magi." From the title you might think it is a religious story, but it's not — except for its message of true love. But decide for yourself. May I present O. Henry's classic—"The Gift of the Magi."

(DELLA *is seated DR at a small table. She has just emptied a ceramic vase of its contents of coins. Spreading them out on the table, she proceeds to organize them into countable groups, and she writes down the total. Then she throws down her pencil in frustration.*)

READER 2 (*Stage Right apron*). One dollar and eighty-seven cents. That was all. And sixty cents of it was in pennies. Pennies saved one and two at a time by bulldozing the grocer, the vegetable man, and the butcher until one's cheeks burned with the silent imputation of parsimony[1] that such close dealing implied. Three times Della counted it. One dollar and eighty-seven cents. And the next day would be Christmas.

(DELLA *leaves table, walks in a tight circle, expressing her frustration, then she throws herself down on a sofa at UR to cry and sob.*)

There was clearly nothing to do but flop down on the shabby little couch and howl. So Della did it, which instigates the moral reflection that life is made up of sobs, sniffles, and smiles, with sniffles predominating.

(DELLA *ends her outburst but continues to lie face down on the sofa.*)

READER 1 (*Stage Left*). In the vestibule below was a letter box into which no letter would go, and an electric button from which no mortal finger could coax a ring. Also appertaining thereunto was a card bearing the name "Mr. James Dillingham Young." The "Dillingham" had been flung to the breeze during a former period of prosperity when its possessor was being paid thirty dollars per week. Now when the income was shrunk to twenty dollars the letters of "Dillingham" looked blurred, as though they were thinking seriously of contracting to a modest and unassuming "D." But whenever Mr. James Dillingham Young came home and reached his flat above he was called "Jim" and warmly hugged by Mrs. James Dillingham Young, already introduced to you as Della.

(DELLA *arises from the sofa wiping away the remaining moisture from her eyes and cheeks. She pushes her hair back into place, walks to the UL window, peeks out briefly, then begins to pace the room. She stops and looks at the small collection of coins on the table. She lifts a cardboard-mounted photo of him from a side table, paces,*

---

1. imputation of parsimony, accusation of being stingy with money

and then returns it. She remains deeply preoccupied with her thoughts.)

READER 2. Della finished her cry and attended to her cheeks with the powder rag. She stood at the window and looked out dully at a gray cat walking a gray fence in a gray backyard. Tomorrow would be Christmas Day, and she had only one dollar and eighty-seven cents with which to buy Jim a present. She had been saving every penny she could for months with this result. Twenty dollars a week doesn't go far. Expenses had been greater than she calculated. They always are. Only one dollar and eighty-seven cents to buy a present for Jim. Her Jim. Many a happy hour she had spent planning something nice for him. Something fine and rare and sterling—something just a little bit near to being worthy of the honour of being Jim's wife.

There was pier glass between the windows of the room. Perhaps you have seen a pier glass in an eight dollar flat. A very thin and very agile person may, by observing the reflection in a rapid sequence of longitudinal strips, obtain a fairly accurate conception of oneself's looks. Della, being slender, had mastered the art.

(DELLA, who had returned to look forlornly out the window, suddenly gets a flash idea. She whirls and steps across the room to the dresser, and she takes up her hand mirror and a comb as she crosses to the table. She loosens her hair and it falls down along her back. Slowly she combs out the long strands of her hair as she studies her reflection in the hand mirror. Then she puts the hand mirror and comb down on the table and whirls again to look at her full image in the pier glass strips.)

Suddenly she whirled from the window to find her hand mirror. Her eyes were shining brilliantly, but her face had lost its color within twenty seconds. Rapidly she pulled down her hair and let it fall to its full length.

READER 1. Now, there were two possessions of the James Dillingham Young's in which they both took a mighty pride. One was Jim's gold watch that had been his father's and his grandfather's. The other was Della's hair. Had the Queen of Sheba lived in a flat across the airshaft, Della would have let her hair hang out the window some day to dry just to depreciate Her Majesty's jewels and gifts. Had King Solomon been the janitor, with all his treasures piled up in the basement, Jim would have pulled out his watch every time he passed, just to see him pluck at his beard with envy.

(In sequence with the narration DELLA does up her hair after a pause or two for sad reflection.)

READER 2. So now Della's beautiful hair fell about her, rippling and shining like a cascade of brown waters. And then she did it up again nervously and quickly. Once she faltered for a moment and stood still while a tear or two splashed on the worn carpet. On went her old jacket; on went her old brown hat. With a whirl of skirts and with the brilliant sparkle still in her eyes, she fluttered out the door and down the stairs to the street.

(DELLA resolutely slips on her old jacket and hat from a clothes tree standing in the corner. She whirls around and disappears Offstage. Lights fade or curtain closes.)

(Spotlight appears on Stage Right apron to the side of the narrator. Beneath a sign reading "MADAME SOFRONIE—Hair Goods of All Kinds," a dowdy, middle-age woman stands at a table arranging the curls on a wig resting on a wigstand head. DELLA steps into the scene.)

DELLA. Will you buy my hair?

MADAME. I buy hair. Take yer hat off and let's have a sight at the looks of it.

(DELLA removes her hat and releases her hair. MADAME SOFRONIE walks around her, touching the hair in careful appraisal.)

(Pause) Twenty dollars, and that's it.

DELLA. Give it to me quick.

(MADAME SOFRONIE *is counting out the money from her cigar box cache as the lights fade)*

(During the darkness the actress portraying DELLA *quickly gathers up her hair and pins it to appear short. She may also put on a boy's cap.)*

(Busy music bridges the transition and continues under READER 2's *narration. Moving spotlights criss-cross as* DELLA *is seen pantomiming the actions of a frenzied shopper moving from shop to shop across the entire darkened stage area or in front of closed curtain.)*

READER 2. And the next two hours tripped by on rosy wings. She was ransacking the stores for Jim's present.

(Spotlights stop moving as DELLA *stops at an imaginary store counter DC. She pantomimes looking at a fob chain,[2] which she studies carefully, holding it up to the light. Then she pantomimes* JIM's *action as if the fob were attached to his watch and he was taking it from his pocket to see the time.)*

She found it at last. It surely had been made for Jim and no one else. There was no other like it in any of the stores, and she had turned all of them inside out. It was a platinum fob chain, simple and chaste in design, properly proclaiming its value by substance alone and not by flashy ornamentation—as all good things should do. It was even worthy of The Watch. As soon as she saw it she knew it must be Jim's. It was like him. Quietness and value—the description applied to both.

(She pantomimes paying the store clerk and receiving her change.)

Twenty-one dollars they took from her for it and she hurried home with the eighty-seven cents.

READER 1. When Della reached home her intoxication of joy gave way to prudence and reason. She got out her curling irons,

lighted the gas, and went to work repairing the ravages made by generosity added to love, which is always a tremendous task, dear friends—a mammoth task. Within forty minutes her head was covered with tiny, close-lying curls that made her look wonderfully like a truant schoolboy. *(Lights fade down briefly and up again slowly to indicate a passage of time.)*

(DELLA *steps back Upstage as lights again reveal the set or the curtain opens. She removes the boy's cap [if she's wearing one] and goes to corner, taking up curling irons. She goes through the motions of curling her hair into short, tight curls. She takes up a hand mirror and studies her new hair style from all angles.)*

READER 2. She looked at her reflection in the mirror long, carefully, and critically, and thought, "If Jim doesn't kill me before he takes a second look, he'll say I look like a Coney Island chorus girl. But what could I do—what could I do with a dollar and eighty-seven cents?"

(DELLA *is seen looking out the window. She turns, goes to the table, and sits on its corner facing the door. She waits expectantly.)*

READER 1. At seven o'clock the coffee was made and the frying pan was on the back of the stove. Jim was never late. Della doubled the fob chain in her hand and sat on the corner of the table near the door he always entered.

(She begins to squirm a little. She quickly takes another peek at her reflection in the hand mirror, puts it down, then resolutely faces the door.)

Then she heard his step on the stair down on the first flight and she turned white for just a moment. She had a habit of saying little silent prayers about the simplest everyday things, and now she whispered to herself, "Please God, make him think I am still pretty."

---

2. fob chain, a short chain attached to a pocket watch

(JIM *steps in, takes three steps, sees* DELLA *and stops.*)

READER 2. The door opened and Jim stepped in. He looked thin and very serious. Poor fellow, he was only twenty-two—and to be burdened with a wife. He needed a new overcoat and he was without gloves.

(*Slowly without moving from his place, without moving his head, he removes his overcoat and lets it slide to the floor at this feet. His eyes are still fixed on* DELLA.)

READER 1. He stood as immovable as a setter at the scent of quail. His eyes were fixed upon Della and there was an expression in them that she could not read, and it terrified her.

(DELLA *smiles at him but she's afraid to approach him. Awkwardly, she waves her hand at* JIM *to try to break his fixed gaze or get some kind of movement or response. There is none.*)

It was not anger, nor surprise, nor disapproval, nor horror, nor any of the sentiments that she had prepared for. He simply stared at her fixedly with that peculiar expression on his face. Della wriggled off the table and went for him.

(*At length she goes to* JIM, *takes his arm, and kisses his hand. She steps back a step and pivots so* JIM *can see her new style. She touches it with her hand.*)

DELLA. Jim, darling, don't look at me that way. I had my hair cut off and sold it because I couldn't have lived through Christmas without giving you a present. It'll grow out again—you won't mind, will you? I just had to do it. My hair grows awfully fast. Say "Merry Christmas!" Jim, and let's be happy. You don't know what a nice— what a beautiful, nice gift I've got for you.

(JIM *steps up close to her and looks dumbfounded at her new hair style. Then he walks about the room looking blindly at things, shaking his head in disbelief.*)

JIM (*slowly, incredulous*[3]). You've cut off your hair.

DELLA (*as brightly as possible*). Cut it off and sold it. Don't you like me just as well anyhow? I'm still me without my hair.

JIM. You say your hair is gone?

DELLA. You needn't look for it, it's sold. It's sold and gone, Jim. It's Christmas Eve, honey. Be good to me, for it went for you. Maybe the hairs of my head were numbered but nobody could ever count my love for you, Jim.

(JIM *pulls himself together, turns to* DELLA *with open arms. She enters into them laying her head blissfully on his chest. He raises her chin and kisses her. Both embrace each other.*)

READER 2. Out of his trance Jim seemed quickly to wake. He enfolded his Della. For ten seconds let us regard with discreet scrutiny some inconsequential object so as not to intrude on their privacy. Eight dollars a week or a million a year—what is the difference? A mathematician or a wit would give you the wrong answer. The Magi brought valuable gifts, but that was not among them. This dark assertion will be illuminated later on.

(JIM *releases* DELLA, *reaches to the floor for his overcoat and takes a package from the pocket, which he throws on the table.*)

Jim drew a package from his overcoat pocket and threw it on the table.

(*Turning again to* DELLA, *he holds her at arm's length at the shoulders. When he finishes his speech he turns her to the present and releases her.*)

JIM. Don't make any mistake about me, Dell. I don't think there's anything in the way of a haircut or a shave or a shampoo that could make me love my girl any less. But if you'll unwrap that package you may see why I acted as I just did.

---

3. incredulous, amazed; not believing

READER 1. White fingers and nimble tore at the string and paper. And then an ecstatic reaction of joy; and then, alas! A quick feminine change to tears and wails, necessitating the immediate employment of all the comforting powers of the lord of the flat. (DELLA *tears open the package. She gasps for joy as she studies its contents. Then slowly her beautiful smile wrinkles into an outburst of tears as she puts the package back on the table, and she rushes into* JIM's *arms again for comfort.*)

READER 2. For there lay The Combs—the set of combs, side-by-side, that Della had worshipped for a long time in the Broadway shop window. Beautiful combs, pure tortoise shell, with jeweled rims—just the shade to wear in the beautiful vanished hair. They were expensive combs, she knew, and her heart had simply craved and yearned over them without the least hope of possession. And now, they were hers, but the tresses that should have adorned the coveted adornments were gone. (*She pulls him over to the table as she takes up the combs from the box and holds them up to* JIM *with a smile trying to find its way through the tears.*)

DELLA. My hair grows so fast, Jim! (*She impulsively breaks away from* JIM, *holding the combs up to her remaining hair as she looks at them in the hand mirror. Then, suddenly she puts down the mirror and quickly finds her present for* JIM.) (*Pause*) Oh, oh! You haven't seen your present from me, Jim.

(*She hold up the watch fob for* JIM *to admire. Then she gestures for* JIM *to give her his watch.*)

Isn't it a dandy, Jim! I hunted all over town to find it. You'll have to look at the time a hundred times a day now. Give me your watch. I want to see how it looks on it.

JIM. Dell. You know what? I have a great idea. (JIM *takes the fob and the combs and carefully puts them aside. Again he takes* DELLA *in his arms.*)

DELLA. What, Jim?

JIM. Well, it's that we put our Christmas presents away and keep 'em a while. They're too nice to use just now. (*Pause*) You see, Dell, I sold my watch to get the money to buy your combs. And now suppose we get busy and get our dinner started.

(*She looks up at him with incredulity, smiles, then they begin laughing together as they proceed to get things ready for dinner. Several times they stop, point at each other, and begin the pantomime of laughter.*)

(*Continue actions under the final narration until* READER 1's *final words, during which they embrace once more as lights fade or curtain closes.*)

READER 1. The Magi, as you know, were wise men—wonderfully wise men—who brought gifts to the Babe in the manger. They invented the art of giving Christmas presents. Being wise, their gifts were no doubt wise ones, possibly bearing the privilege of exchange in case of duplication.

READER 2. And here we have lamely related to you the uneventful chronicle of two foolish young lovers in a flat who most unwisely sacrificed for each other the greatest treasures of their house. But in a last word to the wise of these days let it be said that of all who give gifts, these two were the wisest. Of all who give and receive gifts, such as they are wisest.

READER 1. Everywhere they are wisest. They are the Magi.

Discussing and Interpreting
The Gift of the Magi

Play Analysis

1. What do Jim's watch and Della's hair symbolize in *The Gift of the Magi?*
2. This story has been called "one of O. Henry's most enduring works." Do you think it holds up well in our sometimes cynical world? Why or why not?
3. If you were cast as Jim, how would you play the scene in which he first sees Della with her new bob? Block out how you would move, gesture, and speak.
4. Create a four-color drawing of Mme. Sofronie conducting business. Think in terms of using your image to plan a set for Sofronie's shop, props, and costume.
5. **Thematic Connection: Decisions, Decisions** The narrator states at the end of the play that "... of all who give gifts these two were the wisest." Do you agree that the decisions Della and Jim made were wise? Why or why not?

Literary Skill: Adapt a Passage

Read the following Biblical passage from the book of Matthew. Work with classmates to write a script (including stage directions) based upon this passage. Decide how many speaking parts there will be as well as how the action should be presented; then present your play as Readers Theatre. You might want to research how this story ends—how the Magi trick Herod, and what Herod does to retaliate—and add that information also.

> Then Herod summoned the wise men secretly and learned from them what time the star appeared; and he sent them to Bethlehem, saying, "Go and search for the child, and when you have found him bring me word ..." When they had heard the king they went their way; and lo, the star which they had seen in the east went before them, till it came to rest over the place where the child was. When they saw the star, they rejoiced with great joy....Then opening their treasures, they offered him gold, frankincense, and myrrh. And being warned in a dream not to return to Herod, they departed to their own country by another way.

Performance Element: Mime

Mime communicates thoughts and feelings through action, without the use of words. Working with the Readers Theatre script you created for the passage above, chose two or more classmates, one of whom tells the story in words while the others tell the story using mime.

Glossary of Key Literary and Theatrical Terms

accent
the sound of speech in a particular region.

act
1. a major division in a play: *Let's read the second scene in the first act.*
2. to play the role of a character in a play: *My friend loves to act.*

actor
a person who analyzes characters in relationship to a play, memorizes lines, learns blocking, and performs a role in a play.

allusion
a reference in a literary work to an historical or literary figure, happening, or event.

antagonist
the character who gets in the way of the protagonist, or main character; secondary character.

archetype
a stock character who represents a certain kind of person.

arena stage
a stage that is surrounded by the audience; theatre-in-the-round. The stage may actually be a round shape, but it can also be a square.

aside
a side remark a character makes to the audience or another character.

audio
things that are heard, especially recordings.

audition
1. to try out for a part in a play.
2. the actual trying out itself.

backdrop
a large canvas or muslin curtain on which a scene is painted.

backstage
the areas behind the stage that are not visible to the audience.

beat
a special moment; actors and directors often divide scenes into beats.

biographical fiction
fiction based on research about a person. It reveals not only what the person did but what he or she might have done.

block
to arrange the movement of people, sets, and props on the stage.

book
a script, especially for a musical.

box office
the place where ticket sales take place.

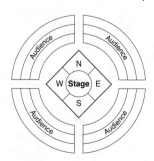

arena stage

business manager
the person who creates the production budget, coordinates publicity and ticket sales, and prepares programs.

call
the time when actors should be on hand before a performance.

callback
an invitation to a second audition.

cast
to choose people for particular roles in a play.

center stage
the middle of a performance area.

cold reading
the reading of a script for the first time.

comedy
a light or humorous play that usually has a happy ending.

comedy of manners
a play that pokes fun at the actions and habits of the upper and upper middle class.

comic timing
pacing comic moments in a scene to create the most humorous effects.

conflict
the struggle between opposing forces that is essential to a good dramatic work.

UR Upstage Right	**UC** Upstage Center	**UL** Upstage Left
R Right	**C** Center	**L** Left
DR Downstage Right	**DC** Downstage Center	**DL** Downstage Left

AUDIENCE

center stage

characterization
the way in which an author reveals the characters to the reader.

choreograph
to design dancing, fighting, or other specialized movements for the stage.

chorus
a group of actors reciting, singing, or dancing in unison, often to comment on the action of a play.

climax
the turning point of a play.

costume
the clothing an actor wears on-stage for a performance.

costume designer
the person who designs and makes or obtains costuming for the actors in a play.

costume plan
breakdown of the costumes characters wear in a play and the scenes in which they wear them.

credits

the list of people who contributed to a production.

cross

to move from one place to another.

cue

a signal, often the last lines spoken by another actor.

curtain

the end (because the draperies open at the beginning of a play and close at the end).

cyclorama

a curved wall or drop at the back of a stage, used to create an illusion of wide space or for lighting effects.

dialect

the way in which people from a certain region or group speak that differs from the standard language.

dialogue

the conversation between people in a literary work or drama.

diction

the words an author chooses to use, dictated by the subject, audience, and effect intended in the literary work. Diction can be formal, informal, precise, complicated, old-fashioned, or contemporary.

direct

to give suggestions to actors and crew members as to how to fulfill their roles in the production.

director

a person who interprets a play, casts actors, develops blocking, and blends performances into a unified production.

down stage

the stage area closest to the audience.

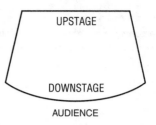

downstage

drama

a play that covers serious topics and may or may not have an unhappy ending.

dramatic monologue

a speech made by a single character that reveals something about the speaker or fills in important circumstances in the story.

dress rehearsal

a final practice of a play before the actual performance.

ensemble acting

a theatrical presentation that focuses on the coming together of all the roles rather than on a star's performance.

enter

to appear on the stage.

exit

to leave the stage area.

fable

a story intended to impart a useful truth; often one in which animals speak.

falling action

the part of a play following the turning point and approaching the resolution of the conflict.

falling action

farce
a comedy with exaggerated characters, physical humor, and a silly plot.

flashback
the interrupting of chronological order in a literary work by relating an event that happened earlier.

fly
a space above the stage, often used for storage.

footage
a portion of a film.

foreshadowing
clues or hints given by the author as to what is to come in the literary work.

fourth wall
an imaginary wall between the stage and the audience.

gesture
a movement that expresses a thought or emotion.

house
the audience, or the place where the audience sits.

house manager
the person who oversees the preparations for performance, supervises ushers, and has contact with the audience.

imagery
the vivid and striking details in any literary work.

improvisation
to make things up as one goes along; to act without a script.

irony
the contrast between what one expects or what appears to be and what actually is.

lighting
the illumination of the actors and the set during a performance.

lighting designer
the person who creates and carries out a lighting plan.

lobby
the area where the audience waits before a performance and during intermissions.

makeup
the cosmetics, hair styling, masks, wigs, etc. used by performers.

makeup designer
the person who designs and applies makeup for all the actors.

mime
1. to communicate through movement and gesture rather than words.

2. a person who communicates in this way.

monologue
a story or speech performed by an actor speaking alone.

mood
the atmosphere or overall feeling presented in a literary work.

motivation
a character's reasons for doing or saying something.

multimedia
using several forms of communication, such as acting, dancing, painting, audio, video, and computers.

musical
a play in which song and dance play an important part.

musical theatre
a play incorporating songs and dances throughout.

myth
a story that seeks to relate historical events in order to explain the world and its events to a people.

objective
a character's goals in a scene or play.

off book
having no need of the script.

pacing
the rate at which a play progresses.

pantomime
mime; to act out without using words or sounds.

papier-mâché
a technique for making props and masks out of torn strips of newspaper and glue made from flour and water.

physical comedy
comedy that uses such physical stunts as pratfalls and slapstick to elicit laughter.

pitch
the high or low sound of a voice.

play
a story created for performance.

plot
story line, generally including rising action, climax, and resolution.

point of view
the relationship of the teller of the story to the characters in the story.

posture
the way in which one holds one's body.

producer
a person who chooses the play, obtains the space, and sometimes casts actors.

production
the performance of a play for an audience.

project
to make one's voice loud and full enough to be heard in a big room.

prop
property; moveable objects used by actors on stage.

prop designer
a person who obtains or makes props.

properties
props; moveable objects used by actors on stage.

prop table
a place offstage where all props are kept when not in use.

protagonist
the character who moves the action of a play forward, usually the "good guy" or the character with whom the audience identifies.

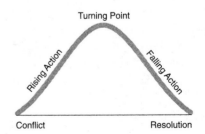

typical **plot** structure

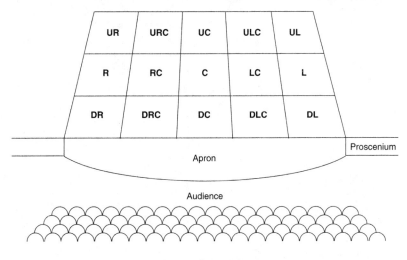

proscenium stage

---

proscenium stage
a "picture frame" stage; a stage that allows audience seating on the front side only.

rake
to incline a portion of the stage from the perpendicular.

Readers Theatre
a dramatic reading of a story or play script.

realism
a style of writing or acting that attempts to be as lifelike as possible.

rising action
the middle part of a plot, including complications leading toward a climax.

role
a part in a play.

run
a period of time over which a play will be presented, typically four to six weeks.

satire
a literary form that ridicules human foibles and vices.

scenario
a plan or outline for a plot.

scene
part of an act; segment of a play that does not require a change of scenery.

scenery
large background pieces that create a sense of place on-stage.

science fiction
a kind of literary work that is set entirely or partly in an unreal world. Events are usually based on current science, but are beyond what modern science can do.

screenplay
a film, video, or television script.

script
the text of a play.

set
the combination of scenery, furniture, and props.

set designer
a person who designs and creates sets, and obtains or makes set pieces such as furniture.

set pieces
large pieces of furniture for the stage.

setting
the location in which a play takes place.

shoot
film something.

sound
all sound-producing elements of a production, including live voices, music, and sound effects.

sound designer
a person who creates and carries out a sound effects plan.

spoof
a light, humorous parody of a piece of writing.

stage
performance area. See **arena, proscenium,** and **thrust** for various types of stages.

stage manager
a person who holds auditions, schedules acting and technical rehearsals, and keeps track of administration for a production.

stage right
the stage area to an actor's right when he or she faces the audience.

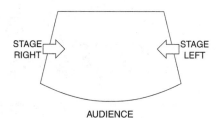

STAGE RIGHT   STAGE LEFT

AUDIENCE

stage left/stage right

stereotype
an oversimplified representation of characteristics of members of a certain group.

storyboard
a series of sketches showing possible scenes in a play.

UR Upstage Right	**UC** Upstage Center	**UL** Upstage Left
R Right	**C** Center	**L** Left
DR Downstage Right	**DC** Downstage Center	**DL** Downstage Left

The performance area of a **stage** may be divided into 9 distinct parts.

stage crew
the people handling sets, lighting, sound, costumes, or makeup.

stage left
the stage area to an actor's left when he or she faces the audience.

style
an author's way of writing; the way an author writes about a subject.

subtext
the layer of meaning beneath the actual words in a play or novel.

suspense
the way an author maintains the reader's interest, creating a mood of anxiety and uncertainty.

symbolism
words and images that represent something more than their ordinary meaning.

teleplay
a television script.

theme
the underlying meaning of any literary work.

thrust stage
stage surrounded on three sides by the house, or audience.

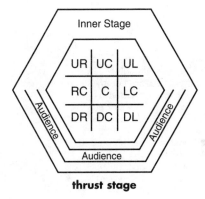

thrust stage

timing
the pacing of particular moments in a scene.

tone
the author's attitude toward his or her subject and toward the reader.

tragedy
a form of drama in which the main character comes to an unhappy end.

turning point
the decisive moment in a literary work in which the central problem of the plot must be resolved.

understudy
an actor who learns a role in order to substitute for an actor who is absent.

upstage
the stage area toward the back of the stage.

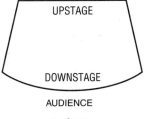

upstage

ushers
the crew members who seat the audience, hand out programs, and clean up the house after each performance.

video
things that are seen, especially recordings that can be seen on television.

voice
the intelligence, heart, conviction, and feeling of an individual writer that comes through in his or her writing.

voice-over
a recording of a voice that plays while action or other sounds are taking place, often indicated as VO in stage directions.

wings
the offstage areas to the right and left of the stage, where actors often wait before their entrances and after their exits.

Acknowledgments